Tribune of the People
A Novel of Ancient Rome

Dan Wallace

© Copyright 2016

By Branden Books

Library of Congress Cataloging-in-Publication Data

Names: Wallace, Dan, author.
Title: Tribune of the people: a novel of ancient Rome / Dan Wallace.
Description: Wellesley MA: Branden Books, 2016. | Includes bibliographical references and index.
Identifiers: LCCN 2015039859| ISBN 9780828326049 (pbk.: alk. paper) | ISBN 9780828326056 (e-book)
Subjects: LCSH: Gracchus, Tiberius Sempronius--Fiction. | Rome--History--Fiction.
Classification: LCC PS3623.A359753 T75 2016 | DDC 813/.6--dc23
LC record available at http://lccn.loc.gov/2015039859

   ISBN 9780828326049 Paperback
   ISBN 9780828326056 E-Book

Branden Books
PO Box 812094
Wellesley MA 02482

www.brandenbooks.com

To Ivey, love of my life.

into a plain, grey metal goblet, which he brought back to the consul. The other military tribunes in the tent drank wine and water.

"Carthage has nothing left. We never really needed to be here at all, if it's supposed to be about any sort of threat to Rome."

"Then, why are we here, Consul?" Tiberius asked. The others looked at him as if he were mad, brother-in-law or not, still one of the most junior officers in the tent daring to interrupt Scipio with a question. Bemused, Scipio assumed an indulgent expression. "Why, for the goods, boy, the gold, the ivory, the slaves, everything. That, and because the indomitable Cato the Elder, may his spirit rest with the gods, said we should be here: 'Carthage must be destroyed,'" Scipio intoned, raising a finger to the tent roof, "and the members of our most august Senate concur." He dropped the finger, "Of course, they concur on the gold, the ivory, and the slaves, too."

The tent filled with laughter, and Tiberius raised his voice to be heard, "If that's true, Consul, couldn't we simply ask for more tribute rather than waste time, money, and our good legionaries? If we destroy Carthage as Cato insists, won't we be killing the goose that lays the golden eggs?"

Fannius kicked him in the side of the calf, but the damage had been done. The laughter died out, and Scipio stood up, surprisingly short, but plainly spry and sharp. At 39, only a bit of grey had invaded his curly aura of hair and beard. His dark eyes sparkled as he spoke.

"My dear boy, perhaps your naiveté is a result of having lost your honorable father so young. Or, it could be an understandable consequence of your education at Diophane's knee, who teaches the old values, including thrift. Nonetheless, there are still certain ineluctable facts in life that trump even these considerations. One of them is politics. If the Senate wants us to destroy Carthage, Carthage will be destroyed. No matter what the trumped-up excuse might be, the horror of Hannibal relived, the refusal of these Phoenician renegades to yield unconditionally to our rule, or any other irrational assertion, we will do as the people of Rome wish—the people of Rome who count, that is. We will pluck this little sea-side bird clean. We will roast it, eat it, and shit it out so that it is indistinguishable from the offal of the other wild animals roaming this fecund land."

Tiberius remembered how the rest of the tribunes cheered, while Fannius pulled him into the background. "Brother-in-law or not, you're lucky he decided to be funny."

Never far from the surface, the thought of his sister Sempronia's unfortunate marriage washed over Tiberius again. "How can he say such things so freely, so openly?" Tiberius asked.

"By the gods on the mount, you are naive. He's Scipio Aemilianus, hero of Macedonia and adopted grandson of the great Scipio Africanus, who alone defeated Hannibal. And, if he has his way, he'll soon be a bigger hero than his grandfather. Great Mars, they elected him consul five years before he reached the proper age, he can say any damn thing he wants!"

"That doesn't make me wrong," Tiberius said, petulantly, he knew, but he couldn't help himself. He was right, this war was a waste. Yet, here he was.

He wished he was back in Rome. Impossible, he thought, with his mother there. His mind traveled back to the day before he left for Brindisium to board the transport galley that would take him to Carthage. His mother had summoned him to her chambers. Reluctantly, he entered her bedroom, where she sat in a curule chair in low light.

"Tiberius," she said, "tomorrow, you leave for your first war. In a few months, when you are about to scale the walls of Carthage, Rome's great enemy, I want you to remember who you are. You are the oldest surviving son and namesake of Tiberius Sempronius Gracchus, twice consul, once censor, the conqueror of the Hispanic people, Rome's greatest man. I, Cornelia, daughter of Scipio Africanus and member of the oldest and most noble patrician family in Rome, married your father, a plebeian. To me, it mattered not that he was a plebeian, but that he was to be great. My only regret is that he did not live to see this day.

"Now, your father gave me twelve children, Tiberius," she said to him, "and only your sister, Sempronia, you, and your little brother, Gaius, have survived. It has been hard. Your sister has done her duty in marrying Scipio Aemilianus, and now it is your time. In the memory of your father and your lost siblings, you must abide by the Greek lesson that Polydius has taught you, that of the Spartan mother's instruction to her son: 'Come back with your shield or on it.'

"Come," she said, "embrace me, and go win honor."

Now, he awaited the order for the final assault. The engineers had switched loads for the mangonels, back to throwing heavy stones at the fortifications instead of the bundled firebrands. Great shards of stones cracked off parts of the walls from the constant pummeling by the machines, and the Carthaginians had to crouch low to try to avoid the heavy missiles. They, too, must know that the end loomed.

Centurion Primus Manius Casca came striding up, a boulder of a man on a frame of average height. His helmet looked as though he'd propped it on top of his head, then used a rock to beat it down to fit. Hence, his cognomen Capito, big head. But he was as good a centurion as any Roman legion would know, with experience against the Macedonians and for the last three years, the Carthaginians. Although Fannius and Tiberius ranked Casca technically, they would never think to challenge him on the basics rules of combat.

"Check your arms, again, boys. Don't tighten your loricas too much, you've got to be able to move. And, if you didn't do it last night, be sure to trim your beards tight. Don't want any of those dog-loving, burnt-skinned pirates grabbing your whiskers to cut your throat. Your mother won't like it, your head flopping around while you're pounding away at her again, trying to get back into the womb."

The soldiers laughed, the younger ones nervously. "Remember, above all, be sure the stalks of your beautiful Hispanic flowers are sharp on both sides." Casca pulled out his gladius spina, the long sword adopted by veterans after encountering them in Hispania long ago, and caressingly ran his finger down one edge, then the other. "Like I warned you last night, this battle won't be won by pila, it'll be close-in work, heads flying about, the sky and the sea turned red." He caressed the blade of his sword again, looking at it fondly as he said, "My dear Hispanic gladiola is ready to sip the moisture of Rome's enemies all the way to their taproots."

The veterans smiled, used to Casca's constant reminders before a battle and the pun nickname he had for his sword.

Later, Tiberius asked him quietly, "Soon?"

Casca stepped closer to him, "I saw Scipio leaving his tent and head toward the line. The augurs were with him, carrying fowl. They'll dispatch them quick, the auspices will be favorable, I'll wager, and the consul will give the order. I've seen it a dozen times before. The gods always smile upon Scipio's battles."

Casca had begun to smile himself when the trumpets blared the call to assemble.

"That's it, lads, to your posts. Let's get this over fast, and to the wine-drinking."

Fannius and Tiberius looked at each other, eyes wide and round. They jointly commanded a cohort charged with pushing two of four siege towers forward from the main blockade mole across separate levees thrown up to the walls of Carthage. Other towers and rams would be moved forward simultaneously on land, stretching and squeezing the remaining defenders beyond their limits, if they hadn't been already by the constant bombardment.

Tiberius shouted to his men to begin pushing the great wooden tower forward, admonishing them to stay in its shadow. The huge wheels creaked and groaned as a hundred men manned long timbers yoked to the lower walls, nudging the massive structure forward. Carthage loomed ahead, less than a quarter of a mile away. Fannius urged his men behind another tower on the jetty parallel to the one Tiberius walked. Both of the towers and that of the two other junior tribunes on the remaining dirt levees moved forward in unison, making reasonably good progress. The soldiers behind those pushing the towers pounded their swords against their shields in time, creating a fearsome din aimed at filling the Carthaginians with dread.

Casca yelled out a verse, and the legionaries began to sing a vulgar song of death, rape, drink, love, and honor. As they reached the halfway point on the bulwark, the Carthaginians fired their ballista.

At first, the projectiles thudded into the wood of the towers, harmless to the soldiers beneath and behind. They hooted and cried obscenities in ecstasy as the large pila and stones bounced off the tower walls. Casca howled, gesturing them forward with his gladius.

A rain of arrows poured out from behind the walls, arcing high over the towers into the ranks of the soldiers below. Expecting the tower to protect them, they hadn't raised their shields overhead in the protective turtle formation, and many of them were impaled as a consequence.

Those hit screamed agony, clutching at shafts buried in their shoulders, in their arms, their necks. One legionary was forced into a split with a leg pierced through by an arrow, blood pumping out from a severed artery. Tiberius watched him go pale, slump over, and die, his hands still wrapped around the arrow's shaft.

"Get your shields up!" roared Casca as a second flight of arrows descended. "Press tight to the tower," he yelled, raising his shield as an arrow struck him. "My God Mars, I'm killed!" he said as he sat down on the packed earth and fell back dead.

His jaw slack, Tiberius ran over to the body. He saw that the arrow had pierced Casca in the notch of his breastbone just above the edge of his lorica, angling down into his heart. Like Achilles killed Hector, Tiberius thought oddly as arrows pounded the ground around him. He turned quickly to the men. "Push the tower forward!"

Glancing over to the other levee, he saw Fannius staring at him. Tiberius waved his sword, and Fannius returned to shouting his men to go forward.

They were just a hundred feet from the walls when the Carthaginians launched ballista arrows into the towers, their points covered with burning rags soaked in lamp oil. Flames started to course up the front, but still the towers moved inexorably forward. The Carthaginians intensified their fire, arrows, pila, ballista, stones. Tiberius thought they had a good chance to reach the walls before the flames consumed his tower when a large boulder smashed into the lower left corner, knocking one of the great wooden wheels into a dozen pieces. He heard a sharp, cracking sound, and looked up at the structure as it shook, shuddered, and lurched horribly to one side.

"Get out, get off!" Shouts raised from the ranks as the tower leaned over, men leaping from it with abandon. Tiberius watched it hold still for a single instant at an impossible angle, then slowly fall sideways, slipping down the edge of the levee and dropping into the harbor with a thunderous smacking noise, sending twin spouts of water angling up from its sides.

A withering cascade of arrows flew down from the walls as the defenders concentrated fire upon the exposed Romans. The soldiers scrambled for cover on the narrow levee, crying out as they were struck, some of them beginning to turn toward the rear.

Tiberius crouched on one knee, his shield angled up at the walls. Across the half-submerged wreckage of the tower, he saw Fannius exhort his troops, glance at him, then back to his soldiers. Three arrows struck Tiberius's shield in rapid order, almost driving him into the ground, and he wondered if Scipio had sent him out here to be killed.

Tiberius jumped up and yelled to his men, "If you want to die, stay here or turn your backs. If you want to live, follow me!"

He dashed to the side of the levee, dropped his shield and plunged into the water. The men close on his heels stopped short, until they saw him splash and paddle to the tower wreckage, then clamber onto it, running toward the other end as fast as he could. The others followed closely on him, many of them punched off the tower wreckage by pila and rocks from the walls.

Tiberius reached the end only to realize that he was a good 30 feet from the other levee. Fannius stood on the edge and motioned them down. Tiberius's men dropped low on the tower wreckage, cringing for cover. On the other side, archers sent flights of arrows up toward the enemy walls. Tiberius snapped to his men behind him, "Drop your shields and helmets, cut away your loricas. If you want to live, swim!" he roared as he plunged into the water. He covered the ten yards quickly, worked his way halfway up the mole's bank, and crouched to look back at his men behind him. Many floundered in the water, desperate to reach the other side. Others still stood on the broken tower, feinting to jump; then hesitating at the last instant, terrified of drowning. Tiberius watched as scores of them fell to arrows. He glanced down to see others struggling, pulling on shafts in their bodies as they disappeared beneath the surface. He wheeled around to shout for help from Fannius when he saw men forming human chains down the embankment. Ignoring the fusillade of bolts aimed at them, they reached out with their hands or threw lengths of rope out to the splashing men and pulled them in. As soon as the last man reached the bank, everyone scurried for their lives behind the standing tower. Leaning against a bulwark, breathing heavily, Tiberius gazed back at his command. Out of 300 men, fewer than half had survived.

"Jupiter's balls," Fannius snarled, "I'll slit the throat of the first woman with short hair I see in there!"

"We've got to get off of this levee, Fannius, we've got to move!" Tiberius gestured to his men to press in with Fannius's troops on the tower. With Tiberius's men helping, before long the tower had been pushed to the end of the mole onto the permanent docking area in front of the wall. But the storm of projectiles grew worse, and the men huddled close together in the tower's shadow.

"Tiberius, the tower is starting to burn!" Fannius cried out. Tiberius looked up and saw that the flames were beginning to work their way inside the structure. He bit his lips, then licked them. He started to look out; then stopped himself. His stomach felt leaden. Finally, he pulled around the edge of the tower and looked over to the other moles. The other two towers were stalled, and one seemed to be burning badly.

He quickly ducked back in. "Fannius, the other two towers are far behind us. They might not make it at all."

"Hades gods, what'll we do? Maybe we can wait; maybe Scipio has taken the city already, from the other side!"

Tiberius shook his head, "We can't wait. This tower is about to fall in on us. We need either to fall back or go forward."

Fannius peered up fearfully at the tower, then back at the body-strewn levee. He looked in panic at Tiberius.

"Why are we here, Tiberius?" he gasped, "Why us?"

Tiberius almost whined his low reply, "I don't know! Someone had to attack across the mole."

He grimaced, his expression darkening. He sprang up and yelled, "Where do you want them to find us, Fannius, skewered here while cringing, or on the walls?" Then, louder, he shouted, "To me, let's go!"

He bolted inside the tower and began pushing it forward. The men around him shouted, and began to heave again. Slowly, the stalled wooden beast moved forward, staggering, until it gained momentum. Fannius summoned a small troop around him and sprinted in front of the tower, shield raised, to clear any debris away from the path to the walls. He and his men barely careened out of the way and back around as the tower accelerated. Before the city's defenders could throw any more impediments down, the wooden tower crashed hard against the stone, bouncing some of the pushing soldiers off balance and back on their hindquarters.

"Up!" yelled Tiberius, who ran up the ladder to the first, the second, and the top level of the siege tower, ignoring the flames around him. Fannius had bolted up the other side, gingerly sidestepping the burning ladder that halted his ascent on the second level. He ran to the ladder Tiberius had used and joined him at the top of the tower behind the heavy wooden platform in front, held in place by stout ropes and ready to be dropped to bridge the wall.

They heard the thuds of rocks and beams smash against the wooden parapet as the defenders tried to dislodge the tower. Tiberius darted a glance through a crack between the timbers of the platform, then motioned to Fannius. They both positioned themselves at the ropes, swords poised. Tiberius nodded his head, and they slashed the hemp. The platform dropped, Tiberius sweeping across it before it struck the top of the wall. When it hit, it bounced once, which helped propel him up over and past a line of archers, arrows notched to strike down the first wave of soldiers. Pivoting quickly, he hacked ferociously down on the bowmen, killing two before they could turn. Fannius leaped from the tower to the wall as the other bowmen scattered through the ranks of the Carthaginian foot. Fannius ran to Tiberius to meet the charge of spears and swords aimed from both sides at the two Roman invaders.

Tiberius parried a spear thrust, quickly blocking a sword stroke almost in the same motion. He stepped in and attacked furiously, beating them back and into each other, packing them too close to fight effectively. So many, he thought, as he sliced the air with his sword.

He felt a sudden, sharp pain in his lower back, and ducked low and left to see Fannius backhand his assailant off the wall, who screamed as he fell. Tiberius swerved back in front to snatch the haft of a spear as it jabbed past his head. Pulling the soldier close with surprising ease, he stabbed him in the breast, and twisted the spear to flip him off the wall. The edge of a heavy sword drove his blade down, sliding off to cut him high on his left arm. He dropped his sword and instinctively butted the Carthaginian with his forearm and shoulder back into the mass of attackers. He knelt to retrieve his sword and slashed at the legs of soldiers forging forward. A ringing blow sent his helmet flying from his head. Tiberius skipped, leaning back to dodge the sweeping arc of a curved blade.

He bumped into another back and cried out, "Fannius!"

"Ho!" yelled Fannius at his shoulder. This is it, then, Tiberius thought. He gripped his sword tightly and pressed his back against Fannius's, ready to strike again. The Carthaginians howled and surged forward, and suddenly were intercepted by a group of legionaries jumping from the tower.

Tiberius relaxed momentarily as the legionaries beat back the Carthaginians in front of him. Another group of Romans dropped over the wall, running past Tiberius and Fannius to battle on the other side. Tiberius had a chance to look further down the parapet, where he could see that another tower had made it to the wall intact. The legionaries were bounding from the far tower in numbers, pressing the Carthaginians hard on both sides. The enemy defense was beginning to disintegrate around them.

"Look, they're leaving the walls," Fannius said in a thin voice. "They're almost done for."

"Over there, Fannius," Tiberius pointed to the interior of the city, which was full of Roman soldiers. He realized that to have gotten that far, the resistance at other points along the city must have collapsed precipitously.

"It's almost over," breathed Fannius.

"I think so," said Tiberius. He watched the legionaries in the city cutting down anyone in their way, killing running Carthaginian soldiers from behind.

A tumultuous roar went up from the walls, startling Tiberius and Fannius. The survivors of their cohort shouted out again, their swords and shields raised high, clattering one against another. The wall had been swept clear, the victory was theirs.

A cry welled up, "Hail Tiberius Gracchus!" It grew in volume as the soldiers shouted out their praise, "First over the wall! Gracchus! First over the wall!"

Tiberius raised his hand in acknowledgment, first one way, and then the other. He whispered to Fannius, "Do you think it's true? We were first?"

"You, Tiberius!" said Fannius, "You were first!"

Tiberius gave him an incredulous, almost ridiculing expression. "I don't see how it could be," he said, "it took us so long to get here."

"Long?" Fannius said. "Look at the sun. We've been here less than an hour. We fought up here for perhaps fifteen minutes at the most."

Bewildered, Tiberius gazed at the sun, then at the city. Fifteen minutes?

"Still and all," he said, "we couldn't have been first; we're still where we started, while the rest of the legions are deep into the city itself. Someone else must have been first."

"Perhaps so," Fannius conceded. "In any case, look at you, you're a mess!"

Tiberius looked down at himself, and for the first time he felt the dull pain in the small of his back from the spear puncture, pain from the cut in his bicep, and the throbbing of his head. He turned his gaze to Fannius, "Well, you're not ready for a wedding party either."

Fannius sported a jagged slash across his clavicle just above his molded lorica. A few inches deeper, and he would have been another lifeless corpse spilled on the wall. He had a gash on one forearm, and a slight stab wound in his thigh. Fannius grinned and slapped Tiberius on the shoulder, "We'll live. What now?"

"Call the troops to order, I guess, secure the wall, and move down into the city."

Fannius nodded sadly, "That's what Casca would have had us do."

Tiberius grinned a tight smile, and barked a command to his men. They left fifty legionaries on the wall to prevent any escapes or sorties. The remaining 350 soldiers descended the steps where Tiberius and Fannius formed them up for a sweeping action through the streets. Before they could begin, however, a troop of horse pulled up in the small plaza between the walls and the buildings. Scipio Aemilianus pranced in front of the group and shouted out "Tiberius Gracchus, Gaius Fannius."

The two tribunes stepped forward. Scipio riding his horse, mused Tiberius. The battle truly was over.

"Tiberius, Gaius, first over the wall?"

Fannius shouted, "Tiberius, Consul, Tiberius was first!"

Tiberius looked at him with a puzzled expression, but the cries of approval from their men shook the air.

"Tiberius Sempronius Gracchus," Scipio declared in a raised voice, "First over the wall, winner of the Mural Crown!"

And the city rang with the blood-thickened voices of the legions cheering the young officer, celebrating the final conquest of the greatest enemy in Rome's history, Carthage.

In the physician's tent, Tiberius and Fannius lay exhausted as Scipio's surgeon tended their wounds. He had stitched up the gash above Fannius's collarbone, and had placed herb poultices on the sword cuts. The herbs were good enough for Tiberius's cut on his bicep, and he held a compress to his head. But the surgeon felt that he had to cauterize the spear wound in his back to ensure that the poison wouldn't enter. Tiberius lay prone, waiting for the iron to sizzle.

With his head hanging slightly over the edge of the table, he stared at his hand dangling close to the ground. He was tired, sad. Visions of the battle and aftermath crowded his aching brain. Once the invasion had succeeded, Scipio ordered a march through the city. Tiberius and Fannius were charged with cordoning off the streets in the wake of the first wave of legionaries, easy duty to acknowledge their triumphant sacrifice in leading the attack.

Tiberius instructed his men to form two lines, and begin to move slowly behind the rest of the troops, who had broken up into informal gangs. As they walked, the exaltation from the wreathing by Scipio and the army's acclaim had faded by what he saw then.

The ganged Romans broke into each home and building, and turned out all of their inhabitants. In the street, they forced the men to their knees and killed them, slashing their throats, taking off their heads, or simply hacking them to pieces. Old men and women, infants, and babies were dispatched as quickly as possible so that the conquerors could go about their business of taking everything.

Women and girls were dragged out, some clutching scraps of cloth to their bodies, some naked, some already dead from repeated, brutish rape. Those alive were tied together by their necks and marched off along with any boys too young to wield weapons, back to the harbor to await sale to the slavers.

Most were killed. After a brutal, three-year siege, the Romans exacted their revenge as expected. But, something else was going on, Tiberius realized. He watched as a woman of 30 or so, a comely young matron, he thought, was pulled out by three soldiers. She was thrust on one knee to the cobblestones, her arms jerked straight out to steady her. She looked up at Tiberius, dark brown eyes dead already, and an optio sliced her head from her body with one measured stroke of his sword. As her head fell, Tiberius noticed her hair, closely-cropped, almost to the skull. He quickly fixed his sight on Fannius, who witnessed her death with an expression frozen in shock. Fannius glanced at Tiberius, then averted his eyes, almost guiltily.

The sudden, searing pain from the red hot blade in the small of his back brought Tiberius back to the physician's tent.

"Well done, Tribune," said the surgeon. "That ought to heal nicely." He proceeded to bind it in a soft bandage, asking if it was too tight, instructing Tiberius to return the next day to ensure that infection hadn't set in.

Tiberius looked at Fannius, who pulled lightly at the bandage wrapped around his chest and shoulders like a linen lorica.

"How do you feel?" Tiberius asked him. "Lucky," replied Fannius. "Fortuna kissed us upon the lips today, Tiberius."

Tiberius nodded, but said, "A kiss not so loving for many legionaries," he said, "or for Carthage."

Fannius's shoulders slumped. "I know we are new to war, but I didn't think we would see what we saw today."

What they had seen had been repeated endlessly throughout the rest of the day deep into the night. As they followed behind the troops stalking from street to street, house to house, without even the most impoverished dwelling being overlooked, Tiberius gradually realized that the rape and massacre he witnessed was precise, engineered. Scipio had transformed the exultant, furious pillage of his conquering legionaries into a killing maneuver meant to expunge the entire population of Carthage.

What was left of the population, anyway, thought Tiberius. During the death march, the shock of battle faded from him. He now saw the lethal enemy whom he had fought as the few remaining residents of the other great city in the world. They were ambling sacks of bones painted in tones of mottled flesh and skin. He noted bodies filling the streets before the killer legionaries had gotten to them, dead from disease and hunger. Of course, in the tradition of his grandfather, Scipio first starved Carthage for the better part of a year before committing his troops to the assault. Tiberius could see how he and Fannius had been able to keep the Carthaginian soldiers at bay on the walls, and why they had been so easily tossed from the parapet. Though they'd still fought as valiantly as they could to defend their families and their homes, the Carthaginians in their horribly emaciated state were no match even for two green tribunes. Just as Scipio had planned, thought Tiberius.

After being relieved near midnight, Tiberius and Fannius staggered back to their tent to await a call from Scipio's own surgeon to check their wounds. Fannius wandered off to find wine, but Tiberius fell across his bedding face down to avoid the pain from his wounded back.

Scipio entered the tent alone and pulled up a stool to sit at Tiberius's side. "How goes your healing?" he said with a wry smile.

"I'll live," Tiberius said, "no thanks to you."

Scipio laughed, "Now, why would you say that, dear brother-in-law? Why tempt the gods?"

"That mole was a rat trap, running all of us right down a funnel into a Carthaginian grindstone. It's a miracle of the gods that any of us made it to the walls in one piece, never mind surviving the assault itself."

"Yes, it was a tall task," Scipio said, his expression momentarily reflective. "But, you are tall, Tiberius, and someone had to distract them into centering their forces at the wrong place."

"Distract them?" Tiberius asked, stunned. "We were a distraction? But, the order of the day was for a general attack."

"The order," said Scipio, carefully, "was amended."

"We were never expected to succeed," Tiberius moaned. His face became a mosaic of anguish. "You did want me to die out there. Do you really hate us so much, Sempronia and me?"

Scipio straightened up; then relaxed again. "Don't be foolish, Tiberius. Who else should I have sent in your place? You're a Gracchi, your father's namesake, and son of Cornelia. You're here to win glory, aren't you, to burnish the family reputation, just like every other scion of a noble Roman house? Yes, you could have died, but you didn't. You lived and you won the Mural Crown the only way you could, by being sent first, the chance that greatness demands. So, don't whine to me about your life or my wife. You got what you wanted."

He rose to leave, but paused to say, "The attack from the levees was the most difficult of the engagement and you executed it successfully, surprisingly so. You've earned honor today, brother-in-law, which qualifies you for future prospects. Even I admit to that and will act accordingly. May the gods go with you," he said, as he turned and left the tent.

"They say that once the citadel falls and the last of the Carthaginians are finished," Fannius said when he returned, "Scipio intends to raze the entire city. He plans on being here for as long as it takes to wipe Carthage from the face of the earth. Nothing will be left of the greatest foe that Rome has ever known."

Tiberius rose to a sitting position, then to his feet. "It doesn't matter to me. I've done what was expected here, and I'm done with it. Tomorrow, I return to Rome."

"But Tiberius," Fannius, almost plaintively, "the worst is over. Don't you want to be here for the division of the spoils?"

Tiberius shook his head, "I'm sure that Scipio will protect my interests in exacting measure. But, I'm finished with killing skeletons and the walking dead. I'm going home, home to Rome."

Chapter 1. 138 B.C.E.

Claudia slipped out from under the covers and pulled a robe at the end of the bed around her shoulders. She walked softly from her room to the door across the hall, carefully nudging it open to see if Tiberius had awakened. Even after this many years together, she still smiled a prayer to Fortuna as she did every morning, thanking the goddess for the strange and wonderful turn of the wheel that had made her his wife.

"Antistia, I have wonderful news," her father had said as he burst his way into their vestibulum. "I've just betrothed Claudia to the most outstanding young man in Rome."

"Oh, Appius," her mother had cried out, "Why are you so impetuous? No young Roman is good enough for Claudia, none of them, except for just one, Tiberius Gracchus."

"Tiberius Sempronius Gracchus," her father had said, nodding his head, "that is whom Claudia will wed."

Claudia laughed silently to herself as she recalled her mother telling her how she had run to jump into her father's arms. As affectionate as they were toward each other, she doubted that either of them would have engaged in such a display. No, she thought, the story was just that, a story. More likely, the contract had been closely negotiated, especially with Tiberius' mother Cornelia guiding the Gracchi interests. Tiberius Sempronius Gracchus, she acclaimed, the oldest living son of his great father, who twice was elected consul, twice triumphed in Rome, and who finished up his brilliant public career as censor. Behold his eponymous son, Tiberius Sempronius Gracchus, winner himself of the Mural Crown at Carthage, and son of a Cornelii, one of the most celebrated families in Rome. But, after all that was said, the Gracchi were plebeians with average holdings who required marriages of status and wealth. The Claudii could offer both, the trade-off being that Tiberius would marry Claudia.

She knew that she was not beautiful. Too thin by far, too tall, and almost vulpine in her features, Claudia knew that she would be married to some noteworthy suitor, and she would bear children. She imagined loving her family, her children deeply. She would love her husband, too, as much as he would allow.

Then, stark terror would overwhelm her, the thought that she might be barren and never have any children to love, none to love her back uncritically. If she could bear no heirs, in time even the most patient of husbands would divorce her. The thought petrified her and threw her into wild despair about being disgraced for her entire life, utterly useless to her family and Rome, and utterly alone.

She shook her head to dismiss her past fears. She had married and had borne two children in quick succession, a boy and a girl. Heirs were assured, and she was a dutiful wife. She had achieved all she had ever asked for, never asking for more.

Yet, Tiberius loved her.

Her face flushed at this well-worn realization. She hardly could believe that this tall, Roman demigod of a man, in truth the most outstanding young man in Rome, could love her as much as he did. But, he did, and he showed it in a thousand little ways, and in just as many grand gestures as he could afford. She knew that it didn't matter that he was not the richest man in Rome, and not yet a senator. His star would rise without question, even his begrudging brother-in-law Scipio Aemilianus couldn't deny that. What thrilled Claudia here and now was Tiberius's unfailing devotion to her and the children. In her heart of hearts, she believed that if he could choose, he would rather stay at home with her than do what was necessary to rise in Rome's service. But, Rome must be served.

He stirred just as she was about to close the door. He rolled over and lifted his head to gaze at her, and she bounded across the tiles to pounce on him.

"You're caught!" she cried.

"Blessed be the gods, woman, you are killing me. Let me breathe!"

"Not until you do as I say as my bought and paid for slave."

"Your slave."

"Indeed. You must obey my every whim, or it will go badly for you."

"Obey you. I am your husband. Shouldn't it be you who heeds my beck and call?"

"Not here, not now. I am in command. Do as I say!"

He collapsed backwards. "What would you have me do, oh cruel, brutal Mistress?"

"Love me. Love me now."

"I love you always."

"Show me, then. Show me how you love me."

"Isn't this house, this family, enough? What more can I do?"

"Give me more!" She groped beneath the covers until she found what she was looking for. "Give me all, all over again!"

"Claudia," he squirmed, but she insinuated herself under the covers, then under him.

"Come, pleasure slave, do your work."

"Claudia, I have a busy day. Can we wait until we have more time?"

"No! What I have hold of says no, too. That's two against one, hah!"

He groaned, "If your parents ever heard the things you say now. They would disown you and prosecute me."

"As they should. Look what you have turned me into."

"I could never turn you into anything. I am powerless around you. I am your slave, the slave to your heart."

"Ah, poetry," she said sprightly, but she turned her head into his shoulder to hide her blushing face.

"No, it's true, just the unadorned truth."

Tiberius worked his arms around her to hold her close. He embraced her that way, still. She hugged him back, and they lay quietly for what seemed to be a long time.

"What must you do today?" she asked.

"I must go to the Forum. The Senate will take up Numantia. Our dear brother-in-law Scipio will castigate the generals who failed, and push for a return in force. He'll win. It's the only way."

"And, what will you do?"

"I don't know. I'll have to talk to your father. He'll want to suggest a candidate at least to share the command. I just need to know what role Father Appius has in mind for me."

"You'll meet him at the baths?"

"Your father loves the baths."

"All Romans love the baths, especially Roman men."

"The elders. Young men still train first, then bathe."

"So where do you fall?" she asked, digging him in the ribs.

"Why, somewhere between. I like to go to watch the young men train, then bathe."

She laughed at the conceit. Tiberius trained diligently, usually with Fannius, who acclaimed his friend as no shooting star, but a man among men. Claudia knew it was true from looking at him, his lean body and long muscles. He was known to be quick and strong, but it was his intelligence, too, that separated him from the other citizen warriors. Maybe he should be leading the legions to Numantia.

"Love me," she said.

"I thought we had finished that conversation."

"Love me now, before you must go."

"Claudia, don't you want us to have more time together?"

Staring deep into his clear blue eyes, she swayed her head back and forth, no. She reached to pull him above her.

As she left, barely pulling her robe around her naked back, Tiberius shook his head, wondering how he could love her so. Other men might overlook her, but he had never known another woman so perfect, so beautiful. Her eyes were so deep, violet wells of unquenchable question, highlighted as if a full moon shone upon them. Her deep chestnut hair was thick on the whole, often pulled to one side in a twist, yet each strand seemed as slender as a thread of the finest Egyptian linen. And her white skin carried a darker cast beneath, almost a royal purple to go with her royal eyes. Her figure was willowy full, narrow at the waist, but curved like a young, supple olive tree. Other women were more ample and blatantly desirable, but Claudia rushed desire in him through and through. She was beautiful in a way no other woman was, or could be, because there was only one Claudia. And, she loved him.

A knock on the door broke his reverie. "Come," beckoned Tiberius.

Polydius slipped into the room. "Are you ready, sir?"

"Ready for what? To pray to the gods, to kiss my wife and children, my mother? To see to the croplands, the pastures? To meet with my clients? To cross the river."

Polydius smiled, a warm, winning smile that saved him grace upon many an occasion.

"All these things are worthy of your attention, and your priorities seem to be in order, particularly leaving the last to last. However, I speak more of the quotidian, of observing the session in the Senate today, and all that therewith might occur. Pardon my prosaic inquiry in light of your poetic pondering, Master Gracchus."

"That's twice this morning I've been accused of committing poetry, Polydius, though the first time was much more satisfying. And, yes, of course I know you meant the Senate session. I know I've been a vast disappointment to you as a student, Polydius. However, I'm not that oblivious to what presses the day. Whether I'm ready for it or not is a question I am not yet ready to answer."

Polydius laughed, and Tiberius said, "I need to wash quickly before beginning the day. Call for Philea, and I'll jump to."

Polydius stepped forward, "If you wish to save time, I could wash you."

Tiberius, a tall man, looked up at the thin man towering above him. "Good Jupiter, you are a tall creature. But you will have to defer your base Greek ways, Polydius, I'm in a hurry."

"Master Tiberius, I have a woman who has gifted me with several children!"

"And who knows what you do with those vulnerable little ones, especially the boys, given your perverted inclinations. Quite some gifts, indeed."

"Sir Tiberius! I am a judicious father. You do me harm and wound me deeply."

"Laugh, Polydius, you are the butt of a joke rather than the butt of one of your aberrant countrymen. Know now how it feels to be in the middle of the melee rather than on the periphery, cooking it up."

Philea entered the bed chamber with a wooden stool and a jug of water, a thick, linen cloth draped over one shoulder. She stepped up on the stool and poured the water over Tiberius' head, who stood naked before her. She drenched him completely, then began wiping down, after which he threw on undergarments and a long house robe.

"Call the children to the Lararium for worship."

Tiberius left the bedroom to cross the house atrium to his mother's room. He hesitated, then scratched on the door.

"Mother, it's time to pray."

"Come."

He sighed, and opened the door to her room. She sat on a stool, gazing at the mural on the wall, Diana running with a stag through a meadow at the edge of a forest. Cornelia wore a deep blue robe, almost black, cut to the ankle and accentuating her slight, slender form when she stood.

"Mother, we are gathering for the morning devotion."

"Yes," she said. "Let us pray on this propitious day. Then, to the baths."

"Yes, mother, as is my habit daily, to train and cleanse myself."

"And to meet with your other mother Appius Claudius Pulcher."

"Mother, he is my father-in-law, and most distinguished senator."

"He prattles like a woman. Go to Scipio, Tiberius. He is a man among Romans."

"But not the only man, Mother, and not the only favorite. Too many resent him."

Cornelia looked up at her son for the first time, and sunk him with her unworldly beauty, her perfect skin, as cool a marble as any god's effigy, but alive with those green gem eyes that could see through to any man's soul, anyone's. A strand of her hair had escaped from the side of her hood, proving she was human, spun gold though it was, flecked with platinum.

"You speak of Sempronia."

"She is unhappy with Scipio."

"Many wives are unhappy with their husbands, Tiberius. Roman women do not marry for happiness."

"Were you unhappy with Father?" he asked.

Cornelia's eyes half closed in long held sorrow. "No, no. I was not unhappy with your father." Then, opening them wide, she said, "No woman could be unhappy with the man he was. He was first in Rome! A true Roman, your father. There was no one like him."

Nor ever will be, thought Tiberius.

She paused, then said, "Sit with me, Tiberius, just for a little while."

He searched around, and pulled up a servant's stool next to her chair. She took both his hands in hers. "You could be like him, Tiberius, the next great man. You could outshine all of them, even Scipio. Oh, I know that your brother-in-law is bold and sly at the same time, but perhaps too much for his own good. I know, too, that Sempronia is unhappy, and that makes you unhappy. You're such a good brother that way. But, if you take your chance, you will surpass Scipio, I am sure of it. Once you do, Sempronia can divorce him. For now, though, your future is at sea, and Scipio is a necessary stepping stone to your success."

Tiberius marveled silently while she talked. His father had married the right woman for his ambition, and not just because Scipio Africanus had been her father. If she had been a man, she would have outrivaled her husband for honor. As fate would have it, she had been his greatest counselor.

"Numantia," Cornelia said. "You must go to Numantia. After the dog's dinner that Pompeius, Servillianus, and Caepio made of their campaigns there, the Roman people are incensed. They want Hispania brought to its knees, and the Senate hears them. Conquer Numantia, and Rome is yours."

She referred to the mishaps of the recent governors of Hispania. Servillianus had been thoroughly out-generaled by the tribal leader Viriathus and was forced to sign a peace treaty. Servillianus' successor Caepio immediately scorned the treaty only to be soundly thrashed in turn himself, though he did manage to arrange to have Viriathus assassinated by his own tribesmen. And Pompeius proved to be so incompetent that the best he could do was make a deal with the various Hispanic tribes, trading peace for a bribe to fill his personal coffers.

"Mother, dearest, my father triumphed after his conquest of Hispania, and look where we are now. In any case, I can't conquer Hispania, I've never been more than a military tribune. Someone else will have to do it."

"Scipio, of course. He'll be sent to crush the Numantines. And you must be quaestor to Scipio's legions."

Tiberius frowned. "Scipio will not be sent to Hispania. I promise you, he will not get the support."

"Oh?" she said, eyes askance. "Appius is stirring up the pot, I suppose. That might not be the wisest course. If Scipio doesn't go, who will? Without Scipio, reducing Numantia could be a difficult proposition."

"Nonsense, Mother, there are plenty of capable military men in the sdenate besides Scipio."

"Really? As good as Servillianus? As good as Caepio? Certainly not Pompeius again. Perhaps you think your illustrious father-in-law would do the trick."

Tiberius fidgeted impatiently. "No, of course not. Appius knows his limitations. But there are others, excellent candidates."

Again, Cornelia gazed at him skeptically. "You need to be quaestor in Numantia." She grimaced, "If Appius thinks he will win out, fine. But, visit with Scipio, too. He likes you, he hasn't forgotten your courage at Carthage."

"Mother, that was almost a decade ago."

"He hasn't forgotten. You should not forget him, either."

Tiberius rose to his feet. "Mother, it is time to pray."

"Indeed," she said.

Although situated halfway up the Palatine, the Sempronii Gracchi house presented a modest, traditional appearance among the newer, more imposing residences. A heavy door opened up upon a narrow, open-aired vestibulum flanked by four simple columns encircled by flowering vines. At the end, another door led to a larger foyer for receiving visitors and guests. Tiberius' office and library were off to the left, opposite to the reception and dining room on the right, with the kitchen behind them. The atrium in the center displayed flowers in narrow beds and trellises next to stone benches, and tile paths on either side of a small pond in the middle led to a fountain, a statue of a youth pouring water from a curved pitcher in the Greek style. The bed chambers flanked the atrium, Tiberius's in front near his office, with Claudia next to him, and the children's room next to hers. Gaius occupied the bedroom across from Tiberius, Cornelia's was next to his, and Polydius slept in a corner room closest to the other servants' quarters, a row of three rooms in the back. It was crowded, and they sometimes talked of moving to a larger home. But, the humility taught him long ago by Diophanes prevented them. Because of this, they had been forced to locate the Lararium and the family shrine in the hall connecting the kitchen and the servant's other workrooms.

Everyone took their place in front of the Lararium. Tiberius' brother Gaius passed him, brushing his shoulder hard as he walked by. Tiberius looked back at him sternly, and the youngster, also tall with dark hair, smirked as he took his place. Claudia and the other women gathered to Tiberius' left side, the servants and other men to his right, the children directly behind him. Cornelia entered the long hallway that served as their sanctuary and moved slowly to his side to sit on a small stool.

Seeing that all were present, Tiberius turned away and hooded his head with his robe. He raised his arms in supplication as he faced the small shrine, a marble tabletop filled with the figurines of the gods of Rome. He chanted a brief prayer to Vesta, the goddess of the hearth, then to Jupiter Maximus. He prayed to the Lares, the household gods. Then, he stepped to either side of the table and opened the small cabinet doors to reveal the masks of the family ancestors. He opened his father's last, and as soon as his countenance appeared, Cornelia left her stool and knelt before the waxen image. Slowly, she prostrated herself in front of the first Tiberius Sempronius's mask, weeping silently as she did every day. Tiberius the younger sighed to himself, stepped back to kneel and bow, praying this time to the goddess Fortuna.

Chapter 2. The Paullian Baths

Polydius trailed Tiberius by a few paces, quiet in the wake of his preoccupied master. Behind Polydius came the house slave Lysis, who carried a bag slung over his shoulder containing Tiberius's gear for the baths. Tiberius absent-mindedly stepped around the refuse and waste in the street, no doubt deep in thought about the upcoming meeting with his father-in-law Appius Claudius Pulcher. He had spent the morning with his business manager, trying to grasp how he could ring out a few more sestertii from a very small holding north of the city. Towering in the background, Polydius shook his head imperceptibly as he listened to his master ply the foreman with question after question. Plant more crops; the land will be worn out and yield nothing after five years. Rotate to pasture; your current yields will be halved. Make up the difference by raising more livestock; you can't grow enough to feed more animals.

Polydius knew that there was only one solution to his master's troubles, more land. Unfortunately, he didn't have the capital to purchase more land, and he couldn't generate it because of the tight budget mandated by the modest earnings from the farm. Polydius sighed to himself, Tiberius had been an excellent student, an enthusiastic explorer of the aesthetic of austerity. But, now he was a practitioner out of necessity. The only thing that would change this dynamic was the Roman way, war, conquest, tribute. Tiberius needed to go to war, which is why he would meet with Appius today.

They made their way out of the shadows of the large apartment buildings flanking the narrow street into an open space, the front of a large plaza with a grand facade of brightly colored columns, different hued, marbled walls, with three arched entryways, the middle one a third larger than the flanking two, signifying it as the main entrance to the Paullian Baths. Tribute from the first Macedonian War 30 years ago had funded the impressive building complex, sponsored by one of the consuls at the time, Lucius Amelius Paullus Macedonicus. Paullus's natural son Scipio Aemilianus also distinguished himself at his father's side in the war. Thereafter, Scipio Africanus adopted him, making him Tiberius's cousin, while his ensuing marriage to Sempronia made him his brother-in-law as well. Ah, the tortuous lineage of the Romans, Polydius laughed to himself.

Of course, Macedonia always had been generous to Rome, he mused ironically. Twenty years later, the new Roman conqueror Quintus Caecilius Metellus triumphed again in Alexander's native land, which earned him the honorific Macedonicus as well. Not to be outdone by Paullus, Metellus used some of his spoils to fund Rome's first ever temples constructed entirely out of marble, one for Jupiter and the other for Juno. He decorated them with statues of Alexander's generals on horse, also procured from Greece.

The three men headed toward the main entrance, past vendors with sweet cakes and hot meat on sharp sticks, others selling hot water and honey, or wine if preferred. Street prostitutes beckoned from near the grand doorway, kept at a distance by the private guards, who simultaneously accepted regular bribes from high-priced courtesans for access. Tiberius usually headed to the apodyterium to change, and then to the paleastra to train, but this time he sped directly to the hot pool where he knew that his father-in-law would be lounging, no doubt his feet dangling in the hot waters. Lysis took his place in the changing room to guard Tiberius' belongings, while Polydius followed the young scion down the passageway toward the caldarium. The walls of the arched hallway displayed cheerful murals of family life, and athletes boxing or throwing the javelin. One wall presented a vivid depiction of a lively boar hunt. As they reached the doorway for the hot baths, Tiberius patted a stone phallus on one of the columns for luck.

They peered through the rising steam, searching for Appius among the dozen or so men sitting in and around the rectangular pool. "Tiberius," Polydius said, pointing to a corner where Appius Claudius Pulcher sat wrapped in a white linen sheet, his feet indeed soaking in the soothing water of the pool. Flushed from the heat, Appius naturally was as brown as a nut, his black hair just barely touched by grey. A handsome man in his day, he shaved regularly to show off his fine features, now lined somewhat by the creases of time and experience.

Tiberius marched over and Appius slowly raised his eyes and opened his arms. Tiberius stepped into the water to embrace the older man, kissing his cheeks as he said, "Dear Father-in-Law."

"Tiberius, my son," responded Appius, who kissed him heartily in turn. Tiberius then greeted the other men grouped around Appius: the two brothers, Publius Lincinus Crassus Dives Mucianus, lean and craggy with something of a hangdog face, a princeps senatus like Appius who embraced fastidiousness both in fashion and in political deliberations. His older step-brother Publius Mucius Scaevola impressed in exactly the opposite way, a short, arrogantly handsome and sleekly muscled man who whenever possible enjoyed displaying his physique in short tunics. He also possessed an attraction to money, even though the Crassus family owned one of the great fortunes in Rome.

Gaius Blossius, the philosopher from Cuma, who had studied with the Stoic Antipater of Tarsus, greeted Tiberius warmly in turn. The only one sporting a beard, its reddish tinge and his pale eyes caused Romans to wonder if Blossius's family blood hadn't been tainted somewhere along the line by barbarians from the north. Being fair-skinned with black hair, Tiberius was more than familiar with such speculation, though speculation about his origin centered on the Hispancic tribes located in the Alps.

They all took their seats around the pool, Tiberius sitting in the middle next to Appius, noticing that only Diophanes, the rhetorician exiled from Mitylene, had yet to appear. Polydius assumed a standing position just behind his master.

"Your arrival is timely, Tiberius," said Appius. "We were just discussing the situation in Numantia, and how best to address
Scipio's obvious ambition."

Tiberius nodded.

"It's a difficult matter," Crassus leaned in to say "since Scipio's reputation casts the longest shadow in Rome." The gangly senator's few remaining strands of hair clung to his skull from perspiration. Still, it was all brown hair, and the hollows in his cranium plainly had little to do with the sharpness of his wit.

"Yes, but we have resources of our own," Appius said. A robust man in his day, Appius wore his pedigree with elan, comfortable in the spread of his body from the good life that accompanied age. No one doubted the iron within this man's soft exterior, or his will to prevail. But, the grey of his hair and the laugh lines at his eyes proposed a gentle demeanor, too, a promise of mercy that would temper his power.

"Now, we expect that blowhard Rufus to set the stage for Scipio, raging on about the Numantine transgressions, the need to subjugate them, and so forth. Thereafter, another stooge will stand up for a resolution, followed by the cry for Scipio. That's when we must interject our own man's name."

"All well and good," said Scaevola, "except how will we persuade the others that our man is more of a general than the Hero of Carthage?"

"We have the Hero right here," Appius said, slapping Tiberius on the knee.

"Please, Father-in-Law," Tiberius said, "I'm hardly a hero. Some would say I left before the job was done."

"Before the butchery was done, you mean."

"Yes," said Scaevola, a slight, dark man with dark, corkscrew hair over all of his body, his head capped by an equally dark crown of curls. His fitness belied his profession, explained better by the intensity of his black eyes when he spoke. "But Tiberius is right. He won honor in Africa, but he has never run a campaign."

"No, but his father did, successfully, in Numantia. He is his father's son and should follow in his footsteps to tame today's rebellious Numantines."

"Certainly, we all are in agreement on that," Crassus said impatiently, "but how do we deflect Scipio from being chosen?"

Just then Diophanes arrived, gliding in as though he floated rather than walked. Without a word, he sat at the far end of the pool next to Scaevola.

"Ah, Diophanes," Appius said, turning to the small man, "you've arrived at last. We are discussing the disposition of Numantia. Do you have a stratagem to put forth?"

Diophanes wore a dark blue robe with an even darker, squared-off border, and simple sandals. His grey-streaked hair had been pulled back hard from his crown and bound at the back of his head like a thick shuck of wheat. Despite the heat of the pool, he seemed cool compared to the others.

"My words shape thought, not worlds. It seems I've come at an inopportune juncture. Thus, I take it, it is time to take my leave."

The others chuckled, "Your leave-taking accomplishes nothing except perhaps the departure of the best mind in the room," Appius said. "But, we wouldn't want you indicted by thoughts of ours that you have not shaped. If you could be so kind, and also have Tiberius's man Polydius accompany you?"

Tiberius frowned, but Polydius nodded and walked with Diophanes back toward the front of the building.

"So," said Appius resumed, "how do we stop Scipio from marching to Numantia?

The men drew closer together to speak in low voices, the steam from the pool obscuring their features as they planned.

Tiberius found Diophanes and Polydius sitting on a wooden bench that encircled a large, shady elm tree, sipping a fish broth from fired-clay bowls.

"Your breakfast, or an early midday meal?" Tiberius asked.

"Nourishment, no matter when," replied Diophanes without raising his eyes. "Although my beard does seem to be dining better than the rest of my body. And how went the skullduggery?"

"There is a plan in place." Tiberius shook his head no at the bowl proffered by Polydius. "And, its execution begins today."

Polydius put down his bowl without finishing, and began to rise, but Tiberius stopped him, "No, no, finish, finish! We still have a few hours before the Senate convenes. I'm going back inside to train. I have to do something to keep my mind occupied."

Polydius stood up with Diophanes, who said, "I'll be going home then, Tiberius."

"Nonsense. Sit with Polydius, talk to him about Greece. You've been there most recently, you can tell him the latest about your homeland. He'll want to return some day after his manumission."

"You are kind," said Diophanes flatly. "Let the gods will he lives so long."

Tiberius frowned. "Of course he will. If he keeps to his duties, it will be sooner rather than later."

He turned and went back into the baths.

In the palaestra, Tiberius found a small army of men exercising in various ways, some tossing the heavy ball, others running short sprints, while others practiced gymnastic maneuvers. The sun shone between the ribs of the grills on the narrow windows at the top of the stone walls, causing a ripple effect on the sandy floor. Where it fell, the sand was warm, though it remained cool in the shadows closest to the walls. As with every part of Paullus's baths, the palaestra seemed endless in length and size, marveled Tiberius, fit for chariot races. Indeed, at intervals of fifty paces, indented alcoves housed the most exquisite copies of Greece's most beautiful statues, Jupiter casting his thunderbolts, Mercury spiriting across the sky, Apollo shooting his bow, Diana leaping after an invisible hart, Hercules grappling with the horns of the Cretan bull.

Tiberius handed his tunic to Lysis, and began to stretch. As he did so, he heard a commotion from a circle of men a good hundred feet away. Bent over his right leg, he peered at them as they hooted and howled. Gradually, he made out who they were, young and middle-age men of affluence, plebeian and patrician alike, all vying for various positions on the cursus honorum, the highest offices on the path to prestige in Rome. One happened to turn and see him, and smiled. Marcus Octavius could smile, Tiberius thought, enough to warm up a mountain stream. Dark-haired and dark-skinned, with a shaggy black beard to boot, it was a wonder they hadn't nicknamed him Nubius; perhaps his smile forestalled such a jibe.

He started toward Tiberius, revealing a hitch in his gait as he walked, which made Tiberius frown. In Macedonia, Marcus had caught an arrow in his calf which must have been dirty. The infection shriveled up his leg, causing him to limp. But, he never complained, and he refused to allow it to keep him from pursuing the art of combat.

"Tiberius, come save the day," he said when he arrived. "Your cousin Nasica is destroying all competition."

Tiberius allowed his gaze to drift over to the large circle of men. Publius Cornelius Scipio Nasica, consul with Brutus Callicus, and also his distant cousin through Sempronia's marriage to Scipo Aemilianus, squared off with another man in the center. A follower of the Hero of Carthage, Nasica was distant in more than one way, thought Tiberius.

"I've just arrived, Octavius. I've barely begun to warm up. And, in any case, I'm no wrestler."

"But, he's cutting a ruthless swathe through all of the good men of Rome! No one can stand up to him!" laughed Octavius.

"What about you, Octavius? You're good for a throw or two."

"He's dropped me on my ass twice already, in less time than it took to tell you. Only you can save our honor, Tiberius Gracchus," and he began to raise the call, "Gracchus, Gracchus, Tiberius Gracchus!"

Others in the circle heard him and turned, then joined in, smiling as they cried out his name. Tiberius pressed his lips together, and continued with his stretching, annoyed. Nasica had always been keen on athletics, winning many a laurel wreath in his youth for various sports and skills. Now, here he was, a consul of Rome, carrying on like a common tumbler, and all his sycophants lining up to roll over for him. And, Tiberius would have to lose, too, even if he had a chance to beat him. Nasica was consul.

He had no stomach for the entire farce. Let the braggart toss the others around. He would not take a fall for his fatuous cousin even if he was a consul of Rome. He began breathing in and out, swinging his arms around and into his chest. But the shouting went on and on.

The group of chanting men parted and Nasica walked through, his sun-browned body glistening from sweat mixed with oil, his curly black hair held close to his head by a leather band. He stood as tall as Tiberius, but his shoulders were wider, while his waist was narrow. He posed with his fists on his hips and smiled as Tiberius continued with his stretching.

"Salve, cousin, are you next to submit to my might?"

"I am not, Consul Nasica. You must excuse me, but I have my routine, and it's best for me to keep to it."

Nasica frowned. "What, are you running from me, Gracchus? You're acting like you did when you bolted from Carthage, just because of a little blood."

Tiberius felt a burn begin to rise, but he forced himself to maintain his outward composure. He gestured to Lysis, who left for one of the equipment racks against the wall.

"Oh, now, you can't say that, Consul," Marcus admonished lightly, "Tiberius won the Mural Crown at Carthage, first over the wall."

Nasica seemed to consider the point. "True. But, they were all starving scarecrows by then, thanks to Scipio's brilliant strategy in cordoning off the city. They were so weak. Anyone could have been first, even you, Marcus, gimp and all."

Marcus grinned, pulling himself up straight, "Oh so, Consul? Then, we must wonder why you weren't first at Carthage? How did a seventeen-year-old like Tiberius beat you to the Mural Crown?"

Nasica scowled, raising his head as if to look further down at Marcus. "I attended Scipio as ordered. Otherwise, Marcus, I assure you I would have been first over the wall and first into the Citadel. The latter was an opportunity lost to Gracchus because of his too fastidious nature when faced with the realities of war. But, let's not stray too far from the matter at hand, Romans. Gracchus refuses a match," he said, gesturing to Tiberius, who had begun throwing the heavy ball back and forth with Lysis. "So, I guess I must subdue you, again, Marcus. Are you ready?"

Marcus smiled and said, "Oh, yes, Consul, this time I'm ready to upend you."

He charged at Nasica, who met him with his chest, grappling his arms under Marcus, then rolling his back sideways to lift the smaller man off of his feet. Nasica threw him hard to the sand, and stumbling, stepped on his bad leg. Marcus' head snapped back as he cried out, almost in rage at the pain. The others rushed to him as Nasica stood, looking down at him.

"Sorry, Marcus," Nasica said, "I lost my footing."

Tiberius tossed the ball hard to Lysis, who stepped back to keep his balance before lobbing it back.

"If you're all right, Marcus, come, get up and I'll throw you again."

Marcus exhaled, and said, "All right, but I won't be that easy again."

Girding himself, Marcus stood, his face set hard, until he lurched to one side.

"Are you sure? You look a little drunk on your feet," said Nasica, and the other men laughed.

"Come, do your worst," said Marcus.

"Seems I already have," Nasica said, bringing more laughter from the men.

"Attack, Consul!"

But before Nasica could close, Tiberius broke in. "Enough wrestling, Consul, you've clearly swept the field. Why don't you play catch with me instead?"

Nasica turned to Tiberius and looked him up and down. "You'll make a fabulous lawyer, Tiberius. All right, do your best. Throw the ball."

Tiberius nodded to Lysis, who heaved the ball to him, then moved out of the way. Tiberius raised the ball and lobbed it to Nasica, who caught it easily, then half-turned and catapulted it back. Tiberius took the full brunt of the heavy ball in his midsection. It doubled him over and sent him staggering backwards, nearly falling to the sand. The men around them shouted their surprise, then clapped and cheered as they saw Tiberius regain his balance.

Nasica laughed, then said, "I guess it's your turn again, cousin. I suppose now you'll do your worst. Very well," he said, crouching with his arms spread, "send it."

Tiberius paused, frowning. Abruptly, he lifted the ball above his head and charged, roaring. Nasica blinked as he saw the crazed man rushing down on him. He put his hands over his head to take the brunt of the coming blow. Still screaming, Tiberius closed with him brandishing the ball high up, until suddenly, he stopped, and said, "Here," gently placing the ball on Nasica's outstretched hands. Nasica fumbled, trying to control the ball's weight at the awkward angle; he lost his footing, and fell back sitting in the sand.

The group of men stilled themselves, and Tiberius held his breath, ready for anything without being ready at all. Nasica peered up at Tiberius looming over him, and quietly laughed, almost a giggle. The rest of them broke into a howling wave of laughter, almost hysteria of mirth.

"By the gods, cousin," Nasica said, "you are a slippery one. Remind me to stick to wrestling next time." Tiberius stretched out his hand, and Nasica reached up. He made a sudden stabbing move with it, "Hah?" and Tiberius pulled back. "Hah!" said Nasica, holding his hand out again. Tiberius pulled him up, and they embraced as the other men applauded and cheered.

They kissed each other on each cheek, and broke. "Good Romans, it's time to prepare for the afternoon session," said Nasica. "You'll join us soon; I'm sure, Tiberius, in a few years. Vale," and he strolled away with the other men.

Marcus hung back. He threw an arm around Tiberius' shoulder, and squeezed, whispering, "Slippery indeed. More like a fox than a snake, I'd say."

"I'm faint," Tiberius said, "I need a nice, long soak in the caldarium myself."

"But, surely you'll be attending the Senate today? They will debate the Numantine problem without question."

Tiberius. "I've had enough excitement," Tiberius said, turning to walk away, his head down. "I'm sure I'll learn soon enough about Numantia, just like everyone else. Lysis, to the tepidarium. I need a good scraping and a glass of wine."

Chapter 3: The Curia Hostilia

Polydius made his way from the baths through the side streets to the Via Sacra, which soon brought him to the southern end of the Forum. Across the busy causeway flanked by the basilicas he could see the curia that the ancient Hostilius had built, where the Senate would meet soon, his final destination. First, though, he thought to visit the Vulcanal and offer a prayer for his master's success in the coming session. He slipped around a side of the dust-colored, stone hump of the horseshoe-shaped shrine and crossed the black marble path at its entrance to stand in front of its ancient stone altar. Next to it, the god stared down at him from its blood-red marble pillar, bent, ugly, but fierce in its inspection of mere mortals. Polydius bowed low to Vulcan, the Roman god of fire, really Hephastus, of course. The Romans stole everything from us Greeks, including our gods. They changed their names and called them their own, but every Greek knew, and sent their prayers from Rome to the true home of the gods, Olympus, in Greece.

Though, Polydius was devoted to Gracchus, a kind man who might someday set him free, but mostly because the master was so gentle to all around him. So, he prayed for him in this old, weird shrine. It struck him as some arcane altar where who-knew-what was sacrificed by the barbaric chieftains of these violent people's violent ancestors. As he silently recited, he found it difficult to keep from peering around at the dark sanctuary, his eyes drawn to the archaic Lapis Niger and its inscriptions of Roman Kings summoning the gods to protect the city. He admonished himself, thinking that he could have gone to any other temple of the many nearby. He could go to Concordia's, to Saturn's, to that of the glorified heroes Castor and Pollux. Or, he could walk a little farther afield, to the glorious marble edifice newly built for Jupiter Strator on the Campus Martius. But the work today called for a fiery, earthbound spirit to shake free the gods from their conventions. Fire could do that; it was fire that was needed. That is, if a god could be roused to do anything at all for any man, he thought.

Polydius heard the herald from the steps of the Curia call the midday hour, and knew that the session would begin soon. He concluded his prayer, and hurried across the square toward the Senate building, passing amid the wedged stalls of food, wine, and other goods on sale, dodging the barkers popping up in front of him to push their wares. He hiked quickly up past the Rostrum festooned with the prows of Carthagian ships sunk in battle, and past the graecostasis, the Rostrum for foreign orators, where his own, free countrymen would speak, or wait their turn until the Senate summoned them.

At last, he reached the Curia Hostilia, and just in time. He found a good place at a low window that looked in on the great Roman seat of power. Literally the seat or seats, he acknowledged to himself, as he gazed at the rows of chairs and benches set high upon six sets of concentric stone steps curving around the ornately decorated marble floor. Opposite the ziggurat of rows stood the two curule chairs for the consuls. Some of the senators had arrived early to discuss strategies and form pacts, but most would drift in, still digesting their second repast. It would be a long wait, but Polydius understood that to find the best vantage point for witnessing the session, he had to be the first there. True, any citizen could supplant him, which would make the effort all for nothing. However, he had to trust to luck and his relatively good tunic to deter this from happening. Upon that thought, he lowered his long frame to cross his arms on the window sill, and waited.

As soon as the two consuls, Scipo Nasica and Junius Brutus walked to their chairs, Nasica, also the Pontifex Maximus, arose to conduct the blessing of Rome and the Senate in its work. He sat, and Brutus, the presiding consul for the day, stood to open the afternoon session. He then gave the floor to Publius Rufus Faba, a short, fat, pasty man who perfectly fit the nickname that they called him in the streets, "Rufus Fava Bean." Rufus began to address at last the topic that had all of the windows and doorways of the Curia overflowing with people, and more spilling out back into the Forum square.

"Senators of Rome: our city prospers, our people flourish, our star nears its zenith." The members all applauded in unison, but Rufus quelled them with his outstretched hands, pressing them down in front of him, "Near the zenith, citizens, near, but not there yet. For Hispania still defies us, especially the Numantines."

He paused for effect.

"The Numantines flout Roman rule and flaunt their independence," cried Rufus, his feet planted apart on the checkered marble floor. "They refuse to submit their tariff, they pillory Roman collectors, and they incite their neighbors to join them in defying Rome!"

The other senators grumbled and barked their agreement and discontent.

"I say that we cannot accept such impudence from a conquered people. We cannot allow them to set this example for our other provinces to see. Think of what the other barbarian tribes must be thinking. Think of what the Italians must think!"

The grumbling turned into a loud chorus, "No!" "An outrage!" Sedition!"

"There is only one response to such blatant defiance of Rome. The sword!"

The chamber burst into riotous noise, and Rufus raised his voice to be heard above the tumult. "I say to you, fellow senators, we must act and act now to bring Numantia to its knees before the other tribes join them! We must send the legions to Hispania to make a lasting example of them for all to see!"

Another senator, Marcus Livius Drusus, lifted himself from his seat and stepped onto the floor. His satin hair, sharp eyes, and his quarter-moon curved nose highlighted a countenance common to many of his illustrious Drusii ancestors. A recent convert to Stoicism and the causes of Rome's neediest, Drusus represented the most extreme member of the Populares faction. Appius and the Mucius brothers stood with Drusus, though more as centrist Populares. Together, though, they constituted the arch opponents of the patrician Otimates, the "Good Men" who thought that the order of things in Rome was correct, proper, and blessed by the gods.

Drusus hiked the crimson edge of his toga further up his shoulder in a deliberate signal of his rank and dignity, and began.

"Senator Rufus Faba," stated Drusus in a clear, calm voice that, for all of its even modulation, carried well throughout the large space. "Why do you insist upon extreme measures for the slightest offense? When a child of yours steals a sweet, do you slice off his offending thumb and finger to make your point? The greater issues of blood and hatred are of no consequence to you? They will be to Rome, if we determine to go to Hispania and destroy this small nation.

"The great Tiberius Sempronius Gracchus Major defeated the Numantines, a remarkable feat."

At the mention of his master's father, Polydius shrunk against the window, momentarily feeling as if all eyes turned upon him. But, of course, they paid him no attention at all.

"More remarkable, he made a peace with them that they could accept as honorable, not onerous. Most of the Hispanic tribes complied without incident for decades, a wondrous record for such warlike people, true barbarians. But the greed of the praetors who followed Gracchus undermined his working peace. Lucullus and Galba's atrocities, Caepio's treachery, Pompeius's indiscretions, and many other transgressions have shamed Rome. Worse, they left an unstable region in their wake despite subsequent victories by Metellus Macedonicus. We are untrustworthy in peace, senators.

"Should it be surprising, then, even for a small tribe to rebel? They have reason to rise up. And, if they foolishly challenge Rome's might again, should we scorch the earth and thereby destroy the possibility of any future gain from them?"

"What would you do, then, Drusus," Rufus said scornfully: "relieve them of their responsibility to Rome? What would the barbarians learn from that?"

"Hardly," rejoined Drusus blandly. "In the tradition of Gracchus, let us send a peace contingent to Numantia to see if they can be persuaded to mend their ways. After exercising bravado for their neighbors's sake, the Numantines might think twice about engaging our formidable forces. Through a deliberated offering of sweets with the sword suspended overhead, our emissaries might be able to bring them around without shedding blood or destroying property."

"Ludicrous!" shouted Rufus. "They will laugh in our faces. We cannot go bent-backed and craven to these savages and ask them please to behave!"

"Thank you for interrupting me, Senator Rufus. As I was proposing, we need not depend solely upon a diplomatic venture. While our representatives endeavor to induce the Numantines to submit, we can bolster our legions at the same time in case force becomes necessary."

"They're all the same, these Hispanic rebels, due to their inbreeding," scoffed Rufus. "How long do you think that the Lusitanians or any of the other Hispanic dogs will sit still if they see Numantia flick their chin hair at us with impunity? Furthermore, reinforcing our legions will take too long, and only get the savages' blood up to attack us first. No, patriarchs of Rome, I say we cannot wait on sniveling diplomacy, or the fancy of adding more legions, as if that would be necessary. Our matchless Roman legionaries are not at fault, it is the leadership that is lacking. I say we must punish the Numantines now, with the superb army that we have in the field under the best general that Rome has to offer. I call for a division!"

The great hall of the Curia Hostilia burst into furor as the senators shouted out their support or derision, until Brutus pounded the floor with his staff.

"To order, senators, to order. Recognizing Senator Catullus."

"I second the call for a division," Catullus called out.

"A call for division has been seconded," Brutus announced. He peered around to Nasica, who sat still. Brutus raised his voice, "All in favor of immediate military action against the Numantines, to the right. All opposed, to the left."

Polydius watched as more than two-thirds of the Senate took positions on the right, including Appius Claudius Pulcher and most of the other Populares. Only fifty senators joined Livius Drusus on the left.

"The motion is passed. Rome will march upon Numantia, gods be willing."

Even from his obstructed view, Polydius could see Rufus preening over his victory.

The senators returned to their seats, and Appius stood up. "Consul, may I have the floor?"

Brutus nodded, and Appius continued. "Senators of Rome, we have determined to assert our rights in Hispania overwhelmingly. This is a noble day for this sacred body. Let the gods smile down upon our endeavor. But the gods shall not execute this war for us. No, the sinew and blood of our valiant legionaries again will be risked for the greater glory of Rome. Let us not chance wasting them against the Numantine brutes through indifferent leadership, as has happened too often in the past. No, Roman patriarchs, it is our duty to send the most capable of generals to destroy these rebels once and for all."

Polydius held his breath; here it was coming, Appius Claudius Pulcher's nomination of Hostilius Mancinus to command in Numantia, the key to Master Tiberius's future.

"Fellow Romans, senators, there can be only one champion sent to Numantia: Publius Cornilius Scipio Aemilianus, conqueror of Carthage. No one else will do."

Tiberius sat in the peristylum with Claudia and his mother, eating some fruit and sipping from a small pot of vegetable broth as he pondered his fate.

"Tiberius, you are picking, not eating."

"Yes, Mother. I'm not ferociously hungry."

"But, you just exercised," she pointed out.

"True, but my appetite fails me. Too much on my mind, I suppose."

Claudia leaned into him, her beautiful eyes again riveting his attention with their loving concern. "Don't worry, Tiberius. It will work out as designed."

"I wish I could be so sure," he sighed.

"Now, now," she said, placing her hand on his forearm, "it will, and if it doesn't this time, it only means you'll have to stay here at home with me a little longer. Is that so terrible?" she said, smiling. But, he could see the worry behind her eyes. She'd much rather he stayed at home than go to the wilds of Hispania.

He smiled wanly, "Of course, my love. Either way is good for me."

"Huh!" Cornelia expelled. "Either way is not good for you; you must go to Numantia. These opportunities do not come as often as they used to, Rome has been too successful in its domination. If you don't go now, you may never go. No, Numantia is the key to your future, not lying around this house with your wife, creating more mouths to feed. You must go to Numantia!"

Polydius burst in, breathless from his run-walking pace to get there as soon as he could.

Tiberius shot up from his bench. "Well, Polydius? How did it go?"

The tall Greek bent over to grasp his knees, pulling in breath as fast as he could.

"Get him wine, Lysis. Sit, Polydius, sit and tell us what happened."

Polydius gulped, and said, "You won't believe what I have to say—an amazing, bizarre mash of events. Amazing!"

"All right, enough theatrics; tell us what happened," snapped Cornelia. "Is Tiberius going to Hispania or isn't he?"

"No, Mother, let him tell it in his own way, from the beginning." She glowered at him, but he held up his hand and shook his head. Sullenly, she sat back to listen.

"Astonishing," said Polydius. "Well, then. I made my way to the Senate building early, to get a good vantage point...."

As the Senate members roared their approval, Polydius almost fell over the ledge of the window into the Senate chamber, so stunned was he by Appius's nomination. Scipio! Tiberius' despised brother-in-law, the last one he would want as his commaner, and the last to have him as quaestor in Numantia. What was Appius thinking? It was unthinkable that he would betray his beloved son-in-law.

The uproar went on, almost riotous, with some senators virtually frothing at the mouth and grinding their teeth in excitement. The tumult subsided, however, when Nasica rose to his full height. "Senators, I regret to inform you, in anticipation of the possibility of such a series of events, that the great Scipio Aemilianus has asked me, on his behalf, to humbly thank the Senate for this honor," and he paused while Polydius cringed, "which he cannot accept."

The Senate's celebration dissipated as though it swirled down a drain in the marble floor, while Polydius' bewilderment mushroomed.

Nasica quieted the ensuing murmurs in the building, and the shouts of "No!" and "Scipio alone!"

"Senators, senators, Roman fathers, please stay your dissent. Scipio gratefully declines this honor due to personal promises he has made that conflict with his devotion to the Republic. He begs your forbearance, but previous service to Rome has led him to neglect domestic duties. Also, the Destroyer of Carthage firmly believes that his past glories suffice, and that subduing Numantia should be an opportunity given to one of Rome's many other capable generals, of which our great city has a surfeit. Indeed, Scipio asks this noble body to grant him a moratorium on his service so that he may straighten out his private affairs while cheering on our other worthy sons of Rome."

"Now," said Tiberius, interrupting Polydius's account, "why do you think he did that? And why did Appius propose him in the first place?"

"I haven't an inkling," said Polydius, cooled off after his dash home from the Curia Hostilia, and now looking reflective.

"And, in the name of Jupiter, why did my father-in-law propose Scipio in the first place?"

"Simple, Tiberius, my boy," said Appius as he swept into the peristylum, "Nasica told me that Scipio wouldn't go, though he wouldn't tell me the real reason. You should have seen our glorious consul's expression, as though he'd bitten down on a bitter herb. Dour, dour he was! And things didn't get better for him after that when I nominated Hostilius Mancinus as the only possible replacement for Scipio. Nasica nearly spit!"

Appius allowed his rumbling laughter to shake all the way through him, causing his generous body to ripple like a walking lake. "Of course, with Scipio out of the running, Mancinus was recruited straightaway. It was like a dream," he exulted. "And, you, most beloved son-in-law, are going to Numantia as his quaestor! The notices will be posted for the Comitia Centuria assembly to vote for the coming year's offices in one week. Mancinus will be elected consul, and you will grab hold of his toga to be elected quaestor at the same time. It has been arranged!"

The household broke into shouts and applause, and Tiberius felt his face flushing, looking at them all as they smiled and congratulated him. Gaius punched him in the arm, which hurt, and little Tiberius and Cornelia rushed to grab his legs, happily oblivious to what was being celebrated. Claudia smiled broadly, too, though he could see the apprehension in her eyes. But, she tossed her head and beamed at him her happiness for him and her pride. He grinned and laughed, gripping Appius and Gaius' hands awkwardly over his son, Tiberius, and tiny Cornelia. He swept his eyes around the applauding people in the room until his sight rested upon his mother Cornelia. She sat without even the slightest effort to disguise her disinterest. Tiberius's smile froze, all of his pleasure washed away by the impatient expression on her face.

"A celebration!" exclaimed Appius, "Daughter, if I may; Lysis, run to my house and tell Mistress Antistia that we dine with our son and daughter tonight. Then, go fetch Crassus, Scaevola, Blossius, and Diophanes. See if Drusus wants to come, too, though I doubt it. Philea, to the market for the best of everything! Have them send the bill to me. Falnerian wine, pigeon eggs, lake eels, a suckling pig, and whatever else you can think of. And a cake—a glorious cake!"

Philea turned to leave, but Claudia stopped her to give more specific instructions.

Tiberius watched as Cornelia arose and quietly headed toward her chamber.

"I believe that should do it," said Appius, "but, while we wait, how about a libation for the gods and ourselves now?"

"We have no Falernian, Father," Claudia said, "just ordinary table wine."

"I'm sure it will be delicious!" he said. "Tiberius, if you will, we can thank the gods for our good luck."

Tiberius nodded, and led the way to the Lararium to pour wine onto the floor to Jupiter, Juno, Apollo, Mars, and Fortuna. All the while, he wondered what had spurred his mother to leave the fete that marked the great success that she had been urging for so very long.

The party had become mildly riotous due to the good spirits of his friends. Others had been invited, Fannius, who had survived Carthage with him, and Marcus Octavius, his cheerful goad at the baths that morning. Even his revered mentor Diophanes came to dine, though not to drink.

Before the night was done, Hostilius Mancinus himself made a grand entrance. Dark and tall, well over six feet, he gripped arms with Appius, who then formally presented Tiberius. Mancinus eyed him up and down, "So, you're to be my quaestor, the gods willing, and me. Well, come to the Campus, tomorrow, and we'll see if you're up to it. I'm no potentate and I bear no fools on my marches, no matter who sponsors them."

He turned and chatted with a few of the men and women in the dining area, which ranged from the peristylum into the atrium, overflowing to the very edge of the house vestibulum. Appius lowered his head muttering, "Pay no attention to his churlishness, he's merely flashing his feathers for the hens in the house. Mancinus knows your reputation and is happy to have you in his service."

Appius went off to catch the new general tasked with subduing the Numantine barbarians. Tiberius watched him go, then looked for Claudia, who was in a deep, animated conversation with her mother Antistia. His brother Gaius flirted with Scaevola's daughter, who had come with her parents. All were flushed with excitement and happiness.

So, why did he feel so uneasy in the wake of his mother's absence? Why did that old woman roil him so? Bitterly, he drained his wine cup, set it down, and stalked toward her room.

"Mother," he shouted, knocking on her door, "let me in and tell me why you're sulking like this. This was your idea in the first place and you did get your way."

Cornelia opened her door. "You are drunk."

"Not yet."

"Well, you better stop now, you're not very good at being drunk."

"That's your opinion of me in general."

"Oh, don't pout, Tiberius, of course you possess talent and skill," she said, turning her back as she left the door, "you're simply too green right now."

Tiberius closed the door behind them and pulled up the small footstool to Cornelia, perched on the end of her bed, one knee held up with her arms wrapped around it, like a young maiden.

"Mother," he said earnestly, "what is wrong? Why are you not out there leading the festivities? This is your victory as much as mine and Appius's."

"Appius," she said, shaking her head. "How is this a triumph for me, too?"

"I will be Mancinus's quaestor on his campaign in Numantia."

"In whose stead is Mancinus going?"

Tiberius paused, then said, "Scipio."

"And why isn't Scipio marching to Numantia to secure all the gold and silver in Hispania?"

"He has personal affairs to address. And, he wants to give another noble Roman the opportunity to achieve glory."

"Really?" she said in a singsong of mock surprise. "How magnanimous of him. A first, I believe, unless he means to give you the same kind of opportunity when he sent you first to climb Carthage's walls."

She leaned back. "However, that did work out to your benefit. So, let's not talk about it anymore. How many legions will the great Mancinus command in Numantia?"

"The better part of four, the two stationed in Hispania Citerior and Ulterior, and the two that just returned. They'll be remustered, bringing the total to just under 17,000 troops."

"Less than those commanded by Caepio and Servillianus, both of whom failed."

"Yes, but everyone says their failures came from poor leadership."

"Perhaps, Tiberius, but even poor leaders have a better chance of succeeding when they have enough legions. To win with inferior forces, you must be a genius, like your father."

Tiberius held back his reply. What was the use?

"Even Hannibal succumbed to the overwhelming forces of Scipio Africanus. Your brother-in-law learned well from the example of your grandfather."

Seeing the morose look on her son's face, Cornelia moved forward to grab his shoulders by both hands. "Tiberius, don't you see? Scipio declined the generalship in Numantia because he knew that he wouldn't have enough legions! The barbarian tribes in Hispania number in the thousands, maybe hundreds of thousands."

"Mother, they're divided into hundreds of tribes. They war among themselves all the time."

"Tiberius, you've never been there. Four legions is barely enough to garrison the holdings we have now," she said, "much more conquer the Numantines, who have proven able to stand up to superior numbers in the past."

"That was the Lusitanes, Mother, and they were subdued after Caepio saw to their leader Viriathus's assassination."

"They remain subdued for now," Cornelia said. "Who's to know what they'll do after the example of the Numantines."

Tiberius rose up. "Mother, what would you have me do? The first thing the Senate did was to designate the campaign force as the standing legions in Hispania. That is the army that we have at hand, and the one we will use to subjugate the Numantines."

"Under Mancinus," she said. She seemed to look off into the distance, absently twirling the blood-red carnelian stones of her necklace. Said more as a spoken thought, she uttered, "It should be Scipio, but he's no fool." She raised her eyes back to Tiberius, "All right, then: it's Mancinus. You will be his quaestor, Tiberius," she said, suddenly smiling as only she could, the light of Apollo dancing around her green eyes, the heart of the earth suddenly at her feet. "The rest is simply a matter of details."

Caught in the spell of her sudden warmth, Tiberius smiled himself. "Come out to the celebration, Mother. It's as much for you as any of us."

She shook her head, "No, Tiberius, it's for you and your comrades. I'm just a widow in the way. You go, enjoy yourself. Be sure to tell Claudia to retire along with the other women and children. Now, go, now."

Still grinning, Tiberius stood and headed for the door.

"Oh, and Tiberius," she said. "Could you ask Appius to call on me? I want to thank him for all he's done."

Tiberius pulled up, wondering what intrigue she intended to hatch with Appius now. He nodded, "Certainly, Mother."

He smiled at her as he left the room. He paused before turning back to the men carousing in the peristylum, resigned to drinking more himself and the inevitable headache to follow. Appius sat in their midst, no doubt regaling them with his own exploits as a young officer. He would not relish being interrupted, much less so for being summoned by Cornelia. He would be more miserable than me, at least, thought Tiberius, some small consolation. He laughed, and headed toward his now ill-fated father-in-law.

Chapter 4. The Campus Martius

Chaos reigned on the campgrounds as Mancinus marshaled his troops for the march to Ostia, from where they would sail to Hispania. Officers at every level shouted orders, assembling legionaries with their arms to drill them, an endless exercise until the final order was given for departure.

"We cannot laze around thinking of how we will crush the Numantines, Tiberius," Mancinus said, leaning in full armor against a pole at the opening of his tent, his legs crossed, popping an occasional grape into his mouth.

"We must act swiftly, forcefully, before they can find their own Vitharius to be their military chieftain. So, I will take the Fifth and the Eighth by sea to get this campaign off to a running start. We'll join with the Second and the Third in Hispania Citerior and head straightaway to Ulterior to harass the filthy dog lovers. Your father-in-law says that you commanded a cohort ably at Carthage, and it is true, you won the Mural Crown. You must be brave enough, so I'll give you another cohort to march up the Via Aurelia through Etruria, where you will raise another legion. You can train it on the way overland to join us in Numantia."

Tiberius gazed at him with sharp eyes, again wondering if Cornelia had cajoled Appius into bringing about this diversion, a clever stratagem to keep her son out of harm's way until the troops she felt were needed had been raised to even the field of battle. No doubt, Appius persuaded Mancinus of other benefits he would gain in delaying the novice Gracchus by sending him off to northern Italia.

"But I'm your quaestor, Consul," Tiberius said evenly. "Who will maintain the lists and the payroll if I'm recruiting in Etruria?"

Mancinus didn't hesitate. "I've asked Quintus Fabius to handle them while you're away. Before he became my first military tribune, he served as my quaestor in Greece. He'll be able to manage the books until you arrive."

"That's an unusual arrangement, Consul," Tiberius said.

"I know, I know, but it should work, and it gives you the opportunity to form your own legion. After your record in Africa, you should rise quickly, Gracchus. You've earned the right and the opportunity."

Tiberius wondered about Mancinus's magnanimity. It would be no easy task to raise a full legion on the fly, and where was he to find the funds to supplement the needs of 4,000 new legionaries? In the meantime, the rolls and the army's treasury would be far away from him, the elected quaestor. Fabius had been Mancinus's quaestor during the Achean War, true, and the general had grown rich when Corinth had been razed. Did the consul's plan to harass the Numantines translate into grabbing what wealth they could before Tiberius managed to meet them in Hispania? Maybe Mancinus didn't want the brother-in-law of his main rival Scipio Aemilianus to track him too closely on this campaign. In any case, now he had to travel north to find soldiers.

"Once you arrive," Mancinus went on," we should be able to squeeze the Numantines between our five legions like a press making fine wine."

Mancinus demonstrated his simile by forming a fist with his hand holding the grapes, which caused purple juice to course thinly over his knuckles like so many little rivulets. He gazed at the sticky, thin streams running between his knuckles down his hand, saying, "Ye gods, what a mess!" wiping them on the leather flap of the tent.

"Twenty thousand men," Tiberius said. "Caepio had that many and lost."

"Caepio didn't know how to gain an advantage," Mancinus said. "It is apparent that he proved to be much better at subterfuge than military strategy, tactics. Anyway, the Numantines are not the Lusitanes."

Tiberius held his tongue. From what everyone had told him, including his mother, all Hispanii were difficult to pacify. His father's success seemed to have stemmed from that understanding, in that after he had conquered them on the field, he hadn't asked too much from them in the way of tribute or subjugation. Mostly, he had asked for and received a loose sort of fealty. But Mancinus had returned from Achaea with a solid reputation as a capable officer. Perhaps his experience there drove his actions now. In any case, Tiberius's fortunes were now tied to the new consul, and his own interests required him to do whatever he could to ensure his success in Hispania.

But, it wasn't going to be easy. The cohort assigned to him came from the Fifth, a blooded legion, a gift from Mancinus. ("Better you should have seasoned troops; I'll be better able to break in a new cohort from the home guard.") But, even the seasoned warriors from the Fifth had gone sloppy during their hiatus. All of their Greek pay and booty was gone, drunken up, gambled away, or spent whoring, and they were itching to replace it with Hispania treasure. But, they needed to be whipped into shape, along with the raw recruits he was supposed to dredge up in Etruria. To do that, Tiberius would need centurions.

"Bring me," cried his brother Gaius, "Make me a centurion. I don't need to be a tribune, centurion would be good enough."

"You're too young," Tiberius said impatiently, as he scrambled to organize his gear. His mother had given him a new lorica, a fine piece shaped to his torso without embarrassing embellishment. Greaves, too, though he hated wearing the damn things. And Appius had gifted him with a massive bronze helmet, ornately decorated with two strange horns coming out of the top. "It's an exact facsimile of Alexander's, worn while he conquered the world! I could not think of any more appropriate war headdress for you than this, Quaestor!" As he thanked his father-in-law profusely, Tiberius wondered that if he wore it, would he risk outshine the finery of Mancinus himself. He laughed, thinking, that was unlikely.

"You laugh at me!" cried Gaius. "You think I'm not man enough. But you were a military tribune when you were my age."

"I was a year older, and the most junior tribune Rome ever saw. Anyway, I'm not about to take you to Hispania and chance that your mother would have to light funeral pyres for two sons, her last two sons, after having lost nine other children and a husband."

"He was old," Gaius said, and Tiberius turned on him.

"Don't ever say that again!" he shouted, seizing Gaius's shoulders in his arms, hard enough to leave thumb marks on each bicep. Gaius shrugged himself loose and stepped back.

"Don't you ever grab me like that again!" he yelled. "You are not my father, just a glory hunter of honors all for yourself!"

Philea slipped into the room and whispered in Tiberius's ear.

"No, no, everything is all right, Philea. We're quarreling, but not killing each other. Go tell your mistress that we'll come see her soon."

She left, and Tiberius sighed, gazing at his younger brother turned away from him, his hunched back clearly revealing his disappointment.

"Gaius, come sit next to me."

Tiberius cleared a place on the bed and patted it. Sullenly, Gaius sat by his brother. Tiberius looked at him, his beard barely wisps upon his chin, a red flush to his cheeks so pronounced that it looked like an actor's paint. Young Gaius knew nothing of arrows cut out of a breast to free bubbly blood from a pierced lung, or a cauterized gash low on the calf still slowly turning green, then black, finally requiring the leg to be cut off, often too late. And the smell, Tiberius remembered, of rotting dried blood and putrefying gore, of flesh burning from a thousand fires, the oily smoke that would blot out the Sun God Apollo himself. All Gaius knew was of the glory of war told to him by old men who perhaps had forgotten the rest.

"Gaius, even if I wanted to, I could never capture all of the honors or glory, not with you growing so strong. You are too irrepressible. I struggle to attain the proper dignitas of a noble Roman; it comes naturally to you. I work diligently to achieve, while you seize your birthright. I must go to war, now, but you must take care of mother and our family. In time, and not long from now, you will lead the way. When that time comes, I prophesize that you will outshine me by far. But, today, you must wait."

Gaius began to weep silently. "Tiberius, I ache to go with you. I know you're right, but I want to honor Rome and our family, and it is hard to wait, too hard."

"I know, I know." Tiberius put his arms around his brother's shoulders. "Your time will come. But, remember, there are only three of us left. Think of how hard life would be for Mother and Sempronia if they had only each other."

Gaius buried his head into Tiberius's breast. "You're right, Tiberius, you are right. I will stay home. But, what will become of us if something happens to you? If we lose you, we have each other. But, what of Claudia and your children?"

Tiberius frowned. "If she loses me, Claudia will be the widow of a citizen-soldier in the service of Rome. She will act accordingly, and she will raise our children to do the same."

Cold comfort for his loving wife, he thought, as he sat at the field desk in his tent. But, he could do nothing to change that. And, he still needed centurions. He gestured to the clerk to send in the next candidate on the roster, another veteran of Macedonia.

A huge hulk of a man strode into the tent and saluted. He looked vaguely familiar to Tiberius, the barrel shape of his body and the powerful legs, except he was tall, too. Slowly, it dawned upon Tiberius of whom this soldier reminded him, even as he asked him his name.

"Casca, Quaestor Gracchus."

"Casca," Tiberius muttered softly, and a chill coursed through his body. Then, impulsively, he said, "Remove your helmet."

The Centurion snapped off his helmet, while saying at the same time,

"You won't find an arrow hole in the notch of my chest, Quaestor Gracchus. I'm not killed dead like my brother."

"Your brother," muttered Tiberius.

"Manius Casca Capito, Quaestor. My older brother. While he was fighting in Carthage, I was mopping up in Macedonia. I am here to serve Rome again."

Tiberius gazed at the large man standing before him, whose eyes were fixed on some point in the distance. Unlike his brother, this Casca carried little fat on his broad frame. He looked to be inches taller, too, if he remembered the long-gone centurion correctly after all these years. Tiberius wondered if this one wanted to join his legion so that he could kill him.

"Do you blame me for your brother's death, Centurion?"

"Sir, I do not. My brother drew the short straw and the Fates cut his thread."

Tiberius paused, mulling over the motivation of the large soldier standing before him, knowing full well that he really couldn't know the deeper reasons, if any, that brought him here to apply for a position from the officer who saw his brother die.

"If he had lived, do you think your brother would have been first over the wall at Carthage?" he asked.

"Sir, my brother was too fat, sir."

Tiberius burst out laughing. "He was a barrel of a man."

"Yessir."

"So," Tiberius said, rubbing his beard, "Your brother was Capito, the head. Who are you, younger Casca?"

"Lucius Casca Naso," he said.

Tiberius saw it at once, the large misshapen proboscis hanging over his mouth and spread across his face like its own continent.

"All right, see the scribe. He'll sign you on as a centurion in my cohort."

"Yes, sir. Thank you, sir. I'm honored to serve."

"Only the Fates can determine that."

As Casca saluted and turned to leave, Tiberius said, "Oh, and Casca. If you know of any other centurions who wish to win glory in Hispania, send them to me. We will be raising another legion on our way to Numantia, so I will need other seasoned officers."

"I know four more, Quaestor. We fought together in Greece. They are hard men and as broke as I am, in need of new coin quick."

"Very good. Send them to me after you've signed in."

Casca saluted again, and left briskly.

Four more experienced centurions, thought Tiberius, an excellent start. But, where was he going to find 4,000 new legionaries?

After the ox, pig, and sheep had been sacrificed to Mars in the Temple of Jupiter Strator, and white bulls to Juno Quiritis at her temple on the Campus, the people of Rome lined the Via Ostiense to cheer Mancinus and his legions. They formed up to begin their march to Ostia, fourteen miles away, to board transports to Hispania. Tiberius had his cohort lining both sides of the road at attention to honor their comrades. As they passed by, the older legionaries in each group exchanged insults.

"Sorry there won't be anything of worth left when you mules arrive."

"That's okay, we'll be happy enough bedding your wives when you're gone."

"You can have the old witches, we'll be having sweet Numantines every night soon enough."

"That's right, we hear those Numantine men are as good as Greek boys; when we get there, we'll try out their women."

"As if you could tell the difference!"

"Gracchus can!" shouted one, and they all laughed, followed by choruses of "Mancinus can!"

And on it went, until the last of the legions passed down the road, disappearing among the flanking trees. The people who had come to watch and cheer turned and strolled back to the city gates.

Tiberius nodded to Casca, who formed the men into ranks and marched them back to their barracks just outside the city walls. After they'd trooped off, Tiberius removed his crested helmet and turned to Appius. "Mars's bastards, I'm glad Claudia wasn't here to listen to that. I wouldn't be able to look her in the eyes!"

Appius smiled, "She would have taken it in stride. She knows how legionaries carry on."

Tiberius blinked at the older man, "Of course, Father-in-Law."

Appius blinked himself. "I'm sorry, my son, the sound of the war horns always stir me. I miss my old soldiering days."

"I understand, Father Appius," Tiberius said, looking down the road at the empty place where the last of Mancinus' troops had tramped out of sight. "I imagine you were even more inspired by the parade today. They marched as if in a triumph already."

"That's just Mancinus's confidence flowing in them, Tiberius. Yes, we finally have a good plan for dealing with Numantia, and perhaps all of the Hispania hosts."

Tiberius looked at him askance, "Let's start with the Numantines."

Appius looked back and laughed, "Of course, you're right. One step at a time."

They began walking to back to the city, Tiberius holding his helmet in the crook of his arm.

"So, you leave when?" asked Appius.

"In two days," Tiberius said, "sooner than I thought, thanks to you. Truthfully, I didn't know how I was going to find the funds to leave at all. The Senate excels at providing money for grain, even oxen and carts to haul provisions, but not one sesterce for the contingencies of war, nothing for bribes. You did me a great service, Father-in-Law. You shouldn't have, but you did, and you saved me."

"Oh, think nothing of it. In the end, it's all for Rome, isn't it?" They had just passed through the gate inside the walls, where crude stands stood propped against the heavy stones, hawkers selling sweetbreads, dried fish, vinegar and wine, and even toy swords for the children excited by the swagger of the recently departed legionaries. Appius grabbed Tiberius' elbow, "I have another surprise for you, too. Come this way."

He steered a wary-looking Tiberius down several alleys and across major avenues into other crooked streets until they arrived at a small square in the Aventine. Shops flanked each side, and people milled about, but Appius paid them no attention, taking Tiberius directly to a stable in the center of the far side. He stopped, grinned widely, and yelled, "Strabo, front and center, bring him out."

A big man with wild black hair stuck his head out of one of the two stable doors, then ducked back inside. After a moment, he pushed one of the doors open ahead of him with one hand while pulling a short rope with the other. He stepped out into the square leading a grey horse mottled white, some four cubits at the haunch. Tiberius stared at it, uncomprehendingly.

"Well?" said Appius. "Get on it. It's yours!"

"Mine?" Tiberius's hacked out the word, almost in a panic. "A horse?"

"Of course it's a horse. Every quaestor needs a horse, and here's yours!"

Tiberius gazed at the huge beast, feeling a little sick to his stomach. "Appius, I don't know anything about horses. What am I supposed to do with this one?"

"Ride it, Tiberius, ride it to Numantia! Get up on it. You must have a horse!"

Tiberius sighed, "Father-in-Law—"

"Come Strabo, bend your back. Up, Tiberius, up, up, up."

Tiberius gritted his teeth, and stepped up on the back of the big stable man, obviously a freedman, perhaps even a former gladiator. He swung his leg over and settled in on the grey's broad back.

"Give him the reins, Strabo. There!"

Holding the reins loosely, Tiberius sat on the horse, which did nothing.

"It seems docile," he said hopefully.

"It is a gelding," Appius admitted. "We weren't completely unaware of your limited experience with horses."

"I see."

"Go ahead, give him a nudge with your heels."

Tiberius grimaced, then prodded the horse gently, which still did not move.

"Harder!" said Appius.

Tiberius gave it a solid dig with his sandals, and the horse slowly moved forward. "What do I do now?" he cried out.

"Pull your reins, not all the way back, that'll stop him. Pull them to one side."

Tiberius did as he was told, and the horse began to walk in a circle. Once around, and Tiberius was smiling, "Well, then."

"Strabo tells me he's a good warhorse, blooded in the slave uprising near Brindisium."

"What's his name?"

"That's for you to decide, Tiberius, he's your horse!" Appius shouted with a laugh.

"Not yet, he isn't. I haven't paid for him yet."

"Oh, no, he's a gift. He's your horse, all right. So, what do you want to call him?"

Tiberius slid off his back. "He cannot be a gift, Father-in-Law. I cannot continue accepting all these gifts from you! It's inappropriate and unmanly. I must pay my own way."

Appius grabbed him by the shoulders. "Tiberius, we are very, very proud of you, and we know that you are a proud man, too. Until you have your chance, you cannot be expected to afford the expenses of making your name in Rome. But Rome doesn't want to lose the talents of such a gifted young man as yourself because of a sesterce or two. We've all had help in the past, which always has been repaid tenfold. Why, I consider this an investment in my daughter's husband, in her well-being. We anticipate great things, wonderful things from you, Tiberius, and we know that you will succeed!"

Tiberius marveled at the wide-open assurance beaming from Appius's eyes. It was hard to believe, he thought, that this round man with the sun-drenched face once was a young noble on the rise himself, or a Roman officer who had fought the Celts to a standstill, and had helped conquer the Macedonians with Paullus. His belief in his son-in-law was almost overwhelming, more than Tiberius's confidence in himself. He shrugged his shoulders, and walked back to the mottled grey.

Just then, a tall angular figure stepped through the gateway. Dark-haired but fair-skinned, he was lean, muscular, and taller than Tiberius by an eye. He moved with a cocky stride, as though he'd already conquered the worlds in front of him.

"Oh," said Appius, "this is Sextus Decimus Paetus, a noble of the horse class and the breeder of your fine mount here. In fact, the Paetae are the finest horse-breeders in all of Rome, in all of Italia!" exclaimed the old senator.

Without any evidence of humility in his features, Sextus said, "You make me red like a virgin, Senator Claudius."

"Not at all. Sextus, my son-in-law, Tiberius Sempronius Gracchus."

"Honored," Sextus said, smiling broadly as he reached out his hand, though to Tiberius, the look in his eyes seemed unchanged, a glint of challenge blended with ambition and high self-esteem. Tiberius shook his hand, though he couldn't help leaning his head back slightly.

"You praise me for a simple act of survival," Tiberius replied.

"Don't be ridiculous," Sextus said briskly, "everyone knows the story, no surprise, given your stock. I'd like a shot at a Mural Crown myself someday." He shook his shoulders loose of the reverie, "It still would be a privilege to serve with you."

Tiberius could only wonder at such open ambition and the ego that drove it. Without question, Sextus's aspirations had won out over challenging the new quaestor, at least temporarily. "Privilege?" he said.

"Oh, yes," Appius interceded, "Sextus has asked for a commission among your auxiliaries. He's a fine horseman and an excellent soldier, I'm told."

By whom? Tiberius mused. No matter, there it was. He examined Sextus up and down. Nineteen, he thought, maybe twenty, though he was big, big for a horse soldier in fact. Then again, who can be choosy when there were no other auxiliaries to join? This rope-like reed from a family of horsemen had the arrogance to talk easily about wearing a Mural Crown. He expected to wear it. Does that mean he would jeopardize his comrades in pursuit of it?

"You could join my auxiliaries, Sextus," Tiberius said, "if I had any. But, I do not. My orders are to raise another legion in Italia on the way to Hispania. I believe that includes the usual complement of auxiliaries."

"I understand," Sextus said, "and I can help you. I'm not the only one who wants to ride with you. Fifty strong, all of good horsemen families, all well-trained and well-mounted, ideal for your needs."

"Really?" Tiberius said. He mulled the offer over. Fifty trained Roman horsemen would be an excellent core for his legion's cavalry. But, would they be beholden to Sextus as their leader? Maybe so, but not necessarily for the entire campaign. Some judicious reorganization of their numbers and the addition of other auxiliaries directly under the Quaestor's command would restore order in the ranks. Yes, he was brash, Tiberius concluded, but he was available.

"Report to Centurion Casca Naso on the Campus Martius first thing in the morning. Travel light, and tell your friends the same."

Sextus broke into a beaming grin, saluted, and turned to march out of the gateway.

Tiberius glanced at his father-in-law, who also smiled broadly. He pivoted back to the forgotten horse, and happily saw that Strabo had grabbed hold of him close at the halter.

The size of the beast took him aback again. "He's huge," he muttered.

"Yes, Tiberius," agreed Appius, staring up at the big horse's head, "but his stature will give you your best chance to win."

"Maybe so," Tiberius said, not completely convinced. He inched forward to the horse and lifted his hand to the side of the gray's head just beneath his eye. The horse snorted and Tiberius moved his hand back.

"My best chance," he murmured, stroking the horse on its neck. "Then, Chance you shall be."

"He liked the horse?" Cornelia asked.

"He did," Appius said, "after getting used to it. When he first climbed up, I thought he might swoon."

Cornelia frowned, "He never really liked trying new things. Now, Gaius, he would have been up and away, racing through every bread stand in Rome. But, Tiberius, no," she said.

"Well, he seemed fine with it by the time we left. And, it's a steady horse, steady in a fight. Strabo guaranteed it."

"That's something, I guess. No matter, Tiberius is cautious, but he will do his duty. He is brave that way."

Appius stopped looking at the flowers in the peristylum and faced Cornelia. "Why didn't you tell him that you bought the horse? Or gave him the bribe money, for that matter? Why create this fiction that I sponsored him so?"

Cornelia shook her head, "He's a grown man. He cannot have his mother paying his way. Better his father-in-law be his benefactor. Aside from the obvious association with Claudia, he can think that you backed him for political gain when Numantia falls."

"I would have given him the money, if you hadn't" Appius murmured.

Cornelia smiled, "Now, what makes you think I would have allowed that? He needs to be his own man when he returns, too, Appius."

Appius sighed his frustration. "But the horse. At least you could have openly given him the horse. That wouldn't have been too much for his mother to do."

Again, Cornelia shook her head, slowly this time. "No. He must stand alone. He must see himself achieving glory by himself, without the support of his mother or anyone else who might indulge him. He's a Roman quaester, now."

Agitated by her words, Appius said, "He's already achieved glory! Can't you take any joy in what your son has done? You've had twelve children, and lost all but three of them, two if you consider Sempronia lost to Scipio. Tiberius is your oldest living son, and he's going off to war. Can't you enjoy him at all? "

Cornelia said flatly, "My joy died with his father. Now, it is only duty that moves me to go on."

Chapter 5. The Via Aurelia

Tiberius dragged himself out of bed and over to the chamber pot. He relieved himself for what seemed like the thousandth time that night. Too much wine again, he knew, for one who seldom drank at all. No matter, he wouldn't have slept that well anyway.

The stars were still out on a clear night, their light casting the city in a soft, pale glow amid dark shadows that seemed to promise peace rather than fear. Yet, Tiberius felt a few vague, timorous pangs. The day promised to unfold in such a way that he could expect his nerves to be on end, knowing himself.

When morning broke, he and his cohort would leave for the north to raise the rest of his legion. They were ready, he had seen to that. Casca and his brethren had driven them hard for the past month, marching the wine and bad victuals out of them, bringing back the muscle tone usual to veteran legionaries. Three other centurions had signed on, Didius from Sicily, Ulpius, from the city of Lucca in northern Etruria, which should be helpful, and the most interesting, Shafat. Shavat was the son of Carthaginian slaves who had declined taking a Roman name, although his reputation as a Roman soldier in battle was outstanding. The fourth that Casca had suggested could not join up, having had his left arm nearly slashed off in drunken brawl.

"If the arm heals up well enough for you to raise a shield," Casca had told him, "you can join us in Numantia. Otherwise, brother, you'll need to find a job as a guard. Don't become an assassin, their life span is too short, often ended by dangling on a cross."

Casca and the others worked on squaring away the soldiers and supplies while Tiberius went home to see about his own packing, and to sit at a final dinner with his family. Claudia tried to insist upon several more layers of clothing, winter trousers, and fruit, as if it would last all the way to Hispania. After Tiberius had objected repeatedly to no avail, he mentally made a note to tell Lysis later to quietly remove the excess garments. He'd told Casca and the others that he did not want the usual baggage and camp followers to trail the march, that they had to move as swiftly as possible to reach Mancinus before the consul had ended the war. So, it wouldn't do for him to show up with a cartload of camp luxuries while his men slept in little more than their cloaks.

Appius and his family joined them for dinner, as did his old comrade Gaius Fannius. The meal was superb, too much, Tiberius thought, and the wine flowed freely. Appius took his leave early, knowing enough to allow for Tiberius to spend time with his children, his mother, and Claudia. Fannius lingered, however, until Claudia finally said goodnight, and withdrew.

Fannius watched her leave, then said, "Well, old mate, you're off to war again. How does it feel?"

Tiberius rolled his head, "I can't fool you, Fannius, I'm nervous, scared even."

"Oh, you'll be fine once you're underway. I've seen you, Tiberius, you stand up when there's a need. Don't worry so."

"I'm more afraid of the trip than the actual war," said Tiberius. "Raising troops is new to me. Where do you find them, anyway?"

Fannius nodded thoughtfully, stroking his beard. "Locating men who own land is not easy these days. Too many killed in the past few years. I say don't spend a lot of time near the larger towns, Piso, Firenze, that sort. Sweep farther afield in the smaller villages, places where other recruiting officers couldn't be bothered."

"Yes, but 4,000 men?"

Fannius shook his head, "It's a formidable task, all right. Easier to find cattle. But, I'm sure you'll be resourceful." He looked toward the bed chambers, hearing some noise. "I better go, now. No doubt, your wife would like to see as much of you as she can before you march off."

Tiberius walked him to the door, an arm around his shoulders. He hugged him and kissed his cheeks, then sent him walking down the street following the lamp in his body slave's hand. After seeing him off, Tiberius headed for his bedroom, swaying between the hall walls, and realizing that he'd had more to drink than he'd thought.

Claudia awaited him in his bed, and they embraced silently, their passion tinged with a hollow, open-ended sorrow. Afterwards, she left him to sleep, also not to feel her tears.

Now, here he was, ready to leave his family and home for a year or more. Little Tiberius, and Cornelia. Tiberius would be close to school age by the time he returned, and his baby girl would grow, too, and perhaps forget her father a little bit. Claudia had gripped him tightly before she'd left last night, saying in a harsh voice, "I hope this night brings me another child. I want more to remind me of you if the gods command the worst, and you do not return."

He consoled her, naturally, saying of course he would return, in victory. But, he remembered those who hadn't from Carthage, their bodies darkened and bloated in the brutal, African sun. Their families wore ashes and torn, black linen for the longest year of their lives, and then what? Destitution, disease, deaths of their own? This, in victory?

A scratch at his door. He draped the bedcover over his legs, and pushed his hair back with both hands.

"Enter."

Cornelia slipped into the room, looking almost deferential for the first time in his life.

"Mother," Tiberius said evenly.

She sidled up to him and stretched out her hand. In it was a long dagger, beautifully crafted of the best Hispanic steel, with an ivory handle carved in an elaborate scene of battle and conquest.

"Your father's," she said, "presented to him by the Hispanii chieftains when peace was reached. I give it to you now, to wish you your own success."

Tiberius felt a little stunned at the gesture. He was surprised by his mother's emotion, something he couldn't remember seeing since he was a child.

"Thank you, Mother. I will bear it with honor."

"I know you will. Tiberius, your father told me about the Hispanii people. They are not fur-swathed, long-bearded barbarians, they've been trafficking with all parts of the civilized world for more than two centuries. Your father remarked upon their skill as warriors and their valor. They shouldn't be taken lightly. Mancinus will need every man he can get, and certainly every man that you can bring."

"I understand, Mother. Don't worry, I will enlist a full legion."

"I know you will."

Then, Cornelia leaned over to hug him, murmuring, "May the gods be with you."

She gathered herself and swiftly left the room, leaving Tiberius still sitting on the edge of the bed, astonished.

In full armor, Tiberius walked briskly from his room to the front of the house, Polydius at his side.

"Do what is necessary to keep this household together. Pay attention to your mistress, but also exercise your own judgment. If she and my mother disagree, do not attempt to mediate. Simply leave the room until the dust settles. And, try to keep track of Gaius. Make sure he continues his schooling and training." He turned and put one hand upon Polydius' shoulder. "I'm counting on you, Polydius. If all goes well, when I return, you shall no longer be in my service, only in my employ, if you wish."

Polydius flushed, "I would serve you anyway you desire, in any fashion."

"Spoken like a true slave on the brink of freedom," laughed Tiberius. "Well, just try to keep the peace around here, and don't let any hawkers or our property managers steal us blind."

They stepped outside the door, where Philea and Lysis let loose a covey of doves. As they furiously flapped away, Tiberius craned to watch them, shading his eyes from the sun with one hand, murmuring "If an eagle doesn't take them now, I guess we'll know that this effort isn't ill-fated, at least."

Before Mancinus marched for Numantia, the priests had sacrificed two white bulls to Mars, and signified that all had gone well, that the campaign would be successful. Now, Tiberius was leaving to a flight of mourning doves.

Lysis came up to him, "All is ready, Master Tiberius."

Tiberius looked at the slender young Greek and sighed. He gazed at the slight youth, so fair and slender of frame that he looked more like a river sprite rather than a half-grown man servant. Ever since they'd purchased him five years ago or so, Lysis had kept his eyes in the stars. Philea and Polydius forever had to bring him back to the firmament to do his chores. Yet, his constant, wide-eyed, warm demeanor charmed everyone, so much so that they couldn't stay angry at him, never mind punishing him. The children loved Lysis, too, playing with him all the time. He sang to them and told stories, plying a wild gift of imagination in such an utterly enchanting way that many of the adults found themselves caught in the net of his fancies. Yet, it had been decided that Lysis would be Tiberius's servant at camp instead of Polydius, who was too old and could be so much more useful with the family. Everyone left at home would miss Lysis, Tiberius thought, maybe more than their master. Certainly, the children would miss him more.

Lysis greeted the decision with wide-eyed fear, one slave who didn't dream of winning his freedom on the battlefield, Tiberius thought. When they headed off to the baths, the boy could barely hike up Tiberius's training bag to his shoulder and stagger after him. How on earth would he be able to lug around a full military kit? Tiberius wondered.

He glanced away and said, "All right then, let's go." Claudia, red-faced from crying, hugged him one more time. His mother Cornelia waved her hand wanly while Appius cheered and clapped his hands. The others who had wished him well at the farewell feast last night—Fannius, Marcus Octavius, Crassus, Mucius Scaevola, and his old teacher Diophanes—must still be sleeping, Tiberius thought. He waved his hand at those in the vestibulum as he walked toward the house gates, only to turn and abruptly stop.

In front of him, the cart requisitioned for his personal belongings stood loaded almost to the height of the house's roof tiles.

"What in the gods'? Lysis!" The slight Greek youth hurried to his side. Tiberius struggled to control the volume of his voice. "Lysis! What is this? I told you to take away most of this, this detritus. Why is this cart still buckling from this extraneous stuff?"

Lysis began to stutter until Claudia stepped forward to save him. "I ordered him to return these necessities to your wagon. I'll not have you conquer the Numantines only to have you succumb to the elemental gods. I won't have a hero husband taken away by a fever or an attack of ague. You need to care for yourself well enough so that you can resolve upon the best stratagems to defeat the Numantines. A sick, cold man is no effective praetor."

Tiberius looked at her in complete exasperation and said, "I'm not a praetor. Oh, very well."

He turned and marched to where Casca was holding his horse. The centurion kept a stern expression, though his dancing eyes betrayed his enjoyment at the scene. As Tiberius reached Chance, he whispered to Casca, "First thing in camp tonight, give all of this to the men. I'm not going to have them think of me as some spoiled son who cannot leave home without his pillows. At once!"

"Your tent, too, sir?" Casca said sardonically. Tiberius stared at him fiercely, then scornfully said, "I didn't know you to have such a sense of humor, Centurion. Give away all, except for that which I need to keep from freezing my ass off."

Casca nodded as he held out his clasped hands for Tiberius to mount.

Tiberius swept up onto Chance, pulled the reins to turn his head, and nodded to his family, saying "Salvete" as he rode out onto the street.

At the Campus Martius, the men of his cohort immediately snapped to attention when he arrived. Casca handed the reins of the cart he was driving to Lysis, and jumped off to take his position at the front of the rows of men. Sextus and his retinue of young horsemen rode up to the front of the column in split ranks on both flanks, and reined in.

Lysis handed the reins of the cart to a drover, and climbed down. The drover flicked his long whip to prod the oxen toward the other carts and mules at the end of the column.

"Are we ready, Casca?"

"Ready to march, sir," Casca said.

"Then, get them moving."

The centurion turned and bellowed the order to move forward. Tiberius walked Chance to the front of the slowly advancing column and took his place next to Sextus up front to lead the column of men north.

The chill of the early spring morning had given way to a pleasantly warm day, occasionally cooled suddenly by a slight breeze from the purple mountains in the distance. After crossing the Pons Aemilius over the Tiber, the column stepped lively along the Via Aurelia, one of Rome's oldest roads. It was a perfect day for marching, and the men were thrilled to be on their way at last, so much better than constant drilling and endless haranguing by the centurions and optios. Never mind that they had hundreds of miles to travel and other recruits to press into their ranks, the men sang their marching songs with carefree spirits in the exquisite spring air.

Tiberius felt exhilarated himself by the day's warmth. He'd dismounted to stroll in front of the marching legionaries, with Lysis leading Chance behind him. Casca walked next to Tiberius, ready to send back orders as instructed. Instead, Tiberius preferred to chat.

"Did you ever see a more beautiful day, Casca? A brilliant day, full of promise!"

"I did, once, sir, on the island of Capri." Casca said. "It is a wondrous place, with cliffs covered in beautiful foliage all around, and amazing birds. Apollo himself blessed the island, bringing it closer to his level so that he could more easily reach it to rest. Thus, the reason for its miraculous height, so the locals say."

"Amazing. And, what were you doing in Capri, Centurion?"

"Fishing, to pay off my gambling debts. But, I didn't do any better at fishing than gambling. War ruined me for everything else but war."

"Indeed," said Tiberius. "Still, this is a spectacular day to start a campaign. The only way it could be more promising is if we could see a falcon beat to the sky with its prey in its claws. That would seal our success."

"Yes," mused Casca, "unless the catch is a snake that bites the bird on its breast. That would be a bad sign for both hawk and snake."

As if summoned, a small raptor flapped hard up in the air with a huge rat in its talons. The rat struggled fiercely, twisting until it was able to latch onto a wing with its teeth. The small bird began to pinwheel in a parabola caused by the uneven weight of the rat. They both plunged into a stand of cypress trees, flushing a flock of starlings into the blue, then away across the meadow.

Both men stared silently at the sight. Finally, Tiberius glared at Casca sourly and said, "Apparently, you have a much greater ability than I do to divine the true sentiments of the gods."

"I wouldn't say that, sir. After all, it was a rat, not a snake." Seeing Tiberius glower, he said, "Shall I go back and check on the order of the carts?"

"By all means, you do that."

The day grew hotter, unseasonably so this early in the spring. The men's singing had stopped, and only the drum beat could be heard, and the occasional bark of a centurion or optio goading a legionary to keep up. Tiberius himself grew peckish because he knew that every mile took him closer to fulfilling the single promise that he'd made to his mother, the idea of which he utterly loathed. But, the seasoned troops had made good time despite their layoff, which meant that they had covered ten or more miles already. This meant that they would soon reach the place he'd selected for their midday halt, the destination he'd promised to his mother, the estate of Scipio Aemilianus. He hadn't had much to do with the Hero of Carthage during the past ten years, he hadn't seen his sister Sempronia very much either. When he had run into him in the Forum or the baths, Scipio had been more than congenial, asking after Claudia and the children. Such solicitude galled Tiberius, of course, knowing how unhappy Sempronia was and how utterly ruthless Scipio could be when it served his purposes. But, he had to keep the pleasant pose to maintain the peace, particularly with his mother. Paying his consular brother-in-law a courtesy call on his march to Hispania was one of these occasions.

The men sprawled on either side of the road, drinking water from their wineskins while munching on their crusts of bread, a few of them layering on pig lard left over from breakfast. No wine or beer would be issued until the evening's camp had gone up. A few men called for vinegar, but most stayed with the water because of the unseasonable heat of the day.

Tiberius gestured to Lysis to bring his horse to him. As he stepped upon Lysis's back to mount Chance, he issued his orders to Casca, then rode off followed by Sextus and another auxiliary. They trotted up the flat stones of the Via Aurelia in search of the gate to Scipio's estate, tucked away somewhere along the tree-lined lane. Clattering ahead, they almost missed the stone pillars that marked the entrance, with visages of Neptune staring empty-eyed out from the top of the columns. Tiberius wheeled his horse back and around, and urged him through the gate down another, narrower path between towering elm trees. As he rode, the trees gave way to vast fields on either side dotted with apple and pear trees, acres and acres of them as far as the eye could see. Hundreds of small figures worked the orchards, trimming branches and cultivating the ground. As they rode on, olives replaced the fruit trees, and in the distance, Tiberius could see outbuildings where the olives would be turned into oil. Beyond them, trellises stretched almost to the horizon, bare now, but ready to grow soon, together to form raised carpets of purple, fuchsia, and ivory from a blended plethora of grape vines. Past them, he saw the main villa, an enormous tile-roofed alabaster structure, with wings on both sides of a central, three-story building nestled in an old stand of trees that seemed to surround it. The three riders approached the front of the villa, which spurred a flurry of activity. Three stewards in short tunics suddenly appeared to grasp the reins of the horses, which Sextus and his subordinate immediately pulled back and out of their reach. Two guards crossed their bodies with their spears and stepped forward from the huge, ornately carved, wooden front doors, while a third thumped a panel with his fist three times. One door opened, and an officer appeared who strode to the edge of the rounded stairs in front of the villa mansion.

"Who rides here?"

Tiberius pulled himself up high over his horse's head and said, "Tiberius Sempronius Gracchus, Quaestor to Hostilius Mancinus, Consul of the Hispania legions. Where is your master?"

The officer snapped to attention. "Salve, Sir. Master Scipio is within."

"Announce us."

The officer saluted, wheeled, and marched into the villa. While he waited, Tiberius also snapped the reins out of the attendant's hands. He turned Chance around to view further the enormous scale of the estate, teeming with hundreds, maybe thousands of workers.

Scipio Aemilianus emerged from his house in a lively gait, clapping his hands and raising them to Tiberius, "Brother-in-law! A delightful surprise! Come, come, off your horse and into the house for refreshment. Quintillus, see that his companions are well-fed, and the horses watered. Vulcan's balls, it's hot enough already, isn't it?"

As the officer nodded and began issuing orders, Tiberius slipped from Chance's back into Scipio's embrace. A quick hug, and Scipio held him out at arms' length.

"You look fit, Tiberius, fully the man everyone thought you would be. And, now a quaestor, a soldier of Rome again. Congratulations!"

"Thank you, Publius."

Scipio looked fit as well, a bit of gray around his head, but solid otherwise, a short man who always seemed taller, thought Tiberius. And, though he was 49 now, his sharp, dark eyes still pierced with a vital sort of searching energy. He wore a simple long tunic, a muted burnt-orange in color, cinched by a leather belt with a sheath that held a small pruning knife.

"Come, let's get a drink and a bite out back where it's cool."

He turned to Sextus, now standing next to his horse. "You must be Sextus Decimus Paetus, Tiberius's equitus. Welcome! Perhaps you will join us for some refreshment?"

Tiberius's brows furrowed, and he shook his head almost imperceptibly.

Sextus had started toward Scipio, but halted when he saw Tiberius's gesture. "Thank you, sir, but I think it better that I stay with the horses."

Scipio gave him a momentary glance, then turned to escort Tiberius into the villa. He led the way through the vestibulum, open to the top of the roof, into a long hallway supported by glorious columns of marble painted a muted green, like the countryside in fall. Between each column stood a magnificent statue, Venus in her bath, Diana stringing her bow, Apollo in repose, holding the reins of his astrophysical chariot, and a dozen more on the men's way back to the end of the corridor and the broad doorway leading into the peristylum. Sweeping past and forward among the columns and statues were long, white curtains, made of the finest

Egyptian linen, wafting over the statues and around them from the breeze flowing through the open doorways. Just before they stepped outside, they came upon a magnificent rearing horse, his mane flying in exquisitely twisted strands as though defying the wind god Aeolus himself. Astride the astonishing marble horse, a general in the style of Alexander brandished his sword at the sky. Tiberius was amazed to see that the general's armor, sword, and helmet were of pounded gold, and more astounded when he realized that the figure astride the stallion looked exactly like Scipio himself.

"Yes, I know," Scipio sighed, "it is completely embarrassing, but what was I to do? Mithridates himself sent it to me in honor of our victory at Carthage. So, I had to keep it, but, I certainly couldn't display the ridiculous thing at the house in Rome. The only place I could think of putting it was out here. I don't receive a lot of guests, this is a working farm."

"But, you don't have it stored away, either, do you," Tiberius said, still gazing up at it as they passed by and outside.

Scipio's voice revealed just the slightest flinty edge as he said, "It's too heavy to move back and forth, should Mithridates visit Rome. Besides, the ludicrous pomposity of the thing keeps me humble in some contradictory way. I say, 'Is this what glory is?' Laughable!"

"True, too, the work is first rate."

Scipio smiled at that.

The peristylum bedazzled Tiberius, 300 yards long surrounded by ivy-covered, white marble columns that supported a tiled walkway. Flowers in ornate ceramic pots and finely painted stone boxes added rich colors and essences to the vista. In the center of the pond stood a fountain statue, a lithe nymph balanced on one foot, the other leg extended behind as if steadying her while she poured water eternally over her shoulder from a vase held in the crook of her arms. Water lilies and other aquatic exotics covered the pond, which was populated by turtles and frogs, silver waterbugs, and dragonflies. Swallows and swifts occasionally swooped from above down to water level in search of a quick meal, then soared up and out over the house.

"Here, sit here, Tiberius," said Scipio, gesturing at an unusual set of chairs, wooden with cushions, with slightly slanted backings. Tiberius sat in one, and was startled by the comfort.

"Gallic. At least, that's where I was told they were from when I bought them. But I don't know where they were built, really. Wonderfully comfortable, though. I swear, Somnus visits me every afternoon when I sit in one of these chairs. It's become a terrible daily habit of mine, sleeping the day away. I'm not getting much done around here because of it."

"There's a lot to do," said Tiberius.

"Oh, endless, more than any campaign I've ever commanded."

A servant arrived with a tray of bread, vegetables, olives, and a pitcher of olive oil. Another placed two cups on the table, while a third held up two pitchers sweating cool liquid.

"Ah, food and wine. How do you mix yours?"

"Mostly water, I'm on the march."

"Of course." Scipio gestured, and the steward poured wine and water in equal parts into the cup. He turned to Scipio, who said, "Just water for me."

Tiberius frowned inwardly at that, but the first sip dissolved his ire. "This is delicious!" "Isn't it?" beamed Scipio. "Our own vintage—I swore to out-Falernian Falernian wine. And, I think we've come pretty close, don't you?"

"Gods above, yes!"

"Wait until you try the olive oil."

They sat and ate quietly for a time, except for Tiberius's exclamations about the wonderful flavors he encountered, and Scipio's purring thanks. Finally, they rested, virtually exhausted from the surfeit of sensations.

Eyes closed, Scipio said, "Does Somnus beckon you, too, Tiberius?"

"I wish. I haven't had such good things to eat since I left Rome."

"Oh, and when was that?"

"This morning."

They both laughed out loud, Tiberius stuttering at the same time, "I meant that, even in Rome it's been a long time since I ate so well."

Still laughing, Scipio said, "You don't need to apologize. I understand, this is different fare, very simple, but so good in the country air. That's why I enjoy spending time here more than in smelly old Rome."

"I see," said Tiberius, his laughter gone. "Is that why you declined to be considered for the campaign in Numantia?"

Scipio opened his eyes. "For the most part. Did you look around you when you rode in?"

"Of course."

"What did you see?"

"Vast holdings. Orchards, vineyards, olive groves."

Scipio nodded, "And, there are large grain fields behind the villa. Fortuna has blessed me, my estate is substantial, even more than that. What else did you notice?"

Tiberius thought for a moment, then said, "Workers. You have hundreds, maybe even a thousand."

Scipio said, "Yes, more than a thousand. It takes that many to keep this farm going."

"Farm? It's quite a bit larger than a farm, don't you think? So, where did they come from, your numerous workforce?"

"Former legionaries," Scipio said, "mustered out and settled on land that they proceeded to lose in short order, gambling, drinking, whoring. After so many years, soldiering is all they really know. So, I hired them on. They respond much better to a beating than slaves."

Tiberius nodded, "I have a cohort full of them, resting out on the via awaiting my return. And, if I hope to have them in camp by nightfall, I need to leave you now." He stood up, and Scipio arose with him.

"Thank you for the delicious repast, Brother-in-law. An unexpected pleasure."

Scipio clapped him on the shoulder and walked him toward the front door, "A delight for me, too, Tiberius. As I said, I don't get a lot of visitors out here, and it's a joy to have a member of the family stop in. Especially you, considering your pressing business for Rome."

"Ah, well, my mother wouldn't have it any other way," he said dryly. "Speaking of family, is my sister near? I'd like to see her before I leave Italia."

Scipio's features took on an exaggeratedly serious cast. "Sempronia? You didn't see her in Rome? She left for Rome yesterday to see you off."

"Really?" Tiberius felt a flush coursing up his neck. "I didn't see her. I'm surprised I didn't pass her on the Via Aurelia on her way back."

"Oh, what a pity," said Scipio. "She likes to take in the scenery. My guess is she dawdled on the way and had to stop for the night. You probably passed the inn before she left. She'll be so disappointed."

"As am I," Tiberius said evenly.

They had reached the front of the villa where Sextus and his subordinate awaited, already astride their horses. A steward held Chance's reins, which Tiberius grabbed, then stepped into the steward's cupped hands and mounted in one fluid motion.

"You plan on continuing up Aurelia, then?" Scipio asked.

"Yes. I need to recruit a full legion on the way to Hispania."

Scipio grimaced, "You'll have a hard time, I'm afraid. Servillianus and Caepio scoured Italia to raise their legions, Brutus and Metellus, too. What few eligible men left are probably hiding in the barley. You might have better luck diverting to Via Cassia. They might not be expecting you there until it's too late."

"Sound advice, brother-in-law. I'll certainly give it some thought. Vale."

"Vale indeed. Jupiter Strator bless you, Mars guide you, and Fortuna be with you," Scipio said, waving as Tiberius wheeled Chance around and headed down the lane.

As he trotted down the long road past the vineyards and orchards, he fumed. Sempronia was hidden in that house, he was sure of it. Leave it to Scipio to spite both of them while acting out his little hospitality charade. What a fool he'd been to fall for any of it. For all of his championing of the high Greek philosophies, his brother-in-law was still a twisted, posturing lout, he'd proven that in Carthage, and again, here. A common bully raised above his station by a lucky roll, his true nature couldn't be hidden forever. Tiberius glanced at the workers in the field as they rode, seeing them carefully prune and cultivate the various plants. For drunken, whoremongering veterans, they seemed to know their way around fields and crops well enough. So, why would working for Scipio be better than tending their own farms, public land that was the best in Italia? He couldn't even believe Scipio in this respect, he decided, further proof that he couldn't trust him about anything.

In short order, the riders reached the cohort, the men dozing by the side of the road.

Casca strode up to them, his hand on the heft of his sword, looking up at Tiberius inquiringly. Tiberius dismounted and handed the reins to Lysis.

"Roust the bastards," he snapped to the centurion. "We march on."

Chapter 6. Spring Seeding

The cohort from the Fifth finally found their stride, on flat stretches of road covering as much as 25 miles a day. Of course, much of the Via Aurelia crawled over steep hills and plunged into deep vales that shaped the fertile curves of Mother Dea. No matter to the men on foot, after the first week of marching, they began to sing again. While rolling along, they split the air with spirited songs about skewering Numantine warriors on spits to roast alive while they screwed their women by the fire's light. The weather held, and they made relatively good time, especially under the able prodding of Casca and his fellow centurions.

Tiberius was dismayed, however. He signaled to Lysis to bring his mount, then trotted Chance up and down the line. He repeated this throughout the day, reviewing the marching troops, the baggage train that trailed them, and situated in the middle of the ranks, the new recruits that he'd managed to find so far. They'd been through every town, big and small, anywhere near the Via Aurelia—Alsium, Caere, Graviscae, and Tarquinii itself—only to enroll a pitiful number of men, not enough to form a single maniple. They were headed up to Cosa, but Tiberius didn't have much hope of filling the ranks there, or anywhere all the way up to Pisae. He hated admitting it to himself, but Scipio was right, there seemed to be no landholding citizens left on the road to Hispania to recruit. The ones they had managed to reel in were reluctant, to say the least. For this reason, they were relegated to the middle of the column to keep them from running back home. Italians, he thought. But maybe the praetor in Cosa could offer some relief. Otherwise, he was going to land in Hispania with barely more than the cohort with which he'd started. He'd be the laughing stock of Mancinus's army, and maybe that was the consul's point.

Agitated again, he pulled on Chance's reins to wheel back toward the baggage train where Shafat prodded the oxcart mule drivers and the camp servants with his vitus. As soon as the centurion spotted Tiberius, he redoubled his efforts, shouting, "Step off, you blockheads! Move your asses, and the ones you're riding!"

Tiberius walked Chance next to Shafat, a dark man with black eyes and a thick, black beard, his limbs wrapped around with corded, ropy muscles, typical of Carthaginians. Shafat wore an old Spartan style helmet on his head and a leather lorica, with a long spina, the famous Hispanic sword, strapped to his waist. He carried his vitus loosely, switching hands to whip it around on any soldier who looked to be straggling. Despite his own exasperation, Tiberius said to him, "Easy, Centurion, these men have to last all the way to Numantia. We're making good time as it is."

"Yes, sir," Shafat said, "but they also need to be pushed to maintain our pace."

Tiberius turned and looked back, "I suppose it's the camp followers?"

"There are always women trailing along with their sucklings. We shoo them away, but they straggle back. That's army life. But the true impedimentae are these others hangers-on who were here on the road already, before we arrived. Quite a few more than I've seen in past marches."

"Huh," said Tiberius, turning again to cantor to the column's head. Now that Shafat mentioned it, there had been more people on the road out here in the countryside than expected at this time of year. Some standing, some squatting, he hadn't noticed them before because they hugged either side of the road when the column marched past. This was very strange; though they seemed thin, he didn't recall a pallor among them that might indicate a blight or plague. No bodies in the road, either. He hadn't seen any smoke anywhere, which ruled out civil strife or any sort of raid. So, why were they here? Perhaps they were on some obscure Etruscan cult pilgrimage. It certainly wasn't Roman. It was a mystery, he thought.

Just then, he spied Sextus riding hard down from the top of the road cresting the hill.

"Quaestor, Cosa is within view from the other side of the hill."

"Good," replied Tiberius. "Maybe we can pull in some real numbers there."

The column wended its way up a high hill, so steep that Sextus dropped off his horse and led it up by its halter to give it a rest. Tiberius reached the high point and cupped his eyes against the setting sun. He looked out at the murky blue-green of the Tyrrhenian Sea to his left, the great body of water that separated Italia from Hispania. Between high ridges covered with trees, he could see the sandy coast and parts of a little village, Olbia, partially encircling a gorgeous, placid lagoon. Out on the water, a few small, black dots gently rocked back and forth ever so slightly. Fishing boats, he realized, a key part of the Cosan economy. He liked fish, he thought, brightening at the prospect.

The road dropped steeply away again for perhaps one or two miles, then climbed once more up a smaller hill, 150 or more steps high. Cosa hugged the top of the hill, an old Etruscan fort taken over a century and a half ago. Built in the old style, it featured an arx for a citadel, and the old original city wall, a massive piling of multi-shaped stone and masonry. The new governors had added a few forums since then, though Cosa continued to present itself as a modest town. Fishing, a few olive trees, and a bit of trading on the Via Aurelia had kept Cosae bodies and souls together, but luxury was not part of their lives. Winning glory and booty in Numantia could change all that for a poor fisher-farmer, thought Tiberius, the basis for his hope of filling out his ranks.

Appius had told Tiberius that a Samnite named Lucilius Sentius was the praetor of Cosa. A veteran of the Macedonian wars, Lucilius probably had won the post for his ability to fight in the hills, and also as a way to keep him from fomenting trouble among his own Carricini mountain people in the South. He'd have no loyalty to the Cosae, which would allow him to do whatever was necessary to maintain order. He could be the keystone to producing recruits.

Tiberius turned to Casca. "Instruct Shafat to take all of the men except the auxiliaries down to the water's edge and have them set up camp. Secure the new troops and the perimeter, but otherwise allow the men to bathe and rest."

"And the auxiliaries?" Casca asked.

"They'll accompany us to Cosa. I need to balance a show of force without seeming to be overbearing."

Sextus and his fifty horsemen joined Tiberius, and they proceeded to walk up the steep road toward the gates of Cosa. Behind them, the rest of the cohort cheered and carried on as they worked their way down to the beach. Only the newly recruited men remained glum.

They reached the gates of the town, iron-trussed beams of hardwood pinioned between two massive stone towers joined by a stone parapet. The old walls winded their way around the hillsides upon which Cosa perched. They could see the old arx-style citadel and its battlements on one hill, flanked by the Capitolium and a smaller temple. Another visible hill hosted Cosa's main forum and several houses.

A sentry called down to them, and Sextus shouted out their identity. The Cosan sentry immediately snapped to and ordered the gates to be opened.

Tiberius and Sextus rode into the town, followed by the rest of the auxiliaries. They headed directly toward the arx where Sentius headquartered. As they moved slowly up the main avenue, people moved to the sides, out of the way of the large troop of cavalry. Passing by, Tiberius realized that Cosa was small, a few hundred houses for perhaps 2,000 residents or so. The old Etruscan fort with its ancient arx still loomed formidably, signaling Cosa's importance to controlling traffic on the Aurelia. Beyond that, it was not an imposing community. Where were the men? Tiberius wondered.

A man on foot approached them from the arx. Wearing a plumed helmet and a handsomely carved lorica, the officer saluted them, "Praetor Marcus Lucilius Sentius Caricini at your service, Quaestor Sempronius." Sentius stood several inches lower than Tiberius. In his mid-thirties, he was broad and muscular with little fat on him. His hair was as black as lava rock, his skin colored an eternal brown. Yet, he had vivid, blue eyes that intimated a sharp intelligence and, to a certain extent, wariness.

Tiberius slipped off of Chance and said, "My equitus, Sextus Decimus Paetus."

Sextus, who also had dismounted, traded salutes with Sentius. Stewards took the reins of the horses and led them off, followed by Tiberius's auxiliaries. Sentius turned and motioned with a wave of his arm for Tiberius to proceed to the arx. They fell into step together.

"Cosa's decurions hope you will be able to join them for a banquet during your stay," said Sentius. "They're very excited to find out about Mancinus' plans for subduing the Numantines."

Tiberius grimaced, "I'm afraid I might have to disappoint your council members. I cannot stay long, I'm to meet Mancinus in Hispania on the spring equinox."

Sentius cast a slightly exaggerated sorrowful frown, "Oh, they'll be crushed. A shame."

They had stepped through the equally formidable gates of the Cosa arx and through a broad hall to a fortified door at the back of the wall to their right. Inside, a rough-hewn table covered with documents lit by an oil lamp stood in the middle of the room, an old stone and mortar structure warmed by thick wall coverings. Round-backed wooden chairs also covered with furs and wraps surrounded the table. Sentius gestured to one and circled the table to sit down opposite Tiberius. He signaled his orderly, who placed a tray with a kiln-hardened pitcher and two cups on the table. Sentius poured red wine into one cup and handed it to Tiberius, then poured himself another. He glanced inquiringly at Sextus.

Sextus leaned casually on the back of one of the chairs and said, "Thank you sir, I respectfully decline."

Sentius shrugged, "Well, you can sit, can't you?" Sextus worked his way around the table and draped his long frame in a chair. Sentius returned his attention to Tiberius, who was pouring water liberally into his cup. The Cosan praetor did likewise, and they raised their drinks in a common salute.

"Now, Quaestor Sempronius Gracchus, how can I be of assistance?"

"Simple," said Tiberius. "I need recruits. Lots of them."

Sentius closed his eyes, nodding, "I thought so." He opened his eyes, his expression grim as he said, "I'll help you in any way I can, Quaestor, but I'm afraid you won't find many on the Via Aurelia."

Tiberius kept himself from slumping in his chair. Even though he expected as much after seeing the sparseness of Cosa, he still had hoped that somehow enough men could be found.

"Why do you say that, Sentius?"

The dark-haired Samnite finished a sip of his wine before answering. "Because Caepio and Servillianus were through here before you. The legions quartered in Hispania that Mancinus intends to join were filled out by replacements from Western Italia recruited just a few years ago, half of them, at least. That's part of the problem."

"And the other part?"

Sentius smiled wryly, "Even before you left Rome, the news of Mancinus's campaign sped up the via faster than wildfire, and back down again replete with fresh rumors. When they heard you were coming, every eligible man in northern Italia disappeared into the hills."

"I see," said Tiberius.

"Now, if it were Scipio leading the campaign, it might be a different story. But, most of these boys don't know Mancinus. And, although your name is certainly illustrious enough, what with your legendary father and you winning the Mural Crown at Carthage, it seems that they still would rather hide out until you move on, so that they can stay here and take care of their land."

Scipio, again, Tiberius thought.

"This is an unwelcome assessment of the situation, Sentius."

"I know. I've rounded up a dozen or so that didn't run off fast enough, but that's about it. That's all there are."

Tiberius's voice deepened, hardened. "I could take your troops. I have that authority."

Sentius nodded, "You could, that is within your purview. However, Quaestor, I have but a few hundred men at my command, not even a full cohort. Most of these are triarii, old grey heads at the end of their final tours. Still, they would serve you well, but I can't guarantee for how long, especially in the wilds of Hispania. And, to raise a full legion, you would have to strip every fortress on the Via Aurelia, leaving the entire northern coast of the Tyrrhenian Sea defenseless against pirates, bandits, and other such brigands. Considering how this action might be perceived in Rome, raising a reserve legion for Mancinus at the expense of the safety of one of Italia's most important trade arteries …." trailing off, he shook his head slowly, "I don't think this is a viable solution to your problem."

Sextus stirred, and Tiberius quieted him with a gesture of his finger. Something about Sentius told him that he only spoke the truth and that the last thing he wanted to do was to antagonize a quaestor embarking on a popular war.

"Perhaps you have a suggestion, then, Sentius, for solving this problem?"

Sentius glanced at his orderly, and the soldier slipped over to the door to close it, then stood in front of it with his arms crossed.

"As I said, the Via Aurelia is barren. You won't find a decent recruit from here all the way to Pisae. They're all gone, or hiding because they know your marching orders."

Sentius wore an expectant expression, and Tiberius said impatiently, "Yes?"

"They do not, however, expect you on the Via Cassia."

"The central road," Tiberius said thoughtfully.

Sentius nodded, "My guess is that you will find plenty of healthy young warriors ready to march to Hispania to tame the Numantines."

Tiberius turned his eyes to Sextus, whose expression changed ever so slightly, as if saying silently, Who knows?

"Capeo and Servillianus did not recruit on the Via Cassia," Sentius said, "they didn't have to. They found the troops they needed here."

Exchanging looks again, Tiberius and Sextus stood up together.

"Thank you for your hospitality, Sentius. I'll be returning to my camp, now."

They all rose, with Sentius saying, "I'm sorry you cannot stay. The decurions will be disappointed. Can I not entice you with our baths? We do have simple, but very comfortable bathing facilities here. No? Well, then...."

Sentius jerked his head to the orderly, who opened the door and disappeared, probably to roust the stewards into bringing out the mounts. Before Tiberius could leave, Sentius grasped his forearm, and gently pulled him closer as he spoke lower. "Quaestor, don't mistake me. Although this is a rotten situation for you, it is for me, too. I'm not happy at sending you away empty-handed, but what I've told you is true. I wish you Kerres' blessing, and that Mamerte brings you the soldiers that you need, I swear."

Startled by the intensity of the blue eyes staring up at him, Tiberius paused. Then, he said, "I believe you, Lucilius Sentius."

The Cosan praetor smiled, and followed Tiberius and Sextus out the door.

In the evening after supper, Tiberius stood over a map of Italia on his camp table with Sextus, Casca, and the other three centurions. Ulpius, the native of Lucca in northern Etruria, spoke, using his dagger as a pointer. He was the oldest of the centurions, wearing his silver hair long and wild beneath his helmet, which was dimpled with old dents and creases from battles long past. Tiberius noticed that his forearm, typically strong and scarred, bore a great number of cryptic tattoos, perhaps signs of some mystical cult. That was odd, thought Tiberius, he seemed the most irreverent soldier of them all, famous for his outrageously vulgar marching songs, a clear camp favorite who never lost his good cheer.

"As the crow flies," said Ulpius, "the Via Cassia is fifty miles from here. If we leave the wagons behind, we can march most of the men to Vulsinii in three days."

Casca grunted. "Three days. In that time those oily-feathered Etrurian magpies will flap their way up the via and warn the rest to fly the coop long before we can get there. It might be better not to rush to Vulsinii only to find the same kind of idiots we did on the Aurelia, too slow to escape."

Tiberius frowned, and said, "Let us hope that isn't the case. It is possible that Sentius is right. Perhaps Servillianius and Caepo did pick the cupboard clean on the coast, making it hard on local farmers. But, Italia is fertile. There are bound to be many young tyros left eager for a chance to win Numantine spoils rather than sweat their scrotums off digging in furrows. We should have known—I should have known—before we left Rome that our best chance to raise a legion would be up the Via Cassia, not the Aurelia."

He looked down at the map for a time, chewing his lower lip. "All right. We can't afford to march back to Rome and start over, we're more than halfway to Pisae. The baggage train will slow us down, too, you're right about that, Ulpius. We must move fast. So, Shafat, you'll take the supplies and the recruits we have now straight to Pisae. I'll give you a letter commanding the praetor there to secure them until we return. Ulpius, you will lead us directly to the central road overland. Didius will incorporate any men that we conscript along the way. Sextus, take the auxiliaries back to Veii. Cross over there to ride north up the Cassia. See if you have any luck, but don't delay. If we all do our part, we'll catch any possible recruits in the grid we've fashioned between us. I expect us all to meet in three days at Vulsinii with a good 4,000 new recruits among us. Any questions? All right, ready your men, we leave at dawn."

The centurions saluted and left the tent. Tiberius motioned to Lysis to prepare his bedding. This will work, he thought as he sat, waiting. Plenty of young bulls will be keen to find glory and riches fighting in the farthest reaches of the world. Little would they know of war's toils and tolls, caught up as they were in the phantasm of its maddening allure. Better to be bored on the farm, dipping bread made from home-raised grain into olive oil pressed from garden trees. Wash it all down with vinegar wine left over from the last harvest festival. Better by far than suffering from hunger, thirst, heat, and cold while marching farther and farther away from home, many never to return. But, he sighed, this was Rome's glory, and a chance for young men to serve her while thriving in a way they otherwise could never have known.

Lysis stood next to the small cot and swept his arm over it to show that it was done. Tiberius gazed at the slight figure standing before him, slender, black-haired, weighing no more than a mina. If found along the Via Cassia, he would never be enlisted, not soldier stock at all. As far as he knew, Tiberius thought, Lysis wasn't Greek in the Greek way. But, what did he really know about the youngster? For that matter, how young was he? He didn't even know his age. Looking at him, though, he could picture him standing and pissing into a fountain while his likeness was sculpted on the statue of a young faun reveling in his mischievousness. He shook his head, he never should have brought this reed on campaign. He should have brought Polydius. But, he was too old, and needed at home to help Claudia run the house. Who, then? Who was left but poor Lysis. Tiberius shook his head again, and said, "Tomorrow, Lysis, when we leave, I want you to take Chance and go with the auxiliaries."

Confused at first, Lysis expressed surprise, beaming as he realized what this could mean. "But, Master, how will you travel?"

Tiberius said, "I'll march with the men. You'll ride Chance staying close to Sextus."

"Why, thank you, Master!" Lysis said.

"Yes, well, I don't want to risk the horse going lame by traveling cross country. Better he keeps to the roads for as long as possible. There'll be no choice on the terrain soon enough."

"Yes, Master."

The young Greek retired from the tent, and Tiberius watched him go, a slip of a lad slipping into the night.

Chapter 7. Pastoral

Lysis chased goats over the rocky hillsides when he was a very little boy. Everyone loved him for his unworldly beauty, but his father roared at those who said so out loud. His father, rugged and squat with lean, braided muscles, loved him, hugged him, but made him work as he did all of his children. There was Amphios, the oldest and tallest, dark like their mother. Olus came next, slightly smaller than Amphios, but dark and handsome, too. Zoe was the oldest daughter, golden-haired, followed by Niobe, beautiful and round, then Penelope, brown-haired and lovely. Lysis was next, with obsidian black hair, and the youngest was Kleitos, a tiny version of his bigger brother.

They lived in the small village of Pios on the side of the mountain above Kleoni, south of the great city Korinth. To live, they ate goat cheese with herbs that Mother made, the olives, fresh bread, and, on special occasion, meat served in grape leaves cooked in olive oil and wine. The grapes grew behind their home, a four-room wooden hut built by Lysis' grandfather. The family spent most time together in a large common room that separated three smaller cubbies, one on the west side for his parents, and the other two for the boys and girls on the eastern side, which were warmer in the cold weather. They were too poor to own any slaves, but Lysis' father was influential in council meetings called by Orestes, the Pios headman. Lysis could remember the last one his father went to, a late spring night. He came back a little drunk on wine, but also looking worried. Lysis overheard him talking to Mother, saying that Korinth wanted soldiers to rise up against the Romans. Kleoni had sent a herald to Pios, summoning the town's men to join them on the march to Korinth. Orestes had called for a general meeting at the temple the next night to debate and decide.

Lysis's father took Amphios and Olus with him down the mountain pathway. Lysis and Kleitos followed, hiding in the dark. The townsmen sat on their haunches in a circle in the only temple in the small village, a tiny stone and wooden structure that honored an ancient statue of Apollo, with smaller open-window alcoves for the other important gods: Artemis, to bless the hunt, Dionysus to bless the grape, Hera, queen goddess, and, of course, Zeus, god of gods, all important to the survival of Pios. The villagers prayed to each in turn for rich harvests, good hunts, safety from animal, man, and monsters, and for wisdom in this time of peril, the prospect of war with Rome.

Young hotheads wanted to go right away, and though thought of as a hothead himself, Lysis's father argued against the war. So did the other older men who knew of the Romans's brute strength, their willingness to use it, and the fact that they never gave up. Other men, younger men, wanted to fight. They had never seen a Roman legionary, and couldn't fear what they hadn't seen. They argued that if they agreed to help, the Kleonites might reduce the tribute Pios needed to send every harvest, if in turn Korinth forgave Kleoni's tribute. Lysis' father added, "If we win, which we won't."

The others countered with the fact that Korinth was already at war, soon to be joined by the men from Kleoni and other outlying towns. If they won, they wouldn't forget that Pios had not joined them. But, if they lost, and the Romans were as ruthless as the old men had described them, the consequences would be that much worse. Better to join the Korinthians to give them the best chance to win. The men of Pios voted to join the uprising.

As Orestes closed the meeting with a blessing, Lysis grabbed Kleitos by the arm and tried to run quickly and silently ahead of his father and brothers back up the mountain path. But Kleitos kept tripping and crying, and in trying to shush him to be quiet, Lysis made more noise than he liked. Abruptly, Amphios and Olus jumped out from the side of the path, having looped ahead to catch them. They held the howling boys up by their armpits, but their father did not whip them with his stick.

"Put them down," he said. "It's late. We all should go to bed in peace."

Fifty men from Pios left the next morning, including Lysis's father and his older brothers Amphios and Olus. Hiking his sword behind his back, Lysis's father hugged and kissed all of his children one by one, giving Lysis an extra squeeze as his best-loved son. His father stood, stared at Mother, and walked out the front door without a backward look. Amphios and Olus trailed him, carrying thick staffs sharpened at one end, and knives in their belts.

While his father was gone, Lysis ran the goats up the mountain with Kleitos. While they foraged, the boys played soldiers. Lysis insisted on being the Pios warrior, though Kleitos cried at always having to be the Roman. They played and fought and died, and jumped back up to fight and die again until they were tired. Kleitos refused to be a Roman, so Lysis said he could be Athenian, and fought him again as the brave Pios citizen-soldiers did centuries ago.

They played this way for weeks, breaking off now and then to look to the goats, then re-engaging their armies. Frequently, their battles and rests took them far from the herd.

As usual after a morning meal, Lysis mounted a brisk attack on his little brother, pushing him back with left and right blows of his staff. Kleitos grew angry and suddenly charged like a mad stag, surprising Lysis so that he stumbled and fell backwards. Kleitos stood over him, brandishing his staff as if ready to crown his bully brother once and for all. He froze at the top of his arc, and both heard the crying of the goats in the distance. Panic filled them as they imagined what the cries must mean.

The boys ran as fast as they could down one bluff and to the top of another, looking down on the herd in horror. Three dead goats, their bodies ripped open, lay in a line leading to the rest of the herd, at bay under an outcropping of rock, cowering in front of a female wolf that growled at them, canines gnashing revealed by the severe curl of her lips.

Horrified, Lysis ran down the slope, shaking his staff above his head as he shouted as loudly as he could. The wolf turned her head, then shifted toward him, revealing teats full of milk for a brood of pups hidden somewhere in the mountains. As soon as she turned away, the goats bolted from the rocks down the slope. The wolf gathered itself to leap, and Lysis lowered his staff, pointing it in desperate hope of holding the beast off. In a blur of motion, the wolf reached her head around to clench her jaws on the end of the staff. With a snap of her head, she wrested the staff from Lysis's hands and tossed it behind her. Kleitos cried out.

The wolf lowered its body, almost rubbing its belly on the stony surface, and began to slink toward the terrified boys. Step by step, Lysis moved back, grabbing blindly behind for Kleitos's staff. He felt it and yanked, pulling Kleitos off his feet to pile into him. The wolf gathered itself to spring, and Lysis held his forearm up above Kleitos, trying to get up as he did.

The wolf stopped. Her ears pricked up, and after a second's pause, straightened and whirled to lope to the top of the ridge.

Stunned, Lysis and Kleitos watched her disappear over the ridge even as they began to hear noise behind them. The noise turned into muffled yells, shouting, thumping, panting. They looked behind them, and saw a man emerge running from behind the crest where the boys had been fighting and resting before. Then another man came over the top, and another, two more, then an entire group, running as fast as they could, carrying nothing, pounding down toward them. The first man flew past the two boys, and as the others reached them, Lysis shouted at them.

"The Romans!" cried one man over his shoulder, a man Lysis recognized from the village. Others darted by, some familiar, some strangers. Lysis nudged Kleitos, and they both started running. They headed off in a different direction from the fleeing men, down a goat path that led to a vantage point above Pios.

Once there, they crouched behind a small growth of bushes and watched. Men in strange clothes walked through the village, poking swords into doorways and windows. Behind the soldiers, the boys could see smoke billowing out of the old Temple, and occasionally a lick of fire. Perched on the edge of the mountain, all of the dwellings of the small village of Pios faced one way, out to the valley where Kleoni lay beneath a dark cloud of smoke.

Lysis grabbed Kleitos' arm and began working the two of them across the ridge toward their house. He told his little brother to hide between two rocks, then started down the slope to the back wall of their hut. Inside, he found Mother dead by her own hand, and in their cubbies, Zoe, Niobe, and Penelope, also dead, laid out with care by Mother afterwards. Crying silently, Lysis slipped out the back and stealthily worked his way up to the rocks where Kleitos waited, unawary that Mother and their sisters had left forever, and that they would never see Father, Amphios, and Olus again forever.

Just as he reached Kleitos, who looked up at him, puzzled by his expression, Romans on horses rolled over the hilltops and down the side, their mounts daintily picking their way. Lysis screamed for his little brother to run. But Kleitos turned to look at them slack-jawed, making it easy for one of the hairy riders to scoop him up by the waist.

Lysis ran and ran. He darted down the slopes and through narrow crevices to leave the horsemen's shouts ever more distant as they searched for ways to reach him. He ran for the better part of an hour, crying as he scurried between sharp blades of stone cutting the earth to the sky. The sun began to fall, and he looked for a place to sleep. He hid beneath a rock ledge.

He was hungry and alone, shattered and lonely. His family was gone, and he knew now that he would never see them again. Even Kleitos had been taken from him. He cried.

A hard grip around his leg awoke him. He was yanked out from under the rock, scraping his back as he tried to hold on. The man grabbing his leg cracked Lysis on the side of his head and yelled at him to stop struggling.

The man, a few inches taller than Lysis, wore a leather chest guard and chaps, but no other armor. He pulled Lysis roughly to his feet and brandished his fist when the youth tried to pull away again. Lysis stopped, but the man hit him anyway. Knocked down and senseless, Lysis vaguely noticed the man tying a leather rope around his neck. He jerked it, and Lysis rose as fast as he could to prevent from being strangled. The gruff man walked him down the hillside to a path where other men waited, some on horseback, others on foot, marshaling a long line of bound people. Men, women, and children all stood, waiting, their heads hanging in despair.

Lysis was walked to the end of the line to be tied in, and there he found Kleitos, also bound by his neck. The two boys fell together in a long, sorrowful embrace until the guard pulled them roughly apart. They stood a body's length away from each other, crying and crying, while the others in line stood waiting for the last captives to be tied in.

After an hour on their feet, swaying with exhaustion, they turned their eyes to a bustle at the far end of the line. A troop of horsemen pranced up the narrow road, the leader wearing ornate golden armor and a matching helmet with stiff, red horse hair on top. Lysis instantly realized that this was a Roman general. Next to him, Lysis saw an officer from his land, wearing a leather breastplate and a huge plume of feathers sweeping back from the crest of his helmet. The sides of his helmet covered his nose and cheeks to the tip of his chin. The Roman talked to the other officer briefly, who nodded. He turned and barked an order to the men guarding the line of captives. Immediately, they began flicking their prisoners with short whips, wheeling them around to begin the descent down the mountain. Lysis craned his neck back to stare at the Roman general, a dark-haired god with a stern countenance who, with one quiet order, could change the world for all of the people in the village of Pios.

Two weeks later, they arrived above Korinth, a strange, massive place to the boys, full of man-built stone mountains that were now burning. As they walked down to the city, they almost forgot their own misery when gazing at the corpses in the street and the burnt-out shops and houses. Kleitos began to whimper, and Lysis shushed him to keep the guards from using their whips. The eerie nature of the vast tumbles of stone and smoldering wood frightened them, destruction caused by the terrifying monsters called Romans. The smell of charred wood mixed with that of decaying flesh brought them close to retching. They held their hands over their mouths and noses to hold it back, though some were unable to, adding to the stench.

Eventually, the string of prisoners made its way through the destroyed capital down to the harbor. There, they found the warehouses and piers intact, saved by a general command so that the plunder from Korinth could be shipped to Rome. The captives from Pios were marched to a stone pier where a large ship was tied up, and were told to sit. As they lowered themselves, they looked at the ship, then hid their eyes to cry. Lysis weeped silently, knowing that they might never see their mountainside home again. Kleitos was too young to understand, but he cried out loud for Mother, and that he wanted to go home. Lysis hugged him and rocked him, humming while he secretly wiped his own tears on his brother's tunic.

In the morning, the guards prodded them with the handles of their whips until everyone was awake and standing. The guards ordered them to face forward, which they did, waiting. In the distance, they saw the Roman commander emerge from a giant house with two enormous doors swung wide open to reveal a tall, black mouth of darkness. The Roman, again flanked by various soldiers and officers, mounted his horse and cantered toward them. But, first, he stopped to lean down and talk to the foreman of a gang of dock workers. He gestured at a large stock of amphorae and other goods, the foreman nodded and turned to shout at his crew. They jumped into action, and the Roman commander continued riding toward the prisoners, the Greek officer taking long steps to stay next to him.

When they reached the string of prisoners, they stopped and began talking to each other. The two men seemed to reach a decision and turned to face the long line. The Greek, a Macedonian, murmured the grown-ups in line, began tapping captives on their shoulders with the haft of a short spear. The guards then cut those tapped free from the main tether, looped individual ropes around their necks, and led them off. Occasionally, the Roman officer would utter something. The Macedonian would reply and proceed on, though sometimes he would stop the guards from cutting out some of those being inspected.

Many of the prisoners started to cry out as family members were cut out and led away. The further the two officers progressed down the line, the louder the hue grew, until the Macedonian officer snapped a sharp order. As one, the guards fell on those crying, shutting them up with a series of thudding blows with their whip handles.

The Macedonian worked his way down the line until he reached Lysis. He looked back at the Roman and said something that Lysis couldn't understand. At the same time, he clasped Lysis by the sides of his arms and rubbed them gently, then turned him around to rub his back, bringing his hands down to the sides of his hips.

The Roman called out, and the Macedonian dropped his hands, but replied in a sharp voice. The two of them argued for a while, until finally, the Roman commander pointed down with his ivory and gold baton. The Macedonian followed with his eyes back in the boy's direction. After a moment's thought, he shrugged his shoulders, and cut Kleitos out of the line.

A guard put a tether around the little boy's neck and started to pull him away. But the officer stopped him and took the tether himself.

Kleitos shrieked, pulling against the looped rope, which strangled his scream as he reached open-armed back to his brother. Lysis jumped at him, and was immediately laid out by a guard's whip handle. Lysis heard the Roman shout loudly at the guard and vaguely felt him flinch and shrink away. He could barely raise his head to watch his brother crying inconsolably as the Macedonian steadily dragged him back toward the big dark house. As Kleitos's cries diminished, the Roman spoke again, and the remaining prisoners were marched toward a gang plank. Lysis was lifted up by those closest to him, and helped over the wooden plank as he gazed behind him to where Kleitos had disappeared.

Occasionally, if the wind was favorable, the captain would order the sail to be set as a boost to his rowers. The little shade it provided was welcomed by the captives, who were chained to rings on the top deck. Otherwise, Helios punished them mercilessly as the ship mirrored the coastline on the long, tedious voyage from one tiny port to the next. The guards fed them regularly to have as many reach the market alive as possible. They received enough water to survive, but never enough to quench their thirst, constant on the glassy summer sea known as the Roman Lake.

Even so, Lysis found it difficult to eat or drink. The loss of Kleitos had sapped him of interest. Instead, memories drifted through his mind, of Father and Mother, his brothers and sisters, now happy, joking while they worked, then slain in their house, or marching with the Kleonis to vanish forever.

An old man nudged Lysis by his elbow. Lysis, curled up on his side next to the bulwark where he was chained, gazed up, blocking the white sunlight with his hand. The man looked familiar, drawn, but still someone Lysis had known. He tried to turn his head back to the deck, but the old man pushed him again, harder. Lysis turned to face him. It was Orestes, the village headman. He had agreed to send the men of Pios to war, but was too old to go himself. Now, he lived to look forward to the rest of life as a slave who had led his loved ones and his village to destruction.

Lysis rolled back away from him, but Orestes wouldn't leave him alone. Instead, he forced him to eat and drink. Then, he began to teach him common Greek, the dialect spoken in Korinth and everywhere else after Alexander's rule. He also started to teach him Latin.

In every port, the captain of the guards cut loose some of the captives and dragged them down the gangplank. They never returned, though sometimes strangers were brought onto the ship, though always fewer than the number taken off. Many times, the officer came back alone. Orestes explained it as part and parcel to the slaving business, selling as you go, but always trading up, too, in hopes of bringing a better quality of goods to the premier market, Rome, where the prices would be highest and profits the best.

But some died on the way. Exposure carried some away, among the older and younger captives. Others seemed to die of despair, ignoring food and water until their shrunken bodies were tossed over the side. Orestes had saved Lysis from that fate, and he tried to rally other survivors from Pios, though he failed to save everyone. Slowly, though, Lysis gained strength. Gradually, he began to understand what some of the Roman guards were saying to each other in their own tongue.

On the last leg, the vessel slowed against opposing currents. Food ran out, and they were beginning to starve. Even the sailors and the oarsmen complained, and the ship's captain began to look very nervous. Orestes told Lysis that if the water ran out, there would be trouble, an uprising. The captain would be killed and thrown overboard, followed by the slaves to whom he had given the last of the food in an effort to preserve his investment.

Lysis could care less, as sick and miserable as he was. But, Orestes refused to allow him to drift off into oblivion. Instead, he cajoled him and gave him most of his own food until there was none to give. Still, Lysis languished, and the beautiful dark-haired boy grew gaunt and jaundiced lying in the foul waste of the dead and dying captives.

The ship docked at last in Ostia. The officer of the guards yelled for them to stand in a line. Orestes lifted Lysis to his feet and held him up. The guards released them from the deck manacles and tethered them again by their necks to lead them off the ship. The men, women, and children left alive lurched and staggered across the deck and down a broad gangplank. If one fell, several would be pulled down as well, halting the line until the guards came to untangle them and jerk them back to their feet. Eventually, they all made it off the ship and onto the broad pier, and continued to shuffle up a wide avenue.

The size of the port dwarfed Korinth's and the others they had seen. Orestes explained to Lysis that Ostia served all of Rome, its warehouses were vast and endless. The bustle and noise of the crowded wharfs beat upon Lysis' ears almost painfully. The captain of the guards paced back and forth the length of the line, clearly bearing a concerned expression as he surveyed the sad condition of the property in his charge. Looking at the broad man's familiar, sun-darkened face, furrowed by long wrinkles from his temples to his chin, Lysis felt that he knew him now after traveling with him so long. He imagined seeing him sitting with Orestes and the other elders at the fire-lit meeting, deciding whether or not to go to war. In his weary mind, Lysis mused that he would remember the captain's face for the rest of his life.

The avenue eventually opened into a squared forum surrounded by two- and three-story houses like the dark one in Korinth. These vast buildings were fronted by food stalls and wine shops. A raised platform stood at the far end of an open courtyard, flanked by a series of pillars with iron rings interspersed around each one. The eyes of the roped captives fixed on the little fountain in the middle of the forum, where a relief of Cupid spewed water from his mouth into a small pool. Instinctively, the line of prisoners moved toward the fountain, moaning unevenly from their thirst. The captain yelled to the guards to find food and water for them at once. They were jerked and whipped back into line and forced toward the nearest pillars, some crying in anguish as they passed the fountain.

The guards tied them to the rings on the pillars and pushed them down to the ground. Slaves soon showed up with ceramic jugs and ladles, and moved among them portioning out water to each as they passed. A second wave of slaves came through with bread, tearing off sizable chunks for the ravenous captives. Orestes made sure that Lysis received plenty of water and food, but also held him back from drinking too much too fast. Soon, the emaciated boy's glassy eyes began to clear, and he gazed dully at the surroundings around them.

Somewhat revived, the roped captives were prodded up by the guards and herded to the end of the square. There, they were untied and separated by the officer in charge. The captain still looked unhappy at the state of his charges. Wearing an expression on his face as if he'd just eaten bitterly sour grapes, he barked at his men to hire carts to take the select slaves to Rome. The rest would be sold here.

To his surprise, Lysis found himself in a group apart from Orestes, who gazed at him with deeply sorrowful eyes as the young boy was lifted into a cart pulled by a donkey. As the cart carried Lysis away, he stared back at the old man, who called to him to live, to stay alive and work for his freedom.

A thousand times bigger than Korinth, a million times the size of Pios, Rome did not awe Lysis. He was too tired, cold, and worn out from the long journey to the capital of the world. The tall columns topped by self-assured heroes astride snorting steeds, the unearthly huge temples gilded with gold and a riot of other lush colors, the glut of clay brick and wooden houses cascading down the closely packed hills, everything wedged in behind age-darkened walls stacked centuries ago by giants, the confusion of it all acted to dull his senses, except for the feeling of wanting it to be over, whatever it was.

As hot as the summer air blanketed the city, Lysis was cold and damp. Once they'd reached the outskirts of the city, the guards had taken them from the carts and had thrown them into the river. What little grime washed away was replaced by a heightening of the dank, sour smell of their filthy clothing.

No matter; when they reached the slave market, the rags were stripped from each of them in turn as they were displayed to potential customers. Lysis watched as each stood before the crowd to be sold; men, women, children, some he'd known from Pios, others from different villages and towns around Korinth. Held by a lead around the neck, a male's tunic or a female's shift was loosened to drop to their ankles. They were pulled by the tether to rotate, stopped again face-front to the crowd. Some tried to cover themselves, while others simply stood arms at their sides, looking down, lost.

The captain, now the auctioneer, came down and put a tether on Lysis while the other guards released him from the line. He pulled him up the steps onto the stone stage and showed him to the buyers. Naked, Lysis turned slowly around to the tension of the leather leash, and tripped over his tunic. The captain gave a sharp tug, half trying to prevent the fall, half out of frustration. He struggled to his feet again to face the crowd, and the captain called out for bids. At first, no one stirred. The captain shouted louder, and used his fingers to open Lysis's mouth to show his perfect teeth. Does not anyone want this exotic boy, this pleasure boy?

More like a cooked chicken, yelled some wag in the back, causing the crowd to laugh. The captain's expression turned darker. He cried out again, No one? Disgusted, he pushed Lysis to the stairs. Lysis descended, and a guard tied him up to a ring on one of the pillars.

Lysis threw himself on the ground. He wondered if he would be taken back to Ostia to be sold there. But, what difference did it make?

He heard a noise, a boy loudly, "There, over there. That's the one," pointing his finger at Lysis on the ground. A Roman boy stood over him, looking down at him, still pointing. He looked to be roughly the same age, Lysis observed, and he, too, had pitch-black hair. He wore a plain tunic made out of fine linen cinched by a gold-colored cord, and a pair of beautifully crafted, leather sandals adorned his feet. Behind him stood three other Romans, a tall, handsome man, also black-haired, also exquisitely attired; an older man with a mottled black and grey beard, not quite as well dressed; an older woman, of goddess-like beauty, though small, dressed in deep green robes that matched her cool eyes.

"But, he's a toy, Gaius, not a work slave at all," said the tall man, some years older than the Roman boy. "He's supposed to be my personal servant. Now, how can he do that?"

"He looks like a drowned cat," said the woman. "You'd think they'd throw them some bread now and then."

"Gaius," the tall young man said, "he's pathetic."

"No, no, Tiberius, he's the one. He'll be good, I know he will."

Tiberius turned to the older man and said, "Polydius, talk to him."

"And, what makes you so sure that this poor chicken bone of a boy can be a good body servant, Master Gaius?"

Young Gaius pulled himself upright and poked his chest with his thumb, "Because he looks just like me!"

The others laughed, shaking their heads, but Tiberius whispered to Polydius, who left. Soon, he returned and nodded his head. Tiberius grimaced slightly, then reached down to Lysis, "Okay, boy, come with us. Gaius, give me a hand, he's a bit unsteady."

"He can barely stand," said the beautiful woman. "Quite a buy, Tiberius, a real steal."

"Yes, Mother, well, let's hope he works out."

"I obtained him at a good price, Mistress," said Polydius.

"You better have."

Lysis rose between them, and they guided him up and down the streets of Rome to their home. The other servants washed him, gave him a clean tunic to wear, and fed him in the kitchen. When night fell, they put him in a small storage room on bedding made of old blankets stuffed with straw and wool. Lysis laid down and felt as if he floated on a cloud.

In the middle of the night, his eyes popped open. He listened, but heard nothing. Slowly, he gathered himself and crept to the door. He nudged it open, and listened again. Then, he slipped out and down the servants' hallway in the back to the kitchen. Silently, he rooted around until he found vegetables, dried fruit, jerky of some kind, and water. Hiding beneath the big, wooden butcher's table in the middle of the room, he ate, taking one bite here, one bite there of the different, wonderful foods that he had found. He would stop to drink, then ate more.

A light in the kitchen froze him. Panicky, he thought to throw the food and run, but before he could move, the lamp dropped beneath the level of the table, exposing him to the figure stooped over and peering in to see him.

Polydius motioned to him to come out. Slowly, Lysis put what was left of the food down and came out from under the opposite side of the table. Sick inside, he realized that there was no place to run; Polydius stood between him and the doorway.

"Do you speak Latin?" the old man asked in common Greek.

Lysis slowly raised his thumb and finger above his head.

"Just a little," said Polydius. "Then, I shall teach you more." But before Polydius could continue, Tiberius entered the kitchen.

"What's this, Polydius? Why is everyone up at this hour?"

"Not everyone, Master, just your new man servant, helping himself to another bite to eat."

Tiberius took in the scene, then rolled his eyes. "For the love of Gaia ...." He pulled a stool away from a work bench and whipped it around the table. "Sit, young Lysis. What are you hungry for? No more? I see by the remains on the floor that you have had another balanced meal. Well, then, Polydius, get him some wine. Maybe a drop will get him to sleep so that we can."

Tiberius left.

Polydius opened a cabinet and pulled out a jug of wine. He poured a cup, and handed it to Lysis. As the boy sipped cautiously, eyeing the old Hellene over the cup's rim, Polydius spoke.

"You need not steal food here, Lysis. The Sempronii are kind. They can be stern and demanding, but they do not beat slaves, nor starve them. The gods have smiled upon you by leading you here. That, and making you look like Master Gaius."

Lysis thought he saw a trace of a smile on the old Hellene as he turned to leave. Before he went out the door, however, he turned his head back to Lysis and said, "Make sure you clean everything up thoroughly after you're finished, including the mess under the table."

Chapter 8. The Pedites

Tiberius had divided the men into two groups, one long line evenly spaced apart that beat across the meadows and groves, and the other into small bands sent ahead with Ulpius and Didius, ready to intercept any potential recruits that might have slipped behind the sweep. For three days they climbed over stone walls, sidled through vineyards, tip-toed through grain fields, and otherwise slogged through low brush thickets, tree stands, streams, ponds, meadows, marshes, and an occasional rutted farm road. Still, recruits eluded them, even with the long line of seasoned soldiers searching under every rock and tree. It was bizarre, Tiberius thought, tramping through the heartland of Italia without finding the cornucopia of children that had supplied Rome's armies for so many centuries. Instead of a landscape of small farms tended by former legionaries, he and his men marched across vast plantations similar to that of Scipio's, but without retired soldiers tending the fields and orchards. They traversed huge tracts of rich soil where grapes, grain, and livestock looked ready to flourish from the cultivation of slaves, vistas broken only by overgrown woods and thickets on ground deemed infertile. Every now and then, they would come upon a falling-down hovel, abandoned by the small farmer who once had lived there. Where had he gone? Where had all the settlers gone?

Mid-morning of the third day, Tiberius's line broke through a thick bramble into a clearing where a grand villa the size of Scipio's stood, its stone façade a blinding white in the spring sun. Grunting, Tiberius flicked his head, and Casca fell in with him as they set out for the front of the villa. A magnificent marble portico wrapped around the building at a height that required climbing a dozen steps to reach the level of the door.

"Cursed shades of Hades, it looks like a city basilica!" exclaimed Casca in a whisper.

"With as many goods inside, no doubt," replied Tiberius.

When they reached the top of the stairs, a core of guards rushed toward them, half of them retired soldiers, half freedmen gladiators, Tiberius estimated.

"Stand off, boys," warned Casca. "One shout will send four hundred from the Fifth up your asses before you can cry 'Kiss my mother.'"

The guards pulled up.

"I am Tiberius Sempronius Gracchus, Quaestor to Gaius Hostilius Mancinus, Consul of Rome, on legitimate business. Who is your master?"

"Tiberius Gracchus," a familiar voice said, "you march to Numantia."

The guards separated and Publius Rufus Faba emerged, much smaller than the warriors around him. Chins trebled down from his bulwark lips, and a thinning wreath of sandy hair crowned his head. Despite the country setting a hundred miles from Rome, he wore a full scarlet-hemmed toga, something of a personal reminder of his high station, and certainly full notice that others in his presence should not forget his status.

"Rufus, what a surprise," Tiberius said flatly.

"Equally as pleasant to me, Gracchus. What are you and your assault troops doing mashing around in my fields and vineyards?"

"That's the surprise to me, Senator. I thought that these would be public lands, settled by veterans and their families." "Trolling for recruits, are you? You'll find none here, Quaestor. This land is my land, hard-earned through long service to Rome and legitimately purchased. A good thing, too, since its previous tenants barely broke ground. They wasted Italia's gift of fertility granted by the great grain goddess Ceres herself."

"All drunkards and laggards, no doubt?"

"Without a doubt!"

"Including women and children, I suppose?"

"They all come from somewhere. You know, it's a shame your brother-in-law isn't running this war, Gracchus, he'd have Numantia straightened out in short order, bring plenty more land into the ager publica."

"Indeed," Tiberius said dryly. "It is a shame that he could not serve, engaged as he is with other priorities. I visited his estate earlier, by the way, and his orchards and vineyards look splendid, too."

"Yes, it should be a bumper year all around," Rufus replied, "just like last year. My granaries are bursting from last fall's harvest! Even as we speak, I'm off to Cosa to discuss arrangements and transport to deal with the surplus. I understand that the east did not have a bountiful harvest last year, and they might be interested. Wouldn't that be an irony, selling grain to the Egyptians for once?"

"One for the historians."

"In any case, I'd adore inviting you in for a proper feast in your honor, Quaestor, but I must be off before the goods rot away. You understand, of course?"

"Absolutely, Senator, absolutely. Please do not allow me to impede you. I'll just gather my cohort and be on my way."

"Thank you for your understanding, Gracchus. I promise you, upon your triumphant return from Numantia, I will fete you at twice the expense as recompense for my churlish hospitality this day. You and your entire family, including, of course, your most beautiful and forbearing matron."

"You mean my wife?" said Tiberius.

"Ye gods, no, I mean your mother, of course!"

"I see. But my wife can come, too?"

"Certainly. I invited the entire family, didn't I?"

"You did for certain. I'll look forward to receiving your message regarding the date as soon as I return from Hispania."

"Excellent! All right, then, I must depart, as must you," Rufus said, waving.

"Right, Rufus. May the gods be kind to you. Casca, please form the troops."

As they continued their march into the brush again, Tiberius hissed, "What a jackass turd he is, Casca."

"Yessir."

"And, if you ever repeat that, I'll deny it and have you thrashed with your own vitus."

"By what I saw today, sir, if I ever do such a thing, I'll hand my switch over to you personally and ask you to strike the first blow."

"You can count on more than one."

"Yessir, thank you, sir. So, that's a senator? With all due respect, I mean, sir."

"Don't ask me for respect, Centurion, I'm a plebeian, thank the gods, and I'm no senator."

They pushed on, fighting through the brush as Tiberius thought that unless Casca had found the Hydra of recruit reproduction, Mancinus was going to be seriously disappointed at the strength of his new legion.

Rufus watched them disappear into the trees and bushes surrounding his villa, then signaled to his headman.

"Call up a full guard," he said, "we leave at once."

"Yes, Senator. Do you want the litter?"

"Gods no, we need to move! Bring up the carriage. Horse the guard, we have to hurry."

"To Cosa, sir?"

"You are an imbecile! Mice have more brains! We go to Scipio full speed. He needs to know what his idiot brother-in-law is doing!"

With a constant, cacophonous percussion of hooves on stone, Sextus led the cohort's auxiliaries to the Via Cassia and up to Vulsinii in two and a half days, as estimated. Along the way, they had rousted men out of Baccanae and Sutrium, inducting as many as they could, another century of malcontents. Sextus hoped that Tiberius was doing better. He wheeled his horse about to survey the land around them. A walled town of several thousand farmers and merchants located in the saddle of the lower slopes of the Italian spine, Vulsinii and the surrounding fields was not much to look at except for the large lake to the east. Sextus decided to make camp west of Vulsinii and halfway up the escarpment where the original, ancient Etruscan city had perched. In this way, he figured he would be able to see Tiberius and the rest of the cohort approach from the direction of the Via Aurelia, which should bring them close to the lake. The Vulsinii people would see the cohort approaching, too, possibly spurring those of service age to flee up the mountainside to hide in the old city site, right into the arms of Sextus and his waiting auxiliaries.

He gave his orders, cautioning the men to move stealthily up the hillside in a circuitous route to avoid alarming their Italian allies. When they reached an elevation that allowed him to see the city and the shores of the lake, Sextus told the men to make camp, no fires, cold meals. He dropped from his horse and handed the reins to Lysis.

"Brush the horses down, Greek, and don't be mating with any of the mares. If you get one with a foal, who knows what we'll get when she drops it, maybe a poet with a back kick."

Lysis smiled as he walked them away, always happy to groom and pet the big quadrupeds. Born to them, the little slave was, marveled Sextus. Except for Rome's horsemen, most only rode because they had to. Though, he thought, most weren't quite as shy of horsemeat as Tiberius. Sextus thought of him humping cross country through fields and woods rather than riding easy up flat stone roads. Maybe that was leadership, but it struck him as a bit crazy, too. Well, to work, now, or fear the outcome.

Sextus grabbed a waterskin from an orderly and silently slipped down the slope from the camp to a line of tall evergreens. He slung the plump bag over his shoulder and proceeded to climb a tree, easily rising hand over hand to a limb with an unobstructed view of the surrounding area. He could see the lake in the distance, and farther on, low forests that began at the edge of the fields and pastures dotting the landscape. Tiberius would emerge from those woods, Sextus figured.

As he watched, he noticed campfires near the lake, and wondered if Tiberius had arrived first. Immediately, he realized that the quaestor would never encamp while his small force was divided. The fires must be for locals, and he wondered if they fished there, or trolled for freshwater shellfish. Seemed like a lot of campfires though, he thought, many of them concentrated at the southern end, a good number of miles from Vulsinii. He decided to scout them tomorrow. Right now, the sun was setting, which made it harder to see anything. With a grunt, he climbed down from the tree.

"Send out some men before dawn tomorrow to scout the campfires below," he said to Decimus, his first decurion when he arrived back in camp at dusk. Lysis handed him a cold goat shank and a cup of vinegary wine, and gestured to a rough resting place next to a fallen tree trunk. Sextus threw himself down against it and began to eat and drink. He paused, and said, "Did you eat?"

Lysis nodded his head.

"Good. Go to bed. We don't know what tomorrow will bring, so it's wise to save our strength tonight."

Lysis slipped to the ground and pulled his bedclothes around him. Sextus glanced at him, then continued eating and drinking. He gazed about at the muffled figures of soldiers in their sleep and the silhouettes of guards melded to the trees, and felt content, as content as he could feel, anyway. This hardly compared to lounging at home on a plush couch, alternating sweet figs with fresh bread dipped in warmed olive oil and sampling the most exquisite of roasted cuts. Repasts rivaling the ambrosia of the gods, he reminisced, complemented with wine like nectar. That was the life, he thought, as he drifted off propped up against the fallen trunk.

Tiberius and his cohort emerged from the woods north of the lake near Vulsinii with only another handful of recruits. Weary and long-faced, he ordered his men to form up even as Sextus thundered up with a small troop of riders behind him.

"Salve, Quaestor!" he shouted, saluting.

"Hello, Sextus," Tiberius said wearily.

Sextus slipped off of his horse in a fluid motion. "I've just come from Vulsinii."

"And?"

"They've barricaded the city and stand armed on the walls."

"God of lightning! Are they mad?"

"Clearly, they are."

"Orcus have them. Lysis! Bring me Chance!"

They arrived at the gates of Vulsinii, which sat on the saddle between the hills and the rise of the mountains. A town really, rather than a city, it was walled with ancient tufa stones topped by more recently placed bricks and mortar. Fearfully, the Vulsinii militia peered down from the narrow embrasures at the Roman contingent standing before the gates. Tiberius roared.

"Praetor, do you wish us to raze your town and sell your women and children into slavery? You and your brave citizen soldiers will be dead, of course. Is that what you want?"

The praetor of Vulsinii stuttered, "No, Quaestor, no. We are loyal to Rome, and we do not defy you."

"Then, what is this?"

"With abject respect, Quaestor, we have no more young soldiers to send to Hispania. Those we sent with Caepio never returned. The harvest was hard in those years, and harder still on the mothers of our lost Vulsinii boys. We cannot send more, and if we must die, we will all die together at home, not in some strange, cold land."

Tiberius sat back. Chance rumbled a sneeze, and Tiberius leaned forward.

"Praetor ... what is your name?"

"Julius Paulus Clavicus, your honor."

"Praetor Paulus Clavicus," Tiberius said, "you are an honorable man, and a brave man. But, what am I to do? I need a legion to take to Hispania to fight this righteous war against the impudent Numantines, as my father did before me. Vulsinii is an ally of Rome, and subject to the laws that require allies to provide troops in the Republic's defense. I need legionaries, Clavicus. What am I to do?"

The praetor, a small, skinny man who appeared to Tiberius as someone who might make his living selling wine pots, shivered before him. Then, the pot-seller, or maybe linen merchant, stiffened and stood taller than his actual height.

"We have sent enough boys far away to die. We have no more to spare. Go to the lake, and take their young men to fight Rome's wars. They have nothing to lose, and there are as many of them as birds in the air."

Tiberius gazed up at the insolent man, whose near bitterness in his declaration surely would bring Rome's wrath down upon his town. All around him, though, the citizen soldiers didn't flinch at their magistrate's defiant statement.

"I can bring up the troops, and we can have the town in a couple of hours," Casca said.

Tiberius scratched his eye beneath his gaudy bronze helmet. "And how is that? We have no siege weapons and only a cohort. Seeing that, they might sally from the city and chase us back to Rome."

"Doubtful, sir. They won't stand up to seasoned soldiers from the Fifth. I could have ladders made in an hour, and we could sweep the walls in two."

Tiberius said, "Perhaps, but even if we could bring them down, what good will that do us? We can destroy the town, but only at the cost of killing all the recruits that we need."

"True," Casca said, "though we'll be richer for it from the slaves and goods. It's within your rights."

Tiberius looked at Casca almost condescendingly, even though he knew better than to underestimate his centurion primus. "Casca, how do you think Rome will feel about our conquest of an ally like this, when we haven't even left Italia?"

Casca shrugged. "It's up to you, Quaestor, but no matter what you do, Rome will find a way to fault you for it."

Tiberius laughed, "True enough."

He turned back to the Vulsinii praetor and his soldiers, all who seemed to have sagged somewhat just in the past few moments from the tension of waiting for the inevitable. Tiberius squinted, then said to Casca, "Do you see those soldiers on the walls? How do they look to you?"

Casca raised his eyes to the walls, then said, "Old men, and a few boys. There are no young soldiers of military age on that wall."

"Exactly. Casca, I think Paulus is telling the truth. They don't have any young men left to recruit."

"Can you be sure, sir? This might be a ruse, hiding the young warriors to make us think that their cupboards are bare."

"Perhaps," Tiberius said, shaking his head, "but, really, how many do you think they have up there, in the wake of Caepio's predations? This is a desperate act of despair, and they fully expect us to crush them. The

Vulsinii people know that they can't win in any way, yet, there they are."

Casca didn't respond as he tried to think of an alternative course.

Tiberius thought some more, then called up to Paulus.

"Why should we go to the lake, Paulus, so that you can run into the hills? That won't work. My equitus has our auxiliaries stationed in the foothills to intercept any who try to escape. What could I possibly find at the lake that will save Vulsinii, Paulus?"

"The pedites!" cried Paulus, "hundreds of them, thousands. Allies of Rome who have no place to go, nothing to eat. We had to turn them away, too, because we have only enough for ourselves. They're at the lake, on their way to Rome to find new lives or death, whichever comes first. You'll find all the recruits that you need there, Quaestor. Go to the lake."

"The pedites? The lake?"

Paulus pulled himself straight up again, and raised his voice in stentorian style. "You can kill us all, Roman quaestor, and still march for Hispania without your legion. It doesn't matter to us, we are ready to die either way."

Tiberius tightened his mouth. Impudent Etrurian. He thought about sending Casca for the cohort after all, to knock the stiffness out of that little factotum's spinal column.

"Shall I call up the lads, sir?"

Tiberius sighed, exasperated. "No, Casca, do not call up the lads."

He shouted to the praetor. "Paulus, I'm leaving, now. But, I promise you, if I find nothing of interest at the lake, I will bring down Vulsinii. And before I have you crucified, you will watch your wife and daughters raped, then sold into slavery if they survive."

Paulus himself sighed, and said, almost inaudibly, "May the gods be with you, Quaestor."

Tiberius wheeled Chance around, confused by how this officious little man could make him feel almost powerless. He sped off toward the camp, growling at Casca.

"Prepare the men to move silently tonight. I want a cordon around the campfires at the south end of the lake so that no one can escape. One or one hundred, I want to be sure that we confront everyone who is there."

"It is done, Quaestor."

The cohort swept down on the campsite without incident. They met no guards, not even one soul tending a fire. Instead, smoldering embers trickled smoke up into the lightening sky as bodies slowly stirred from the prodding of the legionaries's pila shafts. Dazed men, women, and children stumbled out from under lean-tos, makeshift tents, and cloaks pulled over them.

The soldiers herded them together into a group, several hundred of them. Tiberius looked on, puzzled by their lethargy. Rather than act fearfully, most of them stood with their eyes lowered, as if indifferent to their fates.

Tiberius noted them shivering on this cold, spring morning in thin shifts and cloaks. The youngest children cried out, their noses runny with green mucus, their faces an unnatural ruddy shade from fever.

"These people are starving, Casca," murmured Tiberius.

"Yessir, they look to be so. Weather's not doing them any good, either."

"No," replied Tiberius thoughtfully. He studied them for a time, watching as some of them simply sat down and refused to rise, no matter how much the legionaries goaded them.

"Didius, hold the men back," Casca called out.

"Yes, Primus," said the wolfish centurion. He bellowed an order, and the soldiers stepped back, though still at the ready with their short spears.

Tiberius sat up in his horse, and in a raised voice, called out, "Is there a headsman among you? Anyone to speak for you?"

The people in front of him milled about, some searching behind them and around, until a tall man with a staff walked to the front. He, too, was thin, though the long muscles of his arms and his thick calves evidenced a full life of labor. A veteran, Tiberius assessed, old, maybe even fifty, yet kept lean by working his plot of land. Tiberius nodded to Casca.

"Who are you, soldier?" Casca said, "What legion?"

"Sacerdus Quarto, Centurion Primus, Cohort Praetoria, Fourth Legion, Emeritus."

"The Fourth, eh, and a centurion primus. Who was your general, Centurion?"

"Quintus Opimius."

"Master of the Oxybian Ligures," said Tiberius, "Well done, Centurion. So, why do we find you now on the side of the road instead of at home cozy in your bed?"

The tall man leaned on his staff and spit. "What home? What bed?"

Slightly taken aback, Tiberius said, "Fallen on hard times, have you, Primus? A bad toss of the dice?"

Quarto looked to spit again, but held back. "My pardon, Quaestor, but do I look like someone who plays out his life, his honor, with a toss of the dice?"

Tiberius and Casca remained silent for a time, taking in Quarto's bitter defiance. He glared at them, his black pupils shining.

"No," Tiberius said quietly, "you don't."

He gestured to Lysis, who ran forward with a wineskin and a bag of bread and fruit. Quarto solemnly shook his head, no.

Tiberius flicked his head, and Lysis retreated.

"So, what happened?"

"What happened? The same as with all of these people here, Rome's allies, mind you. My land—all of our land—was taken from us by fat cat patricians and their wormy lawyers."

"Careful, Centurion," said Casca, and Tiberius frowned at him. He turned his attention back to Quarto, and said, "I don't understand, Quarto. Your land was allotted to you for your service, is that not correct? From the public lands."

Quarto nodded, "I received my forty iguiera, all right, not more than fifty miles north of here. Good land, where me and my woman could put in a vegetable patch and some grain for the beasts, a few dates and olive trees. We lived well, if not high on the hog. Hard work, but our kids grew, we were content. Until the magistrate showed up, telling us that there was a superseding claim to our land. I told him he was wrong, but he showed me paper. I can't read, neither can the woman. He said we needed to move off. I told him to kiss off. After he left, I went to the crawl space to find my sword and sharpen it.

"The magistrate returned with a bunch of bully boys, used to knocking poor peasant farmers about, not a centurion primus last blooded in Marseila. I flicked open a couple of legs, and they left. A few days later, I woke up to our date trees cut down at the base, same with the olives. The pigs were dead, even the litter. So was the donkey and the milk cow, skulls crushed, throats cut. The birds were all dead, poisoned I think. A burnt torch had been stuck in the ground in front of our home.

"I went into the village looking for the magistrate, who was nowhere to be found. I went back home and barred the door. At night, I hunted, slept days. We didn't have much to eat. A fortnight later, mounted troops arrived at Sol's rising, the magistrate thick in the middle. He read a dictum that told me I was trespassing, the men dismounted and started toward me with swords out, twenty of them. I backed away, my woman and the kids behind me, until we were out on the road. Three months ago.

"Others here have walked the road longer, many of them and theirs have died since. We'll die, too, soon enough, since there's not much left to forage in the countryside. The new patriarchs of our land keep close guard on their vineyards and olive groves, and they're out looking to kill poachers. After wandering up and down the Vias, we set camp here by the lake. At least we have water, though the Vulsinii have warned us not to fish."

Quarto shrugged his shoulders, "We do, anyway, but don't get much, not enough for a real meal. Just something to keep us going, for what, we don't know."

He fell quiet, resting on his staff, looking down at the ground.

Tiberius felt paralyzed. He could feel Casca's and Didius's eyes on him, and those of the starving crowd around him, hopeless as they stared at him. Roman citizens and allies, he thought, thrown out of their houses and left to starve or to be cut down like barbarian rebels. This was worse, he realized, than what he had seen at Carthage under Scipio. At least those victims had met a quick end to their misery. But this was torture, Tiberius thought, his mind blackened by the sight in front of his eyes. As a youth, he'd thought he never would see such an order of cruelty as the deaths meted out to the Carthaginians, men, women, children. He hated Scipio for it. Now, he witnessed an even more insidious, more despicable form of conquest and murder. For what? Extravagant estates farmed for profits, food taken out of the mouths of their own people to be turned into coin by slave labor, the rich getting richer. The greed! Rufus, and his gang of "Good Men." Scipio.

"Quaestor Gracchus?" Casca said softly.

Tiberius refocused, glanced at Casca, then back at Quarto.

"How many are there of you, Quarto?"

Quarto answered, "A thousand more or less, mostly women and children."

Juno comfort us, thought Tiberius, a thousand. He looked at them, back and forth. Mostly women and children, sick from hunger and the cold. A women with stringy hair, skin tight against her cheekbones, held a baby close to her chest with one arm while holding on to the hand of a small boy with the other. The boy whined softly what sounded like an endless prayer that had lost its meaning. The bundled baby never moved, and Tiberius wondered if it was still alive.

He slipped off his horse before Lysis or an orderly could assist him and walked up to Quarto. "Tell your people to build fires. They will eat today."

Around the praetorian mess, the centurions ate without their usual boisterous good cheer. Instead, they chewed their bread thoughtfully, sipping at the vinegary wine rather than gulping it as usual. Now and then, Tiberius felt them glancing at him almost surreptitiously. He could imagine what they thought, their commander desperate to raise a legion, falling further behind the appointed time for arriving in Hispania, never mind training on the way. And, they were right, he thought. He was three weeks into the march with a handful of malcontents to show for his trouble, while praetors from two different allied cities defied him. Wait until Rome heard about this, Rufus and his ilk. He was ruined before he'd even left the shadow of Rome's walls. The humiliation would be total. How could he ever face Claudia, Appius, or his mother?

His stomach lurched. "Lysis, take my plate. I'm off my feed."

The young Greek seamlessly slipped in to take away the plate and utensils.

Tiberius gazed around at the hard men seated before him, all proven in combat. He wondered if they had second thoughts about him, about the truth of his Mural Crown at Carthage. Maybe they thought that honor had been prearranged by his cousin the consul. He laughed bitterly, of course it had been in its own way, an accident of timing, not courage. Now, here he was, leading a corps of scarred veterans who likely had bets going on how long he'd last. Who had wagered on the shortest time, he wondered? Casca? Didius? Ulpius? Shafat? Had Sextus joined in? Disloyal bastards.

He compressed his lips.

"Shafat, send for Quarto."

The Etrurian first seemed surprised, then left the tent. In short order, he returned with the tall veteran.

"Quarto, sit with us, have a glass of wine."

"I don't drink, sir. Not for years."

"No wonder you were able to keep a farm," said Ulpius, and the others laughed out loud.

"You're right, brother," said Quarto. "I knew that if I didn't quit, I'd be gone long before now. But, who's to know what the better life is now?"

"Salvete," the men said, lifting their cups in a common salute, then drinking.

"Quarto, you tell me there are a thousand dispossessed people out there, good citizens and subjects of Rome."

Quarto lowered his head in assent.

"The great number of them are women and children, no?"

"Yes, Quaestor, roughly."

Tiberius acknowledged Quarto with a nod, then paused for a moment, as if ruminating.

"That means that three hundred or so of these displaced are men, correct?"

"Yessir."

Tiberius leaned in, "Are any of them veterans?"

Quarto's head moved back. Then, he smiled. "Almost to the man, Quaestor."

"Three hundred veterans. Soldiers of Rome missio."

"Hungry, but handy with shield and sword, Quaestor."

The other centurions looked back and forth at each other after every exchange, their mouths open in surprise.

"I imagine so, Centurion Primus." Tiberius sat back. "So, do you think these men would consider becoming evocati?"

Quarto grinned, a stunning change to his demeanor since they'd met him twelve hours before. "I do believe they'd dance at the chance, Quaestor. Most of them still have their gear, too. That's the last to go when you're on the road with your family."

"Interesting, Centurion."

"That does bring up a thorny one, sir. None of them are likely to leave their women and kids in the lurch. A few maybe, but those are men you don't want. The rest, they'll stay and starve with their kin first."

"Yes, of course," Tiberius said quietly. "One more question, Quarto. Are there others like you on the vias?"

Quarto spit an explosive laugh. "More like us? There are so many, they call us the pedites. There are thousands more like us, Quaestor. This royal robbery of people's land has been going on since the Macedonian Wars. I was a donkey to think I could keep my little plot by myself. There are pedites on every road in Italia looking for handouts, stealing what they can when they can, dying if they don't. Many go to Rome to try their luck there. But the citizen-soldier farmer of Rome has become like a shade in Hades."

"Pedites. Very well, thank you Quarto. You can return to your fire."

Quarto snapped to attention and saluted Tiberius smartly, his fist cracking across his breast. Tiberius saluted him with the same formality. Quarto reversed, and marched out of the tent.

Except for Casca, the centurions stepped all over themselves crying out their objections. Sextus sat in his chair quietly, almost bemused as he heard them shouting.

"They have no land, they cannot serve in the army!"

"The gods will punish us!"

"The senators will banish us!"

"All right, all right," Tiberius said loudly, "stand to!"

The men quieted at once, though they all looked truly shaken, except for Casca.

"What else can we do?" Tiberius asked. "We have barely a century and a half of recruits who will desert the first chance they get. And we are looking at a thousand Roman citizens and allies expiring within our sight for lack of food and shelter. Families of retired veterans from Rome's greatest legions, starving right before our eyes! I have never seen anything like this before, ever, and I cannot let it happen right in front of me. I must do something."

Didius spoke. "We cannot save them all, Quaestor, and we will be condemned if we try to enlist men who do not own land!"

"They owned land, Didius, and lost it. Unlike you and your fellow centurions here," Tiberius looked around the tent, "their land was stolen from them. Under those circumstances," and he slowed, faltering a bit, "we can enlist them as evocati. When we have defeated the Numantines, they will be landed again, as is the case with all honored veterans."

"Oh, what senator will accept that?" said Didius despairingly, "and who will champion that argument for us? We could be decimated!"

"My father-in-law will champion the argument, Didius," Tiberius said, "and so will Rome's consul, Gaius Hostilius Mancinus. If we arrive in Hispania with a legion solid with trained veterans, Mancinus won't say one word about their pedigrees. He will welcome them with open arms."

The centurions looked doubtful and glum, all except Casca, who kept his opinion hidden behind a stone face.

"Centurions, this is my decision. We will enlist the men available here at the Vulsinii Lake, and we will comb the Via Cassia for more 'pedite' veterans until we have a full legion for Hispania."

They still appeared skeptical, which made Tiberius unsure. He breathed out, and said. "Now, I know this seems unconventional, but we will sacrifice to all of the gods that could possibly care for our success. I know that good soldiers that you are, you will follow orders as best you can. But true success can only be achieved if you believe in your commander's vision, and I ask you for that conviction. Do I have it?" he asked. "Do I?"

Sextus raised his arm languidly and said, "You have my vote."

Didius grimaced, but said nothing. Finally, he arose and saluted Tiberius as stiffly as Quarto. Ulpius stood and saluted in the same fashion, and Shafat followed suit. When they had finished, Casca performed a slow, elegant salute to Tiberius, "Hail, Quaestor Tiberius Sempronius Gracchus."

"Hail!" the others shouted.

Eyes darting, Tiberius smiled confidently and dismissed them to their quarters. As Casca was leaving, however, Tiberius told him to wait. Sextus remained seated, having made no move to leave with the others.

Tiberius gestured to the field table in the tent, and Casca sat down. Tiberius glanced at Lysis, who hurried away. Tiberius sat down between the two men.

Lysis returned with a pitcher of wine and three cups, which he laid out on the table. He poured the cups half full of wine. He looked at Tiberius questioningly, who waved his hand to continue, then filled the cups to the brim. Tiberius signaled to Casca and Sextus to pick up their cups while he raised his own. The men each took long sips, and put their cups down. Tiberius looked at Sextus, who hesitated only for a second, then said blithely, "They are right, of course. If you do this, you'll bring the Senate down on your neck."

Tiberius turned to Casca. The primus flashed his teeth in a pained expression, moving his head back and forth as if debating within himself. Finally, he picked up his cup while saying, "You are right, Quaestor, this appears to be the only way to fill out the legion. But, the boys are right," he said, then tossed his head at Sextus, "the equitus, too. The Senate will hound you for this."

"I expect so," Tiberius said, "but they won't get far. Those men out there are evocati, for the love of Venus. Whether they gambled their land away and had to re-up, or they were robbed by a bunch of patrician thieves, they are honored veterans who will hump their campaign gear again to help us punish the Numantines. Who will argue with that? The fat cats sitting on the ager publica? Not likely."

Casca, pulling on his chin, said "True enough."

Sextus simply opened his mouth in a wordless smile.

"Even if they do object," Tiberius said in a bitter tone, "I'm not going to let these men starve. They're better off taking their chances in Numantia than slowly dying next to a lake where they're not allowed to fish."

"Yes," said Sextus, "but what about the women and their brats? The men will feed while their families perish? Most of them won't have that."

Tiberius grimaced. "I won't have it either."

He stood up, and began pacing back and forth in the tent. Then, he spun around to face the other two. "We'll feed them. We'll give them enough to survive through the campaign season. If we don't return, we'll have Quarto tell them to go to Rome for the winter. That's the best we can do, but it's better than starving right here, right now."

"True again," Sextus said. "But, where are we going to get the provisions? We're almost out ourselves just by feeding them once today. Where will we find enough to supply them and the legion for six months?"

Tiberius rubbed his mouth with his hand. "There is a place."

Rufus rode slowly between his men back to his villa, glumly thinking about Scipio's response to his concern. "Gracchus is following consular orders, you can't fault him for that."

Following consular orders, following all his orders, Rufus moped, such as traipsing about in the brush and the woods, disrupting honest stewards of the land. If he has been charged with finding recruits, why doesn't he stick to the roads like all good tribunes in the past? And, of course Scipio would side with his brother-in-law, the politics of the marital bed. Rufus shook his head, I had thought Scipio to be more constant and fair. Not so, apparently.

His bitter reverie was interrupted by a tumult taking place in front of him. He could see dust rising above his vanguard, and he shivered, What? Brigands?

The row of horsemen split, and Rufus watched as Maro, his headman came running through, filthy-looking, and exhausted.

"Maro, what is this? Stop and stay where you are."

"Master, they came back! They sacked the storage barns!"

"They came back? Who came back?" As the rest of Maro's statement dawned on him, he shrieked, "Sacked! Sacked my storage barns! By the gods, Polemo! Draw your sword! They've sacked my storage barns."

Polemo, the greying, white-scarred Anatolian captain of Rufus's guard called down to Maro in a rough, Eastern accent, "Who sacked the barns?"

"Tiberius Gracchus!" cried out Maro, "Mancinus's quaestor came back to take everything!"

Rufus shouted, "Call the rest of the guards, Polemo, and track them down. Bring me back my bounty!"

"Master, we can't," said Polemo. "We can't. Quaestor Gracchus claimed the goods by order of procurement. Even if law is not on his side, he's 600, we are sixty."

"More, Master," Maro cried, "he must have had a thousand men at arms."

Rufus's face turned wine red. He stood on the carriage to beat the front bulwark with his fists. "Dis Pater and all of the gods of death and destruction, I will have you flogged and crucified if you don't go at once to bring back what belongs to me!"

Polemo sat back in his saddle and said, "Master Rufus, I serve you and would be ruined to lose your work. And, you might win to have me flogged and crucified later some time. But, I promise you, if I try to stop Gracchus now, he will flog and crucify me in no time, no question."

Another rider loped up to stop next to Polemo, and began speaking to him in some Anatolian language, complete gibberish as far as Rufus was concerned. Palermo turned to him and said, "Gracchus was generous. He only took a quarter of the goods."

Rufus exhaled some relief, though he was still outraged. "He's a sly fox, that Gracchus. No doubt, he's done the same to every legitimate estate owner up and down the vias. I can't very well lodge a complaint against his pillage if he's assumed a mantle of equanimity. I wonder if his even-handed pillaging extended to his dear brother-in-law."

The pudgy senator churned his features in a remarkable display of displeasure and anger. Finally, he said, "All right, on to the house. Maro, I want a complete inventory of what was taken. Be thorough, Maro, or it will be your hide. Someday the haughty quaestor will pay for this robbery and affront, sesterce by sesterce."

Maro dashed off down the road as the troop of guards flanked the carriage again on its slow way to the villa. Rufus sat silently, deep in his thoughts of revenge. Polemo led the way, warily self-satisfied that he hadn't told Rufus everything reported to him by his scout in their native tongue. The little master would have burst like an overripe tomato if he'd learned that Gracchus planned to distribute the confiscated goods to Pedites clogging the roads. Wasted on pink-skinned vermin, the little master would say. Yes, nodded Polemo to himself, better little master finds out when his captain of the guards is away on patrol.

Chapter 9. The Poet-Seers

Smoke curled from the large, two-story stone house, blending with the cold, grey river of clouds that filled the sky above. Avarus stood some distance from the building, his beige linen shirt peeled down to his waist so that he could splash water on himself from the big, iron bowl set on the firewood stump. The water was freezing, and he wished he could be inside, next to the fire while he waited for his wife Sicounin to serve him breakfast. Maybe she'd serve him some hot, thick bread with a good number of pine nuts, perhaps even an egg and salted pork, a cup of watered wine to wash it all down. Or dried fruit, the dates from that Roman trader, perhaps, mixed with a good, grain porridge. As he rubbed his round belly, the grey hairs twined in a wet ridge down the middle, he ruefully thought maybe just thick bread and hot water for a while, until this went down.

He scratched the place where his belly button was supposed to be, replaced by the scar from the sword slash he'd taken during the war against Nobilor. So long ago, it seemed. The Numantines were ready to protect their homes as were their allies the Segedans, who had come to Numantia seeking refuge from the Roman invaders. The people had been solemn, hiding their fear of the six Roman legions encamped at their city doors. Things couldn't have looked worse when the famed soldiers approached with three elephants in their center, elephants! The city's women and children began to cry when they heard about the destructive monsters. Then, Megaravicus ordered flaming arrows to be shot at the elephants' eyes, which terrified them. The massive brutes turned and ran. When their handlers tried to stop them and point them again toward the city walls, the beasts crushed them with their heavy feet, or grabbed them with their trunks and tossed them. The legions panicked, and fled the walls. Without hesitation, Megaravicus rallied the Numantines and the Segedans, and called for other strongholds of the Arevaci to join them in routing the Roman horde. Six thousand legionaries were killed, including the one who stabbed at an over-exuberant, young Avarus rushing in to extinguish personally the Roman might. The point of the legionary's short sword opened him up, and would have been fatal had Avarus not jumped back just in time while swinging his own spina to split the head of his unlucky foe. Avarus collapsed, and waited for six hours until his father found him, curled like a baby and holding the wound together with his hands.

They burned the center of the puckering wound with an iron poker, causing him to scream like a dying horse. Then, while he whimpered, his father sewed him up with leather sinew. As his father pulled the leather through, he told his son that every stitch was a painful warning to be cautious in war, to wait for the right moment before committing everything. Wait, because everything meant his life, the lives of his family, and those of all the Numantines and the other Arevaci peoples.

The wound festered, requiring his father to reopen it to clean out the green seepage, and cauterize it again, more excruciating pain, more stitches. Avarus had finally healed, but scar tissue had grown over his navel, as though he had never been born of humans. His star had risen because of the weirdness and his bravery, until ultimately a high priestess blessed him as a poet-seer. Now, along with Rhetogenes, he was second only to Megaravicus, the high chieftain of the Numantine Druid warrior priests. In time, he also learned to plan and negotiate rather than rush into battle.

So long ago, thought Avarus, sixteen years. He was middle-aged, his father was gone, as were his first two wives, Stena in childbirth, and Ana from a chill. Sicounin was hale, though, had borne three children of her own, and seemed to have no problem handling Stena's stout sons. Fine warriors in the making, they were, but no match for Sicounin, mostly because they worshiped her. In the meantime, she was making him fat, but how could he complain about that?

He pulled up his shirt over his arms and shoulders just as Sicounin stepped out of the house with a cup of broth. Avarus reached for it and drank, throwing his head back.

Sicounin, a comely, golden-haired woman of thirty years, grabbed his arm, "It's hot!"

"I'm cold," said Avarus, then sputtered as the hot broth burned his tongue. "Curse the nether gods, woman, what are you trying to do, murder me?"

"I told you it was hot, you brainless goat!" she said, trying to disengage her hand from his arm. He snatched it quickly, and drew her to his chest, "Well, then, cool it down with water!"

"Oh, yes, then it will be too cold, you oaf!" She jerked away with the cup, but not before he swatted her on the backside. "I'll take my chances."

She huffed into the house in mock anger, and Avarus watched her with open affection as she disappeared.

"A handsome woman," a deep voice sounded behind him, "and wise to be wary of your goatish nature."

"Rhetogenes," said Avarus as he wheeled around, "always a kind word. And what tears you away from the meseta, noble chieftain, run out of ewes of your own?"

Rhetogenes sat tall on a small horse so that his leather-wrapped feet almost touched the ground. He sat stooped over, leaning on his arms crossed over the neck of his steed as it nibbled at a lone patch of grass on the path's edge. "There are women enough on the tablelands. No need to climb up to this lumpy pile of rocks."

Avarus laughed, "Then, Long God of Love, why did you leave them?"

Rhetogenes pursed his lips sourly, "You know why."

Avarus sighed, "Ah, yes, the Romans. I thought this peace might last."

Rhetogenes shook his head, "Fool, lucky to have such a wise wife."

"Well, off your horse. Let's see if we can find something to drink that dims the past and clouds the future. No reason to face any of it until the council meets."

They made their way into the house and sat at a long pinewood table, pushed halfway between the hearth and the door in acknowledgment of the warmer spring weather. In the summer, the sons would carry it all the way outside to catch the breeze while they ate.

"So, what do you know?" Avarus said. He sat resting his forearms on the thick, pine planks of the table top, his hands curled around a flagon of warmed mead. Rhetogenes did the same, hunched over more because of his long frame.

"The Romans send a new general as usual. Mancinus is his name, victorious in Greece, and ruthlessly greedy. Made his fortune from slaves."

Avarus frowned. "How many legions?"

Rhetogenes shrugged, "I'm told four right now, the two garrisoned on the coast and two more made of veterans from the Corinth campaign."

"Oh," said Avarus, pushing out his lower lip, "Not so bad. We've handled more than that before."

"Aye," said Rhetogenes, "but we laid a lot of our own slain warriors out for the birds to carry their souls aloft." He peered at Avarus admonishingly, "We almost had to lay you out."

Avarus nodded, "True enough."

"Also," Rhetogenes went on, "I heard that another legion is on its way."

"Another one? Oh."

The tall man leaned in, "Led by Tiberius Sempronious Gracchus."

"Sempronious Gracchus?" Avarus looked bewildered, then understood. "His son?"

"Yes, his son."

"The gods are testing us. Five legions, one with the great Gracchus's son at its head."

"Maybe," Rhetogenes said, "maybe not. Sometimes the tree's nut doesn't grow into a tree. Sometimes the squirrel eats the nut first."

Avarus replied, "Yes, but even if Gracchus isn't the general his father was, we still have to deal with Mancinus, who beat the Greeks."

Rhetogenes sat back, tall again on the bench."Mancinus has not fought the likes of us before. We are not Greeks. We have horse, we have warriors, we have courage."

"And they have five times as many men."

"We are Arevaci, Numantines, Segedans, the Lusones, and Pelendines."

"Yes," Aravus said wryly, "all eight thousand of us."

In the Nemeton, the shadows from the oaks and chestnuts cast the priestesses in weird light, accented by the fire flames in front of them licking at the twilight sky. The Druid warrior chiefs sat cross-legged in a semicircle flanked by the young troops standing behind them, spears held straight to the gods. Inside this arc, a smaller one was formed by the three poet-seers, Rhetogenes on the right, Avarus on the left, and the High Druid Megaravicus in the center. All of them faced the singing priestesses, one of them in the back Sicounin. A stranger to me, Avarus thought, as he watched her step lively and sing to the gods, immersed in her spiritual duty. Like the others, she wore a simple shift and no sandals, her hair braided and tied with ribbons the color of the new spring.

The glorious harmonies and the spirited dancing stopped. High Priestess Aunia stepped forward. Megaravicus raised his hand to her, palm out, eyes averted, and cried in an aged singsong, "Oh, High Priestess of those on high, what have the great Matres whispered?"

Aunia keened in a deep, melodious voice.

"The moon is veiled,

> Lugh plays at havoc.
> Fight the Romans, but hold.
> The new old wolf is cruel,
> the cub dangerous.
> Defeat the wolf, save the cub,
> save the people."

She stepped back and disappeared into the shadows of the deep forest with her retinue of priestesses.

Megaravicus turned and said in a firm voice, "The council."

The young soldiers sidled away to the edge of the great trees, out of ear shot while the sitting warrior chiefs rose to group themselves around the poet-seers. Full darkness enveloped the sacred meadow except for the dying fire.

"Go ahead," said Megaravicus, "speak out."

Thurro, chief of the Lusones, called out, "Megaravicus, you are the High Priest and Poet-Seer. What does the High Priestess's prophecy mean?"

"It means that the Romans are coming again, and we must fight," he said almost bitterly. "Instead of the Matres, the three mothers, we hear from the gloomy prankster Lugh."

Thurro, a boulder of a man with his brown hair bound into tails behind his head, grunted, "We don't need a prophecy from Lugh to know that."

"Oh, really? Some have given up fighting the Romans. Some have betrayed their own people. Remember Viriathus was slain by his own men."

"The dogs," Thurro spat, "murder for money."

"They were frightened, too," said Avarus.

"Craven. And look what it got them. Nothing!"

Rhotegenes said, "That is the Roman way. If they cannot beat you at first, they will promise you rich rewards while at the same time threatening you again."

"They wore the Lusitanes down," Avarus said.

"And Caepio never gave them what he promised," said Megaravicus. "Better they should have fought and died, or killed themselves if they could no longer fight."

Thurro nodded his head, "The honorable path."

Silence overcame the meadow for a brief moment.

"Better to fight," Megaravicus said. "Better to die fighting. Who agrees?"

The council raised their voices as one in hoary assent.

"Very well, it's decided. Praise to the holy Matres on high and praise Lugh for showing us the path to triumph, victory or a good death."

The entire assembly grunted their approval.

Megaravicus arose and gestured to the chieftains. "These are the orders for battle. We shall defeat them as we have for the past sixteen years, little by little. First, all chieftains will send one third of your warriors and horses to Numantia. There, I will assemble our main force with Avarus as my second, Rhetogenes as my third."

Megaravicus paused to survey the chieftains. Avarus saw a few of them stir, long traditional enemies of both the Numantines and Lusones when not at war with Rome. But, they all swallowed their objections. Megaravicus continued.

"Each chieftain will form ten forward troops of three riders. They will spread out to scout the Roman horse. When a party comes upon the Romans, they will divide thus: one will ride back to his clan, then to Numantia. A second rider will go to alert the other scouting parties, which will gather together to be lead to the Roman force. The third rider will continue to shadow the Roman horsemen until joined by the main scout group. Avarus, you will lead the scouts troop and harass the Romans as you can, either horse or legions themselves. Slow them down until we can bring our main army to bear. You will be told when we are ready, and where to lead the Roman attack."

Avarus nodded his assent, and no one objected, knowing well his heroic past deeds fighting the Romans.

Megavaricus returned his attention to the chieftains.

"Except for the scouting troops, the rest of your warriors will stay with your clans to defend them as you see fit, under the chiefs of your choice. Those who come to Numantia ride under your direct command, or that of your other chosen chiefs, who are answerable only to me, Avarus, and Rhetogenes. Your first duty is to defend your own people and homes."

The chiefs and men all shouted fiercely, Megavaricus chiming at the end, "Is it agreed?"

"Agreed!" they all roared, and the young warriors on the edge broke into dancing, singing the tunes learned at their hearths.

"Then, we are done," shouted Megavaricus. "Back to Numantia for drink and food to celebrate the coming destruction of the Roman invaders!"

The men screamed and shouted as they wheeled to march out of the dark woods up toward Numantia, singing and dancing all the way.

Avarus slept slumped on the table until Sicounin pushed him awake. He groaned, and she said, "Breakfast?"

He groaned again and vomited on the floor.

"I suppose not," she said. She began bustling around the house, preparing to bake and cook for the sons upstairs and the warriors sprawled in front of the house.

Avarus cleaned up the mess on the floor and returned to the table, cupping his throbbing head in his hands. "Bring me water, please, Sicounin, quietly."

She brought him a cup of mead, saying, "This will do you better."

"Ough," he mumbled, sipping slowly, wincing at any movement.

"So," Sicounin said, "how went the council?"

"How do you think? You and your High Priestess painted the picture for us, didn't you? We go to war with Rome. Again."

"Really," Sicounin said, "did you think it could be any other way?"

"Yes. No. I don't know," he said. "Maybe."

The two didn't speak. Sicounin busied herself getting breakfast, though quietly so as not to cause Avarus more pain. He sat holding his head above the mead, as if trying to keep his crushing headache still within his skull.

"One of the new Romans is Tiberius Sempronius Gracchus."

"What?" Sicounin said, wheeling about.

"The son. He's not the commander, just another officer."

Sicounin shook her head, "Time passes."

"But not the Romans, or their greed and treachery." He took a sip of mead. "I wish he was the commander. I wish we could make a peace with him like his father. There was an honorable man, even in victory, rare for a Roman. I'm tired of war, I'm tired of fighting the same war over and over again."

"You're just getting old."

"And the boys? They're young. Do you want to see them carried out to the stones?"

Sicounin frowned. "Every good Numantine woman wants to see her sons find the warrior's way to heaven, the good death."

"Before they've had children of their own? Before you can dangle your grandchild?"

"What else would you do than fight?"

"Negotiate a peace!" he bellowed. Then, quietly, "A lasting peace."

"What kind of warrior are you?" she said, half sneering, half startled.

"A tired one with no belly button, nor much belly for it anymore." He followed with a laugh, "Despite appearances to the contrary."

"Oh, you're still drunk!" Sicounin scoffed. "Drink your mead, I'll have a porridge for you in a moment. It'll help you regain your senses."

"No," mused Avarus as he watched her move off toward the bubbling pot in the hearth. "We need a peace like before. Gracchus isn't the commander, though. But he could be, maybe. Twists and turns happen in warfare. Turns and twists."

Chapter 10. The Mare Sardoum

Tiberius sat drinking well-watered wine with the outgoing praetor of Hispania Citerior, Marcus Popillius Laenas. He eyed the erstwhile commander, reminded of his meager accomplishments during his tenure in Hispania. Popillius's only significant act had been to ship his predecessor Quintus Pompeius Aulus back to Rome to face the Senate. Pompeius had fared as badly with the Hispanic tribes as Servillanius and Caepio, Sextus Brutus, and the rest of the past, failed Roman commanders. Pompeius had separated himself from the others, though, by negotiating and signing a treaty with the Numantines without Senate knowledge or approval. He denied it later, of course, when the Numantines demanded their rights under the agreement. The Numantines produced witnesses, however, that essentially cooked Pompeius's goose.

Rather than adjudicate this tempest in the midst of the overall mess that he'd inherited, Popillius sent Pompeius home to plead his case to Nasica. Unfortunately for Pompeius, he sent along the Numantine witnesses, too.

While Popillius awaited Rome's decision about Pompeius, he made a few feint-hearted stabs against the Lusones, who were allies of the Numantines. The Lusones quickly scattered his expeditionary force, so Popillius decided to conclude his campaign safely behind the walls of Tarraco while waiting for his successor. The end sum, Tiberius reflected sourly, resulted in Gaius Hostilius Mancinus marching to face the Numantines next, with his quaestor Tiberius Sempronius Gracchus not at his side. So, here he sat.

"You made good time, Quaestor, you follow Mancinus by just a few weeks."

"We came by sea," Tiberius said, "the fastest way."

"Indeed, in early spring no less. Quite adventurous of you to take a chance with Neptune, not to mention the wind gods."

"Corus was good to us," Tiberius replied, "perhaps a bit too good."

He thought back to what seemed like years ago when they arrived back at Cosa, now 4,500 strong. Quarto did not lie, the Pedites were everywhere, starving or stealing and poaching as they drifted down the viae toward Rome. Everywhere they went, Tiberius's troops found deserted homesteads next to vast fields tended by hundreds of slaves from the farthest of Rome's provinces. The constant scowl on Tiberius's face grew darker as they moved up the Via Cassia toward the border of Italia. How could Rome thrive or even survive, he wondered, if the backbone of its strength, the farmer-soldier, was replaced by slaves who had no loyalty to anything but hope for their own freedom?

The growing column of men crawled along the via because of constant distractions and interruptions. As word flew up and down the road, the disenfranchised veterans and their families flocked to the burgeoning legion. Tiberius instructed his centurions to pick out the most seasoned soldiers while giving their women and children rations enough to travel as far as Rome. To be sure that they didn't steal back in the night to be with their paters familia, he ordered half of the auxiliaries to ride rear guard.

Still, they were at least three weeks behind schedule, and doomed to fall further back if they marched their way up and around the mountain coast down into Hispania. Also, even though they now could afford to cream the bumper crop of Pedites for their recruits, they still had to be trained into a single, cohesive fighting unit. The campaign could be over by the time they arrived, Tiberius fretted. There would be no honor in arriving after the war, the laughing stock of Mancinus's troops, probably fated to monitor the defeated Numantines by garrisoning some forlorn mountain reach. No wreaths, no share of spoils, just derision that would travel all the way back to Rome. And, he was the quaestor, responsible for inventorying whatever was found in Numantia. What would Mancinus have left to be accounted for by the time he arrived? Intolerable.

He ordered out the maps. Except for the stone-faced Casca, the officers watched nervously as Tiberius traced his finger across the etchings of mountains, streams, valleys, and roads.

"We will never march over land in time to join in any decisive action with Mancinus. We have only one chance, to go by sea."

Didius let out a groan, while Ulpius shifted his weight in discomfort. Even Sextus seemed somewhat daunted.

Casca said, "Now, how are we going to do that, Quaestor, stuck in the middle of Italia?" He didn't appear to like the idea any better than the others.

"Thus," said Tiberius, pointing down with his finger. "We march posthaste from here back to Cosa and sail from there," he continued, moving his finger, "between Corsica and Sardinia by the Taphros Strait, across the

Mare Sardoum directly to Tarraco. We can be in Hispania Citerior in a fortnight, even less if Corus smiles upon us."

He looked up to see his centurions frozen in stark stares of horror. Appalled, Casca spoke without thinking, "The plan of a man who has never been to sea."

Tiberius pulled back. "What are you saying, Centurion?"

Casca immediately came to himself. "Sir: aside from the known natural dangers of crossing open water in spring, attempting the hazards of the Straits of Taphros in just one vessel is tantamount to pulling the beards of all of the sea gods. To try to wedge 100 or just fifty ships through would be catastrophic. You would lose at least half, and many of those that did squeeze through would require so much repair, the weeks you hoped to save would be lost."

The other three centurions chimed in their agreement, "Oh, listen to him, sir, he speaks the truth!" "There are demons in the water, Pater, who crush ships and eat men!" "Drowning is bad, Quaestor, a dishonorable and horrible way to die!"

"Quiet," Tiberius said, and the din of their cries ceased at once.

He was furious, but unsure. The legion they'd raised was solid, thank the gods, and with rigorous training, they could be crack. It would be infamous to lose them all to a watery afterlife. But, time was honor's enemy, too!

He waited. He breathed in and out.

"What do you suggest, Centurion Casca?"

Casca expelled his own breath in relief. "Continue to Pisae and sail the coast. It will be faster and safer. We can be in Hispania in two months."

The other centurions eagerly shook their heads in agreement, even though it was clear that they really wanted no part of ships and the sea at all. But, if forced to, this was by far a better alternative. Well, too bad for them, thought Tiberius.

"No. I intend to be in the province of Hispania Citerior no later than one month from this day."

The faces of the centurions collapsed. Casca pressed his lips together and said, "All right, then let us sail north and around the tip of Corsica, and on to Barcino. With the proper wind, we could travel as fast as a passage through the Straits. And, it would be much safer."

Gazing at the fearful men in front of him, Tiberius weighed Casca's suggestion in his mind, back and forth. Finally, he said, "You were a seaman, Didius. Have you ever sailed through the Straits of Taphros yourself?"

"No, sir," said Didius, even darker and more dour than usual. "I saw ships sail off into the Straits, never to be seen again."

"And, voyages around the Corsican northern promontory?"

"I've sailed past it on the opposite coast of Italia, never in the open sea."

Tiberius nodded, "All right. Here are the orders. Sextus, you will take the auxiliaries to Cosa and inform Praetor Sentius that we are on our way with a full legion and will be there in one week. By that time, he shall procure 125 seaworthy ships and crews in the lagoon at Olbia, fully provisioned. You will assist him in any way you can to assemble these ships."

He turned to Casca and the others, "You centurions will strike camp at once. We begin marching in one hour, double speed. We'll cross over to Cosa to board the ships. From there, we will sail the coast to Pisae. If the winds favor us, we will continue around the coast. If not, we will sail directly across to Barcino. That is all."

The ravening Sextus was in his element, prodding Sentius to produce the ships. He enjoyed racing his auxiliaries up and down the coast to collect any extra supplies that the legion might need for the journey. The provisions procured earlier from the estates of Rufus and his compatriots had disappeared among the families of the evocati, which made these raids critical to their success, and Sextus rode hard.

Praetor Sentius didn't need much prodding, either. He was so relieved that Tiberius had found his recruits in other places rather than Cosa that he felt no compunction in bullying merchant ship captains to anchor at Olbia and offload their cargos. Sextus then would go through the freight with a fine-tooth comb. Some of the captains spit in rage when ordered to reload commandeered goods that had once been theirs. But, swords were swords, and the seafarers swallowed their bile in a try at making the best out of a bad deal.

Tiberius and his centurions experienced little in the way of impediment, except for one stretch of land through a forested valley cut by a river. In this section, just east of Cosa, an elevated road over a swampy edge of the slow-moving waters had collapsed. Tiberius surveyed the mess, knowing full well that a standing obligation of any officer was to maintain or repair as necessary any part of a road that needed it. Only by keeping these arteries sound and in good staid could the life blood of Rome course between her and her provinces. But, he didn't have time to send his soldiers out to find new stone and gravel to build a proper road. Worst of all, he had no immunes, no engineers who could direct the men and measure the stone so that the road would meet the standards expected of a military reconstruction.

He frowned, looking at the swampy path in front of him. Even with immunes, reconstituting this road the proper way would take a month or more. Shaking his head, Tiberius said, "We'll have to make do for now. Casca, round up any woodsmen in the legion, and laborers to help them. We're going to have to put down a temporary log road for now. When the campaign is finished, we'll return by this route and rebuild it to last."

Casca and the other centurions jumped, knowing that Tiberius chafed at the delay, and also realizing that the longer it took, the more likely they would sail to Hispania on the open seas. The four centurions lashed together a party of woodcutters and workers in no time. These men bent to the task full-heartedly, as they possessed no more desire to chance Neptune and his denizens than the centurions. By the first night, they had cut down enough heavy timber to cover the full 100 kilometers of mire with supporting cross beams. Placing them strategically on the sunken stonework as a foundation, they then laid smaller trunks lengthwise on the cross beams, forming a series of land rafts. The finishing touch was shoveling sand over the entire structure to create a smoother surface for the legion when it crossed. The entire operation was completed in two and a half days.

As soon as the last shovel of sand hit the wood, Casca roared the order to march. When the last of the rearguard stepped onto solid stone, he called for double time as if they were already rushing to engage the Numantines.

Tiberius sat leaning over the neck of Chance, perpendicular to the rapid-paced legionaries trooping past. In the distance, he could hear the cries and shouts of the followers as they tried to keep up. Casca appeared on a high rock, swinging his twisted vitus ominously, as if ready to wither the back of any slacker who would hold them up.

"We'll get them there, by the gods, if I have to paint all their backs red!"

"Go easy, now, Centurion," Tiberius said wryly, "or we'll be delivering a dead legion to Mancinus."

"I'll bet my monumental snout that the great number of them would choose this death rather than being dragged by sea devils down through dark water to Hades!"

"Perhaps, but it's most likely they won't have any choice. So, why should they die both ways?" He laughed at Casca's glum expression and trotted off to see how the other centurions were faring.

When they arrived at Cosa, Tiberius was amazed to find a hundred ships anchored on the Bay of Olbia. Sextus and Sentius had outdone themselves. Each ship was well provisioned with food, water, vinegar, and wine. Ten vessels had been refitted with stalls for the auxilaries's horses, and stocked with plenty of hay and oats. The fastest ship of them all, a sleek bireme with two masts was designated Tiberius's flag ship. A simple covered hutch at mid-quarters served as his cabin, while Chance was stabled in the back with Sextus's horse to keep him company. Lysis asked if he could stay with the horses in case the ship foundered and they needed to be freed. Tiberius reminded him that his first duty was the care and needs of the quaestor. Seeing the sorrowful expression on the slender Greek's face, however, caused Tiberius to relent. The boy beamed as he ran off to see to the horses, Tiberius thinking it wasn't that big of a ship that the young slave couldn't see to the needs of both horse and master. Which came first? he wondered with a laugh.

The ships were nearly full and ready to cast off when Sentius asked to see Tiberius. Grateful for the work done by the Cosan praetor in gathering and preparing the fleet, Tiberius ordered his adjunct to usher him in.

"Praetor, welcome. Allow me to offer you some wine," Tiberius said, clasping his forearm.

Sentius said, "You are too generous, Quaestor, and I know you chafe to push on to Hispania, so I won't delay you long."

"By no means, Sentius, I certainly can spare some time for a true ally and friend."

"Nonetheless," Sentius said, "I'll be brief. You have been generous to Cosa, Quaestor Sempronius Gracchus. You have been reasonable when presented with reason rather than rapacious as some of your predecessors have been with their Italian allies. Cosa could ill-afford to lose any more young men to foreign wars, we barely have enough to fish and farm to feed our people. Instead, you found a way to build your legion that benefitted the people of Italia." Seeing Tiberius's eyebrows furrow, Sentius moved his head up and down, "Oh, yes, some of the men that you used to fill your ranks are Cosan lads, back from war and at loose ends, no value to our town now. You've saved them from brigandry, many a father and mother has told me. We are all grateful."

Tiberius was beginning to wonder what this was all about. He'd acted only in his own interests, he thought, and that of Rome's, of course. What in Hades was Sentius up to?

"So," the Samanite praetor said, "we have brought you a gift, a donation to your success in Numantia. If I may?" he said, gesturing to the cloth that covered the entrance to the hutch. Tiberius nodded, and the cover was pulled back. In marched twelve legionaries in basic armor, older men with grey in their beards.

"Twelve veterans? I have my legion, Sentius, I'm afraid we need no more evocati."

Sentius smiled, "These are veterans, yes, and they are volunteering for your service," he paused, "but they are not legionaries. They are immunes."

Immunes? Tiberius shook his head and looked at the twelve men standing front of him, older men, older than he was, and almost casual in their parade rest stances. Immunes, he realized, engineers that would have made the road repair a few days ago as simple as fixing a child's toy. He breathed a sigh of exasperation, thinking of the time he could have saved, but also of the immeasurable value that these men meant to his legion in Hispania. Ballista, mangonels, battering rams, and siege towers, all of these could be built under the direction of these gifted men, mechanical magicians. No wonder they were exempt from all other duties of the common foot soldier, they were priests of a practical cult.

Tiberius stepped over to one grizzled old man, his lorica an old leather vest studded with oblong metal buttons to deflect phantom blows. His helmet was the old copper pot style, worn for decorum's sake rather than protection.

"You volunteered, is that right?" asked Tiberius quickly.

"Sure, Consul," the old man winked, "why not?"

"I'm not a consul," Tiberius said, "and it is dangerous in Hispania, and hard work."

The old man pushed out his lips and the tip of his tongue, furrowing his nose. "Hard work here in this little shit-hole town is banging together tables and benches. On campaign, I don't work, I think!"

Tiberius stepped back, grudgingly respectful. He eyed the others and raised his voice, "All of you? Volunteers?"

"Aye," they all shouted cheerfully.

Tiberius nodded, and gave Sentius a sidelong glance. The praetor smiled slightly, hardly controlling how much he was enjoying the tableau in front of him.

"All right!" shouted Tiberius. "I am Tiberius Sempronius Gracchus, Quaestor to Consul—" he stared at the grizzled immune, "—Hostilius Mancinus, who is in Hispania at this very moment mounting his campaign to subdue the Numantines. I intend to join him presently to add our legion to his force before he assaults their city walls. Thus, we sail at once. I am happy to have you in our ranks and commend your safety to the gods and to Centurion Primus Lucius Casca Naso, who will add you to the rolls and put you on a ship. That is all."

The knot of men followed Casca down the deck and off the gangplank. Tiberius watched them go, then turned to Sentius.

"I'm not sure how grateful I can be with that lot," he said.

Sentius smiled, "They're good at their craft, I made sure of that."

"Then, thank you, Sentius, with all sincerity," Tiberius said, reaching out his hand to grasp Sentius's forearm. Sentius gripped Tiberius's arm firmly, "You are an honest Roman, Tiberius, we respect you. May all of the gods favor you above all others."

Sentius took his leave as Casca returned.

"You have them situated?" Tiberius asked.

"Spread out across the fleet. They griped about being separated, but we don't have to worry about losing them all because they were on the one ship that goes bottoms up."

"Good. Tell the ship masters to feel free to use the immunes's skills to patch up their ships if needed. Maybe we can keep them all afloat long enough to cross over. Signal them to set sail at once."

Casca nodded and left.

When Tiberius felt the motion of the ship as it moved out of the bay, he remembered that the sea gods were fickle and loved toying with the ambitions of silly mortals. Storms would arise, even in summer, and ships would founder, and all would drown, captives, rowers, and captains alike. Pirate ships might fly out of some hidden cove, and the ship captain would exhort his rowers to burst their hearts pulling the oars, or face death or enslavement if the marauders overtook them. And, of course, the most perverse of the gods might send monsters to torture the sailors with fearful death. Neptune sent Cetus to wreak havoc on great heroes of men such as Perseus. For puny fragile merchant ships, though, he might send an ordinary sea monster, ship-length with iron scales and serrated teeth for chewing through the thickest of beams. Men drowning in the frothing wake of the sinking vessel were soon scooped up in the creature's cave-like maw to be cut asunder by its wicked teeth. Oh, yes, said the sailors, they had seen it themselves, bits and pieces of wood and men floating in a sickly, oily red sea after the monster had writhed away. Tiberius barked a laugh out loud at the thought.

This voyage saw no storms, pirates, or monsters. Instead, the gods seemed to admonish the fearful sailors with drumming boredom. The winds held steady and they sailed above Corsica straight across the top of the large land mass toward Barcino. After clearing Corsica, though, the wind shifted, fortuitously allowing them to take a hard southwest tack directly toward Tarraco. Corsus blew so steadily and friendly that the rowers were told to ship their oars to keep from creating a drag.

Tiberius ordered immediate sacrifices to Neptune and Corsus. He then commanded his centurions to drill the men on deck to ready them for the march to Numantia and also to keep their thoughts off of tentacled ship-eaters. For those waiting their turns, or when they were off duty at night, the ship masters produced a few traders that they had hidden away. Thinking that they could try to salvage some coin at least out of this profitless, dangerous voyage, these procurers parceled out women, girls, and boys to the legionaries. The centurions, of course, were serviced for free to keep them from subsuming the entire enterprise.

Some of the legionaries passed, either for lack of money or desire. Many of them were the old evocati and young recruits who watched their wives, children, and mothers crying on the shore of the Olbia lagoon, left there literally in the wake of the departing legion. Leaning on his vitus as he stared out over the side of the ship at the wailing people, Sacerdus Quarto looked solemn, but he didn't cry; this had always been the way with soldiering. His family would have to survive without him until he came back, if he came back. If he did not, they still would have to survive.

Tiberius finally had rid himself of the legion's impedimenta, but at a cost. He knew that old spears like Quarto would swallow their bitterness and take it out on the enemy, but the new young recruits would hate him for his heartlessness. It was up to the centurions to whip these young wolves into shape, to concentrate their misery and hatred on the rebellious barbarians that had forced this campaign. By the time they sailed into Tarraco, they would be visiting the whores and also would own a keen-edged desire to cut into a Numantine.

Chapter 11. Post

Aprilis was drawing to a close, the crops were in the fields and growing, and the weather in Rome turned toward warmth, leaving only the shadows of the buildings chilled before Apollo, passing in his chariot, kissed them with his light. Claudia loved this time of year, loved coaxing her new babies in her garden to blossom as early as possible, then sitting back to watch the bees embrace them with their busy flight. She would bring the children out to see them, explaining how wonderful the world was, the goddesses Ceres, and Diana and her two sisters, blessing us all with nature and their ways. Philea would watch, and even her ever-solemn features softened at the pure joy of her mistress in spring.

Mother Cornelia never celebrated the rites of spring, sighed Claudia. She loved her grandchildren, but kept them distant, as though that might protect her from their loss, should that occur. Claudia knew better, that nothing could protect a mother from losing a child, like a knife to the heart everyday she lived after that terrible day. Like losing a husband would be, she thought, a husband a wife loved and who loved her, duty or not.

Philea could see the flicker of pain in her mistress's expression, a slight, fleeting disturbance to a countenance so stunning, perfect, that anyone viewing it would rush to restore it to its former image of pure joy. Before the old house slave could move, however, Claudia arose from the flower beds surrounding the pool and motioned the children toward her.

"Please, Philea, have them eat their breakfast, then get them on their way. Polydius should be here soon to give Tiberius his lessons, and I'm sure little Cornelia is ready to practice her stitching."

"I am not!" Cornelia shouted. "I hate stitches!"

Claudia turned and, hands on her hips, stared at her daughter in mock surprise. "Why Cornelia Sempronia, you love your stitching. And, you're so good at it!"

"Not today. Today I am much better at digging up truffles. I'm a big pig, today, and I want to snuffle up some truffles."

Claudia gazed at her daughter, glanced at Philea, then threw her head back and howled laughter. At age three, Cornelia Sempronia was tall and dark, like her father, but had more the temperament of her uncle Gaius, feisty and fiery. Claudia felt ashamed sometimes when she thought that she loved her black-haired, wild child the best of her children. But, then, son Tiberius would tell her something in his serious way, and she knew that she loved them both to death.

They had been to one of the farms for a few days to see how the planting had taken hold. All of the fields looked robust, a relief with Tiberius away in Hispania. Generally surly for having to answer to Claudia, a mere woman, Buccio the hefty farm manager, had fallen in love immediately with little Cornelia Sempronia. As a treat, he brought out his favorite pig and led her on a rope to the nearby woods with the little girl and her mother in tow. Soon, the pig snorted and sniffed until she began to push at the earth near a tree with her snout. Buccio pulled her away and tied her to another tree. While the pig squealed her anguish, causing Cornelia Sempronia and young Tiberius to stick their fingers in their ears, Buccio dug into the ground where the pig had burrowed with her nose. He exposed what looked like three oval, black clods of dirt. The farm manager lifted one up for Cornelia Sempronia to smell, which caused her to wrinkle her nose. But she knew that when they were washed and readied to eat that they were delicious. She smiled and said, "Lunch! I want them for lunch!"

"Oh, no, Cornelia," her mother said, "they are treasures, these truffles. We eat them only on occasion, as a special treat when we have enough. Today, we must send as many as we can to market. Right now, truffles are scarce and dear."

Philea glanced at Buccio, and said to Claudia, "I'm surprised we found these. Our good manager has told us that the main season is much later."

Claudia shrugged, "Who knows, the way our calendar works."

Buccio spoke up hurriedly, "These might be a few missed from last year, Mistress, a rare find, I'm sure."

"Really?" said Philea in just a slightly skeptical tone, "the pig seemed to find them fast enough."

Buccio ignored her, focusing his attention on the mistress of the Gracchi estate while her husband was on campaign. But Cornelia spoke up.

"Philea is right. Oh, if you could find some more before we leave, I love them so much!"

"I like them, too, Mama," said young Tiberius, nodding his head almost judicially.

"Well, then, if Buccio can find some more, you each can have them at your lunch."

"I'll do my best, Ma'm," Buccio said, bowing his head.

"And throw in a pig, too," murmured Philea. Seeing his expression of horror, she said, "Oh, not the truffle pig, farmer, some other hog. A suckling, perhaps." She leaned into him and whispered, "It's the least you can do, don't you think? Oh, yes, I know your little game—and it better stay little, farmer, if you want to stay."

Buccio didn't reply to Philea. He turned to Claudia instead and said, "I have the nicest suckling pig for you to take back to Rome, too, as soon as you are ready to return."

And that was the way it had been every day since their return. Cornelia did not want to do her crafts, her singing and musical lessons, or anything else. She wanted instead to snort around the home sniffing for truffles. Meanwhile, Tiberius had made a pet out of the little pig. No wonder, thought Claudia, that Mother Cornelia seldom left her room.

Polydius arrived with Gaius from the baths. Gaius rushed to Claudia and swooped her up and around in his arms.

"Post, Sister-in-Law, post! Tiberius has sent us letters!"

At first resisting his unseemly exuberant dance, Claudia froze. "Letters from Tiberius? For me?"

Polydius stepped up and bowed slightly as he held out a leather-wrapped packet. "Your letter, Mistress."

She took it from the tall Greek and clutched it to her breast as Gaius went on. "All of us got one, Sister Claudia, even Mother. Yours appears to be the biggest. Mother's is the smallest, of course. Open yours and read it to us, why don't you?"

"Not today or ever! Read your own, this is my letter from my husband Tiberius Gracchus!"

"Oh," said Gaius, mocking, "'This is from my husband Tiberius Gracchus,' hero of Carthage and now Numantia I suppose. Very well, I'll read my own and you can wonder what secret things he told me that he wouldn't tell his wife."

Claudia paid him no mind as she told Polydius and Philea to take care of the children. She then rushed to her room and shut the door behind here, leaning against it as she held the letter close in her folded arms. She put it up against her mouth and breathed in.

She began to cry, almost uncontrollably, thinking that she could smell him, his particular scent. Maybe it was her imagination fooling her all this way from Hispania, but not her memory. She could smell Tiberius as if he were in the room, she missed him so much, she ached for him.

Sighing, she went to her bed and sat down. At least he was alive long enough to have written this letter.

Delicately, Claudia untied the leather sinew holding the packet together. She pulled out the rolled vellum, unfolded it on her lap, and read.

>My beloved wife Claudia Sempronia Gracchus:
>
>Salve from Hispania! I'm writing to you from camp near a small town called Malia which is not far from our objective Numantia. We arrived on the day that Consul Mancinus began his assault on the walls of the town, so we received a rousing welcome. The Arevaci within, a tribe allied with the Numantines, put up little resistance and the fortress fell quickly. None of my legionaries nor myself suffered any injury, since Mancinus graciously held us in reserve after our long march. We did, however, engage the enemy several times during our journey from Tarraco. These Hispanics are tricky, preferring ambush to open battle, and many times we had to fend them off while we followed the Iberus River north to the Numantian region. Our soldiers were ingenious in their defensive actions, however, and we suffered few casualties while driving the pesky Numantine horse away every time. So, all is well here.
>
>I will say that Mancinus was very pleased to see a full legion added to his army. That brings his force up to 20,000 plus 4,000 cavalry. He has immediately reassigned all duties, responsibilities, and privileges of quaestor from Quintus Fabius back to me. I am also to remain the military tribune of the newly named Ninth Legion, which I admit, is very gratifying. The god Mars has smiled upon a Gracchi again, even the lesser one known as Tiberius Gracchus Minor.
>
>I forgot that I haven't written to you since we set sail from Italia. I hope you didn't worry your lovely head, the passage was remarkably peaceful. In fact, the gods of the wind and sea also seem to favor this campaign. We made up all of the time lost trying to find recruits. You recall I told you what a challenge that had been in the note I dashed off before we sailed. They are all well-trained soldiers, now, Casca saw to that, he and that valiant old primus Sacerdus Quarto. What a lucky find he was. Without question, all of the gods are smiling upon this venture. The auspices

are brilliant!

What more can I tell you? I'm fit, almost fat. Lysis is thriving on camp life. He is in love with Chance. I believe I will never be able to figure out the Greeks, how they love horses. Lysis dotes on Chance and rides him at every opportunity, which is fine with me. I still prefer my own two lanky legs for getting around. Unfortunately, the troops expect to see their tribune nobly perched on a horse. So, I sit the horse and hope that the nobility will follow, though unlikely considering how I sit the horse. Let young Lysis have his fun. He's become a solid man servant, and he's well-liked by centurions and legionaries alike.

The weather has been surprisingly cool, most likely because we sit on a high table between distant mountain ranges. The land varies from wooded rivers separated by scrubby plains with hills and mountains jumping up in the most unlikely places. Numantia itself is a fortress town built on a small mountain next to the Douro River. Apparently, it has posed a formidable obstacle in the past, but Mancinus is confident that he can lay siege to the town and reduce the Numantines by the end of the campaign season. I was fortunate enough to have twelve experienced immunes enlist in the Ninth, so we can add their skills to the consul's preparations. We expect to move toward Numantia in the next day or so, which means that you will receive this letter long after the engagement. Indeed, all major hostilities will be done most likely by the time you read this. Really, it shouldn't be much of a contest, we have five legions to their 8,000 or so warriors, and they'll be penned up in their town. It could be a very simple matter of waiting them out. Of course, that might mean that I won't be home as soon as I'd like.

My hours are filled day and night with the duties of war, Claudia, but never do I stop thinking of being home with you and little Tiberius and Cornelia. I never stop yearning for you, your gentle sweetness. I long to hold you, to caress you. I dream of sitting with you and the children in the garden, watching Sol's sunbeams pass over our dial. These are what I miss the most.

To keep Rome strong, war is inevitable, and I will serve her wherever she needs me and for however long. Yet, in my heart, you are Rome to me, Claudia. I serve because I love you. Whatever happens, my love for you is forever and it will last as long as Rome itself. Know that I love you, Claudia, more than the gods and Rome.

Amor,
Tiberius

Claudia clutched the vellum in her hands, crushing the edges together. Carefully, she straightened them out and flattened the letter on her lap to read again. He started so buoyantly, with such good cheer, as though this struggle in Hispania was a stroll in the country. After learning about defeat after defeat of Roman generals and armies during the past fifty years, she knew that Hispania was a dangerous, wild land full of brutal barbarians. She couldn't recall ever before receiving such a heartfelt expression of love as in the last part of Tiberius's letter. What would move him so if the campaign was routine?

He was protecting her from the truth. The campaign was not going as well as he would like her to believe. Why? What was happening?

Claudia folded the letter and put it back into its leather cover. She tied it tightly with the sinew, rose, and hid it away at the bottom of her jewelry chest. Then, she left her room for the vestibulum. She walked out to the peristylum where Gaius sat across from Polydius, talking about his letter from Tiberius.

"He's doing magnificently well!" Gaius cried happily. "He showed up with a brand new legion trained for immediate battle!"

"Gaius," Claudia said gently, "let me read your letter."

Surprised, Gaius turned to his sister-in-law and said in a broad, blustery voice, "Well, I thought it was private, like yours!"

Polydius immediately arose and said with a twinkle in his eye, "If you'll excuse me, Mistress, I'm sure I heard Philea, or someone, call my name."

"By all means, Polydius." Claudia turned to Gaius, "Beloved brother-in-law, my letter is private, as any correspondence between husband and wife would and should be. Yours, however, might be considered more general in nature and thereby also for general consumption."

"Oh, I don't know about that," Gaius huffed, making an out-sized movement shifting in his chair to avert his eyes from Claudia. She slipped up behind him and twined her fingers into the feathery curls of his hair at the nape of his neck. Gaius tensed into stillness.

"Now, Gaius, you know how terribly I miss your brother. You wouldn't be so cruel as to deprive me of any bit of news from him. I'm starving for any little morsel!"

"Then, eat a sweet," Gaius barked, and she pulled hard on his hair.

"Ouch!" he said, laughing as he sprinted out of the chair. But Claudia followed, not letting go. "Gaius, your letter!"

"All right, all right, you vicious sorceress. I'm amazed that my brother fell for such a siren as you. Or, maybe I shouldn't be amazed at his enchantment. Here, here, the letter. Now, let go of my hair!"

Claudia released him unthinking as she tracked the letter tossed on the chair by Gaius. She scooped it up, smiled prettily, and said, "Thank you, Brother Gaius. You are a thoughtful young man."

"Yes, and barely in one piece, no thanks to my harpy sister-in-law."

"I love you, too," she said as she paced off to Tiberius's den to read his brother's letter.

She sat in his favorite chair, a curved wooden peasant seat from Thebes with Persian pillows sewn to the arms and the back. A betrothal gift from her father, Claudia loved sitting in it when she missed Tiberius the most. She unfolded Gaius's letter again to find that familiar hand. He had dated it a week later than hers, she noticed with a frown as she began to read.

> Greetings Gaius,
>
> I miss you, little brother and wish you were here. Yet, I'm glad to know that you are taking care of our family, which is more important. Our roles will flip soon enough, you forging new paths of glory for Rome and burnishing the Gracchi name while I mind hearth and home as all grey heads should do. In the meantime, I miss you, though I am well and the campaign goes well.
>
> You will be happy to know that we successfully attacked the Arevaci in the town known as Malia. It's a small hilltop fortress on the path to Numantia. The town is fortified by fifty-foot wooden walls with seventy-five-foot towers spaced every hundred yards or so. The scouts estimated a force of perhaps 4,000 warriors defending the town and perhaps a civilian population three times that number. Our general Consul Mancinus held a war council the day after we arrived with our new legion, now named the Ninth.

His reports convinced him that Malia would fall to a direct assault—you know, siege towers and battering rams with mangonels and ballista covering the attack. The head of his immunes suggested sapping the walls as well, but Mancinus rejected this suggestion, stating that it would take too much time.

Some of the other military tribunes complained that too many men would be lost in a direct assault, soldiers that would be needed for what promised to be a much heavier undertaking, the siege of Numantia itself. Mancinus calmed them by promising to double or triple the number of rocks and other missiles fired into the town so that fewer men would be at risk while humping over open ground. He also said that fiery darts would be shot as well, but with precise calibration to inflame only those parts of the walls where our towers would not be driven. The tribunes seemed satisfied with this proposal, and the planning continued. I must admit though that the Ninth's centurion primus Lucius Casca Naso, attending as my second, whispered in my ear that Mancinus must be on intimate terms with Vulcan if he can command fire to burn wood only in places of his choosing without spreading all over. I swear, I almost laughed out loud, except Casca's crack made me wonder, too.

Mancinus issued his orders, and we were unhappy to learn that the Ninth would be kept in reserve since we'd just arrived from a hard march and were likely to be in an exhausted state. I objected furiously, saying that the Ninth was more than ready to fight, our legionaries hungered to fight after the shipboard tedium, then marching and training for weeks without any action or distractions. Mancinus reassured me by saying that the Arevaci were vicious, trickster warriors who almost guaranteed the need of reserves in the upcoming battle. He would call upon the Ninth, he said, no worry about that.

And he did, indeed, need us to press the attack. As Casca had divined, the burning bolts were not choosy in what they struck. Those that reached the Malian walls were quickly doused, while many fell short right into our troops carrying ladders and the battering ram before they had reached the town. Velites and hastati fell over themselves getting away from the burning shed and ladders, centurions flaying away with their sticks trying to stiffen them up. Rather than throw in the principes or triarii in this little dust-up, Mancinus gave us the nod, and we roared across the field and up the Malian walls. The Averaci accounted well for themselves, but were no match. Our boys swept them from the parapets before you could spit.

Young Sextus Decimus won the Mural Crown, though he was wounded during the feat. He rode his horse full speed to the gates, taking arrows on his shield and into his mount's breast. He slammed the stricken animal sideways into the wall and scrambled to stand straight up on his saddle. With the speed of Mercury, he began grabbing arrows stuck in the wall to lift himself before his mount collapsed. Sextus climbed fast, reaching higher for new holds while the arrow shafts snapped beneath his weight. He threw his shield arm over the wall, and an Arevaci warrior slashed at his shoulder. Sextus lunged and drove his sword into the Arevaci, driving him back. He then leaped up and over the parapet, wheeling, carving, and slicing until he was joined by Centurion Shafat and his men. Shafat, that wily Carthagenian, also proved his bravery with fierce fighting. I have to admit, it's gruesome to tell, but at one point he made me laugh. With savage courage, he moved to strike a ferocious Arevaci by whipping his sword above and behind his head. Unknown to him, another Arevaci had run up to strike him from behind. But such was the force of Shafat's backward swing that he split the rear attacker's head and without any loss of force, struck down the huge warrior facing him. Shafat cut down two defenders with a single swing of his sword!

The rest went as you can imagine. Mancinus praised the noble Ninth in the aftermath when he crowned Sextus with his wreath. I cannot tell you how proud I was of our new legion, already showing the stuff of legend in its first engagement. Of course, many of the men are evocati, so it was their first blooding only in a technical sense. A lot of hoary heads in our ranks have seen plenty of action for Rome before. Still, they came together quickly in a new force to win a solid reputation and the respect of Mancinus's seasoned legions.

I should tell you that Sextus's wound was not serious, no muscle, sinew, or bone cut. The surgeon cauterized it, which caused our young equitus to cry out like a throat-cut pig, don't tell his mother or his school mates. He should be fine in no time, up and around on a new horse and with a fine scar that ought to give him plenty of chances to brag.

I know it could have been you first over that wall, Gaius, probably faster than Sextus could have imagined. And, I'm sure you would have defeated twice as many of the Arevaci. But, I also know that the cut to Sextus's shoulder could have been to your heart. Then, what would I have done? How could I explain this to Mother that one of her last boys had died under my command? And, what if something happened to me, too? How cruel this would be to a woman who has lost nine children before, to lose her husband's only heirs. How cruel it would be to Claudia and the rest of the family. So, I had to leave you at home, even though I know how bitter a decision it was for you. It was necessary, to protect our loved ones and the Sempronii family line. Your time will come, dear Gaius, you will outshine all of the Gracchii, certainly me, and even our godly father. The difference is that I will be the one safe at home so that our mother need not think about the possibility of suffering the loss of us both at one time. Think of this, Gaius, be patient, and be the man of the house. Soon enough you will be free to master the world!

Vale,
Tiberius

Claudia laid the letter down on Tiberius's desk, again overcome by a wave of yearning for him. She admonished herself to stay with the task at hand. Picking up the letter again, she scanned it quickly. Again, her husband had styled the missive to his audience, a young lion anxious to hear about great military feats and individual glory. Only the first and last parts hinted at the serious nature of the campaign. Nothing pointed to any danger to Tiberius, though who knew? His description of Sextus's and Shafat's exploits seemed to be very detailed for him to have been at any great distance from the melee. Yet, he penned not a line about his own actions.

She shook her head in frustration. This man, she thought, was showing some of his mother's deftness at maneuvering around the edges of matters.

A loud commotion pulled Claudia out of her reverie. She tied up the letter and tucked it away in her gown as she arose and left for the vestibulum.

"Polydius! Get me a messenger!" Cornelia stood in the middle of the hall shouting, "Polydius!"

Claudia approached her and said, "What is it, Mother?"

"Your husband, my son! Look at this pathetic scrap! Two months he's been gone and he sends me this nine-stitch account! If he were here, I'd crown him with his own helmet! Polydius!" She turned to Philea, who had just emerged from the kitchen. "Philea, where in Hades is that Greek featherbrain?"

"Off shopping, Mistress. For tonight's dinner."

"Oh, for the love of—Philea, run next door and borrow a slave. Ask for a swift one to carry a message for me."

"Yes, Mistress." Philea quickly disappeared.

Claudia hadn't seen her mother-in-law so exercised for a long time, since before Tiberius had left. Her emerald eyes cast even darker, and an extraordinary crimson color had crept up her throat, almost obscuring her famed ivory skin. Her eyes darted, too, Claudia noticed, a sign that she wasn't agitated only out of anger. She was worried, too.

"Why are you so upset, Mother?"

"Read this and you'll seen soon enough."

Cornelia thrust a short piece of vellum toward Claudia. She took it and flattened it out between her hands.

>Salve, Mother,
>
>I miss you and the family very much. I hope you and the grandchildren are in good health and thrive. There is not much to report since I wrote you last. Our trip from Cosa to Tarraco was surprisingly and happily uneventful. We made record time with fair winds throughout the entire voyage. The centurions spent the time usefully, training the new legionaries in close maneuvers, which made sense since quarters on the galleys were quite constrained. When we arrived, the men were well along in the formation of solid maniples.
>
>The former governor of Hispania Citerior welcomed me in Tarraco, though on the whole, I found him to be a disagreeable man. I was soon free of his company, however, since I was keen on marching the new legion to join with Mancinus before he

reached Numantia. Fortuna favored us again, as we found him in two weeks at a small Arevaci stronghold called Malia. We made quick work of the town and intend to march on Numantia tomorrow. If the gods continue their good will, we might be finished with this campaign by the end of the month, two at the outside. I will be glad of that and eager to come back home to Rome as soon as possible.

Please give my love to all. I hope you stay well, Mother dear.

Your devoted son,
Tiberius

When she finished reading, Claudia drew her head back, surprised. She stuttered, "He doesn't want you to worry, Mother, that's why he's brief."

Cornelia looked at her with mild scorn and said, "I understand how he feels about me, but he's not paying attention. I can be of some help to him here if he reports what's going on."

"Well, here, Mother, here's his letter to Gaius. It's much longer and details a battle at Malia."

Cornelia whisked up the proffered letter, unrolled it, and read. Even as Claudia marveled at how fast she parsed the words, Cornelia crushed the scroll between her hands and pushed it back toward her daughter-in-law. "Heroics. A minor epic, devoid of any genuine information."

The small woman turned to Philea, who had arrived while she was reading. "Did you bring me one?"

"Yes, Mistress, he's here." Philea stepped aside to reveal a dark, curly-haired youth in a simple tunic.

"What's your name?" Cornelia said as more of a command rather than a question.

"Hermes, Mistress."

"How appropriate. Do you know the Claudii house on the Palatine? Do you know where it is?"

"Yes, Mistress," said the little boy.

"All right. Fly there and tell them that Matron Cornelia Scipio Africanus sent you. Tell them she wants at once the letter that her son Quaestor Tiberius Sempronius Gracchus sent to the Senator Appius Claudius Pulcher. Brook no delay, Hermes. Show them this if they balk."

Cornelia pulled a gold chain from around her neck until an old ring appeared, bulky, its heavy gold dulled and dark from age. She draped it around the boy's neck, where it hung down to his waist. "This is the signet ring of my dead husband Consul and Censor Tiberius Sempronius Gracchus. That should get the letter from them in dark magic time. Bring me back that letter fast, and the ring, too, Hermes. Don't be too fast for your own good."

The boy ran off, and Cornelia paced. Claudia refolded Gaius's letter and asked Philea to put it in his room. Then, she retired to Tiberius's room to lie on his bed and dream of him.

Chapter 12: Appius's Letter

Salve, Father Appius,

This letter tells you that I am alive for now. I trust this doesn't sound too dramatic to you since it is a statement true of any soldier on campaign. But, I must admit, there have been moments when I wondered if we would even make it to Numantia, never mind back to Rome. There are events I must relate to you in this letter, dear Father, that will give you pause about the outcome of this entire campaign. But you must know them, so I must write of them.

I last wrote you when we were embarking from Cosa to sail to Tarraco. This was the last peace that we have enjoyed since, though the men stayed on edge throughout the voyage. If they weren't throwing up their grain or their vinegar, they stared wide-eyed at the waves, dreading to sight a coiled, fanged monster hiding behind the sea foam. Even the centurions kept looking over their shoulders for fear that a sea imp would fly by and snap them up. As for myself, I confess some queasiness in the stomach, though I'm not sure it wasn't from the motion of the sea, perhaps eating some poorly dried fish, or bad humors in general.

But, there was no time to pamper myself like a Rufus, we needed to whip the men into shape before we landed in Hispania. The centurions picked optios from the evocatis and had them swung over to other ships by rope lines, not an easy maneuver. The ship captains and sailors that we conscripted turned out to be exceptional, more favor from Fortuna. They managed the transfer of the optios with only one mishap. Two ships collided and the optio was killed, crushed between their hulls coming together. Both ships lost quite a few oars and incurred many injuries among their oars men. The ships themselves did not founder, however, and were repaired in short order. We held a service for the lost optio and burned incense to the gods. The smoke rose straight to the sky, and we cast his body to the sea with coins affixed to his eyes. I am not sure how he can cross the Styx while deep in the sea, but the gods seemed appeased. Our voyage continued apace, winds favorable all the way, and we lost not one of our fleet's 100 ships.

The transferred optios were charged with forming lines for maniples, sorting out the young cubs from the scarred old lions, then putting them through their steps. With such a good cadre of immunes on board, I was willing to sacrifice pila to the sea to have the new men learn how to throw them correctly. The senior immune, however, a man named Titius, suggested tying fishing string to the end of the pilas so that they could be retrieved. He promised that any awkwardness created by the strings would soon be ironed out on land with a few days' practice. The centurions agreed with him, so I let him have his head and the innovation worked perfectly.

This Titius, a brown toad of a man with razor-sharp eyes, strikes me as the kind who would think up such an ingenious scheme so that he and his comrades wouldn't have to organize the manufacture of another 8,000 pilas to replace those lost at sea. His notion was extraordinary, god-like in inspiration. It wasn't the last he came up with, either. He told me that he had in mind to create tiny ballistae that would be easier to carry around because of their smaller size and lighter weight. They could make many more of them, too, which would make them as effective, or more so, than full-size ballistae. He called them wasps because of their sting. Of course, I haven't seen anything like them from him, yet.

In Tarraco, I met the retiring governor Marcus Popillius Laenas, a long-tongued creature of an entirely different order. Since I saw him last in Rome, Popillius has not changed an iota except perhaps to be even more unctuous and dangerous. I considered it our good luck that he would soon be departing Hispania for Rome. We did not dawdle in Tarraco, either, thank the gods, since my goal was to catch up with Mancinus before he began the final assault on Numantia. Popillius assured me that I was only two weeks behind Mancinus's army, which would move slower due to its size and impedimenta. Of course, I was skeptical of any information from this odious man. Still, I had to shore up the men and myself with the possibility that he spoke the truth. With that good thought in mind, I charged the centurions to prepare the legion to march at once. They were to streamline our baggage impedimenta as much as possible to allow the utmost speed to catch up with Mancinus. Only necessary provisions and weapons of war would be acceptable. The men snapped to and proceeded to execute the order with single-minded purpose.

We left Tarraco after just a day, marching up the northwest side of the Iberus River, wagering that any chance of harassment might be less on this border of Hispania Citerior. We followed the Iberus banks as close as possible while still keeping to firm ground. As I'm sure you know, despite nearly a hundred years of pacification, the roads in Hispania range from the rudimentary to completely unformed. The terrain consists of relatively even plains vegetated with grasses, and scrub brush, intermingled with hearty woods, followed by more grass, brush, and woods, most of them near the river or around streams flowing into the mighty Iberus. One common trait marked this part of Hispania, no matter the seeming symmetry of the land. That is, as we marched, we climbed.

We tramped as fast as we could up toward Salduba, our friends, as you know, since the wars with Carthage. Once there, we intended to replenish our provisions and cross the Iberus at that point, knowing that the entire meseta leading up to Numantia would be completely hostile. Even so, it would take us some days to reach Salduba no matter how fast we moved or how much we lightened our kits. The last measure turned out to be my first mistake.

Spring must be beautiful in Rome, now. Plants must be spiraling their little, pointed green leaves out of the soft soil, stretching to Sol's rays as if after a long nap. If you take a ride out to your country farm, I don't doubt that you have to break out your old campaign boots to deal with the mud in the fields. Well, here on the rising tables of Hispania, spring is a different creature. Any ground out of the sun god's path is still mostly cold and frozen unless you lie on it, hoping to rest. Only then does it melt, making repose a cold, wet affair. At night, though, there wasn't much sleep because the temperature dropped off the end of the earth and the wind gods cried their pain. It was during these severe nights that I wished we had kept more cloaks and linens to keep us warm.

After the third day's march, we halted to erect the camp as usual, and sent out the wood-gathering parties, ten men each. But they didn't come back, not a man. That night, the men quivered from the cold, but also from the specters of those missing soldiers. We searched for them the next day, but found no one, nothing, not a body, not a trace.

At the end of that day, we sent out twice as many men in each party. This time, they came back, at least, those who could. Out of a hundred men, twenty-three returned, some impaled by arrows, others with ugly wounds from stones thrown by slings. One man came back with half his head crushed from the blow of some great cudgel. I mobilized a full cohort under Casca Naso's command who, using one wounded survivor as a guide, retraced their route to the forest stand where they had gone to hunt firewood. In the grove, they found their corpses hanging from the trees, some with limbs removed, others their heads. Casca told me the poor soldier leading them back to the massacre dropped to his knees and cried out for his fallen friends. Working quickly, they retrieved the bodies, seventeen, and grabbed as much wood as they could, bringing all back directly to our camp. That night, the men warmed themselves for a short time over the flames of their fellow legionaries's funeral pyres.

In the morning, the legion was assigned by cohorts to retrieve the remains of the other missing men. They loaded another fifty of their massacred tent mates onto the wagons. In just two days, our legion had lost more than 100 men without one enemy falling. I immediately called a halt to our march and ordered camp. The fossa was dug and the agger thrown up in no time, and as soon as I saw that the stakes were in place to secure the castra, I convened a meeting of the centurions, the auxiliary equitus Sextus, that river wharf rat of an immune Titius, and even old Centurion Primus Sacerdus Quarto, since the recruits hold him in great respect, as do I. Then, I summoned the ambulatory survivors from the wood parties to report to us what happened.

In spite of a chorus of inchoate, sometimes hysterical accounts, a basic pattern of the enemy attacks took shape. Men on horse appeared from nowhere on all sides, pounding directly through the ranks before our legionaries could reach for their pila, never mind throw them. Wielding long swords and light axes, the riders struck hard, cutting down almost half of our men in their first pass, while others positioned on the edge of the woods fired arrows and stones to cover their riders as they rode back. The horsemen then wheeled and charged again. Instead of riding directly at the remaining legionaries, however, who by then had formed a hurried front with spears extended, the attackers circled, slinging stones or casting their arrows from horseback. Their archers fired from high ground or tree limbs, shooting down into our men without hitting their cavalry. Finally, the surviving troops ran, and many of them were cut down from behind. As I wrote before, only a fraction from each party made it back to the legion.

We thanked these soldiers and ordered them back to the surgeon or to their tents if they were well enough. The officers in my tent looked grim. Shafat spoke first, saying that the attackers without question had been Arevaci, some probably Numantines themselves.

"This far from home and across the Iberus?" I asked, almost in disbelief.

"They ride, and they ride light, he said. Distance isn't an impediment to them."

Sextus spoke up, saying, "I thought that Mancinus's auxiliaries would be keeping them busy."

Shafat shook his head, his shining black ringlets turning back and forth. He said they most likely are harassing Mancinus, too. The Arevaci are a slippery lot, they can do much with just a few. Look at what they've done to our force in just two days.

"Now that we know their tactics, we can stop them, "Sextus said, "and defeat them."

"They'll change their tactics," replied Shafat.

"Then, what do we do, Shafat?" asked Didius. "How do we protect our legion until we join Mancinus? Huddle together in some gigantic testudo all the way across the Iberus and clear to

Numantia?"

"Impossible," said Ulpius, "we'd never make it before winter. Then, what would we do?"

Casca raised his fist, and bellowed, "You jackasses! The Quaestor wants us to join the main army in days, not years! We cannot cringe like a tortoise because of a scroungy band of barbarians. We must kill them for massacring our comrades!"

And Shafat said, "True, Primus, but they are formidable foes. They come and go like foxes."

"Then we must outfox them," Sacerdus Quarto said.

Everyone looked at him in surprise. All of them had the same question plainly written on their faces, Father Appius, but were reluctant to ask it in deference to the

tall, old warrior. So, I asked. "How, Centurion Primus? How do we outfox the fox?"

"By setting a trap, of course, with a chicken as bait." He said no more after that. He merely leaned on his staff and stared at me.

"Of course, Centurion Quarto," I said, steady on his eyes, "Why didn't we think of that?"

That evening, the men again ate cold gruel and slept as best they could in their thin cloaks. The farm boys that we had saved from the roads in Italia looked as though they would shrivel up and blow away with the next gust. In the meantime, I poured over local maps with my officers, bent on setting that trap of Quarto's. As you know, of course, the maps were horse dung, but Sextus and Casca had rounded up a few shepherds who helped us gain a better feel for the lay of the land. Recognizing that some might give us the wrong information deliberately, we asked all of them the same questions separately, and considered those answers that matched to be fairly accurate. They had another compelling reason for being forthcoming, Casca's insistence that they accompany scouting parties to verify their descriptions while their families remained as guests of the Ninth until their return.

We learned from these sources that this part of Hispania is a riot of mismatched terrains, plains, rivers, hills, valleys, and mountains intermingled in some wicked stew cooked up by the impish spirits of the earth. After comparing the maps and the most common of the shepherds' descriptions, we resolved upon a plan.

Sextus picked a small corps of his fastest auxiliaries and a local who said he could sit a horse. They left in the night, first walking their horses quietly out of camp, then riding close to tree cover to keep the moonlight, little as it was, from silhouetting them against the horizon. After they left, I ordered the centurions to ready for a quick break of camp before sunrise. Then, I ordered the annonae optio to bake two days' worth of bread and distribute it to the men along with the same amount of water. Casca addressed the auxiliaries left behind by Sextus while the other centurions circulated among the rest of the men, quietly telling them what needed to be done before dawn.

Sextus returned to camp two days later just before sunrise. I called for an immediate meeting of the centurions and optios in my tent, where the equitus quickly reported his findings. Some twenty miles away from our present camp, he had found a place in the roadway that narrowed between the Iberus and a string of low, heavily wooded foothills. The hill closest to the riverbank stretched for about half a mile. The hills on the other side were interspersed by a series of ravines that looked difficult for wagons to negotiate, though groups of men and horses could pass through them. In other words, Father-in-Law, it seemed the perfect setting for an Arevaci ambush. Indeed, it occurred to me that their chieftains might think of it as an opportunity to reproduce Hannibal's massacre of my ancestor's army at Trebia.

The debate began. Didius, ever the pessimist, argued that we should find a safer way through or around the hills. Ulpius was inclined to side with him, while Shafat and Sextus disagreed vociferously. Casca and Quarto held their peace, as did I, waiting for the others to begin repeating their arguments. When they started going over the same ground again, I spoke.

I told them that we couldn't afford the extra time it would take to find another route through the hills. I suggested that we could heighten our security measures when we came upon the narrowing of the riverbank, sending strong patrols to the closest hills beforehand, stationing them there until we had passed through safely. Or, I said, we could gamble to see if we could snare the barbarians in their own rabbit trap.

The plan I proposed meant dividing our legion into three forces. For it to work, we would have to expose our supplies and many of our brothers in arms. We would have to act with stealth in a land completely foreign to us without its native warriors detecting our actions and our purpose. It truly was a game of chance, a play for decisive success or utter disaster. Never would we need Fortuna's favor more. I outlined the plan, and after much discussion of details, the officers embraced the stratagem.

Nothing much needed to be said after that. Our equitus left to meet with his horsemen while everyone surged into action. Each of the centurions went from tent to tent to wake their men without noise, and instruct them with specific orders. At the same time, Sextus mobilized a number of his auxiliaries brought with him from Rome. They quietly led their mounts out to the front gates in the waning moonlight. Gradually, legionaries began to appear near the horsemen, wearing no helmets or loricas, carrying no shields or pila, only their swords wrapped in cloth. Once everything was in order, I nodded at Sextus and Shafat, who silently guided their men out of the camp into the night. Sextus returned just before morning, his men again taking their horses quietly to the corral for fodder and water.

The next morning, we struck camp and, as originally planned, marched north near the Iberus toward Salduba. We put in a good ten miles, and set camp as though nothing had changed. But, on the following day, our march would take us onto the tapering riverbank flanked by the steep hillsides.

Once we set out, our pace began to quicken as the ground next to us began to rise. As planned, the auxiliaries stayed close to the marching legionaries, running up and down the column in hope of confusing observers tracking their number. Gradually, the distance between us and our baggage train began to stretch out. Indeed, parties watching from afar might have thought that we were hastening our step, almost in a hurry to traverse the hills to reach the next camp site and safety. After marching until Apollo raced Sol at the height of the sky, our baggage train trailed the main force by almost an hour.

Since the main body of the legion traveled in good discipline, with velites openly patrolling the hillside, no marauders harassed us. I must admit, the lack of any hostilities caused me some concern, wondering if they would take the bait. No matter, the bones had been thrown, I thought.

After another hour's march, the river began to bend away from the hills, and the surrounding terrain broadened and sloped down. Once clear of the confined riverbank, we slowed our speed, until I called a halt. We issued orders for men to draw water from the river and allowed others to relieve themselves in the nearby brush.

In the meantime, Father, the lagging baggage train entered the constricted pathway between the hillside and the river where we had been. As fast as we had marched the legion, the impedimenta dragged ever so slowly, until the entire array of wagons and weary men plodded on the cramped roadway.

As expected, the Arevaci attacked at this point. They could not resist the opportunity to strike a devastating blow by destroying our legion's entire supply train. I must tell you, Father-in-law, when I heard the distant, muted sound of the tumult on the riverbank behind us, I was much relieved. Though many of our men and all of our supplies were at great risk, I knew then that we at least had a chance. As soon the cornicens from the supply train bleated the alarm, I gave the order.

Our own horns blared, and the men dropped all pretenses and formed up facing back the way we had come. They shed their packs and camp stakes as previously instructed, and on command quick-stepped back toward the sound of the battle along the river. As fast as our men ran, though, Sextus and his auxiliaries surged past us.

We were told later by those with the baggage train that, without warning, a band of horsed warriors had attacked from the rear. Meanwhile, another throng of barbarians on horse had raced through the narrow passage on the opposite side of the hill to the front of the supply train to hem in our wagons and men. Finally, Arevici foot soldiers descended from the hillside where they had been hiding since the night before. While they brandished their long swords and cudgels, their marksmen shot arrows and slung projectiles in terrific numbers into our wagons. Our troops took cover amid the wagons, though many were downed before they could reach them. The Arevaci foot soldiers reached the base of the hill and charged wildly, ready to push our men into the river.

I learned that it was at this point that Casca, whom I had put in command of the baggage train, ordered his men to let fly their pila. In alternating waves, the soldiers whipped their shafts point blank at the front mass of charging Arevaci warriors, piercing many of them like onions on skewers. Still, at the outset, our legionaries defending the wagons were severely outnumbered and pressed.

That is when a century of our legionaries surged down the hillside behind the Arevaci foot to attack them from the rear. These were the men that Sextus and his horse had secreted to the hills near the river two nights before. In charge of these men, Centurion Shafat silently led them that night through the ravine on the opposite side of the hill next to the river. They climbed to the next hilltop and hid in the woods on the other side without fire or light, for the next two days. Shafat later told me how he and his scouts had watched the Hispanii warriors position themselves on the next day to rush over and down the hillside to attack our supply train. The centurion told me they could barely contain themselves in waiting.

Finally, as planned, as soon as they heard the horns sound distress from the baggage train, they rushed down the hillside across the ravine and up over the hill next to the river. With only their swords in hand, our men fell with a fury upon the rear of the barbarians attacking our supply train from the hillside.

At the same, our auxiliary force was closing in on the Hispanii horsemen blocking our wagons in the front. Again, as planned, our cavalry divided forces, with Sextus and a hand-picked contingent heading straight at the enemy horse. Sextus and his troop rode hard to the riverbank, slashing the Arevaci with their blades and stabbing them with spears. In the meantime, his second officer Decimus led another company through that very same ravine between hills used by the Arevaci to encircle the wagons on the riverbank. Decimus was charged with engaging the barbarian riders at the far end of the riverbank, thereby completing our envelopment of all of the Hispanii warriors.

When I heard the first peal of our horns, I jumped onto Chance and raced to catch up with Sextus and his men. As I have already related, they had charged straight back to harass the Arevaci cavalry blocking the front of the river road. Confused and stymied by the sudden assault, the Arevaci turned tail and raced toward the wagons. We followed and saw the enemy horse on the far end also running toward the wagons with Decimus and his men close on their heels. Any Arevaci on foot running from us were being hacked to pieces by our riders as they galloped by or stabbed to death by the legionaries flowing down the hillside, revenge for their fallen comrades.

Just as it looked as though we would slay them all, however, a leader among them shouted out an order that immediately reversed the tide of their fleeing horse. Sextus commanded his men to be ready for a counterattack, and the Arevaci riders did seem to charge directly at the auxiliaries, who outnumbered them two to one. Instead of actually closing with our cavalry, however, they instead pulled up and whirled around, each picking up a running warrior and hoisting them behind onto the back of their horses. They then rode up the hill as fast as they could. Our horse and foot tried to follow them, but they could not match their speed and agility climbing up the steep slope angling between the trees.

Through this feat, I would say they managed to save more than half of their remaining warriors. As they reached the hilltop, I saw the chieftain who had saved them suddenly halt his mount, turn, and look back. He was round and grey-haired, wearing a fur vest with round metal disks sewn to it, and on his head a simple, round bronze helmet without a crest or the horns that some of them affix. Then, and I swear this by the good graces of Jupiter and Mars, Father-in-Law, he seemed to look straight at me, as if we were next to each other. Involuntarily, I raised my sword slowly in the air. Without a gesture, he pivoted his horse and rode off.

By then, the rest had escaped into the farther hills. I reached Sextus, who had halted his troops out of arrow range. Spent, he sat on his horse resting his hands on its neck, gazing up at the hill. Nearly breathless, he said to me, "Those barbarians do know how to ride." After which he asked me in almost a bemused tone, "Pursue, sir?"

"No," I said. "Guard the perimeter while we reform the legion and tend to any wounded. Then, form a detail to return the shepherds and their families to their villages."

He looked at me in amazement, so I tried to educate him. "The barbarians will be amazed, too, Equitus," I said. "They will be grateful and happy to tell their countrymen of our fairness. It might keep some of them from pressing our flanks."

Sextus didn't strike me as being convinced, so I added a cautionary corollary. "Even so," I said, "when you return, keep to the foothills so that even should they want to, they cannot attack again. Meet us at the specified campsite. We'll march to Salduba from there tomorrow."

And, that's what we did. Our men raised a shout of triumph, and we celebrated that night, sacrificing to Mars and Fortuna liberally, and also to the moon goddesses Diana and Luna, for hiding their light during the two nights that Shafat and his men hid away. We had been victorious with but a handful of men slain or wounded. The Arevaci suffered the loss of perhaps a hundred warriors, including many Numantines, who Shafat identified by their distinctive clothes and armor. To us, such casualties are considered significant but not crippling. Apparently to the Arevaci, however, the losses mean more. I'm not sure I understand why, since all former commanders have estimated the enemy forces in the tens of thousands. Of course, those numbers could have been predicated on an alliance of all the Hispanii peoples, while an individual tribe such as the Numantines might only field a little more than a legion of soldiers, though on horseback. As I've written, they are remarkable horsemen.

But, they failed to attack us again during the rest of our trip to Salduba. Of course, we took away any advantage of surprise afforded by the woods, being sure to encase our advance with a large array of scouts. Firewood became no problem, either, since the scouts doubled in their duty by bringing back what we needed when relieved. The wagons always presented a problem, but I drove the men to move fast, and we built roads where we needed them, and bridged many a stream with the speed of Mercury.

We arrived in Salduba in a fortnight, slower than I had hoped, but as fast as possible considering the enemy harassment early on and the difficult terrain thereafter. Salduba is an actual town that features a mixture of stone buildings and the wooden structures expected in this wild country. The praetor, one Vibius Curius Triarius, struck me as a lean, hard soldier from his look with plenty of experience warring in Hispania. Curius was solicitous but nervous, of course, when he welcomed our motley, gaunt legionaries standing at ragged attention in front of his walls. I did my best to assuage him, and he was quite generous with the town's victuals and potables. I allowed the men to eat and drink themselves to sleep that night because granting leave to Salduba was out of the question, considering our terribly compromised timetable. How would I ever have been able to round them up? I'd have to search every bed chamber in Salduba!

I admit, I was so discouraged at this time, I even whined to my poor boy orderly Lysis about being too late, now, to join Mancinus in front of the walls of Numantia. Slight and shy as he is, to his credit he did the best he could to buck me up, telling me that Mancinus was likely to have met similar resistance and obstacles in his march. He swore to the gods that Mancinus would be relieved to see our legion no matter when we joined him. I was secretly bemused by my little Greek slave acting the heroic augur in my tent. He hadn't been with us at dinner that night so long ago in Rome, when Mancinus eyed me for the first time, taking my measure. Lysis could play act as much as he wanted in his mind's fantastic world, but he didn't know how much rested on our success. Mancinus had sworn publicly that he would not be joining the endless ranks of generals who had failed in Hispania, that he would win or come home with coins on his eyes. Without ever saying so, the consul had made it resoundingly clear that if I in any way impeded his vision, large or small, it would be to my detriment. Young Lysis does not know this about Mancinus, though I will say this, the boy certainly can ride Chance. He's a natural, surprising for one who was only a Greek goatherd before being a house slave. But on that horse he looks like a miniature, black-haired Alexander.

Salduba would be another ten-day march to Numantia, and I feared that I would arrive too late. No matter, I could only do what I could do. Praetor Curius did his best to advise us and to give us reliable scouts. Their families lived in Salduba, so I supposed they would be truthful to some extent. I ordered the centurions to make preparations to leave in the morning. During a farewell dinner that evening, Curius showed us maps and traced the route that Mancinus had taken, one directly toward Numantia. He cautioned us again about Arevaci and Numantine attacks, but also said that good time could be made by taking a more southerly route where the terrain was better.

We left at dawn, keeping as rapid a pace as we could while hewing close to the hills where Sextus could watch out us from high ground. Occasionally, we saw riders, the enemy, no doubt, prowling at a distance, anxious to attack but leery of the whereabouts of our own horse and the thrashing they'd received at the riverbank and our tight formation since then. Young, wild warriors would rush forward now and then to show their bravery to their clansmen. They would fire an arrow and flee, chased by a flight of twenty of our own bolts. A few bold ones drew too close and suffered the consequences. Unfortunately, an arrow of theirs struck home as well. Centurion Ulpius caught one in the meat of his thigh, an almost spent arrow that did not penetrate too deeply. Our only surgeon extracted the pointed shaft and sealed the wound, calling upon Vulcan to bless him with his fire. The surgeon said that, barring corruption, Ulpius should survive. Whether or not he'll be able to march a full campaign again remains to be seen. But, we stuck him on a wagon, and he continues to command his men from afar with good cheer and appropriate invectives. If anything, his attitude promises him a speedy recovery.

The march was rugged but swift. The men responded well to our urging. They especially excelled in erecting and striking camp, perhaps motivated by a sense of self-preservation as much as by our continuous cajoling. But the shifting terrain presented many challenges, and we averaged just ten miles a day. By the fifth day, I was nearly distracted by our slow progress and my concern that Mancinus and his men at this very moment lounged in the Numantine chieftain's great meeting chamber, eating the last of their winter stores and drinking their wine and ale. We would arrive as an afterthought and, behind closed doors, be a laughing stock. Worse yet, I envisioned Mancinus commanding us to garrison Numantia, and end up being stuck in Hispania for two or more years.

With these thoughts plaguing me, I paid little attention to Sextus and two adjutants loping toward me, a broad grin creasing his face. Nor did I wonder that he was here instead of at the head of his auxiliaries, ensuring that the pernicious Arevaci were kept at bay from our legion.

"Salve, Quaestor," he greeted me, still smiling broadly.

"What brings you here, Sextus?" I asked, a bit peeved at his cavalier manner. "Who's keeping track of the Arevaci wild men?"

"They're in their place, sir, well out on the fringe and unhappy about it," he said in the smug way he had perfected. He said, "Decimus is in command for now. I felt it necessary to bring this news myself."

"And?" I said. I was truly becoming irked, impatient for him to quit dancing around his news.

"And," he said, "the Numantine town of Malia is just miles away."

"Malia?" I said out loud. "That's the town that Pompeius secured some years ago, hostages and all. So, it's just a few miles away? We might be able to re-provision there."

"Not immediately," said Sextus. "At present," he said flatly, "the town is under siege." His reply puzzled me until he went on. "Mancinus and his entire army has surrounded Malia, and look ready to attack."

Of course, I was more than surprised, I was stunned. A host

of emotions assaulted me, relief and joy that we had caught Mancinus before he'd conquered Numantia, confusion from the knowledge that he had not even reached the Numantines' city, and slight bafflement at his siege of Malia, a town from all reports subservient to Rome. Perhaps its status had changed, hardly an unusual occurrence in Hispania, as I'm sure you know. Then, it occurred to me that Mancinus had reduced Numantia already and was returning to Hispania Citerior and Rome in triumph. In all likelihood, Malia had broken its treaty with Pompeius, thereby requiring the consul to delay his celebration until he'd brought this last Numantine stronghold back under control. Woe to the hostages, I thought gloomily, plunged again into depression as dark as Hades.

"Then, let us go and hail the consul, Sextus," I told him. I then placed Casca in command, cautioning him to keep the legion steady and alert on through to Malia, where we would rejoin them.

We cantered the five miles to Malia without incident, reasoning that the harassing Numantines had melted away when realizing how close they were to the full force of the Roman army. The camp praetor welcomed us and sent us immediately to Mancinus's headquarters. I presented him with a formal salute. To my surprise, he came up and greeted me warmly, grasping my arms with his hands. "Welcome," he said, "to Hispania, Tiberius Sempronius Gracchus! Look, Quintus, young Tiberius has joined us, and none too soon."

"Welcome, Quaestor," said Fabius, a handsome figure of a man who presents himself as the perfect model of Roman masculinity. "I am delighted to see you in camp, he said cheerfully, and relieved to be relieved soon of my extraordinary duties."

I thanked Fabius, telling him it was my pleasure to be there. Then, I congratulated Mancinus on his brilliant successes to date. He replied, "You celebrate me too soon, Quaestor. I haven't done anything brilliant just yet. But, I will with your help. The Numantines still defies us. But, now that you are here, we can dispense quickly with Malia and move on to Numantia itself. Have you raised your legion?"

Father-in-law, I was flabbergasted. We pushed our men and

they did their best, but we did not meet my goal of reaching Mancinus in two weeks. It took us three weeks to meet him, and he was barely ahead of us, while the Numantines ranged freely, scorning the Roman mandate.

"A full legion, Consul," Sextus told him. "Five miles away and on the march," he boasted, slyly distracting them from my confoundment.

Mancinus turned to me then and again clasped my shoulders. "Now, that is brilliant," he said. "Five miles away? Then, we will attack Malia at dawn."

Our men arrived and were folded into the main camp. Mancinus informed me that our legion would be kept in reserve since we'd just arrived after a long journey. I imagine he decided this, too, after seeing all of the old evocati and farm boys in our ranks. When our men learned that they would be reserves, they were incensed, and I did my best to assuage them. They ate and drank well that night, and slept until the cornicens roused them with their assembly call.

Father Appius, I cannot express how bewilderment turned into concern as I witnessed the assault unfold. Completely sacrificing any element of surprise, Mancinus brazenly formed the troops in front of Malia's gates, barely out of ballista range. With a loud klaxon, he sent his cherished Fifth legion directly at the walls and ordered the siege towers to advance. Before his men had marched a hundred paces, a wave of enemy cavalry swept around the walls directly at the advancing troops. The legionaries readied their pila, but the enemy horsemen ignored them as they raced their mounts to our siege towers. The pila struck many of the barbarians down, but a few rode abreast of the towers and threw leather bags that burst oil all over the wood. By this time the siege towers were within arrow range, and flaming shafts curving from the city walls lit the oil. As our troops tried to douse the fires, arrows struck them down. Seeing the towers consumed, the front line faltered. The Numantines wasted no time in sending out another flight of cavalry to attack the milling legionaries, while survivors from the first group of Arevaci horse flew to the ram to kill our men moving it to the gates.

Without question, the front line needed support, as their ranks collapsed and the triarii were already engaged. I had mounted Chance at the beginning to see better, while Lysis held his reins since the horse had become agitated, being in his first battle in a long time. Lysis himself looked pale as he gazed toward Mancinus and the other officers just a few paces away. Seeing the first rank slowly give ground, I jerked the reins from Lysis and walked Chance over to Mancinus.

"Consul, the first rank is flagging," I said, and he did not reply. Instead, he twisted the leather reins of his horse with both hands. "Consul, I said, the Fifth needs reinforcement."

Mancinus never looked at me as he muttered, "Why aren't they sweeping the field?"

"Consul Mancinus!" I shouted, "The Numantine horse are too mobile for them. Let me send in my auxiliaries, please, sir!"

Mancinus bit his lip, and nodded briskly to me. I turned Chance, and slashed the air with my left arm. Sextus cried out, and our auxiliaries galloped across the field. They were on the Arevaci before they knew it, and the enemy horse sprinted back behind their town fort.

Sextus roared to the front rank, and they followed him with their ladders. The bold young warrior urged his horse to the walls, where it died beneath him. No matter, he made it up and over, winner of the Mural Crown. Seeing the first rank climbing the ladders, Mancinus took heart and called to me, "Follow your equitus's lead, Gracchus, and take down Malia!"

I shouted at Casca, and the men formed a column with shields up. They rushed the gates of Malia where the ram stood unmanned, legionary bodies strewn around it. Before long, the gates came crashing down and Malia fell.

We suffered 400 casualties in this assault, and our victorious troops took their spoils with Mancinus's blessing. I tried suggesting to him that a show of restraint might erode the will of those in Numantia awaiting our arrival. He would have none of it, however, swearing by Jupiter and Mars that the pernicious Numantines and their fellow Arevaci tribesmen constantly defied Roman hegemony and require suppression again and again at great cost to the Republic. The consul said that he would not put up with it, that he would vanquish this centaurian race once and for all. On that vow, he ordered all surviving Malian warriors to be crucified at once, and the women and children to be sold into slavery. Malia itself would be burned to the ground and those in Numantia would quake and sue for peace.

As I watched, the surviving five or six hundred warriors in Malia were stretched and hanged on crosses fashioned from the wooden posts of their city's breached walls. I witnessed three thousand of the town's people crying as they were sorted out and roped together according to sex and age, then saw the old and infirm driven out on the high plains to die. I feared that word of this action would have the opposite effect on the Numantines than that which Mancinus intended. While his legionaries gambled away the measly plunder to be had from Malia and fought drunkenly over the women, girls, and boys they expected to have that night, I volunteered my men to tend to the funeral pyres of our noble dead. Newly named the Ninth by Mancinus, and I its acting military tribune, my legion of old soldiers and farm boys grumbled slightly under their breath at this somber duty compared to the pleasures they were missing. Then, they saw the souls of nearly 400 legionaries ascend to the gods. They honored their fellow soldiers at attention, while I thought of how easily these lost men had perished in such an ill-conceived, poorly executed attack. And Numantia looms, Appius.

We march in two days. I trust that I will send you another letter in due time. But, if I don't, dear Father-in-law, know that I love your daughter far beyond the honor of marrying into the Claudii. I love Claudia as the essence of my own spirit, a gift from the goddesses Juno and Venus for some good deed of mine that I cannot imagine ever could warrant such favor. She is the burning star in my sky, Apollo's gift of love, the glory of all the gods. I love her and the children she has given us; please protect them always.

Vale,
Tiberius

Cornelia crushed the letter in her hands as she turned her eyes to Appius. "Curse the dark shades of the underworld, he sounds terrible!"

Appius nodded his head solemnly. "He's in a tenuous position. If what he says is true, we can only hope that what happened at Malia will prove the same at Numantia. Despite Mancinus's mercurial inclinations, Roman soldiering may prevail."

"Horse manure! Better generals have lost in that Hispania sinkhole than Mancinus, and with more men. We need to get another army to them. To win, an inept like Mancinus must use overwhelming force."

"And how can we do that, Cornelia? They're marching on Numantia even as we speak. They may already be there, the battle could be over now, won or lost. We can't get an army there in less than two months! What could they do then?"

"Save the survivors or exact revenge for my son!"

Appius sighed. "How are we to achieve this?"

"First, by going to the Senate. Philea, my cloak!"

Cornelia dropped the crumpled letter on a side table next to her bed. As she emerged from her chambers with Appius beside her, Philea wrapped an exquisite lavender cloak patterned with gold embroidered flowers around her shoulders. On her way to the front door, Cornelia turned her head to Claudia, who had just come out of her own room.

"Claudia, your father and I are going out. We will be back for supper." The light in Cornelia's green eyes struck Claudia like the moon reflecting on the black surface of a summer lake.

After Cornelia and her father had left, Claudia stood in the vestibulum alone. She casually walked over into Cornelia's room. Standing in the doorway, she gazed around until she saw the crumpled letter on the table. She glided over and slipped it into the folds of her dress. Calmly, she left the room and returned to Tiberius's study. Once inside, she locked the door and stepped over to settle down again in his favorite chair. Then, she pulled the letter from her clothing, flattened it out, and began to read.

Chapter 13: The Numantine War

Sextus scratched at the still fresh, scabrous wound running over his shoulder. A noble symbol of his bravery, true, but a pain in the rump nonetheless. He'd been lucky, the Arevaci's blow had barely penetrated after cutting through the leather strap of his lorica. But, now he'd need a new lorica and a new horse.

After their vigil over the fallen troops, the Ninth finally had been allowed to stand down and pick over the few, remaining Malian goods still left. A paltry selection, indeed, sighed Sextus, a few faltering hags, some broken pottery and furniture, and a couple of sickly looking goats and pigs. The men didn't care, they slaughtered and ate the animals and passed around the hags along with any wine that they could find. Sextus took a quick turn with one scrawny girl, the right of an equitus redoubled by winning the Mural Crown. The act was mechanical and boring for the most part. He was too tired and the girl was terrified, so after a weak tryst he told her to go. Then, he drank a cup of wine and fell asleep.

Now, here he was at the base of the wall where he had achieved his trophy. Behind him, six of his auxiliaries stood in a half circle awaiting his orders. They looked beat and almost bewildered at their bad luck in being chosen by the Equitus for the gods knew what, instead of being asleep back in their tents. Well, Sextus thought, pedicabo eos. He turned his attention back to the wall where his great mount Triumph lay in a heap. Big black birds flapped around him, alternating between pecking at each other and the dead horse beneath them. Sextus pulled his sword and swung at them half-heartedly. They flew out of reach while he stung his arm by inadvertently striking the shafts of arrows sticking out of Triumph's breast.

Ah, what a good horse you were, he thought, a noble beast worthy of your name. Never once did you falter until the last when the night shades spirited you away. He pressed his lips together as he gazed, slowly swinging his head back and forth at the sight.

Gradually, he lifted his eyes. There were birds everywhere, in flight over the town walls and on the ground feasting on Arevaci corpses. Let them pluck out their staring eyes, they wouldn't feast on my Triumph.

"All right," he barked. "Get ropes and spades. Drag him out of here over to that glade. Bury him deep so that nothing can get at him. And, make sure you get all the arrows out of him before you put him in the ground."

The men looked stunned, which fueled his anger. But by Mars, he would have sent Triumph to the gods by fire if it wouldn't have scandalized him in the eyes of the entire army.

"Dig, you stinking curs! I'll be back to make sure you did it right!"

They cowered and began moving toward the big horse's body, which had begun to smell, spilled blood always first to foul the air. Flies buzzed around everywhere, further accentuating this dark Hades on earth. No place to eat breakfast, Sextus mused as he made his way back to the camp perimeter.

He watched the hung-over legionaries striking tents and bundling equipment, complaining the entire time of how their heads hurt. Now, the men were supposed to be readying themselves for the critical march to Numantia. But, they moved slowly, less injured from wine, Sextus thought, than by the idea of leaving this safe place to face a stronghold that housed three times as many warriors as this little town, warriors who were likely to fight to the end when they learned the fate of their fellow barbarians. The centurions were sure to dismiss these misgivings by smacking a few backs with their vitae. As for himself, he was starving, now feeling no ill effects from his wound or from his carousing last night. He wondered where he might find something to eat.

Sextus reached his tent and sat down on a camp stool in front of the open flaps. Food, he thought, where will it be? Not at the Ninth's hearth. The way things look, that had been packed up long ago. Leave it to Gracchus to kick his legion's ass. Wasted though they all seemed, the legionaries of the Ninth seemed much farther along than Mancinus's lot. Then, it hit him: Mancinus's ovens. If the consul's army dragged in forming up, most likely his cookery dawdled as well. He stood up and stretched his long frame to the heavens. Then, he started his long legs in motion toward the Via Principalis where Mancinus's praetorium was situated, not too far from the quaestor's quarters.

As he walked, Sextus thought what a strange bird was Quaestor Tiberius Sempronius Gracchus. While every Roman soldier did his level best to get blind drunk and laid, Tiberius Sempronius sat in his tent hand writing letters home. He didn't even call for a scribe, he wrote them himself! Sextus shook his head; if he tried to write a letter in his own script, no one would be able to cipher it at all. They'd think he was a spy, or a sorcerer, or worse. No, he was not much at letters, Sextus admitted to himself. But Gracchus wrote to everyone—his father-in-law, his mother, his wife! For all Sextus knew, he might even be sending post to his house slaves! Strange for a fellow plebeian, Sextus mused, even one of Gracchus's lineage. But, you couldn't fault him as a military man. He'd proven it early on with his own Mural Crown, and his behavior on this campaign had been a model of efficiency and tactical ingenuity. Sextus smiled wolfishly as he recalled those Arevaci bastards running from them by the river, and the other lot just caught in Malia and now hanging from crosses. If you concentrated, you still could hear them crying out on the plains next to the smoldering town. Maybe the Numantines could hear them, too. They were next.

He reached the via principalis and turned left toward the praetorium. Sure enough, he could see the smoke rising from the cook fires. He also could see the annonae packing up, so he broke into a trot. Before they could put all the victuals away, Sextus swooped down and grabbed a loaf of bread and what was left of a lamb's haunch. He tore the loaf in two, then pulled the final scraps of meat off the leg and tucked it between the two halves of bread. The annonae optios complained at the interruption, but he ignored them, deciding instead to check in with the quaestor.

He found Tiberius pouring over the payroll scrolls. Tiberius looked up at Sextus and said, "These rolls were a mess when I received them. Fabius's handling of them was a disaster. Nothing was accounted for, and the legions haven't been paid for months. Mancinus and Fabius must have been distracted in the extreme to allow affairs to reach such a state."

"Perhaps these distractions led to lapses in the numbers in more than one way."

Tiberius sat back. "Surely you would not disparage the consul, Sextus, by accusing him of avarice?"

"Not avarice, just enterprise, Quaestor, a genius for it. Both he and Fabius returned from Macedonia and Corinth as wealthy men. Heavy in the slave trade, I understand."

Tiberius nodded, "Leave it to one of your station to give a nod to Mancinus's business acumen. Not quite consular, though."

"True enough, Quaestor, but it's one way to solve the dilemma of having patrician blood but not the million required to join the ranks of the Senate."

Tiberius gave him a steely look, "Be careful, Sextus. Don't allow camp comradery to lead you too far."

Sextus spread a vulpine smile. "I speak theoretically, Quaestor Sempronius. I meant no insult, certainly not of anyone above my station, of which there are many, even in this camp."

Tiberius was about to retort when a crashing noise and tumultuous cries rose from outside their tent. Both men gripped the hafts of their swords as they bolted out of the tent. They saw a throng of legionaries milling around in front of the Praetorium, blocking their view.

"Out of the way!" shouted Sextus, pushing the soldiers aside. Tiberius followed him, stepping in front to see what was going on.

In the middle of the camp forum before his tent crouched Mancinus, holding one hand at his throat, a trickle of blood seeping between his fingers. His other hand held a dagger at the back of the neck of a small figure pinned to the ground by the consul's sandal on his head. Sextus noticed a small boy appear behind the consul from inside the tent, then bolt away, hugging the canvas side until he was out of sight.

"Demons of Hades," cried out Tiberius in a whisper, "that's Lysis!"

Sextus was confused, until he realized that Tiberius meant the youth under Mancinus's foot, not the fleeing boy. Lysis, Tiberius's man servant, he thought.

"This little Greek maggot tried to assassinate me!" roared Mancinus. "I'll cut his head off with his own knife and hang it from my standard as an example!"

Mancinus moved his foot between Lysis's shoulder blades, and grabbing his hair with his free hand, pulled his head up and brought the blade to his throat.

"Lysis!" Tiberius shouted out at the top of his voice.

Startled, Mancinus held up. Sextus and the rest of the onlooking crowd of soldiers turned their eyes to Tiberius who shouted again, only this time in a language unknown to them.

Lysis cried out a muffled sentence from beneath Mancinus's sandal.

Mancinus stared at Tiberius, dumbfounded. Then, he gathered himself and slowly started to bring the blade back to Lysis's throat. But Fabius stepped in and whispered into the consul's ear while gently grasping his forearm. As he whispered, he glanced toward Tiberius.

The blood left Mancinus's face, and he raised the knife from Lysis's neck. "All right. Tribune Gracchus, this little Greek is your, yes?"

Sextus watched Tiberius step further forward in front of the crowd, which seemed to number every legionary in the army.

"He is my slave."

"Then, deal with him."

Mancinus pulled Lysis halfway up by his tunic and flung him at Tiberius's feet. Lysis peered fearfully up at his master, but Tiberius stared straight ahead.

"Casca!" shouted Tiberius.

"Sir!" snapped Casca, who had quietly moved to Tiberius's left shoulder.

"Crucify him. Put him with the Arevaci."

Casca grabbed Lysis by the neck and marched him stumbling off in the direction of the gate. Mancinus nodded briskly, dropped the knife, and swept back into his tent.

The men drawn to the tumultuous scene gradually turned back to resume their duties, helped along by the vitae of their centurions. Tiberius stood still in the middle of the camp forum until Sextus suggested they return to his tent.

"Wait!"

Fabius slipped up to the two men. "This is yours, I believe, Quaestor?"

Wearing an unctuous half-smile, Fabius held the knife thrown down by Mancinus by the blade, the haft resting on his forearm. Tiberius resisted the immediate reflex to reach for his scabbard as he recognized the knife. Its beautiful engraving and gold finish marked it as the blade given to him by his mother, his father's knife. He hesitated, then took it from Fabius. Instead of putting it in his empty scabbard, however, he headed back to his tent holding it in his hand.

Fabius looked at Sextus and smile smugly. Then, he pivoted and entered Mancinus's tent after a perfunctory knock on one of the wooden poles.

Sextus could not believe what he had just seen. Why did that crazy Greek sliver of a slave try to kill Mancinus? And why did Tiberius shout? Did he really cry out to save the slave? Maybe he wasn't just writing letters when he was hiding away in his tent. Even so, to risk defying a consul, what enchantment did this slave hold over him?

Sextus shook his head, still flabbergasted by the weirdness of it all. Well, that was the end of Tiberius's military career for sure, he thought. It might be a good time to request a transfer to another legion. My Mural Crown might stand me in good staid for that, he thought.

Time to check on the interment of Triumph. They should be close to finishing, now, or they better be since the camp was fast disappearing onto the backs of the legionaries. Sextus hiked over to the stable and picked out a horse to ride to the grove. He galloped as much as he could, but his mount was a nearly worn-out nag, good only for transporting men with leg wounds on the march. But, he made do.

The men burying Triumph had just finished putting on the last few spades of earth when Sextus loped up. Good, he thought, they knew their officer well enough not to dawdle.

He jumped off the horse, which did its best to bolt away. A couple of the exhausted men ran stiffly after it while Sextus walked to the head of the grave. He reached into his tunic and pulled out a twist of hay and a small pouch. From the pouch, he took flint and stone and started a small fire with the hay. Then, he laid some incense on the small flame, causing a feathering of smoke up to the sky as he prayed.

"Mighty god Mars and goddess Diana, take the spirit of my wonderful warhorse Triumph to your breast and away from the black shades of Hades. Let him run hard among the clouds, and introduce him to Pegasus's mares and fillies to start another great line of warhorses. For, he was a great one himself, second only to Alexander's Bucephalus. Bring me his colt so that I may honor you both again in the field of combat and hunting the hart."

That was as good as he could do, he thought, but fat chance that he'd see another horse like Triumph. Still, he owned the Mural Crown.

He left the grave and saw that the two men, bent over and breathing hard, had been able to run down the old nag, which stood behind them nibbling grass. Without a word, Sextus strode over and mounted the horse. As he started to ride, he told the men to return to their posts to get ready for the march.

The horse walked back toward the camp, Sextus allowing it to have its head as he thought deeply about today's occurrences. He still couldn't dismiss the strange behavior of his commander. Bewitched, perhaps, by some satyr or imp, he mused. And what had he said to him in that bizarre tongue, clearly the speech of demons. The boy had spoken back to him in the same language.

This was too much, he thought, his brow furrowed. He pulled on the reins and dug his heels into the nag, pulling her away from the camp and its hay and wheeled toward the field where they had planted the Arevaci prisoners and the deserters.

Approaching the grove of crucifixes, Sextus found the smell to be almost overwhelming. He yanked the neck of his tunic up over his nose and wandered around through the forest of hanging men. Birds pecked at them, crows at the eyes of both the living and the dead. Eerily, it was quiet with very few plaintive voices crying out their mortal misery. Most of them were dead or dying, he thought, quick to go with almost all of their energy sapped by the battle itself. As he passed by men who until recently had been fellow legionaries, he averted his eyes, hiding the sense that a flogging would have done the army better rather than Mancinus's queer form of decimation for desertion.

Eventually, he saw a small group trudging back to camp, soldiers he knew from the Ninth. As he passed them, he saw one figure standing opposite a cross. On the cross hung the Greek slave.

Sextus dismounted and walked up next to Casca. The Ninth's First Spear was a hard man whom he didn't like much for both his forwardness and silent disrespect. Despite his heroics, Casca Naso could never match the valor of an equitus, being stuck on foot as he was. And, he was the son of a slave himself, not so far removed from the one hanging above them. Yet, he had his airs.

Sextus gazed up at the slave, seventeen he supposed, but still not a much of a figure of a man. Striking, though, with his raven hair and those sorrowful eyes. Understandable that he could be attractive to those who went for that sort of thing. Tiberius, though? And, the lad could sit a horse pretty well, he recalled, better than Tiberius on that massive gelding of his that the boy exercised. Done with all that now, he thought. So, what was it about him?

Casca started to walk away when Sextus called to him, "Centurion."

The broad-backed man halted, allowing his shoulders to drop, and swiveled. "What?"

"A sad day, eh? Tiberius's man servant and all." Casca pivoted to go, and Sextus hurriedly said, "What do you think made him do it? Shout, I mean, to stop Mancinus?"

Casca stalked back to Sextus and planted himself inches away from his face. Sextus stood a good six inches taller than the Centurion, but somehow Casca seemed to look down upon him.

"Sextus, you're a self-centered, ridiculous jackass. A good soldier, but a jackass nonetheless. Tiberius had that boy in his household since he was nine years old. Slave or not, he was a member of his family. And, now this."

"Oh," said Sextus.

Again, Casca made to leave when Sextus said, "So, what did he say? I mean, when they spoke in that barbarian language, what did Tiberius say to him?"

Casca sighed, "It was Greek, you fool. Tiberius asked him why he'd attacked Mancinus."

"And?"

"The boy said the consul had killed his family and taken away his little brother." Sextus appeared completely bewildered and Casca continued. "Mancinus and Fabius fought in the Corinthian war when the city was razed. Lysis is from the Corinthian peninsula. The timing is right."

Shaking his head slowly, the centurion seemed to muse sadly. "Perhaps he'd recognized Mancinus when we first joined up. But, seeing the consul with another young boy like his lost brother …." Casca trailed off.

"Gods above," murmured Sextus.

"Right. No matter, our tribune is Roman and does what is required." He looked up at Lysis, silent in agony. "Orders are orders or I'd finish this for him. But, I must do my duty, too, of course."

Casca left.

Sextus peered up at the youth struggling for breath, his huge eyes cast down, unfocused but imploring. The equitus mounted the nag and yanked the reins to turn, then jerked them again until he'd done a complete circle, glancing once more at the slave on the cross.

Then, he said to himself, Well, it's not my duty. Wheeling around once more, he drew his sword, thrust it through the little slave's heart and galloped back to camp.

The army was on the march at last. Sextus trotted up to his horsemen, who rode on either flank of the Ninth as they awaited further orders. The five legions were strung out over several miles, with both the head and the rearguard in the hills, out of sight. Sextus was surprised to see that the auxiliaries he could see flanked their legions closely. He would have thought that they would be out scouting for ambushes and other enemy activity.

"Ah, here you are, Equitus."

Sextus twisted around to see who called him even as he recognized the voice. Tiberius walked his horse up, holding the reins of another trailing behind him. Something struck Sextus as odd, until he realized that Tiberius wasn't riding as high as he usually did. Then, it dawned on the young equestrian that the quaestor-tribune wasn't on his dappled warhorse, but on a smaller bay mare. The horse he led behind him was his big war horse Chance.

Tiberius smiled, though Sextus could see deep wells of pain in his eyes. He looked drawn, too, worn out.

"You're the Ninth's equitus, Sextus, and a good one, a brave leader. You need a good mount beneath you to do your best, like you did at Malia. The survival of the legion could depend on it. So, here," he said, handing the reins to Sextus.

"You're giving me your horse?" Sextus said, completely baffled.

Tiberius shrugged, "I've never been much of a horseman. This sweet mare is good enough for me. I know you'll make good use of Chance in defending the honor of the Ninth. So, ride, Equitus."

He smiled at Sextus again, and walked the mare away to the front of the legion.

Sextus could not believe his good fortune. Maybe he prayed to the gods better than he knew. He shook his head again at the thought of Tiberius. What a strange one he was. But, here was his horse.

Sextus slid off the nag and jumped up on Chance. The horse reared uneasily for a second until it recognized the sitting of an old hand.

What a steed! exulted Sextus, balls or not. He slapped its flank and bolted out in front of the auxiliaries at a quick gallop, then curved around and back, thinking to himself, Maybe I'll hold off on that transfer request for a bit.

Chapter 14. Numantia

Avarus and Rhetogenes sat under a large tree taking turns sipping from a wineskin. They wore glum expressions on their faces, not looking at each other as they spoke.

"And the Malian heroes?" Aravus asked.

"We cut them down and laid their bodies on the sacred stones," said Rhetogenes. "We left the Romans hanging. Let them rot until they fall."

"Why would they crucify their own men?" Avarus said.

"Deserters, cowards, something like that."

Avarus nodded. "Any survivors in the town?"

"None that we could find. Those that lived must have fled, both from the Roman murderers and to find water and food. The earth was scorched."

Avarus bit his lower lip. "They stormed Malia."

Rhetogenes dipped his shaggy head up and down, "According to the few who escaped, the Romans were on their heels until they sent in another legion. It seems one horseman rallied them, and they swept up and over the walls. From his description, I thought this chieftain might have been Gracchus the Son himself. Instead, it appeared to have been a man much like him in height, though younger from what I heard."

Avarus said, "Yes, Tiberius Gracchus is almost as tall, but a little bit older—not nearly as old as we are, of course. The other man is the captain of his cavalry. I saw them both when we were surprised at the riverbank. The young horseman led riders around our flank to attack us fiercely from behind at the same time that Roman foot soldiers surprised us on the hillside. The young Tiberius rode with more riders and the rest of his foot soldiers back upon us from the far end of the riverbank. We barely got out. I saw Gracchus leading his men into the middle of the clash. He rode a giant grey horse and raised his sword when he saw me. I swear by the great gods, he was the image of his father."

Rhetogenes grunted. "Maybe we're lucky he isn't leading all of the Roman soldiers."

Avarus said, "It was a simple maneuver, but we rushed right into it. How he managed to get those soldiers past us into the hills without our knowing . . . . The Romans are such poor fighters in our land, terrible on the hoof. What they are good at is sending more and more soldiers to bludgeon us. They're good on foot, and at bringing down walls."

"And, they are closing on Numantia."

Avarus scratched his belly scar. "True. A week, maybe a little longer. They march slowly, slower than the other Roman armies."

"Have you been pressing them?" Rhetogenes asked.

Avarus grimaced, "It's harder now. That cavalry captain of Gracchus's? He has his scouts riding in numbers around the ridge tops. It's difficult for us to gather without being seen and chased ourselves."

"So, what do you do?"

"We draw back and wait. They'll get sloppy and slack off. Then, we can go after them again."

"But, won't they arrive at Numantia before that happens?" Rhetogenes asked, puzzled.

"Yes, and that isn't necessarily a bad thing. Besieging the city will occupy their horse even more, which will give us a better chance to chew on their flanks again."

"Meanwhile, the Romans could bring Numantia's walls down. They're good at that, I've been told."

Avarus looked for the first time in the conversation directly at his old friend. "Megavaricus and Thurro agree, the only way to defeat the Romans is to have them think that the battle is for Numantia. While they turn their forces to breeching the city walls, we will turn on them and drive them out."

"You think this is a good strategy? You think it will work? Is it worth the risk of losing the town, of risking Sicounin and your family?"

Avarus appeared unnerved by the question, which he quickly covered with an expression of resolve. "It's the best chance we have. Remember, Numantia has never fallen, not to the Romans or anyone else."

Then, he stared straight ahead into the afternoon light.

At last, the forward Roman units reached Numantia. Velites emerged from a shallow woods that covered a low hill in front of the elevation where the great Numantine stronghold town was situated. Hastati followed, and as soon as they saw the walls above them in the distance, they spread out into loose maniples. The sight in front of them was daunting. Numantia covered a hill only a few hundred feet in height, and the fortifications seemed rudimentary, two twelve-foot walls constructed of stones and wooden beams wrapped around the slope in concentric rings. Timber towers covered with shingled roofs bolstered the walls, though these, too were of modest height, maybe fifteen to twenty feet each. A seasoned architectus might surmise at first that siege towers could dominate the walls in short order. Slowly, though, details began to register with the Roman scouts.

Two rivers, the Durius and the Tera, met on Numantia's left side, severely compromising any assault at their juncture. On the right side of the city, the hill fell off sharply, clearly impossible to traverse without fixed ropes or railings. The middle part of the hill formed a V that led up to the gates, a high arx itself with towers on both sides. The approach sloped steeply up and lay directly in the path of missiles, arrows, and spears. Nothing but scrubby grass grew on the promenade, bare of any other cover except for occasional outcroppings of sharp-looking rocks. This was the place where every other Roman army had failed, where elephants brought by Nobilior to crush the Numantines were stampeded instead back on their own troops, causing an outright panic. Shaken, Nobilior retreated to a former camp where his legionaries froze or starved to death during the winter. Another campaign lost.

Sextus rode up with his auxiliaries and spurred them around to the left of the fortress-town galloping on the outside bank of the Durius River to the far side of Numantia. As he disappeared around the hill, an occasional arrow flew from the stronghold into the middle of the river, scarcely noticed by the pounding horsemen.

Mancinus and his entourage emerged from the woods in front of Numantia even after Sextus had ridden out of sight. Fabius rode at his side as did the tribunes of his legions. Tiberius took up the rear, partially because of the newness of his commission, but mostly because of the debacle of his slave's attack on the consul.

"There it is, men, the thorn in Rome's side, a jumble of stick huts clinging to an anthill."

"An African-size anthill, Consul," said Fabius, "surrounded by a well-disposed set of ring walls. Going up that slope will challenge the resolve of any legionary."

Mancinus screwed his lips into a sour pout, as if someone had thrust a lemon in his mouth. "Our troops have proven themselves at Corinth, and now again at Malia. They'll march up this hillock like it isn't there and roll over those bowlegged chicken herders. Tribunes, form up the line. Make camp, then make ready."

Just then, Sextus came storming back at the head of his flying horsemen and rode straight to the cluster of officers. Tiberius watched him pull up directly in front of Mancinus and Fabius, the consul's senior tribune, without even a gesture or nod in his direction.

"What have you, Sextus?" Fabius asked.

"No getting in from that side. A sheer escarpment, deadlier than the Tarpeian Rock. Looks like it'll be up through the front door, sir."

"Well, the men are up to it," Mancinus said dryly. "You are dismissed, Equitus."

Sextus walked his horse past Mancinus back to Tiberius. "I can see why this little bump has been such a tough nut to crack."

"Mancinus seems confident that he's the one to crack it."

Sextus looked at Tiberius skeptically. When he realized that nothing else was forthcoming from the tribune, he moved his horse away toward where the stable area of the new camp would be set up.

The army, now 24,000 strong, pitched camp with an efficiency and cheer that must have been daunting to the Numantines watching from their parapets. The Roman soldiers sang bawdy songs as they dug the big, square trench as the perimeter of the camp. Once completed, they rushed with equal enthusiasm to hammer in the camp stakes of the palisade and to help to raise the gate and corner towers, singing all the way. For, their goal lay at hand, Numantia itself. Hispania was not Greece, there would be little in the way of silver, gold, or other rich spoils, Malia had proven that. But, there would be wine, women, slaves, and glory for being the Roman army that finally forced the Numantine renegades under the yoke. Most likely, too, there would be new land for the taking.

Mancinus didn't wait for his praetorium tent to be raised, he called for field tables to be put up in front of the camp construction. Surrounded by the tribunes, immunes, and architecti, he began plotting out his assault plans just out of arrow shot from the Numantine walls. The public strategy gathering was simple posturing, another deliberate ploy to demoralize the Arevaci tribe, another massive Roman army at their walls, another threat to their freedom.

Mancinus posed as the hard-jawed master of Rome's relentless forces, sometimes defeated but never vanquished, never turned away. The Numantines could worry this knowledge in their minds as they watched the purposeful chaos of the Roman preparations. They could wonder if it was worth it to fight again because they only had to lose once in order to lose everything. Surrender might mean hostages and tribute, maybe even the execution of their leaders. The loss of a battle meant the loss of the war and the likely razing of Numantia, the death of most of their people, and enslavement of the rest. Remember what they did to Carthage; look what they did to Malia.

A lot for them to chew on, Tiberius thought. Despite the Consul's playacting, he would be delighted if the Numantines simply capitulated without a fight. Tiberius was much more skeptical after his experience marching to Malia. Since then, he had learned, too, that the Hispanic tribes were warlike people who cherished death in battle. He found out that the rocky places where the bones and weathered scraps of skin and flesh had not been a dumping ground for slain foes. Local tribesmen had told him they were shrines to the warriors, that the birds that picked their bones lifted the spirits of these valiant heroes to their rightful seats next to the gods. Tiberius wondered at this elemental belief and the fierce, almost careless way in which they fought. Could death in battle be a goal as much as winning? If so, these renegades had an intense advantage over their enemies, perhaps even the Roman legionary.

In time, the camp was up, the watches assigned, and the legions in bivouac stared into the cooking fires warming their grain mash, plying vinegary wine as they waited. A few broke out instruments to play a tune and others joined in, singing bawdy lyrics with their tribunes's, centurions's and optios's names replacing those of the original satyrs in the old songs.

The officers' mess was the same, spirits soaring and invectives flying through the air. Mancinus had opened up his private wine store to toast his tribunes and their troops ready to serve Rome.

"To the Roman legions destined to destroy the Numantine stronghold," he shouted out, and the rest roared. Tiberius turned to Casca and said, "Who has the last watch?"

"We do, Quaestor Tribune."

"Good. Make sure they're up to the task. No drunks."

"Absolutely, sir."

Tiberius took himself off to the latrine, and among those in the trench, found a spot to squat. A shadow moving to stoop next to him blocked the torches from the camp.

"Salve, Tribune," a voice from the dark said. Tiberius turned his head to find Ulpius scrunched down next to him. "Centurion. How goes it?"

"The wound is healing, sir, but too slowly. I'm still unable to step to.

The surgeons say another week or so. "

"Enjoy it while you can, Ulpius. You'll be back humping with the rank and file before you know it."

"True enough, but I do get bored." His voice trailed off. "And, how goes it with you, sir?" the grey-haired spear asked.

"Everything seems to be in working order, here."

Yes," laughed Ulpius, "it's good to evacuate before a battle."

Tiberius didn't reply.

"When my guts feel a bit balky," Ulpius said, "I like to distract myself by trying to think up little ditties for marching. It keeps the boys' spirits up, I think."

"A useful pursuit," Tiberius agreed.

They were silent for a time. Then, Ulpius sang.

> "I once met a beautiful lady
> who, sad to say, was very hairy.
> When plying my stiff prick so precious,
> I got all caught up in her tresses.
> It took a barber and his knife to free me,
> Now I'm a lesser man when I wee-wee."

Tiberius stared at the dark, stooped shape next to him. Even in the dark, Ulpius must have felt his eyes on him. He said, "I know, I need to work on the last line the next time I'm here."

As ordered, the immunes had made a score of thick-planked wooden barriers on wheeled sleds for the legionaries to push up the slope. In the middle was a shed with a V-shaped roof made of thick horse hides set on wooden wheels. Inside, the trunk of a large tree stripped of limbs swung from meter-wide, tanned leather straps, a half-dozen in all. The end of the trunk facing the city-fort had been hewed to a point and covered with a metal cap. Mancinus called up his beloved Fifth and Eighth Legions to man the ram and the blinds, with archers filling in behind them.

Tiberius's immunes assembled their catapultas and ballista under the seasoned eye of Titius. They placed the machines next to the heavier mangonels with Tiberius's Ninth Legion in support. Sextus joined the other army auxiliaries on the right flank to stave off any attacks by horse outside of the Arevaci stronghold. The Fourth Legion also was held in reserve, and the Seventh manned the camp's palisades.

Mancinus rode his horse across the lines, ignoring the occasional arrow that fell around him. He barked a curt command to Quintus Fabius, who signaled the cornicens to sound the order of the day. As if one, the catapults, mangonels, and ballistas fired in concert while the Fifth and the Eighth slowly pushing their wooden walls and rams up the mountain hill to the walls of Numantia.

Tiberius watched with grudging admiration. Whatever his misgivings might be about Mancinus's casual approach to campaigning, the training of the Roman legionary looked to promise victory by default. Good or bad generalship aside, the Roman soldier might win any engagement simply for being the Roman soldier.

At first, the advance progressed deliberately in order. With the hail of projectiles and rocks raining on Numantia, not a soul could be seen above the parapets. One of the towers supporting the gateway to the city-fort took a direct hit from a mangonel boulder, exploding in a cloud of wooden splinters and dust. Muted cries of pain could be heard even at this distance, which caused some of the troops to laugh. Mostly, though, the stones and spears arched over the walls to plow into the city behind. They were less likely to hit the defenders, but they cleared the streets while terrorizing the people, always a desirable effect. The soldiers on the walls might not be able to help turning to look back to see if any of their family had been injured. Worry like this was sure to shake an enemy soldier's resolve. In any case, not one Numantine missile had been fired in kind since the Roman's barrage had begun.

The ascending troops, however, had slowed in their climb. The navigable ground to the city's gates had begun to narrow, a natural funnel that caused the wooden walls to crowd together. The centurions called for them to take turns and form columns rather than lines, but the changeover had brought the massing legions to a crawl. Nearly brought to a standstill, the Fifth and the Eighth suddenly found themselves in the shade of a flight of Numantine arrows.

Without warning, hundreds of Numantine horsemen pounded out from around the left side of the fortress, appearing as if out of the air.

"Sextus said there was nothing but cliffs in that quarter!" exclaimed Tiberius. "They've come out of the two rivers!"

The Numantines swarmed around the backs of the wooden mantlets, slashing any Romans within reach or casting their short spears into their bodies. When the legionaries turned to face their assailants, arrows from the walls struck the soldiers in their backs. The Numantines completed their run behind the Roman lines, and wheeled around before they came too close to the auxiliaries. Barely losing any momentum, they galloped back to make another pass at the confused and wounded legions in the front line.

Mancinus roared out another command, and the cornicens blew their signal. With Fabius and Sextus in the lead, the auxiliaries immediately charged to pursue the enemy riders. As they rode by, the Numantines took a few more strokes at the crippled legionaries, then simply ran east, away from the city toward the wooded hills.

Tiberius squinted as he watched the action unfold before him. Aside from the near disaster with the forward legions, who were now regrouping behind their wooden walls, something seemed wrong. Even as he realized this, a cloud of dust rose from behind the right side of the Numantine fortress.

"Casca, form up the men! Shields up, pila ready. Testudo! March them out to support the assault!"

Casca shouted above the din of the battle, and the other centurions picked up his call. The men moved into action, hurrying in a smooth, practiced motion. Tiberius spurred his horse as they marched to close the distance between them and the frontline troops.

But, it was too late. Another column of Numantine horsemen tumbled down from around the right side of the city walls straight at the troops pressed hard against the wooden barriers. The riders spun their swords and spears into the packed mass of legionaries, cutting out large gouts of flesh and spraying blood as they sped by. They turned at the last to fire a parting volley of arrows point-blank at the huddled soldiers as they passed the end of the Roman line.

Casca ordered the pila cast, but the distance was still too great. Tiberius reined his horse to a stop. "Cack!" he shouted out as he saw the second Numantine cavalry group gallop behind the Roman auxiliaries running headlong in pursuit of the first group of enemy horsemen. Even if he couldn't see beyond the forested hills, he could picture graphically what would happen to the Roman riders caught between them.

"Send them up, Casca. Get the survivors off of that hill!"

"Aye, sir," shouted Casca, who turned his head to roar orders at the Ninth. The men held shields in front and above their heads, ignoring the arrows and spears slicing toward them from Numantia's walls. Finally, they reached the beleaguered Fifth and cautiously passed them beneath their shields held higher so that the rescued troops could carry their wounded mates back with them.

Mancinus rode up to Tiberius.

"Jupiter's bolts, what happened?" Mancinus cried out.

Without thinking, Tiberius said, "A minor massacre. I'm guessing several hundred casualties, maybe more."

"Where did they come from?" Mancinus said.

"Two hidden passages on either side of the fort. One by the brush near the river junction, the other high up on the hill above their burying grounds."

Mancinus set his jaw, muscles flicking at the edges. "That's a trick they can't use twice," he said.

"They won't need to. Look," Tiberius said, gesturing with his head.

Sextus came back in a slow gallop at the head of perhaps half of the army's auxiliaries, many of them riding wounded, barely able to keep their mounts. The crippled cavalry rode into the camp too fast, knocking aside several legionaries slow to move out of their way. Sextus pulled up in front of Tiberius and Mancinus, and only then did they see Quintus Fabius clinging to the tall equitus's back. Fabius slowly slid off Chance's rump, crumpling into a ball.

Tiberius was off his horse at once to kneel next to Fabius opposite Sextus, who held the tribune's head under his thigh. Fabius gazed up at Tiberius with imploring eyes, opened his mouth, yawned one bloody bubble, and died.

"He was far out in front of the charge," Sextus said, "when the entire Numantine host suddenly reversed and attacked. He didn't have a chance, they speared and hacked him off his horse before we could reach him. As it was, they rode right through us, we were so shocked. Then we were hit from behind by a second force. It took no more than a few minutes for them to cut down half of us, and they were gone. I gathered together those that could ride, picked up what wounded we could, and made it back here."

Tiberius looked up at Mancinus. The consul's face was flooded black with fury. "Form up your legion, Tribune, and bring back our fallen Romans. Equitus, are you up to leading the way?"

"At your command, sir," Sextus said, "but, I'll need a horse." He turned his gaze to Tiberius and said softly, "Chance took a spear point in the breast. Not deep, though. He should survive, Goddess Diana willing."

Tiberius nodded, and shouted to Casca to bring up the men with wagons and oxen teams. The Fifth assembled in short order, though the wagons seemed to take forever. In the meantime, the few surgeons traveling with the army did their best to treat the legionaries wounded in the assault. Many moaned from the pain, sending up constant lowing like livestock before a storm. A few shrieked loudly as an arrow was cut out or one of their limbs was removed. For those mortally wounded, the surgeons gave them opiates to ease the pain on their journey across the River Styx.

Once the wagons pulled up, Sextus road up on a small roan to join Tiberius at the head of the troops. "It's not far, maybe a mile past that hillock."

"I know," said Tiberius," I saw you all dash after the Numantines like dogs after a baby rabbit."

Sextus's lips formed a pressed white line. He said nothing.

The men marched quickly, able to direct themselves by the horde of black birds looping back and forth just beyond the hill pointed out by Sextus. The velites signaled the hill cleared, and the main body scurried over the crest and halted. Again, the scouts encountered no resistance, and the legion marched on. Eventually, they reached the killing ground in a meadow on the other side of a ragged stand of trees. The velites had run off the vultures picking at the bodies of their dead comrades. Even so, the sight of their twisted bodies in rictus was hard to take. Tiberius was surprised to see that, except for the disfigurement caused by the ravens, the corpses seemed not to have been mutilated by the Numantines. Killed only, he thought, except for the handful found still alive, fewer than a hundred.

Their comrades gently laid them into hammocks made by stretching capes between four pila tied together, and took them to the front wagons. The dead auxiliaries were piled into the rest of the wagons behind. Tiberius did a quick count—there must have been close to 500 casualties. His legion would be hard pressed to bringing them all back if the Numantines decided to attack again. Some 4,000 enemy cavalry still ranged freely in the field, essentially a one-to-one ratio. He seriously doubted that they would return to the city when they could inflict much more damage on the Roman army through ambush and harassment. He'd learned that much on the march to Malia.

"Casca," he said to the primus sitting on a wagon. "Make sure the velites spread wide, and not just in front and rear, but on both sides up on the hilltops, too."

The burly centurion nodded and strode off to pass the order.

Sextus cantered up to walk his horse next to Tiberius.

"Sextus," Tiberius said, "the consul will need a true equitus, now that his de facto cavalry captain is dead." Shaking his head, he murmured, "Fabius had a penchant for taking over duties beyond his grade's purview. This time it cost him his life." He gazed up at Sextus and said, "My guess is that you'll be the new head of horse."

Involuntarily, Sextus's eyes lit up.

"If he does choose you, and you lead the same way as your predecessor, you'll soon follow him to the funeral bier."

A flash of anger crossed the equestrian's face, and Tiberius continued in a more ameliorative tone. "Sextus, don't you understand that this is how the Numantines have kept Rome out? You saw it on our march here. They never took us on directly, they always nibbled at our heels until we tired and make some critical mistake. You can't chase after them in their land, they're the masters of ambush. That's the only way they can win, there are too few of them to confront us directly."

Sextus's angry expression gradually shifted to a begrudging, wary look, almost that of a petulant boy who knew that his lecturer was right, but didn't like it anyway. "Unless they all come together under one leader, like Virithius," he muttered.

Tiberius nodded, "Well, yes, that's true. But, they never seem able to stay together long. Too many squabbles among tribes. I'm merely trying to caution you, Equitus, to ride clear of what they do best."

Sextus grunted and spurred his mount ahead. Tiberius sighed as he walked his horse along.

The funeral pyre for Quintus Fabius burned high into the night, the white ash rising above the flames as if to join the other stars in the cosmos' firmament. Mancinus stood rigidly, almost at attention as he witnessed the freeing of his most trusted officer's spirit and body from common corruption.

Tiberius entertained other thoughts. There goes the only witness to that part of my quaestorship when I was absent in Etruria. Who knows what creative accounting might have been accomplished between Mancinus and his right arm Fabius? Aside from the consul himself, only the gods know now. Pray they keep their peace if misdeeds have been done.

Fires ringed Fabius's mounded bier, the funereal flames of those who died with the senior tribune, plus those who died beneath Numantia's walls. Except for the guards on duty at the camp's walls, the entire army stood in honor of their fallen comrades. Once dismissed, they would straggle back to their tents to eat cold fare as the evening's last meal. A swig of vinegary wine might wake them up long enough to wonder what tomorrow would bring.

As soon as the priests finished their offerings and prayers, Mancinus snapped around to Tiberius and said in a low rasp, "Come with me. I have something to show you."

They walked off among the troops falling out and plodding into the encampment, exhausted from the day's events. Mancinus led Tiberius on a circuitous route through the back lanes of the camp close to the palisade walls so that they remained mostly in the shadows. Only Mancinus's adjutant accompanied them, trailing behind.

Soon, they arrived at the camp stables. Mancinus walked into the corral, past the strings of horses on either side toward the stable hands' bivouac. Beyond them was a log lean-to which looked to be where the work was done to repair the auxiliaries' riding gear.

Tiberius noticed a small open hearth burning charcoal just outside of the structure, white hot heat hovering over top. Two large, bear-like men wearing leather aprons and nothing else shifted metal rods and blades in the white coals of the fire, something he expected to see in the armory rather than here.

And the smell, sickening and familiar. As they skirted the forge to stand behind it, he realized that he'd just smelled a more corrupt version of it at the funeral fires. Burnt flesh.

Behind the forge beneath the lean-to, a naked man lay stretched out on a wicker raft. Or, what was left of the man. His feet were gone, his eyes burnt out, his ears and nose pussy messes of blood and charred skin. A Numantine warrior from the look of his hair, he moaned softly, plaintively.

Mancinus stared at him, as if measuring him for the next step in his ordeal. He said to Tiberius, "He's one of the Numantine horde who failed to escape or die, sadder for him. But, listen to what he says." He nodded at one of the men at the fire.

The man slipped a long, white-hot blade from the fire and laid it on the

Numantine's already blistered and scarred chest. The howl of pain almost caused Tiberius to cover his ears reflexively, but he resisted the urge.

The quaestionarius turned to Mancinus, waiting. "Ask him," said the consul.

He turned and spoke to the supine man, first in Latin, then in the Hispanic tongue.

"Who are the Numantine allies?"

The Numantine warrior slowly swung his head as far as he could on the rack without speaking. The quaestionarius turned to his partner, who handed him the burning iron blade. He faced the man on the rack again and proceeded to saw at one of his wrists until the left hand fell away. This time Tiberius put his hands to his head to dull the screaming.

Oblivious to the horrible din, perhaps because he still wore his helmet, Mancinus told the quaestionarius to ask again.

"Who are your allies? Where are they coming from? Come on, your sword hand is next, then your manhood. Who are they? Docius, the blade again," he said.

"No, no, no!" screeched the crippled soldier as the white hot blade separated his tendons until his other hand dropped to the floor. The shriek that followed roiled through Tiberius's stomach.

"Your allies!" shouted Mancinus in Latin.

The Numantine's eyes rolled back, and the quaestionarius doused his body with water, which sent him into a torso-wrenching spasm.

After arching his spine several times, a silent howl shaped in his mouth, he subsided into an unsettling stillness. The quaestionarius leaned over and whispered to him, then moved his head around to bring his ear close to the wretch's mouth.

"The Beroni, Peledoni, and the other Arevaci. The Turmodigi, and Vacceci. The Vettoni and the Lusitani."

Mancinus looked shocked. "The Vacceci and Vettoni? The Lusitanes?"

The quaestionarius nodded.

"Dispatch him," Mancinus said, as he turned his attention to another Numantine warrior, who hung, tied to the low crossbeam of the building in a makeshift crucifixion. The quaestionarius drew the hot blade across the neck of the maimed man tied to the rack at the same time that Mancinus said, "Did you see what happened to your brave comrade? Do you want to suffer the same, and die the same?" Mancinus said, the second quaestionarius translating quickly the consul's words into the Numantine tongue.

The hanging Numantine smiled a bloody smile of his own and spoke.

"What did he say?" Mancinus demanded.

"A bhás álain," the quaestionarius said, "a beautiful death."

Mancinus scowled. "Kill him."

They walked by the shimmering heat of the forge and past the line of horses out into the welcome, cool spring air, Mancinus mumbling as he took long strides.

"These Numantines have inspired a general uprising. We need to take down their fortress tomorrow, or we'll be facing the entire Hispanic horde."

Tiberius gazed at him, startled. "You think that warrior told you the truth? They're likely to tell you anything while being dismembered."

Mancinus briskly shook his head, "No, the story was the same from the other captives questioned before him. They all said that the Arevaci had united, which is natural, of course. But, the Vaccaci and the Lusitani? And all the other tribes?" He swung his head, "No, we must win tomorrow."

After a moment of self-reflection, Mancinus jerked his head up. "Prepare your troops, Tribune. We storm Numantia at dawn. No reserves, five legions full force."

He pounded his fist into his hand and strode off toward his tent. Tiberius watched, then hurried to his own quarters to call attention to Casca and the other centurions of the battle looming.

Chapter 15. Assault

In the dark just before daybreak, all of the legionaries mustered behind the camp palisade. Rain poured down on the troops, chilling them as they awaited the call to march forward. Except for the cold, they didn't mind the change in the weather, thinking that the darker it was, the harder it would be for the Numantines to target them. The priests had performed a rather perfunctory sacrifice before the battle, struggling hard to keep the sacred flames afire long enough for the battle auspices to be deemed good. Even as the holy sacrifices sputtered, the immunes sighted in their mangonels and ballistas to pummel the Numantine defenders and demoralize their families. Mancinus had split the auxiliaries, putting them on the flanks to blunt any soirees by the Arevaci horse, either from the city or the surrounding woods.

This time, Mancinus had decided on speed as the only way to storm the walls. Therefore, the immunes had worked all night crafting new, lightweight ladders for the troops to climb the relatively low walls of Numantia. They would run up the mount with the ladders over their heads, which would protect them somewhat from the defenders' arrows and spears.

When Mancinus laid out his plan of attack, the tribunes never changed expression, though Tiberius figured that they all contemplated the same thoughts. If they could take such a drubbing the first time, with men well-protected behind wooden barriers, how bad would it be running to the walls in the open slowed down by ladders made unwieldy by the rain and wind? No matter, the consul had spoken and the Roman legions would follow through. It wouldn't be the first time that the grit of the legionary had succeeded despite overwhelming odds. But, the cost would be high.

Tiberius had dismounted and sent his horse to the rear. He stood in front of the maniples of the Ninth, which occupied the left wing next to the Fifth, which shared the center with the Eighth. On the far side, the Second held the right flank. A single legion guarded the camp, mostly made up of wounded men from the last encounter who were mobile enough to man the parapets.

Sextus's half of the auxiliaries rode on the right flank with the Second, where the steep grade made it difficult for them to maneuver their mounts near the walls. The left flank fell away to the two rivers, presenting the other cavalry contingent less in the way of physical obstacles, except for a dangerous narrowing of ground near the water's edge. Given these obstacles, Tiberius didn't expect the Roman horse to play a telling role in the attack, outside of keeping Numantine riders at bay. The success of the assault hinged, then, on a frontal charge of 20,000 soldiers up the mountainside and over the walls.

The thought caused him a ripple of memory, the mad rush across the mole at Carthage, Fannius at his side, the death of Casca Capito, and all the others falling around them amid chaos. Since that time, he'd often relived that harrowing charge, feeling stark fear set in even while sitting around the fountain in his placid peristylum. Then, he would get up and look for Claudia or the children, anything to distract him from that time. Now, that ambient fear had returned in full force. The dread he felt as he readied himself to plow up that slope cut his breath short. He'd come full circle, back into the nightmare horror where he had never wanted to be ever again. At Carthage, he sweated in the burning sun before they crossed the mole. Here in Numantia, he sweated again, this time in the dreary cold of a wet, spring dawn on the high plains of Hispania. Again, he could never show such dread in front of the Roman troops surrounding him, men who expected him to lead. Craven instinct would pull at him to run with fear, but honor dictated that he race full out toward the plane of death.

Gorge climbed up his throat, which he forced down with several swallows. He glanced over at Casca Naso, who gripped and regripped his sword. The centurion's broad face seemed twisted with resentful anger, as if he hated the Numantines even more for daring to threaten him at all. Tiberius clamped down on his teeth, hoping that determination would win out over the sense of panic that he barely could quell within him.

The cornicens sounded the order and the Roman mass began to move forward as one, quick-marching up the gentle part of the slope, slapping their swords against the sides of their shields. Mancinus had commanded the shield beat, declaring that it never failed to strike fear in the hearts of Rome's enemies. The tribunes wondered if the troops would be better off doing their best to slip up the slope silently under cover of darkness. No way of knowing now, Tiberius thought as he turned and nodded at Casca.

Casca, bellowed leonine-like for the Ninth to advance. The men shouted back with a ragged roar, hoisted their ladders up and started trotting forward as fast as they could. Tiberius paced himself up the hillside, trying to breathe evenly. As they advanced, he noticed the lines of his men closing ranks involuntarily as he knew they would from his first survey of Numantia's seemingly natural defenses. Rock outcrops with jagged edges funneled the lines of the Ninth into the path of the left flank of the Fifth's line, slowing their progress. Still, no missiles flew over the Numantine walls. Tiberius could see the advantage for the enemy to wait until the entire Roman force had been crowded together.

He stopped running and called out an order to Casca, "Form column!"

Casca relayed the order, soon followed by the other centurions, and the Fifth shifted from their three-line maniples into a narrowing column of fours, Velites trotting loosely on either side. The pace of the Fifth immediately picked up, causing them to move slightly ahead of the long legionary line. As soon as the other tribunes saw that the Fifth was breasting the line, they ordered their troops into the same formation. In the middle of the shift, the hailstorm of fire began from behind the Numantine walls. Rocks came first, then bolts and arrows pouring down on them, appearing suddenly out of the dark rain like wraiths turned into hardened snakes. The men staggered, slipping on the slick surface back into the men coming up behind them. Tiberius urged them forward, and Casca whipped them with his vitus from behind. The men rallied and forced themselves up, encouraging each other, helping to their feet those who had fallen.

Even so, the columns formed by the four legions were closing in on each other again. Tiberius barked to Casca and Shafat to double the pace. The men responded by bounding out ahead of the front lines of the legions, some dragging their ladders, some holding them in front as they ran. The first chain of Numantine walls was just 300 feet ahead, the rocks and projectiles flying behind the Fifth's charging mass. Arrows still sliced through their ranks, though, filled quickly by men behind. Without an order from Tiberius or the centurions, the column spread naturally in front of the wall, throwing up their ladders with shouts of triumph. In a matter of seconds, they would be up and over the short wall, raging to destroy their tormentors cringing on the other side.

Tiberius stood back, waving the rest of his men on with his sword. He glanced back and saw that the Fifth and the Eighth would soon reach the crest. They'd join the fight in an instant, and it all would be over in short order, Tiberius thought. No equal force, much less a smaller one, could stand up to the might of Roman legions. Numantia would fall. He joyously turned back to the fray.

The cornicens suddenly sounded their horns. Retreat.

Tiberius looked back again, unsure. The curved horns blared again, and he realized that he had heard right. The Fifth and the Eighth had halted their ascent. They milled around, some going ahead hesitantly, others reluctantly stepping back, flinching as a boulder fell among them, others dropping from bolts striking them. The horns called again, and the legionaries seemed to melt away.

"No!" cried out Tiberius. "No, no!" he shouted again at the disappearing legions. Casca ran up, bellowing, "What's happening? Where have they gone?"

Tiberius raised his voice above the din, "They've retreated. Pull those men off the ladders, we've got to get them back down!"

Horrified, Casca scowled as he pivoted and rushed up, bellowing at the top of his voice to fall back. Shafat and Didius soon picked up the cry, and the men began to come down. Tiberius ran up and down the base of the wall, dodging missiles thrown from above. Sacerdus Quarto was halfway up a ladder, his shield above his head when he heard the call to withdraw. He started down the ladder when a boulder knocked his shield aside followed by another that smashed his head, knocking him into his son on the rungs below. Quarto's son cried out, cradling his father in his arms at the bottom of the ladder. Tiberius moved over to them and saw immediately that the old centurion's head had been crushed.

"He's gone, Quarto Minor, you can do him no good. Get up and get back."

The young Quarto, Severus by name, glared at Tiberius. Before his tribune could say another word, he stood up, lifted his father's body over his shoulder, and trotted down the hill. Tiberius slipped under the ladder against the wall to avoid the plummeting projectiles. He watched the young man and his burden fade down the side of the mountain under the eyes of the gods, no doubt, arrows falling all around without striking them.

The ladder crashed to the ground, prodding Tiberius to move out before he was hit by anything from above. By this time, Casca, Didius, and Shafat had moved the men back, some carrying wounded comrades on their ladders. Others fashioned a haphazard testudo overhead to protect them from the missiles piercing the engorged, black sky above Numantia.

As the Fifth legionaries scurried down the incline, Sextus appeared on the summit trailed by his auxiliaries.

"What in the name of the gods happened?" Tiberius shouted to him.

"The Numantines attacked our camp at the farther gate. Mancinus signaled for the recall."

"Did they breach the palisade?"

"No, but the men inside panicked and ran for the front portal. As soon as they opened the gates, a gang of Numantines rushed inside. They had the rear portal opened in no time, and their horsemen overran the compound."

"Dis in Hades!" Tiberius cursed. He looked around, realizing that the roar of the battle had faded. Sextus's men had formed a ragged line to shield the descending troops, but by this time, the Numantines had stopped firing, unwilling to waste more of their arrows on the few Romans left clinging to the slopes.

"What about Mancinus and the main force?"

"The last I saw, they were heading into the woods to the south."

"What? Why? We almost topped their walls; we had them!"

"I don't know," Sextus said, "after I heard the recall, then saw you up here, I rallied my men to your side."

"Curse the Fates, we need to get down from here and see what we can do at the camp. Ulpius and the other wounded are inside that palisade."

Sextus reached down his arm and Tiberius used it to swing himself up behind him. The equitus reined his horse hard over and down the incline while shouting for his command to follow. The two men skittered down the steep slope, almost pitching over the horse's head. The horse leaned back so much on its haunches trying to keep from falling that Tiberius's sandals dragged on the muddy incline.

Back down on level ground, they were surprised to find a legion formed into a square, pila at the ready, swords drawn in the interior lines. Tiberius quickly saw Casca and Shafat in position next to their standards, one facing the Numantine mountain again, the other fronting the Roman camp, Didius centered in the interior lines. Enemy horsemen rode between the Fifth's first line and the palisade. The gates had been closed, the parapets now were manned by Numantines and other Arevaci warriors, catcalling down to the last of the Roman legions. The grim-faced legionaries heard screams within the compound and saw a yellow glow rising behind the camp walls.

Tiberius didn't wait any longer. He dropped from Sextus's horse and started running toward the legion, barking as he loped, "Run off those Numantine dogs, Sextus, then cover our rear."

Sextus and the auxiliaries thundered off while Tiberius moved up to the Ninth.

"Halt! Password!"

"I'm your tribune and quaestor, soldier, open ranks."

The optio squinted, unsure, until Shafat whacked him out of the way with his vitus as he spat, "Tiberius Gracchus, you onion head." He whipped around to attention, "Sir! Orders?"

"Defensive column, Shafat. Quick-pace to the east woods."

Shafat raised his voice and spit out the command even as Casca approached.

"We have to move, Casca," Tiberius said, "before they come down from Numantia to join forces with the troops in our camp."

Tiberius looked at Casca intently, who nodded, his face drawn. Casca knew that, while his orders did not state so directly, Tiberius considered the skeleton legion inside the camp lost, including their old comrade Ulpius. "I'll send for your mount, sir."

Tiberius walked before his horse slowly at the head of the column. They moved deep into the forest that grew up to the banks of the river flowing southeast from Numantia. No one knew its name, a tributary of the Durius, perhaps. Night had fallen at last, after another day full of attacks and ambushes by Numantine cavalry. They had been marching for a week, trying to find Mancinus and his missing army.

They did their best to use the tactics that earlier had brought them safely to Malia. Traveling at night when they could, the Ninth hugged the high ground as much as possible, resting during the under forest when available. But, in trailing the passage of Mancinus's army, they frequently were forced to travel on lower ground, which invited fierce, slashing attacks by Numantine horsemen. Although most of the army's auxiliaries had bolted with Mancinus, Sextus's old company had followed him. They did their best to shadow the legion, and managed to beat back every thrust by the hounding barbarians. Still, soldiers were struck down.

The fallen wounded were quickly placed on stretchers in the middle of the column. The dead were left behind. Worse, on Mancinus's trail they came across other fallen legionaries, some of them seemingly left behind before they had died. It was clear, the campaign had become a full-blown disaster, like so many before in cursed Hispania. Another Roman army had been defeated by the Numantines, and now they ran in full flight for their lives. Tiberius wondered if any of them would survive.

On this day, the troops of the Ninth trudged through the muddy banks of the rivulet, taking their chances that the enemy cavalry wouldn't find them. The rain resumed, a brutally cold downfall that soaked men and animals. The men ate what few grain cakes they had left in their kits while they marched, sharing with those who had none. Tiberius felt a continuous chill up his spine not only from the stinging rain. Again, he thought of Hannibal Barca's brilliant stratagem at Trebia, and how he and his men had adapted it to surprise the Numantines on the Iberus. If they discovered the Ninth now, creeping along the river shore, they could just as easy annihilate them in the same fashion.

But, the legion needed some respite from the constant harassing attacks. Knowing this, Tiberius resisted every panicky impulse to rush his men again to higher, solid ground. Instead, he crept along with them, nerves strumming without relief. Eventually, they came upon a small knoll rising out of the riverbank that offered cover and a dry area for the exhausted legionaries to sleep. The centurions passed along orders for silence and no fires. They dared not construct fortifications, so they posted a perimeter of guards 300 feet out from the rest. Where there were any high trees, lithe velites slipped up and onto limbs with good vantage points for possible infiltration by Numantine scouts or assassins. After seeing that all of the men and beasts were bedded down, Tiberius picked a spot three-quarters up the hill facing away from the stream and toward the most likely point of attack, and laid down on his cape. He used his ornate helmet as a pillow, and tried to sleep, which wouldn't come. Instead, that terrible, endless day the week before ran through his head, again and again. They were on the verge of cracking the Numantine town fort when Mancinus abruptly abandoned the assault. Many a soldier had fallen in the retreat for no good reason. The men in the Roman camp had been slaughtered or enslaved, the supplies, wagons, livestock, all gone over to the Numantines. Worse of all, the army's account ledgers had been in Tiberius's camp tent. Now, they too were gone. All evidence of his forthright discipline in paying the men, procuring necessary supplies, and otherwise greasing the wheels of war for Mancinus's army, was gone. Without proof of his scrupulous accounting, he could be called in front of the Senate for any number of trumped-up charges, especially by Rufus and his ilk. His career would be ruined, he thought. That is, if he survived. He hacked a rueful laugh, and quickly covered his mouth.

Nothing moved. He could hear the deep breathing of the exhausted men, and the occasional ninny in the distance where Sextus had the mounts tethered. Tiberius knew that a large number of auxiliaries would be on duty through the night to keep them quiet. But, a horse is an animal, and sometimes they called to each other. The beleaguered Romans could only hope that the Numantines assumed that any noise from a horse came from one of their own.

The rain finally abated just before dawn. Small groups of men slipped down to the river to draw water, which they brought back to rest of the troops, parched from the forced march despite the drenching they'd endured. The horses slurped thirstily and noisily, which couldn't be helped. The centurions and optios had the men up, ready to move on in the dark. They muffled weapons and animals and slowly began to ease their way off of the knoll back into the brush along the river. The sleep and water had revived them, but their stomachs still churned from hunger.

By dawn, they came upon velite outposts from the main army. Tiberius saw fear jumping in the scouts' eyes, and it was by the grace of Fortuna that they didn't sounded an alarm or try to kill any of the Ninth's men. As soon as they recognized their fellow soldiers, they almost swooned with relief, as though the arrival of another harried, worn legion would tip the balance and save them all. Tyros, thought Tiberius.

"Where is the consul's headquarters?" he asked.

The velite pointed behind him, "Two miles back toward the river, in the center of a defense perimeter."

Tiberius nodded, turned to Casca and told him to form a square, and signaled to Sextus to accompany him. The equitus passed on orders to Decimus, while Casca picked six seasoned men to act as their guard. Tiberius secured the password from the young velite, and they left.

They worked their way through the brush and rushes near the river until they came upon a three-meter agger hastily thrown up in a long curve out from the bank of the Durius. The bank sloped down from a small string of heavily wooded hills that rose perhaps a mile from the river. Stakes spiked the agger at the top to form a makeshift castra, with sentries looking out between them. Tiberius saw no towers or any evidence of catapulta or other artillery. From the look of the soldiers on watch, they had no parapets to stand on behind the castra. In fact, he couldn't see any gates anywhere along the line of defense. If they needed to evacuate the compound, it looked like they would have to climb over their own stakes. He shook his head in dismay.

Casca called out the password, "Haven," and they scrambled up to the top. A grizzled centurion of the Fifth named Gabinus greeted them, expressing particular warmth toward Casca, whom he knew from a previous campaign. As they talked, Gabinus led them down the side of the mound onto the makeshift parade ground. There were no tents, and the men huddled together under their cloaks, crowded into small groups around their standards in the sucking mud. To keep warm, they had started fires that smoked liberally from the green, scrubby cottonwood and evergreens the troops had stripped from the muck at the river's edge. After a ten-minute walk, they saw Mancinus's headquarters, a ragged collection of capes tied off to spears and standards, with the four legions's eagles serving as the entranceway supports. The army's tribunes, Horatius, Nicomedes, Secundus, and Cadmus, lounged in front of the shelter's opening. Others stood or sat around them, though no one spoke. Instead, they waited while the officers passed around a wineskin. Tiberius approached them, and Horatius said, "Salve, Gracchus, back from the dead?"

"Close enough. Where is the consul?"

"Why, in his quarters, Quaestor, planning our next maneuver."

"I see it's not vinegar in the skin, Horatius. Why don't you give it to the physicians for the wounded?"

"Wounded? I don't see any wounded in this camp. Do you, Secundus? Nicomedes? How about you, Cadmus? No, there are no wounded here, Gracchus, just the walking dead."

Tiberius brushed past him, saying, "Take heart, Horatius. We're not dead yet."

Hardy words, he thought, though he felt as black as a moonless night in his own heart, as black as Vulcan's lair. An agitated slave ran past him as he stepped into the consul's tent, ducking folds of the cloaks draped from the spear shafts. He worked his way through an improvised vestibulum into a round area just a few meters across. Mancinus sat on a low bed, apparently fashioned from bent, green wooden limbs with capes and linens stack on top. The consul wasn't wearing his lorica, which hung from a tree-branch tripod. He wore only a scarlet-bordered white tunic turned grey with grime and sweat. Yet, to Tiberius's amazement, he still wore his greaves above his sandals. Elbows on his knees and head held in his hands, Mancinus sat, staring at the ground. Eventually, he slowly looked up to see who had entered. He recognized Tiberius, then allowed his sight to fix upon the ground again.

"Before I embarked on this campaign," he said evenly, "before I'd even boarded my flagship at Ostia, I saw two serpents quickly slither up the gangplank onto the ship and disappear. Everyone stopped, my adjutants, guards, the tribunes, even Fabius. You should have seen the looks on their faces, shocked, utterly horrified by the omen.

"So, what could I do? That sourpuss Horatius urged me to consult a soothsayer, and the others joined in. But, I couldn't do that, what would happen if the oracle said the entire campaign was ill-fated? The day it was to start, before I'd even left the shadow of Rome? No. I lifted my head and said, 'No pair of wiggling worms will divert me from doing my duty for Rome, not even those the size of snakes.' Then, I walked up and boarded the ship. My men followed."

He glanced up. "I'm not a fool, you know, tweaking the beards of the gods. I consulted secretly with a high priest. He told me I should have had auspices taken before I stepped onto that ship. I had the ship scoured to find those damn snakes, and nothing. Nothing! I moved my flag to another ship and sailed on that one until we reached Hispania. On land, I felt better. We didn't lose a ship or a man on the voyage, so why would I worry? No matter, I sacrificed daily, generously, all the way to Malia. The campaign was going so well!" he cried out in a shout, pounding his knee with his fist. Then, he seemed to deflate again.

"The gods punished me," he said, "But, what could I have done? Of course, I chose Rome before the gods." He dropped his head again to gaze into the muddy floor.

Tiberius stood still, controlling himself. Mancinus's dark face, lean and brown with lines that usually made him look handsome and virile, now seemed creased, embittered if not petulant. Tiberius's mind skipped to Claudia waiting for him to return, his children, perhaps a new one on the way, he might not know with no post for a month. Gaius, Appius, too, even Polydius and Phalea, all waited for him. His mother, for Jupiter's sake. Now, it appeared that they waited in vain because of this man's vanity, this self-pitying, patrician prig disaster of a man. Tiberius had the urge to brain him, except he couldn't, not with the mothers and wives of the pedites and his other Roman legionaries pining for them to return. No, he thought, they could not give up without even an attempt to salvage the situation.

"Consul, the campaign isn't over. We still have more than four legions essentially intact. The Numantines and the rest of the Arevaci can't stand against four Roman legions."

Mancinus lifted his eyes, looking incredulous. "Can't stand against us? They won't stand against us, they refuse to fight like real soldiers! Fight and run, fight and run, that's all they do, until they wear us down, wear down the spirit. Then, when we're stunned and vulnerable, they bide their time in their impenetrable fortress. At last, when we try to execute a strategic withdrawal, they nip at our heels and bite our flanks to bleed us into exhaustion. That's why we can never vanquish Numantia, ours describes the fate of all the Roman armies that have faced that rock on a hill!"

Tiberius clenched his teeth again to avoid blasting Mancinus with his sure knowledge that they'd had the walls won, the city in their grasp until the retreat had been ordered.

"We can still defeat them, Consul, we have the army. It will be more difficult, now, since they've taken our camp, which we will first have to win back. But, then we can start again, starve them out, or attack them after a siege has softened them up."

"No, we stand here."

Tiberius froze. "Here? Against the river?"

"That's right. Let them break their army on our defenses."

"But, Consul, we have no provisions, the camp is barricaded by a dirt wall. How can we last if they simply decide to hem us in until we starve?"

"We won't starve, we can fish the river. We can send out silent patrols. The Numantine barbarians aren't the only ones who can move with stealth. We'll wait them out. Until they're ready to fight like men, we'll sit and wait."

Mancinus folded his arms and sat back on his bed to punctuate his resolve. Tiberius thought that he had gone completely mad.

The slave who had run away before reentered the tent and headed directly to Mancinus's lorica and began applying some kind of grease to its surface. He started polishing the little metal sculptures on the breastplate, cupids, Tiberius thought, with horses just above the abdomen. The smell of the grease seemed familiar, but he couldn't quite place it.

"At last. That's it, shine it up. I don't want to look like a country thief when I step out to fight them. Shine it until it glows, so they know that it is a Roman consul who vanquishes them."

Tiberius recognized the odor, now, animal fat. From what animal? He couldn't venture a guess.

"Well, Gracchus, where's your legion?"

"Not far from here."

"Good. Then, you'll be bringing them into the camp. It'll be cozy, but we'll all make due, as Romans do." He issued a vapid laugh.

"You don't think it will be too crowded, Consul? You have the better part of 20,000 men concentrated here. Perhaps it would be better if the Ninth found a position outside the palisade to ensure that the main force isn't flanked."

"What's the matter, Gracchus, your boys aren't up to a fight?"

Tiberius fought to hold himself in check, and Mancinus could see that he'd stung the quaestor tribune.

"All right, hunt around for a better place. But, don't come weeping to me after you come up with nothing. You and your reluctant heroes will find themselves bedding down next to the entire army's latrines."

"Yessir," Tiberius said as he saluted, and left before the consul could change his mind.

Outside the tent, he smelled more of the grease, cooking this time, making his stomach roil, but not from hunger.

"Horatius, what is that smell?"

"The latest in fine Roman rations, Gracchus, horsemeat. Faced with the choice of having a cavalry or feeding three legions, the great consul decided we didn't need auxiliaries riding around anymore, since we will be defending this ground. Hungry?"

"Not yet, Tribune."

He rounded up his contingent and made for the camp perimeter at the water's edge. The late spring morning had brightened the river bank beautifully, with delicate pale green folded leaves appearing as if out of thin air. For Tiberius and his small squad, however, it was a dangerous time. But, he could not wait. They waded around the mounded walls and ran bent over to the nearest bushes outside of the earth fort. After reconnoitering, they began to work their way back to where they had left the Ninth.

By sunset, they'd made it to the outpost guards. Quietly, they uttered the password and slipped in through the squared lines. Tiberius quickly gathered his centurions around him.

"Make ready, we're marching at nightfall."

"To join Mancinus and the other legions?" Didius asked.

"No. Mancinus plans to make a stand with his back against the Durius. We will lend support from higher ground." He turned to Casca and Sextus, and spoke softly. "Get me Titius. I want him to ride with you, Sextus, and you Casca. Guide them to the group of hills opposite Mancinus's fortifications. Tell the immune to find the best point to defend closest to Mancinus. Shafat, Didius, and I will follow with the Ninth at nightfall. We're going to finish in Hispania where we've done our best, Romans, taking the high ground."

Chapter 16. Survival

The men of the Ninth kneeled in a crouch behind the massive tree trunks that formed the major part of their fortifications on the high foothill overlooking Mancinus's earthen camp nearly a mile away. Titius had galvanized his fellow immunes and the troops to Herculean feats in a matter of a few days and nights. Scores of men wielding only their swords took turns hacking, slicing, and cutting down trees with diameters as wide as a foot each. As a result, a solid, six-foot barricade of green tree trunks lined the hillside just below its apex, reinforced by logs hammered into the ground. On the far corners of the long log wall stood square towers twice as high. The thick wooden boxes commanded the flanks and also served well for watching both the movements of the enemy and of their fellow Romans squeezed in together against the river bank.

    The heavy wall continued up and around to the top of the hill, closing at the peak of the high ground. Two more towers on each side looked out over the back, which fell off into outcrops of sharp rock with brambles growing around small rivulets and springs coursing down the incline. Another, shorter log wall ran further up the hill parallel to the front wall. The interior wall was punctuated by narrow corrals attached behind it. Nearly 1,500 feet in length and half as long at its width, the size of the complex defied belief in the fact that it had been raised almost overnight. The Ninth had been spared attacks for those three nights because Titius had reversed convention by ordering the men to leave a number of trees intact around the encampment. Those trees felled had been cut in a pattern that left tall saplings and others unsuitable for construction standing as a screen. The head immune explained that leaving trees in the way also would help diffuse an attack by an overwhelming force. The spaces between would allow archers and artillery to narrow their target areas, thus creating lethal barrages when they let loose their weapons. Tiberius wasn't as sure about these innovations, but the cocky little engineer was absolutely sure.

    "And, wait until you my wasps. The Numantines will regret the day they decide to fight us here!"

    "Let us hope so. Pray to the gods, Titius, that your new machines work their magic. Our survival could depend upon them."

    The troops themselves were spent, exhausted from nonstop labor for three days and nights while barely eating enough to survive. Because of the springs on the far side of the hill, water was not a problem. Food was. Soon they, too, would be eating their horses, though Sextus was doing his best, raiding nearby settlements for sheep and goats, anything they could butcher and eat. Amazing, thought Tiberius, how short a time it took to bring an army to its knees when it has lost its lines of supply. Just a matter of weeks, he thought. Why would the Numantines attack at all when they knew that the Romans would fall and die on their own?

He imagined the Numantines's glee at the suffering of these young warriors, their death ordained for doing Rome's bidding. He thought of Quarto Minor, grieving over the loss of his father, not yet aware that his life itself would soon be over. Every one of the farm boys that he pulled off the land to fight for Rome's glory and tribute soon would face the worst death for a soldier, alone in an alien land. All of them were destined to die as things stood now, the Fates had decreed their deaths. He shook his head, this was not right, but it was imminent.

The line of his jaw hardened as he envisioned the terrible images. He would not let it happen, not without trying. He would engage the Fates themselves if needed. Death be assured or not, he would drag as many Numantines to Hades with him as he could.

The fight wouldn't be long in coming, he soon learned. As he mused standing near one of the corrals in the back, he heard a sentry cry out. A troop of Numantine riders had appeared on the hill behind the camp. They were close, just a few hundred feet away as the crow flies. As rugged as the terrain was between the two heights, carved by a stream below on its way to the Durius, there was no fear of an immediate clash on either side. Still, the barbarian horsemen stood so close that the legionaries could see the strange emblems painted on their shields and breastplates, plaid-patterned linen shirts, the flourish of horsehair looping out of their round helmets, and the wild striations in their light-whiskered beards. The men on the opposing slopes stared at each other, silently weighing the portent of the sudden encounter and what it would bring.

Unsettled, a few Roman archers shot arrows at the Numantines, which the horsemen easily avoided with a few deft moves of their mounts. Others legionaries tossed pilas that fell harmlessly into the gully, until an optio cursed at them to stop wasting spears.

Sextus snapped an order and his auxiliaries ran and jumped on their horses, sped out of the compound, and down the slope. The Numantines watched the Roman cavalry hurtling down and around in search of a way up to their position. The Numantine riders waited for a few more moments, then wheeled about and disappeared below the other side of the opposite hilltop.

Tiberius stepped away from the wall and signaled with his arm to Casca. All of the centurions and optios began to trickle from their command points to the center of the square situated beneath a large evergreen. Sextus joined them from the corral in the northeast corner of the compound.

"Is everyone here? All right. Now that they've found us, the Numantines, their Arevaci brethren and the rest, they will attack us first. If they intend to destroy the Roman army barricaded against the river, they cannot leave us at their rear. So, they will come for us. They don't need to commit their entire force, which means that Mancinus won't be able to relieve us."

As they absorbed his words, a pallor seemed to descend upon the already grim visages of his men. Shafat kicked dirt at his feet. Sextus's usual wry smile now seemed fixed in rictus.

Didius spoke up bitterly, almost caterwauling, "Why attack us at all? They know they have every one of us caged up. Why don't they simply starve us into surrender?"

Before Tiberius could answer, Casca shook his head and said, "We're too close to Mancinus. The Numantines do not want to risk a desperate, simultaneous attack from both positions, which would be likely. Any soldier would rather fight and die than starve to death. The Numantines will attack us as soon as they can, probably at first dawn."

He turned to Tiberius and said wearily, "Orders, sir?"

Tiberius watched as the others gradually straightened to listen.

"Assemble the men in center square. When I finish, put them at their posts. They sleep in armor tonight, and every night until the Numantines attack."

Except for guards on watch in the towers, the men of the Ninth gathered around the middle of the hilltop fort. Some leaned on wooden posts spaced around the square, others sat splay-legged, leaning back on outstretched arms to keep upright. Still others simply stretched out on their sides, cupping their heads in hands propped up on their elbows, gazing cockeyed at the center where their tribune was likely to stand. They looked tired and gaunt, Tiberius noted, which heightened his anxiety. He didn't like speaking to a lot of people under any circumstances, and his words this time would be vitally important.

Yet, what could he tell them? Fight for your lives, which are likely to be lost anyway? Strike until you surrender and become slaves forever somewhere far from home? Die for Rome's ambition, because those who lose are shamed or forgotten. Punish your enemy for keeping you from ever seeing your loved ones again. Lose everything because it is the will of the gods, fall bravely to save your place on the boat across the Styx. Or, he could lie.

Tiberius motioned to an orderly, who positioned a stump in the middle of the square. Wearing full armor and the horned helmet given to him by Appius, he put his hand on the shoulder of the orderly and levered himself up onto the stump. A slight breeze whispered past him, and the light was failing as nighttime began its descent. He turned his head and spoke softly to the orderly, who quickly brought forth two torches on long staffs and planted them to Tiberius's left and right so that the troops could see his face clearly.

He cleared his voice and began. "Men of Rome ... sons of Italia ... soldiers of the Ninth. We've come this long way to Hispania, to the walls of Numantia itself, only to fall short in our quest, with great loss of our comrades. The gods have not smiled on our efforts for reasons known only to them, and they have ordained more trials for us in this barbaric land. But, Fortuna can change luck, and time and again she will do that. She will change our luck if we remain stalwart. We can change our fate ourselves if we fight like the Furies in the coming clash.

"Now, we await a larger force. To any ordinary man, to any ordinary warrior, we yaw and pitch on a sea of calamity. Blood drains from the face, fear gnaws within like a white plague. But we are not ordinary men, we are not ordinary warriors. We fight for Rome, we fight for the Ninth, we fight for our birthright, to win! Let us meet the tribes of the Numantines, the Arevaci, the Lusitani, and any other Hispanic horse-loving goat herders on these wooden walls and stain them ruby red with their blood. Let us meet them hard, blade for blade, and bring them to their knees for the death stroke. We'll crush them and send their survivors howling back as a lethal lesson of what comes from fighting Romans face to face!"

He ended on a crescendo, joined by Casca and the other centurions and optios in a ragged, roaring cheer. But, only a few men joined in. The rest seemed as fixed-eyed as they had been at the beginning of his speech. Spent men, he thought, men too tired to be afraid and perhaps too tired to fight.

He jumped off the stump and headed for his quarters. "Deploy the troops," he said in clipped words over his shoulder. "Attend me when you're finished."

Rain rolled in with the dawn. The sky grew somewhat lighter above the trees, but the shadows in the wooded hillsides remained deep, still. Even so, every now and then they heard the far-off sound of a horse snorting or a coughing neigh from the dark tree line below them. They were here, thought Tiberius. He crouched near the western corner's lower tower, bent so low behind the barrier that only his eyes cleared the wall's edge. The conditions favored the Numantines; we can't see, so they can attack. Well, he thought, we're as ready as we'll ever be.

Titius had shown him his latest contraptions, tiny ballistae that fired large, arrow-shaped projectiles. Wasps, he called them, fashioned by himself and the other immunes during the brief lull after the palisade had been completed. Tiberius was skeptical, but the engineer's glib promises about their capabilities, true or false, hardly seemed likely to affect the outcome that they faced. Because of their small size, the immunes had been able to produce a good number of them. They could fire quite a flight of them at the enemy, if the little machines did work.

A dull bellow, like a cow, could be heard coming low on the hill. Another answered, then several more, signal horns. Suddenly, a thousand horsemen burst from the thick trees and rode roaring up the hill. They weaved deftly through the patchwork of trunks left in their path, closing on the Roman wall quicker than possible. Behind them, a thousand more riding warriors galloped out, followed by a thousand more. When the first line was 300 feet away, a flight of arrows flew over their heads at the Roman fort from the tree line, followed by spears from the riders as the range shortened.

Even as he rose up to shout to the men near him, Tiberius could hear his yell echoed up and down the wall by the centurions and optios, "Down!" "Get down!" The Roman troops clung to the interior of the wall as the projectiles flew above them, and the pounding of the hooves grew louder, closer. Tiberius turned his torso back to the second wall and the corrals behind them, where a hundred miniature ballistae, the wasps, stood poised to be fired. "Titius!" he thundered.

Titius signaled, and 100 darts flew straight down the hillside, over the

Roman walls and into the breasts of the horses and men who had just reached the wall.

Tiberius heard the screams of the wounded horses, high and shrill like women, and saw gouts of blood pour from a rider struck in the chest by a four-foot arrow. The second line crashed into the first, stalled before the wall when Didius sounded, "Pila!" and a line of legionaries whipped them into the air from the second wall, devastating the first and second wave of Numantine riders. Still, they came, met by a hundred more bolts from the wasps and more pila from the second wall, with the Romans up front rising up to thrust eight-foot spears down at the horses and men trying to breech the palisade.

The next flight of wasps flew over the milling mass of horses and warriors at the front of the wall pounding into the third line of Numantine cavalry. The horsemen barely flinched as they pressed up the slope to join their comrades, war cries filling the air as they surged up to attack. And, they began to find openings, hurdling over the wall, past the legionaries flailing with their long spears, and pivoting their horses hard to assault them from behind.

Tiberius didn't hesitate. He leaped to the top of the wall and ran across it, slipping and sliding on the slick logs, but also swinging his sword freely at the horsemen now within range. He sliced the shoulder of one man, slapped away the swing of another's long blade, thrust at the head of one of the Numantines inside the compound, and shouted at the top of his voice for Didius to attack. Didius yelled out an order, and the troops behind the second wall scrambled over and started in on the rear haunches of the Numantine horses that had jumped the front wall.

A stinging blow to the head knocked Tiberius off the wall headfirst into the compound. He sat up, shaking away the cobwebs while grabbing at his helmet. He pulled it off to find an arrow stuck in the raised metal cleft of one of his horns. Flipping the helmet aside, he stood up and climbed back onto the front wall rampart. The Numantine riders outside had retired to the tree line. The few left inside turned and twisted their mounts as the Roman troops ganged up on them from all quarters. A few managed to vault over the wall on the run as their companions fell to the legionaries' spears.

"They've packed it in," yelled Shafat, "they're done." The men who heard him raised tired shouts out at his words, until they heard the horns again and the pounding hooves. "To your posts!" bellowed Casca, and Tiberius called to Didius to return back to man the second wall.

Titius let loose another volley of bolts, and Didius's men threw more pilas, but the Numantines were quicker to the walls this time. Shafat and Casca led separate squads of men into the alley between the fortress walls to attack a new wave of Numantines inside. They attempted to hamstring the horses and kill their riders, but more and more leaped over to slash down at the Roman soldiers.

Tiberius glimpsed a small band of legionaries surrounded by Numantines. He picked up a shield from a fallen soldier and raced over to join the pressed soldiers. Three men had gone down by the time he reached them, and the enemy riders circled quickly, closing in as they swung their long swords. Two men on either side of Tiberius fell, while he and the last two deflected blows with their shields and stabbed upward at their attackers.

Suddenly, one of the horses screamed and nearly fell on them. They jumped sideways to avoid its flailing form, kicking and biting at the spear sticking out of its belly. The horse snapped teeth at its attacker, Casca, the bloody haft of the broken spear in his hands. Casca reached back and smashed the horse on the head, which went still. He straddled its carcass and thrust the jagged edge of the broken shaft into the helmet of the rider.

Tiberius spun around in time to ward off a blow from another Numantine horseman. The other two legionaries had fallen, and the Numantines crowded their horses together trying to reach him. As he stepped back next to Casca by the dead horse, he recognized one of the enemy warriors, the small, grey-haired man he'd seen leading the retreat from the riverbank ambush back beyond Salduba. The grey-haired chieftain shouted at the riders, who pulled up and spread out, waiting for the command to attack again. Water splashed up from their horses pawing the saturated ground, their blood high, impatient to thunder ahead again. Slowly, the Numantine chief raised his sword, almost in salute, before dropping it like a counterweight cut loose from a gate. But, before the band of horsemen could charge, Sextus bolted out of the rain with the last of his auxiliaries.

Seeing the Roman riders, the grey-haired chieftain jerked at his horse. He gestured to a rider close to him who pulled out a curled ram's horn and blew three deep, short notes. Without a moment's indecision, the chieftain and the other Numantines inside the perimeter broke off the battle and rode for the wall, grabbing up any unhorsed companions they could on the way.

In just a matter of seconds, they gracefully glided over the front of the palisade and disappeared into the thundering rain, all gone except for their dead and wounded.

"Sound assembly," Tiberius said, breathing heavily between each word. "Get the wounded to the surgeon immediately. Have the annonae optios butcher any wounded horses to roast for the men. Get these dead barbarians out of here and away from the perimeter. Prepare the Ninth's fallen for funeral biers. But, first make sure that the towers are manned and the walls have sentries. We're the key to the survival of Mancinus's army. They'll have to attack again."

The centurions and optios left at once to carry out their orders. At first, the din from the wounded men groaning and the dying horses shrieking compounded the thudding that Tiberius felt in his head from the arrow strike to his helmet. Soon, though, the cries began to mute as the horses and the enemy wounded were dispatched. The rain began to taper off.

Tiberius rubbed his temples. "How many lost?"

"Two hundred dead, another 300 wounded," reported Casca. "Of the wounded, a hundred are mobile and can return to the walls. The others look like they might be joining their brothers across the River."

Tiberius blew out a heavy breath. "And the enemy?"

Casca curled up his mouth, shrugging, "Maybe 500. It's hard to say, they take as many of their dead with them as they can. Still, we dragged a good number of them out of the fortress and away from the wall."

Tiberius nodded. "You collected pila and bolts?"

"We did. Titius's baby ballistae worked well. They must have been a big surprise to the barbarians."

"All right. After you have everything situated, have Shafat, Didius, and the optios meet at my quarters."

Casca saluted and walked off. Tiberius turned to Sextus."Do you think you can get through to Mancinus's camp tonight?"

His black hair falling over his brow, the handsome horse soldier smirked, "Without a doubt."

Tiberius nodded, "Very well, but you better go down the back way and skirt the Numantine lines."

Sextus frowned. "That'll take a lot longer."

"But it's surer. I need you to get through and back before dawn."

"That's a lot to do in very little time," Sextus said.

"Then, you better start now. Mercury speed you, Equitus."

"Let us hope so," Sextus grimaced, "since no horse could make it down that precipice."

"You're long-legged," Tiberius cheered him, "be your own horse."

As Sextus turned to leave, a legionary approached Tiberius. He handed him his helmet, which had been bent by the arrow's impact. Tiberius pulled on the shaft, but it wouldn't give. He took out his dagger and worked on prying it loose. The arrow suddenly popped free. Tiberius tossed it aside and resheathed his knife. He tried to pull the helmet on, but it had been disfigured slightly so that it didn't sit comfortably on his head. He took it off and examined it.

"It seems I won't have my father-in-law's fancy present for Mancinus's triumph, Casca."

Casca said, "I'll find you a good, plain legionary's cap to wear."

"A soldier's piss pot? I doubt that would flatter me very much, Centurion."

"You looked as good today as any Roman mule, Tribune."

Surprised, Tiberius glanced up. But, his centurion primus had turned and walked away.

Before the coals from the Roman funeral fires had cooled, the Numantines attacked again, this time on foot with ladders. First light had yet to come, so the battle began in the dark. The Roman sentries were vigilant, however, and spied the crouching, darting figures before they made the walls. Archers fired several measured flights of darts at the front that proved effective at first, from the shouts and screams of surprise they heard on the walls. The following rounds were less so, most likely hitting raised shields and covered ladders.

The legion followed with pila, knowing that it didn't matter if they struck flesh. Every legionary understood that every barbed head of a pila bent through a shield would impede the marauders' mobility, making them easier to strike. And Tiberius ordered up scores of torches on high posts that cast light into the area immediately in front of the walls.

The Numantines had committed thousands upon thousands of troops to the assault. Once the torches went up, they abandoned stealth and charged straight ahead like demons from Hades. Behind them, archers on horseback fired waves of arrows at the walls to keep the defenders's heads down. Their ladders thumped against the wall in a matter of minutes, and they surged up to the top of the logs to meet short, Roman blades thrust at their heads or into their sides, some slicing their arms. The long spinas of the Numantines were unwieldy in these close quarters, and the Romans killed throngs of them as soon as they reached the top of their ladders. They threw them down dead or screaming onto the next warriors trying to clamber up the ladders. Legionaries manned the walls shoulder to shoulder, slashing and stabbing at the legs and underbellies of the Numantines suspended on their ladders. There were too many, however, and soon they were spilling over the wall in the gaps where legionaries had fallen away.

Tiberius smashed with his shield, then stabbed beneath, aiming for the crotch. If he missed, he pulled back and went over top for the eyes. He struck one man in the chest, wrenched free his sword, and stabbed him under the chin. Blood sprayed from his punctured carotid, and Tiberius pushed him back off of the ladder, pulling his sword free as the dying man fell.

Tiberius turned and signaled to a cornicen by his side to sound a withdrawal. The horn blasted over the clashing din of the battle, and slowly the Romans left the walls, fighting backwards to the second wall. Tiberius called to Shafat, who ordered his men to throw pila directly at the front wall, knocking down the Numantines as they reached the top. Arrows and wasps flew after the pila, killing more Numantines as they exposed themselves.

The fighting between the two walls turned into truncated cuts and stabs, as the close quarters forced men in the opposing lines together, shoulder to shoulder, screaming and shouting as they thrust and slashed. Slowly, the Roman line fell back, until they were but two feet from the second wall. As the optio pipe whistles sounded, Tiberius stepped back, replaced by a hoary triarii who immediately chopped down two Numantines in front of him.

Tiberius looked to both sides, then nodded to the cornicen, who sounded his horn loud and high, like a stag raging in the night. Upon that signal, Didius's corps hurdled off of the wall above the Numantines, their short swords swinging. At the same time, Shafat led men from the left while Casca charged with his men from the right. They slaughtered the Numantines in the alley between the walls, then climbed back onto the fortresses front ramparts and swept the Numantines off from both sides. Tiberius joined his line again and raged at his men to cut down the enemy interlopers, widow their women, orphan their children.

Tiberius rested sitting on a stump. The slaughter was over, but the toll had been great. Casca reported another 300 casualties, this time most of them dead. The Numantines now had lost at least 1,000 warriors in their three tries at the wall, and likely had to tend to as many wounded as well. But, did that matter? The Numantines could throw thousands more at them until all of the Ninth fell, one by one.

Sacerdus Quarto Minor had fallen, trampled down in the second attack. This saddened Tiberius. His prediction about the son of the old centurion primus had come true. Yet, Tiberius wondered how could he dwell on the loss of this one soldier recruited from the pedites when all of them faced the same fate? How could he mourn when mourning of his own death could be at hand? Appius would be helpless at his loss, his mother would feel another sharp shaft sting her in the heart after having lost her beloved husband and nine children. Polydius and Philea would be sorrowful for his sweet little Tiberius and Cornelia, confused at the loss of Pater, never to see him anymore again. And Claudia, how she would grieve, keening a silent lament so as not to upset the others. But, her loss.

"Tribune."

Tiberius slowly raised his eyes. "Sextus, you return."

The tall equitus nodded his head.

"And, what of Mancinus?"

The young knight paused. "Mancinus will not move. He cannot move. They are out of food and fever is running throughout the camp. Morale is low. A coordinated attack will not be possible."

"Possible," Tiberius said automatically, harking back to Blossius' teachings. "Anything is possible, but this, improbable. All right, refresh yourself. We all must rest while we can."

Sextus left. And, before he knew it, Tiberius fell asleep, still sitting on the stump.

Chapter 17: The God of Dreams

Tiberius's features tightened into an expression well-known to her. He spoke with the authority of being right: Never forget that we are plebeian, that is our virtue and our strength. We are no different than other common men, no better than any common man.

Cornelia rolled onto her side. Drousing on her bed just before sunlight, it was easy to lose track of her place in time. Half awake, she could easily find herself once again back when she was the young wife of Tiberius Sempronius Gracchus Major, conqueror of Numantia, proconsular and likely to be elected consul again, the father of her children who sternly reminded them of their proud heritage as plebeians.

Of course, he had been mistaken about being common, no matter what he said to little Gaius, who gazed up at him in begrudging, open-faced awe. Tiberius was special, unique. He was a great man of Rome, and a great man at home. War did not destroy his compassion or his passion, she laughed to herself, flipping again to her back to look up at the blue sky creeping into the room. Where are you little Gaius, where did you go?

The spring sunshine fell victim to a passing cloud, and she could hear Gaius's father again:

"Get out of bed, sorceress," he said. "Attend to your wifely duties."

He picked her up and she giggled crying out faux fear like a little girl herself. The children rushed in, Decima, Marca, Aulus, and the rest, all wearing horrified faces.

She laughed out loud, "Your father is a beastly lion, look how he mauls me!"

They all shrieked as Tiberius dropped her back on the bed, bared his teeth and growled at them, chasing them from the room. Publius stood in the doorway with a smirk, too big for this sort of horseplay. He turned and left.

"Why don't you stay, today, Tiberius?" she asked.

"I'm to address the Senate on the state of affairs in Hispania. You know those old women, they have to be assured that their interests are protected without a scintilla of trouble. Clearly, none of them have ever been to Hispania."

She'd seen him first in the Forum, already a famed warrior, and she so young, so young. He owned a stunning shock of hair, as black as obsidian, almost shining when reflecting the sun's rays. His eyes, laughing blue crystals, bounced in time to the glory of his smile, made more vivid by the burnished tan seemingly all over his body. She felt a flush, seeing his stout arms bursting out of his plain, olive tunic, cinched at his waist to emphasize his broad shoulders. His legs seemed like those of a tumbler, so muscular and hairy! She hid behind her mother like a toddler, not a thirteen-year-old girl soon to be matched, soon a matron.

Why was she acting this way? He was old, not much younger than her father, but old!

Her mother grasped her hand and wheeled her out to meet this laughing, godlike man. "He will be consul," her mother whispered, "for his many victories in battle. An amazing hero, rarer than rare for a plebeian. Salve, Tiberius Sempronius Gracchus," she said when he approached.

Introduced, when he saw her, he lost his endless smile for an instant—"Why, what a little sprite you are, the gods must be fighting daily over those eyes. How many emeralds were crushed to dust to fill your eyes with the most beautiful colors of the meadow? Any husband of yours will kiss those eyes twice every morning and twice at sunset, cherishing the priceless treasures of the family."

She glowered and he looked again, and said, "But it is you who animates those precious gems, your spirit is the catch! How ever will you find a match for her?" he said to her brother-in-law Publius, who beamed as did her mother.

You, she said to herself, you, you, you will be my husband, kiss my eyes, and my lips every night and every day. You will treasure me above all things, and I will treasure you all of my life; may the gods on Olympus hear me and make us one.

From that day on, she ran off to the Forum to see the new consul, propriety and personal slaves be damned. Leaning casually on the Rostrum above the beaks of the sunken Carthaginian ships adorning the Comitia, he spoke to an adoring public about the issues of the time, land, food, games. And he saw her. When his turn was done, replaced by an august senator, he took his seat in the back, but gestured to an aide, one of his veterans, no doubt. Soon, she was surrounded by burly men with knives on their hips instead of short swords, men who lingered ten feet away from her, but whose presence discouraged any and all common idlers from approaching a well-bred girl standing alone in the Forum. The speeches done, he disappeared. Disappointed, she went home, her new guards shadowing her at a respectful but effective distance.

She came again and again, and every time the veterans skirted her in a protective parameter. Gracchus spoke, often looking directly at her, while never coming to meet her. Finally, after weeks of this close distance between them, she grew angry. When the senators finished spouting their palliatives to soothe the mob, she marched straight to the Rostrum steps. Surprised, her silent guards hurried to catch up to the quick-striding girl. At the steps, she halted, her hands on her tiny hips, and waited for the consul to descend. He came down and stopped, halfway.

"Why don't you come to me?" she said sternly. "Don't you care about me? Don't you want to marry me?"

Taken aback, he settled himself and stepped down. Grasping her by the elbow, he escorted her away from the Rostrum and said quietly, "I do, but it will never happen."

"Why? Because you're too old?"

And he laughed in such a way as to make her swoon on the spot, she, who never swooned. "Ask permission from your brother-in-law," he teased.

"I will," she said, "and if he says yes, will you marry me? Will you?"

"Sure," he said easily, "but he won't say yes."

She huffed, "You don't know. You don't know me and my brother-in-law."

"Still, he won't allow it."

Why? Why do you say that?

He shrugged, "You come from an illustrious family. I'm a plebeian."

"He's a plebeian!" her brother-in-law shouted, pacing throughout the house.

"I love him!" she yelled. "He is to be mine! The gods ordain it!"

"Praise the gods, sister, you don't believe in the gods! You are a realist, and realists know that you don't marry a plebeian."

"He's consul!"

"A plebeian!"

"He's mine! He will be mine forever!"

"A plebeian!"

"He's my plebeian. My consul-of-all-Rome plebeian. More than that, he is a god himself, the god of my dreams. I will marry him, brother-in-law, I want to marry him and have a dozen plebeian demigods with him! Think of the bloodline! Our children—your blood—will dominate Rome! We will fill every cranny with our capable, lovable children. No one will challenge us!"

"You are mad, mad with lust! What makes you think he wants to marry a harpy-in-the-making such as you?"

A little smile crossed her mouth, the one that had melted her father's heart a thousand times before. Seeing that her brother saw her smile, she watched him shrink before her eyes.

"You already asked him," Publius said. "He's already agreed."

She laughed, "Only if I could persuade you, brother-in-law. And, I have, haven't I? Haven't I?"

He sat down on the nearest bench, shaking his head, "He'll marry you, sister, and still think he's the only one with a phallus in his house. He'll be wrong."

She stopped laughing. Solemnly, she said, "No, Publius, I will be a good Roman wife. I just needed to find the right man. And he is the right man to make me a proper Roman matron."

Her brother-in-law simply shook his head.

Later, Publius came into her room and had her sit quietly. He said to her in gentle terms, "Sister-in-law, I have made the match for you. Tiberius Sempronius Gracchus has agreed to marry you."

She threw her arms around his neck and buried her head in his shoulder. He cleared his throat, "There is a stipulation."

She pulled back, suspicion in her eyes.

"He wishes to marry you in three years' time."

She laughed now as she remembered how Publius had pulled his head down into his toga after she yelled at him. If he could have, he would have flattened his ears for fear of her boxing them. Well, an exaggeration. His avocation was to make her happy. How funny life is, my devotion became the same for Tiberius. Poor Publius.

She drowsed, and was running again down the Palatine to the Forum, her guards and attendants racing to keep up. But Tiberius was not in the Forum. Then, she ordered her guards to rent a chair and carry her up the Caelian Hill to his home. Not waiting for the head bodyguard to put the chair down, she leaped from it and dashed to the front door. Pounding on the thick, wooden planks, she cried out, "Tiberius, let me in! Let me in to be your wife! Open this door!"

The door opened to reveal a somewhat surprised but mostly bemused Gracchus standing only in a tunic and sandals. "My dear Mistress Cornelia," he said, "What brings you up to the heights of the Caelian? The view, perhaps?"

"You told my brother-in-law you won't marry me!" she shouted. "Why? Why did you do that?"

She thought about how his smile had faded, which sent a bolt from Jupiter through her heart. Too far, she'd wondered?

"Dear Cornelia," he said, "I will be happy to marry you when you become a woman, which from the look of you will happen as I forecast, in three years."

"I am a woman now! Many of my friends have married younger. I want to marry you now!"

"Oh, yes," he said, "I can see you running a consul's house, staging a grand dinner, sitting in your chair, engaging the King of Numidia in spirited repartee, your feet dangling above the floor."

Her fear turned to fury as fast as Mercury flew. She jumped at him and beat his chest, "Don't mock me, I am a woman in full, and I love you. I love you to death and forever!"

He gently grabbed her wrists and brought them to her waist. "And I love you. Let us make a pact that we will love each other to death and forever, but in three years' time. You will see things differently, then. You will be different, I hope. That's as long as I can wait, anyway."

He kissed her on the cheek, maneuvered her outside, and softly closed the door.

She had cried all the way home, laughing now as she remembered. Cried, cried, cried, for three full years. After every formal occasion, the betrothal dinner, the courtship calls, every time she saw him, she would be ecstatically happy, and when he left, brutally depressed. And, she would cry.

Then, the day she took the veil arrived. She cried again, this time in apprehension. Suddenly, he looked like an old man again. A hairy, scarred, crinkled-eyed old man with darkish hair, or was it grey? Tears coursed down her cheeks until the wedding had been sanctified.

As they walked toward the dining area, Tiberius suddenly pulled her into his office. He lifted her veil and kissed each of her eyes. "Don't cry, Cornelia Sempronia Scipionis Africana. You are the mistress of my house now, and of me. Let us dine, drink, sing, and laugh until we sleep. Our marriage will be long, there will be time enough for everything."

He kissed her again. She threw her arms around him, burying her face in his neck. He gently unwrapped her, then held out his forearm, upon which she gently rested her tiny hand.

She laughed in her bedclothes, crying at the same time, laughing and crying, and missing him, the old man. Now, she was the old woman.

The wedding night left them little time for the sleep he'd promised. She attacked him like some kind of rabid ewe might assault a lion. He was shocked, then full of passion, careful, though, because she seemed so slight.

But her slight size deceived. As it turned out, she had a knack for childbearing. By turn of fall, little Tiberius was born. To everyone's surprise, she was up almost immediately after his birth. They were even more surprised when she brought in the Pontifex Maximus to bless him and place around his neck a bulla filled with phalluses and other male talisman to ward off evil and ensure success. Cornelia, famous for her irreverence, hewing to the conventions of religious Rome? Of course, she didn't believe in any of it, all hokum pocus as far as she was concerned. But, she said, shrugging and crinkling the exquisite ivory skin above her nose, "Why take a chance?"

Numeria followed, then Aulus, and Publius. Twins came, Marca and Marcellus. Five years, six children. Number seven, little Caelus arrived in 164, and they were all gone by 163.

She raised herself from the bed clothes and swung her legs over the side, where they dangled. She propped herself on both arms, leaning forward a little as the memories came pouring back.

She saw little Tiberius marching off in the morning, a little replica of his broad-shouldered, thick-armed father, his golden bulla full of those cute, tiny phalluses bouncing back and forth across his little man's chest. Even his dark hair tousled the same as his pater, and his skin glowed that golden brown from the sunshine. Numeria, a stranger, darker-haired beauty even as a toddler, cried the morning her older brother left for school. She wanted to go, too. Cornelia saw no kinship in her first daughter's features or figure, but she knew that hunger for knowledge oh, too well. Numeria would have to learn on her own, as her mother had. No harm in leading her to the right books, though.

Aulus and Publius were just baby toddlers, both fairer than their father by far, the color he was as a child, so he claimed. They ran and laughed, happy little ones whose own personas had just begun to spring forward. The twins were so sweet, clinging together in their big cradle built by Tiberius himself out of pine wood brought back from the northern mountains. Baby Caelus had his very own cradle, but he slept in the twins' nursery for company. Another dark-haired child, Caelus smiled sweetly every day of his sweet, short life.

Rome in the summer burned from the heat, and so did children. The fever struck Tiberius first, coming home from Polydius's teachings. She'd never seen such a pallor seize him before. Even his startling blue eyes became milky. He was burning up, no matter how much cool water she laved upon his skin. At midnight, Numeria came into his room, shaking, and said, "Is Tiberius dying?"

Cornelia started to say "No, not at all—". She rushed to Numeria, grasped her, and let go. Her lovely, dark beauty was on fire.

Cornelia made a bed for her in Tiberius's room, but as she moved her into the bed, she heard shrieking in the nursery. Running toward the noise, she nearly piled into her husband holding both babies in his arms, desperation in his face.

"They're sick! We need to move them out of this pestilent place!"

Cornelia nodded. "Where is Caelus?" she said as she took the two miserable children from her husband.

"In his cradle, sleeping," Tiberius said.

"Go get him. Philea, get water, lots of cold water and wipe the children with it. Get one of the other slaves to run for ice, as much ice as he can find, I don't care how much the cost, tell them it is for the children of the consul and Cornelia Scipionis Africanus. Have the rest prepare a cart with food, clothing, and water. We depart for the mountains at first light!"

But, Tiberius, Numeria, and the twins died that night, swept away by the heat and disease. The rest were dead within the week. Caelus, Aulus, and Publius slipped away before they could move them out of the city and the ill humors of summer in Rome.

Cornelia wept again at the memory of each of them. In her mind, she bundled them all up again in their soft, white linen wraps, tucking the girls' lunula amulets and the boys' golden bullas close to their hearts so that the gods would protect their souls even so, though they could not save their lives. But, she kept one bulla and hid it away. When they walked next to their children as they were carried to the funereal grounds outside of the city, she kept her countenance somber and sober, though she feared for the one child's spirit who, missing his bulla, soon would be sent to the Styx and Hades' gates without the protection of every other beloved Roman released from mortal life.

Again, in 163, Tiberius won the consulship. Cornelia bore another child, another baby boy whom they named Tiberius Tertius. His father then left for his governorship in Sardinia. When he was gone, Cornelia stealthily slipped into her room and dug deep into her jewelry chest. She found little Tiberius's golden bulla, and hid it in her bodice. Then, she walked quickly to the nursery, ignoring Philea's wondering eyes as she passed, barking to her to prepare lunch.

Cornelia tiptoed into the nursery where Tertius slept. She took his bulla from around his neck, and replaced it with that of his lost, older brother. "Sleep, Tiberius Tertius," she said like a prayer beneath her breath, "under the protection of the firstborn. Live until your time comes."

She calmed the baby boy, long and lean, not a thing like her husband or his dead brother. But, he would be Tiberius's first son no matter what.

Sempronia was born the next year with Consul Tiberius fighting in Sardinia. Dangling her on her hip while Tiberius leaned on her whining softly, she read the letter from her plebeian hero, her brow furrowed.

> Dear Cornelia My Love,
>
> I miss you very much, and the war drags on. We trap these Sardinians, only to see them run for it over the hills. Next thing you know, they're dogging our rearguard again. Still and all, we have them cut off from the rest of the island, and it's only a matter of time until we hunt them down. As you know, I am not one for crucifying rebel leaders, it only makes them martyrs and brings them new recruits. I like the tiered governing approach; make them your agents with healthy stipends and a notion of freedom, and they think peace with Rome isn't so bad. But these thick-curled, thick-brained Sardinians don't care. So, I'm stuck. And, my consulship is running out. I could have this wrapped up in two months, yet I have less than one left. If I could get a little more time, I wouldn't have to turn it over red-faced to the next consul, who of course will reap all the glory for the work my soldiers have done. I'm going to

have to think about this. Maybe there's a way, something religious. Well, we can talk when I get home. I'll be back within the month, and I can't wait to hold you and the little ones again. Until I do, you must squeeze them all for me. Give my regards to young Tertius. I look forward to you all.

Amor,
Tiberius

Of course, it didn't taken her long to solve his dilemma, something only a Scipio could do. A word to the head Vestal Virgin, who then invited the Pontifex Maximus to dinner, and due to astrological irregularities, the feast of the Saturnalia was pushed to the end of December. This threw into consternation those scheduling the election of the new consuls, which traditionally took place in January. With the adjusted calendar, the new consuls could not take office until February. The Senate was confounded because the Lupercalia was celebrated on the Ides of February, leaving no time for the proper lustrum, the ritual cleansing of the Senate building by the outgoing censors and the ensuing installation of the new consuls.

The Pontifex Maximus ordained that the rituals and Lupercalia must be observed. All of the goat-skinned priests behind him nodded their heads in vigorous agreement. Lucius Claudius Strabo suggested legislation that would extend the current consulships one more month. All of the senators agreed to this solution except for Publius Cornelius Scipio Nasica Corculum. Cornelia's brother-in-law, who had matched her with Tiberius, was one of the fairly elected consuls for 162. Now, by the religious decree, he would be forced to resign before he had served one day.

"You left me out!" he shouted at Cornelia, his lean, bony body shaking as though he had the chill. "Not one iota do you care about my career, as long as the great Tiberius Sempronius Gracchus isn't embarrassed in Sardinia."

"Nonsense," Cornelia said evenly. "He'll be back in Rome for his triumph in a matter of months."

She continued trimming the stems of some lovely forsythia found near Brundisium and barged up the Tiber to Rome.

"Why, Cornelia, why did you have to do it this way? If you'd come to me, I would have extended Tiberius's service in Sardinia as praetor. How could you ruin my career this way, for no reason at all?"

"Your career isn't ruined by any measure, Publius," she said, still whittling away at the forsythia until their blossoms looked more suitable for floating in bowls. "It was chancy to leave Tiberius's term in Sardinia up in the air like that," she said. "You very well would have been loyal, most likely, but your fellow consul Marcius Figulus? Very chancy."

Publius Scipio came close to exploding. "Your arrogance is unmatched! Just a woman, and you act like the next king of Rome! By the gods, you're insufferable!"

"Oh, don't go on so. I would be the queen of course, if gender matters as much as you say it does. You are right in one respect. I will do anything I can for my husband. Anything. Keep that in mind, brother-in-law, and that I am a Cornelii. But, let's not fight. You'll lose your consulship now, but suppose you are elected censor? Say, in two years? We don't want people to think of your victory as an outright trade, do we? That would ruin your reputation as much as anything, wouldn't it?"

He went for it, she remembered, though begrudgingly. That explained the nasty hostility of his nasty son, Scipio Nasica, especially to his cousin Tiberius. This might explain why she and Appius had no luck in prompting the Senate to raise more troops to send to Hispania. Nasica opposed the proposal at every turn, he and his toady Rufus. She wondered if Scipio Aemilianus had anything to do with it. He certainly hadn't gone out of his way to support Tiberius in the past, but neither did he oppose him. The opaqueness of the man galled her, he, the great conqueror, content to sit on his ass in his villa and make wine.

But, Scipio Nasica had no reason to complain. His father had made censor in 159, and consul twice thereafter. Still and all, Publius Nasica never seemed to forgive her for the Saturnalia matter. He wouldn't have had to do much to poison his son against them, not even covertly. An unguarded sentence, an offhanded curse at dinner would have any boy mimic an adored father. Yes, she acknowledged to herself, she'd made an enemy in her nephew, perhaps for life. But, it was worth it to see her husband triumph again.

His smile beamed, almost as broad as his back, she recalled, when he walked into the vestibulum and grabbed her up, literally hugging the breath out of her. He turned and embraced his young scion Tiberius as well, and Sempronia, who threw her arms around his sun-leathered neck. Then, he came back to his wife, held her hands in his at arm's length, looking at her in pure joy. She remembered that night, caressing his hair as he slept, the black color of it now streaked with silver. At his temples, it had became white, now truly like white gold, she mused.

More children followed; the new twins twins Servius and Servilia, and Sempronia. Servius was a fat little boy who owned the famed frame of his father. Servilia and Sempronia took after their mother, dark-haired with dark green pools for eyes. They seemed to have their father's jovial humor, though, giggling and laughing together as they grew. The last to come was Gaius, a temperamental version of his siblings, always howling as a baby, always fighting as a boy. The only one in the family that had any sway with Gaius was his oldest brother, Tiberius. Even his father seemed to make no impression on his youngest child. Hence, the lecture, relived as vividly that day again, behind her closed eyes.

"Never forget that we are plebeian, that is our virtue and our strength. We are no different than other common men, no better than any common man."

He said this to Gaius, who stood before him, five years old, yet defiant, his fists on his hips, legs spread like the Colossus's.

"You are better than common men," Gaius said, "better than all other men."

"I am not."

"You are too."

"No."

"Look at what you have done," the boy said, "twice consul, censor, two triumphs, the greatest general of all time."

She'd covered her mouth to hide her smile, but Tiberius could see it anyway, which maddened him more.

"I'm not even the best general in the family! Or, the second best. Don't forget your grandfather Scipio Africanus, and his adopted son, Scipio Aemilianus, a man younger than me and much more accomplished. Humility, Gaius, humility."

"I could give a fig for humility," Gaius said, "I am Gaius Sempronius Gracchus, plebeian, yes, but one meant for great things."

Tiberius grabbed him by the neck of his tunic, turned him around and gave him a swat on his rump, which only caused Gaius to yell out in indignation.

"You exasperate me, knothead! If you haven't a mind to follow my lead, look to your older brother Tiberius as a model. He's a modest, composed young man who, too, is meant for great things."

Gaius quieted down immediately. She shook her head, amazing how that firebrand of a boy idolized his older brother, such an opposite to himself, admiring him almost more than his father. But, his father was indeed the greatest of all Romans, even if he didn't know it.

Cornelia finally left her bed, threw on a robe to walk out of her room. At this hour, everyone else was still asleep. She sat on the bench next to the small rain pool in the atrium.

She gazed into the water and saw her reflection. Old, old, old, she thought, but not from the years gone by. She'd grown old in one day, in a single day.

Tiberius had been home for only a few months. Snow had fallen, a strange occurrence, especially at this time of year, coating the riotous colors of the city in a pale white shroud. Even the filth along the Aventine turned into a crystal sculpture of inchoate shapes, and the stench of the city subsided, replaced by a fragrance, the taste of metal.

Everyone had pulled out their heavy, wool leggings and heaviest cloaks, hoods up even inside their domiciles, the chill ran so deep. A fire was ordered by Tiberius in the big room, and everyone huddled around it, wondering what was going on.

"The gods are up to something," Tiberius said.

"Don't be silly," she said. "Just a little snow? Look, our family is fine. Everything is fine. Look, everyone's warm and playing."

And they were, Servius and Marcus fighting with Gaius, while Tiberius Tertius read, occasionally glancing at the boys. Sempronia cooed over the twins, who laughed and giggled at the attention. They didn't seem to mind the cold as much as the adults. They looked happy, safe.

"The gods have been good to us, Tiberius, they have blessed us with another family."

He smiled that winning smile of his, with just a hint of sweet sadness about his eyes. "No, Cornelia, they have their ways to play with us. What we have today, they will take away just as quickly if the whim strikes them. They've done it before—"

"No!"

"—They will do it again. Sooner or later."

"Don't say that! The gods aren't real! They don't have any control over us!"

"If that's true, then why are you so upset?"

She said nothing, but she felt looming terror.

Tiberius shook his head. "I will bring in a priest to appease the gods. If the gods don't exist, as you say, what harm will it do?"

She sighed. At that time, she had a window cut out of her bedroom wall so that she could look out at the gorgeous flowers in the perystilum whenever she liked. People thought it strange that she had a window cut into the wall of her bed chamber. Many Romans had frescos and outdoor scenes painted onto their walls, but a real window to the outside? That simply welcomed evil vapors into a home. At that time, Cornelia didn't care; vapors be damned, vapors be welcome.

Tiberius came home with the priest, who mumbled-jumbled as he solemnly marched through the house. After blessing each bed room with the smoking stalk of a river reed, he entered the kitchen and the pantry. More incantations, and he turned toward Tiberius's office just off the vestibulum. Tiberius followed him in.

An ungodly cry came from the office. Cornelia jumped up and ran into the hallway to hear Tiberius roar, "Stay where you are!"

She froze. The children tumbled out of their rooms, high voices a cacophony of bird chirps asking what was wrong.

"Silence!" she shouted severely. "Go back into your rooms!"

Stunned, they turned and ran without another word. She returned to straining her ears to learn what the two men in the office talked about, but too soft to hear.

The priest emerged, white-faced. He waved his stalk as he came out. Behind him came Tiberius with his arms held out in front of him. In one hand, he gripped the strangled corpse of a snake, an asp? In the other, the live snake writhed and twisted, trying to bite its captor. But the soldier's strength of Tiberius held it firm. The priest led him to the front door. Opening it, he gave the former consul a wide berth. Tiberius walked out the door and immediately cast the corpse of the dead serpent aside. Then, he carefully placed the living snake on the road, where it quickly slithered away and down a hole into the sewers of Rome.

Tiberius nodded at the priest and walked back toward the front door. Cornelia stood in his way.

"Never speak of this again," he said, and moved past her.

She looked at him as he went back into his office, then back outside at the priest, who frantically waved his smoking stalk in a wide half circle tracing the silhouette of the house. He quickly scurried away.

Despite constant, plaintive questioning, Tiberius refused to discuss what had occurred in the office. It was clear to Cornelia that the two snakes had slipped into the house to find warmth, a natural impulse. But something more had happened in that office than the surprise of the snakes. She had to know what, but her imprecations failed to move him.

Tiberius became distracted. He smiled and played with the children, met with his clients, and went off to the Senate. But, something was missing, something seemed to be slipping away from him. His smiles for her appeared incomplete, as if a niggling problem inside kept him from beaming that glory of his wide-open joy at seeing her. After some weeks of this, she could wait no longer.

Polydius, Tiberius Tertius's new tutor, accompanied her to the Temple of Juno Sospita. There she found the priest who had come to their home. He blanched again when he saw her, and at first refused to speak to her. She dangled a large pouch in front of him, shaking it so he could hear the clink of the coins. More likely, though, the look in her dark eyes was the true incentive for him to talk.

They had found the two snakes, one of each sex, in the day bed where Tiberius sometimes napped, a male and a female. Tiberius asked the priest to divine the meaning. The priest prayed, and Juno revealed to him that not both snakes were to be killed, but only one. If he killed the male snake, Tiberius would die. If he killed the female snake, his wife would die.

The priest dropped his head into his robes when he uttered the last, using the faintest of voices.

"You fool!" she cried. "Why did you open your mouth?"

"Juno Sospita spoke to me!" he whined.

Cornelia hit him in the face with the bag of coins. He fell down amid the shower of gold that spilled from the split leather.

"Why didn't you keep your mouth shut, or make something up? Hades, if anything happens to him, I swear I'll force feed you to the snake that survived!"

It was too late, though. She tried to cajole Tiberius out of his funk, but he wouldn't have it. A fever came on him, and he wasted away. She brought the children in to cheer him, and at seeing them, he would light up for a short time. But, the fever grew worse. The surgeons bled him and purged him. Even the crazy Egyptians couldn't cure him with their outlandish, foul-smelling poultices. Tiberius Sempronius Gracchus was dying.

In his final moments, each catching breath a struggle, she clung to him, curling up against his racked frame. At last, in the dawn of a winter day, with snow again on the ground, the darkness drew over him, and he breathed his last.

Cornelia closed his eyes and stood by the bed for a time. She cried, then stopped. Tearless, she left the room and crossed the vestibulum to the boys' chambers. There, she roused Tiberius Tertius and led him into the bed chamber. As the boy looked down on his dead father, she grabbed him by the shoulders and turned him to face her.

"You are no longer Tiberius Tertius. Now, you are Tiberius Sempronious Gracchus, master of this house. Prepare to honor your father with your life."

Philea came silently into the atrium with a cup of heated water flavored by squeezed lemon. Without a word she handed it to her mistress, bowing her head as she did. She's as grey as I am, thought Cornelia, and just as bony. Her weathering had been earned through hard work though, and worry. She worried about her demanding, oft-times cruel mistress, whom still she treated with respect, and love. Love unearned, Cornelia thought, pressing her lips in silent self-rebuke. She had written the manumission document, but forgotten where she put it. She should dig it up and give it to her. Not that she really believed that Philea would want to leave. Where would she go after all these years? And if she were to leave, what would her harsh mistress do?

Philea withdrew, and Cornelia sipped.

Young Tiberius did his best, but his father was dead. Gone with him was her own heart. Now, she made no sound even when by herself in the cold loneliness of the night. Night after night she lay awake, listening, hearing nothing. No birds calling, no cats rutting, nothing. She never slept, and she was never tired from fatigue, just of being awake, alone. Philea cared for the children because her mistress never got out of bed. They would come to see her, cry for her to get up, but she wouldn't. Instead, she was intent on missing the man who had been and still was her life. The last time she left her bed chamber was for his funeral.

They built the pyre outside of the city walls at the Carmenta Gate opposite the old Temple of Apollo. They chose the site not for religious reasons, but to accommodate the enormous crowd expected to mourn one of the greatest heroes of the Republic, struck down too soon even though his years were long. Cornelia herself couldn't complain, for her Tiberius was an Apollo himself.

All of Rome surrounded the bier, with Tiberius's body swaddled at its top. Farmers, milners, vintners, olive oil sellers, butchers, potters, horse traders, textile dealers, candle makers, iron smiths, goldsmiths, jewelers, and thousands of veterans, his legions, tears striking scars wherever they were. Indeed, years later it was said that all but one dog left the city to wail at the loss of Tiberius Sempronius Gracchus. The dog remained behind, so the story went, because it was deaf, blind, and dying itself.

The senators, adiles, tribunes, praetors, consuls, and censors sat according to station in a stand built across from the pyre in front of the gate. The equitii sat with other wealthy merchants in lower stands situated around the pyre stage. Soldiers ringed the pyre to keep the mournful crowd at bay, their circular cordon waving and ebbing with the back and forth rippling surge of the grieving crowd. Within, standing on the slightly raised platform supporting the bier, the hooded priests burned incense and hummed their arcane prayers to the gods.

Dignitaries from around the world had traveled to pay their respects, Masinissa from Numidia, Deemtrios I Soter from Antioch, Mithridates IV Philopator from Pontus, and Menandros of Bkatria, though his counterpart Agathokleia remained at home to keep the recently won peace. Even the Egyptian Pharoah, Ptolemy VI Philometer, known as "Mother-Friend," had sent his high priest to preside for himself and his queen, Cleopatra II. Of course, his brother Ptolemy VIII Euergetes Physcon of Cyrenaica attended personally to push his claim on Cyprus. The various luminaries were seated in two stands on opposite sides of the main Roman contingent, divided to keep separate any parties embroiled in territorial disputes that could disturb the service. Hence, Ptolemy Physcon sat nowhere near the high priest sent by his brother Ptolemy Philometer.

Cornelia and the children sat in the middle of the Roman stand, with Scipio Amelianus to her right, and Appius to her left. Publius Scipio and his family sat afar, including his petulant stringbean son Nasica. All of the other notable families, both patrician and plebeian, radiated out and around the surviving Sempronii, who clung together in their dark, torn robes of mourning.

Cornelia sat dry-eyed. Tiberius had been dead for a month, his corpse in the temple awaiting the arrival of the foreign state officials, though the farmers and old retired soldiers who had traveled here would have pleased him more. She missed him still, like a deep stab wound had been opened in her breast, aching always without a lethal flow of blood. She had no more tears, either, she was cried out. Within, she wept as the sky embraced the rising ashes of her lovely hero, weeping, as the love of her life disappeared into the clouds forever, with the knowledge that she would cry silently this way every day for the rest of her life.

Meanwhile, the fickle gods laughed at her, the girl who had refused to believe in them because of her willful ways. Coming down from the stand, with tiny, soft feathers of ash still wafting around their heads, Cornelia ushered her confused little children in front of her while young Tiberius did his best to help, despite his own stunned countenance.

A huge, black mass suddenly blocked their way. Startled, she looked up. Ptolemy VIII Euergetes Psychon stood before her—Ptolemy Potbelly, Ptolemy Bladder, Ptolemy Sausage—the other Pharaoh, but not of all Egypt, though he looked as though he'd eaten his way through half the land of the Nile. The fragrance of his perfumes staggered her as much as his glorious, gold-threaded, ruby-hued raiments. His beard looked like a dark honey confection twisted into filigrees that no Ramses had ever seen, punctuated with a tiny pearl in every curlicue. Without looking, Psychon reached back to a slave who handed him a short linen square that he used to wipe his mouth and his hands. Apparently, he'd been eating during the funeral.

"Mistress Cornelia Scipionis Africanus," he said, "please accept my deepest condolences. Your late husband was a great man, a hero worthy to sit next to the Olympic gods."

"Thank you," she said evenly.

"And these must be your beautiful children, gloriously transcendent like their mother, famous throughout the world for her otherworldly magnificence. You must be very proud of them, I'm sure."

She nodded and tried to move around him, but he spread himself so that they couldn't pass.

"As you know," he continued, "I have been occupied as of late in asserting my rights to the throne of the two Kingdoms of Egypt."

"I understand this to be true," she replied, hiding her impatience as best as she could.

"Indeed. Of course, I traveled all of this way to pay honor to Rome's greatest citizen, but also took this opportunity to present my case to the august Roman Senate."

"Yes, I heard," she replied, Gaius whining and tugging at her robe. The other children started crying, too. Her eyes flashing, she said, "Yes, Cyprus is the chicken bone of your contention, is it not?"

Psychon brushed off the remark. "It was, but that has been settled. The Senate has agreed to support my claim again. All it took was the baring of the scars from my wicked brother's assassination attempts. Would you like to see them?"

"No."

"In any case, my venture has been a success, a silver lining to this sad day, wouldn't you say? And I hope to make it even less sad by bringing joy to you, your fine children, and to me, all in one Jupiter-like stroke of lightning. Cornelia Scipio Africanus, would you do the honor of becoming Queen of the next Pharoah of Egypt? Will you be my wife?"

Cornelia clapped her hand over her mouth to keep from shrieking. She kept it there to stem the hysterical laughter welling up inside her body. With inhuman control, she lowered her hand to her side and spoke, completely composed.

"Thank you, Ptolemy Euergetes, you are truly well-named, your beneficence knows no bounds. But I must reject your most generous proposal, for I have just lost the father of my children. And, in his memory, I am obligated to raise them to honor their father and to strive to add to the distinction of his name. Only this keeps me from accepting, and I vow you this, that I will never marry again."

Ptolemy VIII Euergetes Psychon grunted, "Huh. Very well, if that is your decision, unwise though it is. I shall easily find another wife while you spend your life drifting away with the memory of your dead husband, and your loss of one equal in magnificence."

Pyschon wheeled his enormous heft around and marched off toward the Carmenta Gate. Cornelia barked a laugh, the only one since Tiberius had died, and the last one for a long, long time.

She laughed now. Old Ptolemy Potbelly did rule Egypt after all, for a short time. But he was long dead and gone, forgotten now after all these years, except by a few stuffy historians. Meanwhile, the name Tiberius Sempronius Gracchus lives on, still evoking cheers from the Roman people. Of course, she had worked diligently to ensure that, using her own considerable fortune to attach him to many a holiday celebration gifted to the masses. Nothing that he wouldn't have done himself, of course.

Yes, the gods had played her for a fool and made her laugh at the same time, at the hardest time. Then, before the laughter had stopped echoing in her mind, they showed their cruel black hearts. Servius came down with it first, his nose running, coughing, accompanied by a horrible, spreading rash. Servilia soon followed. While trying to comfort them, Cornelia saw that they were finding it more and more difficult to breathe. Gradually, Servius closed his eyes. She watched him, his black threadlike lashes drooping down, until she realized that he was unconscious. She blanched white and shouted for Philea to run for the physicians, and the priests.

"Bring them all, promise them anything!" she screamed.

She didn't wait for Philea to return. Frantically, she ordered Tiberius to strip. She inspected her embarrassed son closely: no rash. She followed with Sempronia, who cried while she went over the girl's body. She was clean, too. Then, she examined Gaius.

Cold rippled through her back, down her arms. Gaius had traces of the rash. Of course, she thought, he shared the old nursery with the other children. As the oldest, Tiberius and Sempronia both had their own rooms. But little Gaius was infected.

She called Polydius to the atrium.

"Pack clothes for Tiberius and Sempronia, and take them to the pig farm. Stay there until I summon you back."

Despite their tears, she pushed the children out of the house and into the cart, seeing them off before Philea had brought the physicians and priests back to the house. The oldest, a grizzled Greek with a grey beard and little hair, carefully looked at all her little ones, Tiberius's last gifts to her.

After examining each one in turn, he motioned Cornelia to the hallway.

"They have Morbilli," he said, "the fevers, exuding noses, coughing, red eyes, and, of course, the rash. You can comfort them, hope for the best, but there is very little that you can do at this point."

She nearly collapsed, held up by Philea.

"Nothing? Nothing?"

The old Greek shrugged. "It might pass. Keep anyone who shows no sign of the disease away from the afflicted, including yourself. If you stay within their reach, the bad humors could infest you."

"But, they are my children, the last I shall ever bear!"

Again, the Greek lifted and dropped his shoulders. "You have other children that you sent away, no? Send in your slaves to care for these. Don't risk orphaning the ones still healthy by succumbing to the malady yourself, then bringing it to them. Live for those who will live; bury and mourn those who cannot survive."

Cornelia's lips curled. "Philea," she said, "pay the physician."

Once Philea had handed the old Greek his gold, Cornelia spat the words, "Get out!"

He left, followed by his lesser colleagues. Cornelia then turned to the priests and said, "Pray. Pray to the gods that they save my little ones, because if they don't, you will have to pray twice as hard to save your own skins!"

She turned to go back to her children, held up by Philea's hand on her arm.

"Mistress, you can't! The physician's warning! I'll go in and tend to them. But, you must be here when Tiberius and Sempronia return."

Cornelia shrugged off Philea's arm, "You must be mad. These are my babies. I will take care of them no matter what that sniveling necrophiliac says."

Then, her fierce expression turning into utter bewilderment, she gazed at Philea and said, "You think I would let you go in there? You are mad. I'm not as heartless as that hack, or the gods. They are my children, live or die."

Philea displayed sharp anger in her eyes. "They are my children, too, the only ones I have!"

Cornelia seemed startled for a moment. Then, she turned and walked into the sick room, calling back scornfully as she entered, "Suit yourself. What's one more death, more or less?"

She slipped off her nightgown, and examined her bony frame. Age steals all beauty, she could see. The reflection in the polished bronze told her that the green eyes were still there, and some of the symmetry of the face. But, the rest was gone. She folded the gown and put it into the ornate wooden chest at the foot of the bed, extracting at the same time one of her ever ready brown robes, forever in mourning. She pulled it over her shoulders. Of course, as expected, they died, all but Gaius. The rash developed, but somehow he'd proven immune to the lethal part of the illness. He carried a fever, but nothing like the others. She buried her twins, her little boy and her tiny little girl. The priests ceremonially burned out the house, after they had removed the irreplaceable, of course, the ancestral masks. Tiberius and Sempronia came back, and the crying-wailing display started all over again.

The house became so empty after that, so lonely. It lasted for decades, worse when Tiberius went off to Carthage to fight with Scipio. Things only improved after he married Claudia, something of a mouse, skinny, too. But, a good wife and mother, nonetheless. Soon, the old place was crowded again with grandchildren and the new slave Lysis, and Polydius returning to teach a new generation. But, her life remained the same, her morning ritual of waking and remembering as she forced herself to rise for prayer before the Lares and the visage of her only love, in waxen death. She sighed.

Muffled voices sounded outside her room. Someone banged on her door.

"Cornelia! Cornelia? Open the door, it's me, Appius. Open quickly, please! I have news, news of Tiberius!"

Cornelia leaped to her feet and moved to the door.

""What is it?"

"Oh, gods, the cruel gods!" Appius said, wringing the edges of his toga, his face contorted with worry and fear.

"Tell me Appius, now!"

He moved quickly to her chair and sat. He dropped the edge of his toga and wrung his hands together.

"Appius!" she hissed, looming over him.

He looked up, this time with worry and sorrow.

"The Numantines have won! Mancinus is routed with his entire army!"

Chapter 18: Hispanic Dawn

The walls of the Ninth's camp bristled with long spears, pila, swords, and arrows. Titius had his wasps loaded and ready for a final onslaught. Tiberius knew that this time the full weight of the Numantine army would be brought to bear, and none of the tactics, traps, or tricks that he had used during the first day of battle would work again now. The only thing left was to fight for life, even if it only lasted hours or minutes longer. This time, he made no speech; the men of the Ninth knew what they faced, they were soldiers, and they would show so until death called.

He stood at the center of the front wall, his helmet singling him out more than any other soldier in the line. Titius had banged out the dent from the arrow. Though it didn't fit as well as before, the repair allowed Tiberius to wear his father-in-law's lavish headpiece once again. For this final battle, he wanted to be easy to find.

A familiar, deep-throated horn broke the silence of the morning. A beautiful morning, thought Tiberius, the first one during their entire time in Hispania that seemed like a true, late spring day. Even the cool breeze that felt icy to the cheek seemed fleeting, followed by sunshine breaking through, warming the very same skin briefly chilled before. A wistful day to face an enemy bound on our deaths, he thought. Summer wouldn't be far off.

Five thousand mounted Numantine warriors walked their horses out of the lower woods, line by line, crowding the space available to them. They stood holding long spears in their hands, their other hands gripping their swords belted at their waists. This time, they stood before the Roman camp quietly, more like they were on parade rather than ready to ride over the walls again to sweep the Ninth from their land.

A contingent of horsemen abruptly broke out of the front line and walked up to the middle of the wall. Tiberius could see by their ornately decorated helmets and breastplates that they were chieftains. In the center, he saw the grey-haired man with the metal discs on his chest. The grey chief eased his horse forward a few steps, separating himself from the others. He raised his open hand slowly and held it still.

Tiberius stared at him for some time, then slowly raised his hand in the same way. The rider drew closer to the wall where Tiberius stood. The

Numantine spoke.

"General Tiberius Sempronius Gracchus," he said in heavily accented Latin, "we offer you peace."

Tiberius drew back his head. What was this?

"What kind of peace, Numantine? Lifelong bondage? If so, we will die first, after we have slain many more of you."

The grey-haired chief shook his head, "We offer you peace with honor. We wish to save our men, and yours. The battle has been well-fought, but," he said, then swept his arm at the host of warriors behind him, "the outcome is assured. Why sacrifice so many stalwart soldiers on either side to produce the same result, only bloodier?"

Tiberius hesitated. He was of half a mind to tell the Numantine that if he didn't want blood, why not leave the field altogether? But, the barbarians didn't have to break their army on the walls of the small fort. They must know by now about the grim ground occupied by Mancinus and his sick and starving legions. The same could be imposed on the Ninth. All the Hispanic tribes had to do was wait. At worst, when desperation forced the emaciated Romans to try to break out, they could cut down either body of legions, smashing them on their defenses. No, a bold response would win nothing but a crueler death. He pressed his lips into a stern expression.

"What terms?"

"Simple. You will leave Numantia, promising never to come back."

Tiberius hesitated. He held his breath, parsing the words in his mind for the secret meaning.

"That's all?"

The chief nodded. "You will be allowed to keep your swords and shields, but not your bows, your spears, or your siege engines. You can reprovision. An escort will accompany you to the border. And no Roman will step on Numantine land again, ever."

Tiberius sensed warmth rising within him, a glow of hope that he and his men might survive this disaster. They all might be able to go home after all.

He stifled the emotion. Mancinus would never agree. This would be the end of the consul's career in Rome. Rather than face that, he might choose to fall on his sword after he had sacrificed his legions. The grey-headed emissary was right, any further fighting for the Romans would be a massacre. No matter, the Ninth would do its duty.

"Your terms are generous, Chieftain, but we follow orders from our commander, the Consul Hostilius Mancinus. I am not the general of this army, he is. You must go to him with your proposal."

The chieftain shook his head. "It is you, Tiberius Sempronius, with whom we wish to negotiate. You are the only Roman with whom we will negotiate."

"Me? Why me? I'm but a quaestor, and barely a military tribune, not even the fourth in command."

The Numantine grinned broadly, and turned back to utter a rapid-fire phrase to the other chieftains. They all roared a quick burst of laughter. He returned his attention to Tiberius and said, "You don't fight like a clerk, Quaestor. We want you, scion of the great Roman whose name you carry, Tiberius Sempronius Gracchus, the only general who ever won a war against the warriors of Numantia, that Roman general who negotiated the fairest, longest peace between our two peoples in history. He created a peace that lasted for decades, until a pack of new Roman jackals broke it repeatedly, including your Consul Mancinus. No, Sempronius Gracchus, we want you for the fierce warrior chief you've shown yourself to be, and for the fairness promised through your legacy. It is you whom we trust."

Tiberius stood on the wall, shocked through and through. A murmur rippled through the ranks of the Ninth at hearing this unadulterated praise for their tribune. They also realized that he was talking of a truce with the barbarians that might see them all going home to their wives and children. Soon, the ripple had turned into a torrent of loud comments and calls.

"Silence!" bellowed Casca. The troops immediately quieted down, but all eyes were glued on the two men opposite each other at the blood-stained walls of the Ninth's encampment.

Tiberius gathered himself. No matter what the Numantine chief said, the Roman chain of command presided. "Thank you for the flattery, Numantine, but I cannot sue for peace. I am not this army's general. What he decides dictates the fate of this legion, he and the good gods above who cause everything. Go to Consul Mancinus now, and if he agrees to accept your terms, we will abide. But if he determines that his army must fight for honor, we will fight until we die honorably on your swords or on our own. Go, now."

Suddenly, Casca huffed deeply, shouting sarcastically "Vale, Numantine!" Didius followed him, joined by Shafat, "Vale," and finally, Sextus. Then, the entire Ninth thundered, "Valete, Numantines!"

The greying chieftain swung his head slowly, wheeled his horse around and joined the other chieftains. But, instead of riding back to the thousands of horsemen behind them, they stayed where they were, appearing to carry on a spirited conversation. Then, the chieftain returned to the wall.

"You, Tiberius Sempronius," he said, "you bring our offer to Consul Mancinus. We promise you safe passage to and from your camp no matter what. But we want you to convince Mancinus. Make a good argument for peace, Sempronius, for all of us."

Tiberius stared out at the chieftain. After some minutes, he said, "What is your name?"

The arduous march to the Roman camp against the river seemed to last forever for the two exhausted, hungry men. After climbing down through the tree line on the hill, they found the going easier in the hollow of the river valley. The grass grew high, just a couple of months away from seed ripening, which would mark the close of the campaign season. Instead of wintering in Numantia, or just building a permanent camp, Tiberius realized, they either would be making their slow way back to Rome, or their bones cracked open by scavengers would lie bleaching in this wilderness. Not much of a choice, though he was sure that the Pedites who had formed the Ninth would feel otherwise. For their sake, he had to see this peace through.

Crickets shot up and bounced around as the two men brushed the grass stalks while traversing the river valley. They hadn't see any Numantine warriors since coming out of the hills, though they imagined that the riders were about, keeping an eye on them during the entire trek. As they closed in on the river bed, horse flies swooped down on them, buzzing and biting, another reason, perhaps, for the Numantines keeping their distance.

When they arrived at the earthen barricade, a sentry called for the password, causing Tiberius and Sextus to exchange glances. They didn't know the password. Sextus stood in his saddle and shouted out, "Stand at attention, soldier, this is Tiberius Sempronius Gracchus, Quaestor and Tribune to Consul Hostilius Mancinus. Give way or never see another payday."

The gaunt guard shrugged and waved them up over the mound. As they passed over and down into the fortified camp, they saw the legionaries huddled together, some standing, others sitting. All looked desperately stressed, hungry, and suspicious, betrayed somehow in some unfathomable way.

Some of the legionaries changed as they slowly recognized the quaestor and the equitus walking toward Mancinus's headquarters. Their expressions showed surprise, an odd reaction, thought Tiberius, until Horatius uttered his greeting.

"Salve, Quaestor, you're not dead yet. From what we heard during the past three days, we thought surely your head occupied the point on a Numantine spear."

Tiberius stopped in his tracks, his hand resting lightly on the butt of his sword. "If your head was missing, Horatius, I don't doubt your body would still fight on."

The other tribunes laughed loudly and Horatius's grin steeled into a death mask. Seeing Tiberius's calm demeanor, he eventually began a barking laugh of his own. "Well said, Gracchus. What brings you to our matchless leader? Permission to cut and run?"

"Peace, Tribune," said Sextus over his shoulder.

"And prosperity?"

They came to Mancinus's makeshift praetorium and noticed that there were no sentries out front to challenge their entry. Again exchanging glances, they stepped into the tent. Mancinus was alone in his camp chair, resting his chin in the cup of his hand. His beard looked to be several days old, maybe unshaven since the beginning of the Numantine siege. He wore only his tunic and no sandals.

"Salve, Consul," Tiberius said in a brisk tone.

Mancinus didn't respond. His eyes stared into an unknown distance.

"Consul Hostilius Mancinus, we are here, at your service. Where are your sentries, your adjutants?"

The consul remained still. Tiberius looked at Sextus and gestured with his head. Sextus strode to the table in the back of the tent and poured a cup of wine out of the pitcher sitting on the table top. He brought it over to Tiberius, who took it and held it to Macinus's mouth. The touch of the liquid stirred the Roman general. He grabbed the cup with both hands and drained it greedily. Tiberius motioned to Sextus to bring the pitcher over from the table.

As Tiberius brought the pitcher and refilled Mancinus's cup, the consul said, "Gracchus? You're here? I thought you were dead, you and your legion. The quiet—no more crashing sounds from that mountain, day and night. You won? How could you have won?"

"We did not win."

He watched the spectrum of expressions flick across Mancinus's face until he saw dark realization building in the consul's features.

"You surrendered?" Mancinus said in low fury.

"Sextus, mind the entrance."

Sextus strode to the front to block the way into the tent.

"You took the coward's way out, you bowed your head to the enemy."

Tiberius pulled up another camp chair and sat opposite Mancinus, almost knee to knee. "We did not surrender, Consul, we bowed our heads to no one."

"Then, why are you here? Why aren't you back in your camp fallen on your sword? Where is your legion?"

"Back on the mountain, waiting for me to return with orders."

"What orders? Fight! Fight to the end!"

Tiberius's mouth tightened. "It is the end, Consul. The campaign is lost. The Numantines can destroy us at any time, either by attacking or waiting for us to attack after we've run completely out of food and water. Any way you look at it, we are done, left only with our choice of how to be slaughtered."

"No!"

"Yes, Consul, yes. Everything is lost, except for our lives. Whether we die now or not is immaterial. The Numantines have won, they know it, and they know that we do, too. So, the question they ask is, 'Do we want to waste more lives denying this truth?'"

Mancinus lowered his head, unwilling to face Tiberius with an answer.

"Consul, you are a brave Roman who has won honor in war before. This time the gods, for whatever godly reasons, have denied us victory. You and we tribunes will have to accept this terrible, black mark on our records. It is inevitable. The only maneuvering room we have is to determine how bad this mark will be. Shall we accept defeat and retire from the field, as the Numantines have proposed? Or, shall we also be responsible for the death of five legions, tens of thousands of good fighting men who are not culpable in any way? That is the only choice left to us—to you, sir. We can lose this war and our dignitas, but still show our Roman resolve through bravado by fighting and dying to the last man. But if we do this, we align ourselves with the worst of Roman generals, my ancestor Pallus and Varo at Cannae. Better to be scorned as Fabius Cunctator than the other two. Remember, every other general who came to Hispania has lost here at one time or another."

"Except your father, Gracchus."

Tiberius dropped his head. "That will be my shame to bear, that I could not preserve his honor. But, I would rather carry that shame knowing that the men who fought with me were allowed to go home to their wives and children. I'd rather return to my own wife,"

He said the last quietly, as if thinking out loud. He returned his eyes to Mancinus.

"The only way we can do this, Consul, is if you agree to the peace that the Numantines propose. It is a generous peace. All we need do is go home."

"And be ambushed along the way."

Tiberius shook his head, "They will escort us, but we can keep our swords and shields. No pylas, no bows, no other weapons. But, in a tight column formation and with our swords and shields, we would be safe from a surprise attack."

"We'll starve before we get to the coast."

"They will allow us to restock. We will owe money as part of the treaty."

"Tribute."

"Payment for goods and passage."

Mancinus sighed, agitated. "It's simpler to fall upon my sword than deal with all of this subterfuge."

Tiberus drew himself up. "If you think so, Consul, I'll hold your gladius for you. You can run onto its blade, die with honor, but it won't change anything. In your staid, I will have this peace."

Mancinus stood up. "Nonsense. Horatius is the ranking tribune, not you. Why, you're the most junior officer here."

Tiberius rose, again shaking his head, slowly this time. "Horatius is an insipid drunk, scared out of his wits. He'd lie down and roll over at the prospect of survival. So will the others, they're all dogs. No, it will be me, Mancinus. The others will jump at the chance to have me save their asses, then bray at home how I caved in to the Numantines, that in your absence, your ill health, you appointed me to deal with them. Who else could be at fault but Tiberius Sempronius Gracchus? Think of the irony, think of how Rufus and the other Good Men would love it."

Mancinus collapsed back in his chair, his head down in his hands. "So, I can honorably take my own life or I can accept the Numantine's peace and be pilloried all over Rome. Not much of a choice."

"You don't have that choice, Consul."

Mancinus peered up at Tiberius, white-faced. "I don't?"

"No. Whether or not you commit suicide, the Numantine chieftains insist that I represent Rome in this peace. Again, it has to do with being my father's son."

The consul squinted, then gradually relaxed his features, as if in mid-epiphany. "Yes, Quaestor, I agree. You are the only one who can manage this. I insist, too. You fashion this truce with the Numantines." He shook his head up and down firmly. "I order you to do so."

Tiberius sought out Horatius after the meeting.

"Well, Gracchus, going back to your mountain stronghold to face the onslaught?"

"Listen to me, Horatius. Mancinus has agreed to terms proposed by the Numantines. We will receive food and water and be escorted to the border."

Tiberius watched as Horatius's usual sneer dissolved. He swallowed nervously and said, "We're getting out of here?"

Tiberius nodded, "Yes, but it isn't over yet. You need to get these men into shape. We have no idea what will happen on the march, so we have to be ready to defend ourselves."

Horatius nodded.

"Get them all to shave, and when the grain arrives, feed them. And clean yourself up, too, Horatius, and the others. Be sure Mancinus is ready in his armor."

He turned on his heel and headed toward the perimeter, praying to the gods that Mancinus's army would be ready to move.

As they crossed the long, grassy river valley on their way to the Ninth's outpost in the hills, a troop of twenty horsemen rode quickly up and surrounded them. Again, the two Roman officers put their hands on their sword butts, standing back to back.

"Pax, Romans, we won't harm you," the captain of the troop said in accented Latin. "I have been ordered to bring you to the chieftains as soon as you left the Roman camp."

The horse commander was a large, long man in dun linen pants and a thick gray shirt with a long sword belted over his shoulder, and a knife in front. His hair fell down on both sides of his head, parted by a leather band. He looked familiar to Tiberius for some odd reason.

"You're Avarus's son."

The man nodded, "I am Caciro, his youngest. My two older brothers were killed during the siege."

Tiberius nodded slowly.

"Here are horses. My father told me to escort you. If you would mount, please, we can be there in short time."

The two horses appeared from behind the men as the young warrior spoke. Tiberius eyed the horses, while Sextus went straight to one and flipped his leg over its side.

"Before I meet with your chiefs, I will return to my legion," Tiberius said, his left hand still on his sword.

The young son of Avarus nodded, "It is all the same way. You'll pass through us to get to your camp, sir."

Sir. Tiberius hiked his leg over the horse's back, and squirmed astride. The young horseman led the way across the wide meadow toward the line of hills where the Ninth waited. In a matter of a few hours, they found themselves in the midst of the Numantine force.

The bearded warriors eyed them curiously as their horses walked past. Tiberius noted the long, two-handed swords some of them carried across their backs, the small, round wooden shields others held next to their shorter but formidable spinas. Bowmen stood staring at them as well, and he couldn't help tensing as he rode by, expecting at any moment to feel a shaft entering his back. But, he refused to show signs of nerves or fear. He rode calmly up to the abbreviated barricade that formed the forward wall of the Ninth's camp. Standing with one sandal at its top, Casca peered out at the two approaching riders. A rough smile barely creased his mouth as he recognized the two Roman officers astride the Numantine horses.

Tiberius raised his hand in salute and said, "Prepare the men to march, Casca. The campaign is over. We will leave for home with honor."

The men of the Ninth sent up a ragged roar of approval as Tiberius and Sextus dismounted, tethering the two horses to a beam of the wooden wall. They scrabbled tiredly up the side, helped up by leather-armored arms of the legionaries. On top of the parapet, Tiberius and Casca silently took stock of each other. Then, the quaestor tribune motioned for his centurion primus to follow him to his headquarters.

The assembled officers listened carefully as Tiberius recounted the events in the main camp.

"Mancinus is not fully capable of leading a withdrawal. His soldiers are close to collapse. Their resources are nearly exhausted and they possess little will left to resist enemy hostility they might face on the way back. We cannot leave to join them now and risk the entire army's destruction."

"What do you wish us to do, sir?" asked Casca, straightening up almost at attention.

"Mobilize the men, but be sure that they understand the threat. Discipline will mean everything. See to it that we gather plenty of fresh water from the hill streams to carry along. I'll insist that the Numantines replenish our food stock now to renew the men before the long march itself. Until we're in possession of these supplies, we defend this camp. I have been asked to meet with the Numantine chieftains which might give us a chance to strengthen terms. Otherwise, nothing has changed. We are the only force between them and the destruction of our army."

Tiberius nodded at Sextus, and the two made to leave the lean-to. As they left, each centurion and optio saluted them, one by one.

When his large-limbed son Caciro flipped the tent flap up to present the two Roman officers, Avarus smiled. He stopped scratching the long-healed scar on his belly and stood, raising his hand to his forehead and bringing it down in an open-palmed salute.

"General Sempronius Gracchus, welcome, welcome, and welcome to your adjutant."

Tiberius grimaced involuntarily, "Quaestor, Chieftain Avarus, or tribune at best. This is my equitus, Sextus Decimus Paetus."

Sextus languidly bowed his head.

"Yes, yes, of course, a good horseman, this one, we've heard of his deeds at the walls of Malia. You're a brave one, you."

Sextus stared straight at the chieftain, silent.

"Yes, sit, sit," Avarus motioned to some stools in the large, linen tent. Beautiful moss-green drapes fell from the four walls to guard against the wind rounding the hilltop. Knotted rugs tied together with linen bits in dark earthen colors covered the floor. At the far end, two piles of perfectly tanned sheepskins over woolen blankets sang a siren song to the worn-out Roman officers wavering trance-like in their stances.

"With respect, Chieftain Avarus," Tiberius said, "we need to return to ready our troops to move out. Can we discuss the protocol for peace?"

Avarus raised his hands as he looked down, "We can discuss, but it will be a waste of time. The entire matter must be consecrated by the high priests and priestesses in our sacred grove. Otherwise, the gods will not sanctify our agreement." He shrugged his shoulders, "Also, not all of our chiefs are in camp. We will need to strike an accord with them, of course."

Tiberius frowned, "And where is your sacred grove?"

"In Numantia. As are the other chieftains, for that matter."

"Numantia."

"Yes, General. I am inviting you to travel to our city to execute this peace before the gods with all proper ceremony and circumstance. That is the only way that it will last in their eyes."

Tiberius sighed his exasperation. "Chieftain Avarus, wouldn't a delay be potentially costly? Don't you think our immediate withdrawal would be best?"

He saw a hard glint appear in the Numantine chieftain's eyes. "We would like to see you leave at once. We wish you had never come." Then, his usual affable expression returned. "But, we must do these things correctly, Quaestor Tribune. The gods must approve of our actions or we shall suffer later."

Tiberius raised and lowered his head solemnly.

"Now, you can inform your men, don't worry about that. We shall be but a few short days, no more."

"Very well." Tiberius turned, motioning to Sextus, who exhaled slightly, wearily. Avarus slipped over to the tall equitus and gently clasped his upper arm. "Let the young officer stay and rest," he said. "He's welcome to eat and drink, and sleep here. Caciro will accompany you back to your camp."

Caciro smiled and stepped forward. Tiberius looked at them, and at Sextus's drooping eyes. "Very well."

Sextus tried to rally and object, but Avarus steered him to one of the sheepskin covered pallets. "Go, go, he'll be here when you return." He uttered a staccato sentence in Celtic to his son. Caciro gestured to Tiberius and the two tall men left the tent. They mounted their horses and slowly trotted toward the top of the steep hillside. As they approached the camp, Tiberius saw a large wooden wagon near the front wall. Again, his hand involuntarily sought out the haft of his sword. But, then, a familiar figure dropped from the stockade and began walking in their direction. Didius, the Sicilian centurion, met them beneath the wall.

"Centurion," Tiberius greeted him, his arm held out.

"Tribune," saluted Didius.

"What goes here? Where's Casca?"

"Food supplies, sir. From the Numantines. Casca is supervising distribution. He's making the drivers taste each parcel before sending it over. Bread, mutton, even some wine. The Numies don't mind taking a bite at all."

Tiberius turned to Caciro. He beamed a smile at Tiberius, "My father sent the wagon. More are on their way down to the main Roman camp. He wanted to make sure that you accepted his invitation to Numantia, and he knows that you would not if your men continued to suffer."

Tiberius stared at this giant boy-warrior, wondering if he wasn't looking at a future chieftain of these formidable people. He turned back to Didius.

"Tell Casca to be sure that all of the men have a full meal, but that some of the supplies are kept in reserve. Inform him that Sextus and I will be traveling to Numantia to formalize the truce. We will be back in four days. Have him send a messenger to Consul Mancinus to report the same."

Didius jerked his chin down and saluted crisply. Tiberius motioned to Caciro with his head to lead the way.

When he arrived at the chieftain's tent, he didn't bother loosening his lorica. Instead, he fell face forward on the sheepskin-covered pallet next to Sextus.

Chapter 19: The Blessings of the Nementon

They rode for two days, over ground that should have looked familiar, Sextus thought, grassy rises turning to wooded knolls, the river never far away. He should have been able to figure out the time it would take to retrace their tracks, but he was having trouble focusing. In the aftermath of the fighting, he could distract himself by watching Tiberius ready the Ninth to march back to Hispania Citerior. The tribune instructed Casca to plan on shadowing Mancinus's main force from high ground to enable the Ninth to protect the exposed ranks of Mancinus's four legions from ambush. The Numantines had demanded that all remaining horses be surrendered in exchange for oxen to pull the wagons. Since every horse in the Roman camp had been eaten, it was almost a generous stipulation. Nonetheless, Tiberius countered by insisting that the Numantines allow the withdrawal by the Romans be executed in two contingents. Some of the chieftains grumbled, but Avarus agreed. Still, everything had to be sanctified by the Celtic gods in their sacred groves, the destination of Tiberius and Sextus now.

Sextus assumed that, like so many religious ceremonies in Rome, this would be a matter of routine after the politics had been settled. Of course, who really knew what barbarians did in their rituals? Romans gutted a few birds, maybe a lamb, even a bull now and then. Suppose the Numantines sacrificed humans to their gods? If so, who would they sacrifice? Not their own when they had enemy captives on hand. He and Tiberius might be opened up after all, by the Numie priests. He shuddered at the thought, then gritted his teeth; he wouldn't go easy.

He wasn't fond of what the Numantines called a horse, either. His feet almost dragged on the ground, his mount was so sway-backed. It clopped along at its own pace, its bony frame hitting him in the wrong places. Apparently, it covered the ground, though. After another half day of riding, they emerged from a wood into a clearing at the foot of a rising hill. On top of it stood the city-fort of Numantia, and though the battle at the city-fort had taken place just a few weeks ago, Sextus was stunned by the change he saw.

The wooden beams of the stockade surrounding the city showed some scorch marks from the incendiaries fired at it, but everything else had been removed. Not a corpse remained, not even a horse. Not one vulture spotted the sky above the Numantine bastion. Every arrow shaft, broken pylum, sword, shield, and siege engine had been removed. More astonishing, not a trace of the Roman camp could be seen. It was as if the bloody battle hadn't occurred, that the legions of Rome had never been there at all. Instead, sheep and long-haired steers grazed before the back-switching walls of Numantia.

"Shades of Dis," uttered Sextus. He glanced at Tiberius and saw that he was equally amazed, taking in the pastoral panorama before him.

"Where are the bodies of Sacerdus Quarto and his son? Where are the remains of Ulpius?" uttered Tiberius, aghast.

"Over there." Sextus pointed to the far side of the city. Well beyond the walls on the west side of the city, a flock of black birds slowly looped around each other in the sky. Now and then one would waft down while another rose to replace it, in perfect unison it seemed.

"Isn't that where they have their necropolis? The place where they throw out their dead for the vultures to pick apart," said Sextus.

"They believe the birds fly the souls of their warriors to the heavens. Their gods are vested in the scavengers, so they say."

"Really? How bizarre. Where did you learn that?"

"I don't know, somewhere," Tiberius murmured distractedly. "Someone told me."

But, he always looked distracted now, thought Sextus, since the end of the war. Brooding over it, Sextus supposed, just like he did himself. Twenty thousand stout legionaries, five full legions with topnotch auxiliary support, and they had lost. Lost to a bunch of bearded wild men in crazy-colored long pants who slept with their horses. Lost because of horrible generalship. He shook his head, bad enough to be a part of such a disaster, but he hadn't drafted the war plan. Maybe he would have another chance in some future campaign. But, Tiberius, he thought, a ranking officer who had surrendered the army, where was he to go after all this mess was over?

Their horses placidly followed the head of the column as they zigzagged their way up the ramp to the gates of the city. Closer in, they could see the scars and gouges from Roman missiles in the wooden walls, broken arrow heads and pyla shafts cut off close to the surface. More work would be done to dig them out, and to rub out the lightest scorch marks on those otherwise sound beams. Some of them more badly burned had been cut out for replacement, not a daunting task considering the vast tracks of forest growing throughout the countryside.

They rode through the gate and found themselves in a small forum-like marketplace, just a few thousand feet in area. More than a thousand Numantines stood in a semicircle, men leaning on long spears or the hafts of their sword, with women next to them wearing solemn expressions on their faces, and children craning their necks, curious to see living Roman soldiers up close.

"Children," said Tiberius. "I can't remember seeing any children since we left Hispania Citerior. Do you think they send them away before battle?"

"We found a few in Malia," Sextus replied. He shrugged, "Maybe they did send them off."

"They were ready to fight and die to the end."

"With any luck we would have obliged them."

Tiberius turned to Sextus. "They could have done the same to us," he said sternly, "but they offered us peace instead."

"All the more fools them. We'll be back. Romans always come back. It might be Scipio next time, let them see how they like a taste of his cooking. It won't do any good to send their brats away then. Scipio would make sure that they'd be serving some Roman patriarch somewhere or another."

Tiberius stared at Sextus. "I'm sure you'd serve well under him yourself, Sextus, if given the chance."

"General Gracchus, Equitus Sextus, welcome to Numantia."

Dressed in an intricately embroidered, stunningly hued shirt that ended just above his knees, with a green sash cinched at his waist, Avarus waved his arm in a flourish and bowed slightly to the two Roman officers. Next to him stood many of the other chieftains also resplendently decked out, and behind them stood their women, wearing ankle-length dresses of the finest linen. They had tied off their long hair with exquisitely dyed ribbons, some in braids, some in long ponytails, while others merely reined in lightly their shining, thick tresses. Golden, red, raven, all the colors of the northern clans lived in those locks, rich jewels of the Hispanii on display.

"Come, you will be guests in my house until the ceremony tonight. We have refreshments waiting."

Tiberius and Sextus dismounted, and a slight, backwards ripple of movement coursed through the wary citizens of Numantia. Wary of the Roman monsters, Sextus thought.

Avarus led them to his house not more than 150 feet from the open market at the gateway. A plain, two-story wooden and stone structure, the house surprised Sextus in its simplicity. Large compared to other houses in the city, it was too small to accommodate the number of Hispanic chieftains gathered for the ceremony. A score of long, plank tables and benches line up in the front yard confirmed his observation.

"Do they expect us to eat with them?" he whispered to Tiberius in a strained voice.

"I don't know," Tiberius sighed. "We have to eat sometime."

"Please," said Granacus, one of the other chieftains said,"our gods demand us to be hospitable to strangers. It is part of our obedience to them, no more."

The two Romans exchanged glances. Sextus started to fidget, and Tiberius began to restrain him with his arm when Avarus stepped forward.

"Our Roman guests are tired from the journey. They will rest in my house until they feel that they have recovered. My regrets to the great chiefs of the Numantines and the Lusitanes. Please sit and have the priest bless the repast. I will join you all shortly."

Avarus led them into the front room of the house, closing the door behind Caciro and Sicounin. He gestured to the table inside, "Please sit."

Tiberius and Sextus slowly, uneasily, took seats at the table.

Avarus spoke briskly to his wife in his own language, then joined them at the table.

"I'm very sorry for the way our customs might have made you feel. Our way is to celebrate a warrior's good death, and many good warriors died in this war on both sides. Honor is our meaning, not humiliation, the same honor given to us by your father decades ago."

Tiberius paused before speaking. "I can see now how you defeated our commander."

Sicounin appeared with trenchers of mutton steeped in herbs covered by large ovals of brown bread. Caciro followed with four clay mugs of mead, and sat at the table.

"Go ahead," Avarus said, raising a mutton shank from his plate, "Pray to your gods and tuck in. You must be hungry."

In the middle of the night, Sextus stirred on the bed of furs beneath him.

They slept on the second floor above the house's main room. Windows had been opened to allow cool breezes from the hilltop to freshen the air in the room. It also allowed the sound of the last revelers' voices in the front yard to rouse those trying to sleep inside.

"Are you awake?"

Tiberius rolled away from Sextus.

"Tribune?"

"What do you want, Sextus?"

"When we rode in today, did you survey the city?"

Tiberius didn't answer.

"It's small, a small town. Fifty, maybe a hundred villages this size would fit inside Rome's walls."

"We've always known Numantia was small."

"They can't have that many people living here, they can't have that many warriors! How could they possibly beat us?"

Tiberius rolled away. "But, they did, and they have for years, decades. We win a battle, they win a battle, no one wins the war. Rome has been here for decades, maybe a hundred years. The Hispanii have been here for thousands of years. They may not possess great numbers, but they won't give up and they know how to fight." He mumbled as he pretended to drowse off, "Maybe my father saw that in them. Maybe that's why he knew enough to strike a fair peace."

The night turned hot, almost breathless in the loft where they tried to sleep. Summer was coming on in Hispania, and even the elevation of the hill town did little to offer relief from the occasional hot winds blowing.

A knock on the beam brought them fully awake. Sextus craned his neck to see Avarus at the head of the ladder at the edge of the loft.

"It is time," said the Numantine chieftain. He dropped out of sight below.

Sextus and Tiberius exchanged glances, then quickly rose to dress. After inspecting each other's tack, they descended to the first floor. There, waiting for them, were the three high chieftains of the Hispanii tribes, Rhetogenes, Avarus, and aged Megaravicus, the old high Druid Poet-Seer. Thurro, chief of the Lusones, had been killed in the assault on Numantia, his bones already glistening white on the sacred stones, polished by the gods' feathered spirits.

They all looked at the two Roman officers without emotion, though it was easy to imagine their deep-seated hatred for this newest set of invaders. Sextus and Tiberius stepped closer to them warily, their near hands grasping the hafts of their gladii.

Grey and lean, Megaravicus spoke in a raised voice to be heard both within and without the house.

"We proceed to the Nementon, the Sacred Grove of the Gods, to give thanks to the holy spirits for the peace—pax—they have brought to friends once foes."

He turned and walked slowly out of the house, followed by Avarus and Rhetogenes. Though uneasy, Tiberius and Sextus allowed their hands to drop to their sides and fell in behind the Hispanii chieftains. The rest of the warriors marched out after them.

Even at this dark hour in the morning, the people of Numantia lined the buildings to watch the procession pass by on its way out of the city fort. They were silent, almost eerily so. Sextus saw solemn faces in the crowd. Even the children wore sober expressions. This would be no ceremony for show, he realized. These people prayed that their gods would bless them with peace everlasting. Good luck, he thought.

The long parade of chiefs and warriors slowly made their way to the western wall, somewhat surprising to Tiberius and Sextus, since the city gate stood at the top of the rise at the south of the city. However, as they came closer to the wall, they detoured into an interior redoubt where they walked down a flight of stairs and traversed 150 feet to an oak door reinforced with iron bands. A guard lifted the heavy beam barring the door, and pushed to open it. It refused to budge until Caciro and several other young soldiers put their shoulders to it to shove it open. They drew their swords and passed through the doorway.

The others waiting inside soon heard the sounds of wood splitting and brush being thrashed. Finally, Caciro stuck his head in and nodded. The High Druid and the head chieftains led the party through the doorway into an underground passage, emerging outside the wall after a short walk.

Inside the city, the light from the moon had been deflected by the closely spaced buildings and walls. Outside in the open, it spilled everywhere in some unearthly white cast that washed out all other color. Sextus turned his head to Tiberius and thought he gazed upon the countenance of a man just raised from the dead, his sea blue eyes milky from the piercing light. He glanced at his own snow-white arm and realized that he must appear the same, and he felt a chill run through and through him.

Wending his way across the rise of the hilltop, Megaravicus raised his palms to the stunning, full moon and chanted a mournful dirge, and the chieftains joined him in deep harmony. The aching beauty of their song haunted the Roman equitus, though he could not fathom why.

They came up parallel to the necropolis, which caused the Hispanii to cease singing abruptly. The High Druid held his flat hand before him like the edge of a cleaver, as though he divided the way safely for the holy entourage behind him. As the men solemnly passed, they gazed about at the remains of the fallen warriors, their shields and ceremoniously broken swords propped against their remains resting on large, flat stones, hundreds of them. Some were black, desiccated corpses with little left for the birds to pick at, while others were nothing but white bones, whiter yet in the almost blinding moonlight, piled in small, informal pyramids. Soon they would be removed to be entombed in individual ceramic vats, the final part of their final journey.

As the procession moved slowly past the necropolis, men left to visit particular stones, dropping to their knees and calling to the heavens to care for and honor their fallen father, brother, son, or friend. Three times they would call above, then slowly rise and rejoin the snaking parade of warriors and priests leaving the dead behind. As they prayed, the notes from a pipe sounded in some unseen distance, evoking depths of sorrow unheard of before by the two Romans. Seeing the surprise and pain on their faces, Avarus came to them and placed a hand on each of their shoulders.

"They pray to Epona, Protector of the Dead, and to Dagda Ollathir, Father of All, to take care of our lost sons. He is above us in full tonight, a special night." The old chieftain saw the discomfort of the two Roman officers, and said, "We know that your ways are different. We sent your lost warriors to their gods honorably, on funeral biers. Unfortunately, we had none of your priests among us, but we prayed to Dagda to speak to Jupiter and Pluto, asking them to accept and honor the spirits of the Roman warriors in death."

Tiberius hesitated, then nodded. They began to walk again, when he stopped. "You lost two sons in this war. Are they here? Don't you wish to pray for them?"

He saw deep sadness fill the Numantine's eyes, quickly replaced by appreciation. "They are here. But, sealing our peace together is most important tonight. I'll come back when the Moon God visits us again and supplicate for my young boys."

The Romans nodded, and Tiberius said, "When we return to Rome, we will sacrifice to our gods for your sons' safe passage."

They continued the slow march to the Nementon, and, in the bloodless light of the moon, Sextus couldn't help but wonder once more if they'd ever see Rome again.

The giant trees of the Nementon shattered the brilliant moonlight into shafts of light impaling the ground like a volley of pila. The clearing in the middle of the ancient grove bathed in the moon's full light. There, in the center, Sextus and Tiberius could see an old stone altar in high relief framed by deep shadows. Caciro gestured to them to enter the meadow and to sit at the base of a huge tree, an oak, grey from age or color, Tiberius could not tell.

The Numantine and other Hispanii chieftains file in, followed by their aides and the other warriors, and sat in a wide half circle around the edge of the clearing facing the old stone altar. Megaravicus stood in front and raised his hands to the heavens. He sang.

Women moved from behind opposite sides of the altar in step to the High Druid's song. String instruments and flat drums joined in from the shadows, and pipes like the ones they had heard in the necropolis, only now keeping time with the drumbeat. The women formed a line in front of the High Druid and began dancing vigorously, their arms twisting and twining languidly in the moonbeams, their shoulders and heads unmoving. They pivoted in the earth, occasionally kicking bare feet up from their knees, then crossing their legs back and forth, dancing in a flurry to the growing fury of the instruments. Curiously, they dressed plainly in long linen gowns, adorned by the slightest embroidery in a strange confusion of interwoven designs. Their hair fell to their shoulders, bouncing as they jumped straight up in the air, single silver runic amulets flying high, too, from slender leather cords. A far cry from the bare bodies of the priestesses of Cybele, Sextus thought.

The women's voices began to harmonize with Megaravicus, gorgeous as they phrased undecipherable chants, and the organized frenzy of the din grew around them, the Numantine warriors rising to their feet to begin singing and joining in with the dancing priestesses. If only to see better, Tiberius and Sextus rose to their feet. Avarus and Rhotegenes had joined Megaravicus in front of the altar, dancing and singing along with the old Druid and the other chieftains. Like a miracle, pots of drink seemed to materialize out of the moonlight, though the Romans thought they glimpsed the slender forms of young girls flitting around with armloads of weighted earthenware jars.

Two were thrust from different sides into the hands of Tiberius and Sextus. "Drink!" cried out Caciro. They both hesitantly took sips.

The liquid burned like silver in Tiberius's mouth and down his throat all the way to his belly. He coughed at the same time as Sextus. Caciro gazed at them madly, shouting out above the singing and dancing, "It's called the water of life. Drink!"

They sipped again, and knowing what to expect, managed the fiery drink better as it burned down again. "I have never drunk such a potent beverage in my life," Tiberius said.

"It's strong enough to take your life," uttered Sextus.

They drank more sparingly, surveying the wild carouse whirling around them. Some of the young men chased after the girls, who outran them to the shadows of the trees. Others danced together, working to outdo their partners in their ferocious joy. Still sipping, Tiberius leaned over to Sextus and said loud enough for the equitus to hear, "They're celebrating. Celebrating their great victory with their gods."

Silently, the two men watched the revelers smiling and crying, singing, and dancing.

Caciro put his head between theirs and said, "If it was up to me, I'd have cut both your throats. You'd be watching us dance, each of you, hanging from a tree. You came to take our lives, our souls, to own us. You killed my two brothers, and you should die for it."

Tiberius and Sextus half-turned to face Caciro, their hands on their swords. The young Numantine grabbed each by a shoulder and squeezed with his massive hands, almost causing the two Roman officers to buckle.

"When we took your camp, we found how you questioned our captured warriors. We should have done the same to you. But, we're Numantines, we don't stretch our captives over a forge fire. We don't stick our enemies's heads on spikes." He shrugged, "And, you're my father's guests. Apparently, your father," he said, jerking his head at Tiberius, "spared us years ago, gave us a fair peace when we were at his mercy. We can only do the same. Enjoy yourselves, drink up. You'll soon be on your way home."

The tall Numantine warrior slapped them on their backs and disappeared into the crowd. Tiberius and Sextus glanced at each other, all the while keeping their hands on their swords.

Avarus appealed to them to stay longer, but Tiberius insisted that they had to leave to ensure that the Roman army was ready to march out of Numantia.

"We had hoped to show you greater friendship in the Numantine way. We want you and your countrymen to know that we can be good neighbors in peace."

Tiberius said, "I truly appreciate your gracious hospitality, Honorable Avarus, but we have stayed too long. The treaty has been signed. Better we should leave now than chance the renewal of hostilities that could be disastrous to us all."

Avarus dropped his head almost to his chest. "That would be unfortunate."

"Let us go, Avarus, let us go home."

The short chieftain pressed his lips together, and said, "Of course. Caciro, please see that the tribune's and equitus's horses are prepared. Bring up the warriors escorting them back to their camp."

He turned his attention back to Tiberius, "I do have one last bit of business to take care of, however. Please, follow me."

Uneasily, Tiberius and Sextus followed the chieftain out of his house on to the street. They walked past several cross streets until they came to a large, beige building, built with heavy blocks of stone, and bare of any windows. A contingent of guards kept watch around the building, two at the thick, front door. Avarus walked past them without a word, pulled out a large cast-iron key and thrust it into a huge padlock. The lock sprung, and Avarus removed it from the door. He gestured to the two soldiers, who exerted themselves pulling the massive door open. Avarus motioned for Sextus and Tiberius to follow him into the building.

After torches were lit, the Romans walked behind Avarus into the dark, narrow opening. The light from the flames revealed a jumble of furniture, rugs, rolls of fabric, shelves of silverware with some golden bowls and flasks mixed in, and a substantial collection of weapons, spears, axes, swords of different lengths and sizes, shields, even some armor. Fine earthenware covered the edges of the floor next to the walls, and in the back, they could see the silhouettes of a couple of war chariots, one looking like it was from Egypt, another from Pergamum. Tiberius imagined them to be trophies from their days allied to Carthage. Next to them were other armaments easy to recognize, loricas, pila, shields, and helmets from fallen Romans. Clearly, the two Romans had been invited into the Numantine treasury. Modest by most standards, certainly Rome's coffers, the Numantine spoils nevertheless showed their outsized success over the legions of the Republic.

Turning, he saw from Sextus's dark expression that he had come to the same realization. Tiberius faced Avarus.

"Why are we here, Avarus?" Tiberius asked the question in a constrained voice, trying to tamp down his rising anger at being so shamed.

Avarus could see it. "We wish you offer you some gifts, Tiberius Sempronius Gracchus, to honor you for keeping with the peaceful tradition of your father in the heavens."

"I don't see anything here that I wish to have."

"I understand," Avarus said, "but you will want these."

He gestured to a small wooden table behind him upon which lay a sheepskin sack that bulged at the sides from its contents. Tiberius hesitated, then walked over and opened it.

"The ledgers," he said aloud. He quickly pulled out several to examine, eventually saying, "my ledgers of the army finances." Tiberius looked up at Avarus, incredulous. "They were lost when you took our camp. The camp burned, so I thought they were gone forever."

Avarus shook his head, "No. After the camp fell, riders headed directly to the officers' quarters. They found them in a large tent with the body of a centurion, who apparently succumbed to his wounds. The riders brought them to me. It didn't take long to realize what they were and to whom they belonged. It was my hope that we would be able to restore them to you."

In spite of himself, Tiberius smiled. "Do you know what this means?"

"Yes, I do." Avarus stated it plainly. "With your ledgers in hand, no Roman can charge you for stealing public funds. The tablets will lay out all of the campaign's expenses."

Except for the interval when Mancinus and Fabius had hold of them while he tramped throughout Northern Italia scrounging around for new troops. Still, he would be able establish that he had been separated from the main army on Mancinus's orders, with the ledgers out of his control during that period.

Avarus leaned in, "We might seem like a simple people with our livestock and horses, and our long beards. But we know about these things, Tribune Quaestor Sempronius. We've been dealing with Roman patriarchs in Hispania for many, many years. Take these ledgers in good health."

Tiberius nodded his head, "I will Avarus. Thank you."

He turned to leave, and Avarus said, "Take anything else you want. Gold, silver, whatever we have, what little we have, is yours."

Sextus looked at Tiberius anew, his interest piqued. Tiberius shook his head, "Nothing. We can take nothing, unless we want to be accused of accepting bribes."

Avarus came to his side, "One small item. I want to give you a personal present, Tiberius, from me alone. Please."

Tiberius searched around until his eyes lit upon another small table covered with small leather bags. He leaned over and sniffed. "Frankincense. I'll take this bag of frankincense to sacrifice to the gods for saving us all, Roman and Numantine alike."

Avarus smiled. "A noble choice," he said.

Chapter 20. East of Cosa

The morning rain had left a chill on the streets, causing Appius to shiver all the way from the baths to the Forum. The columns loomed darkly overhead, the statues of the gods and Roman heroes at their tops lost in the hazy mist of the low clouds. He squinted at the sky, wondering if the sun would break out on this dull, grey day, or would he have to suffer through its gloom all day long. The thought that this was only early fall, with the prospect of winter to come made him even glummer. Not a good place to be in times of crisis like this. Sure enough, two jackdaws flew above, interweaving as they screeched some god's displeasure at the ministrations of the men below. But, which men?

The army had returned, or what was left of it, from the debacle in Numantia. Hostilius Mancinus was under house arrest, Quintus Fabius was dead, along with an entire Roman legion, a loss the Republic could ill afford. It seemed that every speech in the Senate and throughout Rome raged against Mancinus, the Numantines, and Tiberius Sempronius Gracchus. Tiberius! His son-in-law, blamed for the ignominious peace with the upstart Numantines! But what choice had he with the men starving and putrefying, their backs up against a raging river? And, where was he now?

"Your point is sound, Appius," Mucius Scaevola said, "though it might not carry much weight in the court of calumny." The sharp little lawyer had been leaning against the pedestal supporting a statue of Mercury at the southern edge of the Forum. He wore a mid-calf tunic that didn't hide the bronze color of his skin bathed by the sun after summering in Herculaneum. Appius wondered how the slight man stayed warm in such dress, but the wind and rain didn't seem to bother him at all. Appius pulled the fold of his toga closely around his shoulders.

"Don't bait me, Scaevola," he said impatiently, "just tell me the truth of the situation."

Scaevola shrugged, straightening up at Appius's side as he walked into the Forum.

"Nasica is in the Hostilia Curia readying the senators to condemn Mancinus and his officers. Rufus is on the Rostrum pleased to be charged with working up the crowd against the disgraced consul."

Appius cringed, tightening his lips over his clenched teeth. "All right.

We'll go to Rufus first."

"Gracchus! Gracchus!"

The name came out like a screech, an angry epithet spit by the small, round-faced man turned red by his fury, brandishing his fist like a cudgel in the air. "Where is Gracchus? Why is he not in custody to pay the price for his incompetence, his greed, his treason! He not only betrayed the Republic in Hispania and gladly consorted with our mortal enemies the Numantine barbarians, he also raped and pillaged his way through all of northern Italia! While raising an undisciplined mob of brigands, a virtual horde of future slaves and condemned murderers to fill his legion, he helped himself to all of the fruits of the hard work of honest farmers, leaving them and their families to starve! But, where is he, this infamous, capital criminal? Where is he? No one knows!"

Rufus stepped back from the podium for a moment, using a silk cloth to wipe the copious sweat that had formed on his brow despite the chilling breeze blowing through the Comitia. Without looking, he took a flagon of water from the slave to his left and drank long. Then, he tossed the flagon backward in the direction of the suddenly scrambling slave and stepped forward again.

When Rufus first had climbed up onto the Rostrum, a handful of men stopped to listen, merely out of curiosity. Fifteen minutes into his speech, more than a hundred had gathered around, with others following to see what was going on.

Appius and Scaevola had taken their places on the Senate building side near the back. The clouded sky muted the flashing colors of the ramming prows taken from wrecked Carthagian ships after the first Punic war. They had been mounted on the Rostrum as trophies. Now, they appeared to be the brooding visages of birds, raptors waiting to pick apart the flesh and bones of the shrouded men below.

"His commander Hostilius Mancinus awaits trial under house arrest. Many of the centurions and optios present at this horrific retreat have been disciplined most decidedly. But, where is the mastermind of this unparalleled humiliation of our republic? Where is Gracchus? Hiding in some sin pit in the bowels of Rome, shaking from fear of the proper punishment for his treason? Where is Gracchus? Still in Numantia cozying up to the Hispanii scum who love traitors in their midst? Where is Gracchus? Cavorting in northern Italia with his cutthroats and slave rebels? Where is Gracchus?" he bellowed, "Where is Gracchus?"

"Bacchus' balls," whispered Appius, "will he not shut up? If he keeps going on, this crowd could riot. My daughter Claudia, my grandchildren, and Cornelia all could be in danger! Where in Hades is Tiberius?"

"Maybe Sempronius Gracchus has scampered to some prurient bordello," Rufus continued, "on some Greek isle, perhaps, where he can cavort with sluts and satyrs, spending freely the funds that he was supposed to safeguard as quaestor."

"Jupiter's beard!" Appius muttered.

"While our soldiers wasted away from lack of food, Quaestor Gracchus had at his disposal thousands of sestercae to do with what he pleased. What did he do with that coin? Where are the ledgers he was charged with safeguarding, even with his life!

"No," Rufus shook his head ruefully, "a coward of his kind would not present proof of his embezzlement any more than he has produced himself to answer to his capital crimes. Where is this scavenger, this carrion-eater, this 'gracchus,' Tiberius Sempronius Gracchus?"

Rufus raised and shook his hands at the heavens. Appius spun to Scaevola. "All right, this has gone on long enough. Scaevola, you must go up there and blunt the pig's slurs."

Scaevola's mouth split into a cat grin, and Appius sighed, "I'll pay you!"

"Ten thousand?"

"For Laverna's sake, yes. Now, go!"

But, before the famous lawyer could climb the Rostrum steps, another figure bounced up them, tall, lean, with a head of long, thick, black hair.

"You are wrong, Lucius Rufus Faba. Gracchus was not a traitor in Hispania. He did not betray Rome or pocket the army payroll. In fact, he saved the legions from certain destruction, 20,000 men and camp followers. Instead of slandering him, you should be demanding that he receive the Grass Crown."

He looked familiar to Appius, but he couldn't quite place him.

As he talked, the tall horseman closed in on Rufus, towering over him, making him to appear noticeably uncomfortable. "If you have reason or right to know the whereabouts of the quaestor's ledgers—"

"I have every right as a dutiful senator of Rome!" Rufus said sharply.

"—I suggest you go see them for yourself. They have been deposited in the city treasury under consular supervision, as witnessed by the Vestilium Maxima."

"Consular supervision?" Rufus quickly asked, "Who?"

Appius whispered rapidly in Scaevola's ear, "It can't be Lepidus Porcina, he left Rome rather than deal with the Mancinus mess. It must be one of the new men, Scipio's man Philus, if Rufus has his way." Then, he said "I know this fellow. But, I just can't place him."

"Consul-elect Serranus, I believe," said the dark, looming man, "though I'm not sure. I have met neither of the new men."

Rufus tried to hide his sudden defensive position by puffing up his chest, "And the money?"

"Alas, the strong boxes were lost to the Numantines."

Rufus sneered, "How do you know of all this?"

"Because I was there," the tall man said. "I am Sextus Decimus Paetus, equitus of Mancinus's cavalry."

Of course! thought Appius, the young equestrian who had sold him Tiberius's horse.

"I was at the side of Tribune Sempronius Gracchus," Sextus continued, "when he covered the flank of our army and struck a peace with the Numantines that allowed us to withdraw without harassment or further loss. In the course of negotiations, he was able to secure the army ledgers and also some incense to sacrifice to the gods for our safe passage."

"Gracchus sued for peace? A quaestor not a tribune? By whose authority?"

"Consul Mancinus's, who during the course of the campaign, commissioned the quaestor as tribune of the Ninth. I was there for that conversation, too, little bean."

Muffled laughter ran through the crowd, and Appius felt himself breathing more easily.

"You should stick to slandering men in your own class, Rufus. Or, would you like to compare your military record with Gracchus's?"

Rufus blanched, but before he could reply, the heavens opened up, scattering the crowd to find shelter under the eaves of the adjoining marketplace.

Sextus fixed Rufus with a withering stare, then trotted down the steps of the Rostrum, hopped over a side wall, and jogged away through the rain.

Appius and Scaveola hurried toward the Hostilia Curia where the Senate met to discuss the fate of the disgraced Mancinus. Scaveola took up a post near a column beneath the high porch ceiling, while Appius rushed through the open front doors. He held up abruptly in the vestibulum to shake and squeeze the moisture out of his toga. Then, as best as he could, he sauntered into the Senate chamber in stately fashion.

The tall building with its round central floor was filled with gloom despite the long, iron sconces sputtering flames and smoke above from their oil fires. Even the ever-present pigeons were not flying about to release their good-luck droppings on the senators below. Instead, they clustered together for warmth on the ledges of the high, open windows, which had been designed to let in light, but now served as apertures for the blustery wind and rain.

The senators huddled together, too, or held their togas close to their bodies with crossed arms, some covering their heads with folds as though at a religious ceremony. Others slumped as far down as they could below the waist-high marble walls separating the floor from the front row of benches as if the chill was being blown inside the building. Still and all, more than half the senators were in attendance, somewhat surprising on such a cold day. Consul-elect Lucius Furius Philus presided today, so of course, standing in the middle of the black marble floor stood Scipio Nasica holding sway.

Immediately as Appius entered, Scipio Nasica turned his head around. "Well, now we can begin in earnest. Appius Claudius Pulcher has arrived to guide us with his shining light."

The senators all laughed, and Appius smiled as well. "Alas, Scipio, I am not Diogenes. But, then again, you are not an honest man."

Once more, the men in the chamber laughed, louder, thought Appius. Even Scipio himself grinned.

"So, what mayhem are you proposing now, Nasica? A grain tax on plebeians? Or, would it be salt?"

"No common subjects today, Pulcher. Today we discuss how best to deal with the Numantia debacle and the perpetrators of the same."

"I see. And, if I might be so bold, whom do you count among the so-called perpetrators, oh so noble Nasica?"

"Why Gaius Hostilius Mancinus, of course," the tall, sinewy senator said, "Quintus Fabius, postumously, of course, the Tribunes Horatius, Secundus, Nicomedes, Cadmus, and," Nasica smiled his skull smile, "to our regret, your kinsman the Quaestor Tiberius Sempronius Gracchus."

"I see," Appius said calmly, fighting to maintain his composure. "Your list of culprits is long, Nasica, creative, and extreme."

"All those complicit in the greatest defeat in Rome's history, yes, all responsible must answer to the people of Rome. Indeed, extreme measures are warranted."

Appius made his way past the benches where the senators sat, out onto the floor. "Extreme enough to desecrate the memory of a fallen warrior in the service of Rome?"

A collective gasp echoed throughout the airy hall, followed by a murmur of voices barely whispering the surprise and speculation in every corner. Everyone knew that Gracchus was missing—was Claudius Pulcher privy to new information? Was his son-in-law dead? What did he know? How did he know what every Roman wanted to know?

Nasica drew himself up straight to his full, imposing height. "Many a good Roman has fallen to the barbaric swords of Numantia, Claudius Pulcher. It is in their memory that we have assembled this inquest."

"But you besmirch one who died a hero, Nasica, absent to defend himself from these scurrilous charges."

Nasica paused solemnly. At length, he said, "You speak of your son-in-law Gracchus?"

Appius held close to his answer, dragging out the drama of the moment while as one the members of the Senate leaned forward in anticipation.

"Why, of course not! I have no idea where Tiberius is, I speak of Tribune Quintus Fabius, of course, slain while leading a cavalry charge against the Numantine army. How can you prosecute this noble Roman hero, who because he made the ultimate sacrifice, is unable to defend himself?"

Voices groaned from the benches, senators waved their hands in disgust, and shouts carried above the milling men, "Tricks as usual, Pulcher!" "A skunk never changes its stripes!" "Neither does a tiger!" shouted one of Appius's supporters. "Rat-trapped, Nasica," laughed Crassus, wealthy beyond measure and beholden to no one.

Nasica drew back his head, and said, "Fabius died bravely but foolishly. This does not acquit him of his crimes, plundering the army's war chest and abetting Mancinus in his cowardice."

"If Fabius Quintus plundered the payroll, that relieves Tiberius Gracchus of any guilt, no? And, how did Fabius abet Mancinus when he was already dead? By summoning evil spirits from Hades?"

"You are impertinent and sacrilegious, Pulcher. It is common knowledge that Mancinus and Quintus pilfered coin and tribute on a regular basis, wealth that rightly belonged to Rome. And, who was in charge of the army script when it disappeared? Tiberius Sempronius Gracchus, that's who. If you know where he is, Pulcher, you could be charged as an accomplice."

"To what? Saving 20,000 Roman legionaries from massacre?"

"Hah!" Nasica sneered. "As if you could save anything. Review your own hapless performance as praetor at Salassi."

Appius reddened, and out of gritted teeth, snapped, "At least I won in the end, Nasica, a far cry from your ignominious role in the destruction of our legions by the Pannonians. Interesting that the same Hostilius Mancinus whom you are bent upon punishing can brag of a better record in Macedonia than yours."

Nasica's face filled with dark blood. Appius believed the Pontifex Maximus and former consul would have killed him right there, on the spot, on the Senate floor, if he'd had a sword. As it was, Appius wasn't sure that Nasica wouldn't just launch himself and use his bare hands.

"But, I digress," Appius said before Nasica could move. "The question is whether or not we can condemn a Roman officer in absentia, as Scipio Nasica hopes to indict Fabius Quintus, a noble, fallen warrior who cannot defend his own honor. He would do the same to one who proved his courage as a tyro at Carthage, first over the wall, winner of the Mural Crown, a man worthy of the Grass Crown for saving four legions from certain destruction, legions that live to fight for Rome another day."

Appius paused, then took a step toward the middle of the floor and turned to the seated senators, his hands held out wide from his sides.

"Of course, I speak of Tiberius Sempronius Gracchus. True, he is my son-in-law, married to my beloved, only daughter Claudia. Also true, no one knows where he is. For all we know, he might be holed up somewhere between here and Numantia, recovering from wounds suffered while defending his men. Indeed, he may have succumbed to these wounds, and will never be able to ward off Nasica's cruel attack. No one knows. But, I put it to you, august members of the Senate of Rome, we must not pass judgment on men such as Fabius Quintus or Tiberius Sempronius Gracchus without ascertaining exactly what happened in Numantia and whether or not they share any responsibility for this terrible outcome."

He waved one hand in front of him and away as he said, "Pass sentence on Hostilius Mancinus, no one can defend his colossal failure. Question the tribunes and pass sentence upon them if found wanting. But, allow the memory of Fabius Quintus to rest with his bones. And defer any judgment of Tiberius Gracchus until his whereabouts have been determined. If alive, bring him to the Hostilia for a full accounting. If dead, dead let him be."

"But, how will we know?" shouted Marcus Octavius, leaping to his feet unsteadily, Tiberius's old friend whose anguish could be heard in his words.

Appius gathered his toga around his shoulders and said, "Members of the Senate, I will find Tiberius Sempronius Gracchus myself. If he is alive, I will bring him here. If dead, I will grieve his loss and sacrifice to the gods. One way or another, you will learn his fate."

"And, how long do you propose for this noble quest to last?" Rufus Fava said. After his disappointing experience at the Rostrum, he had returned to the Senate.

"Give me two months, "said Appius. "If I cannot locate him, the Senate can do as you see fit. Two months is all I ask. Those in agreement, please join me for the division." He looked at Philus and said, "With your leave, Consul-elect."

Philus, a prune of a man with a long patrician pedigree, glanced quickly at Nasica. Nasica's expression remained a stone enigma, and Appius seized the moment by saying, "Please, Consul Philus, for the sake of Roman justice."

Appearing extremely uncomfortable, Philus nodded slightly.

The members of the Senate left their seats and formed two groups, one standing with Appius, the other with Scipio Nasica. Rufus stood at Nasica's elbow, while Octavius joined Appius.

Philus counted, as did several other officiating members. Finally, Philus spoke,

"Against Appius Claudius Pulcher's resolution, 179. For Appius Claudius Pulcher, 182."

Just a three-man margin? Appius almost collapsed.

"The senator's resolution has carried. From this day forward, he will be given two months to search for Tiberius Sempronius Gracchus. Within this time period, he either will bring Gracchus before the Senate, or his son-in-law will be declared dead. So be it."

The senators all stirred, murmuring their opinions when a clap of thunder cracked overhead, causing them all to duck reflexively. The interior of the Hostilia Curia grew even darker.

"All right, senators, let's move on," Philus said.

Glancing only once at Appius with a countenance of utter hatred, Nasica Scipio said, "The business at hand is the disposition of Gaius Hostilius Mancinus."

Exhausted, Appius made his way to the exit, ready to go home. As he reached the vestibulum and looked out the double doorways, he saw that the sky of Rome was black as night, the rain coming down in a waterfall. This at midday, he thought, terribly ominous.

He drew his toga over his head and started to march out into the rain toward the Palatine. Scaveola fell into step with him, ignoring the pounding rain.

"The door is still open, but barely," Appius warned. "Unless Tiberius returns soon to defend himself, he will be exiled in absentia or declared dead."

Cornelia sat in her usual posture, on the edge of her chair as if ready to leap up at any moment. He always wondered how she could look so relaxed yet poised to pounce at the same time. Sort of like a cat, he thought.

"He must come home. He must be found and brought home to defend himself. Where could he be?"

"You have no idea, some special place where he might like to go?" Appius asked.

"No," Cornelia said, her voice a mixture of scorn and anxiety, "he wasn't the kind to go daydreaming off."

"Huh," Appius grunted. He dropped his eyes in thought. He looked up, "What about Claudia, has she said anything?"

"She is crushed with worry. I do not think she knows anything."

He shook his head, "This worries me. Now I'm wondering if Nasica, Rufus, and their band ambushed him on the way home."

"He was supposed to return by sea," she said, exasperated. "Do you think they attacked him between Ostia and Rome?"

"Ah, but he didn't arrive by sea!" Appius said. "His legion landed in Ostia, true enough, but none of the centurions or optios said he was on any of the ships."

"Then, he couldn't have been surprised by Nasica and his lot. They don't know where he is any more than we do."

Appius paced, rubbing his chin in thought. "Nasica and Rufus had no reason to waylay Tiberius. They intend a much more humiliating demise for him."

He ruminated some more. "We don't know where he is. There is one, however, who might know. At least, he seemed to know more about Tiberius than anyone else in Rome."

"You're talking about the Equitus at the Comitia. Sextus Decimus, the man who sold us Tiberius's horse."

"That's right, Sextus Decimus Paetus!" Appius almost shouted. He looked again at this amazing woman, who seemed to have more knowledge of men's doings than any man he'd ever met, including himself.

"I met him briefly after his father and I closed the deal, the big stallion in exchange for his son's commission as Tiberius's Equitus. Sextus was there when Tiberius and I took possession of the horse. Apparently, the young horseman did well in Numantia, better than everyone else, at least."

"But no better than my son." She almost pierced him with those sharp green eyes of hers.

"No, of course not," he said.

"You should visit him, Appius, see if he knows anything of Tiberius's whereabouts."

"Yes, Cornelia, I'll go this very day."

He might have married Cornelia, if he hadn't been so devoted to his wife Antistia. Of course, Cornelia was somewhat older than he, though never less than beautiful all her life. In any case, Cornelia never would have had him, and he loved Antistia.

Sextus Decimus Paetus lived beyond the walls of Rome, slightly north of the great city on a small mountainside. His villa was not small, however, but huge and sprawling, surrounded by miles, it seemed, of orchards, vineyards, and grain fields. Further up the small mountain, Appius could see another complex, a vast covered structure made of stone commanding the left side, with pens on each long wall. A road separated the building and a series of small pastures on the right, neatly laid out in perfect rectangular patterns. He noted what he thought to be several horses grazing in the grass, though at this distance it was hard to be sure. It made sense, however, since the Decimi fortune rested upon the buying and selling of equine flesh. From there, they had expanded into salt, olive oil, wine, vinegar, dates, figs, sun-dried fish, grain, flax, linens, semiprecious stones, and of course, slaves.

Appius was rich. He and his family never had to worry about means or even living a life of bounteous excess if that was their choice. Like most modern men of his time, he espoused the teachings of the Greek ascetics, and had sent his children to be taught by Diophanes and Polydius, just like Gracchus. Thus, he cared little for the life of Croesus, thinking of coin only as a tool to achieve what he wanted, the power in Rome to effect good. Most prominent Romans felt the same way, though their concepts of good varied greatly.

As he and his entourage entered the gates of Sextus's villa, however, Appius started to wonder. Two rows of marbled columns ran 200 feet down both sides of what looked more like a lake than a pond. Pedestals seemed to climb from the water bearing magnificent, perfect bronze statues—by Phidias himself? Appius halted like he'd looked Medusa directly in her eyes. The head house slave leading him to Sextus now stood waiting several feet ahead. Appius attempted to hurry and catch up, but the marvelous tile mosaics on the walls slowed him again. Among flying fish and serpents, a luscious Venus arose out of blue-green sea foam, colors so vivid they almost blinded him. Across from her stood Vulcan, smiting his mighty forge, sending hot sparks into the air, the background black except for the glowing aura around his intense, craggy face.

In another mosaic, Diana sent an arrow toward an antlered hart amid a richly dark wood of green and gold foliage. A lean, grey dog with teeth bared at her prey crouched beside the goddess. Appius saw a score more of such mosaics hanging along the long passageway between the columns, and he imagined the opposite passageway bore similar masterpieces. A domicile for the gods themselves! he thought.

"Master," the slave called out, and Appius moved quickly toward him.

Again, in the main house's peristylum, the furnishings, art, and other appointments were meticulous and fabulous. Near a bubbling fountain of a Greek youth pouring water out of a jar, Sextus lay stretched out on a couch, reading. As soon as the slave announced Appius, he stood up and reached out his hand to clasp Appius's.

"Greetings Consul Claudius, I am surprised to see you. Welcome."

"I'm long removed from the consulship, Sextus Decimus, just an ordinary senator, now. But thank you for the courtesy."

"Yes," said Sextus, taller it seemed than when he spoke on the Rostrum, and even more striking with his long black hair. "Can I offer you anything? Would you like something to eat, or a drink, perhaps?"

"Thank you, no, I've eaten all the way here, I'm afraid. Boring, travel is so slow, there's really nothing else to do." He patted his girth, "I believe that's what has banished my lean warrior profile."

"Yes," said Sextus slowly, seeming a bit puzzled and somewhat impatient.

Appius hurried to the point, "But, I don't need to keep you with idle prattle, Sextus, we all have busy schedules. May I sit?"

Sextus barely glanced at his slave, and another couch appeared instantly. Appius sat down as Sextus reclined back on his couch. "What can I do for you then, Senator Claudius?"

Appius took a deep breath to begin. He was used to beguiling people from whom he wanted something, whether it was a better price on a toga, or a vote in the Senate for one of his pet projects. This Sextus threw him, though, calm all the time as if his wealth set him aside from other humans' meager concerns, as if he were an immortal. However, he was being polite enough.

"Sextus, you know who I am and our families have had dealings together before. I've been around for a long time. I've tried to serve Rome well, which means I could never be coy or shy. My family name and my own actions precede me wherever I go. I am easy to find, easy to know."

"Of course, Senator Claudius."

"But not my son-in-law, Tiberius Sempronius Gracchus."

Realization spread over Sextus's face, and he curled his lips in what could have been perceived as a small knowing smile, almost smug. He nodded his head slightly, "Your son-in-law, of course." He stretched on the couch, "How can I help you, Senator Claudius?"

"I saw you in the Comitia yesterday, on the Rostrum contradicting Rufus. You did a masterful job of dismantling him and discrediting his slanderous statements, sheer obloquy on his part."

Sextus pursed his lips as if he'd tasted something sour. "Rufus is a baboon. I know, I saw one in Utica once, in a cage."

"He's a dangerous baboon. Mancinus is not the only first man he's brought down with his huge lies. I fear that Tiberius will be next if he isn't here to defend himself. You saved him yesterday with your plain truths. But, you're no longer in service. Why did you defend him against Rufus?"

Sextus sat up, "Because by attacking our tribune's record, he attacked the reputation of the entire Ninth."

Appius bored into him, "And your reputation as well."

"The Ninth fought well in Hispania. Your son-in-law fought well."

"And you, too, Sextus Paetus," Appius said quietly. "We read of your courage in letters from Tiberius. All of Rome knows of your remarkable feats, your Mural Crown."

Sextus slumped back down on the couch, his head turned away from the older man. "No little turd like Rufus should be allowed to insult any soldiers. What war was ever he in? He's just getting back at us for procuring goods from his estate. We should have done with him then, rather than have him nipping at everyone's heels now."

Appius ignored the seditious nature of the remark and said, "Do you know where Tiberius is?"

Sextus turned his head to look at the older man. "I do not. Tiberius discharged his legion in Tarraco except for the cohort given to him by Mancinus in Rome. The remains of the Ninth embarked from Tarraco to sail for Ostia and Rome. Tiberius marched his cohort north. I haven't seen him since."

Appius fretted, "Even on foot, he and his men should have arrived in Rome by now. Or, we should have received word from him, at least."

Sextus shrugged, glancing away.

"Sextus, I ask you, can you remember anything of where he might be? Is it at all possible that he left Hispania safely, that we still can hold out hope of his survival?"

Sextus frowned, "I'm sorry, Senator Claudius, I don't think I can be of much help."

Appius shrank a little, his breathing a bit shallower.

The tall young man then twisted around again. "Maybe one possibility. Up near Cosa, when we first marched for Hispania, the legion came upon a bad road. A good part of it had disappeared into a morass. Whoever built it in the first place should have been flogged and crucified. In any case, the tribune was very worried about being late to join Mancinus in Numantia, and he couldn't spend a great deal of time properly repairing the road. So, they used logs as a temporary fix, which worked well enough. However, he vowed that after the campaign was over, he would come back this way and repair the road properly, for good." Sextus fixed eyes on Appius's. "That's where he might be. The gods know Cosa isn't much anymore, and there isn't much around it either. It could be a good place to lick his wounds. That's where I would look."

"Thank you, Sextus," Appius said as he shot to his feet. "You may have saved Tiberius from utter catastrophe."

"Yes, maybe so. He was a pretty good officer, all in all." He eased back on the couch and closed his eyes, draping his arms above his head to block out the light from the setting sun. "In any case, I'm out of war forever. Too ludicrous to have the likes of Mancinus as a commander and types like Nasica and Rufus giving him his marching orders. I'm finished with all that. I'll stick to raising horses."

Appius had reached the door leading out of the peristylum when he stopped. "One last question. What became of the big horse we gave to Tiberius?"

Sextus shook his head, "Gone. Lost."

Chapter 21: Remorse

The dying fall leaves dropping from the trees whipped around the horses. The chill air driving them this far north reminded Appius every time of how he hated the cold, the winter, freezing to death even though he was still alive. Tucked in behind a group of mercenaries hired for the trip, he still felt every cutting blast of wind, every icy raindrop, the utter inadequacy of his trousers, wool socks, heavy tunic, wool shawl, and sheepskin wrap in keeping him warm. What a horrible way to celebrate the autumnal equinox, he moaned to himself over and over.

He longed for home, for Rome, for the hot baths near the Forum. Time and again he thought of turning back. Time and again he saw Cornelia's expression when he faced her, having returned without Tiberius. He rode on.

He felt lonely, too. Though ten former legionaries surrounded him, they weren't much for conversation, at least, the kind he enjoyed. Amiable as they were, discussions of where they'd gotten this or that scar entertained only for so long. He wished he had asked Scaevola or Diophanes to come with him. But, they probably would have said no.

The gloom descendant upon him wasn't helped by what he had seen traveling up here. In the shadows of the trees lining the sloping road, he saw shadow beings huddled close in the underbrush. A stab of panic rushed through him at the thought that they could be shades from Pluto's dark world—had they come for his spirit? Then, Ajax rushed them on his mule, waving his sword, jeering, "Get out, dung bugs, or I smash your pointy heads!"

They scattered deeper into the underbrush. Spirits of the dead? The party rode on.

Later in the day, the ghostly creatures appeared again at the road's edge where the woods gave them cover for a quick retreat. Ajax moved to dig his heels in his mule's flanks again, when Appius held him back with his hand, "Wait."

He looked more closely at them, and realized that apparitions they might be, but most of them were women and children. He failed to see one grown man among them, not even an old grandfather. The sight troubled him, though he wasn't sure why. They kept riding slowly up the road.

Some of the children crept closer to the roadside. Like cats stealing their way up onto the dinner table for scraps, he thought, darting their eyes around, skittish and ready to jump at the first sign of being shooed away. So were these tiny wastrels, their oversized eyes popping out of their heads, with skin so tightly stretched as to make their heads seem like skulls.

Appius halted his horse. He leaned over it, his arms holding on to its neck, and gazed at the small children staring up at him. One black-haired boy nudged forward the little girl next to him. She tried to turn back, but he pushed her again, this time giving her a good shove. She stepped up to Appius, her face a mixture of terror and hope.

"Master, can you spare something? Some grain? Oats? Something?"

"Why, you little witch," Ajax yelled, "get you and your band away from here!" Pulling his sword, he maneuvered his mule between himself and Appius, who shouted, "Stop, Ajax!"

But, it was too late. Immediately after Ajax opened his mouth, the children scurried back into the woods. Appius marveled that they could move so fast, as frail as they appeared to be.

They continued up the road, Appius pulling his cloak close again against the chill breeze, which now felt even colder as he thought of those hungry children. As they traveled, he saw their silhouettes in the woods, including a few taller ones further back in the brush. But none of them came out again. Word had raced ahead, it seemed. They apparently had encountered men with swords before, not a good thing for any poor peasant. He shivered once more, hoping that this miserable trip would soon end.

After two days of climbing up and down hills and mountains along a seemingly endless, wooded road, they turned a bend and came upon a bustling camp of legionaries. Guards stood watchful in the towers flanking the castra gates. The doors were open, though, allowing soldiers out of armor to lead oxen pulling carts to and from the palisade. Piles of squared-off blocks filled the carts leaving the fortress, while the entering carts brought in rough-hewn stone for final cutting and fitting. In the distance, they could hear the sounds of men working, shouting back and forth to each other, some singing a cadence song.

After seeing Appius and his party approach, one of the guards in the blockhouse over the gate turned and called down below. In short time, a centurion came out leading a small platoon of legionaries to meet the riders.

The centurion was broad and thick, with a large, flat proboscis dominating a leather face carved into rectangular planes. As he closed on the horseman, he recognized a Roman citizen of wealth and stature, even someone familiar. He saluted across his breast, "Lucius Casca Naso, Centurion Primus, sir, at your service. How can I be of assistance?"

"Senator Appius Claudius Pulcher, Centurion. I'm searching for my son-in-law, Tiberius Sempronius Gracchus, Quaestor and Tribune to Consul Hostilius Mancinus. Can you tell me what corps you serve in? Do you know of Tribune Sempronius's whereabouts?"

Casca seemed to straighten his back even more. "You've come to the right place, Senator. This is the camp of the Ninth Legion, recently returned from Hispania. Tribune Sempronius is here, supervising the repair of the road just beyond the camp." He pointed as he spoke without looking away from Appius.

Appius relaxed, feeling like he was melting in his saddle. He grinned broadly, "Can you take me to him? At once?"

"I would be happy to, Senator." He called over his shoulder to another centurion to assume command, then turned back. "Please follow me."

Appius dismounted and led his horse by the reins as the stout centurion walked around the trench beneath the camp walls. He looked familiar, thought Appuis. But, he couldn't place him, he wasn't sure if he'd met him in Rome or somewhere else. If he had met him, though, how could he have ever forgotten him?

Shortly, they came to another wooded area, and the noise from the work could be heard clearly now. Appius handed the reins of his mount to one of his guards and followed Casca into the trees. Ajax walked behind him with five other guards.

The wood opened up to a space widened where the road traversed the forested area. He immediately took in the engineering of the site. Worn and rotting logs from a past temporary fix lined the roadside. The ends of a series of new culverts drained the road, which had been created with precision: a tamped-down, level earthen bed, covered by heavy stone crushed and carefully evened off, followed by another layer of gravel and concrete. All had been capped off with meticulously measured and cut stone blocks, mortared into place with uniform care, slightly bowed from the middle out to allow for rainwater runoff.

Appius estimated that the newly repaired section stretched for 600 to 1,000 feet, an impressive achievement after only a few month's work. From what he could tell, a few yards remained to be capped and the job would be done.

The toiling troops had stripped off their loricas and pulled their tunic tops down to their waists, not feeling the cool weather because of their work. Other soldiers stood guard looking away from the road site, though a surprise attack in northern Italia seemed a remote possibility. Still and all, it was classic, by-the-book military procedure. In the center of the last section under repair stood a tall figure wearing a short tunic and a farmer's broad, straw hat. He seemed to be working a long staff down in the road trench, as if trying to worry some animal out of a trap. As they approached, Appius could hear the sound of his voice, growing.

"There. That freed it. Let's move it and get the rest sealed up."

For the first time since he'd begun this forsaken journey, Appius felt warmth.

"Tiberius?" he called.

The straw hat snapped up, and Tiberius stared at Appius, who saw a Greek pastoral god before him. "Tiberius, it is me, your father-in-law."

Light seemed to spread around Tiberius's face as he realized who was speaking to him.

"Hello, Father-in-law."

"Tiberius, Tiberius, we've been worried about you!" Appius grabbed both of his shoulders and squeezed. "Your mother, Gaius, —Claudia. Claudia tells your children a story every night about how you are bounding around the stars, having one glorious adventure after another. Soon you will come home, she says, to kiss them goodnight. Are you ready to do that, Tiberius?"

Unsettled, Tiberius shifted his body, looking as though he wished Appius hadn't found him.

"Let's go to my tent, Senator."

He turned and started back toward the camp, shouting out orders as they walked. In just a few minutes they were at the gates, the guards snapping to salute. Tiberius waved distractedly at them, and they returned to their former, casual vigilance.

Down the Via Principalis, they headed for the large quarters in the center of the camp, Tiberius's praetorium. Appius noticed the small layout within the castra, a square that could hold no more than an undermanned company. By the number of tents in the compound, he imagined that there were considerably fewer foot soldiers stationed here than the several thousand that constituted a full legion. He recalled, then, Sextus saying that the Ninth had been mustered out except for the original cohort assigned to Tiberius by Mancinus. After assembling an entire legion, embarking on a full campaign season, winning and losing battles, fighting to survive, and navigating an honorable peace, Tiberius commanded just a few hundred men.

Tiberius held open the flap to his tent, the biggest in the camp, though not very big. Appius entered and saw a campaign table and stools, some chests for clothes and documents, a simple cot in a corner, a brazier for keeping warm at night, and an armor stand opposite to the cot. Appius looked for the helmet he'd given Tiberius, wondering if it had been lost in battle. He saw it, then, on the floor of the tent at the foot of the armor stand. Its highly reflective gloss had dulled, its grandeur blunted by a massive dent that had been roughly pushed out.

"Oh, the helmet," Tiberius said, reaching over to pick it up and prop it on the armor stand post. It immediately fell off. "It hasn't stayed on that post since it was bashed. The balance has been upset, I think. I asked our chief immune Titius to pound out the dent, but he wasn't able to completely restore it. Maybe he was in a hurry."

He picked it up again. "Anyway, I can get it repaired back in Rome."

Appius nodded.

"Have a seat, Father," Tiberius said, gesturing to a stool, "or, shall I have an orderly bring you a real chair? Certainly," he said, before Appius could reply, and shouted, "Drusus, a chair for Senator Claudius. Bring wine, too, and food."

Appius already had taken a seat on one of the stools. He gazed at Tiberius, still tall and graceful, a fully mature citizen of Rome. Yet, he seemed thinner, too, somehow not as robust as the young scion on his way up the cursus honorum. Despite his display of good fellowship and cheer, Tiberius wore a weary look, his blue eyes more deeply so, pained by distant troubles.

A young orderly stepped into the tent, a curule chair held in one hand, and a jug and two cups in the other. He proceeded to place the chair near Appius while Tiberius cleared the tabletop of engineering drawings. The officer set down two cups, filled them both, and slipped a basket from the crook of his elbow to a space next to the jug. He then saluted his commander, pivoted, saluted Appius, and withdrew.

Tiberius removed two cloths from the basket to uncover bread, olive oil, and fruit. Two upright plates flanked the meal, which he put on the table along with the cloths.

"Please, Father, sit in the chair."

Although it seemed like more trouble to get up rather than sit where he was, Appius rose and took his place in the chair. Tiberius sat down and raised his wine expectantly. Appius lifted his in turn, saying, "To the good gods above," as he tapped Tiberius's cup. He sipped, staring over the rim as he drank. Tiberius put his cup down and gestured to the meal.

"Please eat, you must be hungry from the trip."

Appius took some bread, tore off a small piece and put it in his mouth. After chewing a few times, he stopped and swallowed, placing the remaining piece in his hand on the plate.

"Tiberius, why didn't you come home?"

Tiberius raised back, then sighed.

"Why wouldn't you?" Appius said, "We had no idea where you could be. The others had returned, yet you ... disappeared."

Tiberius let go his breath again. "I'm sorry, Appius. Truly."

"Your wife—Claudia was distraught! Oh, she hid it well, like a good Roman woman, but we could see how worried she was. And, your mother—do you know what's been going on in Rome?"

Tiberius barely shook his head.

"It's a wild pig hunt! The Senate is condemning the Numantia campaign as a dishonorable display of cowardice. They're debating how to punish Mancinus and all of his tribunes. They've declared the peace treaty to be an act of treason! They claim that you had no right to negotiate anything, that you had no standing."

"Mancinus appointed me tribune of the Ninth."

"The Senate sees you as a quaestor. They don't care about any battlefield promotion, they want retribution. They are fed up with losing in Numantia and they want to take it out on Mancinus, and you."

"Who in the Senate is leading this charge to reprimand the veterans of Numantia?"

A sour look came over Appius's face. "Scipio Nasica, Rufus Faba, Spurius Postumius, and the other Good Men."

Tiberius smiled cooly and sipped his wine. He lowered his head, seeming to take his time absorbing what he had just heard. After a moment, he shifted his eyes back to Appius.

"Well. I'm sorry to hear this. I suppose I must go back to Rome, now, for honor's sake. Perhaps I can wrangle an exile out of them."

"My dear boy, all is not lost! We can fight them on this. You saved four legions and their auxiliaries! We can rally support and blunt this audacious attack. Oh, they think they are big men, Nasica and the Bean, all of the Optimates. But, they aren't, they are nasty, vicious little river rats who fear change because of what they own. They will back down if you stand up to them!"

Appius caught his breath, and reached for his cup. Tiberius looked at him with fixed eyes, his countenance unchanged by his father-in-law's impassioned speech.

"You burn as hot as the sun, Father." His tone was almost a drone, belying any awe in his words. Appius hesitated, then pushed himself to ask the question.

"Tiberius," he said, almost plaintively, "why didn't you come home? What kept you from Claudia and your family, your mother Cornelia? We worried so much about you! Why did you stay away?"

Tiberius stiffened. He gradually relaxed, understanding that he would have to answer. He took a pull from his wine and said, "I wanted to fix this road. It's a soldier's duty to repair any of the Republic's roads when they degrade. We came to it while marching past Cosa to our ships bound for Hispania. The road was a mess, a bog, much of it under water. I wanted to rebuild it then, but I didn't have time, we were so late in leaving. I was torn, but finally decided to plank logs over it and move on. After withdrawing from Numantia and while we waited to board the ships taking us back home, I realized that I could return to Cosa and repair the road."

Appius looked at him, trying to hide his skepticism. Who wouldn't want to delay returning to Rome after the Numantia fiasco?

"You returned to Cosa with the cohort given to you by Mancinus," Appius said.

Tiberius shrugged, sipping some more, "Some of them and some evocati, too. Old spears who reenlisted because they had nothing left here, nothing left to lose."

"Evocati? Roman veterans?" Appius said, mildly surprised.

Tiberius said, "That's how I filled out the Ninth." He leaned forward on his elbows, "You have to know, Father, what we saw was not to be believed. All along the roads across Italia and back, in Etruria and up past Cosa, everywhere. We saw Romans, men, women, and children starving, no place to go. I talked to them, asked them why they walked the roads, why weren't they home working their land, getting ready for winter?

"They said they had no land, no homes. Their farms had been taken, either by extortion or force. Rich Romans, they said, rich. Now richer, swelling their estates to the size of seas by taking small farmers' plots. So, they wander the roads, looking for work, handouts, miracles to stay alive. Hundreds of them, Appius, thousands, our closest allies, the few men left after filling our armies and fighting our wars, and their families, begging on the roadsides. Starving. They looked like shades rather than human beings."

Appius felt a chill rise through him. He pulled his fur cloak closer, crossing it over his breast.

"Are you cold, Father-in-law?" asked Tiberius. "It's a bit cooler up here. Let me get the brazier going."

Tiberius stood up and called for Drusus to light a fire. The orderly came in with wood branches, which he laid into the iron brazier. He soon had a small fire going, carefully situating it close to Appius upon Tiberius's instructions. He bowed slightly, saluted, and left.

Tiberius sat back down. "I thought I'd seen the worst things possible when I watched Scipio execute the last of the Carthaginians—all the men and boys with more than ten years, and any women who resisted. The rest were sold. Maybe half a million perished, the surviving few sold into slavery. I tried to convince myself, 'this is war.' Still, I left before it was all over and done. Perhaps I was weak, but it turned my stomach." He shook his head, "It was a trumped up war, anyway, Cato the Elder and his never ending magpie calls, 'Carthage must be destroyed. We need to raise the grain levy, and Carthage must be destroyed. Pay honor to the Vestal Virgins, and Carthage must be destroyed.' You know, the poets say that the women of Carthage cut their hair to make bow strings for their soldiers. That's how much of a threat they were.

"But what I saw north of Rome was not war, Appius, it was the slow torture and murder of old men, women, and children. They weren't a foreign enemy, they committed no crimes—bless the gods, they served Rome and this was their reward, to have their land taken simply out of greed, their land lost to the Optimates's, the Good Men's greed."

He drank deeply from his cup. "And, so they wander, wandering until they sit down to die." He dropped clumsily onto the bench.

Appius sipped from his own cup. "I saw them, too."

Tiberius raised his eyes to Appius, surprised. "You saw them?"

Appius said solemnly, "On our way here. We didn't know who they were or what they wanted, so Ajax chased them off."

Tiberius gazed into his cup. "Of course. I'll be chasing off the ones still here soon enough."

Appius looked at him blankly.

"The evocati," Tiberius said. "When we go back, I'll have Casca march the men left from Mancinus's cohort back to Rome to muster out. The rest will be dismissed here, so that they can make their way directly home. That is, if any of them still have a home."

Appius nodded silently. He'd never seen Tiberius so animated before, almost passionate. They had been drinking wine, but his son-in-law's distress at what was happening to the country plebs seemed deeply heartfelt. Of course, Tiberius, too, was a plebeian of sorts, Appius reminded himself. Still, he'd never shown this kind of fire before, this fierce conviction. It surprised Appius and caused him pause.

He looked Tiberius up and down. "You've been drinking a lot of wine since Numantia?"

Tiberius smirked, "This is the first time, an accommodation for you, knowing your appetites."

Appius drew back. He paused, then said, "You're showing me a side of you I've never seen before. I didn't know it existed."

"And what's that?"

"Toughness," Appius said. "Political toughness."

Tiberius glanced at him calmly, wearing an utterly neutral expression.

"Oh, you're stout in battle, no doubt about that. Carthage and this last action tells that truth. But, I never thought you would hold up to the infighting of the political life, the slander based on broad-back lies. How would you stand up to rumors that your wife spread her legs for every wine seller that came to her door? Better yet, she rolled over for their donkeys! Would you kill the purveyor of such filth, or out-filth him in turn? Romans will do anything to discredit their enemies, and every other Roman running for office or floating a popular law is the enemy. How would you handle that, Warrior?"

"What does it matter?" Tiberius said, reaching for his cup. He took a pull, then said, "Even if I am this stunning, political phoenix risen from the ashes of my once promising career, as soon as I enter the city gates, I will be pilloried for my role in Numantia."

Appius leaned his head to one side, "True, first we need to deal with the Numantia problem. But, once that's done, we can get you started, move you ahead."

"Appius—Father-in-law—what makes you think I have any potential left to move ahead in Rome?"

Appius said, "You have excellent breeding, an excellent war record—no, don't look like that, you were courageous in Carthage, and courageous and noble in Numantia. You saved lives."

"Even if people believe that, it's still not enough. Rome has men with the same pedigree lining up outside the Senate."

"True, but you have one other thing that separates you from those climbers."

"And, that is?"

"A cause. You have a cause, Tiberius. I just saw it this day."

Looking bewildered, Tiberius shook his head, his hands apart.

"Why, the little farmers, Tiberius, the simple veterans thrown off their land by the greedy, rich estate owners. You can be the advocate of the wanderers, their champion."

"Really? How so?"

Appius groped around, "By, by defending their rights." He slapped his hands on the tabletop, rattling the metal dishes, "By proposing a comprehensive land reform law."

Tiberius pursed his lips in a sour pout. "How could that work with all the wealth of Rome pledged against it? As I recall, it's been tried before. Did not Gaius Laelius, Scipio Amelius's man, fail miserably and utterly when he tried to enact a lex agraria? When he saw how unpopular it was and withdrew it, that's when he earned his nickname Laelius the Wise, the Prudent."

Appius shrugged, waving his wine cup in the air, "The timing wasn't right. How many Roman veterans walked the roads then?"

"Not that many fewer than now, I imagine."

"Yes, but the Roman people knew nothing about them, either. You will be the perfect witness to sway them with your testimony."

"With respect, Father-in-law, this is a tragedy, not a political opportunity."

"I understand, Tiberius, I understand exactly how you feel. I saw it, too. Others must have seen it. We can testify as well, and others will follow suit. But nothing can be done, nothing will be done without the power of Rome behind it, the political power."

Appius arose and leaned both of his fists on the campaign table. "Tiberius, you are the most honorable man I have ever known. Deceit is an impossibility to you, that's why I matched you with my daughter. In this case, however, you must match honor with the power of the state. If you truly wish to save these wretched creatures, you need to grasp the reins of tradition, the Mos Maiorum, and win the Roman people to your side!"

Tiberius sat silently. He pressed his lips thinly together, wrinkling his nose as if he smelled something bad. At length, he sighed, "Where would we start?"

"With the Senate," Appius went on, "right after we deal with these spurious slurs against your character. Once exonerated, you'll become a hero to the people of Rome and we can build your campaign. To do that, we must leave for home, Tiberius, as soon as possible."

Tiberius sighed once more. Slowly, he nodded his head.

In the morning, he reviewed with Casca the last parts necessary to complete the road. Thereafter, the camp was to be struck. Any extraneous supplies would be divided among the evocati, who would be removed from the legion's roles on the spot. Casca then would lead the last of Mancinus's men back to Rome, where they, too, would be dismissed. Afterward, Casca was to present himself at Tiberius's front door.

They saluted each other in front of his command tent, and Tiberius mounted his horse. With the dented helmet ringing dully against his horse's flank, he slowly passed by and saluted the assembled legionaries on parade, who cheered their retiring tribune. Then, he, Appius, and their entourage rode out of camp.

Chapter 22: Sea Change

Tiberius lay on the forward deck of the corbita that Appius had hired to sail from Cosa to Rome. Not quite as quick as the small fishing boats available, the craft was slightly bigger and safer, more comfortable, and faster than any other ship on the sea, merchant or military. For once, the gods of the winds favored them with a following breeze that pushed them south on calm seas. In two weeks, they would be back in Rome.

Appius whiled away the time outside the passenger quarters on the rear deck, sitting against the swan figurehead, drinking half-watered wine, and trading stories with the ship's captain. Tiberius spent most of his time squinting with slit eyes at the autumn sun as it rode through the sky each day, east to west. The constant rhythm of the rushing water endlessly passing by the ship's hull lulled him into a half-waking reverie. Occasionally, he watched flying fish bound above the waves in flight from some predators in the deep. A pod of dolphins slipped in next to the corbita, enjoying their large cousin surging through the waves, sluggish to them as it was. As twilight began to set in, they peeled off with bright calls to each other, ready to dine for the evening. When at nightfall Apollo turned his chariot toward the earth's edge, Luna appeared fully radiant, illuminating everything in a marine blue light. The last time Tiberius had seen such a moon was when passing through the necropolis in Numantia.

He exhaled slowly. A breeze crossed the deck, ruffling the big sail and swinging the sheets back and forth, causing shadows to ripple over him, blocking the moonlight.

Rome, the clatter of Rome. Red-faced fury at him for who he was. Invectives to the measure on both sides. For what?

"Be a Gracchi!" shouted his mother, "not a man-child clinging to the waistband of the Cornelii!" He grinned sickly as he imagined what she might say now. Maybe she would just keen, pull out her hair, rend her clothes, a son dead to her.

Appius would do his best to cheer him on, Antistia, too. Even Polydius and Philea would welcome him warmly, though he also wondered if he'd be able to see the gaping hole in each of them where Lysis had been torn away. His children would mourn, too, though they were so young, they might not hate their father for letting it happen. Perhaps they would love him still.

Would Claudia still love him?

He roused himself, and made his way back to the passenger quarters. Stooping in front of Appius, he said, "Father-in-law, you are sanctified as an augur of the Salli. How do the birds guide us?"

Appius looked at Tiberius, seeing him troubled, wan even, after a day resting in the sun. He said, "The gulls follow us, eating our scraps, shitting on the sea, the sail, our boat, and once in a while, on us. This is good," he said, "this is good luck, as every augur knows."

He turned his attention back to the ship captain and his wine.

"But, Father-in-law, don't you feel that you should inspect the entrails of one, to be sure?"

Appius turned back quickly to Tiberius, "Ah, but all we have at sea are seagulls. It is bad luck to kill a seagull at sea, very bad luck, the worst. It would be better, of course, to perform the examination. But, then, we would be opposing good luck with bad, you see. The results would be vague at least, possibly mystifying. No, it's better if we wait until landfall. That way," he said, slicing the horizon with his hand, "there will be no ambiguity in our findings and the subsequent determination. So, let us wait until we reach Ostia. We'll perform the augury then, and know for sure what awaits us in Rome."

He finished with a brisk nod of his head in conviction.

"Good counsel, Father-in-law," Tiberius said, a slight fox smile sliding across his face.

In Ostia Antica, the corbita's sail was lowered and tied down, and the big stone was dropped, anchoring the ship to await its turn to dock. When given the signal, the crew would haul the stone up by its rope, and sweep the tiller back and forth to create some momentum. Several small pulling boats would close on the ship to guide it toward the designated pier. There, its cargo would be unloaded with remarkable speed, necessary efficiency for the dock crews to handle as many as five ships per day, each filled with as many as 3,000 amphorae of wine, grain, and other goods. At the same time, the captains talked with the dock master to arrange outbound shipments.

The line looked to be a long one, however, with several other vessels positioned ahead of them, including two of the big grain carriers. Rather than wait, Appius and Tiberius decided to disembark at Ostia, where they would dine while Ajax and his men rounded up a small river barge to take them up the Tiber to Rome, a half-day's journey. Hiring a cart and some horses would have been faster since Ostia was only eleven miles from Rome. But, darkness was falling, which would make traveling by road dangerous even with Ajax and his men around them. Instead, they all could sleep on the barge that night and still be in the city at the sun's apex tomorrow.

After a dinner of fish seasoned in herbs and baked in bread, they boarded the barge. The broad, flat-bottomed boat had long ropes looped from its bow and stern to the riverbank, where oxen and slaves pulled it all the way to Rome. The only amenity on the barge was a large, low-slung canopy covering the deck and a small hold to protect travelers and goods from the elements, mostly from the relentless sunlight. Unable to stand beneath the thick, oiled canvas, Appius and Tiberius stretched out on the deck. Without the breeze from the open sea, spats of inland heat stifled any movement or conversation, even in the fall.

Appius called for some wine, but warm as it was, it did little to quench his thirst. The unseasonable heat continued unabated, which kept the two Romans tossing on the rough planks of the barge. Throughout the night, they heard a baleful, moaning song from one of the slaves on shore. Appius tried to block the sound by throwing an arm across his ears, but he stayed awake through the night. At one point, he sat up, searching for Tiberius, who had disappeared from his side. He soon saw him standing in the hold near the shore side, resting his arms on the ship's railing, as still as the river water.

Appius squinted his eyes. What was the young veteran doing? Listening to the slave's song? Huh. He rolled back over and tried to sleep.

The next day, the barge reached the outskirts of Rome without event. On the noon hour, the passengers found themselves slowly passing familiar landmarks as though they were on a holiday trip—the Campus Martius, the ancient temple of Ceres on the left, the Flaminium racing grounds in the distance, the Temple of Jupiter Maximus on the Capitoline looming over the city walls. Every sighting raised their anticipation of being home, excitement in Appius, and in Tiberius, apprehension.

The barge floated past the Tiber Island and slipped beneath the Pons Aemilius, some of the slaves allowing the lines to go slack while others ran to retrieve them on the other side. They could smell the cattle in the Boarium Forum, now, which meant the barge was just moments away from nosing up to the Aventine docks. The slaves reeled the boat in and while they were still securing the thick hemp hawsers and Ajax and his men were gathering their gear, Appius and Tiberius bounded off the deck onto the pier planks. Running between the long rope lines and wooden cranes, Appius hiked his toga up for a longer stride, pulling his garment's folds into place as he stepped. Tiberius tried to keep up with him while adjusting his own clothes, a military cloak thrown over his long tunic.

Instead of skirting the Aventine, they charged up the steep slope, the most direct route to the Palatine. The usually surly residents on the mount stepped aside for the intense two men rapidly darting back and forth up the crooked route to the top. Once there, they picked up their speed more, hopping down the incline as fast as they could. Appius almost fell head first when he caught a sandal on the hem of his toga, but Tiberius grabbed his elbow and righted him before he tumbled. Once at the base of the Aventine, they headed straight up the Palatine. In a matter of minutes, they stood at the front gate of Tiberius's house.

"Well?" Appius said, looking at him expectantly. Tiberius pressed his lips together and banged on the wooden panel of the gate. They waited until the small port opened that allowed anyone at the front door to be inspected before letting them in.

"Zeus's thunderbolts!" a muffled voice said. The port was slammed shut, and they could hear the scraping of the bolt inside being drawn back. Polydius swung open the gate, opened his arms and said, "Master!"

"Master?" Tiberius said in an irritated tone. "Since when do you call me Master?"

He brushed aside Polydius's long arms, striding through the gateway. As he passed by, though, he quickly patted one of the Greek's arms without looking.

"Zeus's thunderbolts?" Appius said to Polydius, "Going back to Greece soon? Maybe for a visit?"

Tiberius headed down the narrow walled walkway, when he saw two thick men emerge from the main door, staring at him with purpose. Before they could move, though, they were split by a tall, lean man coming at him, equally serious in expression.

Tiberius slowed as the young man stopped, squinting, disbelieving.

"Tiberius?"

"Gaius?"

They closed, wrapping their arms tightly around each other.

"Brother, brother, brother, where have you been?"

They pounded each other on the back, then separated. At arms length, they gazed at one another.

"Little brother, you're a grown man!"

Tears streamed down Gaius's face, "What did you expect? Time doesn't stop."

"But, I haven't been gone a year!" said Tiberius.

"Yet, you've changed as much as I have. I think I could lift you, now, Tiberius." He swung his head toward the front door, "Philea, get food! The master of the house is home, half starved."

But the small, grey-haired woman standing in the doorway didn't move. The brothers dropped their arms and stepped apart. Philea ran to Tiberius like a young village girl chasing lambs in the meadow. Tiberius caught her in his arms. She hugged him as hard as she could, her head tucked into his chest. Tiberius caressed her grey hair, tightly bound to her head. "Mamá mou," he murmured softly, "Mamá mou."

Appius put a hand on Gaius's shoulder, "Gaius, go tell your mother we're here."

Without a moment's hesitation, Gaius turned and headed quickly into the house, followed by the two guards, happy to have something to do, someplace to go.

"Tiberius, let's go in the house!" Appius beckoned. Tiberius turned and followed him inside, one arm still around Philea's tiny shoulders.

He gazed around at the vestibulum; the marble table on the side, the paintings of myths and legends on the walls, the worn, wooden doors, the light cast from the back into the atrium. Nothing had changed. It seemed as though he'd never been gone at all, as though he'd come home one evening as he had done each day hundreds of days in the past.

A shadow figure moved out of the far doorway on the right. Cornelia slowly advanced toward him. Philea slipped away to the kitchen. Tiberius straightened up.

"Hello, Mother. I'm back."

Without a word, she glided over to him, hugged him, holding him just a little bit longer. She let go and said, "I am glad to see you, my son, safe at home. Very glad."

Tiberius said, "I've missed home, Mother. I've missed you."

He saw tears brimming in her eyes, and was about to embrace her again, when high-pitched screams stopped him in his tracks. Little Tiberius and Cornilia Sempronia came running from the kitchen, arms open, screeching peals of excitement as they ran to their father. They knocked him back a step when they reached him, both clinging hungrily to his tunic, looking up screaming and crying, "Papa! Papa!"

He grabbed them both up, kissing them in turn as much as he could, as fast as he could. They squirmed in his arms, trying to kiss him and escape at the same time. But, he wouldn't let them go. Everyone around watched, smiling at the scene, happy to see their hero returned.

Slowly, he lowered the children to the floor where they scrambled a few feet away, then turned back, expecting to be chased. Instead, Tiberius looked at his mother.

"Where is Claudia?" he said.

The din of the celebration trailed off. The children continued to run and shout, while the adults exchanged glances. Finally, Gaius said, "She is in your bedchamber, Tiberius. She's been resting there, waiting for you."

Tiberius whirled around to view his closed door. He held still for an instant, then stepped over. Knocking on the door lightly, he slowly opened it and called her name.

"Claudia?"

She sat on the far side of his bed in front of the window. In the midafternoon autumn light, he saw a glowing silhouette, her glorious raven hair pinned up, exposing the fairness of her delicate neck, softened by a few escaping strands of downy hair.

"Hello?" she said, as if drowsing. He pictured her lips saying the word, lovely, her violet eyes full of life with her every thought. She half-turned to him as she said it, "Hello?" She looked the same as when he had left her, she never looked more beautiful.

"Tiberius," she whispered, every syllable evincing a different sense of relief, regret.

Something was different. Tiberius couldn't tell why at first. Then, he saw her slender shape fuller at the waist, rounder. His brow furrowed with his concentration until he realized what he was seeing. He closed the door behind him and drew closer to her.   Bewildered, he said, "When?"

"The night before you left."

Tiberius stood frozen by surprise. "Blessed be the earth goddesses!"

He went to her and took her hands in his. He kneeled and rested his head against her round abdomen. "Thank you Terra, Juno, Bona Dea, thank you for this gift to a lost servant."

Claudia put her hand on his head and softly ran her fingers through his hair.

"Why didn't you return?" she said, trying carefully not to sound wounded, "why didn't you come home?"

Tiberius lay next to her, holding her hand.

"Shame."

He rolled over to face her, gently laying his arm over her belly. "I'd think of returning, then I'd think of how it would be. I'd finally be in the place I'd always longed to be, among those I love above all others, nothing changed, nothing except everything. The disgrace. Would everyone think so well of me when the full weight of it fell upon them, the public scorn, the graffiti, the threats?" He shook his head. "I was a coward. I knew that everyone would be so relieved to see me they would greet me like a hero. But, of course, I'm not a hero. If anything, I was a fugitive, afraid to come back to face the rage of Rome. Your father tells me the Senate is now considering punishment for Mancinus's officers. That includes me, though he also let me know that I'm at the top of their list because I agreed to peace with the Numantines. As bad as that is, they claim I didn't have the station or standing to do so. So, if they intend to be strict with Mancinus's tribunes, they most likely will have something special planned for me. My fate is almost certainly preordained."

He rolled away back flat on the bed.

"But, you did what Mancinus told you, yes?"

Shrugging, he sighed. "He agreed that I should try for peace. If I failed, he'd be no worse off. If I succeeded, I would take the blame for bowing to the Numantines. He almost as much as said I would be the perfect scapegoat. In front of the Senate now, the knowledge that he charged me to sue for peace could be conveniently forgotten."

"There must be some way to change this," Claudia said. "What did my father say?"

"He believes I'll make it through. His attitude is, 'once you've weathered this storm, we can start planning your future.'"

He exhaled as though releasing his last breath. It all seemed so taxing. Despite Appius's enthusiasm, Tiberius had great doubts about how he would fare in front of the Senate. The Populares might see the disenfranchised pedites in Italia as a great political opportunity, but Tiberius could see only the gaunt faces, the hopeless expressions of the pedites.

He rolled back to face Claudia. As he gazed at her lying on her side, he put his hand on her swollen belly again, and said, "Why didn't you let me know?"

At first, she seemed confused, until it came to her. "I tried to. I sent letters, but never received any back from you, just the one you posted early on. I thought you knew but were too busy to write," she trailed off, "especially near the end."

"Your father knew, of course. But, he didn't tell me."

"He must have thought you already knew, too," she said earnestly.

"The entire time we traveled back to Rome he said not a single word about his new grandchild soon to be. That doesn't seem like him at all, Claudia."

She hesitated, then said, "I asked him not to. I told him that if it seemed like you didn't know, to keep it to himself."

"To surprise me?"

"Yes," she said haltingly, "to surprise you."

"To surprise me," he said again, "with good news."

He stared a moment longer, then reached out to hold her and kiss her.

"How is he?" Cornelia asked.

Appius' expression tightened. "Strong as a bull," he said, "and wounded. He is having a difficult time dealing with the defeat. More so, he feels guilty about the lost soldiers in his command. He feels responsible somehow."

"He always had a sensitive nature," said Cornelia. "I'm not surprised that it's hampered him."

"Yes, well, Numantia hardened him, too," Appius pointed out.

"Yes," Cornelia said, "but what about this Senate problem? How will he handle that?"

Appius screwed up his mouth to his left cheek in thought. "In just a few days they intend to mete out Mancinus's sentence. That means they will use the occasion to repudiate the peace volatilely, including its fabricator, Tiberius. It opens the door for them to go after Mancinus's officers, something the Optimates relish. They always like to make more elbow room at the trough."

"So, what can be done?"

"We can mount a spirited defense. He was acting on Mancinus's orders."

"Any witnesses to that?"

"Mancinus's equitus Decimus Pateus was there. However, before he was the consul's equitus, he was the head of horse for the Ninth, Tiberius's legion."

Cornelia gave him a sour look. "Not quite unimpeachable."

"Yes, but Tiberius also seems to have an unusual amount of support from his former soldiers."

"How is that?"

Appius said, "Well, he recruited many former legionaries in Italia as evocati. It seems they were quite destitute when he found them. Believe me, I saw them myself—in fact, I've never seen anything like it. Begging, all of them with their hands out, men, women, and children—they were like locusts!"

"That doesn't sound pleasant."

"It was very discomforting. But Tiberius seemed to respond to their plight very vocally, almost fiercely. He gave them food, I imagine, and hope. In any case, those who survive are devoutly loyal to him. We can round them up and make a show."

She shook her head, "The Senate won't care, they won't give a fig, literally."

Appius angled his eyes up at her. "They might give pause if enough bodies show up."

Corneliab said, "The decision will be made in the Senate by the Senate. You need to find bodies that can enter the Hostilia Curia, ones that count."

Appius nodded slowly, "Let's hope we can find enough."

Chapter 23: Princeps Senatus

An hour after dawn, Philea entered to rouse Tiberius. Before she could call him, however, he sat up in bed as though he hadn't slept. The Senate met at midmorning. He had enough time to perform a quick ablution, get dressed, and eat a piece of bread on his way down the Palatine to the Forum. No time to honor the Lares this morning, or play with the children. Claudia had left his side for her own room in the middle of the night, a victim of his tossing and turning. Today, he would meet his detractors face to face and learn what his fate might be.

Gaius caught him in the atrium.

"You go now?" his brother asked. Tiberius nodded. "I'll join you."

"No need, brother. I can make my own way well enough."

Gaius said with disdain, "Don't be ridiculous, Tiberius. I'll keep you company."

Tiberius shrugged. "As you wish, but be quick about it. I want to get there and meet Appius before it all starts up."

They started walking briskly down the hill, as much to generate some warmth as to make time. "So," Gaius said, his breath visible in the cold morning air, "what do you expect this morning? What do you think will happen?"

Tiberius gave him a searing look and said sharply, "I expect to be impaled on a spit and turned slowly on a low fire. What do you think I expect to happen?"

Faster than he could bite his tongue he saw the jab sour Gaius's features. Tiberius put his arm on his brother's and said, "I'm sorry. I'm sorry, Gaius. I know you're trying to make it better, I know you're trying to help. I'm just not sure there's much helping to be done here."

Gaius regained his bearings, and said cautiously, "It's that bad?"

Tiberius twisted his face in a quick grimace. "Maybe. I don't know. When we get down there, Appius might know more."

They took long strides down the hill silently for a few minutes. Gaius finally said softly, "Well, if I can help, I'd like to."

Tiberius halted abruptly, grabbed his brother by the shoulders, and said, "Just by having you here brings me strength, Gaius. How could I ask for more?"

"Yes, but I'm a good soldier, too," he said, now almost looking his older brother straight in the eyes. "I've been training hard."

He had grown, Tiberius thought, in just a year, a fully grown man. Soon, he would attach himself to some consul or praetor marching for glory. He prayed to the gods that it wasn't someone like Mancinus.

"I know you'll be a fine soldier, Gaius. How could you not be?"

"Yes, well," said the beaming Gaius, "in case things become physical today, I'll be at your side."

Tiberius smiled, "That warms me to know you'll be with me."

The two brothers continued down to the bottom of the Palatine in a much better mood. In no time, they reached the Forum. Outside of the Comitia, they saw Appius waiting with Scaveola, Diophanes, and Crassus.

"Salvete," said Tiberius, giving each man a quick hug and a peck on each cheek. Gaius followed suit. The men pulled their togas tight around their bodies against the cold air of the fading night. A line of pink peeked above the eastern horizon, but it would be a few hours before the city would warm up for the day.

"Well?" said Tiberius.

Appius replied, "Well, it isn't Mancinus, obviously. Since his fellow consul Lepidus Porcina left for to Hispania to quote, 'hold the line,' the Senate is a bit short on consuls right now. So, Consul-elect Furius Philus has been pressed into service. Scipio Aemilianus will be happy about this arrangement, of course, which allows him to stay put on his rustic little farm." Appius smiled grimly as he continued, "The Optimates are out in strength, however."

Tiberius nodded, "Is Mancinus present?"

Appius dipped his head, "He is, and his tribunes, sitting together behind the great man, I believe."

Tiberius nodded again, up and down. Crassus put his arm on his shoulder. "Don't worry, Tiberius, it's all for show. They want blood, it's true, but not from a Gracchi. They won't dare to besmirch your honorable name. Oh, Mancinus will get his just desserts, perhaps exile to Macedonia or some such rock pile. The tribunes will have their knuckles rapped and sent home. Before you know it, they'll be soldiering again in some far reach themselves."

Tall like Tiberius, Crassus hardly filled out his toga, he was so lean. Graying, his eyebrows were bushy black, accenting the most gentle-looking eyes a person could see, matched by his warm attention, a comfort to all he met. Odd, thought Tiberius, to try and match his congenial demeanor with his practical assessment of Mancinus's fate and those associated with him. Still, this man lost in the folds of his drab, grey toga that seemed to wear him came from one of the wealthiest families in Rome, a fortune increased by every ensuing generation. Apparently, a pleasant disposition could take you only so far, mused Tiberius.

"When we go into the Curia," Appius broke in, "you'll be sitting with Scaevola and Crassus on either side. I'll be sitting just in front of you. There will be no grouping of you with Mancinus' tribunes. In this case, you will be the Quaestor. In this context, the others are no friends of your, Tiberius."

"In any context, Father-in-law."

"Oh, really? Well, then, let us join the Senate's deliberations."

The five men headed for the massive doors of the Curia Hostilia crowded around by a surprising number of onlookers. Evidently, word had spread that Mancinus and his lot would soon have their fates decided by the Senate.

Someone shouted out, "There's Tiberius Gracchus!"

Appius winced and tried to hurry the small group inside, but the expected chorus of catcalls never materialized. Instead, the crowd was silent, almost eerily so, throwing Appius into an internal panic of worry. Why were they so quiet, the usually rambunctious and vocal masses of Rome? What did this augur?

Along with Gaius, Diophanes was about to peel off to find a good vantage point near the doorway, since they were not members of the Senate. Before he could leave, Appius grabbed him by his sleeve and whispered in his ear, "Try to find out why this crowd is so docile. It's quite out of the ordinary."

The Greek mentor nodded, and Appius made his way back to Tiberius and the rest of his entourage. They entered the Curia vestibulum and stopped for a moment to compose themselves. Voices sounded from the main chamber, most likely a procedural matter, since they were too low to be heard outside. Appius signaled for everyone to follow him inside.

Passing a series of large, marble-faced columns, they walked into the main Senate chamber, a vast, rounded room with grated windows across the walls, allowing what little sunlight available this day to shine in weakly. Instead of flying around to bless the senators, the pigeons cooped close together in the window sills to keep as warm as possible.

A marble floor alternated black and white rectangles in the dim light. Oil lamps and lit braziers generated a modicum of heat and slow spirals of smoke twisting up into the rafters. Two rows of wooden seats curved around the front of the floor, with a low marble footing enclosing three levels of stone benches on balconies rising to the outside wall. A stairway in the middle leading up to each level more or less separated the Optimates from the Populares. Across the marble floor, two curule chairs faced the gallery, one empty according to tradition. The other seated the presiding consul Furius Philus. What was unusual, however, was a stool and a bench between the chairs and the rows of senators. On the stool sat the deposed consul Gaius Hostilius Mancinus, and behind him on the bench hunched his four military tribunes, Horatius, Secundus, Nicomedes, and Cadmus. The four tribunes wore simple tunics, their military attire and insignia nowhere in sight. They shivered, though not just from the chill in the air. Their demeanors reflected their unease and anxiety at such vulnerability, like ordinary plebeians. Even at this hour, Horatius looked like he was drunk. He must have come directly from the taverna, up all night.

Tiberius was shocked by Mancinus's appearance. He had wrapped himself in an unadorned toga, and gone was his perpetual sneer of arrogance, replaced by almost a birdlike nervousness. His eyes darted up and down, back and forth, guarding against any sudden movement around him. The network of lines running down his drawn face cast his sharp nose in high relief, furthering the avian effect.

"By the gods, Mancinus brought down!" Appius muttered almost in disbelief. "Notice how his toga is free of any bird droppings. Very bad omen."

Across the chamber stood a tall man in an immaculate toga, off-white with the additional crimson trim of a proconsular senator. He stared at the four men at a standstill in the chamber's doorway. Scipio Nasica smiled a disdainful smile. Seated close to him on a marble bench sat Rufus Faba glowering at the new party.

"We've interrupted his speech," Scaveola murmured. "Let us sit down now."

They moved to the side of the Senate gallery mostly occupied by Populares. Appius took his seat in the front row where Crassus usually sat next to him. Instead, Crassus and Scaveola sat directly behind him with Tiberius in the middle. Tiberius could see Nasica's and Rufus's eyes tracking them as they all sat down, and he could feel the eyes of the rest of the

Senate doing the same.

"I'm happy you could join us, Claudius, and particularly pleased that you brought your son-in-law Gracchus with you to stand before this sacred assembly. Quaestor, please join your fellow officers on the floor with your commander Hostilius Mancinus."

"That's perfectly all right," interjected Appius, "we're completely comfortable sitting where we are."

Nasica's friendly smile froze. "Very well. As long as the quaestor is here to face the consequences of his actions."

He turned to the curule chairs and said to the Consul-elect Philus, "By your leave, I will continue with my summation."

"By all means, Senator, go on. Then we can have a division."

Nasica pivoted and walked to within a few feet of Mancinus. "Gaius Hostilius Mancinus, it has been established and confirmed that you led the Roman army into Numantia where you met utter, ignominious defeat at the hands of the barbarians. In this ill-fated campaign, a legion of men were slain, a Roman camp was stormed and destroyed with all Roman property and personnel within lost, while you fled the field only to have the remains of your force penned in at the mercy of the Hispanii hordes. Do you admit to these failings and transgressions?"

Mancinus gazed up at Nasica hovering over him. He swallowed, and said, "I do. I lost the war and I almost lost my entire army. I am guilty of failure."

One senator in a back row gasped. The others held their breath at this astonishing confession, this total capitulation.

Nasica's eyes shone. "You surrendered to the Numantines?"

"Yes," Mancinus said in the barely audible voice of a mouse.

"And, you consorted with the enemy to negotiate an unsanctioned peace?"

Mancinus allowed himself a hopeful tone, "We were allowed to leave. No more were killed."

"You sued for an illegal peace to save your own skin. Never once did you think of honorably falling on your own sword?"

Mancinus covered his face with his hands.

"Instead," Nasica said, "you conspired to cry for peace."

"Uh-oh," whispered Appius. He shot to his feet and said, "With all respect, Consul Philus, and my deepest apology to Senator Nasica for my interruption. However," he said quickly before either Philus or Nasica could stop him, "it seems to me that you stray from the main argument of this inquiry, that of the culpability of losing the war in Numantia. You have a stark confession from ex-Consul Hostilius Mancinus, I see no reason to waste more time exhausting all of us with the minute details of this catastrophe. Rather, it is time that a judgment be rendered, don't you think?"

A ragged chorus of voices came from the seated senators. "Just so," "Let's get on with it, Nasica," "Crucify the turd!"

Nasica opened his mouth to object, until he realized that Appius's support was coming from both sides of the aisle.

"Why did he do that?" Tiberius quietly asked Scaveola.

"Nasica was sniffing around the legitimacy of the peace negotiation, intimating that it was something of a conspiracy. If he opens that door and manages to denounce the peace, the situation would become very uncomfortable for you."

"Oh," said Tiberius.

Nasica stepped over to the consul's chair to whisper in Philus's ear, who swung his head up and down in agreement. Nasica returned to Mancinus

"You recognize how you have disgraced yourself and Rome?"

Mancinus dropped his eyes and nodded silently yes.

"Then, a fitting penalty should be leveled."

Mancinus nodded again.

"In that case, with your accession, Consul Philus, I call for motions on punitive measures to be carried out on ex-Consul Gauis Hostilius Mancinus."

Senators jumped up throughout the room, "Crucify him!" "Strangle him!" "To the arena!" "Throw him off the Tarpeian Rock!"

Every vicious outcry caused Mancinus to bend further over in his chair, as if trying to assume the fetal position while sitting.

Philus banged his baton against the side of his chair, "Enough. Enough! Let's have some propriety here."

"Thank you, Consul," said Nasica. "Senators, your suggestions seem reasonable under the circumstances. But, how to choose?"

At that moment, Lucius Rufus Faba rose from his seat. "Senator Nasica, if I may make a suggestion."

"Yes, Senator Rufus, all right." Nasica turned to the side so that the entire Senate could see the small round man.

Rufus hiked his toga up over his shoulder in the classic pose and began. "The crimes of Mancinus are multiple and serious. Any of the suggestions this body has made would be fitting. However, what will we gain from them? Will Numantia know that we reject their so-called generosity? Will they know that we shall not rest until this blot upon the very soul of Rome is avenged? No, my fellow senators. I put it to you that we need to send a message to the Numantine barbarians. And, what better way to do it than in the person of Mancinus?"

A rumble ran through the Senate as they wondered among each other what Rufus was getting at.

Rufus barely suppressed a secret smile. "Nearly 200 years ago, Rome was at war with our Samnite allies. How times have changed!" he said. "The fighting was brutal, ruthless, the Samnites a worthy foe, unlike the Numantines. But, I digress. Sad to say, as we all know the Samnites inflicted a terrible defeat upon our legions at Caudine Forks. Afterwards, it was found that the loss was due to the incompetence of our Roman commanders. The Senate acted without hesitation; all twenty officers were handed over to the Samnites to do with them as they wished. The act showed the Samnites our determination in bold terms. Soon, they surrendered to Rome.

"My fellow senators, we should send a similar signal to the Numantines. Only then will they know that they enjoy a very brief respite from the might of Rome. Therefore, I propose that we strip Mancinus of his rank, privilege, and belongings, and have him sent to Numantia in chains to show our unwavering defiance!"

The chamber roared, the senators standing and stomping their feet as they shouted, the outburst startling the pigeons in the windows into flight around the heights of the Curia. Philus pounded his baton against his chair without effect. No one could hear above the din. Finally, the men ran out of steam. Philus beat his baton again, and spoke.

"By your actions, I'll assume that we have support of the motion."

"Consul," said Nasica, "we still should have a division to ensure that this sentence was formally approved before we carry it out."

Philus nodded, and the senators stepped down from their seats to gather for the division. Only Tiberius and a few other guests remained in their seats.

"All those opposed to Senator Rufus's proposed penalty for ex-Consul Gaius Hostilius Mancinus, step to the right."

Not one senator moved.

"All those in favor of this punishment, move to the left."

The entire body of senators moved left, which led to another round of ragged yells.

Mancinus slumped in his chair.

"The proposal is unanimously approved," said Philus. "You may return to your seats, senators." But not a man moved.

Philus turned to Mancinus. "Gaius Hostilius Mancinus, please rise. By the power vested in me by the Roman Senate and the people of Rome, I divest you of all of your offices, your patrimony, and your possessions. You will be taken in chains to Numantia to be handed over to the barbarians to do with you as they see fit."

Mancinus nearly collapsed, but two soldiers stepped out to grab him. They immediately stripped off his toga, his tunic, and his subligaculum, leaving him naked and shivering on the Senate floor. The two soldiers put the shivering man in manacles and walked him out of the chamber while a third legionary picked up his clothes and followed. The senators milled around, ready to go back to their seats when Nasica called out, "Senators, we have not yet completed our duty."

They turned to look at their tall colleague. "We still bear the stain of a repugnant peace agreement with the Numantines, a shameless, illicit state of affairs that Rome cannot tolerate. Now that we have fairly dealt with the engineer of this disastrous campaign, we must undo the damage done to Rome's reputation by repudiating this false peace treaty. Consul, I move that we vote on whether to reject any peace with the Numantine hordes."

Rufus immediately shouted out, "I second Senator Nasica Scipio's motion."

Philus addressed the stand of senators on the marble floor. "Well, men, while we're here—all those in favor of rejecting peace with the Numantines, move to the left."

Everyone moved left, led first eagerly by Postumious at the front of the Optimates followed by the Populares led by Appius Claudius Pulcher.

Tiberius was stunned. Appius leading the way to nullify peace with Numantia, the one he, his own son-in-law, had negotiated?

"Unanimous. The peace with Numantia is null and void."

Cheering again, the senators started to make their way back to their seats. Scaveola dropped down next to Tiberius, who immediately whispered harshly in his ear, "What was that?"

Scaveola pulled back his head to gaze at Tiberius.

"You, and Crassus, and my own father-in-law vote against the peace I made? This is how bad matters are, I must fall on my sword?"

Scaveola frowned and hurried to say, "No, no, that's not it. None of these senators are going to vote for any surrender no matter the circumstances. If we voted for the treaty, we would be standing alone, which would give us no standing at all. We need some credibility when Nasica puts you on trial."

Nasica spoke loudly from the floor again. "My apologies, Consul."

Just having lowered himself into his chair, Philus looked at Nasica in annoyance. "We are a busy bee today, aren't we, Senator?" Seeing Nasica glower at him, he said, "What now?"

Nasica raised his long, sinewy body to its full imposing height, grasping the fold of his toga as he continued. "My brother senators, we have done good work today. We have restored much of Rome's honor defiled by the craven coward Hostilius Mancinus and his Numantine kings. We have rejected this most dishonorable peace. But, we have more to do to remove fully this stain from our great city. The gods will it."

He swept his arm across the men sitting on the bench in front of the gallery. "There sit Mancinus's partners in perfidy. He could not disgrace Rome without the complicity of these men, his tribunes. They, too, need to be called to account for their treasonous acts! And, of all the scurrilous scum in our midst, none can be guiltier than their leader in treachery, the architect of this repugnant peace treaty, this capitulation," Nasica whirled around and pointed directly, "Tiberius Sempronius Gracchus!"

Silent for one instant, the men still standing on the floor and those near their seats broke into a torrent of words, some crying out their dissent, others growling their support. The sound rose as they called back and forth, with Philus whacking his baton again and again on one of his chair's armrests. Realizing that no one could hear him, he turned to one of the guards in the shadows and barked an order.

The guard saluted, and left the chamber, soon returning with another legionary carrying a cornum. Philus nodded at him, and he let loose a blast from the curved horn that quieted the room immediately.

"Good senators, please be silent and return to your seats," said Philus. The men grumbled, not used to being ordered around, but those still on the floor walked back and sat down, all but Nasica and Appius.

"Senator Nasica," Appius cried out, "how can you denigrate the head of one of the great families of Rome?"

"Mancinus came from a good home, too," Nasica said dryly.

"Yes, the demise of the ex-Consul is unfortunate, but you cannot place him in the same category as Tiberius Sempronius Gracchus. The Quaestor's record is unblemished!"

"Except for consorting with the enemy Numantines."

"Not so! He followed specific orders from his consul!"

"He put those orders into Mancinus's mouth!" shouted Nasica. "He persuaded his commander to bow to the Hispanii barbarians."

"What a crass and confoundimg lie you tell," Appius said, "a greater invention I've never heard in my life, even by a seasoned liar such as yourself."

"Oh, really?" said Nasica. He gestured with both hands to the doorway. "Perhaps I should have Mancinus recalled to testify? Or, we can ask the Tribunes sitting here to tell us what they know."

"Exactly, they have no axes to grind," rejoined Appius. He turned to the gallery, "Roman senators, think of who we are discussing here. Tiberius Sempronius Gracchus, natural born son of the great twice-consul and censor Tiberius Sempronius Gracchus Major and his venerated mother Cornelia Scipionis Africana Sempronia. No blood line comes any purer, and the young scion here has proven himself worthy again and again. First over the wall at Carthage, an efficient and well-respected city praetor, and the hero—yes, hero—who staved off fatal defeat at the hands of the Numantine horde."

The catcalls began, and Appius was dismayed to see that they came from both sides of the Senate chamber from more members than he found to be comfortable. Nasica looked smug, a mistake, thought Appius.

"It is odd," said Nasica, "how you can see events so differently from how others see them. How differently you see them from the truth. Gracchus is no hero, he's a cowardly traitor who overstepped his rank to kneel before a disgusting, treacherous bunch of goat herders."

"He was charged by Mancinus to deal with the Numantines!" shouted Appius.

"Gracchus was a quaestor, not a tribune." Nasica drew back and folded his arms over his breast. "Not much of a quaestor, either, it seems. His account transcripts are indecipherable and the silver is gone."

Appius sighed his exasperation. "The Numantines took all when they stormed Mancinus's camp, including the books!"

"And, they were happy to return them to Sempronius Gracchus when he agreed to such a tainted peace. Our ignoble quaestor even took a bribe for his traitorous work."

"You begrudge a small amount of frankincense to sacrifice to the gods in the names of our fallen legionaries? You should applaud such an act of piety, Pontifex Maximus!"

Nasica shook his head slowly, "A bribe. For treason."

The men in the gallery growled again. This was going badly, thought Appius, very much so. What to do, how to get my daughter's husband out of this trial by fire?

He paused and breathed silently, in and out. He relaxed his body, and said "I'm surprised at you, Senator Scipio Nasica. Where are you going with your character assassination? First Mancinus, then the martyred Fabius, and now Tiberius Sempronius. Who's next, Tribune Horatius?"

Tiberius saw the shudder run through the drunken first tribune sitting in front of him on the bench.

"Then Secundus? Does Rome decimate officers now? You go too far, Nasica Serapio, your sense of justice wanders as much of a twisted path as your nose."

A collective gasp could be heard throughout the chamber at the crude insult leveled by Appius. Nasica turned an arterial red at the affront.

"Rather than allow you to bully this genteel group of Rome's most distinguished citizens, I believe they deserve to learn more of the details of this event, especially of the qualities of this great Roman scion that compelled him to act in Hispania."

Nasica wheeled to Philus and said, "Consul, is this appropriate or even necessary?"

But before Philus could speak, another voice sounded in the chamber.

"Consul Philus, I believe that Senator Appius Claudius's proposal is not only appropriate, it is absolutely necessary."

Philus opened his mouth to speak, then froze when he saw who had interrupted Nasica. Standing tall next to Tiberius, Publius Licinius Crassus Dives Mucianus had exercised his prestige as rinceps Senatus to interrupt the proceedings. Philus looked at Nasica and held his hand out in a gesture of concession.

"After all," Crassus continued, "we have plenty of time to decide the disposition of Quaestor Sempronius Gracchus once Senator Claudius has concluded his remarks. The condemnation of any Roman should never be conducted like a horse race. Wouldn't you agree, Senator Nasica?"

Nasica's expression tightened even more, but he briskly nodded his head in assent.

"Very well, then. Consul?" he said as he moved to sit down.

Fidgeting uncomfortably, Philus said, "Senator Claudius, please proceed with your commentary."

While they had been talking, Appius had leaned over the wooden partition in front of the first row seats to whisper in Scaveola's ear. Scaveola jumped from his seat and quickly left the Senate chamber.

"Senator Claudius!"

"Yes, yes," Appius said, "I merely asked Senator Scaevola for a favor. Please forgive me.

"Now, we take up an extremely important task today, good Romans, one that has consequences not only for our beloved city. The reputation of one of the oldest, most honored families in our history is at stake as well."

Scaveola returned with Gaius at his side. Gaius carried a jug with him, and a beaker.

"Ah, my fellow senator returns, thankfully, with the succor I most desperately need."

Gaius stopped next to Appius and started pouring water into the beaker. Appius leaned over to him and whispered at length until Gaius shook his head up and down. He placed the jug onto the low marble wall in front of the first row of benches and bolted from the building.

"Consul, must we?" said Nasica, seated next to Rufus.

Before Philus could respond, Appius turned quickly to him, saying, "I was parched, heavenly gods save me. One must have all of his senses intact when orating in front of the most august assembly in the civilized world, no? Now, I am ready.

"To understand the actions of Tiberius Sempronius Gracchus, one must understand the underpinnings of his noble character. Tiberius's great qualities go far back in his family, starting with his most illustrious father, Tiberius Sempronius Gracchus Major. We all have heard of his extraordinary accomplishments, his victory over the Numantines, his two consulships, his brilliant turn as censor. But, to know how truly great he was, one needed to know the man behind the achievements. I knew Gracchus Major as a mentor and a friend. I met him long ago, when I was a very young man...."

Chapter 24. Wind from the North

Tiberius sat on the edge of the bed quietly, bowed over almost to his knees. Next to him, Claudia slept, occasionally snoring until she could adjust her swollen body into a more comfortable position. She had joined him after dinner, a glum affair without much conversation between the adults in the room. Appius ate with them, though even the great senator picked at his meal. The children chattered away, oblivious to the gloom of their elders. The problem was, thought Tiberius, that there wasn't much to say.

That afternoon in the Senate, Appius had kept up his history of the Sempronii family tree. More than occasionally, though, he digressed to describe the peculiarities of the merchants from the far reaches only Alexander had seen, or the intricate process used by the Hebrew peoples to blow glass. Finally, in accord with tradition Philus was compelled to close the session at sunset. Nasica did not bother trying to disguise his ire, while Rufus shouted loudly his fury. The applause of the senators who had not left for an early repast drowned out Rufus's vitriol. Horatius and the other tribunes almost collapsed with relief, and happily rushed from the Senate chamber to seek out the nearest taverna to celebrate their reprieve.

But, it would all start again in the morning, thought Tiberius. Appius would still hold the floor, but for how long? How long could he last? After dinner, they needed to hire a litter to get him home, exhausted as he was.

Everyone in the house knew it. Tomorrow, his father-in-law would have to yield the floor, either from sheer fatigue or from the cajoling of the senators tired of being a captive audience. Nasica and his band would swoop down, then, to draw the blood of their prey, with Mancinus's failed quaestor first in line.

Tiberius grasped his head with both hands. Why did I ever leave this place? In Carthage, I proved to be no soldier, why did I have to go to Numantia? What ambition was this? Whose?

"My love, come back to bed."

Claudia had awakened, though he couldn't think of how he had roused her. She worked to sit up and began kneading his back, trying to get him to relax. Despite her best efforts, he showed no sensation.

"Tiberius," she said, "you must relax, you must rest."

"It is hard," he said in a low voice. "I'm tired, but I can't sleep."

She gently pulled at him until he fell sideways against her hip, a feat in itself, given her swollen state. She repositioned his head until he was resting while she slowly stroked his head.

"What can happen?" she said. "No matter what, you will always have your family, your children," she went on, lightly touching her round abdomen as she spoke. "You'll always have me, Tiberius, no matter what."

"But, will you have me?" he said sharply. "We have no idea what these vipers might do. Nasica, Rufus, Postumious, they're all vindictive elitists. They sent Mancinus naked back to Hispania, and he was one of their own. By the depths of Hades, they might throw me and the other tribunes off the Tarpeian Rock!"

Claudia sighed. She laid her hands on his cheek, saying, "They are not going to throw you off the Tarpeian Rock. They don't dare threaten death to a Gracchi, son of your father and Scipio Africanus's daughter."

"You don't know them," Tiberius said petulantly.

"The worst that could happen would be to send you away from Rome. Not a terrible fate, when you think about it. We could live a pastoral life on our farm, a healthy life. The children would thrive! Truffles and ham hocks for dinner with plenty of greens." She nudged him, "A little wine, perhaps, and more children?"

"We don't need wine for that," he said flatly, "we seem to be blessed by the gods no matter what."

"Ah, but practice makes perfect," she said, "which is why we have such perfect children. So, we better keep practicing to ensure good results."

"Not in the immediate future, though," he said, running his hand over her distended belly.

"Oh, I don't know, we might find a way."

She rolled over on her side away from him, then reached back with her hand. "Let's be a little resourceful, shall we?" she said, beginning to move her hips.

Afterwards, he lay wide-eyed awake, waiting for the dawn.

The cold spell in Rome continued, accenting the misery Tiberius felt as he made his way down the Palantine He walked alone, Gaius apparently being too tired to stir from his room. He stumbled several times due to his own fatigue, but of course he could not indulge in the luxury of sleeping late into the morning. Fortuna awaited him in the Curia Hostilia.

Barely a soul could be seen in the marketplace. A few merchants began to set up their goods to display, but most people were still at home in bed. Even the early risers might hide in their kitchens rather than venture out into the cold, gray morning. He could see the sun begin to rise, which meant that he was late.

He hurried through the Forum to the Curia where he could see on the side away from the public concourse the smoldering remains of the offerings to the gods. Nasica had done his work, he thought sourly as he smelled the singed flesh of the carcasses smoldering on the altar. The auspices for trying traitors had been good, no doubt.

Inside, he found Crassus and Scaveola sitting where they had the day before, saving the seat between them for him. Appius was nowhere in sight, however. Nasica sat with Rufus and Postumius, the other Optimates in close ranks behind them. As Tiberius took his seat, he saw two legionaries enter to post themselves at each side of the doorway. Philus followed them in and sat in his curule chair.

He glance around the chamber, then said, "I don't see our illustrious Senator Claudius among us, today. Probably still hoarse."

Amidst the laughter from Philus's crack, a voice rang out, "A horse I may be, Consul, but one whose race has not run its course yet."

"I see more carthorse in you than thoroughbred, Pulcher," said Nasica.

"You've backed enough carthorses in the Circus to know, Nasica."

The senators laughed heartily at each jibe, until Philus rapped his baton.

"Enough. We have business to do."

"Thank you, Consul, I'm eager to continue my discourse on the Sempronii clan proving how no member of this esteemed family bloodline could have conducted themselves in the craven fashion slanderously asserted by Senator Scipio Nasica and his fellow halfwits."

The room exploded with noise, laughter from the Populares and outrage from the Optimates. Philus cracked his baton against his chair and signaled to the soldiers at the doors to advance. The senators muted their outcries, though strains of laughter still could be heard from the watchers outside of the building.

"No more slanders yourself, Senator Claudius."

Appius gently touched his breast as part of an exaggerated expression of puzzlement.

"Consul, this is a monstrous waste of time," Nasica said, exasperated,

"Can we not do what we have to do without hearing this irrelevant prattle?"

Philus opened his mouth to speak when he saw Crassus begin to rise to his feet. "Continue, Senator Claudius," said Philus.

"Thank you, Consul."

"But, be forewarned, we won't spend another entire day listening to your elaborate history of the Gracchi. A decision shall be rendered in this session."

"Very well, Consul, but I will object if I am not allowed to state all of the plain facts regarding this false prosecution."

"Proceed," waved Philus.

Tiberius had to admire Appius's endless invention and energy in squeezing every second of time out of his delaying strategy. But, to what end? he thought. Sooner or later, he would have to step aside. Then, Nasica would swoop in and sweep away all of Appius's oratory as pointless.

If they didn't condemn him to the same fate as Mancinus, the least they would do is exile him far away from Rome. And no matter how much Claudia implored him, he would not take his family to some rock far out at sea, or some desert province where vinegar passed for water. He refused to subject the love of his life or his sweet little children to such hardship and ignominy. He would fall on his sword first.

"As aedile, he exercised staggering organizational skills," Appius went on, "that served him well in raising a legion in Italia."

The hours passed, the sun actually broke out in late afternoon, and Appius began to flag. He spoke in a ragged voice, now, barely able to be heard. Tiberius looked at Crassus and saw that he was squirming in his seat, ready to jump to his feet again. But, then, he would become still, as if he, too, knew that they were nearing the end.

Tiberius turned his eyes to Scaevola, who displayed the same calm demeanor as he had in the beginning of this ordeal. Scaevola would remain expressionless no matter what happened.

Appius began to cough uncontrollably. He turned to grab a flagon of water even as Nasica stood up.

"Consul, this has gone on long enough. Only an hour remains until sunset. Do you want us all to endure another day of this?"

"No!" "No!" shouted members across the chamber, "No more!" "Call for a division!" "A division, for Jupiter's sake, let's get this over with."

Appius straightened, his eyes wild, "Wait, Consul, wait," he croaked,

"I have much more to say that will prove the difference!"

Philus stared at Crassus, who gazed back sadly without moving. The Consul stood up and said, "You've said everything, Senator, you've send enough. Your time is up. I ask for a vote by acclaim for cloture."

"Aye!" reverberated throughout the Senate chamber. Even the Populares appeared to be too tired to go on.

Appius sputtered, but Nasica called out, "I move that we vote on a pronouncement of condemnation of Tiberius Sempronius Gracchus for high crimes in consorting with the Numantine enemies."

Little Rufus Faba almost leaped from his seat, "I second the motion."

"Senators, please come to the floor for the division."

Appius leaned hard against the front partition as the senators began descending to the chamber floor. He sat down on the floor, propped up against the wood.

Before he made his way to the aisle, Crassus patted Tiberius on the shoulder. Scaevola was ahead of him, stepping down without looking his way. Tiberius swallowed, finding it difficult to believe that he was about to be judged for a capital offense. All of his worries and fears in the night hadn't prepared him for this. He glanced down at Horatius and the other tribunes and realized that they already seemed resigned to a terrible punishment.

Scaevola and Crassus made their way to Appius's side and helped him to his feet. The three men turned to Philus for the call of the vote.

A tumultuous outburst sounded outside of the building, sustained and growing in loudness. The noise grew as a wave approaching the Curia. Philus turned his head to the vestibulum, confounded by the racket, voices of a thousand at full capacity. All of the senators looked expectantly toward the front of the building. They heard the doors slam open, increasing the crowd noise even more. The two guards at the entrance to the chamber tightened their grips on their spears, half-whirling to face the thunderous cheers.

Several hard men walked into the chamber, followed by Gaius, all stepping aside to make way for Scipio Africanus Aemilianus. As he walked deliberately into the chamber, the chants from outside could be heard clearly now, "Aemilianus! Aemilianus!"

Like everyone else in the chamber, Tiberius stared at the man, not believing his eyesight. He glanced to Gaius, who flashed him a quick, wide grin before assuming a solemn bearing again. Tiberius turned his gaze back to Scipio Aemilianus, who walked to the center of the room and faced Philus. He appeared as he always did, half the age of his peers, among them Appius and Crassus, fit, clear-eyed, and ready to lead the world.

"Consul Philus, if you please. I would like to address the senators before they render a decision of this gravity."

Without saying a word, Philus swept a broad welcome with his right arm. Nasica opened his mouth, but then kept quiet.

"Senators, I understand you intend to pass judgement on Tiberius Gracchus about his actions in Numantia. The argument has been made that he aided Mancinus in making a dishonorable peace with the Numantines. For Mancinus, I cannot speak; he's plowed his own furrow in all of this. And, peace with the Numantines is out of the question. It always has been.

"But what of Gracchus? What has he done? Treason? Overstepped his authority?"

Scipio shook his head almost pityingly. "Hardly. Tiberius Sempronius Gracchus saved 20,000 Roman soldiers and their camp followers. Two legions still serve in Hispania Citerior because of his quick action. Those two legions are why we still have any part of Hispania left to call our own. Those two legions represent the core of the army that ultimately will vanquish the Numantines for good. With your leave, I will take those two legions, and add thirteen more to them. With this force, I will mount a campaign against Numantia that will leave no doubt about who rules Hispania—Rome!"

The building exploded with the cheers of the senators joined by sound tremors from the crowd listening through the doorway and windows. All of the men in the Curia rushed to the floor in hope of being the first to congratulate Scipio, but he raised his hand to hold them back.

"Senators, a division has been called, one I consider a poor exercise considering the facts. Bad peace treaties have been made by Roman generals before, several in Numantia. The Sempronii Gracchi have a good record, however; Tiberius Major as a conqueror, Tiberius Minor as a savior. Let us not make a habit of punishing proven heroes. Let us praise Tiberius Sempronius Gracchus for what he has done."

Scipio turned around to Philus and said, "Consul, do you wish to call the division?"

Philus glanced at Nasica and Rufus, then said, "All in favor of condemning Tiberius Sempronius Gracchus, step to the right of the room."

Not a senator on the floor moved.

"Those in favor of acquittal, please move to the left."

Moving with a flourish, Scipio deliberately stepped to the left to join Appius and Crassus. The rest of the senators almost stampeded to their side.

"The division has been rendered. Tiberius Sempronius Gracchus is absolved of all accusations."

The thundering cheers started again, first with choruses of "Aemilianus," then shifting to "Gracchus!" Tiberius felt thunderstruck himself. Appius sat down on the first seat in the row while Crassus and Scaevola came back up to pound Tiberius on his shoulders. While they sat down, beaming and laughing, Tiberius shifted his eyes to Appius.

The exhausted man sat as though he might never rise again, wiping his forehead with a silk cloth. Gaius came up to him and bent over to kiss his cheeks. They exchanged a few words, smiling. Gaius stood up straight and leaned across the barrier to hug his big brother.

"He sent you after Scipio."

Gaius pulled back and nodded his head quickly, smiling and bursting with pride.

Tiberius hugged him, saying, "You're a fully grown man, Gaius."

Gaius said, "I know, Tiberius, I've been telling you that all along. Our brother-in-law has promised to take me with him to Numantia as his adjutant!"

Gaius turned to Crassus, who reached to embrace him as well. He missed Tiberius's face darkening.

"We still have the matter of Mancinus's military tribunes to deal with," Nasica said.

Scipio turned to him, "Oh, cousin, do we really want to try these men for losing a war? If that's our practice, we'll have no officers left anywhere!"

The senators near them laughed as Nasica's face reddened. "The day is almost done, and I must be on my way. I can trust you to marshal my command of the Numantine war through the Senate, yes?"

Nasica lowered his head.

"Wonderful. Then, I'm off to find an army."

Scipio turned with a flourish and started for the Curia vestibulum. Tiberius quickly excused himself and followed him into the long hallway.

"Scipio."

Scipio pivoted and smiled. "Brother-in-law. Congratulations on your acquittal."

"You mean my escape. Gaius persuades you to save me, and you take him to Numantia."

Hearing Tiberius's tone, Scipio's became flinty in return. "You can thank Gaius," he said, "and Sempronia."

"Sempronia," Tiberius said. "You have my entire family at your beck and call. Appius sent Gaius, I'm surprised you haven't found something for Claudia and my children to do."

Scipio pulled back, his brow furrowed. "You are an ungrateful dog," he said almost humorously. "At best, they were about to ship you off to the Indus. What roles would your sweet wife and children have then, son?"

"I'd rather be in exile than in your debt. How many times must you humiliate my sister, my mother before you're satisfied? And, I'm not your son!"

Tiberius moved to leave when he felt his arm pulled. He looked back to see a genuine look of anguish on Scipio.

"Wait. Wait." he said. He breathed in, and out. "I saved you because you deserved to be saved. Those jackels in there would have done anything to make you pay. For their own failings, I guess, I don't know. I argued what I believed. You were a hero in Hispania. If you weren't too old, now, I'd ask you to join me in Numantia as my first military tribune." He shrugged, "But, you are too old, now. So, I asked Gaius."

"I'm not too old," Tiberius said, "but I'm done with Numantia, and certainly with you."

Scipio sighed his exasperation. "You will never understand. I would have adopted you, just like my father had adopted me, if you had just given me any consideration at all!"

Tiberius turned on him. "You? Adopt Tiberius Sempronious Gracchus's oldest son? Your self-esteem knows no bounds. And, you won't be adopting Gaius, either. Get that out of your mind."

Tiberius wheeled around and walked through the doors of the Curia, where he heard again the cries, "Gracchus! Gracchus! Gracchus!"

Chapter 25. Casca 136-133 B.C.E.

Casca raised the cup to his lips and took a sip. More vinegar than wine, he eased it down his throat, in no hurry to quench his thirst. He'd been in the taverna all day long and had no thirst left to quench. Drinking was just drinking now.

Four narrow windows in the front of the building allowed in the light from the hot, setting sun, piercingly bright in the dark, low-ceilinged room. The light never reached the black walls behind the grey trestle tables and benches. Patrons sat in front of their cups as nondescript lumps, moving slightly now and then, as if to prove that they were still alive.

He sipped some more. As he drank, he used the cup to block the glare from the windows, shifting his eyes sideways to survey the room carefully. In one corner, he saw three men passed out on top of a table. Like him, they'd been here since the place opened. So, most likely they were in deep stupors, not pretending.

Dead across from him sat a man with a woman on his lap, squirming, but in a very constrained fashion. They looked like they were screwing right here in the common room. He squinted to see beneath the table, but he couldn't tell for sure because of the dark shadows.

He swung his head to the right and found what he was looking for, what he had expected.

Four men sat at one table, never touching the cups in front of them. They slouched talking softly to each other, sometimes looking around the room, then back at the tabletop. Casca kept his eyes on them, and sure enough, every now and then one of them would take a glance in his direction, then quickly look away. One by one, they saw him staring at them. In turn, each averted his eyes quickly. Finally, they stood up and left.

And that was his day. Drink, watch, drink. Why not?

The girl came up to him and asked, "More, Naso?"

He gazed up.

"Do you know me, or are you just sizing me up by my nose?" He laid his index finger on the wide, flat, misshapen mass occupying the middle of his face.

She paused. "I don't know your name. What do you think?"

She seemed to be attractive, or at least young. Tough enough to show some iron, too, he thought, an important part of working in this kind of place.

"Bring more," he said.

She nodded, but as she was turning to go, he said, "Lucius Casca."

She stopped. "All right," she said, without looking back. She started for the bar again when he said, "Naso."

She eyed him, puzzled. "Lucius Casca Naso, Centurion Primus of the Ninth legion, retired."

"Oh. Lucius Casca," she said, and before he could say yes, she finished with "Naso," laughing. Casca made a face as he bobbed his head up and down. "And you?"

"Helena."

"Of course. Helen of Troy, always starting a war."

She said, "Just watch me," and left.

His twin brother, Manius Casca, had broken his nose when they were six, fighting over the end of a stale loaf of bread. Always the stronger, although the younger, Lucius wrested the bread from his brother and began to stuff it in his mouth. It was too hard, and while he tried to crush it with his front teeth, Manius hoisted up a three-legged stool. Barely able to hold it upright, he brought it down across the bridge of Lucius's nose, which exploded from the blow.

Covered with blood and cartilage, Lucius coughed the bread out of his mouth and shrieked in pain and fear. Manius dropped the stool and dove for the bread, never minding that it had soaked up Lucius's blood. He popped it into his mouth, and suddenly flew across the table from the blow his mother gave him. She worked him over efficiently, quieting him with four quick punches to the head. Then, she turned on Lucius still crying at the table and hammered his head while he screamed bloodcurdling cries of pain, his mother hitting his nose again and again. She pushed him into a far corner of the hovel's small front room and said, "Shut your face up! I'm trying to sleep here."

The two boys muffled their weeping until she'd lifted the ragged blanket that separated the kitchen from the sleeping space to go back to bed. Their father woke them up that night when he came through the door drunk. The boys began to cry again, and Casca Major mumbled, "What the ...? What?"

He looked at their battered faces and stepped past them to brush the hanging blanket aside. They could hear the yelling until he came out dragging their mother by her hair.

"What's this?" he said, "what's this?"

"They woke me up," she said, and he hit her.

"They woke you up? You almost put them to sleep for good, you stupid donkey!"

He hit her again and said, "Clean them up! Then, get me something to eat."

She grabbed Lucius and wiped his face with the hem of her dress. "Cassius, look." She used her finger to flop Lucius's pulpy nose back and forth, causing him to howl with each touch. "There's no fixing this."

Cassius looked at his bawling son and said, "There isn't. I guess you have your full name now, boy—Lucius Casca Naso. Stuff something into that mess, Eudocia, so he doesn't bleed out."

"What about me, Pa? What's my name?" asked Manius.

Cassius grabbed his oldest son by his shoulders and held him back to get a good look. "You're lumped up, boy. Amazing, your head's twice its size!" Cassius Casca nodded, "Manius Casca Capito. Makes sense."

He let him go and shifted his sight to his wife. "Where's the food?"

"We're out," she said, leaning back.

"Out? Why didn't you go get something?"

"No coin."

"I left you some. You drank it up, you sow."

"Well, give me some now and I'll go get something."

"It's dark outside! There's not a shop open now in all of Patavium."

He shook his head, "Stupid pig sow," and left.

Lucius would be Naso and Manius Capito from then on.

When they were nine, they found their mother dead. Their father was nowhere to be found, off to a war in some far reach. So, they dragged her body out of the shanty across the road to a ditch where they dumped it. Then, they went back inside to find something for supper.

By this time, they had learned how to work together to steal food. One distracted, the other snatched. They also learned to fight back to back against the other, older urchins, pulling out sharp sticks when necessary, cutting and thrusting just like their father had taught them. As they grew older, the others still alive left them alone. Soon, they attracted ruffians to their side, and had the run of Patavium, stealing, selling, and squirreling away their take in separate hiding holes.

When their father returned from a campaign, however, he always found their goods. As soon as he did, he ran out for a binge. He'd bring women home, announcing each one as their new mother. Usually, though, Mater Novo landed out in the street the next morning. One time, when they were twelve, he brought home another woman, a ratty brown-haired tramp with a foul mouth and a foul smell.

"This is your new mother," he said. "Give her a big kiss."

The boys cringed, but Cassius thrust them both at the woman, who laughed and grabbed them in her arms, rubbing them up against them her giant, wineskin breasts.

"That's right, Mama," giggled Cassius, "love them up! Teach them how it's done."

The two boys scrambled to escape, but the woman grabbed Lucius before he could flee while Cassius intercepted Manius.

"Take them, Venus, to Mount Olympus. Here, take the oldest first. Naso can have the second course!"

They disappeared behind the cover, and Lucius could hear his brother yelling and shouting until it all went quiet. After a minute's silence, Manius bolted from behind the blanket and darted out the front doorway without stopping.

"You're next, my boy, soon to be a man. Now, get in there and mount that bitch," said Cassius as he thrust Lucius through the blanket. The cackling woman gathered him up and pulled him on top of her. She stank worse than anything he'd ever smelled, and she was moist, more slippery and sticky than wet.

"Here, lover boy, come to Mama," she said, pushing his head down on her enormous mammaries. She tried to push a nipple into his mouth, but he kept ducking. She gave up and started working up his tunic to bring them together. She slipped her hand down and grabbed his pisser, pulling on it and stroking it. Then, she tried to tuck it within her as she began to move against him, rhythmically.

At first, he struggled, but she was too strong. Then, he became very still. She relaxed, and he squirmed free, skittering off of her, past Cassius, and out the door. He headed down to the marketplace where he found Manius sitting on a fountain wall. He sat next to him, neither one saying a word. When they finally made their way back, they found Cassius asleep on the tabletop and Mater Venus gone.

The brothers grew into stout young men through the years, which made life easier. None of the other hustlers wanted to take on the Casca boys, their double envelopment too much to handle. Because of this, fights with other gangs became rare. They fought each other, however, all of the time, brutal encounters that left blood, scars, and broken limbs. No matter how well they worked together controlling outside threats, the rage between them never seemed to end. They warred over food, the spoils of their thievery, or simple insults. Lucius might have moved to another place, but their safety depended on watching each other's back. With things going so well, eventually they moved out of the falling-down shack of their father's to the top floor of an insula close in to the local market. There, the pickings were convenient and easy.

They eventually found their own way to the carnal side of life, too, first with women they knew, street walkers. Money bought quick encounters and no entanglements. Sometimes an occasional partner demanded more than they were willing to pay. But, a raised fist usually ended that, though sometimes Manius let go with a backhand anyway. A quick trip to a taverna afterwards picked up their spirits, and sometimes another girl or boy.

When they were sixteen, Manius brought a woman home. Her name was Ariadne, a lovely girl from the countryside. Her father had been a veteran, an Italian auxiliary given a small plot of land for services rendered in the first Pydna engagement, when Paulus Aemilianus destroyed the Macedonians. For some reason, though, Ariadne's father had lost the land and the family's livelihood. Her mother said he drank and gambled it away. But, her father had said he'd been cheated by some agent of a rich patrician who had stolen his small farm to add to his huge estate. In any case, her family had moved to Patavium to find work. Soon after, her father disappeared. Her mother looked to her oldest daughter to bring in some kind of an income, which led lovely Ariadne to enter the street trade. Before she'd been at it long, Manius found her.

"She'll be staying with us for a while," said Manius.

Mildly bewildered, Lucius said, "Why?"

"Because I like her. You stay away from her, though, she's mine. If you don't, I'll have your head."

They were twin brothers, thought Casca, draining his cup. How could he stay away?

"More wine?" the bar maid asked.

Casca nodded. He said, "You never told me your name."

"Yes I did. You've forgotten it already? Maybe I shouldn't get you another cup."

Casca disregarded the embarrassment that flashed through him and said, "Tell me again— your name, tell me."

"Hah! Why should I? You'll just use it to try to talk me into bed."

He pouted, "That's not fair. I told you mine. Do you still remember it?"

She laughed fully, charmingly. "You wear your name on your face. For the rest, you needn't have bothered."

"I gave you my full, proper name because I thought you were trying to talk me into bed."

She laughed again, sounding like wind chimes, her eyes crinkling. He was in love, suddenly, with the most beautiful woman in the world.

He had fallen in love with Ariadne, too. She straightened up the rooms as though they were her own little home. She shopped at the market for greens, decent fish, and freshly butchered meat. Then, she cooked them farm meals. For dinner, she placed flowers on the table. She sang.

Manius came and went, sometimes just stopping to eat, other times bringing a full jug of wine that he took into the sleep room with Ariadne. Lucius would leave for the streets then, staying out for as long as he could. When he returned, usually Manius was asleep or gone. If his brother was still in the insula and awake, Lucius could hear them talking, mostly arguing until Manius yelled for Ariadne to shut up. Then, Lucius left again, coming back later or bedding down someplace else.

To keep their business in order, they needed to be seen together, a united front. Aside from discussing their next move, however, more and more the brothers had little to say to each other. Lucius seriously began to think about separate quarters again. Slowly, the situation was sickening him, as though he had a disease that ate away his insides every day. If he didn't rein in his thoughts, his mind would be consumed by the awful irony of Ariadne being with his twin brother who was not like him at all in any way. Better to move, Lucius decided. He began to look in earnest for another insula.

He found one just a block away, an important factor in their mutual safety. Feeling satisfied and relaxed, he sauntered back to gather up his belongings and to tell Manius of his move. When he arrived, he found Ariadne alone, cutting up some peppers, shallots, and other vegetables.

"Where is Manius?" asked Lucius.

Ariadne shook her head, "I don't know. Sit, have something to eat."

He shrugged and sat at the table. She piled mixed vegetables into a shallow wooden dish, then poured olive oil liberally over top. Lucius spooned a mouthful up and began chewing.

"Minerva's tits, this is good! What did you put into it?"

Ariadne put her finger to her lips, "Shhh! I used a little bit of the coin Manius left for a pinch of pepper and some sea salt."

"Pepper! Salt! Fortuna bless you, don't tell him for sure. He'll accuse you of robbing his tuck!"

She laughed as he took another spoonful. She had pushed her hair back behind one ear, holding it in place with a single, yellow blossom. Beautiful, he thought.

Ariadne sat down across from him. "My father loved delicious things to eat, and he didn't care what he spent to buy the best. He shared, too, holding up some delicacy and saying, 'Taste. Life is no good if you don't have good things to eat; taste!' And so, we would try it, me and my two little brothers. My mother, too. He shared even when he was broke. Pheasants eggs, a single stuffed piglet, anything he could find to go with the usual fare. I never got over that," she said, her big brown eyes gleaming. She reached a hand over the table and touched Lucius's forearm. "You remind me of him sometimes. You share."

Lucius felt a wave flood through his entire body, neither a shiver nor a shudder, but a sensation that seemed to change him on the spot.

"Enjoying yourself, brother?"

Manius stood leaning in the doorway. "Such a pretty sight. It's like dreaming the happiest moment of my life. I see my woman feeding, caring, and caressing me, except for the nose. That's when it becomes a bad dream, know what I mean?"

"I was just eating, Manius, no reason to get pissed."

"Oh really? Even when you're moving out? Do you plan on taking her with you?"

Lucius's hand froze, his spoon halfway to his mouth. "What? Where did you hear that?"

"I keep an ear out."

Lucius spun around in his chair. "Have you been spying on me?"

"Don't feel so special, Naso. I spy on everyone, everything. It's my nature."

Lucius raised and lowered his head slowly. "If I find anyone shading me, Capito," he spit, "I'll gut him. Then, I'll come for you."

"Why wait?" Manius said, straightening up, his hand on the hilt of his knife.

"No, no, no!" cried Ariadne, rushing over to grab Manius's hand. "Stop it, you are brothers!"

"Shut your bitch mouth up!" Manius said, pushing her by her face hard to the floor.

Lucius leaped to his feet, his hand grasping his knife.

"That's right, come on," said Manius. "I'll cut your ears off through your throat!"

Lucius started forward, but Ariadne stepped in his way. "No, Lucius, no, he's your brother. Go, leave."

He stared at her furiously, ready to throw her out of his way.

"Please," she said, holding him back by placing her hands on his chest, "go now."

Lucius shook, trying to still himself. He gritted his teeth in a vicious, death grin and began to move slowly sideways to the door.

"That's right, slither like the eel you are. Just look back once and I'll cut your stomach out through your ass!"

Lucius turned, snarling, but Ariadne implored him, her eyes full of terror.

"Crawl out of here, you rat louse. I want to be alone to mount my woman!"

Lucius left, and headed to the nearest drinking house. In a matter of minutes, he drained a full jug of wine. No question about it, he thought, sooner or later, he was going to kill his own brother. In the meantime what could he do? What could he do about Ariadne?

He called for another wine jug, but when it arrived, he slammed it down on the table, smashing it to bloody red smithereens. Ariadne pushed him out to save him, and now she was alone with Manius.

Lucius ran out of the taverna and sped back to the insula. Just as he reached it, he heard a blood-chilling scream. He bounded up the stairs, pulling his blade as he ran, and burst through the door.

A woman sat next to the bed, rocking and wailing, holding Ariadne's hand. She saw Lucius, shrieked like the one he'd heard below, and ran from the room. Lucius ignored her, staring down at Ariadne's still form. She was dead, he thought, murdered by Manius.

But, she stirred. Life lifted him as he closed in on her. She moved her head slightly back and forth, and he could see that her face was bound with bloody bandages. He leaned down and carefully lifted the edge of the wrappings. She moaned from the pain even though she was unconscious.

Her face was a mass of red ribbons where Manius had drawn his blade back and forth.

Lucius sat down on the edge of the bed, his eyes streaming. Beautiful Ariadne, he thought. Please live, he prayed.

"I heard her cry out," a woman's voice said. Without looking, he knew it was the woman who had run. "I was afraid to come in. I saw you rush out, bloody, which made me more afraid. But, I couldn't. I couldn't just ...."

"It wasn't me," he said. "Can you wait here with her? Take care of her?"

The woman didn't respond.

"I won't hurt you," he said. "It wasn't me, it was my brother."

He got to his feet. She sidled by him and sat next to Ariadne.

"Take care of her," Lucius said, thrusting a handful of coins at her. Get her a psychic. I have to go, now, to kill my brother."

He bolted down the dark stairs two at a time, swinging on the bannister as he turned the corners. When he finally reached the bottom, he pulled his knife and burst from the front doorway.

In the blinding sunlight of the marketplace, Manius stood leaning against a vegetable cart, his arms crossed over his chest. Lucius launched himself from the doorway and Manius met him, whipping out his knife. They crashed into each other, stabbing and slicing, sending bloody spray into the hot afternoon breeze. Each tried to grab hold of the other, trying to stab with their free hand. They twisted away from each other in a grotesque dance, pulling an abdomen in at a thrust, rolling away from the arc of a sweeping slice, colliding with their two shoulders trying to dislodge the other's hold while stretching away from the knives in the opposite hands.

A quick pivot landed them both onto the vegetable cart, which collapsed beneath their weight. On top, Lucius tried to yank Manius into the range of his knife. But, Manius used the momentum of Lucius's pull to twist past, turning and tugging his brother toward his knife's point. Lucius ducked down and took the stab in his forearm, slashing up at the same time to open a gap just below Manius's sternum. They pulled apart for a moment, screaming roaring shouts before closing again, the crowd around them yelling at them in approval, calling out savagely for more.

The brothers slapped together and tried stabbing each other in the back, when suddenly blinding light came from pain, numbness. Again and again, Lucius felt blows to his back, side, his legs, and most of all, his head, causing him to roll into a ball on the dusty ground. Petrified, he attempted to edge away, his knife lost somewhere in the street. But, again and again, blows to either side fixed him where he was.

At last, he gave up, failing Ariadne and ready for Manius to finish him off. Instead, the blows tailed off, coming again only if he made any move to leave. Slowly, he pulled his forearm over his face, shading his eyes, which he opened slightly to see what went on.

"This one's done, Severus. What about that one?"

Lucius heard a muffled voice reply, though he couldn't make out what he said.

"Okay, get him up and over here." The man standing over him grabbed his hair and pulled him to his feet. "All right, let me have the other one."

Lucius opened his eyes when he recognized his father's voice, then felt crushing white pain as his head was brought together with Manius's. They both sat down, holding their heads in agony, exhausted.

"You stupid donkeys, bleeding each other in a common marketplace. Well, if you want to fight, you'll fight. You're old enough."

Cassius Casca pushed his sons before him surrounded by his troop of soldiers and his optio, Severus, shouting at the crowd to leave. Since the fight seemed to be over, most of them had returned already to their own business.

Cassius enrolled them both in the militia, making sure that the officer in charge understood exactly what was to be done. They trained. Day and night, they worked on mastering their weapons, pilum, gladius, shield, long spear. The one fast rule was that they were not allowed to fight with each other anymore.

But, it didn't matter to Lucius. He had to know what had happened to Ariadne, if she lived or died. If she had died, so would Manius. If she lived, who knew?

After a good month of training, the militia guards relaxed their watch over the twins. Lucius could tell by the banter between himself and the other men, the building of good will. He waited, though, until he thought that enough time had passed. Then, one evening, he slipped out of the barracks and ran back to their old insula.

He hid in an alley until dawn. Once the sun had risen, he entered and climbed the seven flights to their old place. Outside the door, he knocked quietly. No one answered at first. He knocked again, more firmly, and the door snapped open.

"Yeah?" A man twice his age stood in the doorway, holding a cudgel. "What do you want?"

Lucius casually rested his hand on his knife. "I'm Lucius Casca. I lived here. I'm looking for a girl, an injured girl. She lived her, too."

The man, filthy in a rotting tunic, swung his head back and forth. "Naw."

He moved to shut the door when Lucius put his sandal in the doorway. "Hey, what the...?" the man said, raising the cudgel. By then, Lucius had his knife point pricking the man's neck. "Her name was Ariadne. She was hurt, bad."

"Listen, we've been in this hole for maybe three weeks. There was no girl, here. None. I swear by Apollo's prick!"

Lucius pulled back the knife and pushed the man back into the room. He started down the stairway. Dead, he thought. If not, where could she be?

He had a thought, and went back up to the seventh floor. The man had stuck out his head, but when he saw Lucius coming up the stairs again, he pulled back and slammed the door shut. Lucius could hear the bolt fall as he went to another door. He knocked.

The woman who first had found Ariadne appeared in the doorway.

"You're back," she said. "She's gone. As soon as she healed up as best she could, she left. I told her you would be back, but she just shook her head and said 'No more.' Only the gods know where she is now. Only Juno can say how she can make a living."

Lucius thanked her and left. He walked slowly back to the barracks, crying without tears. When he arrived, they stripped him to the waist, strung him up, and gave him ten lashes for desertion. Manius laid them on.

After he had healed, they marched. Outside of Patavium, they patrolled the roads, ever on the hunt for bandits. If they found them, they would make short work of them, crucifying any who survived. Manius and Lucius excelled in such melees, surprising the cutthroats with their ferociousness and fearlessness.

Manius particularly enjoyed slaughter, loving the soldier's gladius for its range compared to the knife. Lucius dispatched his foes with his great strength, but little elan, opined Manius. Lucius ignored him, knowing well the rules that Centurion Casca had laid down for them, even in his absences. If one of them killed the other, he would die.

Still, the forced peace eventually bred an uneasy truce between them. Manius cajoled Lucius for his coldness around him, even joking about his sour puss. He never crossed one line, however. He never mentioned Ariadne. Her name, her existence, disappeared between them. Fighting back to back again closed over the wound as well, though without ever healing it.

The militia captain began to notice the Casca brothers, not only for their withering attacks in battle, but also for their keen intelligence. They never entered an engagement without gauging the terrain, the strength of the forces before them, or seeking out a good escape route should things go wrong. Before long, both brothers had been promoted to optios.

Cassius Casca returned, this time to recruit for Quintus Caecillus Metallus's war against the Macedonian pretender Andriscus. A praetor, Publius Iuventius Thalna, was first to challenge Andriscus, who had brought the four republics of Macedonia together. Andriscus whipped Iuventius Thalna and immediately seized Thessaly. Metallus intended to destroy Andriscus. In just a few years, he had.

Manius and Lucius proved their worth again in the battle that sent Andriscus running. Afterwards, they sat opposite each other in a tent, drinking wine, talking quietly. Severus entered without announcing himself. He stood between them, his hand on the hilt of his sword.

"Centurion Primus Cassius Casca is dead. We have avenged his death and will send his ashes to cross the River at midnight. You may kill each other now, or you can come to his funeral."

Without another word, Severus snapped to, saluted them, and left.

Manius and Lucius eyed each other across the tent.

Lucius awakened in the middle of the night, stood up, and bumped around in the dark searching for a piss pot. "Cack," he said, and walked over to a corner of the insula to relieve himself.

"What in the gods names are you doing?"

"Taking a piss, what do you think?"

"Not in my rooms, jackass. Go outside. Over the fence."

Lucius shrugged and without bothering to tuck himself away, started to feel around the walls for the door. He stepped out to the railing and started to spray.

"Hey, you stupid shit," he heard from below, "watch where you're pissing."

"Kiss my ass," Lucius said indifferently. He shook off a few more drops in the voice's direction, and headed back into the tiny room.

He dropped next to the curved form under the bedclothes.

"You are a turd," Helena said.

"Yes, but I'm your turd."

"Not for long. I want you out of here come morning."

He fell asleep. The smell of pork awakened him. He left the small bed and dragged himself over to the table and chair a foot away. Helena turned from the small brazier she used for cooking and dropped a plate of steaming ham in front of him.

"Eat, then go."

"Why are you so mean to me, Helena?"

"Because I know you, I know your soldiering kind. You'll stay until it's time to fight some war some place, and you'll be gone. I'll be stuck, and the longer I'm stuck with you, the greater the chances are that I won't be alone when I'm stuck. So, better to avoid all that and say to you 'Go.'"

He blew out, "Whew. You should be heading to war, not me."

"Don't be more of an ass, will you?"

He groped around for something to say.

"Do you have anything to drink?"

She rolled her head and her eyes. "Wine? You want wine after last night? After yesterday?"

He lifted his shoulders, shrugging. "Water?"

She brought him a jug of water, and he drained it. The pork smelled good.

Manius stood next to him as they watched their father being consumed by the flames. The stench seemed worse than usual and the fire lasted forever. Lucius passed the wine jug to Manius, who took a long pull, then handed it back.

"Goodbye, Old Shit. I wish you well across the River, though I don't know why."

Lucius looked at him, amazed. "You send him a blessing, and you're surprised at yourself?" He started laughing.

"Don't," Manius snarled, "I'll run Gladiola into you until it pops out of a pimple on your back."

Lucius laughed louder, harsher.

"I'm glad to see you boys celebrating your father's life rather than crying your loss," Severus said. "He lived the life he wanted and died the death he expected."

They stared at Severus.

"Praetor Metallus wants to see you. Don't worry, it should be good news."

In the commander's praetorium, the celebration was well under way. Equites lounged next to centurions, tribunes next to optios. Musicians filled the air with raucous noise. Not an augur or other priest was in sight, only orderlies rushing in with wine, breads, fruits, and roasted pig. Lucius almost buckled at the knees when he caught wind of the pork, realizing that he hadn't eaten since before the final battle.

Severus ushered them forward. "Praetor Metellus, here are the Cascas."

Manius and Lucius saluted in unison.

Quintus Caecillus Metellus stood in front of them wearing a beautifully made, extraordinarily colorful toga. He was slender and vibrant, with handsome features and sharp, clear brown eyes. His hair, however, had thinned desperately through the years, causing him to comb what remained into an elaborate black filigree above his brow. Holding a cup with one hand, he gestured with the other at the two stout men standing in front of him, still in their blood-stained armor.

"Twins, by the gods, what a blessing. No wonder your reputations as fierce warriors precede you, a couple of regular Romulus and Remus's." Metellus waited, then said, "Well, speak up. Everyone's entitled to bray after victory!"

Manius said, "Thank you, my commander. The honor is all yours for leading the way to your triumph."

"Oh, a golden-tongued warrior as well. Triumph, indeed. I imagine you see yourself in the front ranks marching through the streets of Rome, all of the women lining up hoping to play the lioness with you?"

"Not at all, sir. I'm happy to be where I am," Manius said, bowing his head.

"Indeed." Metellus turned his head to Lucius, "And what about you? Are you, too, a soldier poet?"

Lucius shook his head, "Not really, Praetor. Just a soldier, sir."

"A silver-tongued soldier in your modest simplicity. Your brother will go far, but you'll go farther, I think." Metellus turned away and motioned to the wine steward.

The two brothers grinned at each other, then bowed and took a step back, thinking the audience was over.

"No, boys, I'm not done with you yet." Metellus handed them each a cup of wine. "Drink." He turned again and beckoned to a short man, fit, and wearing exquisite bronzed armor.

Metallus greeted him with an arm over his shoulder.

"Centurions Casca, this is Scipio Aemilianus of the Fourth. His contribution to our success here cannot be calculated. Because of Scipio, Macedonia will be Rome's first eastern province."

Scipio smiled skeptically, "You've outdone yourself spreading the horse dung this time."

Metellus laughed, "True, but you've earned the right to call yourself the second-best tactician in the tent." They laughed sharply together, and Metellus continued, "Rome knows it, too, and they've decreed that Scipio will go to Africa to clean up the mess at Carthage. Carthage must be destroyed, you know." The two officers laughed again.

"This means that Scipio will need good soldiers, men he can count on as his own. He will need seasoned leaders to bring him victory. Centurions, I would think."

Manius and Lucius glanced at each other.

"The Cascas could be good men for the job. Sons of a freedman, right?"

"Yes sir."

Scipio leaned toward them. "Centurion Primus Cassius Casca. Your father died today."

The two brother dropped their heads in unison. "He did, Tribune."

Scipio nodded, saying, "My condolences." He said to Metellus, "I'll take these centurions to Carthage. I'm sure they'll serve well."

"Not both of them, you won't. I want one as primus of the Second, to replace their father."

Scipio nodded, "I can understand that. But, which one?"

Metellus shrugged his shoulders, "Flip a coin."

Scipio yelled, "Crassus!"

A tall, lanky man came forward from a game of chance with various officers. They followed him over, and by this time, the entire host in the large tent had gathered around the two most illustrious Romans in Macedonia.

"You're quaestor, Crassus," said Scipio, "please tell me you have one coin left."

The men laughed loudly as Crassus smiled and pulled a gold coin from his purse.

"Thank you. Just a loan, I'll return it soon," which brought on more laughter.

Scipio then turned to the twins and said, "Who's older?"

Manius raised his hand. Scipio said, "Huh," as he looked back and forth from the two brothers, "who would have guessed? Well, Manius Casca, it's yours to call. Mars, you go to Carthage with me, Galley, you stay with Praetor Metellus. Call it in the air."

He tossed the coin in the air, and as it descended, Manius shouted out, "Mars!"

With easy grace, Scipio caught the gold piece and slapped it on the back of his hand. He lifted the top one, glanced, and then showed Metellus, who nodded his head in assent.

"Mars it is, Manius. You will fight by my side in Carthage."

All of the men roared their approval as Scipio grabbed Manius around the shoulders and gave him the gold coin. Metellus grasped Lucius's hand and shook it up and down, gesturing to Crassus to bring him a coin as well.

And, so, Manius Casca Capito went to Africa with Publius Cornelius Scipio Aemelianus, where he died a year later charging the walls of Carthage on a narrow dirt mole built to bridge the harbor.

Clearly Pluto's agent, Severus once again broke the news to Lucius of his brother's death. "Killed by an arrow during a charge," he said, "led by some glory-seeking junior officer named Gracchus. Seems this little turd won the Mural Crown, too, though he apparently made a dogs' dinner out of the assault itself. Just plain lucky, you know? Didn't have much stomach for it either, packed up and left while the city was being sacked. Can you imagine? All that booty just left there."

Lucius was still with Metellus, dealing with the Achaean League when Severus showed up. From the way the old veteran told the story, it sounded like Manius had died because of some fool junior officer's stupidity or even cowardice. Lucius couldn't say that he missed his brother all that much, but something was missing. Maybe he should look for this Gracchus when he returned from war and kill him, just for the sake of being the only Casca of his lot left.

A decade later, he found himself mustered out of the ranks. Metellus was now Metellus Macedonicus, rich beyond measure, such that he could build beautiful porticos and temples made of marble to Juno and Jupiter. Lucius had marched in Metellus's triumph for his victory at Seraphia, and he had marched with the newly elected consul against the Celtiberians in Hispania. They had won then, unlike their successors, who seemed to lose all the time. Metellus finally retired from war, and Lucius Casca did as well, finding himself now a resident veteran of Rome.

"I'm through with war. Too boring."

"Really?" said Helena, eyeing him with special skepticism saved for liars. "Then, what will you do with yourself?"

Casca shrugged, "Hire myself out. Maybe as a bodyguard, I don't know."

"Or maybe an assassin."

He shrugged, "Sure, maybe." And she cuffed the back of his head.

"You won't stay put, Naso, I know you and your kind. You'll run out of money and vinegar wine, and you'll end up doing the only thing you've ever known how to do, march far away and fight strangers. I'll be stuck here on my own, still working in that swill house slinging foul wine and getting my ass grabbed."

Casca rose up and turned to Helena, who faced away from him. "I swear upon Mars' brow and Juno's breast that I will not leave you, ever. This I swear."

She softened, and he held her in his arms in a long, silent hug.

Then, the word was out that the Consul Hostilius Mancinus was returning to Hispania to deal with the Numantines. Casca could care less until he learned that the consul's quaestor would be none other than Tiberius Gracchus. Just days later, he found out that the new officer was looking for centurions to lead his force through Italia.

Without thinking twice, Casca decided to present himself for service, sure that he would be instated, given his sterling record with Metellus, especially in Hispania. Then, he could kill this Gracchus either right away or on the Via Aurelia, after which he might have a chance to run. He thought about it for a moment, then nodded, his jaw set.

Wearing his old lorica and helmet, he stepped out of their sleeping nook and started for the door. Helena tried to grab his arm, but he shook her off, causing her to drop to her knees. The last he saw of her, she was on all fours heaving between wails of misery.

The new quaestor did not make him wait when he arrived at his papillo. Upon entering, Casca snapped to attention, his right hand on the butt of his sword. He eyed this new officer out of the corner of his eye, knowing that he could extract his blade with ease and slash it across the nape of his neck before a shout could pass his lips. He waited, though.

The man was long and lean, appearing more fit than Casca expected. He looked more like a Hispanii with his black hair and bluish eyes. He also looked older, too, closer to his own age than he expected. Casca knew that this quaestor was a decade younger than he, but still. What really stopped him, though, was when this Gracchus recognized him at once.

"I am Lucius Casca, Manius Casca's brother, it's true . . . he died a soldier's death, no one to blame, Fortuna left his side . . . I'm happy to serve."

Instead of leaving a corpse in the quaestor's tent, he left as Centurion Primus on his way to recruit four more brothers-in-arms to serve this new officer. Oh well, he thought, better to wait and kill him on the road with friends around.

To his everlasting surprise, amazement even, it did not work out that way. Every day spent with the lanky Quaestor was another day in which Casca didn't get around to murdering him. When they marched from Rome, Gracchus sat a giant warhorse wearing a ridiculously ornate helmet, a shiny gold replica of Alexander's headwear when he conquered the world. Yet, after they'd left Rome's gates behind, Gracchus had packed the silly headdress away and sported a farmer's broad straw hat on their march to shun the bright spring sun.

He rode the huge horse poorly, too, and many times he allowed his young slave to ride instead, while he walked next to him, leading the mount by its reins. The slave looked like a slighter, younger version of his master, though Casca didn't think he was having the boy. He just seemed to enjoy the slave's thrill at riding.

Gracchus marched the men hard, but halted so that they billeted early enough to rest. He made sure that they ate well, too, though the gold for it must have come out of his own pocket. The scandalous story of the procurement of the army payroll by Mancinus and his accomplice Fabius moved through the cohort like a brisk breeze riffling a field of grain. Plenty of time to slice the penniless quaestor, though. No hurry, Casca thought at the end of each night.

Then, they bumped into the horde of ousted farmers and broken-down vets, all apparently tossed off their land by Rufus and his fellow, fat senator chums. To Casca's astonishment, Gracchus took on all of those starving plebs, even sticking his thumb in Rufus's eye by stripping his big plantation to feed those starving human cows. Casca grinned, thinking about little Rufus jumping up and down screeching when he learned that his barns were emptied. He was a powerful little turd, though, thick with Nasica and his like. But, Gracchus seemed to be connected, too; Scipio Aemilianus for a brother-in-law, you couldn't do better than that. The Quaestor showed some genius by having all those old legionaries re-up to fill out his legion. Once more, Casca decided to wait and see while they crossed the water to Hispania. Garrote him and dump him into the sea—no body, no murder.

Everything changed. Even Casca thought they all would be crossing the River soon when the Numantine horsemen kept picking them off day and night, every day it seemed. The barbarians hung the flayed Roman bodies from trees by their heels to scare the rest of them back home. Everyone seemed ready to run, even the seasoned mules Mancinus had given to his new quaestor. True, they weren't much as soldiers go, but they had been on campaign before. Yet, the Numantines had them spooked. It looked like the new legion would be heading back to Hispania Citerior before they'd even gotten started. But, Gracchus ordered the attack on the riverbank.

It never would have worked without perfect planning, perfect timing, and every bit of Fortuna's good luck. Also, despite their fear, the men listened and believed in Gracchus's plan. When he laid out the ambush, the first to step up were the evocati, with the old primus Sacerdotus in the front line. Casca noticed then how sheepish the men from Mancinus's cohort were when they volunteered second. Even that peacock horse trader Sextus seemed ready to go.

And, it worked, despite being on enemy ground. It worked despite the odds-on likelihood of tipping their hand while trying to slip a hundred men in behind the barbarians on a neighboring slope. Maybe the Numantines were too ready to finish us off, Casca mused, and paid no attention to obvious signs that numbers for the legion were missing. No matter, they chased the Numies off and slaughtered any still left alive lying in the field. Yes, thought Casca, up until then Gracchus had proven himself to be a somewhat better officer than expected. But, the execution of the rattrap on the riverbank showed him to be one tricky bastard. After that, he owned his men forever. After that, Casca knew that he would not kill Gracchus, he would follow him.

He did, through the brutal victory at Malia and the disaster at Numantia. He saw Gracchus extract his legion from a catastrophic rout after Mancinus had bolted. He watched him position his men up the side of a mountain on the Numantine flank so that they couldn't push the main army into the river. In battle, he witnessed the full-grown version of the young warrior who won the Mural Crown, running across the wooden battlements until a Numantine arrow knocked him off the wall into the ground. Casca blanched then, thinking their only hope was dead. But, the groggy son of a bitch showed himself to be tough, too. The newly minted tribune of the Ninth pulled himself up and staggered forward to rally his men once more. Only his silly helmet looked the worse for wear, Casca laughed to himself, not so fancy anymore.

He also saw him follow the orders of their corrupt consul, crucifying a slave boy whom he loved like his own son.

He sipped the vinegary wine, sweating large beads that dripped from his head like raindrops in the brutal, midday heat. His smile turned sour again. Off went the tribune and the equitus to negotiate Mancinus's peace. Casca thought he'd never see them again, unless the Numantines lined up their heads together in the same row. But, they did come back, and Sextus, forgetting his usual preening cock-of-the-walk strut, described in holy tones the wondrous peace granted to Gracchus. They all would walk out, the Ninth and Mancinus's entire force. When he heard the horse rider tell him, Casca snorted his skepticism in supreme disdain. Yet, they did walk out of Numantia, out of Hispania, and onto ships sailing home to Italia.

When they arrived at Cosa, Gracchus cut loose the surviving old vets and their sons. Casca figured that he and the remains of the Ninth's original cohort would be mustered next. That would be the last he saw of Gracchus. But, the tribune surprised him by settling the old mules in a camp near Cosa to rebuild a road. When Senator Claudius appeared, Casca again thought that Gracchus was gone for good.

Instead, Gracchus ordered Casca to finish the road, march the cohort back to Rome, then report to him at his home in Rome. Then, Casca began to think that the Fates had intertwined their threads forever.

By the time Casca arrived in Rome, the big story was racing back and forth through town: the Senate was trying Tiberius Sempronius Gracchus for making peace with the barbarians of Numantia, clearly a treasonable offense.

Casca presented himself to Gracchus that night. Standing in the vestibulum doorway, as big as he was, he felt small. The Greek who greeted him brought him into the main hall and asked him to wait while he fetched his master. Gracchus swept into the hall grinning broadly. He grabbed Casca by his upper left arm while he clasped his right hand.

"Centurion Primus Casca Naso—Lucius—welcome to our home."

Weirdly, at that moment Casca recognized, somewhat ironically, that he would die for this man.

Gracchus brought him into the main room and introduced him to his stunning wife Claudia. Holding a beautiful child in her arms, she mentioned how much they had heard about the feats of the centurion primus in Hispania. Senator Claudius hailed him warmly as well, and two other little children ran overf to look up at him in awe. Then, Gracchus introduced him to his mother, Cornelia Scipio Sempronia. Even Casca understood the power in this tiny woman, a woman universally known as the most august in all of Rome.

She bowed her head slightly when introduced and said, "I understand that you were brave in Numantia. My son tells me that none of them would have survived without you anchoring the legion. Salve, Centurion Casca."

Casca bent at the waist and kissed her hand and everyone laughed and applauded.

Gracchus moved to him, "Come, Lucius, I have a small matter to take care of."

He ushered the centurion into the peristylum and sat him down on a long couch, one that could be used to recline on and read, or just rest while listening to the small birds in the fig trees. To Casca's surprise, Gracchus sat on the wall of the pond opposite him, their knees almost touching. He leaned over with his hands together and said, "I am so happy to see you, Lucius. You were the pillar of the Ninth, you know? Everything my mother said about you is true. We wouldn't have survived without you leading us or covering our backs. You and your brother legionaries were the ones who saw us through this mess."

"You made the deal with the Numantines," Casca said. "You persuaded them to let us leave without punishment."

Gracchus shook his head. "They made the peace because we had them in a vice. If they ignored us, we would attack their flanks. If they tried to take our position, old Pyrrhus had a lesson for them." He sat up straight. "Do you know what I learned while in the Numantine stronghold? They only had 8,000, maybe 10,000 total in their army. Not 50,000, 10,000! If we'd known that, we could have won."

Casca said, "Not with Mancinus in command."

Gracchus pulled in a little, "Yes, well, we won't know, I suppose." He looked down at his sandals, now quiet. Casca said, "I heard about your troubles with the Senate."

"Oh, yes. Politics."

"They are out of their minds. We could have been massacred. It's that little pig-faced Rufus, isn't it?"

"Yes, he's involved. Still, he is a senator. Senator pig face. Fits with his bean-shaped body," he said offhandedly.

They both laughed, then lapsed again into silence. Tiberius seemed distracted until he briskly shook his head. "No matter, Lucius, I wanted to thank you personally for your service, and also for safeguarding the return of the men to Rome. And, I wanted to find out your plans for the future. Do you have anything in mind? More soldiering? Successfully, this time, of course."

Casca laughed and said, "No, I'm done with that now. Getting grey, you know?"

"I'd say I look older right now. In any case, I wanted to give you something in appreciation of what you've done for the Ninth."

"I can't take anything from you, sir."

"It's not from me," said Tiberius, "it's from our illustrious Senator Rufus."

As he spoke, the old Greek slave came into the room and handed the tribune a small leather bag. "The last of the legion's coin," said Tiberius as he passed it to Casca. "I held some back for you. It's not much, but it should tide you over until you decide what you want to do. When you do have an idea, come see me, if I'm still around that is," he chuckled. "Perhaps my family and I can help you."

When the day of the tribunes's trial came, Casca stood close to the Senate doors early in the morning. He watched as Nasica performed the rites of sacrifice to bless the Senate's actions that day. He saw them all filing in, close in with the other members of their factions. Tiberius finally appeared with a couple of senators whom Casca didn't recognize. Senator Claudius walked with him, too, though. He happened to glance Casca's way and saw him standing at the doorway. He nodded slightly, and went inside.

From what he could hear, matters seemed to be going badly. He slipped his hand into his tunic and fingered the blade of the dolo tucked away out of sight. He knew that he couldn't take on the whole of Rome's Senate and their guard. But, he thought, in case someone inside started something. Just in case.

Hours later, Scipio Aemilianus arrived. As he walked toward the entrance to the Curia Hostilia, he squinted at Casca as if trying to place him. Then, his eyes opened wide.

"Centurion Lucius Casca, by the Gemini stars!" he said.

Casca nodded and saluted, saying evenly, "Consul Scipio."

"One of the Casca centurions in Rome," Scipio said, his eyes staring into Casca's, though his thoughts seemed years away.

"Retired, sir," Casca said.

"Yes," said Scipio, "Of course. We're all growing too old for the long campaign these days, no, Primus? But, I bet it wouldn't take much to bring you back into the field, right?" Casca didn't reply, and Scipio said, "Well, I must go in, Casca, but keep a thought in mind about a return to service. Opportunities might come your way that could get your blood going again, not to mention filling your purse."

Scipio left, and in a matter of minutes, Tiberius Gracchus was acquitted of the Good Men's charges. As soon as he heard the crowd roaring for his tribune, Casca left to find his favorite taverna on the Aventine.

So, here he sat, two years later, still drinking bitter wine while waiting for Helena or Ariadne to show up. Neither did. Scipio had summoned him, preparing for his try at Numantia. Casca ignored the call, telling the messenger to let Scipio know that he was a full-time drunk now. He wanted no part of Hispania anymore, never mind Numantia.

He scraped together a living by doing a little body guarding, some thieving, collecting wagers around the edges of the Circus, even fighting as a gladiator in a few funereal matches. He kept a small room on the top floor of an insula, but most of his money went to vinegar wine. Others might have thought of his life as a waste of time; he only thought of it as waiting, watching.

The heat and the brilliant sunlight caused everyone in the wine house to lay their heads on the tabletops. Casca positioned himself so that he could fix one eye on the door while he rested.

A shadow filled the doorway, framing a figure more wide than tall, but substantial. Whoever it was gazed around, searching. Casca slipped his hand into his tunic to grasp the haft of his dolo. The figure gathered himself, and walked straight into the room, straight at Casca, followed by four other bulky silhouettes. Casca unlimbered his dolo and held it beneath the table pointed at the men.

"Centurion Primus Casca!"

Senator Appius Claudius Pulcher stood before Casca, his hands outstretched. Behind him stood an old vet, maybe a first spear himself at one time. Backing him up were three roughnecks, probably from the same legion as the old veteran.

"Senator Claudius, what a pleasant surprise."

"Indeed! May I sit down?"

"There's only room for one more here."

"That's all we require." Claudius waved to the men standing behind him, who split up to take seats at tables directly behind and to each side of the one Casca occupied.

Appius worked his way around the bench on the other side and sat like a sack of grain hitting the floor. "Ah," he said, "it is hot out there today."

He pulled a silk cloth from his toga and wiped his sweating brow, which immediately blossomed forth an entirely new crop of perspiration.

"So, Casca, how are you? Are you well?"

Casca moved his mouth as though tasting something he couldn't quite identify. "I am alive, Senator, so I am well."

"Good, good, well stated!" Appius leaned in and said, "Making a good living, I suppose?"

"Enough to buy wine. What more do I need?"

"Ah, yes, you've definitely taken a philosophical bend, Centurion, since we last met."

"Blame the wine, Senator, for that and how much I talk these days."

"Yes, I imagine you are a man of few words on any other day. But, to run into you after all these years, well, it does mark a special occasion. Girl!" he beckoned, "More wine for my friend here, and for me."

When she had put down the cups in front of them, Casca watched as Claudius picked his up and drained it without a thought. The old man had been a soldier, he noted.

"So, Senator," Casca said, "did you?"

Appius looked at the centurion. "Did I what?"

"Just 'run into me.'"

"Ah," said Appius. He rested his weight on his arms on the table, which brought him closer to Casca. "Of course, not exactly. You are a shrewd one, you are, Centurion."

"It didn't take a soothsayer to figure it out."

"No, of course not." Appius drew back. "In fact, I was searching you out."

"To introduce me to your fellows, here?" Casca said, gesturing with his head at the four men sitting around them.

"Oh, no, Ajax and his men are precautions only. I learned that you were down in this suburbia, clearly a lively, diverse community. However, one such as myself might look too out of place, perhaps attracting undue attention. Ajax and his men allow me to blend in."

"Yes, they do," Casca said with a straight face, and Appius couldn't help smiling. "So, what can I do for you, Senator Claudius?"

Again, Appius drew closer to Casca across the table. "It's not me you can do something for, Casca, it's your old tribune Tiberius Gracchus."

Casca suddenly showed interest. "Go on."

Appius glanced to his left, then said, "After the difficulties he suffered upon his arrival back from Numantia, Tribune Gracchus determined to tend to his family and his holdings. Now that two years have passed since then, Gracchus has decided to reenter public life."

"How so?" asked Casca.

"He plans to run for office."

"Consul? That seems a reach."

Appius shook his head emphatically, "No, no, that would be impossible. No, Gracchus is a man of the people. He feels that the common people of Rome have suffered losses during the past many years, losses economically, politically, and, as a result, a loss of equality. These losses are egregious and a threat to the very survival of the Republic, so Gracchus thinks. He believes that it is his duty as a Roman and a plebeian to do all he can to rectify this dangerous imbalance of power. Therefore, Tiberius Sempronius Gracchus has decided to run for a position as a tribune of the people."

Appius watched Casca to see his reaction. The centurion sat stone-faced without speaking immediately. Then, he said, "Admirable. I suppose he plans on introducing some laws that might annoy some in the Senate?"

Appius slowly moved his head up and down, "A significant number of senators in a certain faction definitely will find his agenda troubling."

Casca grunted, "Hah." He stared at the tabletop for a time while thinking. "So, where do I come into this?"

Appius said, "We would like you to be his agent in the Aventine and the surrounding suburbias. Find others such as yourself and begin speaking upon your old tribune's behalf. See where the opposition might lie, and let us know. Also, form a core group of men who could be counted on to defend the tribune should an uglier side of the contest present itself. Ajax and his comrades will be your first recruits."

"Reporting to me?" Casca said. "Old Ajax looks too much the part of a primus himself to take my orders."

"Ah, thank you, brother," interjected Ajax. "I was a prior in the Third, never a primus. I know you from Macedonia and the Ninth in Hispania. I'm happy and proud to serve as your man, Primus."

Casca nodded at the beaming Ajax, then turned back to Appius.

"There will be money," Appius volunteered.

Casca shook his head, "I don't need money. I'll do it for free."

Appius smiled, "That's very generous of you, very noble, but unnecessary and not good practice. What you will be doing for the Tribune will be a full-time job, and you will need money to grease the wheels. That's how politics work. Also, we don't want you to have to worry about making a living while serving Gracchus. We want to employ your full attention to the tasks at hand. We prefer that you cease earning your living the way you have been during the past two years."

Casca grinned, "No head knocking, no slippery fingers? Where's the fun?"

Appius said, "Think of those who won't like Tiberius Gracchus being in a position of authority, of being able to tell them what to do. That should be fun enough."

Casca laughed and said, "I can see it would be." He paused for a moment, then said, "You have an agent in the Aventine, Senator."

Appius broke into a radiant smile. "Excellent, Centurion, excellent." He reached out his hand and clasped Casca's. "Tiberius will be happy, very happy. He thinks the world of you, you know?"

"I think the world of him," said Casca.

"Well, very well, then." Appius pulled a leather bag from his toga, shook it, jangling it a bit, and placed it on the table. "Seed money for you. There will be more as needed. Ajax will stay with you to discuss plans. He'll come back and report to me. If you need anything, however, come to me whenever you want."

Appius stood up, again offering his hand, and shook Casca's hard.

"All right. I believe we've finished for today. Vale, Centurion Primus Casca."

"You, too, Senator. Vale."

Appius turned and left accompanied by the other three men. Casca turned to Ajax and said, "Have a seat, brother. Let's set to it. More wine!" he barked as Ajax sat across from him, smiling.

Chapter 26. Toga Candida

A tiny frog jumped from the side of the little pond in the peristylum into the water with a dainty splash. Tiberius watched it spread and snap its hind legs as it disappeared beneath the water. He glanced around and saw another, no bigger than his thumbnail, sitting on a lily pad. Signaled by some arcane summons, it, too, arced into the air and the water. Tiberius shifted around, wondering if the house cat lurked nearby. He lifted his eyes to see if birds were flying across the opening above the atrium. They should be migrating, now that it was the middle of autumn. No, nothing. Maybe they'd already flown away.

Or, maybe he had scared them away. The idea surprised him, he sat so quietly, completely relaxed. He had the pond built in the peristylum after his return from Cosa. It became his place of choice when he wished to be silent, to contemplate the life given to him by Fortuna and the other gods and goddesses. He relished perching on the corner of the pond to watch the living creatures come and go in their small universe. The pond served as their entire world, the frogs, the fresh-water minnows brought here from a country brook, the silverfish gliding faster than Jupiter's lightning from side to side, plant to plant. In the center, a magnificent cluster of reeds and water flowers intertwined like exotic dancers in a glorious, serpentine climb to the nurturing sunlight. Birds occasionally darted in from above searching for a fruit fly or some other juicy bug. The peace of it all, the beauty, made him sigh.

Claudia knew how much he enjoyed this time. She kept the children away from him, though sometimes he asked her to let them come. They ran to him silly with pleasure at playing with their papa, doing their best to push him into the water. Little Tiberius and Cornelia Sempronia were seven and six, now, Gaius was three, and baby Appius barely kept his feet at one. He scooped up the youngest and gave them big hugs, giggles all around. Young Tiberius continued pushing, however, his head down in stubborn concentration.

"Tiberius, stop, please. Please stop. If you push me into the water, I might squash the frogs and fish. Is that what you want?"

The boy slowed down his assault, turning to a deliberate, steady pummeling with his fists, "Papa, play with me, play with me!" his lips shaped in a pout as if he knew already the preordained answer.

"I'm sorry, son, not right now. Soon, I'll have to prepare myself to leave."

"You're always leaving!" whined little Tiberius.

"That's right, you always leave," said his sister, who was walking laps around the pool with her finger on the top of the tiles.

"Now, Cornelia Sempronia," said Tiberius, who screwed up one eye and asked, "what are you doing?"

"Tracing the wall, of course."

"I see." She always seemed to be the smartest. Young Tiberius continued his pounding until his father grabbed his wrists and lifted him straight up into the air.

"How about another kiss? Another kiss and a hug before I go."

In spite of himself, the boy started laughing, even as he pleaded, "No! No! No!"

"Oh, yes, yes, yes," Tiberius said, burrowing his head into his son's neck, punctuating each "yes" with a kiss. The boy squirmed, nearly hysterical now, laughing until he couldn't breathe.

"I want a kiss, too, Papa," cried Cornelia Sempronia.

"Oh, you do, do you? Finished with your measurements?"

"Yes, yes!" she shrieked.

"Well, then, very well." He lowered his son down while the boy said, "No, just me, just me!"

"No, everyone gets a hug and a kiss whether they like it or not," Tiberius said, lifting Cornelia Sempronia up with one arm. He nuzzled her neck to screams of delight while young Tiberius tried to push his way between.

"Po-po go away?" said Gaius at his feet. Tiberius glanced down, then to the doorway just as Claudia strode in carrying Appius in her arms and saying, "What a remarkable din you're all making, barbarians in the peristylum!"

"Po-po go?" said Gaius, looking up now at his mother. She leaned down to her knees and said, "Yes, Gaius, I'm afraid it's time for Papa to go change. He has important tasks he must do."

She had filled out during the past three years, still skinny for a proper Roman matron, but looking even more beautiful than ever to Tiberius. Bearing many children does that to a woman, though most of the grand dames of Rome cultivated a burgeoning shape to accent their station in life rather than the fecundity of their flesh. To Tiberius, Claudia now seemed more like a Venus by Praxiteles; he preferred picturing her as the master sculptor's statue on Knidos rather than Kos. The goddess of love unadorned, not mantled and draped.

"Are you ready to dress?" she asked him.

He cocked his head to one side, squinting his eyes in feigned thought. "You could help me dress."

She smiled skeptically rather than joyfully. "Oh, no. That's how I got this one," she said, tipping her head toward Appius, who took this opportunity to tug at one of her raven black curls. The boy had the same hair, Tiberius noted, and the violet eyes, too. They all took after their mother, little Sempronia and Gaius, too. All except Tiberius, his pale blue eyes clearly marking him as the first-born son. His disposition, though, mirrored that of his impetuous uncle.

"Hylas can help you," Claudia said. "I must get these children fed and put them to bed or they will tear the house down."

Hylas. Brought to them by Polydius to replace Lysis. Short and stocky, he came from Crete of all places. He looked strong enough to grab a bull's horns, but too small, thought Tiberius, to clear its head if tossed. He shrugged his shoulders and said to himself, We'll see if he fits in here. Then, he admonished himself as he walked behind the dark Greek into his bed chamber. Even if Hylas proved himself to be the most incompetent servant in the world, he probably had found himself a home for life. That's how the Gracchi treated everyone in the house. By Orcus's shades, Lysis had stumbled about no matter what he was told, and they'd kept him. Of course, they had loved Lysis.

Hylas turned and gestured to the toga on the bed, "Master?"

Tiberius leaned forward. The toga gleamed from the chalk Hylas had applied to it, almost as blinding as the sun. Tiberius straightened and looked at him with some surprise. "This could not be better. Apollo himself will be jealous."

Hylas smiled broadly, and Tiberius thought then that they might get along. "Here, help me into it."

When he emerged from the room, Claudia saw him and stepped back. "You look," she said with a full voice, "magnificent."

Tiberius grinned, "Perfect target for a rotten tomato or two, anyway."

"No," she said, "you look the part. You look like a man, a Roman man of stature."

"Well, I am, aren't I?" he laughed, "Unless you're saying I wasn't before. That would be disheartening."

She laughed with him and he moved in to embrace her. "No, no!" she cried, scurrying away, her hands held high in front of her. "You cannot touch anything before you leave the house. Who knows where the children have been with their sticky paws?"

"Now, I'm sad," he said, his lower lip pushed out in exaggerated sorrow.

"Yes, well, live with it. You're the one who wants to be a Roman of stature."

"Not really," he said as a tumult was heard at the front door, sending everyone into the vestibulum. He trailed, muttering, "I just want to do some good."

Appius Claudius Pulcher marched into the vestibulum in full senatorial regalia, the crimson stripes bordering his toga signifying his status as consular, a former censor, an augur of the Salli, and a most esteemed patriarch of the city. Crassus followed him, resplendent in his own brilliant toga, and behind him followed a half dozen or more other respected members of the Senate, all Populares, of course.

Appius stepped over to Tiberius, saying as he grabbed his shoulders, "You look stunning." Tiberius turned to Claudia and said, "How sticky do you think his fingers are?"

She frowned, and Appius immediately withdrew his hands.

"Oh, yes, so sorry," Appius said. "Of course, too, as one of your deductores, I must keep distance from you as if you have the plague."

"That far?" Tiberius said.

"All right, only as far as if you have bad breath." Everyone laughed and Appius continued, "Really, though, son-in-law, we do not want to break tradition at any point. Nasica and Rufus would climb all over us if we gave them the smallest reason, though reason would seem to be a foreign notion to them. No matter, when we go out that door, we will be there to walk with you. Otherwise, you will be on your own."

Having run for aedile ages ago, and more recently riding as quaestor, Tiberius knew well the strictures involved in electioneering. Those campaigns had been fairly easy, he recognized, compared to this one. To be aedile, he only had to spend a little money on some entertainments and a few public feasts. Other than promising to be diligent in safeguarding the city's water supply and other public facilities, not much had been asked of him as an orator. The same with the quaestorship; he simpy hung on to Mancinus's toga to win. A good thing, too, he thought, since he could not claim grandiloquent rhetoric as one of his strong suits.

Running for tribune of the people called for much more than a few free feeds and some boxing matches. It meant real ambitus, promises of money, then spreading it around after the vote. This time, too, he would have to sponsor races in the Circus with bread and wine in the stands. Thank the gods for his mother's largesse. Still, this was nothing compared to the hurdles he would have on the Rostrum. While he stood there, trying to gather himself to make his case, the ranks would be full of Optimate plants howling catcalls and throwing rotten fruit. He was supposed to maintain his dignitas no matter what. But, it would be hard, he recognized. Any reasonable man would think either to run away, or to run after his tormenters. But, what could he do? Even if there were no jackals in the crowd, he'd proven himself not much of a crowd pleaser in the past. He found himself comfortable when he spoke plainly and quietly rather than thumping the podium with his fists while roaring exclamations. Tiberius would never admit it to Appius or his mother, but this seemed like an uphill battle to him, and he was tired of fighting.

Just then, Philea came in with a basket of warm bread followed by Hylas and Polydius with cups of honey and cider. The men descended upon the baskets and trays, intending to shore up their energy for the long walk about the city. Appius used the distraction to draw close to Tiberius.

"Your man Casca will be with us as well, along with Ajax and a few of their friends. They'll make sure that no roughnecks interfere with your oration."

Relief swept over Tiberius, though with some guilt. Money, games, and now strong-arming would be the signature of his tribunal campaign. No different than it had always been, he knew, but not what he had in mind when he decided to enter into public service.

"All right, are we ready?" Appius asked the men grouped around the baskets.

Before anyone could answer, his mother Cornelia glided into the hallway. She went straight to Tiberius's side, grasped an arm and pulled him down to her level to kiss him on each cheek, saying under her breath, "We are proud of you. Honor your father's spirit."

She let him go and returned to her chamber. With a startled expression, he watched her leave. Claudia came to him with the children, keeping them at a slight distance. "Say goodbye to your father, children. Tell him to walk with Fortuna. Bye-bye."

She stepped close to him and kissed his lips quickly, "Goodbye, Tribune."

He smiled, and Appius laughed, "All right, let's go!"

They assembled at the door, and Appius led the way with Crassus, followed by Tiberius and the others. Outside the front door, Tiberius spied Casca leaning on the wall near the gate. The old centurion stood up and gave a wave to someone out of sight in the street. He turned, then, and gave Tiberius a slow nod. Tiberius nodded in return, and watched him quickly go through the gate ahead of Appius and the rest. When they reached the street, Casca was nowhere in sight.

They started down the hill together, Appius looking straight ahead while talking quietly.

"We'll head for the Subura first. To win, first and foremost Tiberius must convince the common Roman that he is the man for the job."

The others groaned and murmured, knowing that the Subura, with its towering insulae and close proximity to the burial grounds of the Esquiline would exude a stifling stench melded from both human defecation and death.

"Now, now," said Appius, "let's not allow effete sensibilities interfere with our desire and duty to support the Gracchus campaign. After all, in the course of enacting his official policies, he just might be able to do something about the Subura's wretched stink."

The men laughed, and Appius added, "In any case, we need their vote. Afterward, we will head for the Capitoline. That's something to look forward to."

They headed down the narrow alley toward the street, Appius leaning close to Tiberius, whispering, "It's a shame Scaveola couldn't join us today. I'm sure he has plenty to do on his own campaign, and considering how many of the Good Men feel about you, it might be better for him to keep his distance until he wins."

Tiberius nodded his agreement. Filling Scipio's sandals as consul would be a tall order for Scaveola. Fortunately, Scipio, his only real threat if he were to run had all but disappeared from the Senate. The hero of Africa now spent most of his time preparing for his campaign against the Numantines. Scaveola knew, of course, that Nasica and the other Optimates would do their best to stop him, but he seemed to have momentum on his side.

"So, now we know what he did with the outrageous legal fees he's been extorting from me for years," Appius murmured. "His campaign war chest must be overflowing."

They reached the end of the side street and stepped up onto the hexagonal stones paving the main thoroughfare. Tiberius moved to the front of his entourage, which walked in order four paces behind him. All of them stopped chattering as they focused on the business at hand, marching with great gravity behind their chosen candidate.

Tiberius scanned the sidewalks for potential voters and saw just a few people. He saw two workmen carrying wood into a small shop for some building project.

"Salve!" he called out as he approached, reaching up with his right hand. The men appeared a bit startled to have someone who was obviously a well-to-do in a searing white robe hailing them heartily, his hand ready to shake their callused, leathery paws.

"Tiberius Sempronius Gracchus at your service, hoping to continue serving you as tribune of the people, if I can win your vote." He pumped their hands up and down in turn, grinning broadly at them. The last man allowed Tiberius to raise and lower his hand, while saying, "We don't vote. We own no land, Father."

"Oh," said Tiberius. Flustered, he said, "Well, if I am elected Tribune, perhaps I can change that for you. It is my conviction that every Roman should own land that they can call their own, and be able to vote."

At that, the two workers smiled wide, revealing multiple gaps in their mouth where teeth used to be. They nodded their heads, and bowing, backed away into the shop. Tiberius glanced at Appius and rolled his eyes. Appius shrugged, and Tiberius turned to walk on.

A woman moved up the opposite sidewalk balancing a water jar on top of her head. The party of men passed her without a word, their eyes searching ahead for men who might be able to vote.

Before long they reached the bottom of the hill where they turned right toward the Subura. Soon, they walked amid the tall insulae, some of the apartment buildings well above seven stories, many looking like rickety piles of tinder ready for imminent mass funeral fires. In fact, open spaces occasionally interrupted the series of edifices tightly wedged together, their high horizon broken by a past neighboring structure's immolation or collapse, sometimes both. Before long, another enterprising developer would erect over the ruins another insula of questionable quality to confound the odds of which one would go down next.

A few hundred feet more put them at the edge of one of the largest marketplaces in the vicus where the ironmongers, the wool merchants, the shoemakers, all of the tradesmen and craftsmen plied their skills and wares. Women hawked their goods as well, and strong-arms worked the fringe, hoping to find some inattentive soul walking close to an alley to be hoisted and heisted.

Appius exclaimed "We're here! And, here we go." Oblivious to the disapproving scowls of his companions for breaking the customary silence, he moved toward a fountain in the middle of the square. There, women filled their water jugs while others beat dirty dregs out of their clothes against the tops of the stone walls, twisting and wringing the cloth, then slapping them against the flat slate tiles. When they noticed Appius approaching, however, they all stopped and gave way without a word.

Appius stepped up on the wall and raised his hands. Waving his arms to attract attention, he called out to the people in the square.

"Romans! Romans! Come hear your candidate for tribune!"

Again, the others in Tiberius's entourage were aghast at Appius's violation of traditional protocol. But Appius didn't seem to care, grinning broadly as Tiberius rose up to replace him on the wall.

People slowly gathered around, more out of curiosity, it seemed, rather than a burning desire to hear from some egg-white politician. Tiberius cleared his throat, and suddenly realized that he would benefit if he could spit. He swallowed, and spoke.

"Fellow Romans ... people of Rome who work ... you who are in need."

He could see some at the fringe of the small crowd begin to turn their backs to leave. Heat started to crawl up his neck as he realized that he was losing them already.

"Wait!" he cried out. The men who were leaving stopped and looked back. "Don't leave me to die up here alone!"

The people in the front row laughed, and those in the back drew close again.

"I know you have to make a living," Tiberius said, "but even the hardest working among you need some kind of entertainment. You can always work, it will be there for you always. But, you have no idea of what I might do next!"

A tomato hit him directly on his breast, splattering. The crowd roared their laughter, almost jeering. Tiberius saw two ripples in the crowd, like sea serpents sliding through water. A man tossing a tomato from one hand to the other suddenly went down, disappearing. Quickly, Tiberius rubbed his fingers across his chest and put them in his mouth.

"Ah, at least it's fresh. Toss up some cheese, some oil, and I'll have all I need for a good lunch!"

The listeners laughed, warming to the candidate, not noticing the man being carried away behind them by two brawny men into a narrow alleyway. Tiberius saw him taken away, and started to hurry his speech.

"I won't keep you long. I know you do have to work and can't waste precious time on some egg-white, patrician jackdaw cawing at you. But, I am not a patrician. I am a plebeian like you. I am a veteran and I make my living by growing things to eat. You might be a Roman veteran, but if you work in Rome, my guess is that you do not grow your food. Instead, you live in the city, perhaps finding it hard to feed yourself every day, and your family. For your service to Rome, you were promised land to support you through your own industry. So, what happened? Why are you fighting to get by in the city instead of living on your own land, eating your own home-grown food? Where is the land owed to you for fighting for Rome?

"I am here to ask these questions and to answer them. I believe that every veteran should get the land promised to him. I intend to work to get you that land. That is why I wish to be your tribune."

At his pause, a number of people in the small crowd clapped and shouted their approval. Tiberius went on, "Now, if you have no land, you might not be able to vote for me. I don't care that you cannot vote for me. Rather, I want you to own the land that you deserve, that is my goal. If you believe in me, I will be thankful for your support. Tell your friends who have land of my firm belief in this. Also tell them that I will fight so that no one can take their land ever! Spread the word to other citizens who vote so that we can right the wrong that has cost you your land and your livelihood. I thank you for listening and for your support."

As Tiberius moved to step down, the applause seemed to grow, and various men came up to him to pat him on his shoulders. Tiberius nodded, thanking them, and shaking any proffered hand.

Appius looked at Crassus. "Well, what do you think?"

Crassus screwed up his mouth, and said, "Not half bad for one who's not a natural. He did all right. With a little coaching and polish...."

Appius said, "I agree. To tell you the truth, he did better than I thought he would." As Tiberius slowly worked his way to them, smiling lightly, Appius grunted, "Let's hope he can do as well with men who can vote."

Chapter 27. The Comitia

"Well?"

Appius always felt confounded by Cornelia's ability to turn a question into a command. Maybe it came from the skeptical look in her eyes, forever casting doubt on the subject of her inquiry, either his veracity or intelligence. No matter how long he'd been one of her most faithful confidents, she never failed to unnerve him when she posed such a question.

"Well," he said, "he is doing well. Every day, every speech, he does a little bit better."

"Really?" she said, again in a tone of utter disbelief.

"Cornelia," Appius said patiently, "he's not the hammer of Vulcan as an orator, he never will be, I'm afraid. But, he is ingratiating and his arguments are very rational, very persuasive."

"If anyone listens."

Appius pressed his lips together, stifling a sigh. "They do listen to him. That's where he has improved so much. I actually think that they believe in his sincerity."

"I see." Cornelia sat thinking for a moment. She was propped on the edge of the wall surrounding the peristylum's odd little pond, with its frogs and bugs, and other living things not ordinarily seen in a respectable domus. Usually, they had these meetings in her quarters, but she brought them out here instead. Claudia had taken the children and the rest of the household to the market where some jokester mime was said to have a monkey. Thus, sensitive subjects could be discussed by Rome's most respected matron and one of Rome's few principes senatus.

As if speaking out loud to herself. Cornelia said, "Is that enough to win, though?" She turned her attention back to Appius. "What about this centurion?"

"Casca."

"Yes, Casca. How is he doing with the mob?"

"He's doing very well, very well indeed," said Appius. "Tiberius has seen very little in the way of heckling from the crowd. And the ranks of common supporters swell every day. This Casca is so efficient, I'm surprised he never received some kind of a crown, Grass, Mural."

Cornelia shrugged, "Well, he seems to love Tiberius, though only the gods know why."

Exasperated, Appius said, "That is exactly what I have been trying to tell you! The people who see Tiberius, who hear him, genuinely like him, if they don't love him. Somehow, he builds trust in them. He just needs to keep going. And, he is getting better every time out!"

Cornelia nodded, "Very well." She paused, then said, "Scipio and his lot have put Spurius Postumius up against him. Not a very formidable foe," she laughed, and Appius almost swooned as he heard it. The chimes of her rare laughter, the completely unexpected, stunning smile shocked him. He loved his wife, but Cornelia could win any heart by showing just a glimmer of joy. He remembered how she had smiled all the time when her husband was alive. He could bring her to tears laughing. Then again, Tiberius Gracchus Major could make anyone laugh tears. Since he had left them both, the tears still came, though of a different kind.

"Is there anyone else we need to worry about?" Cornelia asked.

Appius shrugged, "None with the same resources. Marcus Octavius is running. Tiberius seems to be happy about that, they're old friends. He might be an ally if he's elected with Tiberius."

"All right," she said. She thought for a moment, then said, "And the money?"

"Sextus is handling it. He's found fertile ground by tapping his fellow equites to horse trade with potential voters. And, he himself is holding back the funds from all new, voting clients until the election has been settled. With Sextus, we don't have to worry about embezzlement, he's so rich himself. He's an arrogant one, but he, too, has an attachment to Tiberius."

Cornelia took it all in while gazing down at the pond. She ran her fingers across the water's surface, which caused a little burst of frogs to jump to safety. Soon, they would be hibernating for the winter.

"All right, Appius, the campaign seems to be going afoot. It is past time that he head to the Forum and step out on the Rostrum to address the people."

Appius dipped his head, "I know. He's ready now, I think."

"Tomorrow, then?"

"Tomorrow," agreed Appius.

Such a day, thought Tiberius as he gazed out on the garden in the back. Sunshine one minute, grey skies the next. He wondered if the skies would open up on him and his chalk white toga. He glanced down at it in disdain, thoroughly sick of wandering around the city trying to keep it relatively clean. Philea must be sick of it, too, since she had taken over from Hylas, who struggled to meet her standards after Tiberius returned from his first tour of the city. Now, Philea scrubbed and chalked the white toga and its alternate back to its immaculate brilliant purity every day. She never complained, but she might be happier if he bought five more. She'd be happiest, of course, if the campaign and the election were over. He'd be happiest, too.

He heard turmoil at the front door, usual at this hour as his friends showed up to escort him around the city. They all had gone to every part of Rome several times, with Tiberius putting forth his best speech, honing it as best he could at every appearance. During the last few weeks, they'd gone to the Forum to see "how he'd fare in front of the fickle, the feckless, and the fearsome," Appius put it, "though few of the latter there may be." To their surprise and hidden delight, he survived. True, they'd gone early in the morning, or late afternoon when the milling host usual to the Forum and the adjoining marketplace were at their thinnest. Tiberius spoke to them, and apparently caught their attention, since no one threw any garbage or offal at him, not once. Of course, Casca and his companions seeded every crowd, which might have been a factor.

Indeed, presenting to a full Forum constituted an entirely different sort of experience, Tiberius knew. He was likely to vie with some of his competitors, also protected by strong-arms. They would be accompanied by some well-coached hectors crying out catcalls from well-situated seats throughout the Comitia. The net sum was that no candidate possessed an advantage in this ultimate venue; the politicians were, for the most part, on their own.

Soon, the members of his regular entourage arrived, some in pairs, others one by one. Philea and the other servants again offered them a quick breakfast and drink, which Appius curtailed by braying at them that autumn was running away and votes would spoil without being harvested right now.

As they emerged from the house, Tiberius was surprised to see a large number of common people waiting in the street. When this first happened, just a few lounged outside, and Tiberius wondered out loud why they were there. "Hanger-ons, my son," Appius said, "glad-handers and seekers of favors from any politician they can find. Pay no attention to them, they don't necessarily have your best interests at heart."

Now, though, their numbers came close to a century, maybe more. Not all of them could believe that they would profit through his largesse. "If you win, they'll think they will," said Appius.

They set out down the back of the hill, the esteemed members of his party walking in step with the candidate while the rest mobbed around, walking in the street beside them or trailing behind. Some hurried to catch up to Tiberius and he called out to them to hurry up, smiling. They laughed, one lively fellow asking him what he planned to do when he became king. Abdicate! he yelled back, which caused rolling laughter as the question and his answer was passed on.

They walked through part of the Caelian crammed with people, bustling and bartering for goods and services. A few craftsmen recognized Tiberius and chided him for heading up such a soft-bread patrician parade. Tiberius shouted back that he was just a pleb running for tribune, but if they wanted bread, the candidates for consul had plenty.

They traversed the edge of the Esquiline, skirted past the Subura, striding toward the Forum down the Via Sacra, the Sacred Way. The sun signified the tenth hour of the morning, and the marketplace overflowed with buyers and sellers, spilling into the Forum just outside the Comitia itself. Around the Rostrum stood a dozen or so campaign factions made up of scores of noble or noble-looking citizens jealously cordoning off their chosen candidate in his virginal white toga. Seeing the mass of men waiting their nominee's turn, Tiberius stopped and turned to Appius.

"Well, it's a busy time of year," said his father-in-law. "Wait here while I see what I can do." He was off in the wind.

Tiberius shifted his weight back and forth for a time, waiting. Finally, he said to Crassus, "This is tiresome. I'm going over to the Comitia and see if I can find a seat."

"Tiberius," Crassus said in alarm, "that sort of thing isn't done. You certainly do not want to appear to be supporting another candidate!"

"Oh, who will notice, Crassus? Look around, there must be close to a hundred men wearing the dove's white feathers. I'll blend in with the flock."

Before Crassus could complain any more, Tiberius abandoned his entourage and headed down to the Comitia to find a seat. He slipped into a back row in partial deference to Crassus's concerns. On the Rostrum, a candidate for aedile expounded on the need to run Rome's vital service systems like a crack cohort executing a close order drill—only then could we be sure to have clean water and clean sewers.

Someone dropped down beside Tiberius and gave him a quick pat on his shoulder. Tiberius looked over and said, "Marcus Octavius, I haven't seen you since last winter! How goes it, noble Roman?"

"Well, noble Roman, well!" Marcus looked Tiberius over and said, "I see you, too, aspire to serve."

"Oh, yes indeed, Marcus, tribune of the Roman people, if I may. You, too, I understand."

The small, dark man nodded and grinned a brilliant white smile out of the background of his thick, black beard, "If all my hopes and dreams come true." He lifted his stiff leg and placed it across the other one. "And, you are one of my competitors. A formidable one, I think."

"Please, let's not think that way. There are ten posts to fill, let us imagine that we are the two most superior candidates, and that we will win while the rest are but chaff in the wind."

"Like Postumious, you mean?"

"Oh, yes," Tiberius said, "first and foremost the esteemed Spurius Postumius. Quite the man."

"Indeed. He is blessed by the gods, or so he thinks," said Marcus, "and we clearly are not."

"No, no," Tiberius said, shaking his head ruefully, "we could never out-preen that peacock."

"Yet, he campaigns to be a tribune. He wants to help people."

"Oh, yes he does," Tiberius said with a firm nod of his head. He leaned down to rest his chin between his hands, his elbows perched on his knees. "He might win. When I ran for aedile, he garnered more votes than I did."

"Oh, don't say that, Tiberius. Let's change the subject. How's the family?"

Tiberius smiled, and said, "Oh, they're all well, Marcus, and quite wonderful. Four children, now, and perhaps another not too long into the future."

"Outstanding. And how is Claudia?"

"Lovely." He turned his head, "And you, Marcus?"

"Ah, divorced again. That's three times and no heirs."

"I'm so sorry. We need Octavii in Rome."

"Oh, so you're voting for me, are you?"

Tiberius laughed, "Of course, if you vote for me."

"I will, I will. You don't need my vote, Tiberius, but I certainly need yours. Wait until I spread the word, 'Tiberius Sempronius Gracchus is voting for me first!'"

"I didn't say first."

"No, but I will."

They laughed, then grew quiet as they looked out on the candidate gesticulating and shouting his good intentions.

"I guess I was too nice," Marcus murmured. "I didn't bed them enough, and I didn't beat them at all when they turned me away from their beds. Instead, I gave them money." He sniffed a rueful laugh, "Now, I'm close to broke. Being tribune will help a little. But, really, I need to forget the young girls, marry some rich old crone, and adopt a son."

Tiberius said, "Fortuna will find you, old friend. Let's start by winning here. When do you speak?"

Marcus screwed up his mouth and said, "Believe it or not, right after Postumius. That'll give me a leg up. When do you go?"

Tiberius raised his hands palms up to the sky, "I have no idea. I'm new and late to this."

Marcus grunted. "No matter, you'll do well. I've seen your entourage has been swelling."

"Really? I didn't see you until today."

Marcus shrugged his shoulders, "No money, no entourage."

Tiberius lifted his head to acknowledge Marcus's remark when they were interrupted by Appius's arrival. Despite the cool air, Appius perspired profusely from his efforts. He waited to catch his breath, then said, "All right, it took some doing, but it's been arranged. Postumius speaks next, then Marcus Octavius—nice to see you Octavius—then you, Tiberius. I've sent for water. Do you need anything to eat? No? Very well, then, I propose we retire to a place where we can practice."

"Thank you, Father-in-law, but I'm as ready as I'll ever be. I want to hear what foolishness Postumius is up to, then listen to Marcus diminish him in his first sentence or two. After that, I'm sure that this black-bearded demon next to us will make some sage, winning remarks that I can steal liberally."

"Thank you so much for the compliment, I think," said Marcus.

"No practice?" Appius asked Tiberius. He collapsed like a toga dropped on the floor and said, "Very well. You're ready, I suppose. It's too late to do anything now. Drink, please!"

By this time, Crassus had joined them along with Blossius, Diophanes, and the rest of the entourage, including Tiberius's servant Hylas. As soon as Appius spoke, Hylas passed around cups of water poured from a bag over his shoulder. Both Tiberius and Marcus drank deeply, while Appius emptied his in one gulp. "More, please, more."

Hylas poured again, and Marcus suddenly gestured. "Our aedile hopeful has concluded. Postumius is next. I better go down below, empty my bladder, and get ready. Gods be with you, Tiberius."

"And with you, Marcus. We will serve the people together!"

Marcus smiled broadly, and disappeared.

Crassus immediately sat in his place. "Well, let's see what this Optimate on the rise has to say."

Spurius Postumius took his place upon the Rostrum. He was tall, like Tiberius, and comely, too, but fair-haired. That was not the only way the resemblance ended. Where Tiberius was reserved, Postumius was brash. Tiberius preferred to stay in the background while Postumius loved being front and center. Most important difference of all, if Tiberius felt at a lack of knowledge or command, Postumius always acted as though he was fully informed, self-assured, and always in charge. In short, he was insufferable, Tiberius thought. But, his family was wealthy from ship building, and the Senate considered him a proper plebeian citizen. Clearly, Nasica, Rufus, and their lot had championed Postumius for tribune, and relished being his loyal followers on the campaign walks. Now, he would step to the front of the Rostrum and shake down the gods from Olympus.

In anticipation, the Comitia had suddenly filled up. All of the rows were now full to the top of the well, and people stood both in the central floor before the Rostrum and seated in rows all the way to the top. Tiberius watched as Postumius strode to the front where the six prows of the vanquished Carthaginian ships loomed over the onlookers.

"Citizens of Rome," he bellowed. "I am Spurius Postumius, your candidate for tribune of the people. I am the only candidate whom you will see today worthy of this position. I alone possess the ability to do what is necessary to safeguard the Roman way of life. I do not implore you for your vote, I demand it. I am entitled to it. You will do no better than me, just look at my record, look at those who support me, the best of the best, the Good Men of the Senate. Follow my lead and live in prosperity. Squander your vote and suffer the consequences. Disaster always lurks, and only I and my supporters can avert it, with the help of the gods, of course. Talking longer is a waste of time. I direct you, vote for me; it is the right thing to do."

He turned to leave the Rostrum amid complete silence. Tiberius, Appius, and Crassus took turns looking at each other with disbelieving eyes. Suddenly, voices from the crowd began yelling angry curses at the receding figure of Postumius descending the stairs. Garbage flew from the Comitia onto the Rostrum, and some men started moving around as if looking for a fight.

Marcus Octavius stepped up on the Rostrum and walked forward with his telltale limp. Waving his hand to try to get the annoyed crowd's attention, he shouted out, "Romans, Romans. Citizens of Rome."

The agitated throng hesitated when they saw the small, round, dark-bearded man with the hitch in his gait stand at the front of the Rostrum. The noise subsided, and looking his most stentorian, Marcus said, "Citizens of Rome, I am Marcus Octavius, candidate for tribune, and I am the only candidate worthy of this position. Just me," he said.

The milling crowd stopped, stared up at him, and began laughing loudly.

"What?" he said, "I don't look the part? I'm not six feet tall, long, slim, and well jeweled? I'm three feet wide, at least."

Again, the people in the Comitia laughed.

"But, I am, I am the only one worthy of this post. That is, with the help of the gods. Why am I the only one? Because I'm one of you! I'm not a rich Roman prince, I'm not a member of the landed gentry, the only land I own is the mud I make to help build Rome! That's right, I make concrete for the city. The baths of Metellus are sealed with my mud. The flagstones in the marketplace walkways were joined by concrete I made! But, I'm no rich man, the gods know my wives made sure of that."

The people in the Comitia laughed, and he continued, "No, I just want to see a better Rome for people like me. I'm not running for tribune to make my fortune, I'm here to make your fortunes! I want to strengthen Rome by strengthening its backbone, the common people who carry the weight of the Republic on their backs. Only someone who is like you, who thinks like you, who lives the same life can be your man in the Tribunal.

That is why I am the only worthy candidate for ribune of the people, only if I am of worth to the people!"

Marcus raised his arms to the sky, and the people listening raised their voices in approval. He waved, bowed, and left the Comitia. As he passed, Tiberius reached over and grabbed his forearm and gave it a quick squeeze. "Well, done, Tribune," he said, and Marcus grinned as wide as his face could stretch.

He left, and Appius said quietly, "You didn't have to be that enthusiastic."

Tiberius shrugged, "It was a good speech. He's a friend."

"Yes, well, now it's your turn to give a good speech," Appius said, "a better speech."

Tiberius exhaled as he stood. He pulled his toga up around his shoulder, and sidled past Appius to the stairway where he made his way down to the base of the Comitia and up the stairs of the Rostrum. The crowd of men milled about, talking and exchanging jibes while hucksters threaded their way through, touting and selling their wares. The midday sun burned above, and many of them began looking for something to eat and drink. The rising noise level told Tiberius that whatever excitement and energy engendered by Marcus had dissipated quickly.

He walked to the edge of the Rostrum and raised his arm high in the air. He waved his hand slightly, but the crowd paid no attention. After a moment, he called out to them.

"Romans. Romans, heed my calling. Listen to me for five minutes, then go about your business."

"Why?" one wag shouted out, causing a few companions to laugh.

"Because I want to work for you, I want to be your servant."

More laughter followed, but faces started to turn to him.

"I am Tiberius Sempronius Gracchus Minor, son of Tiberius Sempronius Gracchus Major, who was twice consul, princeps senatus, and censor to the people. He also was a plebeian. Yes, my father was a common man who did uncommon things. I am a plebeian, too, but much more common than my father. My father was a great general who vanquished the tribes of Hispania, including those in Numantia. I was not a great general; famously, I did not conquer the Numantines. It has been said that I surrendered to them."

Those in the crowd gave him their full attention, now, seeming to be fascinated by a candidate who hoped to win their votes by listing all of his failures.

Tiberius closed his eyes momentarily and shook his head as he said, "I am not here to burnish my image, you will believe what you believe. I will tell you what I learned of the people along the way.

"In my journey to Numantia, I traveled through the countryside of Rome and Italia. I was charged to raise a legion of men to join our army there. But, when I entered a village, any village, or a town, I found it to be empty. There were no Romans, no Italian allies, no soldiers to be had. Instead, I found the farmers of Rome and Italia gathered on the roadways, begging for food— men, women, and children. These men and their families had been pushed off of their lands by rich men who wished to become richer. Veterans who had earned their small plots of land through their service to Rome stood starving next to their starving children. They subjugated themselves, begging for food for their families while their land was absorbed into vast plantations to be worked by slaves."

At this point, Tiberius's five minutes had passed long ago, but the crowd in the Comitia stood still.

"Veterans," Tiberius said, "men who bore arms and exposed their lives for the safety of their country, now enjoy nothing more but the light and the air. The savage beasts in Italy have their dens, their places to sleep in safety. These Roman and Italian veterans have nothing, no houses or settlements of their own. Instead, they are forced to wander from place to place with their wives and children. I am sure that some of these displaced veterans stand before us right at this very moment."

A low rumbling coursed through the crowd, which pressed closer to the Rostrum.

"Commanders in the field foolishly exhort common soldiers to fight for their ancestors, their gods, and their altars. Yet, not one of these plain legionaries could supplicate the household gods to defend their own ancestors at an altar in a home they once possessed. Oh, they fought and they died, but for the wealth and luxury of other men. Romans are styled as masters of the world, but, in the meantime, these Roman citizens have not one foot of ground they can call their own."

Tiberius paused and scanned the packed center of the Comitia's well. He raised his arm again and waved his hand as he continued, "If you cannot own your own land, why should you fight for the wealth of those who use their power to take yours?"

The massed men at the foot of the Rostrum listened without moving. "Fortuna has blessed me with a good family, a good life, and my father and mother taught me to serve Rome. And I have tried to do so, both in the city and in her legions. I did serve Rome in war, though not as successfully as my father. But, I am not vying to be consul, I hope to be tribune of the people to serve the people.

"To serve the people; to do so means to stop them from being torn from their families and land to fight wars for other men. To do so means to ensure that they have land when they return from serving Rome, as is their right. To do so means to ensure that they keep the land that they earned. If I am elected tribune by you good men, this is what I promise to do."

Tiberius smiled, waving his hand in the air as he retreated from the Rostrum.

Appius tried to get hold of his thoughts as he said, "He's not dynamic, and plainly not bombastic. But, he's earnest. Somehow that seems to come through to the crowd."

Cornelia sat sewing while she waited for him to finish. Her practiced fingers moved fast back and forth, in and out, despite the delicacy of the priceless silk in her hands.

"I think he did all right, I would say. They didn't cheer him along, but they seemed to listen. No heckling, no catcalls, nothing of the sort."

"I'm sure Casca and Ajax saw to that."

Appius waved her off with his hands, "No, no, there were far too many for that. I tell you, it was exceedingly bizarre, quite out of the ordinary."

"I see," she said, her eyes on the seam she was sewing.

"What's that you're doing?" asked Appius.

"A summer robe for little Cornelia Sempronia."

"From silk? Quite a present for a five-year-old. She'll ruin it in no time."

Cornelia tossed her head slightly, "I lost most of my children almost overnight. I can spoil my grandchildren if I like."

"You didn't lose all of your children—Sempronia and Gaius, for example. You certainly didn't spoil them."

"Raising them presented other responsibilities. Grandchildren are different." She sewed another immaculate stitch. "So, how do you think Tiberius will do come the election?

Appius rubbed his hand over his head, his mouth open, gritting his teeth. "I think he'll do well. Perhaps seventh or eighth."

"Or ninth or tenth?" she said sharply.

Appius hurried to say, "Maybe better. He's well liked, he's just not demonstrative."

"Yes," said Cornelia, gazing up. After a moment, she said, "We can't count on his likeability, especially with the Optimates pushing Postumius and anyone else, for that matter. We need to make sure, Appius. Allocate more money to Casca; tell him to search far and wide for more votes. Have Ajax scour the countryside for farmers, tell them they vote for Tiberius or risk losing their lands. That should get them going. Arrange for carts to bring them into Rome. Make sure there's enough of everything to do this, Appius."

"It might not be necessary. Tiberius is making good headway on his own."

Cornelia shook her head vigorously, "I'm not taking that chance. Unbend your efforts, Appius, Tiberius must win."

At the end of the year, when the ballots had been cast and counted, Tiberius Sempronius Gracchus came in first, Marcus Octavius second, followed by eight other men, none of them Spurius Postumius.

Chapter 28. Tribune of the People

Claudia reached over Tiberius's shoulder for a cup of water on the small table next to the bed. She sipped some, and carefully put it back, making sure that none of it dripped on him. The campaign, the election, and the celebration had taken a lot out of him, she thought. Though, he still looked beautiful to her, a craggy sort of black-haired Adonis, if that was possible. Despite his efforts, his tireless toil in the face of adversity and scorn, she knew of his true reluctance, his deep-seated desire to stay at home with his children, his brother and mother, and his wife. But, Tiberius would do his duty, she sighed, Gracchi to the last. Her worry started with wondering when the last would be.

She gazed around his room at the beautiful rustic murals on the maroon walls. Diana chased a stag through a wood full of white birches from the north. On another wall, Salacia blew sea foam at the little fishes jumping out of the waves. And, opposite the bed, she marveled at the exquisite rendering of a window frame. Within it, a distant aureole of Apollo sped his steeds and sun chariot across the brightening, brilliant sky, forever towards Oceanus. Only a real window could cast a more beautiful scene, she thought, even if overlooking just the grimy walls of Rome.

Tiberius stirred, turning halfway over to face her. Reaching out, he pulled her down next to him and wrapped her with crossed arms.

"I have a headache," he said.

"You were drunk," she said.

"Was I? Or am I?"

"Only you can tell."

He pulled back, gazing at her, face to face. "Are you mad at me?"

She turned her head toward the ceiling. "Not mad. Just sore."

"Of me?"

"No. Physically sore. You celebrated heartily last night."

"Oh," he said. "Liber be cursed, I don't feel very hearty this morning. Is it morning?"

He asked, holding his head in both hands, barely seeing her with one eye through his split fingers.

"It is morning, mid-morning."

He groaned. "I can't get up."

"I'm not surprised."

She patted him on the shoulder as she rose from the bed. "Sleep. I'll take care of the morning risers."

He rolled over as she quietly left the room.

Claudia entered her own bedchamber where Philea had left a crock full of water, a rough bramble brush, and some soap. Claudia dropped her night shift on the floor and began to wash herself, first with the soap and water, then scrubbing hard with the brush branch. As she rubbed, she noted how she had changed during the past few years. After bearing four children, she had more curves to show now. Any more children and she would fill out those curves.

Yes, she sighed to herself, no longer the wisp of a girl that Tiberius had married. Oh, he pretended not to notice, and his appetite for her seemed to bolster the fiction. But, her own reality belied his delusion. He loved her, that's all. Sometimes, though, she wondered if he didn't deserve more, a goddess like Venus or Proserpina. But, he didn't deserve to die at the hands of jealous gods, Mars or Diana, he never would deserve to die.

She sighed, pulled on her robe and left the room. Crossing the atrium, she paused in front of Cornelia's door, then knocked.

"Enter," the deep alto of her mother-in-law beckoned. Claudia pushed the door open and swept into the room. Cornelia looked up at her from her chair, sewing again.

"Salve, Mother, how did you sleep?"

"Nice to see you up at this early hour, girl," Cornelia said wryly. "And, the master of the house?"

Claudia shook her head, "Quite dead to the world. He celebrated last night, you know."

Cornelia said, "Men. Only men do this, very few women. Except for those women who drink," she said, pondering the thought. "They drink too much, but seem to enjoy life more, too."

Claudia took a seat across from Cornelia as she said, "Well, they are not matrons of Rome. Nor is our triumphant tribune ready to represent the people of the Republic on this day. Appius is coming? They're supposed to meet with the Senate leaders, no?"

Cornelia pursed her lips as if a sour taste had settled on her tongue. "Appius is a man, too. I'll wager a horse against an ass he's feeling the same way as Tiberius."

Claudia nodded her head. "So, no great meeting today with the Good Men of Rome." Cornelia didn't reply, turning her eyes back to her needlework. Claudia sighed, "I suppose one day won't make a difference. Sooner or later, they will meet, and strut, and threaten, then connive until one lot or the other believes they have the ultimate upper hand."

"That is the gist of it," said Cornelia, her eyes still on her sewing.

"It could be dangerous," Claudia said. "Sometimes, they go too far."

Cornelia glanced up. "They're most passionate desire is to go too far. Depend on it." She returned to her handiwork.

Claudia fidgeted in her chair, crossing her legs, then re-crossing them. She ran her fingers through her hair, then rubbed her shoulders. Cornelia continued to sew patiently, oblivious to her daughter-in-law's restlessness.

At length, Claudia sat still. "Do you ever worry," she said, "that something might happen to Tiberius?" Cornelia stopped and looked up.

"Do you?" Claudia went on. "Look what happened to Mancinus, stripped naked and sent to Numantia in chains."

Cornelia laughed, "He was lucky. The barbarians didn't want him, either. He's lucky they didn't spit and roast him like one of their sheep. Though, they may have mounted him a few times. They do that with their sheep, too."

Claudia nodded, "The senators who sent Mancinus to Numantia, these same men, tried to convict Tiberius of treason. They hated him then, they hate him more now. Aren't you afraid that they might try to do him harm? Do you ever fear that he might die?" Claudia's voice trailed off into a whisper as she uttered the last few words.

Cornelia put her sewing in her lap. "My husband died. Nine of my children died. I am accustomed to dealing with death. It is a part of life."

Claudia leaned closer, "That's what I mean. You've lost so much in life . . . ," she trailed off again.

Cornelia said sharply, "He is a Roman of the consular family Sempronii, a Gracchi, and like his ancestors, he will do his duty. And, we will support him and that's the end of it."

She saw Claudia's mouth pursing into a silent pout. She also saw the worry in her daughter-in-law's eyes. Her own softened, and she said, "Don't fret, child, Tiberius is in a very strong position. He is the most popular tribune of the people, and your father is by his side. Scaveola is Consul, Sextus Decimus has delivered the horsemen, and Casca and Ajax protect his person. The election is won!" she said with a little bit of triumph.

"Yes," said Claudia, "the election is won, just e beginning."

Appius came early to the house the next day with Crassus and Blossius in tow for a strategy meeting with Tiberius. Crassus apologized for his brother Scaevola's absence.

"As the new consul-elect, he felt that he couldn't appear to have favorites. Of course, he does," Crassus said followed by a cackling laugh.

Appius leaned over, "Anyone with gold."

Crassus huffed, "Now, that's not fair. He needed money for the election, you know how expensive it is. It's exorbitant! Now that it's over, he can begin working toward his true friends's shared goals."

"Getting richer," Appius quipped, and Crassus glared. Appius laughed, then turned in front of the men grouped in the atrium.

"All right, let us attend to business. Tiberius, we are at your service. How would you like us to approach this meeting?"

Tiberius blinked, surprised that he had been deferred to by Appius and the others. They all looked at him earnestly, and he said, "All right. We know what we want. I know what I want, and we can be sure that Nasica and Rufus and the rest will oppose us in every possible way. That doesn't matter to me, I will get what I want whether the Senate likes it or not. The people are with us, and there isn't much they can do about that."

He gestured to the chairs brought in by Hylas and Philea, and the men sat down. While Tiberius spoke, Philea gave each of them a cup full of honeyed water and a bowl of figs.

"However," he continued, "I do not want to start a war at the outset. If we could engage them, have them meet us part of the way—."

"The front door would be a major concession," Crassus said.

"That may be true, but let us put them in the position of defying the people's will. Let's offer them a law that even they would find difficult to oppose. We should present ourselves in all amicability, peaceful friends of Rome together."

Tiberius looked at each of the men in front of him one by one, and one by one, they shook their heads in assent.

"Very well. Let us take ourselves to them now."

As they exited the front door of Tiberius's house, Casca moved to his side. Others flanked them as well while Ajax stood at the front gateway near other men in the street.

Tiberius frowned, saying, "This is a show of peace and trust?"

"True, but really, my son," said Appius, "how far do we really want to go with the Good Men? They are at their best when they're treacherous."

Tiberius's lips tightened as he said, "All right. But, can't they at least try to stay out of sight? Casca?"

Casca glanced at Ajax, who shrugged. Casca said, "We will take the periphery as much as possible, sir. In tight places, though, we might have to move in."

Tiberius shook his head, "Understandable, but do your best, yes? Let's not start skirmishing, our men against theirs. If there's to be a fight, let's allow the jackasses in charge be the first to bloody their noses. The god of war would enjoy that the most."

Casca smiled, "Of course, Tribune. We might like seeing it ourselves."

Tiberius laughed, cuffing him on the shoulder. "Then, you have something to look forward to! We're off!"

The route to Nasica's domus led up the Palantine where the most prosperous of the patrician families lived. Nasica's manse perched high on the hill as if presiding over the other homes of the first families of Rome. The two-story edifice seemed larger to Tiberius than the other homes because of its position on a promontory. He could see that, in fact, it wasn't really any bigger. Nonetheless, it appeared imposing.

Polydius grabbed hold of one of the iron knockers and pounded it on the solid, bronze-encased doors. Doors like Jupiter's temple, Tiberius thought, appropriate for the Pontifex Maximus, he supposed. Two well-muscled guards opened the doors, and Nasica's main house slave, Rollo, appeared. An attenuated stick of a man in a dark green, embroidered tunic, Rollo stepped between the guards to appraise the visitors. Tiberius and the rest knew that they were expected, Hylas had been sent earlier to notify Nasica. Still, Rollo looked them up and down as though they were itinerant pot-healers rather than the most prominent of Roman citizens.

"The slights begin," murmured Appius. "This clown has been well rehearsed for the farce."

Rollo waved them inside. Tiberius followed first in line through a long, wide vestibulum unusual in having a narrow pool of water run its full length. At its end stood a statue carved in the classic Greek style of a centaur struggling with a Lapith warrior. The wall of the long pool displayed an elaborate mosaic of a school of tiny fish swimming endlessly toward the perimeter. Though the craftsmanship was splendid, Tiberius couldn't figure out the logic of the artistry's juxtaposition. What did the war of the Lapiths and the centaurs have to do with fish in a circle?

"Perhaps the winner gets to go fishing?" Appius said quietly.

"Perhaps."

The vestibulum opened upon an enormous atrium dominated by a stunning bronze statue of a young Apollo leaning against a tree, insouciantly stabbing the point of a knife at a small lizard twisting out of the way.

"Minerva keep us!" exclaimed Appius. "Praxiteles? Could it be real?"

"Genuine, I imagine," said Crassus, "given Nasica's splendid success in agriculture and other profitable ventures, especially procurement in Macedonia."

They moved past it, staring in awe. Behind the statue stood a large marble altar hosting an outsized array of Lares, with Jupiter rising up almost to the height of a small boy. On either side of the altar stood wooden shelves displaying a host of ancestral masks backlit by small oil lamps.

"Is there no end to this?" Appius said. "He must have every rat-catcher aedile up there his family ever had elected."

"Father, please," Tiberius whispered.

Rollo turned to them and, pointing to a half circle of wooden benches, said, "Please be seated. The Master will be with you presently."

Crassus and Blossius made a move toward the benches when Tiberius held up his hand, "Wait. Let's wait for Nasica first."

They stood patiently for several minutes until Appius said, "Tiberius, my sorry feet hurt. I'm going to sit." He took his place on a bench, and was soon joined by Crassus and Blossius. Just then, Rollo came into the room, giving way to Nasica entering from the peristylum in the back. His tall, lean body moved slowly in a way that signaled inbred confidence. Outside of a streak of silver in his temples, his cousin seemed to be no older or less privileged these days, Tiberius mused. At least a score of other men followed him into the atrium, many of them senators, and all of them Optimates, the Good Men of Rome. Ahead of them walked Lucius Rufus Faba, shorter and stouter than before if possible, but looking even more arrogant. Tiberius recognized others among them—Cato Minor, Milo, Lucullus, Brutus, Bibulus, Manlius, Pompeius, Metallus, Fulvius, even Postumious in the back, his face screwed up like he had eaten a sour lemon.

Rollo clapped his hands, and two slaves appeared with a curule chair that they placed in the middle of the atrium directly opposite Tiberius and his party. Other slaves brought in benches with backs and armrests, and embroidered cushioned seats. Nasica's companions sat in them, with Rufus on his right side, smiling open-mouthed, like a lion.

"What do you want, Gracchus?" Nasica said.

Tiberius looked at him dispassionately and said, "First, two curule chairs for the Principes Senatus Appius Claudius Pulcher and Publius Crassus Dive, who are guests in your home."

Nasica pressed his lips together slightly, but he raised his hand and flexed two fingers in Rollo's direction without looking at him. Rollo turned to give the order when Appius raised his hand.

"No, no, that's quite all right. I'm quite comfortable as it is, sitting on plain, good old solid wood," he said, patting the bench with his hand. "Besides, I would have to get up and sit down again, more work than it's worth to these old bones. Don't you agree, Crassus?"

Crassus shot Appius a quick glance, then nodded briskly at Nasica.

"Very well," said Tiberius. "We have come, Nasica, to apprise you of our plans with the hope that you will join us. We wish to ensure that we can act together to improve the state of Rome's people, especially our veterans. It is our hope and belief that if we can join forces in this effort, we can succeed in satisfying everyone with the outcome while also strengthening and reinvigorating the Republic."

"I see," said Nasica. "And what is the implement that you propose to use that will bring about this miraculous metamorphosis?"

Tiberius breathed in deeply, and said, "A lex agraria. A law that will return the public lands of Rome to its people."

Nasica turned his head to Rufus, who exchanged a smile with him. On either side and behind them, the other senators and supporters smiled silently.

"Didn't you and your august father-in-law bring this notion before the Senate not so long ago?"

Tiberius nodded, "A year ago."

"Oh, and how did that go? My memory fails me," said Nasica, smiling sheepishly.

"The Senate turned it down."

"Well." Nasica paused reflectively. "That's a pity."

Muffled laughter could be heard from the men sitting behind him. Nasica said, "So, if the Senate turned you down a year ago, what makes you think minds will change now?"

Tiberius said, "Because the people wish it. They made that clear through their choices in the past election. More importantly, it is what we should do as the leading citizens of the Republic. It is an opportunity to provide livelihoods for their children, for the starving sons of our veterans and the future citizens of Rome. We need to do this now to restore the legacy of the Republic."

Nasica's benevolent smile froze. "So, now you're arbiter of our legacy."

Tiberius held his hands folded together in front of his breast. "Perhaps not. But, Rome possesses centuries-old traditions that have bonded her citizens together in the union of the Republic. These traditions have been bolstered by laws. In recent years, unfortunately, these laws have been deflected or ignored altogether."

"What laws do you mean?" Rufus interrupted, snapping in disdain, "You should talk, a traitor who consorted with enemies, a common brigand who stole from honest farmers such as myself!"

Tiberius dropped his hands into fists and spread his feet. Appius and the other Populares shifted uncomfortably on the benches.

Tiberius spoke evenly, "All in this room know the truth of my military service to Rome. Every Roman knows of it, and I stand before you as their elected official. I am surprised, too, Rufus, to hear that you still take umbrage at the gracious donation you made to my legion, though the barns of your estate still brimmed with goods. I would have thought you would be proud of supporting the war effort in such a benevolent fashion."

Tiberius raised his hands, palms out, and continued, "In any case, you were in violation of the very laws of which I speak, cultivating without license public lands that had been reserved for returning veterans." He shrugged, "All in all, perhaps it was a fair trade-off. Though, I'm not sure how you knew at the time you took over the land that you would be making such a gracious gift to our legion. Such prescience must stem from your overall tendency toward general generosity."

Rufus sputtered, but Nasica interrupted. "So, you intend to mend these broken laws with another law?"

"We do. We will form a three-man commission to investigate the use of public lands for private gain. Those who appear to be in violation will be asked to rescind their holdings. They will be given a grace period to vacate the properties, and they will be compensated for their development expenses. Compensation will extend to their heirs. Thereafter, we will adjudicate claims by Romans for lands promised to them for services rendered, especially veterans. In this way, we can remedy the plight of the common man who owns nothing and has no means of support for himself or his family. With these newly landed men, we also will fill the gaping hole in our legions due to lack of available recruits."

He paused, waiting to hear their response. The Optimates looked at one another, then back at the Populares sitting before them. After a lengthy silence, Nasica spoke.

"An ambitious plan. Admirable in its aim to reinvigorate our citizen army. And, compensation to current proprietors and their sons, very far-thinking." He paused, then said, "Such a venture will require a bit of money. Might I ask, where do you plan on getting it?"

He leaned forward for the answer. Tiberius said, quite calmly, "Rome will supply the resources necessary to undertake this important initiative."

"Ah, Rome!" Nasica said, sitting back. "Always Rome helping the less fortunate."

"Rome is rich," Tiberius said, "the city coffers overflow with gold and coin from Greece."

"Of course," said Nasica, "and we're to use this wealth to help out the poor wanderers who cannot fend for themselves."

"We'll use our own plebeian coin if we have to," Tiberius said, "Saturn's treasury brims with gold, too."

"Unhuh," nodded Nasica. "And, what about the slaves? The current owners have invested heavily in buying slaves to work the land. What becomes of them when your law is enacted? Oh, yes, you will compensate the newly disenfranchised landowners and their heirs, but the slaves must still eat, they must have something to wear, and a place to live. Who is to pay for that?"

Tiberius stopped for a moment. He then said, "You can sell them to others who need them. You can sell them back to their families. You can contract to free them in exchange for a fair amount to be paid out of their future wages. The praetors and aediles can employ them in the service of Rome. Or, you can simply let them go. You won't have to feed or clothe them, and they can go home grateful for the benevolence of their former owners."

Nasica gazed at Tiberius, idly tapping his fingers on the end of his armrest. After some thought, he turned to his right, then to his left.

"I think, Gracchus," he said, "that this sounds like a great amount of work for us without a sure outcome. It seems to me and my colleagues that all of the risk is on our side, not yours. I believe I speak for the majority—," he looked around again, and the men surrounding him nodded their assent. "I think that we like things the way they are."

The men rumbled their agreement.

Tiberius waited. He said, "Then, we will pass our lex agraria without you, Nasica. We have the people, we have the resources, we have the will. I'm sorry that you cannot see this and won't join us. It would have been better for you to be on our side."

"Oh, now, let me see," Nasica said, turning to Rufus Faba, "it was Gaius Laelius who tried to pass a lex agraria, wasn't it?"

Rufus answered, "Yes, it was."

"That's right," said Nasica, "and he failed, I believe. He introduced the law, but once he recognized that the Senate opposed it, he withdrew it, knowing that it would never pass, not in a millennium. That's when people started calling him Laelius the Wise, the Prudent, no?"

"That is correct," Rufus said in an amiable tone, "Laelius the Wise."

"Yes," said Nasica, "Prudent, too. And, do you know who sponsored him? Why, the most powerful man in Rome, Scipio Aemilianus. Even the great hero of Carthage couldn't get Laelius's land law through—your brother-in-law, Gracchus!" he said, almost bubbling. He leaned over, "Your all-powerful brother-in-law Scipio Aemilianus, the best man in Rome, could not get a land law through. And, he isn't here to save you, Gracchus, or to help you out now. He's in Numantia with your little turd of a brother cleaning up your mess!"

He laughed harshly, and the rest of the Good Men joined in, sniggering derisively.

"So, go ahead, Tribune Tiberius Gracchus, try and pass your little land reform law, however you like. You will never get it through, never! We will do everything to stop it, everything!"

Tiberius and the others said nothing. Appius suddenly rose up quickly, followed by Crassus and the rest.

"Rollo, get them out of my house," Nasica said.

Rollo strolled past them, a smug smile on his face, saying over his shoulder, "This way, gentlemen."

"Nasica must know that he can't stop us," Tiberius said, pacing back and forth in his house's atrium. Appius, Crassus, Diophanes, and Blossius sat in chairs surrounding the pool, drinking watered wine while sampling bread, oil, and olives brought in by Philea.

"He must have some sort of plan," Tiberius said.

"Most likely, he thinks he does," Appius said, "but we cannot dwell on what he might or might not be doing. We simply must follow our own plan, amending it as needed along the way."

"Nasica acted so wildly," Crassus said, shaking his craggy head, "he might do anything."

"That's why we have Casca and Ajax," said Appius.

"Yes, but can they be with Tiberius all the time?" said Blossius. "Outside, I mean, in public."

Tiberius turned and said, "I'm not worried about that. There are plenty of political moves they can make before they consider physical play. We just need to be sure that every contingency has been addressed, we must be ready."

Appius lifted and dropped his shoulders. "Ajax is out rounding up our voters. Sextus has provided carts and horses to get the country tribes here. He also has his fellow horsemen at the ready. Casca continues to scour the streets for landed citizens in the city itself. And, of course, our Crassus has seen to our sympathetic senatorial colleagues."

Crassus said, "They've all been meeting with their clients who will vote as required."

"And you have the legislation drafted, Blossius?"

"He has, and Scaevola has reviewed it. He says it is simple and sound. We should have no problems introducing it."

Tiberius slowly raised and lowered his head, "All right. We are ready, then. Is there anyone we need to worry about among my tribunal colleagues?"

"None worth worrying about," Appius said. "Publius Satureius grumbled a bit, but he might only be jealous. He came in third in the ballots. We might be able to assuage him a bit with a bit of coin." He smirked, turning his head to the others, who smiled back at him.

Tiberius lowered his head, "Very well. Then, tomorrow we publish the edict for the Lex Sempronia Agraria in the Comitia and call for a vote. That will give us three days to get the tribes together."

As one, the men in the room clapped their approval.

Tiberius wore a long tunic beneath his toga in preparation for the cool mornings typical to Rome in the early months of the year. He debated taking a pair of gloves and wearing socks beneath his sandals, but decided that some discomfort was warranted for the sake of decorum. Hylas helped drape his toga, a creamy, grey color offset by the crimson of the tunic that peeked out when he shifted in certain ways. He did a half turn left, then right while gazing at himself in the polished bronze door of his mother's closet. Grunting his satisfaction, he pivoted to face her.

"Yes?" he said.

"Yes," she replied. "You'll start out soon?"

"As soon as Hylas returns with the lunch goods. Any last instructions?"

Cornelia stared up at him for an instant, her green eyes shining for once, he thought. "Just remember, my son, the Good Men are as slippery as snakes, and they will do anything to upset your plans. Anything. Is Casca keeping close?" she asked.

He rolled his eyes, "Mother, you are too dramatic. I'm a tribune, inviolate. And, yes, Casca will be controlling matters in the crowd along with Ajax. Trust me, nothing will happen."

"I do trust you, Tiberius," she said, "you are a good son. It's the Good Men I don't trust."

"Yes, well," he said, bending to kiss her cheek, "you'll know first how it all comes off."

He left her chamber, almost passing Claudia on her way in. "Oh," she said, "I was just looking for you. You're off?"

Tiberius wrapped his arm around her waist and grabbed her close to him. "I am. Goodbye, my love, see you soon," he said, his face barely an inch from hers. He kissed her, and let her go. As he walked away, he could hear the small bell chimes of her laughter.

The morning was cold, he thought, and windy, thank you Ventis. He hurried down the lane, hoping that the lower elevation of the Forum would offer some relief. The Rostrum itself would be as cold as the bow of a ship in a heavy sea. Perhaps the day would warm.

Hylas ran to keep up, the sack of bread, cheese, and fruits banging against his leg as he hurried. Along each side of the street, men watched them closely, alert to any others that might impede the tribune and his servant. In a matter of minutes they descended into the Forum, suddenly but subtly surrounded by a small contingent of men escorting them to the Rostrum. At the front walked Casca, while Ajax took up the rear. Waiting at the steps, Appius, Crassus, and Blossius took turns greeting Tiberius with kisses and hugs.

"May the gods bless you my son," said Appius.

"Oh, they will," Tiberius said, "our illustrious Pontifex Maximus Nasica will see to that, whether he likes it or not."

The other men laughed, and Appius said, "You may be blessed already. Casca and Ajax were very successful in drumming up the Roman citizens!"

"That would be a blessing," Tiberius said.

"We'll be watching in the seats to your left," said Appius. He put his index up to his right eye, smiled, and turned to lead the others away. Tiberius stepped up to the top of the Rostrum and sat in one of the ten curule chairs put in place for the new tribunes. He told Hylas to sit behind him, ready to run if need be. While Tiberius sat officially, maybe even officiously, he smirked, Hylas would come and go as his eyes and ears. Saturieus sat next to him, his own slave at his heels for the same purpose.

The two new tribunes nodded at each other without a word. Tiberius leaned out to look down the row of chairs at the others. He saw Marcus Octavius near the end. Too bad, he thought, he would have been a lot more engaging to sit by than the sourpuss next to him now. Then, again, Tiberius felt too nervous for any distractions.

He surveyed the well of the Comitia where city workers lined up the temporary wooden stakes and rope aisles. The voters would funnel through the aisles toward the tables where their ballots awaited them. Only the plebeians voted for tribunal laws, though the seats of the Comitia were filled with patricians, senators, praetors, quaestors, and aediles who would witness the proceedings. The new consuls Scaevola and Piso sat on high opposite the tribunes on high in reserved seats near the Curia Hostilia. Gazing around, Scaevola looked down at Tiberius and his party, then shifted his sight away.

The floor of the Comitia overflowed with people, up onto the steps of the Senate building and into the streets leading to the adjacent marketplace. Among the columns of the large, rectangular market, men were stacked up in rows, waiting for the vote to begin. Gradually, it dawned upon Tiberius that he barely felt the chill air sweeping across the Rostrum.

Then, curia lictors entered, followed by Nasica leading a corps of priests marching in stately form to temporary altars in front of the Rostrum. Situated before them were the voting tables and the tall, woven cistas where the ballots would be cast. Nasica pulled his hood over his head, raised his hands, and prayed in turn to Jupiter, Mars, Neptune, Vulcan, and Apollo to control the elements and bring forth Fortuna to bless this sacred ritual of free Romans. Braying lambs ceased their squealing abruptly as the knives of the priests dispatched and eviscerated them. Before long, the stench of burnt flesh and guttering smoke rose above to be blown away by the bitter breeze of the day's early hours.

Nasica withdrew with the other priests. Tiberius watched them leave, then noticed something strange happening. Instead of preceding Nasica, his thirty lictors spread out behind the ballot tables and the cistas, where they stood at attention.

"What does this mean?" he said. He turned to Hylas, who had the lunch and water bags slung crossway over his shoulders. "Drop all of that and run down to Ajax. Tell him to have some of his men keep an eye on the lictors behind the cistas. Then, run to Casca and have him send men to reinforce the guard at the treasury doors beneath the Temple of Saturn." Once the law has been passed, he realized, they would need funds to put it into action. No reason to have the good senators thinking about quarantining the people's treasury.

A herald stood at the front of the Rostrum and announced the proposed law and the order of the vote. Roaring a deafening cheer, the men crowded together in lines separated by the ropes that would funnel them one at a time to the tables. Behind each table sat an official who checked the rolls and handed out the wooden ballots. After being marked off the rolls, a voter would pick one of two different colored ballots and deposit it into the cista for later tabulation. As those in the stands watched, the lines moved briskly to keep warm.

Hylas returned, almost breathless and shaking. "I passed on your orders to Ajax and Casca, Master. Both of them said I should tell you that their eyes on the tables have seen countless "yes" tablets picked up and put into the cistas. Your law is passing, Master Tiberius!"

Tiberius sat back, feeling warmer now than he had all day.

Suddenly, Nasica's curia lictors stepped up to the cistas. In unison, each grabbed a basket full of tablets, hoisted it up, and headed toward the nearest exit past the Rostrum.

"Orcus curse you," spat Tiberius, rising out of his seat to shout, "Stop them!"

He pointed at the fleeing lictors, and the crowd began to rumble. The lictors tried to run faster, causing a few of them to trip and fall, spraying a river of wooden ballots in front of them. The shouts of outrage grew louder as Tiberius watched men running along the sides of the roped-off aisles after the panicked lictors. They caught up with them easily, and while two men held a lictor, others picked up the cistas and carried them back. Ajax's men had been alert and ready. The men in the voting lines and the rest of the crowd clapped and shouted their approval.

"Why did you stop them, Gracchus?" A voice on the Rostrum to his right called out loudly so that the crowd in the Comitia quieted to hear him.

"They are the curia lictors of our Pontifex Maximus Scipio Nasica."

Tiberius looked over to see Publius Satureius striking a pose as he cried out his complaint. Apparently, the amount that Crassus had promised him hadn't been enough.

"Surely, they must be on some mission of the gods unknown to us," Satureius went on. Tiberius cut him short, "If it's a mission of a god, it must be Hela's, wicked and deceitful! Sit down, Saturieus, it's over!"

They both looked down into the well of the Comitia as quiet gradually returned to the floor. The lictors had been rounded up and cordoned off by a circle of Ajax's men while others returned the cistas to their proper places. The voters had already begun to form lines again to cast their votes. A third had finished, and it should only take another half hour for enough tribes to vote to reach a majority.

Open-mouthed, Saturieus gazed out at the vast crowd, and solemnly returned to his seat. Tiberius watched him sit down. With hands resting on his hips, he wheeled about to face the section where the consuls sat. Next to them, Nasica slouched in a curule chair, Rufus on his right, and all the others arrayed in rows behind them. Tiberius lifted one arm and waved it deliberately in the air like a signaler on a mountaintop watch tower, sure to be seen. Was that your best? he said to himself. Nasica barely lifted a hand above his armrest and weakly fluttered his fingers in acknowledgement.

Tiberius shook his head, and sat down to continue watching the vote. Hylas brought him water and the bag of provisions. He sipped quietly while nibbling on a fig that he didn't taste. At this point in the vote, the cistas had been emptied several times for the tablets to be tallied by the election judges. Runners sprinted up and back around the entire Comitia as each tribe's final total became known. Hylas showed little fatigue, being young and having only a dozen steps to negotiate to the top of the Rostrum. Other slaves going to the top tiers could be seen halfway up bent over to catch their breath. No matter, thought Tiberius, they could take their time now. The count in favor of his law was close to being insurmountable.

Hylas dashed up the steps again. "The eighteenth tribe has cast their vote, the nineteenth is straight ahead!"

Tiberius tousled his hair, "Well done, Hylas. You've been an excellent courier." The young man beamed.

Tiberius stood up and stretched. He swiveled left to see Appius, Crassus, Blossius, and others on their feet clapping their hands furiously. He smiled broadly, then turned to his right and peered up at Nasica. Nasica arose from his seat and the other Optimate senators followed suit, though the consuls remained seated. Slowly, the Pontifex Maximus made his way across the rows of chairs set up for the vote. At the end, however, he stopped and stared directly at Tiberius.

"Roman citizens," a voice called out near to Tiberius. He glanced down to see Marcus Octavius standing at the edge of the Rostrum.

"As tribune of the people," Octavius shouted out to the crowd below him, "I exercise my right of intercession and veto the Lex Sempronia Agraria. This ballot is at an end."

Octavius yanked his toga up across his chest, and left for the stairway.

Tiberius looked out at the thousands below him, frozen by the announcement. He gazed back up at Nasica, who slowly lowered his chin in a nod, then disappeared behind the seats with the others.

Chapter 29. Intercessio

"Marcus Octavius? Jupiter, who could have imagined this?" Appius nearly cried out his frustration, "I thought he was your friend!"

"He is," Tiberius replied, sitting quietly.

"Then, why did he do this to you? Why?"

Tiberius pressed his lips together and said, "I don't know, Father, I haven't talked to him, yet."

Walking back and forth in front of Tiberius with his head down, almost pouting, Appius stopped after hearing the answer and stared sternly. Tiberius remained still, almost relaxed.

"They must have gotten to him," Crassus said, "Nasica and his gang." He was seated next to Tiberius, seeming to look inwardly as he spoke. "I wonder if they gave him more than we paid Satureius."

They all sat, stood, or paced in Appius's tablinium, ornamented in lavish but somewhat dated furnishings and decor. On calmer days, the princeps senatus graciously greeted his many clients in the spacious, open office, but today, consternation reigned. After the shock of Octavius's stunning betrayal had worn off, they all charged into action, sending a host of couriers with orders for Casca and Ajax, and urging Sextus to keep the rural voters here. Sextus agreed, though grudgingly, to allow them to camp on his estate, and persuaded his fellow equestrians to do likewise. These measures enabled them to keep their votes close at hand, but for how long? How could they deal with this infernal Octavius and his veto?

"How long can we feed and shelter the thousands of farmers sitting around waiting to vote?" Crassus said, suddenly looking alarmed. "We'll be bled dry!"

"That will take some bleeding on your part, Crassus," Appius said. "But, we need to do something, and quickly."

Tiberius breathed in and out heavily. "I'll go to Octavius and talk to him. Even if we can't change his mind, maybe I can find out why he did it."

The others glanced at each other, and nodded solemnly. Tiberius called to Hylas and told him to speed to Marcus Octavius's house to request an audience. Hylas left, and Tiberius retired to wash his face and hands. He returned to Appius's tablinium to sit and await Hylas's return.

In less than half an hour, Hylas came back. "He would be delighted to have you visit him at home, Master Tiberius," Hylas said between breaths, "the sooner the better."

Tiberius stood up. "Very well, let's go."

The Caelian Hill stood behind the Palatine, a long, lean spine densely packed with shops, houses, and insulas, home to a huge number of Romans and friends of Rome. Hylas led Tiberius up the steep grade quickly, so much so that Casca's men had trouble keeping up. Usually, Tiberius took a certain kind of pleasure in leaving them behind, freedom from this new found security. At this point, though, his mind was far from pleasure of any kind.

They darted in and out of narrow streets, up long thoroughfares and around rickety insulas, careful to look for any flying refuse from above. Eventually, they came to a relatively open space with a row of shops on one side, pork, flour, bread, fish, and greens. Between them, they saw a barred, thick wooden door reinforced by iron strips, the entrance to a private domus situated off the street, behind the shops.

Hylas banged his fist on the door until a slot opened at eye level. "Tribune Tiberius Sempronius Gracchus here to see Tribune Marcus Octavius." The eyes behind the slot disappeared as it was closed. The door opened, and a single, aging house slave ushered Tiberius and Hylas inside and led them down a narrow vestibulum into a sparse atrium. Tiberius was asked to sit on a simple wooden bench while Hylas stood apart near the doorway of the vestibulum.

Marcus Octavius hurried in from a room on the side, his arms outstretched in greeting. "Tiberius, it is an honor to welcome you to my humble domus," he said, smiling broadly, then turning his eyes around the barely decorated room, "humble, indeed."

He returned to Tiberius, grasping his hands, "Nonetheless, I'm happy to meet you under any circumstances. Sit, sit with me in the peristylum. There's a small breeze coming through, rippling the water—perhaps we'll see a silverfish or two," he laughed.

Laughing himself, Tiberius followed the small, dark-haired man as he limped his way to two curule chairs angled around a very tiny pond. Tiberius sat down and watched as Marcus lowered himself gingerly into his chair, briefly expressing a fleeting pang of pain until he rested.

"Wine? Water, then?" he asked. "How about watered wine? We've had a long day, I promise I won't let you imbibe too much."

The old house slave brought two cups to the seated men. "Thank you, Prospero."

Marcus drank, and waited for Tiberius to sip. Then he said, "I guess I know why you're here, old friend."

Tiberius genuinely sighed. "For the love of the gods, why did you do this, Marcus? The people want land reform, haven't you seen the graffiti on the walls? The only ones who don't are the Good Men, Nasica's kind. You hate Nasica! Why did you side with that bunch? Marcus!"

Marcus dropped his eyes. "Your feet are white. You're shivering." He turned his head, "Prospero, bring a couple of pans of hot water."

He gazed back up at Tiberius. His dark, brown eyes seemed shiny, warm with affection and imploring, like those of a dog. He took a swallow of his wine, buying time. Prospero came back with the bins of water steaming from their heat.

"Ah," said Marcus, "there must have been some water already on the fire. Delightful!" Prospero unclasped Marcus's sandals, and his master plunged his feet into the pan, causing some water to slop over the rim onto the floor. "Ouch! Be careful, it's really hot."

Despite Tiberius's shifting attempt to dodge the Greek slave, Prospero managed to loosen his sandals and remove them. Left without a choice, Tiberius dipped his feet into the water. After getting used to the heat, he admitted to himself that it felt good. He felt himself warming up.

He shook his head briskly, and said, "Marcus, please answer me. I deserve an answer. Why did you betray me?"

"Betray you," Marcus mumbled. "Betray you, Tiberius? I didn't mean to. I didn't think it really mattered that much to you. I thought it was merely a gesture on your part, a nod at fulfilling your campaign promises. We'd already won the election. Why alienate the Optimates? We need them to get anything meaningful done."

He shrugged his shoulders, and Tiberius leaned back, his eyes slits.

"I don't believe you, Marcus, you're too intelligent to think that the bill wouldn't pass." He moved his eyes around the small, spare domus. "What did Nasica give you?"

Marcus jiggled around in his chair. "This water is starting to turn cold." Tiberius said nothing, and Marcus pulled his feet out of the pan in exasperation. Prospero rushed to dry his feet.

"I know, my house is a dump. Except for old Prospero here, I'm alone and I must look desperate. And why? Because I am alone and desperate.

Guess where I grew olives and grapes to support my family? Sicily, where for the past two years slaves all over the island rose up to scorch the earth while joyfully killing all the farmers and caretakers in their path. No matter that our legions finally destroyed them, I lost everything, my mortar business, all of it!

"And why am I alone without wife and family? Because I begged my wife to allow me to divorce her so that she could remarry to provide for herself and our children. She agreed! So, I lived broke and alone, until now." Pain crossed his face, "Until Nasica made an offer just after the election. He and his cronies knew that the Lex Sempronia Agraria would pass by a landslide, so they needed another tribune to veto the bill before it became law. They were shrewd, of course, they didn't offer me money. They wanted me to be vested in their success." He stopped to take a long pull at his wine cup. "So," he continued," they gave me 5,000 iugera of land, plus livestock."

Tiberius interrupted, "In Campania."

Mucus nodded slightly. "Yes, the public land. The land taken over by the Good Men, the very land you wish returned to the people to whom it was promised by law oh so many eons ago."

Tiberius lifted his feet out of the pan and waited patiently while Prospero dried them. He slipped on his sandals and rose to his feet.

"I'm happy that you see the irony in this, Marcus. I am so sorry for what has happened to you. As your friend, I wish you had come to me long ago. I would have done something to keep you and your family together, anything."

"I could not do that, Tiberius," Marcus said quickly. "I liked you too much to saddle you with my foolishness."

Tiberius paused, and sighed. "Well. Things are as they are. We can talk more about your situation, but immediately I need you to reverse your veto. I want to bring the lex agraria back to a vote as soon as possible."

"I can't do that," Marcus said. He stood up and crossed his arms, wearing a hard, almost petulant expression of determination on his face.

"What? Why not? You know how these fat cats have been stealing land from plain Roman citizens for centuries! Now is our chance to change all this, to strengthen the Republic by benefiting her most important asset, the common people. You should know this, Marcus, you're a plebeian, too!"

"Oh, yes, Tiberius, I'm a plebeian just like you, you backed by the wealth of your esteemed father and the Cornelii on your mother's side.

You're no more common than the Good Men, you're just not good enough. Tell me that this most charitable act of yours toward the common man is genuine. Convince me that it's not just you wearing an actor's mask covering an act of spite against your enemies while fattening your coffers at the same time!"

His brow furrowed, Tiberius pulled back his head. "Of course it isn't! There are much easier ways to gain wealth, Marcus, you must know that now, sailing with the current rather than against it. Do you really think that I wanted to do this? You've known me for a long time, Marcus, you know that I've never been a politically ambitious man. My little brother Gaius would be much better than me at this. I cannot tell you how many times I wished he had been the oldest son. I never had a choice in the path I took until now. After seeing what has happened to our fellow plebeians, the deprivation, starvation, and death, all at the hands of Rome's own leading patriarchs, I had to act. This is a passion for me now, Marcus, not because I want it to be, but because it must be."

Marcus took a half step back. "Well, then, I'm sorry for you, too, Tiberius. We all have our burdens to bear. But, I still must oppose you. I believe in the order of things in Rome, I believe in the Mos Maiorum. And, it also could be my last chance to have a little of what you have, Tiberius. Perhaps I'll marry again one day and have heirs. I must oppose you, Tiberius."

Tiberius scowled, "Very well, Marcus, but you will lose. The people want this change and they will press you until you revoke your veto. And, I will be leading them, Octavius, know this."

"So be it," said Marcus. "Prospero, please escort Tribune Sempronius Gracchus to the door." He waved his hand at breast height, "Vale, Tiberius."

"May the gods be with you, Marcus."

The following day, the crowd in the Comitia roared as Tiberius stepped forward to present his case.

"Tribune Octavius, the people of Rome have made themselves heard: they want the lex agraria to pass. They want the land promised to them by Rome's forefathers. They want their fair share, and you must rescind your veto and vote for the people!"

Thousands of men in and around the Comitia stomped their feet and brandished closed fists in the air. Women and children far away added their high-pitched screams and shouts to the din rising from the Comitia floor. Tiberius waved his own hand high in his familiar fashion, which caused even louder, throaty cries. He gracefully turned aside and looked back at Octavius.

Octavius gathered himself deliberately and slowly made his way to the front of the Rostrum. As he reached front and center, the noise from the crowd subsided as they waited to hear what he had to say.

"People of Rome, I cannot condone Tribune Sempronius Gracchus's disregard of the traditions of the Republic or the Senate leadership with which the gods have blessed us all. Gracchus wishes to change Rome only for the sake of change itself, to rend the fabric of our society only as a means for installing himself and his accomplices as masters of Rome. Therefore, once again, I exercise my right to veto the Lex Sempronia Agraria."

For an instant, nothing broke the silence except the distant cry of a single crow flying low across the city. Pandemonium exploded throughout the Forum as the massed men shouted and surged closer to the Rostrum. Tiberius raised spread arms to them as if silently saying what more can I do? The men started chanting "Gracchus, Gracchus, Gracchus," and "land, land, land."

He lowered his hands and peered at Octavius, who stood like a rock against the closing tide of men screaming and bellowing their outrage. Octavius knew that, as a tribune, his physical person was inviolate, that anyone who attacked him would be stripped of his house and belongings and either be dropped off the Tarpeian Rock or thrown into prison. Tiberius wanted to strangle Octavius himself, but he also realized that he somewhat admired him, too. He wondered what would happen if a tribune attacked a tribune?

The next day repeated the previous, and the one that followed repeated the last. Tiberius would broach one salient after another, and Octavius would stand firm in his opposition. Sextus and the other equestrians gritted their teeth and maintained the camps of rural voters, but even these were eroding despite their efforts. Farmers had farming to do, livestock to raise, fish to fry. Their defection didn't really threaten the Populares majority, but the impasse started to stretch tempers.

"It's been a week now," Crassus lamented, "and still that little cripple goes on and on about the propriety of this radical law. Venus love me, the laws are already on the books, they just ignore them! This goes on, and we bleed dry," he said mournfully.

"We are stuck," Diophanes agreed. "If this continues, the little stone over which our tidal waves break will soon become the massive crater that swallows our ocean."

Appius mused, "The stone in the sandal that cripples the marching legionary."

"The cripple who is crippling us," moaned Crassus.

"He's not a cripple," Tiberius said. "He may have a short leg, but if he's proven anything, he's shown us that he is not at all a cripple."

The other men dutifiully nodded their agreement.

"Tomorrow, I'll try a different tack, see if that moves him."

"Tribune Octavius," Tiberius called out the next morning, then softly, "my beloved friend Marcus, will you not relent?"

Octavius raised his voice, "I cannot, dear Tiberius. I must defend Rome against even the lightest shift in the wind if it threatens the people with illegal and ruinous new mandates."

"You accuse me of wanting to be the master of Rome," Tiberius said. "I harbor no such ambition. Indeed, I would gladly defer and follow you if you would only reject your intractable stance. Please, follow the will of the people!"

A ragged cheer erupted from the men in the Comitia, a much smaller crowd than on the first day, and every day after that. Their support was eroding from the trickle of water flowing from Octavius's obstinacy. Octavius let loose a few more drops by saying, "I cannot. The greatness of Republican tradition is at stake."

"It's all but over," Blossius stated that evening. "He won't budge. We should withdraw the legislation and go after something more attainable while we still have any majority at all."

"Oh, don't be in such a hurry to rush to defeat, Blossius," Appius said, "there's plenty to be done before we reach that point."

"Oh, very good, then, Appius," said Crassus, "what do you have in mind?"

His head cocked, Appius eyed Crassus, wondering if he was being sincere or sarcastic. "Well," he hesitated, "we can master the situation if we just put our heads together."

"I don't think we can," Tiberius said softly. All of them stopped arguing with each other and fixed their sight on him. "I don't think Octavius will ever give up," he said.

"You don't?" Appius said, leaving his mouth hanging open. "Now, wait, we just haven't arrived at the right incentive, that's all. How about we give him money, a great deal more than the Good Men offered him? Or, how about we give him land, land that is far away from any we hope to reclaim for the people."

Tiberius shook his head, "The only incentive that would move him now is a lethal one."

They all stared at him as if they didn't know him.

"Oh, don't gape at me like that, I don't want to see Octavius come to any harm. He's still my friend. We must accept, however, that he simply is not going to change his mind. And, it isn't for the money, the land, or any reward that either we or the Optimates can offer him. Plainly, he's made his decision, and that is that."

"Then, what do you think we should do?" Appius asked.

Tiberius pressed his lips together in distaste. "I have some idea," he said pensively, "but I have to think it through. Let's meet tomorrow early morning. We can decide then, one way or another."

The men gathered themselves together, traded hugs, and left. Tiberius was the last to embrace Appius and leave, followed by Hylas into the darkening streets, shadowed by Casca and his men.

Claudia entered his room late in the evening to find Tiberius sitting on the side of his bed, his back to the doorway. He seemed to be staring at the window painted on the wall, sitting in the same position he'd been in when she'd left him an hour ago. Without a word, she silently glided past the end of the bed and sat softly next to him. She put her arm up and rested her hand gently on his shoulder.

"Tiberius?"

Without looking at her, he said, "It's going badly, you know?"

She nodded, though he couldn't see her, and said, "I know."

"Nasica is a shrewd man. He recognized that Satureius would be quick to switch allegiance to the highest bidder. He couldn't trust him to stand fast in front of a hostile mob." He swung his head, "But, Octavius, he knew. He knew that once given, Octavius would never break his word. To Octavius, it is a matter of honor and a way to show his courage. He would die before he gave either of them up."

He lapsed into silence again.

"So," she said, lifting her hand to stroke his hair, "what will you do?"

He breathed in, "What I have to do," dropping his shoulders as he exhaled. "I wish Satureius had been Nasica's man. It would have made it so much easier."

She dropped her hand away from his head. "Why? What are you going to do?" she said, confused.

He looked at her for the first time. "You're as bad as the others. Though, what I will be doing could be worse than death to poor Marcus."

She appeared to be even more perplexed. Tiberius clasped her hand and shook it rhythmically as he said, "Tomorrow, I intend to sue for the people to strip Octavius of his tribuneship for obstructing their wishes."

She pulled her hand away, now looking horrified, terrified. "You cannot do that!" she whispered. "No one has done that, ever."

"There's a first time for everything," he said calmly. She stood up.

"But, you will be breaking with tradition! Nasica, Rufus, and all of the other Optimates will castigate you for violating the Mos Maiorum. They might try to strip you of your office, they may even ostracize you and seize all you own!"

"Not if the people back me. If they do, the Senate won't be able to do a thing. And, I believe that they will back me."

"Oh, perhaps, but why take such a risk? You could lose everything, your family, your property—you could end up being Marcus Octavius! Why risk everything?"

"Because I must!" he cried out. "If I am able to do this, if we can get the land reform through, we can restore the people to their proper place, as fully vested citizens, not the chattel of the rich! We can change Rome forever by giving back to Romans their dignity and a true say in what becomes of them."

She stepped back, saying, "You would be willing to lose your family, your children, and me?" Without waiting for him to answer, she turned and left the room.

Tiberius turned back to the window painted on the wall and placed his head in his hands.

In the morning, his entourage formed in the vestibulum, uneasy as they waited to leave for the Forum. Tiberius appeared before them looking as though he hadn't slept the night before. Not long after Claudia had left his room, Polydius knocked on his door and said that Cornelia wished to see him. Seeing Polydius at such a late hour surprised Tiberius at first, since he had freed his old teacher after returning from Numantia. The old Greek had set up house on the Esquiline, though he did come to the Palantine to teach the boys. Tiberius quickly realized that Polydius's presence that evening, most likely at his mother's request, portended a more considered assessment of his decision. Sure enough, Cornelia sat in the center of her chamber with Appius on one side and Claudia on the other. Polydius silently moved behind Appius and Cornelia as if adding his de facto authority to their presence.

Without a moment's hesitation, Cornelia said, "Claudia tells me you plan to be a fool tomorrow on the Rostrum."

"My dear mother," Tiberius said, "I might not be the man my father was, but I will never be a fool, either. You have seen to that much, at least."

"You could ruin your entire term as tribune. Give up the lex agraria, and find another way to take down the Good Men."

"And, how do you propose I do that?"

She swung her head in frustration, "I don't know. Offer the people something else, land somewhere else, but don't try to take it from Nasica and the rest of them. Go after them later, separately. Together, they're too strong! Tell him, Appius."

Appius started. He gathered himself and said, "My dear Tiberius, your intentions are so good, so magnificent, but the Good Men are evil. As your most exceptional mother suggests, we must reconsider and find other ways to vex them." His voice became imploring as he said, "Please, my son, let's not wager everything on one roll of the dice. Think of the wellbeing of your family, your children, my daughter your wife."

Tiberius gazed at him with troubled, tired eyes, and said, "Appius, I'm sorry, I cannot. This must be done no matter what personally is at stake for me—my wife, my children," he looked at Claudia for an instance, then back to Appius and Cornelia, "even my most exceptional mother." His eyes hardened as he continued, "Tomorrow, I will announce the posting of two bills, the first asking the people to depose Marcus Octavius. The second will be another lex agraria, though not the watered down version we first presented. In the amended bill, compensation for those who surrender their illegally gained land will be smaller, and their children will receive nothing. Any who resist will be prosecuted at once; they will be the ones to risk losing everything. That's the Lex Sempronia Agraria that the Optimates, the Good Men, will face. I will ask that both bills be voted upon consecutively, immediately after the feast days of Concordia, exactly three days after their posting. Plebeians will roar their wholehearted support, I am convinced this will happen. Regardless, this is what I will do, whether you support me or not."

Tiberius paused, defiantly eyeing each one of them in turn. No one said a word. He resumed, "If you support me, you will rally our followers now. Sextus and the other equestrians need to make sure that the voters assemble today."

Appius said, "Crassus and I will go to the Senate. Nasica may suffer an apoplectic attack. We'll try to keep him and the other vipers in the basket. I'll make a late-night private visit to Consul Scaveola tonight. Perhaps Crassus will come visit his brother, too."

"Thank you, Father-in-law." Tiberius leaned down to Cornelia. "And, you, Mother, will you give me your blessing?"

Cornelia lifted her eyes to his, almost as hardened. "You will always have my blessing, Tiberius, if only for trying. My only fear is that you will fail."

Tiberius straightened up, "I won't fail."

He gazed at Claudia, "And, what of you, my beloved wife? Will you forgive me for creating doubt that I love you above all? If I have caused us to be torn apart by my choice, I am destroyed. But, I must follow this path as the right course to take. Can you accept that it is ineluctable for me, a moral mandate intrinsic to the man you loved and married? Can you forgive me and support me even if it means that I have sacrificed our family in this effort?"

Tears streaming from her eyes, Claudia rose from her chair and raised her arms to wrap them around Tiberius's neck. By then, she was openly sobbing, now, her torso undulating from each deep cry. Tiberius closed one arm around her waist and with the other held her head to his shoulder. Tears coursed down his cheeks as he whispered, "Oh, my love, my only love," and guided her out of the room.

Among the men grouped in Tiberius's vestibulum, no one seemed to express any enthusiasm for the upcoming engagement. Appius fidgeted with worry, while Crassus's face went back and forth between pained concern and almost peevish anger. Blossius twitched nervously. Always the implacable Stoic, Diophanes displayed no emotion whatsoever. Sextus, a surprise visitor, appeared to be no more put out than usual, though the object of his annoyance this time centered on Tiberius. He made that clear in his brusque reply when Tiberius greeted him warmly.

No matter, thought Tiberius, they could be as miserable as they wanted. He wasn't overjoyed either by the prospect of the morning's confrontation. But, none of that mattered.

He glanced out the front door at Casca and Ajax, noticing that they, too, seemed the same as always. Ajax looked the affable night portator, while Casca looked ready to kill. Tiberius turned back to the men inside.

"All right. Let us begin."

They marched somberly out together. Sextus mounted his horse, whirled it around once, and said, "This better work, Tribune."

"Do your part, Equitus."

He rode off, hooves clattering down the stone road. The others walked briskly in his trail.

Halfway down the Palatine, Appius and Crassus peeled off to head for the Senate, passing by the other side of the marketplace. Tiberius and Blossius strode between the marketplace and the Temple of Jupiter to reach the Comitia near the Rostrum. Tiberius trotted up the steps of the Rostrum as Blossius climbed to a nearby seat in the amphitheater on the side opposite the Senate house.

Tiberius made his way to his curule chair and stood before it, gazing around. He was the first tribune to arrive, though it was likely that only a few would actually show up today. As his arguments with Octavius had dominated the Rostrum, some of the other tribunes began to absent themselves. Since today marked the eve of the Feast of Concordia, Tiberius wondered if anyone else would show. Would Marcus Octavius himself show?

Indeed, as he scanned the surroundings, he saw that very few street vendors were setting out their wares, and only a few had fired coals in their braziers to roast nuts or strips of meat for the assembled people. Looking toward the Senate building, he saw a few young priests preparing to render the auspices, with Nasica nowhere in sight. They lit their fires, raised their hoods over their heads, and lifted their hands to implore Jupiter and the other gods and goddesses to clarify their fate through the sacrifices they would make. Tiberius bowed while the birds were dispatched and opened. The priests signified that all was as it should be, and he turned to the front of the Rostrum. As he did, throngs of people entered the Comitia from every entrance and began to fill the seats. More showed to take places on the floor before him, and he could see horsemen on the fringes just outside of the Comitia walls. Sextus had done his part.

Diophanes ran up and gave Tiberius two sheaves of thick paper. He glanced at the title of one, and saw Lex Sempronia Agraria, and knew that the other called for Octavius's removal.

"Copies have been posted throughout Rome," Diophanes said with a solemn face. "Our scribes spent the night getting them ready."

Tiberius nodded his thanks, and Diophanes descended to sit next to Blossius in the stands. At that moment, Marcus arrived.

"Good day, Tiberius, ready to go at it again?" Tiberius didn't respond, his expression one of concern. "Oh, come on, it won't be that bad. I'll be gentle, stick an elbow in your ribs, then send you home to feast and sleep a few days before we do it all over again."

Tiberius replied sadly, "Not today, Marcus."

He walked to the front of the Rostrum and called to the men filling the Comitia.

"Citizens of Rome," he said loudly, "once more we must take up a lex agraria that will restore the land and rights to our brothers who should be citizens again. We must wrest from the avaricious wealthy in our republic the holdings they have illegally wrenched from the destitute veterans of Rome's wars." He held up one of the rolls in his hands and said, "I present to you an even stronger Lex Sempronia Agraria that pays these wicked transgressors only what the land is worth, and not a penny more."

The crowd growled their approval. "Also," Tiberius continued, "their children will receive no consideration; they earned nothing, so they get nothing."

Again the mass of men in the sunken amphitheater shouted their support, this time even louder.

"Furthermore, any who do not comply with the tenets of this law will be prosecuted immediately, chastised, and stripped of all their land."

The throng of men surged to the edge of the Rostrum as they howled and cheered. Octavius stepped quickly to the front and bellowed, "This Gracchus wants to reorder the world! He wants to divide and give away the wealth of the Republic! We don't need new laws, we have good ones already in the canon! Gracchus's ulterior motive is to provide himself and his accomplices with positions of authority that will allow them to rule Rome! They wish to be princes of Rome, if not kings!"

The cheers from the men below began to turn to catcalls. Tiberius listened carefully to their cries of derision, and saw his moment. Half-facing Marcus, he said in full voice, "Tribune Ocatvius, do you intend to persist in obstructing this law so clearly favored by the people?"

"If you refer to this power-grab you hold in your hand, I do, Tribune Sempronius Gracchus," Octavius shouted, "I will oppose it to my grave!"

Tiberius turned to the crowd and thundered, "Then, I have no choice but to introduce another bill." He rolled up the lex agraria, tucked it under his arm, and unrolled the second sheaf of papers. "Upon a special vote by the people of Rome, a tribune may be removed from office when defying their collective will in passing any law, obstructing any...."

He read on, glancing now and then at Marcus, who at first looked stunned, then furious. When Tiberius finished, Marcus sputtered in trying to speak. Tiberius interrupted him while rolling up the stiff vellum. "Both of these bills have been posted throughout the city; the vote will take place upon the day following the Feast of Concordia."

Tiberius then faced Octavius. "Tribune Marcus Octavius, we have come to a serious impasse in this dispute, one of such proportions that it could lead to a greater conflict, perhaps even civil war."

A hush came over the Comitia as though the thousands assembled had simultaneously held their breath at the enormity of what Tiberius had suggested.

"As honorable men in the service of Rome," Tiberius continued, "we cannot allow this to happen. One of us must give way according to the will of the people. Therefore, Tribune Octavius, I will defer to you to ask the people to vote upon my worthiness to continue serving them. If they declare that I am at fault, I will submit to the Lex Impediem and give up my tribunal office. Please, Octavius, for the sake of peace in Rome, summon the people to pass verdict upon my endeavors."

Octavius stared at Tiberius, his face growing darker every passing minute. Finally, he shouted, "I will not be a party to this outrageous violation of our most cherished traditions. This is an illegal act of the highest order!"

Tiberius quickly wheeled around to the crowd and said, "Then, I have no choice. To restore harmony in Rome, I ask her people to ratify the Lex Impediem with the intention of relieving Tribune Marcus Octavius of his office and powers. The vote will be in three days, at the conclusion of the Feast of Concordia."

Without looking at Marcus, Tiberius marched to the stairway and descended amid the rushing ocean of voices screaming, "Gracchus," "Lex agraria," "Lex impediem." At the bottom of the stairs, he was joined by Blossius, Diophanes, and Casca with Ajax and their men. Appius and Crassus soon showed up, straight from the Senate. After they arrived, the entire contingent marched out of the Comitia to the Palatine toward Tiberius's home.

"How did the Senate react?" Tiberius asked in a low voice.

"Oh, Nasica nearly burst like a bloated corpse," Appius said, "mad as a foaming dog. There wasn't much he could do about it, though, once he saw the enthusiasm of the people in the assembly. But, you can count on every posted bill being torn down before the day is over."

"That's all right, we have men at the ready," Diophanes chimed in. "They have enough to replace all of them each day for the duration of the Feast."

Appius swung his head briskly back and forth, "That might not be enough. Casca, please make sure you have men guarding the postings up until the vote."

Close by, Casca dipped his head and dropped back to issue orders.

"All right, then," said Tiberius soberly, "Let us all go to our homes to feast Concordia, the Goddess of Harmony in Rome."

They all pulled their togas around their shoulders against the chill wind whipping through the street and made their separate ways home.

Three days later, all of the Tribunes stood at the front of the Rostrum, watching the tribes lining up in the roped aisles, ready to cast their votes on the two pieces of legislation looming over the entire Forum. At the top of the Comitia, senators and their clients, unable to vote in a plebeian assembly, shouted and screamed invectives and threats at Tiberius. Their attacks were quickly drowned out by the mass of men in the Comitia eagerly waiting to vote.

Tiberius stood apart from the other tribunes, or they stood away from him. Except for Satureius and one or two others, most of them privately had implored every god they could think of to keep them well out of the fray between Gracchus and Octavius. Of course, their waffling left them square in the middle.

Marcus Octavius made his way over to Tiberius. "Hail, noble Roman," he said wistfully. Tiberius grasped his shoulder firmly as he replied, "Noble Roman. Hail."

Marcus cast his dark eyes up at Tiberius, who saw that they glistened with moisture. "This promises to be a spirited day," the small man said, smiling uneasily.

"A hard day," Tiberius said quietly, "one that could be sad for us."

"If so, sadder for me," Marcus said, throwing his head back with a laugh.

"Can you change your mind, Marcus?" Tiberius asked. "Will you?"

"I can," Marcus said, his mouth set firmly, "but I won't. Do your worst, Tribune."

Tiberius slowly lowered his head. He took a half step and peered out at the horde of Roman plebeians in front of him, frozen in anticipation at what he would say.

"Roman people, we come to consider two bills, a lex agraria to return the Republic to the people, and a lex impediem to prevent elected officials from opposing the people's will and thereby violate their oaths of office."

The din sounded by the overflowing assembly caused the other tribunes to cover their ears. Only Tiberius and Marcus neglected to do so as they gazed upon the roiling crowd. Tiberius waved his arm to quiet them, which caused the volume of the deluge to rise. He put up both of his hands outspread, lowering them up and down to stem the tide. Eventually, they quieted as they realized that he intended to say more.

Once the noise subsided, Tiberius addressed Marcus. "Tribune Marcus Octavius, I will put to you the question again. But, in light of the impediem law posed to be passed and enacted, I caution you to weigh your words. Will you now still oppose the lex agraria in dispute?"

Marcus put his right hand across his breast and faced the body of people below. "Tribune Tiberius Sempronius Gracchus, I opposed your first lex agraria, I oppose your new lex agraria, and I state for the gods and the people to hear that you have no right to even utter the words 'lex impediem.' What you propose is a clear and outrageous transgression against Rome's Mos Maiorum, the unwritten law of tradition that has guided this city and its people since Romulus and Remus suckled at their mother wolf's teats."

Grumbling began to rise on the floor of the Comitia, causing Tiberius to snap his arm up high again. "By your own admission, Tribune Octavius, you continue to impede the clear will of the people. Therefore, I call for a vote on the Lex Impediem to determine if your obstinacy forces the people to remove you from office."

He pivoted around as though on parade with his legion and shouted out in full voice, "Stewards, begin the voting!"

The ocean of plebeians thundered their approval and pushed their way to the roped aisles to cast their votes. While they staggered slowly through to the tables, marking their ballots and casting them into the cistas, one by one the tribunes on the Rostrum withdrew to sit in their curule chairs. Only Tiberius and Marcus stood in place at the front, as if each intended to witness the fall of every vote into the bowels of each wicker urn. Before long, they both could see that the dominant color of the ballot chips was white, white for yes.

As the march of Romans continued and, on the far side of the Comitia, the end of the line could be seen. Marcus began to shift from one foot to another. He started to rub his lips with his fingers, trying to wipe away moisture that wasn't there as he watched the torrent of people go by him.

Tiberius could see him slowly losing his composure, he could see the slight sheen of perspiration begin to rise on his neck. How could this have happened? Tiberius wondered to himself, how could he stand here and watch this man, this good man, dissolve before him? What am I doing, he thought, what benefit could possibly come from this? There must be another way, no?

He averted his eyes from Marcus, whose agitation continued to blossom, and looked up to search out Nasica. He was there in his seat, in the midst of his regular pack of wolves, waiting for the chance to tear asunder any helpless soul, perhaps even one of their own.

Tiberius bore in on Nasica, and it startled him to see a rage in the high priest's eyes that he had never seen before, anger that might wither the will of a god. He realized, too, that all of this fury was focused on but one person on the Rostrum, in the Comitia, in all of Rome.

An imperceptible shudder passed up Tiberius's spine, and he shook his head briskly. Marcus had deteriorated dramatically during those few seconds. His eyes darted here and there like a wild animal caught in a snare. Tiberius reached out his hand to pat his shoulder, and the little tribune jumped and nearly lost his balance. Tiberius put his hands up to his own head and pressed, thinking this cannot go on.

The Maceia tribe had filled the voting aisles and was moving rapidly to the tables. Once they finished voting, the Papiria, the eighteenth and deciding tribe, would vote. By then, there would be no saving Marcus Octavius. Tiberius glanced at the aisles, at Appius and the rest of the Populares, who gave him guarded smiles, and up at Nasica and the rest of the livid Good Men, the Optimates. He thought for an instant, then raised his hand and shouted at the top of his voice, "Intercessio!"

Everyone paused, startled by what they heard. "Halt the proceedings!" he cried again. Everything stopped. The thousands of Romans standing on the Comitia floor and in the aisles gazed up at Tiberius, stunned into silence.

"In the name of the good and just gods, I ask you to suspend the people's vote for the beat of a heart, one beat."

Tiberius twisted and grabbed both of Marcus Octavius's arms. "Marcus Octavius, most honorable of all Romans, most courageous," Tiberius said, staring into the shocked, pain-filled eyes of Marcus, "I appeal to you to abandon this terrible course that you've chosen. I entreat you to renege on any vows that you may have made in haste, I promise that no ill will occur to you or your loved ones. Please, Marcus, don't allow this to happen."

Marcus stared into Tiberius's eyes, his expression a mixture of hurt, fatigue, and resentment. Tiberius said, "Marcus, if you just embrace the people's will," and he gestured widely at the host of Romans raptly listening to him, "I swear at risk of the wrath of the gods that I will give you land and livestock from my own estate, as much as you wish. You won't have to worry about any consequences from the lex agraria. Accept my offer, Marcus Octavius, in honor of your integrity and courage, and let us be done with this!"

Only then did Tiberius realize that tears had fallen on his own cheeks. For a fleeting instant, Marcus's expression softened. But, his features turned to stone again, and while gently removing Tiberius's hand from his arm, he said," Don't be absurd, Sempronius Gracchus. I'm in no risk of breaking any law. It is you who have desecrated our most sacred principles. You will indeed suffer severely at the hands of the just gods."

The Good Men picked this time to rise up together and shout, "Treason!" "Treason!" "Sacrilege!" "Treason!" At this outburst, the masses in the Comitia drowned them out with their own overwhelming curses.

Tiberius turned to the people and wearily waved them off with his hands. When relative quiet had been restored, he said in a flat voice, "Tribune Octavius persists in his objection. I withdraw my interecessio. Resume the vote on the Lex Impediem."

As the assembly cheered, the Maceia and Papiria voted in short order. Tiberius said solemnly, "The Lex Impediem has been passed. Tribune

Marcus Octavius, by the people's will you have been removed from office."

The massed plebeians roared their joy like stormy surf breaking over rocks. Sound on the Rostrum barely could be heard, but Octavius did his best, shouting tightly into Tiberius's ear that he refused to acknowledge such an illegal vote and that he would not leave. Rather than try to speak, Tiberius gestured to two guards nearby, pointed at Marcus, and jerked his thumb toward the stairs. The legionaries grinned and grabbed Marcus to usher him unceremoniouslydown off the Rostrum.

Tiberius glanced up at the Good Men, who were filing out knowing that their voices could never make way against the volume of such numbers. Nasica and his entourage had already left.

He turned his attention back to the crowd and waved them down. When the noise subsided, he shouted out, "Marcus Octavius has been dismissed. Are there any other tribunes who wish to raise objections to the lex agraria?" He glanced behind himself at the array of tribunes in their chairs, all wearing wide-eyed expressions like deer driven toward archers. Hearing no dissent, Tiberius called out again to the Comitia.

"Then, let us vote upon the lex agraria," he said, and the eruption reverberated throughout the Forum. The Lex Sempronia Agraria passed without incident, after which Tiberius, weary to the bones, slowly made his way home.

Chapter 30. Nine Obols

Tiberius strolled down the Palatine toward the Forum, ready for a full day's work, flush with energy and the beauty of late summer. Birds were out searching for breakfast for their broods, cats lurked in the shadows, hoping to snare a feathery meal of their own, and street dogs lolled their tongues in anticipation of chasing the cats just for fun. Those in the marketplace setting up their stalls would break off from their work to throw a stone or stick at any animal picking or sniffing at their goods.

The early morning air felt cool on Tiberius's face although he knew that by midday it would be as hot as ever. No matter, he was in fine spirits, healthy, happy, and content with the progress that they had made in implementing the Lex Sempronia Agraria—the silent sound of the formal title always made him smile inside. The law stipulated a three-man commission to supervise and adjudicate the reapportionment of the public lands. Appius Claudius Pulcher had been appointed as had Gaius Sempronius Gracchus, who could not serve immediately, since he was away in Numantia as one of Scipio Amelianus's military tribunes. So, Publius Crassus Dive was appointed as a temporary substitute until Gaius returned from war. Of course, Tiberius had been chosen as the third commissioner. The Populares were in charge.

Livid, the Nasica-led Senate refused to provide the commission with a budget or even a tent for the enterprise. Instead, they instituted a charge of nine obols per day from the commission for incidental expenses. Tiberius wasn't surprised, and wondered that they hadn't passed an edict requiring another obol each from the three commissioners to pay Charon when they crossed the River Acheron into Hades. Most likely, the Senate would be happy to arrange their passage as well.

Funds were an ongoing challenge, he admitted to himself. The final law had reduced compensation to those patrician thieves for reclamation of the public land they had stolen. But, the very object of the other side of the equation, the restitution of land to impoverished veterans and citizens inherently provided no revenue. Coin went out; none came in.

Monies from the plebeian treasury in the bowels of Saturn's Temple had carried them this far, but the stream was narrowing. Plebeians commanded far less of the Republic's wealth compared to the Senate's patricians, especially considering the latter's recent windfall of nine obols a day. Oh well, Tiberius thought, grinning grimly, perhaps we will have to pass a tax on the Senate to carry us.

He reached the entrance to the marketplace and hurried through the eastern entranceway. He passed one of the public fountains burbling amid its circle of carved, marble columns and concave roof. There, women filled their vases from the stone lion's mouth while their children splashed in the cooling pool. As he strolled past, he resisted the temptation to examine the wild riot of goods surrounding him in the market. Fat olives and ripe figs led to bursting purple and green grapes followed by arrays of wine jugs with cups ready for sampling. Succulent meats fresh off the spit hung from iron hooks as burly butchers carved pieces into folded flat bread to sell to passing customers. An adjacent stall showcased a range of roasting fowl, from small songbirds to child-size swans and cranes, plus a dozen different ducks ranging from miniscule to massive in girth. On the other side, a skinny little man wielded a cleaver to dismember pigs beneath a necklace of body parts, testimony to his skill and trade. Next to his stall, the smell of baking bread threatened to cast those too close into an enchanted state. Beyond them, other stalls roasted various nuts amid vendors displaying the most delicious of cheeses.

Tiberius kept moving, though the fulsome fragrances made him want to slow down. Other perfumes did their best to claim him as he came abreast of the flower vendors stationed around the small rostrum for the heralds. Women sat on the steps amid baskets and vases full of lavish blooms, intoxicating in their assault on his olfactory and equally threatening from the riches of their resplendent colors. In stalls further down, jewelers held semi-precious stones in their hands as though they had robbed some eastern tomb, calling out to the well-dressed strollers, gems for the precious jewels of Rome, her matrons.

Tiberius felt himself torn by the wonders of the great goods in the market, and he hadn't even seen the glorious garments and fabrics hawked on the opposite side of the vast, marble-pillared square. There was so much, so many beautiful things—of course, the Forum where the wealthy pols gathered stood next door, and Rome was the richest city in the world! To keep it that way, the common people needed to be reinstated as voting landowners. Still, he wanted to look, he wanted to see lovely things, and buy them for his gorgeous Claudia, once again showing a round belly. He smiled; after the passage of the two laws, another celebration and another child on the way. The commission better find some money soon, he thought, with four and soon-to-be five hungry little mouths to feed, some not so little anymore.

No matter, despite the concerns and the ever-present pressure, it all had turned out pretty well. The commission had situated close to 6,000 Romans on newly reclaimed public land in just half a year. Nasica and the other fat-cat senators screamed as each plebeian had been served, while the divesture of their own lands sent such howls to the Curia's ceiling that the resident pigeons wheeled wildly above. Rufus and Postumius especially expressed their agony as they saw their vast holdings chopped up and handed over to the wretched dregs of Roman society. Never mind the gold pieces clinking one against another in their bulging purses, pay-off for their blatantly illegal land grabs. The Senate lamented constantly, but the new consul Mucius Scaveola kept them at bay.

At least Marcus Octavius had made out well. The ink on the deeds to his 5,000 iugera land bribe had hardly dried when the commissioners claimed it under the new law. Octavius received compensation, however, which allowed him to buy a small winery in Etruria, where his former wife and children joined him. Thus, the plebeian tribune, who had nothing and failed to stem the tide of the Populares, ended up with more than he would have had he succeeded. After the debacle of his removal, Marcus never spoke to Tiberius, not once. Still, it was some solace to know that his old friend had prospered in the end, and maybe even might be happy.

Of course, not all of the plebeians agreed with the lex impediem on principle. When it had been passed, Titus Annius, a well-known headsman in the craftsmen guild, waited until the tumult of the crowd had subsided for his chance. During the long procession of plebeians casting their ballots on the lex agraria, Tiberius stood on the Rostrum watching patiently for the eighteenth tribe to vote. Just as he was about to announce the new order in Rome, Annius called out to him loudly in a stentorian voice.

"Tribune Sempronius Gracchus, how could you violate the sacred laws of Rome in such a cavalier manner? Never in the history of the Republic has a duly elected and consecrated tribune of the people been summarily dismissed by one of his peers. There is no precedent for this outrageous act, Tribune Gracchus, and it is a clear violation of the revered Mos Maorium. You have shamed yourself, and you should resign as soon as you have reinstated Tribune Octavius."

After this curt assertion, it was no surprise to Tiberius that all activity in the voting aisles came to a halt. The plebeians held Annius in high regard as an honorable, truth-speaking leader of the community, a sculptor by trade who produced exquisite work prized by patrician and other wealthy Romans. This could be tricky, Tiberius thought as he readied himself to answer.

"Citizen Annius," he said in a measured, almost quiet voice, "you bring to the surface the very thoughts and concerns that worried me for many days and nights. As ordained by the gods, tribunes are sacred and inviolable. I know this full well, a fact that drives the oath sworn by me and my colleagues, and those that came before us. In that oath is our obligation to execute the will of the people. Yet, what do we do when one of our fellow tribunes, one of our own, defies the people's will? Do we fail in our duty to them in deference to the inviolable sacredness of that one dissenting tribune? Even if that single, sacred, and immune tribune betrays the people? Would this honor the intentions of the gods?"

Tiberius took a step forward and gestured with one hand as he continued, "Suppose a tribune attempts to depose a consul? Shouldn't the people have the right to stop him? Yet, the people brought down Tarquin, the last king of Rome. Was that against the will of the gods? Vestal Virgins who betray the faith of the people lose their stations and their lives. The sanctity bestowed upon them for the sake of the gods is forfeit. You see, Citizen Annuis, no one is inviolably sacred when the gods are offended. It is true that a tribune has never been removed from office before, but that is because no previous tribune in history has so offended the gods. Today, we saw the will of the people, the will of the gods, and the Mos Maorium observed by the removal of Tribune Octavius, who, however misguided, acted alone in his egregious offense to our sacred entities."

The remaining crowd started a chain of remarks agreeing with Tiberius, until Annius waved his hand for attention. "You reason well, Tribune, and no one can refute your logic." With that the throng of people in the Comitia shouted their approval as Annius stepped closer to the Rostrum. "Remember one thing, Gracchus," Annius said, audible enough only for Tiberius to hear amid the roar of the crowd. "What happened to Octavius now could happen to any tribune." He smiled, turned, and walked away.

A truly unsettling moment, Tiberius recalled as he ambled on. He reached the corner of the marketplace just off of the thoroughfare leading to the Comitia and the Curia Hostilia. Immediately next to the entrance stood a tavern and a stairway on its side that led to the land commission's office on the second floor. Men were lined up from the top of the stairs down around to the corner of the taverna, Fortuna's Inn, which sold watered wine to those outside at the end of the queue.

This was the second office for the commission, the first originally being situated on the ground floor. The crowds grew so fast and became so unwieldy that the commissioners decided to relocate in one of the law offices upstairs to control the throng. That they happened to settle above a taverna seemed more of a whim of Mercury rather than of Fortuna. As each day progressed, they found themselves dealing with more and more drunken clients. After some unpleasant transactions, they cajoled the taverna keeper downstairs to sell only watered-down wine to supplicants waiting in line. Thereafter, those who had been drinking seemed much more tractable and mellower on the whole. As for those who couldn't tear themselves away from the taverna, their behavior smacked of poor risks for keeping any land that might have been bestowed upon them. Most of them never made it up the stairs.

Quickly, Tiberius vaulted up to the office door before any waiting in line realized who he was. The door was locked as usual. The other two commissioners apparently found the hour too early to parcel out public land. Generally, they showed up at noon, presided for two to three hours, then headed off to the baths to relax before dinnertime.

Fortunately, Tiberius was never alone. As he reached into his purse for the office key, Diophanes, Blossius, and Polydius appeared together at the top of the stairs. Ah, the Greeks, he thought.

The four of them entered the office where three tables had been set up with various styli, wax tablets, and parchment on top of them. Blossius and Diophanes took their seats at two front tables, and Tiberius sat at the single one in the back. Polydius manned the door, and as soon as Tiberius nodded, he opened it and allowed the first men in line to shuffle inside. Diophanes asked the first man, a haggard, tall fellow in an old but clean tunic.

"Name? Veteran? Over there," Polydius said, gesturing without looking in Blossius's direction. The next stepped up, and Polydius asked the same questions. Most of the men ended up in front of Blossius. Those not veterans faced Diophanes to present claims related to usurpation by the large landowners. Each of them documented the claims, including what proof was available, then gave the applicant a return date to learn the disposition of his case.

For the most part, the two Greeks handled everything, keeping meticulous records of every interview and transaction, with copies made later by scribes. Tiberius seldom stepped in, unless asked to by the extraordinary agents tirelessly working on his behalf, really on the behalf of the principles represented by the lex agraria. Instead, he spent a great time watching the people who came through the door. Many made little impression on him, except that they all were of a kind, a bit worn and harrowed, poorly dressed, mostly bearded, with hands gnarled and curled from labor. They looked hopeful, but also ready to flinch from some invisible blow, maybe from just the threat of a blow. A few looked and acted cocky, veterans obviously. But, they, too, could be cowed by a stern admonishment. After seeing hundreds of them parade in, thousands, perhaps, he occasionally found himself straying in thought from the need to engage the common plebeian in governing the Republic. He'd quickly shake his head to clear out such notions, reminding himself that the ancestors of these very men in need played a major part in building the might of Rome. So, never underestimate them, he thought, scolding himself.

"Tribune Tiberius," Blossius called back to him. When he looked at the Greek stoic, he saw that he had a very young man in check next to him. "I believe you will want to talk to this fellow."

Gesturing with two fingers, Tiberius beckoned the boy. He shuffled over, a very lean young man with dusty brown hair hanging around his head. When he reached Tiberius, he pushed the hair away from his face to reveal extraordinary sharp, deep brown eyes. He looked up at Tiberius somewhat fearfully, but also with a sullen edge as if pushed, he would push back.

Tiberius stared at him for a moment, wondering why Blossius thought he'd want to see this skinny, arrogant boy. He wore a dull brown tunic and carried a common farmer's staff, resting his boney body on it with both hands. When Tiberius saw the eyes, though, he thought he recalled something familiar, which tugged at his memory. Suddenly, his mind cleared and his brow seemed to rise in recognition, in realization.

"What is your name, young man?" he asked, feeling as though he already knew.

The boy straightened and said, "I am Cimon Quarto, second son of Centurion Primus Sacerdus Quarto."

"Yes, you are," Tiberius said, slowly moving his head up and down. As gaunt as this young fellow was, he still possessed a bearing that hinted of an iron backbone. "How did you come to be here, Cimon Quarto?"

The boy lifted his head again in an almost defiant expression and said, "My mother sent me to claim land as is our right."

Tiberius nodded again, "Of course, land for veterans first. Your father and your brother fought fiercely in Numantia. Each would have received their proper portion of land if they had returned. As heir to both of these noble Romans, you are entitled to their legacies, a plot of 160 iugeras each, 320 iugeras in all plus a stipend to purchase an appropriate complement of livestock."

Cimon's sharp eyes softened suddenly, his lower lip quivering. He stuttered a few indiscernible words, then took a breath and said, "I would have fought, too, if I could have. If I'd been older."

Tiberius raised his hand and clasped him by the shoulder, "I know. Then, we would have had three noble Romans in the field." Tears streamed down from the boy's eyes as Tiberius added, "But, your mother and your brothers and sisters need you at home, now. So, go back over to Blossius there. He'll take care of you. You need not wait in line again."

Cimon dropped his head and stepped over to the table where Blossius sat.

Tiberius fell back into his chair, thinking of the old centurion primus who had carried a staff much like his son's when they first had met. He sighed as he recalled how the old man had fallen, and how his older son Severus had lifted him up onto his shoulders, though it was clear that his father was dead. Severus died, too, in that last battle in Hispania, his ashes buried on the battlefield. His father's body had been lost on the field during the Romans' rout. Vultures might have picked his bones clean for all he knew, though it was possible that the Numantines Avarus and Rhetogenes had laid him to rest in their necropolis among the other honored warriors, both Numantine and Roman. If the Numantine priests were correct, the scavenger birds took the souls of the Quarto Major up to the heavens of the gods, maybe in his case to Mount Olympus itself to join his son. He could only hope that their fates had been ordained so fortunately.

Tiberius lifted himself from his solemn reverie and gazed around at the men crowding into the small office. Just as bedraggled as young Cimon had been, these men waiting in line for new land struck Tiberius differently now. They were plain men, ordinary men who wanted a chance to work for a better life. They came from the stock that had built Rome, and they could be those men who would save the Republic.

At noon, Appius and Crassus sauntered into the office, sweating freely from climbing the stairs. Only Tiberius and his three assistants occupied the room, closed for an hour for a midday repast. Appius dove into a chair as he said, "Vulcan's eyes, it is hot out there. I've grown too old for all of this running around. Tell me again, why did we decide to take an office upstairs?"

"To slow the mob down," Crassus said, also taking a chair. "A good idea, too. We can only handle so many of these characters."

"They are not only characters," Tiberius said, "they have character, too."

The two august senators gave him a blank look.

"The son of a centurion lost in Numantia came to claim his legacy. He renewed my resolve," Tiberius said quietly.

"Ah, steeled you, did he?" said Appius, with Crassus chiming in, "Stiffened your back, huh?" They both laughed, and Tiberius smiled and said, "We are doing good work here, friends."

"Oh, absolutely," "Of course," they said hurriedly, gesturing broadly with their hands.

They lapsed into silence.

"But, you must admit," Appius said, "it is ungodly hot!"

Tiberius gave a slight nod, "It is typical late-summer weather in Rome."

"Really? You're sure we're not in the African desert?"

Tiberius turned to Polydius, "Can you ask the taverna keeper for some water?"

Appius's voice trailed him out the door, "The colder the better." He turned his attention to Tiberius. "So, did we give a lot of land away today?"

"Diophanes can show you the map," Tiberius suggested. The Greek rhetorician jumped to his feet and stood in front of a vellum map of Italia and surrounding territories stretched and tacked to the back wall of the room.

"No, no," said Appius, waving his hand, "that's all right, Diophanes, I'm sure you all have done Herculean labor, here. However, Senator Crassus and I need to talk to Tiberius about some pressing confidential matters. So, if we could ask you please to retire for just one half hour, we would be grateful beyond words."

Diophanes and Blossius withdrew from the office.

After they had left and Appius directed his sight at Tiberius. "We need to talk about finances," he said.

"Or, the lack thereof," Crassus murmured moodily.

Tiberius listened, his mouth slightly open.

"We are running out of money," his father-in-law said quietly. Seeing Tiberius's expression frozen in shock, he asked, "How many applicants have we situated in the past few months?"

"I don't know," Tiberius said, rubbing his hair back over his head, "let's say a century a day, for five, six month, perhaps … 6,000 men, and their families?"

"Huh," Appius said, "a legion and a half. How many more in total, do you think, will want to take advantage of this generous state program?"

"Jupiter," Tiberius said, shaking his head, "maybe 100,000—200,000 men. I'm really venturing a wild guess, here, but certainly at least that many."

Appius glanced at Crassus, "Yes, sheer speculation."

Crassus replied dryly, "That's what it will take for us to get us enough coin to see this grand scheme through." And, the two old senators laughed together.

In dismay, Tiberius suddenly saw the full magnitude of the task, at least a decade of long lines of veterans and other men suing for their iugeras of land. With every war, they would have a host of new clients seeking what they had been promised. But, the commission would run out of money long before they reached that point, certainly unabated by a thoroughly hostile Senate. In time, everyone would forget what he and his party had tried to do. Rome would go back to what it had been before the lex agraria. It would be as if nothing had ever happened.

"Tiberius, why so solemn?" Appius asked.

"Yes, young tribune, what brings this ill humor upon you?" joined in Crassus.

"The money," he answered. "We need a king's fortune."

Appius smiled, "Yes, and then some," which caused Crassus to laugh again.

"How can you be so insouciant?" Tiberius said crossly. "Our work has barely begun and soon we'll be out of funds and out of time," he trailed off.

"Now, now, young star, don't burn too bright," said Appius, "Apollo will be jealous. It's true, the coffers are baring their bottom planks. But," he continued, closing his eyes while nodding his head, "there might be something to be done yet."

"Yes, indeed," Crassus chimed in.

"Just give us a little time to see to it," Appius said smoothly, patting Tiberius on his shoulder. "Who knows what might come about?"

"That's right," said Crassus, "who knows? I know that I'm getting hungry. Shall we find a morsel to hold us until dinner, Appius?"

"Excellent thought, Crassus! I smelled wonderful things in the market below. Let's explore."

The two eminent senators lifted themselves up to head out the door when Polydius returned. "My apologies, masters, the taverna had no potable water, I had to go to the fountain. I'm so sorry, it's not very cold, either."

"No matter, Polydius," Appius said, taking hold of the jug in the tall, old man's arms, "wet is wet." He took a long swig, and handed the jug to Crassus, who did the same.

"Let us go, most admired Roman citizen,"

"Lead the way, honorable sir!" said Crassus, passing the jug back to Polydius.

The two men disappeared out the door, down the stairs while the Stoics looked at Tiberius in bewilderment. Tiberius dropped his shoulders, "Send in our next clients."

The three men took up their posts and ushered in the waiting plebeians while Tiberius sat back in his chair, still brooding over the precarious situation facing them.

On his way home at the end of the day, Tiberius fretted about the commission's lack of funds, and he also worried about the short time they had left to keep momentum going. They had been so successful so far, he thought, if they only could continue on, the people would embrace land reform to the extent that the Senate could do nothing about it. The Lex Sempronia Agraria would become part of the Mos Maiorum itself; the gods willing, in time the balance of power in Rome would be restored. Yet, he only had four short months before the year was up, including his term as tribune. By then, he hoped to nominate his successor, even Gaius, to ensure that the commission endured. Gaius could nominate a worthy successor in turn, and his protégé could present another, maybe even his older brother again, Tiberius thought, for a second term. In this way, the commission could win its decade of time and become an institution in Rome. It was possible, he thought, if Gaius came home soon enough to run. But, the money, he thought, they would need it to campaign, and enormous more amounts to keep the commission moving land. Where would they find the money?

The thought plagued him right up to his home and into the vestibulum. His head down in thought, he almost didn't recognize the fluid tones of the woman's voice that greeted him.

"Tiberius."

He looked up to see a vision of his mother as a young matron, her eyes the same emerald green, her hair black and shiny as a raven's wing.

"Sempronia," he said. He stepped forward to hug her. "Where have you been, my sweet sister?"

Laughing, she hugged him back while saying, "At the villa, with the children."

He pulled back. "How are they—did you bring them?"

Smiling warmly, she nodded, "I did, they're in the peristylum playing with your own wild barbarians!"

He huffed a laugh, "They are wild, a threat to the entire city."

She laughed with him, turning to put her arm through his to guide him to the front door.

"I'm so happy to see you," he said, "why didn't you tell us you were coming?"

"I sent Claudia word," she said, and as an afterthought, "and Mother. But, I wanted to surprise you!"

"Well, you did, just about to death."

"Oh, don't be so theatrical," she said as they moved into the atrium.

"Sister, we hardly see you at all anymore, not even for the highest holidays. You must fear the wrath of the gods."

She frowned, "We observe them at the villa."

"Of course," Tiberius said, "and your new-found freedom has nothing to do with your husband being on campaign."

She looked wounded, "Oh, Tiberius, don't tease me that way. All I can do is think of the terrible things that have happened to all of the other generals who have gone to Hispania. I can't bear to imagine what is happening there now."

Surprised, Tiberius replied, "Don't worry about Publius, Sempronia. He's won wherever he has fought." I'll give him that, he thought to himself. "Macedonia, Carthage, he destroyed them all."

"Mancinus was successful in Greece, too. Look what happened to him."

He pulled back, squinted at her, and pulled her into his arms. "He'll be fine, and back soon. After all, Gaius is there, watching his back. He can't do better than having his own brother-in-law as a bodyguard."

"Unless Gaius decides to kill Publius himself," she said wryly. They both burst into laughter. "My husband can bring that out in people sometimes."

"Sometimes?" Tiberius said, and they laughed again.

"No matter, the Fates must be at work, having you mention Gaius's name. That's why I've come to see you."

"Oh, really?" Tiberius said, somewhat wary now.

"Yes." She reached into a small purse tied around her waist and pulled out a slender packet. "A letter from little brother to you!" she said, handing it over.

"Oh," he said, breathing some relief.

"Yes, he wrote one for everyone in the house, even the children. I've already given everyone else theirs. He sounds very jovial and positive about coming home soon."

"That's good."

"Yes, if it's true."

"Well, didn't Publius write to you?"

"Of course. But, he says nothing, except to mind the estate and its manager. Nothing about what he's doing."

"I see, but perhaps that's for the best."

"For you men, certainly!" she said in scorn.

Just then Claudia and Cornelia came in from the peristylum trailed by a horde of children, two of Sempronia's and four of her own. They crowded around Sempronia, pulling at her dress and telling her to come play. Claudia tried to hold them back while Cornelia pretended to scold them. But, the wave was irresistible, and Sempronia was being carried away. As she was swept back into the peristylum, she cried out, "Tell me if Gaius writes about something real!"

He laughed as he nodded. He called out to Philea to bring him some water to his office. He entered and sat down to read Gaius's letter.

Salve, Brother Tiberius,

I trust all is well and the gods smile upon you. I've heard that they have, one victory after another over the Optimates. You have my heartiest congratulations, and, I must say, all the gloating that a man can muster. It is true, I gush about your success to my fellow officers, most of whom can barely stand me, as they generally spring from the same snotty patrician stock as Nasica and his loathsome gang. Oh, there are a few stalwart friends I can count on, solid plebeians who worked their way up like our forefathers, no more than to be expected. Scipio keeps his peace, though I imagine that he's jealous, too, having failed with his lex agraria when Laelius the Wise, the Prudent was forced to drop it. But, you didn't fail, Tiberius, you are your father's son! I am so proud, older brother, I cannot wait to return to join you in tweaking the noses of the Good Men many more times!

And, the auspices look good for my return. The war has gone well. Our brother-in-law has executed an extraordinary campaign. I say extraordinary, but in fact it is a simple plan that he has used many times before, as you know. Bring an overwhelming force to bear, cordon off the enemy, and slowly squeeze them to death. Of course, this is easy to say in theory, but how he does it is a different order of things. I recall the difficulties you had in raising a single legion to bring to Numantia, the ranks of available recruits were so thin and so unwilling. Somehow, though, Scipio has managed to scrape together ten legions and, most tellingly, 20,000 horse. The camp rumor mill has it that he brought legions from as far as Macedonia and Phoenicia to add to those he commandeered in Italia and both Hispania Citerior and Ulterior. Of course, he had his own legion all along working his estate. I'll wager they were happy to exchange the farm yoke for the soldier's. In any case, Scipio showed up at Numantia's gates with an army of 40,000 legionaries and twice as many horse as their standing force.

He immediately set about entrenching the perimeter of the city, including pontoons across the northern rivers that provide the city-fortress with its water. I saw your old friend there, Titius, leading the immunes in their ingenious machinations. The Numantines might have plenty of food stuff saved to endure a long siege, but water is another matter. In time, their cisterns must have been exhausted. Toward the middle of summer, in the hottest days, they rode out several times in an attempt to break our lines. But, of course, our superior numbers, especially the cavalry, repulsed them. They lost many men and horses. Those that we captured appeared to be in desperate straits, if I can be allowed the irony. They suffer from a hot, dry summer here. The prisoners looked gaunt and parched, barely walking corpses. Scipio wasted no time in executing them and mounting them on stakes in front of our fortifications. By the end of Quinctilis, dead Numantines formed an unbroken line around our entire perimeter. In a matter of days, the city surrendered.

Scipio followed his usual practices, decimating their warriors, including the wounded, the weak, and the aged. He organized the rest into separate groups, the men on their way to the mines in Citerior, the women and children back to Rome to the slave markets. Before all of this, of course, he crucified the leaders of the Numantines, most prominently two elders named Avarus and Rhetogenes. I recall you mentioning that you knew them and thought well of them. And, thus they died, grey-haired and brave to the end. I am sorry to have to bring you this sad news. They were all brave, in fact. Even the women and children showed no signs of dejection leaving the city for the long march to the waiting ships and slavery. Though, when they walked past the two old men hanging from the crosses, they weeped.

I'm surprised that Scipio didn't take them back to Rome for sacrifice in his triumph—oh, yes, dear brother, there will be a triumph for Scipio yet again, it is inevitable. Aside from destroying Numantia, he has served cold notice to the surrounding tribes of what resistance to Roman might brings. Hispania is ours, Tiberius, without question. Only the final details will determine the day of full subjugation.

In the wake of this latest victory of Scipio's, I will be some time here while we consolidate the region. Numantia will be razed, of course, and two legions will now occupy this newest part of Rome's territories. The legions summoned from Ulterior and Citerior will march back to their respective headquarters in a show of force. Then, the rest of us go to the sea to return home. I expect to be back in the arms of our family by March of the coming year, ready to stand beside you in defying Nasica and his pack of curs. The gods willing, we all shall be safe—Mars will guide us home, smiling. Until then, dear brother, stay strong against the Good Men's antics. My love to Mother, Claudia, and the children. I long to embrace you all.

With honor and love,
Gaius

Tiberius folded the letter and put it on his desk. He had never talked to Gaius about Avarus's strange generosity in Numantia. No one in Rome would have understood such bizarre behavior from a conqueror, certainly not honor. The old chieftain had thrown the dice on the chances of peace. He would have been better off putting every Roman he could find to the sword. Instead, he helped save the remnants of our legions, the very same soldiers that returned to hang him from a cross next to Rhetogenes, his hard-as-flint, fellow warrior. At least the birds would pick their bones clean and fly their spirits up to their gods in the sky.

He sipped his water, and put the cup down. Gaius expected to be home at the beginning of next year, too late to run for tribune. Even if he had returned sooner, any campaign would have been daunting, given his youth and the fierce animosity of the Senate. They certainly would claim that the Gracchi aspired to dynasty. He shook his head, no, whether he was here or not, little brother Gaius wasn't the answer. So who was?

"Tiberius?"

Claudia entered the office, saying, "Tiberius, Sempronia wonders where you are. She's come all this way to see you, and you hide in your office."

"My deepest apologies, love of my life. I'm a lout. Tell her Gaius sends good news from Hispania. I'll come out soon to share it with everyone."

Claudia leaned over and kissed him. "Love of my life," she said as she straightened to leave. He clung to her hand until it slipped from his grasp as she left the room.

What was to be done? he thought, again and again.

Chapter 31: Philometer's Bequest

In the morning, he arrived at the office, which was already alive with activity. It took him by surprise, since he knew he wasn't late. He angled his way around the men at the doorway, first in the line that, as usual, stretched out from the door, down the stairs, and around the market walkway. Diophanes and Blossius sat at their desks, briskly talking with the supplicants in front of them. As soon as Polydius saw Tiberius enter the office, he quickly closed the space between them and whispered, "Masters Claudius and Crassus are here, waiting for you in the back room."

Tiberius stared at Polydius, shocked and disbelieving. Appius and Crassus here this early in the morning? Why? Polydius nodded his head and gestured again to the back.

Tiberius slowly made his way past, knocked lightly on the back room door, and let himself in.

Appius and Crassus sat on chairs usually stationed in the front room. As soon as they saw him, the two rose up and said heartily, "Tiberius!" "Excellent that you're here, Tribune!" they both patted his arm and back, and shook his hand. "Good man, here at last!"

Bewildered, Tiberius said, "What sorcerer's spell has beguiled you both to be here so early?"

The two senators grinned at each other broadly in a naughty boy sort of way. Then, Appius spoke. "Why, we've come to solve all of your problems!"

"Money problems, that is," Crassus said.

"Yes, of course, strictly financial," said Appius. "Sit down, son, but first ask Polydius to stand at the door and allow no one to disturb us."

Looking somewhat bewildered and also askance at the two antics in front of him, Tiberius went over to the doorway and asked Polydius to watch guard. He returned and sat down across from the still smiling senators.

"All right," he said, "tell me, what golden bounty did you stumble upon?"

Appius and Crassus traded glances again, almost joyfully. Crassus nodded at Appius, who turned back to Tiberius and said, "Pergamum."

"Pergamum? You found a king's fortune in the far reaches of Pergamum?"

Appius and Crassus burst out laughing, "As a matter of fact, we did!" laughed Appius. Seeing Tiberius's confusion rising, along with his ire, he continued, "Actually, the King of Pergamum himself. Past king, that is. He died, Attalus Philometer did. The poor wretch contracted some kind of grippe that took him off..."

"Helped, perhaps, by a potion less than palliative conceivably administered to him by his less than faithful physicians," Crassus said.

Appius cocked his head, "Always a possibility in the eastern world. His beloved nephew Eugenes III has stood poised to ascend the throne for three decades or more. He could have grown tired of waiting to grieve."

"Now, he has even more to grieve about," Crassus said.

"Oh, yes, he certainly does," rejoined Appius, which caused them both to laugh again.

"Very well, Father-in-law, but what part does this play in our turn of fortune?" Tiberius asked in a clipped tone.

"Why, by way of Attalus III Philometer Euergetes's will, dear Son-in-law." Appius turned back to Crassus, "Did you know that Euergetes means 'Loving-his-mother Benefactor?'"

"I certainly did not," said Crassus. "Who told you?"

"Polydius, of course."

"I'm sure Eugenes wished that his uncle had been dubbed 'Loving his nephew' instead."

"I imagine so," said Appius.

"Honored of Rome!" Tiberius said loudly. Startled, they stared at him, which caused him to say gently, "Please."

"Very well," said Appius, "we've kept him in the dark long enough." He faced Tiberius full on, and said, "Attalus Philometer was not as fond of any of his relatives as one might have thought—"

"His nephew Eugenes at the top of the list," Crassus said.

"Yes," Appius went on, "Philometer did not leave his wealth or his kingdom to his next of kin—"

"Not Eugenes."

"Yes. In his wisdom and generosity, Philometer left his kingdom and his wealth ... to the people of Rome!"

Appius slapped his thigh as he joined Crassus in raucous laughter.

Tiberius said, "I don't understand? He left everything to the people of Rome?"

Appius nodded his head up and down, still caught in a silent paroxysm of laughter.

"Could he do that?"

Crassus shrugged his shoulders, "Why not? It's his kingdom, his gold."

"And Eugenes? He won't object?"

"He doesn't know, yet. He's still searching for the will, thinking it's misplaced somewhere in Philometer's vast palace."

"Huh. If Eugenes is as devious as you've suggested and he cannot find his uncle's will, I don't suppose it will take him long to issue a forgery."

"Oh, he's not worried about that right now," Crassus said, "he's too busy celebrating his approaching coronation. His house slaves have been assuring him that it's just a matter of time before they find the will. They have all sworn on their gods, too, who or whatever they might be, that his uncle had left him everything, such was his love."

"What if the will does turn up?"

"It cannot," said Appius, hesitating momentarily for effect, "because it is here, in Rome!"

Tiberius blinked. "In Rome? How did it get here?"

"It was secreted here from Pergamum by Philometer's trusted secretary Eudemus."

"Oh. I see," Tiberius mulled this news over in his mind for a time. Then, he said, "Still, Father, what does this have to do with us and the lex agraria?"

"The will," Appius said fervently, "leaves Philometer's kingdom and massive fortune to the people of Rome! The people of Rome, Tiberius!"

Crassus broke in, "Not to the city of Rome or its patricians, but the people."

His brow knit, Tiberius said, "But why? Why not to the city and its patrons? How can you divide a kingdom and a fortune among hundreds of thousands of people?"

"You can if you turn it into land," Appius said slowly, enjoying as he spoke the slow dawning taking place revealed by his son-in-law's features, "and give the land away to the people."

Tiberius drew back in his seat, splaying his feet out in front of him. He found what he was hearing so hard to believe, like a carrot dangled in front of a donkey. He rubbed his hand across his mouth and said, "What about the patricians? Why didn't they seize upon this enormous opportunity? It is so unlike Nasica and Rufus to pass on a chance to fill their purses, no matter whom was named in the bequest."

"They don't know about it yet. They are as much in the dark as Eugenes," said Appius.

"Or Philometer himself, may the gods celebrate him on high," murmured Crassus.

"And, how did you find out about this?" Tiberius asked impatiently.

"Philometer knew of the struggle here in Rome between the Populares and the Optimates. He also knew that his doting nephew had received a promise of support from the Good Men of Rome should he find himself in position to be king. So, before he died, the king picked sides. He picked our side."

"He was quite a tyrant, I hear, in his early days." Crassus said. "The old boy changed later on, it seems, became quite the scholar and ascetic."

"Eudemus was told to bring the will to one man in Rome, one only."

"Who? Me?" said Tiberius. Appius shook his head, and Tiberius said, "You?" Again, Appius shook his head and said, "Crassus, it is your honor."

Crassus beamed and said, "Consul Mucus Scaevola! My delightful brother!"

Tiberius's mouth hung open while Appius continued, "Scaevola immediately squirreled Eudemus away and sent word to us. We came here directly to tell you."

Tiberius could barely breathe. He kept glancing up and down between the two craggy senators and his sandals. Pergamum, famous in children's stories for its wealth! Of all the other gods and goddesses, Fortuna smiles upon us!

"You will meet Eudemus today in the baths where he will show you the will and consign it to your wellbeing. We have magistrates lined up to inspect it and verify its authenticity, after which you can announce the news of this glorious windfall to the people!"

Tiberius could only stare up at the two senators, stunned.

They were to meet in the apodyterium, Tiberius trailed by Hylas carrying his bathing garments and toiletries. It was early, which usually meant that only a few men would be at the baths, this being the traditional time for women. Even so, Tiberius was surprised to find the dressing room virtually deserted when he entered. Halfway down the long hall, he noticed a large, heavily muscled man leaning against one of the clothing niches, his arms crossed over his breast. Although he wore a regular long tunic with a plain leather belt, his biceps were pinched by curling bands of bronze shaped like snakes. He sported wild, curly black hair pulled back in a ponytail, revealing gold earrings that dragged his ears down, making them look like drooping, eyeless sockets. Tiberius noted, too, the curved knife sheathed at his waist.

Without hesitation, Tiberius walked up to him and said sternly, "Where is your master?"

The man straightened up and said with a heavy accent, "The frigidarium."

Tiberius's brows furrowed. The usual order for bathing was to head for the tepidarium to ease the body into warm waters, followed by a hot dip in the caldarium. The cold rinse in the frigidarium came last. Of course, a good bout of exercise usually preceded all of this, so it was odd that this eastern elite, accustomed to the warmth of the Aegean, would head directly to the coldest room in the baths.

Tiberius shed his toga and handed it to Hylas. Without looking back, he said, "Wait here." Wearing nothing but his subligaculum, he walked purposely to the far door leading into the drafty chamber.

Inside, he saw a man wrapped in an exquisite chartreuse, silk cloak sitting on a bench near the cold pool of water. He wore an elaborate headpiece that allowed his finely pressed array of shiny black curls to flow below to his shoulders where they met his equally resplendent black whiskers, wave after wave of them spilling down to his substantial chest. Beneath his cloak could be seen a fine, beige linen shirt plaited in folds across his breast, covered by row after row of curving gold necklaces. His pants matched his cloak, also of silk, and his sandals gleamed with gold inlays.

Tiberius noticed his long fingernails, cut and polished a dazzling red that competed with the precious gems and gold of his many rings. He held his hands folded together, his head resting on his breast in contemplation as he waited. Tucked beneath one arm was a small chest made of precious wood, also festooned with spangling jewels and gold.

Tiberius stepped up to the man, who raised his head to reveal the deepest, darkest pools that were his eyes. Tiberius could see the pain in them, and gentleness. He said, "You are Eudemus."

He nodded and said, "Tiberius Sempronius Gracchus? Champion of the people of Rome."

Tiberius grinned, clenching his teeth. "Tribune of the people, yes."

Eudemus smiled slightly. "King Attalus was very impressed by you, very much so."

"Really?" asked Tiberius. "A king impressed by someone with completely opposite values? Someone who is seizing wealth from kings in all but name only, and giving it back to the people?"

Eudemus seemed wounded. "You know little of the Attalids, Tribune. Yes, they were kings, but they also gave tax money back to their subjects when they saw them in need. They spent their wealth to bring art, knowledge, and beauty to their people."

"Even your recently departed king Attalus Philometer? I understand that he was quite the scourge of his kingdom."

"He was," Eudemus said, looking thoughtful, "when he was young. He was quite awful, but then he changed. He became a benevolent leader in the end."

"What changed him?" asked Tiberius.

"He learned to pray." Seeing Tiberius's skepticism, Eudemus said sharply, "You do not understand, you do not know. He was a great king, despite his stupid nephew Eugenes, who did everything he could to undermine him. Eugenes wanted to be king, the swine, and he couldn't wait. He tried for thirty years to steal the throne, everything, alliances, assassination attempts, any heinous act under the stars. But Attalus thwarted him at every turn, until finally, our good king had to face the fact that, like every man, the thread of his own life was fraying. He did the only thing he could. Rather than fade away to see from the farther world the destruction of Pergamum, he wrote his will giving his kingdom to the Roman people. Oh, not the Senate, not the Good Men, no, Attalus knew better than that. He gave it to you so that the best of Rome would save his beloved people and land from civil war. And, remember this, Tribune Sempronius Gracchus, the Attalid kings and all of Pergamum were there as allies when Rome face its worst enemy, Carthage. Rome owes a debt to Attalus and his people, don't you forget this. This is not just a giveaway, Pergamum's wealth is yours as a trust, a sacred responsibility. Remember this most of all."

Abashed, Tiberius leaned down to the bereaved man and said, "You are right, of course, Eudemus. I apologize from the bottom of my heart. As a Roman, I vow on our gods and the lives of my children that I will do my best to protect the wellbeing of the people of Pergamum. I also promise to safeguard their culture and honor their gods."

Eudemus drew back and eyed Tiberius as though he were crazy. "No one expects Rome to do this without consideration. You will receive a stipend of 5,000 talents annually for as long as Pergamum thrives. The first payment awaits you not far outside the city walls. You need only give me the order, and I will have it transferred to your treasury."

Tiberius froze as he heard Eudemus's words. The impeccably appointed minister nodded, "That should keep your land reform program going for quite some time. Unless, of course," he said smiling wanly, "some impatient Romans decide to take it from Pergamum all at once. You know, kill the goose—no more eggs."

He stood up, "But, that is your challenge, I guess, and no business of mine. I can proceed assuming that you agree? Good, well, then, here is King Attalus III Philometer Euegerte's will entrusting Pergamum into your hands as I have delineated."

Eudemus handed over the heavily bejeweled box. Tiberius opened it to find an exquisite parchment scroll with beautifully illuminated script on the outside. The parchment was held together by a simple, royal purple ribbon of silk and a heavy gold clasp delicately sculpted with reliefs of god-like visages.

"That is the original, though copies have been made and tucked away in Pergamum, to be released when the people have been informed. I suggest that you do the same here in Rome. And the rest," he said, gesturing toward the doorway. The burly guard Tiberius had first seen outside crossed the chamber toward them. At first alarmed, Tiberius relaxed when he saw Casca move silently through the shadows on the other side of the room. To his left, he noticed another figure, though he couldn't make out who it was, perhaps another guard.

The Pergamum strongman approached them and bowed his head, waiting. Tiberius noticed that he had brought with him a large wooden chest hoisted on his shoulder. Eudemus said, "My man Apogenes." He beckoned with his hand, and the man took a knee and brought the chest down to the sandy floor and opened it up. He lifted out a purple bundle and held it in his hands above his head. Eudemus grasped an edge of the silk wrapping and flipped it back. He then flipped back an inside flap to reveal a large, ornately decorated gold crown and a gold scepter, both bedecked with priceless gems, emeralds, rubies, diamonds, sapphires. "May I?" Eudemus said, sweeping his hand across the crown and scepter.

"No!" Tiberius stepped back as though from a snake or a blighted man. Eudemus looked at him, puzzled. "Rome recognizes kings and kingdoms in other parts of the world," Tiberius said, "but we freed ourselves from servitude to kings almost five centuries ago. No honorable Roman would ever think of assuming the trappings of a king of any kind. I'm sorry."

Eudemus stared at Tiberius again as if he were from some strange land. "You are a peculiar man, Tribune." He shrugged, "No matter, if you wish to rule Pergamum as a tribune, so be it."

"I will oversee Pergamum's liberty and safety," Tiberius said, "along with the other tribunes duly elected as representatives by the people of Rome."

"Very well." Eudemus barked to Apogenes in a guttural language completely unknown to Tiberius. "These go back into the Pergamum treasury," Eudemus said to Tiberius as Apogenes carefully rewrapped the crown and scepter, and put them back into the chest.

"Well, then," Eudemus said, "I suppose I have completed my king's final task. He will look down upon us from his seat next to the gods and bless us. Goodbye, Tribune Sempronius Gracchus, and good fortune."

The Pergamum minister bowed deeply, touching his brow with his hand as he did so. When he straightened, Tiberius noticed his eyes glistening even more so than before. "Good bye," he said, bowing his head once. Eudemus snapped an order to Apogenes, who lifted the chest to his shoulder again and headed toward the door.

"Eudemus," Tiberius called after them. Eudemus turned around. "What will you do now?"

Eudemus pursed his lips in thought and cocked his head to one side. "I will return home, the gods willing. There, I'm sure that Eugenes would love to roast me in the brazen bull, though I imagine he will have to settle for simple assassination." He grinned wickedly, "Unless, of course, Apogenes kills me first and steals the crown jewels."

Tiberius said, "You could stay here under the protection of Rome."

The Pergamum high secretary shrugged, "Why? Life is an adventure, after all, part of which is death." He smiled gently then waved to Apogenes to lead the way out of the frigidarium.

Casca stole up next to Tiberius. Still watching the doorway, Tiberius said, "Take this box to the tribunal treasury. Make sure you have plenty of men at your side. Send for Polydius and tell him to find as many scribes as he can to make copies of the document in the box. Once that's done, have the original hidden well away—no other tribunes must know its location."

Casca dipped his head in acknowledgement. "And you, Tribune? If you are ready to leave, I can assemble another escort at once."

Tiberius shook his head, "No, that won't be necessary. I'm here, I might as well get some exercise and a good scraping. Just leave the other guard with me."

"Another guard? I was here alone," Casca said. Tiberius turned to face him. Casca said, "I didn't want to make them nervous."

"Then, who was the man I saw at the other end of the chamber?"

"I don't know. Perhaps another bather?"

Tiberius scowled doubtfully, "Not at this hour, unless it was a woman."

"I'll search when I leave."

"No, don't bother. Secure the chest."

Casca nodded, picked up the strongbox, and left through another door at the far end of the room. Tiberius headed toward the other doorway, walked through, and called out, "Hylas!"

Tiberius gingerly made his way back to the commissioners' office in the marketplace, his body tender from his shockingly short stint of exercise. Afterwards, he found himself struggling to catch his breath the entire time Hylas spent oiling and scraping him. The hot and cold dips refreshed him to some extent, but really, he realized, his public life had robbed him virtually of all conditioning and agility. The more he walked, the sorer his body felt. As he painfully worked his way up the steps to the office, he swore to sacrifice to the goddesses Salus and Valetudo to force him to train on a daily basis. He understood better Appius and Crassus, too, in their propensity to recline in the office for a time, then take their leave to casually meander down to the baths where they would recline some more. In his current condition, Tiberius found such a guilty pleasure wistfully attractive. But, he was a younger man in his prime, he reminded himself, and he had work to do.

Tiberius sidled past the line of men on the stairs and into the office. He gave Blossius a glance, who nodded and gestured with his head to the back room. Tiberius walked back, and said before entering, "When Casca arrives, send him in to see me directly." Blossius nodded again, and Tiberius went into the back office, closing the door behind him.

Appius and Crassus sat in their usual chairs, drinking lemon water and eating sweet rolls. As soon as they saw Tiberius, they leaned close to him. Appius said, "Well?"

Tiberius nodded his head, "It is done. Casca is securing the will in the plebeian treasury now. Unless this is a very elaborate fiction engineered by the gods-know-who, we are poised to fund the lex agraria well into the foreseeable future."

The two elder senators clapped their hands. "Excellent, Tiberius, that is wonderful news," exclaimed Crassus.

"Yes, but we must move fast before the Good Men get wind of it, if that is at all possible."

"I agree. We must bring the news to the people before Nasica and Rufus can fabricate some sort of impediment."

Appius mulled it over quickly, and said, "Perhaps so. We better act now."

They heard a knock on the door, which then swung open as Casca walked in.

"Salve, Centurion," Appius said, which Crassus quickly repeated.

"Did you secure the document?" Tiberius asked the heavy set man, who out of habit stood at attention. "Yes, Tribune," Casca said, "it is in the bowels of the Temple of Saturn, safeguarded by our best men."

"Very good, Casca. And the scribes?"

"Polydius has them hard at work, two copies to start. As soon as they are completed, the original will be tucked well away in a place known only to me. I will share that knowledge, of course, only upon your order."

"Well done, Lucius Casca Naso," Tiberius said, smiling. "I know I can always count on you."

He turned to the senators and said, "As soon as the copies are completed, they will be posted throughout the city, along with an edict calling for an immediate assembly. There, the people of Rome will vote on a referendum deciding the disposition of Philometer's bequest. If we are lucky, this matter will be done in two days."

The senators nodded their agreement. Appius faced Crassus and said, "I believe it is time for us to return to the Senate, dear Crassus, to ensure a smooth transaction."

"I believe that you are correct, Appius. Why don't we repair first to the baths right now to chart our course?"

"Where else?" replied Appius.

The posting of the edict and the will created an immediate sensation. Plebeians ran through the streets celebrating the riches that soon would be theirs. The horsemen grouped in the marketplace, debating how this might affect their enterprises and commerce in general. The patricians split upon faction lines. The Populares publicly declared their support of the general distribution of this windfall, though, in private, apprehension and disquiet presided in light of the current disorder in the streets. The Optimates suffered no such ambivalence; all of them exploded in fury.

"I tell you, they almost rioted in the Curia," Appius said, wiping his brow from the evening heat. They all sat in Tiberius's peristylum. Crassus, Blossius, and Diophanes encircled the pool on benches, while Cornelia listened farther off, sitting in a chair next to the wall with Polydius standing nearby. Claudia swept back and forth into the garden to be sure that Philea and Hylas had kept the luminaries' water cups and plates full.

"It was Piso's turn to take the chair that day, but when he heard the relentless cries of outrage from the Optimates, he sent for Scaveola at once."

"My poor brother Publius walked into a thunderstorm," said Crassus.

"It was all he could do to call for order—he finally had his lectors brandish their fasces to bring some quiet to the room," Appius went on.

"Even so, no one could complete a sentence without one outburst or another," Crassus added.

"Exactly. We might as well have been standing in the middle of the Circus during a chariot race!" Appius took a long pull from his cup. "You can imagine how Rufus bellowed, though Scaveola managed to tamp down the madness to a certain extent."

"What about Nasica?" Tiberius asked. "What did he have to say?"

"Believe it or not, he was brief," replied Crassus.

"He made a short statement," Appius said, "saying that this attempt to pirate Philometer's fortune without Senate counsel constitutes an unforgiveable violation of the ancient traditions of Rome, the Mos Maiorum. As the Pontifex Maximus, he pronounced the authors of this capital crime to be sacrilegious and its perpetrators condemned in the eyes of the gods and of all men. That's all that he said."

"That's quite enough," said Cornelia, and all heads turned to her. "He is serving notice. If this must be done, you need to prepare to withstand the full weight that the Optimates and most of the other patricians will bring to bear."

"By your account, Father-in-law, it sounds as though we have been condemned by Nasica just for proposing the referendum," Tiberius said. "If so, we might as well proceed with the vote. The people still outnumber the patricians." The men in the room all nodded their heads in agreement. "In any case," he continued, shrugging his shoulders as he looked in the direction of his mother, "we need the money."

Standing atop the Rostrum with the other tribunes, Tiberius wondered if the wasting heat and humidity this early in the day signified the displeasure of Jupiter and the other gods at this gambit. The irony of being an avowed advocate of ascetic ideals who now angled to appropriate vast wealth from the East hadn't escaped him, or many others, he thought wryly. However, the riches of Pergamum would be used for the common good, not to line his purse.

To ensure the gods' blessings, he had preempted the usual sacrificial rites by engaging Saturn's priests. They at least would be neutral in their reading of the auspices, if not openly sympathetic to the Populares cause. The great Pontifex Maximus Nasica could suck the marrow out of this cold chicken bone along with the others. He would not be allowed to impede the people's vote on some trumped-up religious grounds.

The priests at their altars next to the Curia Hostilia raised their hands in praise of Saturn, Jupiter, and the other gods, and consigned the disemboweled fowls to the sacred fires. Before long, white, guttering smoke arose from the flames, blessing the proceedings as expected.

Tiberius pivoted to the front of the Rostrum where thousands upon thousands of plebeians immediately raised their hands and voices in a resounding roar for the first tribune of the people. He smiled, and signaled to the electoral officers to commence the vote. As he did so, he saw Sextus astride a horse just outside the far left entrance to the Comitia. When the tall rider saw the movement of the first tribes, he dismounted and walked his horse behind the curved seats to a fountain in front of the Senate building. A corps of other equestrians trailed him, perhaps a half a century or so, all walking their horses in a line to the fountain. If anyone wished to enter the Comitia, they would have to circumvent the men and their horses, which meant making their way to the far entrances near the marketplace. There, Ajax leaned against the wall along with several other hefty men. Tiberius glanced to the other entrances, and saw a contingent of veterans milling around—Casca's men. There should be no trouble this time, he thought.

Indeed, when the first tribe cast their vote, only the patricians allied with the Populares appeared in the stalls. Apparently recognizing the hopelessness of winning this vote, the Optimates chose to abstain, a sign of protest, no doubt. Even better, thought Tiberius, it will make the vote go that much faster. He waved at Appius and Crassus as they passed through the wooden stalls, beaming their pleasure at actually, physically participating in this vote. Tiberius smiled as they waved back like young schoolboys.

The referendum passed before the noon hour. The crowd bellowed their approval in waves, refusing to allow the tribunes who had endorsed the lex to retire. Every time one would wave, the shouting would begin again and again. After an hour, the tribunes all looked at one another, wondering when it would end. Finally, a small contingent came to Tiberius and asked him to speak so as to send them away.

Tiberius stepped forward, and the sound reverberated throughout the Comitia. He grinned, and raised an arm, trying to lower the noise. The crowd continued on, until he turned to the other tribunes and shrugged. Again, he raised and lowered his hands to quiet the crowd. They roared louder, until at last they seem to have exhausted their voices.

Tiberius smiled broadly, and said, "Faithful Romans," he said, "the gods have sanctified our vote today." They yelled again, but he was able to quell it quickly this time. "Now, it is time to thank the gods and celebrate the future of Rome and her people. Thus, I ask you in the name of the tribunes that you go now to make offerings to Jupiter, Saturn, and all of the great gods and goddesses who have smiled upon us today. I commend you to make libations in their honor, and drink wine in thanks. May Fortuna be with you," he said, waving as he retreated to the stairway. Seeing their chance, the other tribunes scurried to the stairs first, so that Tiberius stood waiting his turn. He happened to glance up at the Curia and saw a flock of pigeons flying around one of the high windows. Squinting, he wondered what had agitated them so. Suddenly, a hawk screamed out of the sun's light to snatch one of the pigeons with its claws. It beat its wings up and away leaving a wreath of feathers from the unfortunate victim stirring in the air. The surviving pigeons cried out in fear and alarm as they flew as fast as they could back into the window of the Curia.

Huh, he thought, a sign from the gods. This was a blessed day.

Chapter 32. Dolo

Tiberius found Appius and Crassus with several other senators at the foot of the stairs, along with Sextus, Blossius, Diophanes, Polydius, and Hylas. As soon as they saw him, they broke into applause. He grinned as he trotted down to the bottom to join them.

"Outstanding, my son, I've never been so proud!" said Appius as he clutched Tiberius in a fierce, warm hug. Crassus shook his hand, saying "Well done, young man," followed by all of the other senators in turn. When they all had congratulated him, everyone paused, until he said, "So, what now?"

Everyone laughed. "Time to go home and thank the gods, as a wise young fellow advised," said Fulvius Flaccus, not a Populares, but known to be a fair and decent senator.

The others agreed, and waving warm goodbyes, everyone dispersed except for Appius and Crassus. "I believe that success allows us to reverse the order of that sage's counsel without ill effect, don't you think?" said Appius. "We should sacrifice to the gods, but first, let us celebrate at Fortuna's Inn!"

"The gods will not punish us." said Crassus. "To Fortuna's!"

They each took one of Tiberius's arms and headed from the Comitia toward the marketplace trailed by the other members of their party, even Sextus and Casca.

In no time they secured a large, round table and cups of pure Falernian wine all around, including one for Hylas, who turned red-faced with embarrassment. "Easy does it, Hylas," said Polydius, "small, slow sips."

The others ignored the mentor's advice, drinking the first cup quickly over half a dozen toasts. Tiberius tried to measure his rate, but the two senior senators did their best to undermine him. He succeeded at least in having the steward add water to the later rounds. But, the raucous party raged on all afternoon into the evening.

Appius and Crassus took turns telling stories of their experiences in politics and in war. The others sat raptly taking it all in. Sextus asked questions continuously, clearly the most interested of all of them in the old men's lives. Bread, nuts, cheese, figs, and dates came at timely intervals, buoying them through the waves of wine washing over them. Eventually, the grape took its toll. First to leave were the Greeks; Blossius, Diophanes, and Polydius all bid their goodbyes and wandered out of the inn. Sextus left reluctantly, knocking into benches and tables on his way out. Hylas fell fast asleep resting his head and arms on the tabletop. Only four remained capable of carrying on, the two grand senators and Tiberius and Casca.

Tiberius leaned over and said to Casca, "You seem to be the only one with his senses about him, Naso. When did you stop drinking the wine?"

"Three years ago, Quaestor."

Tiberius sat back. He looked at the Ccenturion for a moment, then at Crassus and Appius. "Gentle men," he said, "it is time to go home. We must fulfill the other part of our agreement. We must give thanks to the gods."

The senators glanced at each other, then said to Tiberius, "Indeed," "Absolutely."

They put their hands gingerly on the table and stood up. Tiberius walked with them to the door, where Casca stood waiting. "I ordered two litters. Some of our men will walk with them."

Tiberius nodded, "Very good, Casca, thank you." He turned back to the table where Hylas sat, rubbing his eyes. "Time to go," murmured Tiberius.

They left Fortuna's Inn and headed through the marketplace toward the Palatine. The sun had set, and the marketplace stood open and vacant, with permanent shops and stalls shuttered and other temporary stands struck, their goods stored away for another day. Only a few figures lingered along the way, street girls trolling for customers, small-time cutpurses on the lookout for the inebriated, and beggars settling down for the night. Tiberius had seen this remarkable transformation of the bustling center of human activity many times before. Yet, he never failed to be amazed at the complete desolation imposed by darkness. Perhaps he felt more affected this time after such a heady day and fulsome night.

They reached the other side of the marketplace and headed across the square toward the narrow street that led up the hill to his domus. Two men preceded them on either side of the square, coming closer together as they approached the head of the street. Tiberius took a quick look behind him and saw two other men behind them mirroring the men in front. Casca walked a step behind Tiberius and Hylas, now and then searching in front of them, behind them, and to the sides.

They entered the narrow street that wound around the Palatine where Tiberius's residence was situated halfway up. Tired from the long day, he inhaled deeply to start the ascent. After a few steps, he called to Hylas. "Hylas, come help me up the hill."

The young slave came back to Tiberius who wrapped one arm around him. "Where are you from, Hylas? I mean, where in Greece?"

"A little village north of Chalcis," Hylas replied, "Dirrevmata."

"And, how did you come to be in Rome? Was it after the Macedonian war?"

"No," he shook his head. "My father died of plague. My uncle took in our family, six including his sister, my mother. He tried to provide for us, but it was very hard. He and my aunt had four children of their own. He did his best, but it was impossible, especially after a terrible drought ruined his crops and caused him to lose many of his sheep. He came to me one night, and explained to me that our family could not survive the winter without money to buy food. He was crying, and could not tell me what he had to do. But, I was the oldest, I understood. The next day, we left for Athens where he sold me into slavery. Since Greeks are very desirable as slaves in Rome, I was put on a boat the next day, and here I am."

Tiberius said nothing for a time as they slowly made their way up the hillside. Finally, he said, "Yours is a sad story, Hylas."

He felt the young Greek lift and drop his shoulders beneath his arm. "Not so sad. I felt honored to help my uncle and our family. And, I was fortunate that Mistress Claudia bought me first. But, it was very hard for my uncle." He moved his head to look at Tiberius, "I was named after him, you know. I was his favorite nephew."

Tiberius stared at Hylas for a second. "I can see why," he said.

"Attack!" They heard the cry in front, followed by the sharp ring of metal on metal. Tiberius straightened up, straining his eyes ahead. "From the rear!" came shouts behind him. He wheeled around to see Casca's two guards fending off a half dozen figures, arms sweeping above them. Casca was nowhere in sight.

"Hylas!" Tiberius said, spinning the young slave around. "Run! Run home and get more men! Stay low and close to the other houses. Go now!" he said, pushing him off to the side of the street. The boy crouched and ran off.

No weapon, Tiberius thought. One of his men up front went down. The remaining guard gave ground slowly, working his way back and to the side so that his assailants couldn't surround him. But, it looked hopeless.

Tiberius backed his way toward the wall, his eyes darting up and down the street. His men in the back seemed to be doing better, bringing down two of the enemy. But, it was still four against two. Suddenly, Tiberius felt the wall at his back. He pushed around in the dark with his foot to feel for something he could use as a weapon, a piece of wood or a stone. Nothing.

The last man in front went down, and his killers spread out, five of them, and slowly stalked Tiberius. Quickly, he pulled off his toga and spun part of it around both of his arms. A flimsy barrier, he knew, but perhaps he could ward off the blows until help came from home.

A flashing figure bounded out of the shadows and cut two of the approaching men down, then rushed toward Tiberius. Tiberius instinctively held up his arms, and the swordsman slashed down at him. Tiberius blinked, and felt his arms fall free. He peered into the dark to see Casca in front of him.

"Take this," Casca snapped, "and keep your back to the wall."

The centurion held out a long, double-edged knife by its blade. Tiberius grabbed the haft, made of smooth wood with a knobbed end that could be used as a club.

Casca pivoted, feinted, and swiftly gutted a third attacker. The other two paused, then fled. He quickly wheeled around to see that his men below them had dispatched two more of the assailants. The last two had turned and run.

Tiberius glanced back and forth up and down the street, empty except for the carnage of ten bodies strewn about. His street, he thought.

A dozen men came running from above, and Tiberius tightened his grip on the blade given to him by Casca. "They're ours," said the veteran.

Hylas ran up to Tiberius, beaming with relief, and said, "Are you well, Master, are you injured?"

"I am fine, Hylas, quite well. Thank you for bringing these good men so quickly."

The young man grabbed Tiberius in a fierce hug, which caused him to smile. "Now, now," he said, gently disengaging himself.

He turned to Casca and proffered the long knife by its wooden hilt.

"Keep it," said Casca, "and wear it from now on wherever you go."

Tiberius nodded vigorously. "What is it?"

"It's called a dolo," said Casca, "Good for inside work. You can hide it easily beneath a toga."

Tiberius shook his head quickly up and down. He turned away to find Ajax standing in the middle of circle formed by the men facing outward, surrounding Tiberius, Hylas, Casca, and the two surviving guards. Tiberius stepped up to them and shook their hands, "Thank you, thank you for saving our lives."

He then addressed Ajax, raising his voice to say, "Have your men bring our fallen to my domus. They will be buried with high honors, and their families will be comforted and cared for."

Ajax snapped his head in assent. Casca said to him, "Get some of your boys to find a cart for these dead rats. Run them down to the Aventine and dump them on a trash heap. But, first, cut their throats as a warning to the rest of them still skulking around."

On their way up the hill, Tiberius walked abreast to Casca. Just before they arrived, he leaned close to him and said, "When asked, we were attacked by a band of cutthroats after my purse."

Casca eyed him, and said, "If you think they'll believe it."

At home, the family including Appius, who had hurried over as soon as he'd heard of the attack, greeted Tiberius as a returning hero. After Tiberius assured them that the only damage suffered by him was a bisected toga, they laughed and tried to have him sit for a meal. But, he begged off, saying that all he hoped to do was go to bed.

On his way to his bed chamber, Cornelia stopped him outside of the atrium. She held him gently by his chin and said, "You are well, son?"

"I am, Mother, not a scratch on me. Casca made short work of those brigands," he said.

She stared deeply into his eyes, and said, "Brigands. Stay well, my son, and thank the gods."

Once in his room, Tiberius softly closed the door. Before he fell into bed, he found his chamber pot and urinated. Then, he threw up, several times. Finally, he dropped into bed, eventually falling into a deep sleep.

In the morning, he awoke to find Claudia next to him, naked beneath the covers. Her belly was enormous, it wouldn't be long before their fifth child would come into the world, praise the goddess Lucina.

"You're awake at last," she said, her head in her hand propped on one elbow. "It's about time, everyone ate breakfast hours ago. Dear Mother Cornelia had to lead the Lares service."

Tiberius grabbed both sides of his head. "My skull hurts."

"I don't wonder. Father said you all partook of quite a celebration yesterday after the referendum passed. I'm surprised your head isn't bursting forth a little Minerva."

"Don't blaspheme so. I'm no god, certainly not Jupiter."

"No, more like Bacchus. But, you're right, you couldn't be a god. Bacchus would have made it to breakfast."

"Why are you berating me so? I'm a crippled creature here. Please allow me to lick my wounds."

"Your wounds—even the so-called thieves who tried to kill you last night couldn't wound you, or so you say."

Uh-oh, he thought, the crux of the matter.

"Casca saved me. And Hylas."

"He did indeed, though Hylas told us that your survival was a miracle of the gods."

"The gods again," he said.

"Yes, he said that the situation was hopeless when you told him to run, twelve against five. He was very much surprised to see you alive when he and Ajax arrived."

"Yes, well, perhaps the gods did smile upon us, it was that kind of day. Did I tell you that we celebrated at Fortuna's Inn?"

She sat up; her breasts were enormous pendulums resting on her distended stomach, like a fertility goddess incarnate.

"Tiberius, you almost died! We would have lost you forever!"

"It wasn't like that. They were an inept gang of thieves, no more. They thought they'd seen a drunk and his companions, easy prey. Casca and his fellow veterans made short work of them."

"Two of Casca's men were killed. Those men who attacked you, Tiberius, they were not just ruffians, they were assassins. I know it, Father knows it, everyone knows it. The Optimates tried to murder you, Husband. Don't you understand?"

He sat up and took her hands. "I am safe, now, Claudia, and wiser for it. Casca and Ajax will take further measures to protect me. When the people learn that a tribune of the people was attacked, an unthinkable transgression, they will be outraged. Even if they were assassins who attacked me, a preposterous notion, mind you, the Optimates would never chance it again. As tribune, I am inviolable, Claudia, remember that."

"Yes," she said, "but how long will that last? Your term ends in a matter of months. How safe will you be then?"

He reached over and hugged her close to him. "Don't worry, love of my life. I won't allow anything to happen to me or our family. Gaius will assume my post when he returns from Numantia. By then, the lex agraria will be established and the Optimates will have no option but to accept it. The balance of power and righteousness in Rome will be restored, and you and I will retire to our farm to raise our children and truffles."

He kissed her on the cheek. She seemed to relax some in his arms, though he knew that she wasn't fully convinced.

"Now," he said, "why do you honor me by presenting yourself in my bed like Venus emerging from the waves?"

"Hah," she said, "more like Salacia carrying Triton these days. I've come to have you mount me while you can since your future is in doubt."

He drew back in utter shock. "What?" he said. What had become of his demure little wife and mother of his children? Then again, he thought, when was she ever demure in bed? He said sharply, "My future is assured." Then, he stammered, "Anyway, aren't you past the time when you can do this? Wouldn't it be uncomfortable?"

"From the front," she said, raising herself up and turning onto all fours, "but not like this."

The lioness, he thought, like prostitutes. Yet, she looked at him out of innocent, calf-like eyes. "Are you sure?" he said.

She nodded up and down, so he girded himself, and did as she asked.

She had been right, though, as had Casca. As he had said, no one believed that they had been attacked by thieves, and he had verified it that night. During the rejoicing of his safety, Tiberius saw Casca next to the door silently signaling to him. He made an excuse and went to the toilet where Casca joined him.

"Ajax just returned and told me that one of the strongmen they picked up was still alive. He talked a bit before they dumped him on the Aventine."

Tiberius hesitated before saying, "And?"

"The men who tried to kill you were headed by an Anatolian named Polemo."

Tiberius squinted, trying to place the name. "Polemo? Do I know him?"

"You met him once," said Casca. "Captain of the guard at Lucius Rufus's villa." Tiberius stared at Casca, who nodded his head, "that's right, Fava Bean, Nasica's favorite little troublemaker."

After that conversation, Tiberius knew he couldn't rationalize anymore about robbers. Nasica and Rufus had tried to assassinate him. They had become that desperate or at least that mad for blood. He had been lucky to survive.

He shifted on his bed, crossing his legs to lean on his ankles with both hands.

Of course, having Casca and Ajax at hand added mightily to his chances for survival. This attempt might not have been the first, only the one that his defenders couldn't keep from him. No matter how exceptional his security was under Casca's watch, how many more attacks could he withstand? Even after snatching Pergamum's wealth out from under their noses—he laughed again thinking about it—he also recognized ruefully that the Optimates possessed vast resources and would never give up. For as long as he continued to poke them in the eye, they would come after him. Maybe Nasica and Rufus had acted hastily, outraged that the referendum had passed, a near miss that put him on guard. But, they also could bide their time. In less than a year, he would be out of office and new tribunes would preside, many without doubt owned by the Optimates. They could use their new leverage and their power in the Senate to slowly dismantle the lex agraria and its commission. They probably would figure out some trumped up excuse to redirect Pergamum's bequest into their coffers. That is, if they didn't kill the golden goose, as poor Eudemus had warned. In just a few years, it could be as though nothing ever had happened to change Rome. The plebeians would be put back in their place. Time, time was on the Optimates' side.

Tiberius clenched his jaw. He'd hoped to build the momentum of the land reform scheme to the point that the Optimates couldn't destroy it, and he had come so close. If only Gaius could be home to run as his replacement—oh, he was young, technically too young to run, but that wasn't a huge hurdle. Popular opinion could change that, the same way they elected Scipio consul well before he was old enough, to lead the legions in Carthage. But Scipio would now keep Gaius in Hispania until spring. To burnish his already legendary reputation even more, Tiberius thought bitterly, the great Scipio Aemilianus would impede his youngest brother-in-law's destiny. In the process, he also would destroy the Lex Sempronia Agraria and the future of the Republic. Scipio's political leanings remained a mystery to all, but Tiberius couldn't help but wonder if his illustrious brother-in-law secretly conspired with the patricians, if not the Optimates themselves. In any case, Gaius would not be available to replace him. So, now what? Tiberius thought.

Claudia entered, appropriately attired as an expecting Roman matron, carrying a tray with fruit, bread, cheese, and a cup of hot, flavored water. "Do you plan on lying around all day?"

"Not if you plan on keeping your garments on."

She frowned, "That moment has passed. Eat, drink, get up, bathe, and get dressed. The day is half wasted, and you have work to do."

Tiberius did as he was told. He took himself to the commission office that afternoon, and every day for weeks. He busied himself overseeing office activities, which ran smoothly through the work of Blossius, Diophanes, and Polydius. Their extreme competency relieved him again and again to mull over his next course of action.

Even though unsuccessful, the assassination attempt should have scared him away from his work. At the least, as far as the Optimates were concerned, it should have served as a lethal warning. If anything would prompt them to try again, it would be his renewed diligence on the land commission. They had expected him to run for his life.

Running would do him no good, Tiberius figured. Once he left office, Nasica and the Optimates would go after him anyway, just out of spite. It lay deep in their nature. So, he might as well fight. The decision came hard to him, since they seemed to have all of the advantages, while he had so much to lose. He thought of Claudia and his darling children, even his mother Cornelia. He could not afford to lose.

So, what were his assets? The people, he thought, and his string of successes with them. Perhaps this explained further the attempt by Nasica to cower him into hiding. The people were fickle, and would soon forget a less visible Tiberius Gracchus, especially if they were distracted by a diet of horse races in the Circus and gladiatorial matches in the arena. But, if he could keep the people on his side, the Optimates would be powerless. They were the key, he thought, the plebeians, the people of Rome.

He knew now what he had to do.

"I shall run for the Tribunate again for the coming year," Tiberius said.

Utter silence greeted his announcement, as every man arrayed around him stared with shocked eyes and slack jaws. Grouped around him in a tight semicircle in his home office, they sat still, stunned.

Appius was the first to speak, sputtering, "Impossible! You cannot run again, elected positions are for one term only."

"It is illegal!" said Crassus with alarm, "it is in complete violation of the Mos Maiorum."

"It is extremely dangerous at this time," said Blossius.

Others cried out objections, and Tiberius remained silent until the outbursts had subsided. "Is there a written law against running for two terms? Many past Romans have served more than one term as consuls."

"Not consecutively!" said Appius.

"The Mos Maiorum!" shouted Crassus.

"The Mos Maiorum changes as needed over time. There is a need, here and now. Gaius will not be back from Numantia in time to run and there is no one else to run in my place. How long do you think it will take for the Optimates to put one or more of their stooges on the Tribunate to destroy the lex agraria? They'll elect sympathetic consuls, too, with the help of other senators afraid of losing their estates. The only way to stop them is to maintain our popularity with the people. I've been able to do that all along. The people will vote me in for a second term, I am convinced of that."

Appius shook his head, "The people are fickle. A few games, some horse races, a couple of coins for their votes, they will have trouble remembering who Tiberius Gracchus is."

"Not if we call for an election soon. I can campaign on having won them the Pergamum fortune, and offer some other promises that will appeal to them."

"Such as?" Blossius asked.

"A moratorium on forcing them to fight stupid wars against barbarians far from home. Giving the right of appeal to plebeians in judgments by the Senate. Adding equestrians to the bench equal to the number of patricians to ensure fair verdicts. In short, to further increase the power of common Romans in our Republic."

"And further alienate the Senate and all patricians," Blossius interjected.

Diophanes stroked his beard nervously. "They will redouble their efforts to destroy you, Tiberius."

Tiberius said, "They are bent upon that now, though it would be much easier for them if I am no longer tribune, no longer sacrosanct and inviolable. My only chance is to continue as tribune with the people behind me. Perhaps then, the Optimates will back off for a time. By then, Gaius can run for tribune, and the lex agraria will be entrenched."

Again, the grim-faced men in the room grew quiet.

"It is a terribly risky plan," Appius said in a low voice, "almost a desperate gamble. You would do better to save yourself and your family by leaving Rome for a time. We can continue the fight while you're away, we can hold on until Gaius has his chance."

"The Mos Maiorum," Crassus uttered, sadly shaking his head. "You will be accused of thirsting for power, and the Senate might block the election. My brother might not be able or willing to support you on this. I am not sure that I can."

"I understand," Tiberius said, "but I must do this. If it is a gamble, then I will roll the dice."

Appius sighed. "What do you need us to do?"

"Go to the Senate and tell them that I am sick and tired of fighting with them, that I'm even talking of resigning. Rather than have me lose stature, propose an early election at harvest time, a cleansing of bad blood by bringing in a new corps of tribunes."

"Nasica and Rufus will jump at the opportunity," Appius said, "how they will crow."

"Just before the election, I'll proclaim my candidacy and new platform. The people will respond, and the Senate will be hamstrung."

"Then, you can crow," Appius said wryly. "You better have Casca and Ajax fill in their ranks. The risk to your safety will be highest during the campaign running up to the election."

"I'm sure I'll be fine under their watch."

Appius said, "All right." He glanced at Crassus, whose expression twisted as he struggled. Finally, he nodded his head.

"Very well, let us begin," said Appius, and they all left Tiberius alone in his office.

Cornelia came in soon after without knocking. As soon as he saw her, Tiberius suspected that Appius had stopped by her room before leaving. Amazing how such a diminutive woman could seem so intimidating. Those green eyes of hers, though, burned when she was serious about something. This time, however, she seemed ready to flinch, standing before him, almost vulnerable, to Tiberius's surprise.

"Appius told me that you wish to run for tribune again," she said, her voice as steely as ever.

"Yes, Mother," he said, "it is the only way."

"It is not the only way," she snapped, "there always are other possible courses to pursue than just one way."

"Possible," he said, "but improbable. The Optimates are hard after me."

"And you think running for a second term will stop them? They will kill you, Tiberius, and leave your family ruined by grief. Worse, with your death, so too will your dream die. This is the way they are, my son, this is the way they always have been, always. Their notion of the Mos Maiorum is to keep everything as it is, with themselves rich and all powerful. They considered you one of their own until you defied them, Tiberius. You defied them and you frightened them. They will never forgive you for that whether you become tribune again or not."

"Then, if my fate is sealed, I might as well fight them," he said, "I will not bow to these evil men, I will restore the Republic!"

She dropped her eyes in exasperation. "All men are evil, Tiberius. Look at you, you and your hubris; 'I will restore the Republic.' Where is the ascetic ideal in that self-righteous rhetoric? Your phallus is as hard as theirs, Tiberius, your blood is up, you just want to beat them. You've done wonderful things this year, so I haven't interfered. But you play with disaster, you are on the edge of a vortex that would please Neptune. If you allow your pride to drag you in, everything will be lost."

She stood looking at him, her arms on her waist. He turned his head away, scowling in his seat. "You are hard to please, Mother. I thought you would be proud of me."

"I am proud of you, Tiberius," she said, "and I will be proud of you in the future, if you preserve it. Please, don't do this."

He peered up at here, and saw that vulnerable expression in her eyes again. At length, he raised one hand and allowed it to fall languidly, saying, "I cannot. This really is the only way."

Cornelia dropped her hands to her side, and said, "Then, I will miss you, Tiberius. I love you, my son, and I wish I had never guided you down this path."

She turned and left the room.

He sat with his chin in his hand, his arm propped on his knee. All men are evil, she'd proclaimed, except of course, his father. Still, he questioned whether or not he really was driven simply by pride, not just the good of the people. He could only hope that the answer was no.

When Claudia learned of his plans, she had nothing to do with him. The family ate together, she would carry on lively talks with the children and anyone else at the table, but not with Tiberius. He began to wonder if he really did stand alone in this.

The Senate gobbled up Appius's suggestion, and voted for early elections almost unanimously. The dictum had been posted; in three weeks, new tribunes for the coming year would be elected. In the meantime, the general good cheer in the chamber seemed oddly out of place.

"After all," he pointed out, "the very foundation of the Senate is held together by the mortar of acrimony. Of course, when you announce your candidacy, everything will return to normal, madness will rule. Then," Appius said, "the hard part begins."

Chapter 33. Change of Heart

"My son-in-law has had a change of heart," Appius said in a most solicitous tone.

Appius had expected the Curia Hostilia to be half-full on this putridly hot day in the city, typical of late summer. Hot, humid, stinking of garbage and offal, Rome stifled all romantic notions of its grandeur at this time of year. Even the pigeons residing in the rafters apparently felt too logy to defecate on the togas of the denizens below, an omission taken as another ill omen. Thus, those who could afford to had left for their seaside retreats days or even weeks ago, to wait out the gods's seasonal tantrums until they relented, usually on the advent of autumn. The building should have been an empty warehouse, Appius observed, yet here he was, addressing a full house. Someone had alerted the Optimates.

"Considering the fact that the good work he is doing remains unfinished, Tiberius Sempronius Gracchus wishes to serve again as a tribune of the people. Toward this end, he has announced his candidacy; the bulletins are being posted throughout the city and its suburbs at this time."

The packed members of the Senate stared at him in silence. A stray thought occurred to Appius; they gazed at him the same way that he must have been looking at Tiberius when his son-in-law had told him. "To this end," he continued, "Tribune Gracchus petitions you for this opportunity, and looks forward to your blessing."

He could see that no one heard the last part. The Senate erupted in a chorus of violent outcries, ear-piercing howls as though the dogs of Hades had been let loose in the chamber. The thunderous clamor eliminated any possibility of any senator being heard or understood. Piso, the presiding consul, hammered his wooden baton upon the floor as hard as he could with little effect. He pounded it again and again, finally rising to his feet as the uproar continued. He struck the top of his chair repeatedly while motioning to his lictors. Holding their fasces chest high, they formed a line on either side of the consular seats, and the noise finally subsided.

Piso turned his attention to Appius, still standing in place. "This has been done, Senator Claudius? Tiberius Gracchus has posted his name in candidacy for the Tribunate again?"

"Yes, Consul, he has. In fact, I imagine the announcements are up by now. I believe notices have been couriered to Romans outside of the city as well."

"This is criminal!" broke in Rufus, "an outrageous violation of Roman tradition and law!"

The chaotic din began again, until Piso shouted, "Quiet! Remain silent or I will have the lictors escort those interrupting these proceedings to the door."

The outburst dwindled, though grumbling and a few sporadic catcalls spurred more dark looks from Piso.

"You understand that this is highly irregular, Senator?" Piso asked.

"Irregular, unusual, yes," said Appius calmly, "but not without precedent. Why, Tiberius's own brother-in-law Scipio Aemilianus was elected consul at the tender age of thirty-five just a decade ago."

"An exception was made then, Senator Claudius," Piso said, "so that Rome could avail itself of his extraordinary military leadership in the war against Carthage."

"My son-in-law Tiberius performs an equally vital role in restoring land to our wrongfully disenfranchised veterans. Without his efforts, these men could never again serve in Rome's legions for lack of owning land. As a member of the agrarian commission, I can tell you that this program is of critical importance to the wellbeing of the Republic. Yet, land reform is in its infancy and might perish if not properly nourished. It requires the steady hand of its patriarch to ensure that Rome remains robust. As the architect of the lex agraria, Tiberius Sempronius Gracchus has proven himself to be an exceptional man worthy, in this instance, of exception."

"Here, here," "Well spoken," and other shouts of approval came from Crassus and the other Populares sitting around Appius, soon drowned out by the scathing objections of the Optimates and many other senators. Piso opened his mouth to speak, but the sudden rise of Nasica halted him.

"Honorable Consul," Nasica said, "May I speak?"

Piso signaled his assent. Nasica stood tall and imposing, his frame bonier if possible, his eyes now darker than his dark hair, now showing strands of grey.

"Gracchus's actions are illegal," Nasica said, standing tall, "and more egregious, they are sacrilegious. I say this with the knowledge and authority vested within me as Rome's Pontifex Maximus. Elected officials serve one term in Rome according to our most important and sacred tradition, the Mos Maiorum. The reason for this holy, absolute dictum is to prevent ambitious men from becoming demagogues by vying for successive terms. We adopted this hallowed tradition after finally casting off the oppressive yoke of tyrant kings. We swore never to bend to a king again in whatever guise he might assume. Tiberius Sempronius Gracchus possesses the unbridled ambition that Rome disdains. His past actions have proven his intent. It is common knowledge that while in Numantia, he consorted with the enemy for personal gain."

The Populares began to shout out indignantly until Piso rapped his baton.

Nasica continued, "As tribune, he curried the favor of his fellow plebeians by promising land handouts through his deeply flawed agrarian law. He illegally deposed an honorable tribune who vetoed this same illicit law. He illegally appropriated the Pergamum fortune to endow his own designs. All of these acts show that he wishes to have his way at any cost in total disregard of Rome's tradition and laws. And, now he wishes to run for tribune again, the ultimate step in his plan to sap the wealth and power of the Republic's most honorable families. Thus, he can anoint himself King of Rome!"

Tumult burst out in the Curia again, the Populares on their feet raging against the Optimates, who stood roaring their fury in turn. Piso directed the lictors into the rows to forcibly quiet the crowd, when one voice rang out above all of the others.

"I have proof!" cried out Nasica. His piercing declaration brought everyone's attention to him again.

"I have proof, if the consul will permit me," he said in a steady voice. Appius could see sharp anticipation in his eyes, a deeply unsettling sight. He glanced at Crassus, also uneasy at what he was seeing. Piso waved his hand, and all of the senators sat again except for Nasica.

"Senator Pompeius," Nasica said, "if you will, please rise."

Pompeius stood, tall and heavy-set, clean-shaven, his hair a proud, grey mane that framed his rugged features. Wearing his ever-present scowl of superiority, he threw the edge of his toga across his shoulder in a grand gesture.

Pompeius, Appius thought, another scoundrel. His disgusting behavior in Hispania hadn't been enough to hide his colossal failure there. Stymied by the Numantines, instead of marching on, he signed a secret treaty with the Numantines in exchange for thirty talents of gold. The Senate rejected the treaty with prejudice, which led eventually to the last fiasco at the hands of Mancinus. Yet, somehow Pompeius had survived all indictments. Most likely, he had forged some other clandestine, illegal agreement through his willingness to do anything without conscience to tread water. Now, it seemed another example of his duplicity was in the offing.

"Senator," Nasica went on, "a month ago, when the emissary from Pergamum arrived in Rome to announce the disposition of his deceased king's will, did you have occasion to see him at that time?"

"I believe I did, Senator, at the Paulian baths."

"Where in the baths, Senator?"

"In the frigidarium, though the Pergamum character wasn't dressed to go into the pool."

"Oh, no? Curious. Was he alone?"

"No, he had a strong-arm with him, quite an unsavory, swarthy sort of fellow. He rather looked like a wild boar."

Appius felt a sudden stab in his stomach. He sensed what was coming.

"Anyone else, noble Pompeius?"

"Yes. Sempronius Gracchus was in the room as well."

A massive intake of breath could be heard throughout the Curia, followed by murmurs reaching a noise level that caused Piso to hit the floor sharply with his baton again.

"That is even more unusual," Nasica went on. "I imagine this is where Tribune Gracchus struck the deal that allowed him to steal the Pergamum fortune."

The Populares growled again, but stopped to listen to Pompeius's reply.

"I do not know about that, I was too far away to hear anyone speak."

"Of course, an honorable man such as yourself would never attempt to listen in on a private conversation. Then, what did you see, Senator Pompeius?"

"I saw this dark peacock with greasy, black hair and an ostentatiously curled beard, wearing overtly opulent, garments. This clearly foreign fellow handed an ornate box to Gracchus."

"Tribune Sempronius, Senator."

Pompeius sneered, "All right. Tribune Sempronius Gracchus."

The Optimates laughed coarsely, cut short by Piso's baton.

"Could you see what was in the box?"

"No, but it was big enough to hold a will."

435

"You lie," Populares cried out from the benches, "Back stabbing!" "Blatant fabrication!"

Piso called for order, and Nasica continued.

"Did you see anything else, Senator Pompeius?"

"I did," Pompeius said. He faced the Populares, his face a map of scorn. "I saw that barbaric Pergamum popinjay open up another strongbox. From it, he extracted and presented to Gracchus a purple robe and a bejeweled diadem!"

"The trappings of a king! Proof of Gracchus's treason!" shouted Nasica, who continued mouthing inaudible invectives as a storm of sound following Pompeius's accusation swept throughout the Curia. Appius wanted to press his hands to his head, but instead, he rose up.

"Enough!" he bellowed, a voice so loud that it stunned the mass of bickering senators into silence. He paused as all eyes fell upon him.

"I've had enough of this calumny directed at my honorable son-in-law," he declared, his voice full of gravity and the weight of a princeps senatus. "The slanders that Nasica and Pompeius attack him with cover old ground, old news that has been trod and put to rest long ago. I will not put up with this disgraceful display of political maneuvering any longer."

Appius faced Piso. "Everything that has been said today is nothing but unsubstantiated gossip, prattle by the best prattlers we have in Rome." He twisted around, "You, Pompeius, confound us by how haplessly you skew the events that took place in the Paulian baths. Eudemus did not present a purple robe and a diamond diadem to Tiberius. He offered him a jewel-encrusted scepter and a gold crown, you old washer woman, you."

The Senate rumbled in surprise at the audacious statement, some of them laughing in disbelief.

"And, how do I know this?" Appius asked. Sardonically, he answered, "Because he told me. He's my son-in-law." He gestured with one hand casually, "No matter, Tiberius rejected the overture immediately. He harbors no kingly ambition, he is a servant of the Republic and the people of Rome. In any case, he is a duly elected tribune of the people, sacred and inviolable in his station, which makes these despicable accusations moot. You cannot touch him without deposing him, an action that you already have asserted as illegal. He will run for the Tribunate again, and the people will decide if this, too, is a precedent that they wish to support." Appius spread his arms, his hands open, as he said, "Tiberius Sempronius Gracchus's fate rests in the hands of the people, Senators, not yours. I see no point in listening any longer to the contemptible slurs against the honor of my son-in-law."

He looked sternly at Piso, whose lips were pressed into a thin line white with anger. The consul said nothing, and Appius turned to Crassus. Crassus hesitated for an instant, at a loss, then quickly left his seat. Appius started stepping out from the row to the marble floor, Crassus behind him. The other Populares stood and followed them past the consul to the vestibulum and out the door of the Curia.

"There's no doubt about it, now," said Appius, sitting in a chair near the pool in Tiberius's peristylum. "Your only safe course of action is to win the Tribunate a second time. Nasica and his cronies have made it clear that they are out for you and never will relent. It is personal, now. They are fixated on your utter downfall."

Tiberius listened, though somewhat impatiently. He'd been trying all along to tell Appius and the rest that the Optimates were bent on his destruction.

"The best chance you have is to secure your inviolability as a tribune," Appius went on. "That might keep them at bay for a while. You must win, and in a convincing fashion."

"I recognize this," said Tiberius.

"How is Ajax's detail going?" asked Appius.

Tiberius winced slightly, "Not as well as with past efforts. He's out there, beating the bushes with his men for votes, but it's harvest time. Most of them are bringing in their crops. They're sympathetic to our cause, but they see eating this winter as a more pressing priority."

"Uh," grunted Appius, "that's a bit disheartening."

"Don't worry, Father-in-law, we'll win. There are still more than enough votes within Rome's walls to win the election for us, and Casca is doing his usual, excellent job of lining them up."

Appius peered up at the pacing Tiberius. "He has enough coin?"

Tiberius nodded, "Oh, yes. Amazing how lenders are so free with their silver when they know that Philometer's will is collateral."

"Quite so," said Appius. "Their attitude would change quick enough if the Senate stole back the Pergamum gold."

"Too late for that in this election, we already have the money."

Appius pursed his lips in thought. "Well then," he said, rising to his feet, "three weeks will tell the tale."

"Three weeks will tell the tale," agreed Tiberius. He embraced his father-in-law, "Thank you for your help and counsel, Father."

"Of course, you are welcome, Tiberius, and thank you for carrying the shield and spear for us old goats and the people of Rome." He hugged Tiberius, and left the house.

During the days that followed, Tiberius divided his time between the commission's office and campaigning. In the early morning, he would head to the office to check with the Greeks to see if they needed any special assistance from him. An hour later, Hylas would arrive, and Tiberius would change into the pure white toga that his servant brought to the office every day. Then, they would descend the stairs to join up with his entourage of supporters to walk various routes through the city.

Tiberius's party would stop at various neighborhood forums, where most of the people would congregate to draw water from the fountains for their meals, or to wash up. Tiberius climbed the nearest wall or steps and spoke quietly but firmly, eloquently, about the ongoing need of the lex agraria for the people. He then would turn to their new needs, limits on their military service in foreign wars and greater representation in the city's courts. Without exception, his speeches engendered loud and enthusiastic demonstrations from all who gathered. Wherever he spoke, the people would stop what they were doing and listen raptly to Tiberius Gracchus's promise of a better future.

After a week of uninterrupted receptions like this, Tiberius's confidence that he would win began to grow. At home, however, Claudia still kept her distance. Around the children, she would fill the air with light, breezy expressions of love and fun, orchestrating games, plays, and other activities. They all shared their meals together as usual. After every dinner, she would send the children to their father to say goodnight, gently goading the older Tiberius and Sempronia to follow the little ones in giving him hugs and kisses. But, after they'd been put to bed, she would retire herself without a word to him, or a hug, or a kiss. In the morning, they all would assemble for their devotions to their ancestors and the Lares, after which the daylong façade of family harmony would begin again.

Tiberius was heartbroken and forlorn. Yet, he could do nothing, because what Claudia wanted was something that he could not give her. It seemed stunning, in a way, that she defied him so. Throughout their years together, she had always supported his decisions wholeheartedly, doing whatever she could to help him succeed. This time, however, she was adamant. He couldn't quite understand her objections, he thought he had explained his reasoning clearly. The risk of failure existed, he was challenging the Senate and elements of the Mos Maiorum. But, Claudia had never been much of an adherent to the Mos Maiorum, and she had supported him in more dangerous situations in the past. By the love of Venus, she'd conceived a child with him the night before he left for Numantia, and managed their interests the entire time he'd been gone. So, why this now?

He shook his head, bewildered. His mother felt somewhat the same as his wife, he knew, but she hadn't ostracized him like this. Of course, he couldn't ask her to intercede with Claudia, she would just use it as another opportunity to tell him to change his plans. But, he couldn't. He needed to be tribune to secure his standing in advancing the lex agraria and other initiatives that would improve the lot of Rome's people. A strong plebeian populace meant a stronger Republic. He knew this in his soul to be true, and the gods had favored him so far. He had to go on.

He missed Claudia deeply.

The morning sun fought a losing battle to brighten the day with the clouds above. The grey day caused Tiberius to leave home later than usual. He and Hylas trudged their way down the Palatine through the marketplace to the office at its end, Casca's ever-present bodyguards shadowing them the entire time. In fact, the obscured sky made seeing the guardsmen almost impossible. But, they were there.

They climbed the stairs above Fortuna's Inn, still shuttered, until they came to their office door, wide open so that lamp light splashed out, almost welcoming them after enduring the dreariness outside. Tiberius stepped in and greeted Diophanes and Polydius in turn. Hylas followed, the egg-white toga folded in half on his back so as not to drag it in the trash-strewn street. He hung it on a hook in the back room while Tiberius sat down in a chair against the wall in the front office. Blossius hadn't come in yet, so Tiberius started to paw through a stack of documents in front of him, deeds and affidavits related to the current distribution of lands in Campania. If it rained, he thought, there would be little reason to stalk the streets for votes. A lost day of campaigning would be bad, he thought, but he really felt less than enthusiastic. Perhaps the day's weather had dampened his spirits as well.

If it rained, he could stay here and help, another prospect that didn't thrill him. Maybe he felt tired, not just lazy. He sighed and picked up another paper from the pile.

Blossius arrived, walking purposefully through the door, then stopping suddenly. His regular ruddy complexion browned by the summer sun seemed pale, and his blue eyes looked startled. He surveyed the room until he saw Tiberius sitting and poking at the items on the desk. Blossius hurried over.

"Good morning, Gaius," Tiberius said, still looking down at the deed in his hand.

"Tiberius," Blossius said in a clipped tone, "can we go into the back office?"

Tiberius glanced up, and put the deed back on the pile. He stood up and led the way back. "Hylas," he said, "Would you mind …?"

Without a word, Hylas left. Blossius closed the door behind the young man, and turned back to Tiberius, who watched him expectantly.

"Tiberius," Blossius said, "Sextus Decimus has died."

Tiberius stared at Blossius, his mind working to gather in what the Cumian had said. He sat down. "Sextus, dead?"

Blossius nodded up and down, his face white.

"How?" Tiberius asked. "How did he die?"

"No one knows. His house slave found him in his bed. He had taken to it yesterday after suddenly falling ill."

"Did he see a physic? Was he examined?"

"Only after he'd been found this morning. A surgeon confirmed his death. Rumors have it that he was afflicted with some kind of scourge."

Tiberius arose and walked to the door, turning around and back, his head down as he tried to understand. "Pluto have me! Sextus dead! He couldn't be, he was strong and healthy. He took care of himself. Gods be good, he was young!"

"I know," Blossius said, "I know. But it is true. He is gone. The gods have reclaimed him for their own."

"Mars has taken him," murmured Tiberius, distracted. "He was a fearless warrior."

"And, a great ally."

"A friend," said Tiberius. "He was a friend. Hades have him, so many times I found him insufferable to be around. His arrogance knew no bounds. But, he was a friend, a faithful comrade in battle. Every battle."

He wept silent tears, and Blossius touched his forearm, his own eyes large with sorrow.

"Does Casca know?" Tiberius asked.

"I don't know," said Blossius. "I haven't told him, only you."

Tiberius sadly, slowly lowered his chin to his chest. "Summon him, please. I'll tell him."

Blossius nodded, and said, "The funeral will be tomorrow, for fear of pestilence. It will be in the southwest necropolis at the noon hour. His family's home on the Palatine isn't too far a walk from there."

Family, Tiberius thought. He never imagined Sextus with a family. The horseman always had seemed bigger than life, too big to have had an ordinary one.

"He was too young to die, too strong," Tiberius uttered to no one.

In the morning, after a sleepless night, Tiberius donned a toga pulla dyed a deep, blackish-blue color. Philea rubbed ash on his face and hands, and drew a few lines of red down his cheeks to affect open wounds of sorrow rent by his fingernails. Once she had finished, he took himself to the vestibulum and sat on a bench by the atrium pool to await Appius's arrival.

Claudia had come into his room to say curtly that she was sorry about Sextus's death. That was all. Perhaps she meant it as another reproach, the fate of a young man immersed in a political cauldron. Even if she hadn't meant it that way, he reflected morosely, the image had played in his own thoughts. He felt guilty that his grief for Sextus was not all consuming. A tiny part of his mind kept seizing upon the notion that Sextus had died from some fatal flaw or a singular mistake, one he could avoid. The tension, he thought, distracted him from rational thinking. Yet, irrational hope kept rising to the surface.

Appius arrived, his usually bright, round face drawn by long lines of missed sleep. "Crassus will meet us at the market square," he said in a low tone. Tiberius wondered at his father-in-law's capability to feel so deeply about so many people.

"Are you ready to go?"

"As ready as possible," Tiberius answered.

They left the house, and this time Casca fell in step with them, wearing a long, dark mourning tunic. In silence, the men marched down the hill and headed to the marketplace at the foot of the Esquiline. They met Crassus, and walked toward the southwest gate and out to the necropolis where the funeral would take place. When they arrived, the size of the crowd waiting to honor the fallen surprised them. As they approached the altar, the crowd gave away to either side.

A platform had been built in front of the altar, before which a row of wooden benches had been assembled. Saving the front row for the family, Tiberius and the rest of his party lined up in the second row of seats. In the distance, they heard a dirge of pipes, and the loud weeping and lamentations of the mourning family. The slow, deliberate beat of a heavy drum marked the progress of the funeral procession. The drumbeat grew louder as they drew closer. Now, priests could be heard chanting to Cheron to carry Sextus's lost soul across the Styx to the Elysian Fields.

The mourners came into sight, wailing women rending their clothes, clawing at their faces, and tearing long hairs from their heads. After them came the actors and dancers, wearing the images of the revered Decimi ancestors, dozens of them, impressive even for a prestiguous equestrian family. A long line of clients and associates followed, some covering their faces with their hands in a formal pose of bereavement. After them, the parents of Sextus and his younger siblings passed, crying inconsolably, leaning upon each other as they walked by. Behind them stepped the priests, now beseeching Pluto to welcome the warrior entering his realm while imprecating Orcus to allow the young soldier's spirit to pass by the gates of Tartarus. Many of the incantations were too ancient to decipher.

Two broad-shouldered slaves followed, carrying a roasted pig on a spit, to be sacrificed later to Ceres, with portions of it to be consumed by the bereft. Finally, behind the line of mourners came a chair, jerking up and down and sideways as its bearers negotiated its weight over the street stones. Atop the chair sat Sextus Decimus Paetus, propped up as though he still sat among them, wearing on his brow the Mural Crown he had won as first over the wall at Malia. An exquisite, ocean-blue toga fell in careful folds around his body, his forearms resting on the the chair rails, his fingers grasping carved wooden lion heads at the end of each armrest.

Ah, poor, poor Sextus, thought Tiberius, as the bearers turned the chair to face the mourning. Tiberius gasped, joined by a chorus of others as they saw Sextus's body straight on in clear sight. A rumble coursed through the crowd when they saw the equitus's face, purple and mottled with black bruises and open, weeping sores. His eyes bulged from the pressure of the fluids, the skin of his arms blotched and bursting.

"Pluto's curse!" shouted one voice, "Scourge!" "Pestilence!" cried another. "Plague, he died of the plague!" Tiberius heard them stirring behind him, even as the priests raised their hands in an attempt to calm them, trying to restore the decorum of the rites. But, the crowd wouldn't have it. Tiberius twisted around to see them milling about in agitation, some pushing to leave.

"Not plague," one suddenly shouted out, "poison! They have poisoned Sextus!"

"Murder!" "Assassins!" "They have killed Sextus!"

Tiberius glanced at Appius and Crassus. "They're going mad," said Crassus.

"We might want to retire before a riot starts," said Appius.

Tiberius stared at them both, alarmed. "What if they're right?" he said. "How could he die so suddenly, so horribly, otherwise?"

Appius looked at him with concern. "Tiberius, things like this happen."

"Happen? He was in the prime of his life, a demigod among men. How could he die? We just saw him riding a warhorse as though he were a centaur himself." He swung his head bull like, "No, he couldn't just die like that, turned into a festering hulk overnight."

"Tiberius," Appius said, his hand upon his forearm. The crowd began to surge toward the stand, furiously screaming at the priests, who now looked terrified. Tiberius pulled his arm away, and said, "Go home, Appius. Crassus, go home. I won't let them intimidate me, I'll appeal to the people for justice."

He searched around until he saw Hylas standing near the end of the benches. He waved him over. "Hylas, run home and tell Mistress Claudia that I want her to put on mourning robes and to dress the children as well. As soon as she can, I want them all to join me here. Go, fly, as fast as you can!"

Appius and Crassus peered at him as though he had gone mad himself. "I cannot sit still for this," Tiberius said, "I must do something to save us. Go home, now, I'll come to you later."

Looking deeply disturbed and unsure, the two men left Tiberius alone. He watched as they disappeared from the cemetery surrounded by a contingent of men, Ajax in the vanguard.

Alone, Tiberius allowed the massed mourners to sweep around him, brushing past the priests to Sextus's body. They attempted to lift him out of the chair and lay him on a makeshift bier made out of boards and tree branches. But, even as they put him down, his body seemed to explode from the pressure, releasing foul-smelling fluids everywhere. Green effluent splashed upon the men closest to the corpse, who drew back in horror. Then, others lit torches and set Sextus's remains on fire.

Tiberius watched from the benches, which had emptied during the tumult. Poor Sextus's family had fled from the crowd's outburst, quickly followed by the priests, actors, and the women hired to mourn. Sextus's associates and clients had left as well. Tiberius realized that he seemed to be the only official mourner left to grieve for his comrade.

Soon, the vile stench of the cremation began to drive the outraged people away as well. Tiberius sat brooding alone. The shock, the loss seemed almost too much to bear. How had Sextus died? Was his death truly part of a conspiracy? How far would the Optimates go with their mad revenge? And, what could he do now?

"Tiberius."

He raised his head to the soft tones. Claudia stood next to him, bending gently at the waist, her hand outstretched. A few steps away he saw young Tiberius and Sempronia. Next to them, Philea held hands with tiny Claudia and Gaius. Each of them wore grey tunics and capes.

"Tiberius," Claudia said gently, again.

He turned back to her and looked deeply into her rich, violet eyes. Tears came to his as he said, "Sextus is no more. The people think he was murdered. I fear that he was."

"Oh," she said, sitting next to him. She clasped his hand with both of hers. "I am so sorry, Tiberius."

He gazed up at her, struck again by her beauty. He put his hand on her round belly, and stood up. "We need to go," he said, "to the markets and the forums."

Puzzled, Claudia said, "But, we're here. We're here to honor your friend Sextus."

Tiberius shook his head violently, "No. Sextus is dead, gone to us. We must do what we can to be sure that nothing like this can happen to us. Let us go."

He took her by the hand and pulled her up. Still confused, Claudia followed his lead while saying, "You wish to go to the markets? With the children?"

"Yes," he said.

"But, that's too far for them to go, certainly too far for Gaius and Claudia. It wouldn't be safe."

"Casca and his men will watch over us. But, we must go and tell the people what we've seen, to prevent it happening again before it is too late."

"Tiberius," she said as he picked up little Claudia and put her in her mother's arms. He hoisted Gaius up and started for the city gate, Claudia close behind him carrying their youngest daughter. Philea trailed holding the hands of young Tiberius and Sempronia.

Once through the gate, Tiberius didn't hesitate, striding purposely toward the Esquiline. Claudia hurried after him, asking him why they were doing this. He entered the marketplace and took himself and his family directly to the forum. Lowering Gaius to the ground, Tiberius stepped up on the marketplace rostrum and shouted out as loud as he could.

"People of Rome, I am your tribune Tiberius Sempronius Gracchus. You know me as the author of the Lex Sempronia Agraria and the executor of Philometer's bequest to you. I have strived to serve you well, and hope to continue so in the future. But, evil forces oppose me. Evil men who will do anything to wrest from you what is rightfully yours. I know," he said fervently, "because I have just come from the funeral of one of ours, Sextus Decimus Paetus, Equitus of the Ninth Legion and friend of the people of Rome. In the prime of his life," Tiberius voice began to quiver, "Sextus was struck down, slain by some putrid malevolence foreign to natural things. Sextus died defending you, the people of Rome, and your rights. I will do the same if I, too, am not struck down as Sextus was."

Tears began to fall down Tiberius's cheeks as he spoke in anguish. "There are men," he said, "who will do anything to stop me. I fear that they will assassinate me," he cried, "I fear not death, but for the sake of my family."

He turned and waved down at the children and Claudia, who turned her head down and away.

"They will take me from my loved ones, and will stop the work I do on your behalf. I beseech you, Romans," he said, holding out his folded hands, "I implore you to save me and my family from this dire threat. I am your tribune; allow me to be your tribune until my work is done."

The people listening below had grown from a small group of ten or so to a crowd of one hundred or more. When he finished, they all clapped and cheered, somewhat restrained by the gravity of his remarks.

Tiberius thanked them and descended. Without a word to Claudia, he lifted Gaius again and led them to the marketplace in the Aventine. When they arrived, he took to the local rostrum and repeated his speech. They, too, reacted with an awkward but warm show of support.

Claudia watched Tiberius standing on the Rostrum, shedding tears as he gestured toward her and the children while denouncing the rich patricians who intended to destroy him, his family, and the Republic. She had never seen him cry before. So, was he sincere in this astonishing baring of the soul? Or, was it the master stroke of a cunning politician who stood at the height of his powers? She was sure that he genuinely grieved for Sextus, but could she believe this public display from the man who had gone eye to eye with the murderous Numantines? She shook her head in wary admiration. He could be so kind and self-effacing one moment, and so fierce the next. She loved him so.

Tiberius marched his tired, complaining children from one marketplace to another throughout the city. At one point, Philea commandeered the youngest, Gaius and Claudia, and took them home. The others trudged on behind their possessed father. Eventually, they made their way to the Roman Forum and the Comitia's rostrum.

The summer sun still shone high in the sky, but most of the marketplace's regulars had gone home long ago for dinners. The pols had left, too, and the vendors were closing up shop, chasing away the last of the urchins trying to steal and run. It didn't matter to Tiberius, who climbed the familiar steps of the Rostrum and began his oration. Soon enough, everyone still present drifted over to listen, even the petty thieves. When he finished, they gave him a rousing, ragged round of applause.

He stepped down and walked over to the first row in the Comitia where Claudia and the children sat, spent.

"I'll come back tomorrow," he said, "when there's sure to be a bigger crowd."

"Will you be wearing your mourning toga," Claudia said, "and ashes on your face?" He glared at her, and she stood up and grabbed his hand. "Come, let's take the children home."

At home, he ate little. Instead, he kissed little Tiberius and Sempronia, who both had fallen asleep with their mouths full.

Later, Claudia found him in his bed chamber, sitting with his head in his hands, his back racked by his heaving, silent sobbing. She sat next to him and hugged him with one arm around his shoulders. Without lifting up his head, he said, "We will miss Sextus. He was very important to us. Have I ever told you how magnificent he looked seated on Chance? It was inevitable that he would ride that horse, he was born to it." He sighed, "Oh, I was so jealous of him. Except for a whim of the gods, he would have been better striving for position than me. He certainly could be as arrogant as any senator, that's for sure," he laughed roughly.

She squeezed him, "He would have been just another stuffed peacock. Do you really think he would have passed a lex agraria?"

He turned to her, "Don't misjudge him, he was a loyal ally through and through, a true friend every step of the way. We will miss him, and the support of his fellow equestrians."

Claudia watched him dive into his own thoughts again. "Do you really think he was poisoned by Nasica and the rest?"

Tiberius frowned, "Oh, I don't know. He looked ghastly on that chair. If he died of disease, the gods surely punished him in the end." He paused, thinking again. "But," he said, "if the Optimates did kill him, then they have become even more dangerous. If they did that to Sextus, what won't they do?"

Claudia hugged him closely, and he half-turned to embrace her.

Chapter 34. Inviolable

Tiberius sat alone in his peristylum before dawn on the day of the tribunal election. Every now and then he could hear the bubbling of the fountain in the pool, and he could smell the sweet fragrances of the flowers in the beds bordering the walls. Still too dark to see, he could picture in his mind their summer beautiful blooms now fading, the lavenders, deep purples, ruby reds, the delicate white laces, and the gaudy, giant orange blossoms. As the sunlight appeared, he could see the silhouettes of the two little trees, cherry and lemon, which accented the small rectangular garden. The tranquility relaxed him, as it always had since he was a small boy. He imagined that it had soothed his father, too, and all of the ancestors who had made this old-style domus their home. The world outside raged with every human activity, conceivable and inconceivable. But, here peace presided.

Soon enough, everyone would rise, chores would be tasked, gods, goddesses, and ancestors would be honored, food would pass lips, children would play, parents would admonish, servants would glide silently, dogs would bark, the day would proceed. Today, he would don his white toga and appeal to the people of Rome to elect him tribune again, one more turn. If they voted yes, he would serve as well as he could for another year until Gaius or some other Populatus took over. If they voted no, he would retire from public life and sit more often in this garden. Sitting now, just before dawn, he wondered which outcome to hope for more.

He heard stirring in the outer rooms. Philea and Hylas were up, soon to head for the kitchen. He shook his head in memory; Philea had been his wet-nurse, and now she had grown so old. Along with Polydius, he had manumitted her some years ago, since his mother never seemed that she would get around to it. But, unlike the Greek mentor, Philea had no family of her own. A free woman, she served Tiberius as she always had, as if nothing had changed. His family was her family.

He had drawn up Hylas's manumission papers as well, shortly after he had listened to the young man's story about how he had become a slave. The papers were tucked away in Tiberius's office, however. Hylas was too callow to send out in the world just yet. He needed some seasoning and he needed a trade. The young Greek wasn't cut out to be a mentor, either, though he was as good-hearted a person as could be. Finding him a good livelihood would take some thought. Perhaps Polydius could meet with Hylas to see what interested the young man.

Tiberius rose up from the bench and stretched luxuriously in the warm, breaking sunlight. He slowly strolled around the pool absently, taking in the glorious growth and marveling at the intricate architecture of the spider webs glistening from dew in the lemon tree.

A shining reflection in one of the beds caught his eye, something foreign to the plants, something manmade. He stepped closer and leaned down to see a round, coppery object half embedded in the soft black earth between some fern fronds. He reached down to it even as he felt a vague sense of recognition. As he touched its metallic surface, he felt knobs on one end near the edge of the soil. He pulled on a knob as he realized that it was a helmet, his helmet, given to him by Appius nearly four years ago to wear in Numantia. He gave it a firmer tug by the knobs, one of the two horns decorating the top of the helmet. Young Tiberius enjoyed wearing it to play fearsome Roman conqueror, he remembered. The boy must have left it out some time ago, Tiberius thought as he pulled it free. Look at how dull and tarnished it had become.

Several small, black snakes slipped out of the helmet, causing Tiberius to drop it at once. He lost his balance and sat down backwards, watching the snakes quickly disappear beneath the plant leaves. Black snakes, he thought, poisonous? Images of other snakes rushed through his mind, the two that legend tells led to the death of his father, and the two that slithered on Mancinus's ship, premonitions of his disaster in Numantia. Were these snakes ill omens of his own? Tiberius wondered. Or, had they been planted to assassinate him?

The possibilities sent waves of alarm through him until he picked himself up and brushed off the damp dirt on the back of his tunic. The helmet had been in the ground for weeks, maybe months, a perfect nesting place for snakes. They could have been baby black snakes for all he knew, harmless. He laughed uneasily at his own edginess. The times, he thought, a sign of the times.

Tiberius left the garden and headed for his bed chamber to wash and dress. As Philea arranged the folds of his toga candida, Claudia sat on his bed.

"Well," he said after Philea stepped back. "Do I look like a winning candidate?"

He spun around as Claudia said, "I'm glad we kept the candida, though I didn't think we'd need it so soon again."

Tiberius pursed his lips frowning, "Yes, well it turned out that we did. Let's go out for the morning devotion, I'm anxious to get moving."

Philea left the room, but Claudia held Tiberius's arm, "Wait."

She moved around in front of him and pulled him toward her. He wrapped his arms around her, saying, "Now, now."

She hugged him close, and pulled back. "What's that beneath your toga?"

"What?"

"That knobby thing on your left side. If it wasn't in the wrong place, I would have thought I was piquing your interest."

"Oh," he laughed a bit nervously, "that's the dolo Casca gave me. It's a sort of a club-knife sort of thing. I've taken it with me ever since the attack in the street that night."

She frowned, and looked at him darkly. "Do you think you might need it today?"

"I don't. They had their chance, and I am a tribune. If they were to try again, they could lose everything, including their lives. Still, if they are mad, I don't want to be in the middle of things without having some defense for myself."

He could see the anger building in her features again. He held her arms and said, "Claudia, don't fret. In the unlikely event, I intend to use it to fend off anyone wishing to do me harm long enough to scurry to a safe place."

Claudia pressed her lips, the lower one a buttress of discontent. "Tiberius, promise me by the gods above that you will do everything you can to stay safe."

"I promise by all of the gods above," he said, leaning in to kiss her. "Now, let us go give praise to them and our ancestors."

The family assembled before the Lararium, all except for Cornelia. Puzzled, Tiberius glanced at Claudia, who shrugged. Philea spoke up, "Mistress Cornelia will not attend this morning. She wishes to conduct her morning devotion privately in her room."

Tiberius drew back slightly, and then opened the cabinet doors to reveal the venerated masks of the Sempronii ancestors. Then he opened up the smaller shrine within that sheltered the figurines of the household gods surrounding the all-powerful deities of Olympus.

Tiberius pulled the hood of his toga over his head and conducted the service with outstretched hands. Claudia and the children each brought up petite offerings of food and incense to the small altar in front of the divinities, which Tiberius blessed and burned. Beneath his breath, he sent a special prayer to the goddess Concordia asking for her favor in granting harmony during today's events.

After the morning worship, Tiberius sat on a bench in the house vestibulum. Wearing a cloth around his neck to protect the white toga, he ate a light breakfast of honey cake and fruit while he awaited the members of his entourage. Before long, he heard voices outside the open front door. Hylas led the way and announced the arrival of Blossius, Diophanes, and Polydius. Tiberius felt a pang of sorrow at the absence of Sextus, which he quickly dismissed. Past the men in front of him, he could see Casca and Ajax in the narrow courtyard leading to the gates, along with several of their men.

"Well," Tiberius said, "are we ready?"

Blossius answered, "As ready as we can be. The number of plebeians arriving from the countryside has been thin. As we predicted, the timing of the election has kept many in their fields bringing in their crops. But, the turn-out in the city should be strong, considering your new reforms."

"And my father-in-law and Crassus?"

"The Populares senators will meet in strength in the Curia to blunt any outrages by the Optimates. Once the votes have been tallied, they will join you to show their solidarity."

Tiberius nodded, "All right. Let us get under way."

Blossius held up a hand. "Be prepared for what you see outside of your domus. Many plebeians have gathered here to protect you, some throughout the night."

"I know," said Tiberius, "they've been here since Sextus's funeral, a virtual encampment of clients outside my door."

"Oh," said Blossius. "Well, today they have summoned soothsayers from the Temple of Saturn to take the auspices."

"Must we? I'm anxious to go to the Forum and see this finished."

"Your supporters out front would feel better," Blossius said persuasively, "if they knew that the gods smiled upon you."

Tiberius sighed, "Very well."

Outside of the domus gate, a space had been cleared among the tents and lean-tos in the street for the soothsayers and their holy birds, which they carried in woven wooden cages. Again, Tiberius hooded his head with his toga and clasped his hands respectfully in front of him. The members of his party followed suit as the seers began their supplication of the gods. They raised their hands to the sky in prayer, then cast them low, releasing seeds among the street's cobblestones. Novices quickly raised the gates of the cages and quietly attempted to shoo the birds outside.

The soothsayers watched carefully to see how the birds would peck at the seeds, the patterns of which would tell them how the gods felt that day about the pecking order of men.

But the birds seemed agitated, and refused to leave the cages. Instead, they stirred among themselves, flapping their wings and spreading their feathers as they bumped into each other. Nervously, the head seer motioned to the neophytes, who tried tipping the birds out of the cages. Just one came out. It fluttered one wing and stepped toward the seeds, only to turn and fly quickly back into the cage.

"Orcus curse us, this couldn't have gone any worse," said Tiberius, pulling his toga down. "We go to the Forum now."

Wheeling forcefully away, he walked briskly down the street, well ahead of Blossius and the rest, who hurried to catch up. Halfway down the hill, Tiberius felt a sudden searing pain in his foot that caused him to stumble almost to his knees. He caught himself on the curb, his right big toe in agony. Bent over, he could see that the nail was missing, torn off by a stone sticking up in the street. Blood flowed everywhere. Polydius dropped to his knees, ripping linen from the hem of his tunic to wrap Tiberius's toe.

"Aah," Tiberius spat through gritted teeth, "this hurts more than a knife in the gut."

Blossius and Diophanes raised him to his feet, uttering words of sympathy and comfort. A wave of pain caused Tiberius to throw his head back, so that he could see the tops of the house roofs closest to the edge of the street. The sudden motion caused two crows to caw and flap away, dislodging a clay shingle, which fell and shattered at his feet. He jumped back reflexively, triggering another surge of pain from his damaged toe.

His mind raced. This cannot be, he thought, the snake goddess Hela played with him. How could anything go more wrong? If the gods intended to abandon him, this was a day to abandon.

Blossius saw Tiberius's stark expression and the flickering of his eyes side to side. Quickly, he grabbed the tribune's elbow and ushered him out of earshot of the others.

"Tiberius, I know what you're feeling, the signs have been bad. But, they are only bad if you permit them to be so. Old women and ignorant men allow birds, stones, and twigs to rule their lives. But, you are an educated man, a Sempronii, son of Gracchus Major and grandson of Scipio Africanus. You are a tribune of the people who count on you to protect them. For their sake, please, do not give up the day."

Tiberius stared down at Blossius and shook his arm loose. "I might have given up," he said, "but you have shamed me, Stoic, haven't you?"

Blossius flinched, abashed. Tiberius said, "Don't worry, Blossius. I know who I am. I'll save the day no matter what bad fortune comes our way."

He turned and began limping down the hill.

Appius and the other Populares took their seats in the Curia well before the vote was scheduled to take place outside in the Comitia. After much moaning about the Mos Maiorum, Crassus was with them, though, in a fit of pique he'd sat his bony ass a few seats away. No matter, he was here, thought Appius. They would need every man they could find to soldier on in the face of the Optimates's inevitable outrage and fury. Again, both consuls would be presiding.

As he expected, the Optimates also sat in strength despite the early hour. It surprised him, however, that neither Nasica nor Rufus Faba Bean had appeared. This worried him a bit; what mischief kept them away from the grand stage? he wondered. But, everything about this scenario worried him right now, an unusual, unhappy state of being that he found extremely irritating.

Appius didn't have to wonder for long. Nasica entered the Senate chamber with Metellus at his side. Pompeius followed, paired with Rufus, and behind him Spurious Postumius wearing his usual superior, smirking smile. They led an impressive cadre of other prominent senators to the front row of the Optimate section. Appius leaned over to Flavius Flaccus, who sat next to him in Crassus's usual place.

"There they are, the best of the Good Men on parade."

Flaccus laughed quietly, stopping when old Cato Minor, the princeps senatus moderating for the day, stood and called for attention to the consuls. Piso Frugi arose to announce that a quorum had been attained, which caused light laughter throughout the crowded hall. He then asked the Pontifex Maximus if the proper sacrifices had been conducted. Nasica stood to shout "They have, Consul," and immediately sat down. Piso then declared the Senate to be in session.

Metellus bolted up, a surprise, thought Appius, who had been settling into his seat in anticipation of a long, spiteful oration by Nasica or Rufus.

"May I have the floor, Consul Piso?"

"By all means, Metellus Macedonicus!"

Metellus adjusted his stance, spreading his legs just so while hitching a fold of his toga up over his shoulder. "I wish," he began, "to bring to the attention of this distinguished body an unseemly pattern of behavior unbecoming to the Roman sensibility of decorum. When my father served as censor to Rome, his devotion to safeguarding the scruples of the city met no match. His sincerity in this so impressed the people that every night when he returned home for supper, they would snuff out their lights to assure him that they refrained from indulging in feasting and drinking at unreasonable hours. Yet, in today's world, the indigent, the scofflaws, and the reprobates clamor throughout the night, their bright torches brazenly publicizing outrageous behavior of such audacity as to offend every god and goddess in the celestial. And who do they follow and celebrate in their disgusting merriment? The arrogant tribune Tiberius Sempronius Gracchus!"

Augh, Appius groaned to himself, it begins again.

Casca stood high on a nearby street above the Comitia, surveying the preparations for the vote. He could see Ajax and his group on the opposite side, assembled near the Curia Hostilia to keep watch on the comings and goings of the Senate. Casca spotted his own men at various points at the bottom of the Comitia, spaced so that they could rally to any trouble that arise. The plebs had begun to flow into the amphitheater, congregating with their respective tribes to wait their turn to cast their vote. The turnout seemed solid, he thought, though not as sizable as the first time Tiberius had run, or when he had put forth his lex agraria. That vote coupled with the deposal of Octavius seemed to have brought forth every living citizen from every province, town, and village under Roman rule. Today would produce some anxiety among the Populares, Casca imagined, but they needn't worry. More than enough plebeians just living in Rome itself would rally to carry the day for their favorite tribune.

He scanned the Forum and its surroundings again, and just in time saw Tiberius's party emerging from the marketplace to his right. Casca hesitated for a moment, wishing to hold fast to his vantage point until the equestrians arrived. Sextus was dead, but his associates had assured him that they would ride in strength today. They still wholeheartedly supported Tiberius's promise to expand the courts with judicial positions for them. They seemed to be running late, though. Casca shook his head as he started descending the stairs, sorry that Sextus wasn't alive to see this.

Tiberius had just reached the steps of the Rostrum when Casca met him in the Comitia.

"Salve, Primus, how goes it?" Tiberius said warmly, grasping Casca's forearm and hand.

"It goes well, Tribune. The people are arriving now, in high spirits, it seems."

"Wonderful. Any trouble?"

Casca shook his head, "None yet." The tribune seemed pale, leaning to one side. "And you?" Casca said. "Did you encounter any problems?"

Tiberius grinned, though he looked to be gritting his teeth at the same time. "I bashed one of my toes, I'm embarrassed to say. Tore the nail completely off."

Casca nodded. He reached over to Tiberius's left side, patting him until he felt the haft of the dolo beneath the material. "Glad to see you have that with you."

"Yes, well, I don't know what good it would do in a tight spot," Tiberius said. "I haven't used one in years."

"I saw you in Numantia," Casca said. "You'll know what to do."

Tiberius assumed an exaggerated expression of self-doubt, "Let's hope the need doesn't arise." He gazed around and up at the Rostrum. "I believe it's time for me to assume the position."

Casca dipped his chin, "Fortuna be with you, Tribune."

"And with you, Lucius," Tiberius replied as he ascended the stairs.

Metellus finished his windy invective at last. Appius shifted his weight in his chair, yanking his toga away from him. The cool of the early morning was giving away to heat as the day progressed. He wondered if he should answer Metellus's blather, though it irritated him that he had to be the one. Why didn't one of these other young blades with them stand and defend Tiberius as the champion of Rome? Or, for that matter, why didn't Crassus speak? Couldn't he just for once swallow his damn Mos Maiorum and speak out for the people?

Appius sighed, and started to rise, his hand halfway up. But, Nasica stood first.

"Honorable Consuls of Rome, I can wait no longer. Outside these very doors," he said, pointing toward them, "a great crime against the Republic could be perpetrated. In fact, perhaps the greatest crime in the history of Rome is about to take place."

Appius groaned out loud as he sat back down.

Nasica whipped his head around, "Don't you dare utter a sound, Pulcher! Not one grunt! You are as much to blame for this as any man in this chamber! You should pay the price for this travesty as much as its author, Tiberius Gracchus!"

Appius sat silently, taken aback.

Nasica returned his attention to the consuls, his voice raised for all to hear. "In less than a single year, Gracchus has flaunted all of the cherished laws and traditions of Rome. He has forced through an illegal bill that ┐ls land from its rightful owners and awards it to his criminal support-! He did so by illegally deposing a rightfully elected tribune who defied m, thus further breaking the law and violating the sacred stature of his ation. His past actions mark the arrogance and ambition of a tyrannical emperament, pride that allows him to discount the liberties of the people. And, now, he wishes to break another sacred law so that he can continue his crimes for another year!"

As if on cue, the other Optimates bounded up from their seats, screeching and shouting, "No!" "Outrage!" "Sacrilege!"

Nasica started again, and the voices abruptly went quiet. What is going on here? Appius thought, gripping both arms of his seat with his hands.

"Consuls, senators, I am your Pontifex Maximus, the High Priest of all the people of Rome. I took the auguries this day before we met. I dread reporting that the auspices were horrifying. Never have I seen such evil signs! The portents are clear. Tiberius Sempronius Gracchus has been possessed by demons, spirits of Orcus's underworld driving him to the worst of crimes, the highest act of treason: Gracchus wishes to be king of Rome!"

The great hall burst into tumult again, with cries of "Treason!" and "Tyranny!" ringing to the rafters, so loud that the pigeons flew up in a